A Meeting at Corvallis

"Stirling concludes his alternative history trilogy in high style." —*Publishers Weekly*

"A fascinating glimpse into a future transformed by the lack of easy solutions to both human and technological dilemmas." —*Library Journal*

"Exciting and suspenseful.... Blending elements of Arthurian and Tolkienesque romance with down-in-the-muck details of birth and death, farming and herding, building and politicking, Stirling manages to fashion a narrative that acknowledges that humanity is a creature of both soul and body, heart and mind, lust and sacrifice, much in the manner of Poul Anderson.... Stirling has blazed a clear comet trail across his postapocalyptic landscape that illuminates both the best and the worst of which our species is capable." —Science Fiction Weekly

"The ensuing maze of intrigue, diplomacy, and battle comes up to Stirling's highest standards for pacing, world building, action, and strong characterizations, particularly of women." —*Booklist* (starred review)

"Entertaining and satisfying." —*Contra Costa Times*

"[Stirling's] made his heroes real people about whom we care and with whom we identify, and the way they have risen to heroic stature out of necessity and the instinct to survive and to thrive says something heartening about the potential in all of us." —SF Reviews

"An exciting and fitting end to this science fiction thriller trilogy." —Alternate Worlds

The Protector's War

"Absorbing." —*The San Diego Union-Tribune*

"[A] vivid portrait of a world gone insane . . . it also has human warmth and courage. . . . It is full of bloody action, exposition that expands character, and telling details that make it all seem very real. . . . It is the determination of its major characters to create a safe and loving world that makes the book so affecting." —*Statesman Journal* (Salem, OR)

continued . . .

Dies the Fire

"*Dies the Fire* kept me reading till five in the morning so I could finish in one great gulp. It's an alarmingly large speculation: how would we fare if we suddenly had the past 250 years and more of technological progress taken away from us? No more electricity. No more internal combustion engines. No more gunpowder or other explosives. All gone, vanished in the blink of an eye. . . . Don't miss it." —Harry Turtledove

"Gritty, realistic, and apocalyptic, yet a grim hopefulness pervades it like a fog of light. The characters are multidimensional, unusual, and so very human. Buy *Dies the Fire*. Sell your house, sell your soul, get the book. You won't be sorry." —John Ringo

"A stunning speculative vision of a near-future bereft of modern conveniences but filled with human hope and determination. Highly recommended." —*Library Journal*

"S. M. Stirling gives himself a broad canvas on which to display his talent for action, extrapolation, and depiction of the brutal realities of life in the absence of civilized norms." —David Drake

"The Willamette Valley of Oregon and the wilds of Idaho are depicted with loving care, each swale and tree rendered sharply. The smell of burning cities, the aftermath of carnage, the odor and sweat of horses . . . Stirling grounds his action in these realities with the skill of a Poul Anderson. . . . Post-apocalypse novels often veer either too heavily into romantic Robinsonades or nihilistic dead ends. But Stirling has struck the perfect balance between grit and glory." —Science Fiction Weekly

"Stirling shows that while our technology influences the means by which we live, it is the myths we believe in that determine how we live. The novel's dual themes—myth and technology—should appeal to both fantasy and hard SF readers as well as to techno-thriller fans." —*Publishers Weekly*

"Fans of apocalyptical thrillers like Stephen King's *The Stand* will find *Dies the Fire* absolutely riveting. . . . A fantastic epic work." —*Midwest Book Review*

"The character development is excellent. . . . I found myself devouring every page as quickly as I could. I enjoyed the thrill of a world in which so many things we take for granted are gone. . . . For fans of what-if, this is a must read." —SFRevu

Novels of the Change

Other Novels by S. M. Stirling

A MEETING
AT CORVALLIS

S. M.
STIRLING

A ROC BOOK

ROC
Published by New American Library, a division of
Penguin Group (USA) Inc., 375 Hudson Street,
New York, New York 10014, USA
Penguin Group (Canada), 90 Eglinton Avenue East, Suite 700, Toronto,
Ontario M4P 2Y3, Canada (a division of Pearson Penguin Canada Inc.)
Penguin Books Ltd., 80 Strand, London WC2R 0RL, England
Penguin Ireland, 25 St. Stephen's Green, Dublin 2,
Ireland (a division of Penguin Books Ltd.)
Penguin Group (Australia), 250 Camberwell Road, Camberwell, Victoria 3124,
Australia (a division of Pearson Australia Group Pty. Ltd.)
Penguin Books India Pvt. Ltd., 11 Community Centre, Panchsheel Park,
New Delhi - 110 017, India
Penguin Group (NZ), 67 Apollo Drive, Rosedale, North Shore 0745,
Auckland, New Zealand (a division of Pearson New Zealand Ltd.)
Penguin Books (South Africa) (Pty.) Ltd., 24 Sturdee Avenue,
Rosebank, Johannesburg 2196, South Africa

Penguin Books Ltd., Registered Offices:
80 Strand, London WC2R 0RL, England

Published by Roc, an imprint of New American Library, a division of Penguin
Group (USA) Inc. Previously published in a Roc hardcover edition.

First Roc Mass Market Printing, September 2007
10   9   8   7   6   5   4   3   2   1

ACKNOWLEDGMENTS

Thanks to my first readers:

To Steve Brady, for assistance with dialects, and saving me from a couple of embarrassing faux pas about home-brewed beer and other things. As the saying goes, it ain't what you don't know that'll kill you, it's what you think you know that ain't so. Sample the Real Ale for me!

Thanks also to Kier Salmon, for once again helping with the beautiful complexities of the Old Religion, batting ideas on how it might develop in this (thankfully!) alternate history back and forth, giving me firsthand reports and pictures of Oregon locations, and coming up with the great idea about the ox and other nifty ideas.

To Dale Price, for giving me help with Catholic background, and some excellent suggestions.

To all of them for becoming good, if long-distance, friends.

To Bob Noonan, for help with the Gaelic, which I cannot speak. But *déan crónán cupla barraí agus cuirfidh mé bréagriocht air.*

To Melinda Snodgrass, Daniel Abraham, Emily Mah, Terry England, George R. R. Martin, Walter Jon Williams, Sally Gwylan, Yvonne Coats, and Laura Mixon-Gould of Critical Mass, for constant help and advice as the book was under construction. And heck, they were already friends.

Special thanks to Heather Alexander, bard and balladeer, for permission to use the lyrics from her beautiful songs which can be—and should be!—ordered at www.heatherlands.com. Run, do not walk, to do so.

Special thanks to Kate West, for her kind words and permission to use her chants.

Special thanks—am I overusing the word?—to William Pint and Felicia Dale, for permission to use their music, which can be found at http://members.aol.com/pintndale and should be, for anyone with an ear and saltwater in their veins.

Thanks again to everyone from the author of *Amadis of Gaul* on down. Writing is a solitary occupation, but we aren't alone!

All mistakes, infelicities and errors are of course my own.

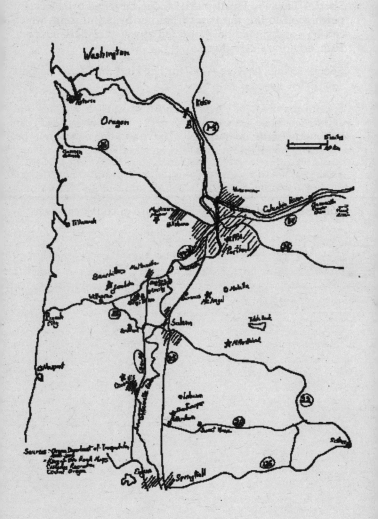

CHAPTER ONE

Norman Arminger—he rarely thought of himself as anything but the Lord Protector these days—stared at the great map that showed his domains, and those of his stubbornly independent neighbors; it covered the whole of the former Oregon and Washington, with bits of the old states of Idaho and northern California thrown in.

Winds racing out of the Columbia gorge howled amongst the empty skyscrapers, and drove rain that spattered audibly against windows hidden by tapestries shimmering with gold and silver thread. The map covered one wall of what had been the main hall of the city's old public library, built in Edwardian times with a splendor of gray-veined white marble and brass inlay. That and the easily adapted heating system were why he'd picked it as his city palace, back right after the Change, and he'd had workmen busy with it ever since.

Then he turned on his heel and walked to the larger of the two thrones that stood on the new dais at the foot of the staircase; his left foot automatically knocked the scabbard of his longsword out of the way as he sat. This hall was the place he'd first unsheathed it in earnest nine years ago, and where he'd first spilled a man's life with the steel. The chairs were massive gothic fantasies in jewels and precious metals, gold for his and silver for his consort's; the materials had been salvaged from luxury stores and worked up by Society-trained artisans. The long stair behind them was black marble carved in vinework, rising to a landing and then splitting in two, curling up to the second story and the gallery that overlooked the throne room.

Outside, day's gray light was fading into blackness under clouded heavens, but the great room was brilliantly lit, by gasoline lanterns of silver fretwork hanging from the galleries around it, and by a huge chandelier salvaged from a magnate's mansion in the center of the ceiling thirty feet above. That burned a spendthrift plenitude of fine candles; their wax-and-lavender scent filled the chamber, overlaying metal polish and cloth and the sweat of fear from the crowd of well-dressed courtiers, clerics, advisors and officials. It was silent except for the occasional creak of shoe-leather or crisp ripple of stiff embroidered cloth from the tapestries, quiet enough that the faint whisper of flame from the lights was audible; the shifting glitter of flame shone on the thrones, on the jewelry and bright clothes of the courtiers, and on naked steel . . .

Spearmen stood like statues about the walls, their mail hauberks gleaming gray and the heads of seven-foot spears bright; their big kite-shaped shields were flat matte black, bearing the same sigil of a red cat-pupiled eye wreathed in flame as stood on the great banner hanging from the ceiling to the landing behind him. Three household knights stood in a line before each throne. They wore black-enameled mail; the golden spurs on their boots and the bright steel-sheen of their swords were the only color about them, besides the Eye on their shields. The weapons rested ready with the long blades on their shoulders; their eyes moved ceaselessly behind the splayed nasal bars of their conical helmets. There were discreet crossbowmen along the second-story galleries as well.

After a moment the woman seated in the other throne reached out and touched his arm. Arminger nodded—Sandra and he had played good cop/bad cop very effectively for years—and spoke:

"You may rise, Lord Molalla, and approach the throne."

The three kneeling figures stood: a man, a woman and a boy

of about nine. The trumpeter beside the throne raised his long brass instrument and blew a simple tune, two rising and one falling note. The herald cried:

"The Lord Jabar Jones, Baron Molalla! The Lady Phillipa! Their son, Lord Chaka! You are bidden to approach the Presence!"

The knights before Arminger's throne stepped aside in perfect unison as the three approached, swinging like a door. Then they swung back and turned, which put them—and their ready swords—within three feet of the petitioners. Sandra's guardians remained facing outward, like iron statues with living, hungry eyes.

Jabar Jones—Baron Molalla—was a big man, an inch or two over Arminger's six-one, and similarly broad-shouldered, though unlike his overlord he'd added the beginnings of a paunch, despite being a little younger than the Lord Protector's mid-forties. His cannonball head was shaved and the color of eggplant save for a few dusty white scars. He'd been a gang leader before the Change; Lady Phillipa was a Junoesque redhead of a little over thirty, and came from the other major element among the Protector's original cadre of supporters, the SCA ... these days known as *the* Society.

The Society's notion of clothing, or "garb" as they called it, had prevailed over the years, at least for the Portland Protective Association's upper classes, as had many of their notions. Phillipa wore an elaborate wrapped and pinned headdress of white silk that surrounded her face and fell to the shoulders of her long blue gown. The dress was what they called a cotte-hardi; jeweled buttons ran up from a belt of gold chain links to the lace at her throat, and down the long sleeves. For men garb had worked out to loose trousers, boots, linen shirt, belted thigh-length t-tunic and flat hats with a roll of fabric around the edge and dangling cloth tails; the only exceptions in the room were servants, clergy of the Orthodox Catholic Church in their long monastic robes or colorful dalmatics, and some foreign guests.

Arminger's clothes were the same, but in black silk, and he added silver plates to his sword belt, a gold chain around his neck that supported a pendant of the Lidless Eye on his chest, and a niello headband to confine his shoulder-length brown hair. That was receding a little from his high forehead; the features below were harshly aquiline, lines graven from nose to mouth, and the eyes were an amber hazel.

Molalla wore no sword belt. That was a political statement just now, as was his willingness to promptly obey the summons to court—some would have thought raising the drawbridges in his barony more prudent, though that was a counsel of desperation. The way his wife's eyes occasionally darted to Sandra Arminger's face was probably political appraisal by Phillipa, too. The women had been friends. She evidently didn't find the stony calm on the face of Arminger's consort very reassuring.

The way the guardian knights stood within arm's reach behind them wasn't reassuring either. It wasn't meant to be.

"You may speak," Arminger growled to the man.

"My lord, I have petitioned to be allowed to explain my error before this—"

"You're lucky I didn't let you come near me until now, Jabar," he said. "I was waiting until I could be sure I could control my temper. I'm not a forgiving man by nature. My confessor and His Holiness Leo tell me it's my greatest fault."

A ripple of chuckles ran through the court, except for a few of the clerics. Arminger grinned inwardly, behind an impassive mask.

Actually, I was wondering what Strongbow or the Conqueror would have done, he thought.

The Norman duchy and its offshoots from Ireland to Sicily and the Crusader principalities had been his area of study, back when he'd been a scholar, before the Change. Playing at knights had been his recreation, a way to live a little of the life those civilized Vikings knew. But the contacts that had given him had proved crucially useful in his rise to power. Society people—at least the less squeamish of them—had been very handy as a training cadre in pre-gunpowder combat and a dozen other skills, but there were problems . . . what had been their slogan?

Silently, he mused to himself: *"Recreating the Middle Ages as they* should *have been."*

They were perhaps the only people in all the world who'd felt *vindicated* when the Change killed all high-energy-density technologies between the earth's surface and the Van Allens in a single instant of white light and blinding pain.

I'm more interested in the reality. With some refinements, of course. Showers and flush toilets are technologies I approve of. At least for me.

"My lord Protector," Molalla plowed on, sweating as he trudged through a speech obviously memorized in advance and probably written by his wife. "I sent the Princess Mathilda back on a well-guarded train as soon as the outposts reported a Mackenzie raid out of the Table Rock wilderness, thinking they'd be safe in Portland before the enemy could penetrate the lowlands—and I sent my own son along. My own younger brother commanded the escort, and was killed in the ambush on the railroad. I admit error, and I beg your mercy for it, but I claim innocence of any malice or disloyalty. Would I have done either if I hadn't thought it the safest course for the princess?"

Sandra spoke, her voice soft and careful: "But it wasn't as safe, lord baron, as guarding them in your keep would have been. Raiders could ambush a train—which they did. They could not storm a castle, which they didn't even try to do. And while the Mackenzies released your son at once, they did *not* release my daughter! For more than half a year, she has been captive among the Satan-worshippers."

A heavy silence fell. The burly black nobleman opened his mouth, and then closed it.

Wise, Arminger thought.

The whole past spring and summer had been a series of disasters. The Mackenzie raid, the failure of his attempt to salvage something useful from the old chemical-warfare dump up the Columbia at Umatilla—those damned Englishmen who'd come in on the Tasmanian ship had been responsible for that, suckering him completely—and then the rescue mission for Mathilda had crashed and burned spectacularly. If it hadn't been for the way the Umatilla expedition had extended the Association's influence into the Pendleton country, it could have been a dangerous blow to his prestige. As it was, land for new fiefs would keep discontent to a minimum.

When he spoke it was to his steward. "Why is Baron Molalla unarmed? Bring his sword at once; it isn't fitting that a trusted vassal should appear without a weapon."

A man came up with the long blade, the belt wrapped around the scabbard and showing a buckle bearing the barony's sigil, a rampant lion grasping a broad-bladed assegai. Molalla donned it; his face stayed impassive, but sheer relief suddenly put a beading of sweat on his forehead, glittering in the candlelight. Servants handed sheathed daggers to his wife and son.

"Use it well in my service, and in the interests of the Association," Arminger said.

He noted how Phillipa's eyes sought Sandra's again, and how her face relaxed slightly at the consort's smile and nod.

Easy enough to see who's got the political brains in that family, though Jabar's a good fighting man, Arminger thought.

Chaka was looking at the Association's overlord worshipfully, too. Arminger suppressed a sudden wave of murderous fury at the thought of Mathilda lost among the fanatics; they wouldn't harm her directly, but every moment she was exposed to that poisonous brew of superstition and make-believe was one too many.

And if you screw up again, Jabar, all three of you are going to spend your final hours hanging from iron hooks on the wall outside!

He smiled instead of snarling the threat. It wasn't necessary; the baron and his family bowed and backed six paces away, among a crowd that didn't avoid them like plague carriers anymore, but Phillipa was looking extremely thoughtful. With an effort of will Arminger thrust gnawing worry aside; he couldn't afford distraction, and could do his daughter no good if he was crippled. Instead he made a gesture. Another trumpet blast echoed.

"Lord Emiliano Gutierrez, Baron Dayton!" the herald called. "You are bidden to approach the Presence!"

Emiliano was in his thirties as well, a stocky brown-faced man in fine white linen and gleaming satin. He grinned as he bowed, and met the Lord Protector's eyes, ignoring the naked blades ready behind him.

Men who can be intimidated easily aren't very effective servants, not as fighting men, Arminger reminded himself. *Irksome, since intimidation is so much fun, but there you are.*

"Lord Emiliano, I'm hereby appointing you Marchwarden of the South, to replace the late Lord Edward Liu, Baron Gervais." He waved aside thanks. "Just see the damned Bear-killers and kilties keep to their side of the border."

Another trumpet blast. "Lady Mary Liu, dowager Baroness Gervais! You are bidden to approach the Presence!"

A slim blonde came forward, sinking in a low curtsey; she wore mourning ribbons around her headdress. The knights did their deadly pavane.

"Lady Mary, I'm taking the barony of Gervais into personal wardship pending the majority of your heir, but I'm making you my steward for it until your son comes of age," he said. "You may appoint a garrison commander from Baron Edward's following. Please inform me before you make a public announcement of exactly who."

"Thank you, my lord Protector," she said, in a high, reedy voice.

Liu's widow didn't have a prescriptive right to rule her husband's personal holding until the heir reached twenty-one. In strict form the land reverted to the Association, and the Protector could have given her a manor as dower house, or apartments at court, installed his own administrator and commander and collected the mesne tithes from the barony and its subordinate knight's-fee manors for himself. That would have given him the income for more than a decade; Liu's eldest was only eight. But Eddie had been one of his personal hatchetmen, and a good one, until his final failure. Besides which, Mary would probably do a pretty good job of it; she knew the place firsthand, and in the long run it would help to have Eddie's kids grow up there.

Though she's not *going to appoint her brother garrison com-*

mander. Sir Jason's too much of a hothead. A pity, since he's intelligent otherwise.

As a gesture, giving her the chatelaine's job would help keep the rest of his baronage sweet, if he had to take action against Molalla. They were developing an irritating attachment to the minutiae of the law, and an even more irritating sense of collective solidarity about their privileges. Step on one, and the others all squalled like scalded cats. He was stronger than any individual noble, but not more powerful than all of them put together.

Less formally, he went on: "Mary, Eddie was a good man, and a friend of mine. I won't forget that he died trying to rescue my daughter from captivity. And you can take it as a promise that I'll see those who killed him pay for it. I'll see that they pay in full—*and to the inch.*"

Mary Liu's blue eyes flared for a moment; she'd grown up in a Society household before the Change, and was only twenty-eight now. He'd noticed that the younger generation took certain things very seriously, particularly those with that background. What their parents had dreamed, they lived.

"I'll rely on that promise, lord Protector," she said. Her fingers curled into claws. "If you take the Satan-worshippers alive, I'd appreciate your turning them over to *my* court for sentencing and execution rather than the Church and the Holy Office. We . . . *I* have some experts as good as any of His Holiness'."

Sandra Arminger chuckled, and Arminger laughed aloud. "That's the spirit!" he said as the crowd applauded. He rose, and caught the eye of two at the rear of the crowd: the merchants from Corvallis. A flick of the head said *later.*

"And now, dinner," he said. Sandra's fingers came down to rest on his arm, and he turned to lead her up the great curving stair.

Dun Juniper, Willamette Valley, Oregon
December 12th, 2007/Change Year 9

The girl drew carefully, using the shoulders and body as much
as the arms. The yew bow bent . . .

"Bull's-eye!" Mathilda Arminger whooped as the shaft
thumped home in the circle behind the wooden deer's shoulder.

"Not bad, Matti," Rudi Mackenzie said. "Not bad!"

It was late afternoon going on for evening, and overcast.
The sudden chill and wet mealy smell in the fir-scented air
meant snow coming soon, rolling down the heights from the
wall of mountains eastward. Rudi finished another round of
practice and then looked up and stuck out his tongue; sure
enough, the first big flakes came drifting down, landing with
a gentle bite and a somehow dusty taste. Snow was rare in the
Willamette, where winter was the season of rain and mud, but
Dun Juniper was just high enough in the foothills that it
could get heavy falls sometimes, though they rarely lay for
long. This would be a big one, by the way the air tasted and
felt.

The two children were the youngest in the crowd at the
butts; they'd both been born in the first Change Year, and
were shooting up with a long-limbed, gangly grace. Rudi was
the taller by an inch or two; the hair that spilled out from
under his flat bonnet was a brilliant gold tinted with red to her
dark auburn-brown, and his eyes somewhere between blue
and green and gray to her hazel, but otherwise their sharp
straight-featured faces were much alike as they began to shed
their puppy fat.

"Willow!" one of the assistants called to a round-faced girl
of ten. "Don't hop and squint after you shoot. It won't help."

The girl flushed as classmates snickered and giggled; she
shot again, then did the same up-and-down-in-place hop as
before, squinting with her tongue between her teeth and the
wet turf squelching under her feet. Today Chuck Barstow
Mackenzie, the Clan's Second Armsman, had dropped in to
observe. Which made everyone a little nervous despite the
fact that he lived here, even if it wasn't as momentous as it

might be at some other dun. Now he silently reached over and rapped her lightly on the head with the end of his bow; she flushed more deeply, hanging her head.

The rest of the crowd at the butts ranged from nine or so to thirteen, children of Dun Juniper's smiths, stockmen, carpenters, clerks, schoolteachers and weavers, and of the Clan's small cadre of full-time warriors. Their work was overseen by a dozen or so elder students in their later teens, walking up and down the line offering advice and helping adjust hands and stances, and four Armsmen oversaw them; archery was very much part of the Mackenzie school syllabus, and much more popular than arithmetic or geography or even herblore.

"And Otter, Finn, don't laugh at Willow," Chuck added. "She shoots better than you do most of the time. Someday you'll have to stand beside her in a fight, remember." He cocked an eye at the darkening clouds. "All right, it's time to knock off for the day anyway; everyone unstring. Carefully!" he added, keeping a close watch on the process, as did the teachers and their helpers, lest cold-stiffened fingers slip.

There were a couple of quick corrections to those doing it wrong. Rudi braced the lower tip of his bow against the top of his left foot, stepped through between the string and the riser, and pushed down against the bow with his thigh while his right hand held the upper part of the stave steady. That let him slide the string out of the grooves in the polished antler tip—carefully!—with his left hand. There were the inevitable throttled yelps and a few tears from those who'd let go too early or put their stave hands too far up, and so pinched their hands between string and wood even through their gloves, but no real accidents. Even a light child's stave could be dangerous if the wielder let it get away from them, and the tip of a grown-up's war bow would rip through flesh and bone like a spear when it slipped just wrong. That was why you always kept it pointed away from your face when stringing or unstringing, something he'd learned years ago.

"You're getting pretty good, Matti," he said.

"I always had a bow," she said. "Not just here."

"Not a bow like that, I bet," Rudi said, grinning.

"Yeah!" she said enthusiastically. "It's great. We heard

about Sam's bows, even, you know, ummm"—she didn't say *Portland*—"up north."

The longbow was one of Sam Aylward's; the First Armsman made Juniper's son a new one every Yule as he grew, and last year's was about the right weight for Mathilda. It was his bowyer's skill as much as his shooting that made him known as Aylward the Archer.

It's funny, he thought. *She learned some things up there— she can shoot pretty good. But not how to look after her own gear. Weird.*

They both wiped their bows down with hanks of shearling wool, slipped them into protective sheaths of soft, oiled leather, laced those tight-closed and slid them home in the carrying loops beside their quivers. By the time they'd put on the quiver-caps—getting wet didn't do the arrows' fletching any good—the snow was thick enough to make objects in the middle distance blurry, turning the faint light of the moon above the clouds into a ghostly glow. The thick turf of the meadow gave good footing, but the earth beneath was mucky, with a squishy, slippery feel.

Most of the mile-long benchland that held the Mackenzie clachan was invisible now from here at the eastern edge; the mountain-slope northward was just a hint of looming darkness. They could hear the little waterfall that fell down it to the pool at the base that fed Artemis Creek and turned the wheel of the gristmill, but only a hint of the white water was visible. Rudi cocked an ear at it, humming along with the deep-toned voice of the river spirit in her endless song, and enjoying the way the snow muffled other sounds: the wind in the firs, the sobbing howl of a coyote—or possibly Coyote Himself—somewhere in the great wilderness that surrounded them, creaks and snaps and rustles under the slow wet wind's heavy passage.

The teachers and their helpers chivvied everyone into order on the gravel roadway, counting twice to make sure nobody had wandered off into the woods and fields. Aoife Barstow hung a lantern on her spear and led the way; she was Uncle Chuck's fostern-daughter, a tall young woman of about twenty with dark red braids, and a figure of tremendous prestige with the younger children. She and her brothers Sanjay and Daniel had been on Lady Juniper's great raid against the Protectorate just after last Beltane, when Mathilda had been captured; Sanjay had died on a northern knight's lance point. Aoife had not only killed the knight who did it; she'd cut off his head and waved it in the faces of his comrades, shrieking and possessed by the Dark Goddess the while. Gruesomely fascinating rumor had it that she'd wanted to bring the head home pickled in cedar oil and nail it over the Hall's front door, the way warriors did in the old stories, but that Rudi's mother had talked her out of it.

Chuck mounted his horse and trotted along, quartering behind them and to either side to make sure nobody straggled.

"School's over until after Yule!" a boy named Liam shouted as they walked, which got him a round of cheers.

"I wouldn't mind school, if it were all like this," someone else said.

"Yup," Rudi said. "Even arithmetic and plants aren't so bad. It's that classwork about things before the Change. *Boring!*"

"Yeah." Liam nodded; he was several years older than Rudi, but far too young to really remember the lost world. "Presidents and atoms and rockets and all that hooey."

Chuck Barstow caught that, and reined in beside them. The other children grew a little silent, but Rudi grinned up at the middle-aged sandy-blond rider; Uncle Chuck had been as much a father to him as any man.

But Lord Bear's your real body-father, he thought, then let his mind shy away from the knowledge. He wasn't sure what he thought of that at all, and he'd only learned it for sure last year at the Horse Fair.

"What about King Arthur and Robin Hood and Niall of the Nine Hostages and Thor's trip to Jotunheim and *A Midsummer Night's Dream*?" Chuck asked.

"Oh, that's different," Rudi said confidently; there were nods of agreement from those within earshot. "That's more like real life, you know? Those are the *cool* stories. They mean something. They're not just weird names like Liam said."

For some reason Uncle Chuck gave a snort of laughter at that, and rode away shaking his head. "People that old are *weird*," Liam said.

Rudi nodded thoughtfully. Of course, there weren't all that many *really, really* old people around at all. They'd mostly all died the year he was born. Uncle Dennis was fifty-eight, and the oldest person in Dun Juniper by a decade. There were only six or seven people here older than Mom, who was forty.

Then he called out to the leader of the little column. "Aoife," he said. "Do you think all the old folks are weird? I mean, you're grown up but you're not old—not *real* old."

"Thanks!" the woman who'd turn twenty-one in a few months said.

The lantern wavered a little as she looked over her shoulder, and paused to brush snow from her plaid. "Not really, sprout," she went on. "I was . . . just a little older than you are now, at the Change. I remember riding in cars, you know? And TV and lights going on when I pushed a switch . . . sort of. We were in a school bus when the Change happened, Dan and Sanjay and me; I can remember *that*. But I'm not really sure if I'm remembering all the rest of it, or just remembering remembering or remembering what the oldsters told me."

That got a chuckle; but then he thought her face went uncertain and a little sad in the white-flecked dimness. "And it gets more that way all the time; more like remembering a dream." More cheerfully: "But they do go on about it a lot, don't they? Even Dad."

There were more nods and mutters of agreement.

"Hey, I heard that!"

Chuck's voice came out of the snow-shot darkness. Rolling eyes and sighs were the younger generation's only defense against tales of the days before the Change. There wasn't much point in talking about it among themselves.

"Let's have a song!" Rudi said instead.

That brought enthusiastic agreement; it usually would, among a group of Mackenzies. They passed a few moments arguing over what tune, which was also to be expected. At last, exasperated, Rudi simply began himself and waited for the others to join in:

> *"The greenwood sighs and shudders*
> *The westwind wails and mutters—"*

There were a few complaints, but the song matched the weather, and most of the youngsters took it up with blood-thirsty enthusiasm:

> *"Gray clouds crawl across the sky*
> *The moon hides her face as the*
> *sunlight dies!*
> *And mankind soon shall realize*
> *The Bringer of Storms walks tonight!*
>
> *No mortal dare to meet the glare*
>
> *Of the Eye of the Stormbringer*
> *For he is the lightning slinger*
> *The glory singer,*
> *The gallows reaper!"*

The road wound along between the muddy, reaped potato fields and truck gardens covered in mulch of wheat-straw and sawdust and spoiled hay; a whiff of manure came from beneath. A rime of ice was forming in the puddles along the water-furrow from the pond that watered them in the summer; they tramped on over the plank bridge, then past fenced and hedged pastures, and other fields where the stems of the winter oats bowed beneath the wet snowflakes. The stock was mostly huddled in the shelter of board sheds, and the herd-wards forked down hay for them from the stacks or walked their rounds. They had thick cloaks and jackets and knit vests and leggings, and booths to take shelter from the worst of the weather; they and hunters in the woods and unlucky travelers were the only ones who'd sleep outside walls this night.

The song wasn't one he'd have picked if he were going to be rolling in a sleeping bag beneath a tree. Not out where wolves and bears and tigers and woods-fey roamed—the fey could be friendly or unfriendly, and were usually tricksey—

and where a stranger met might be anything from an outlaw to a wood-sprite or godling in disguise.

But it was a fine tune when you were heading back to stout gates and bright fires and a good supper. Rudi filled his lungs with the wet chill air and bellowed out:

> *"Upon his shoulder, ravens*
> *His face like stone, engraven*
> *Astride a six-hoofed stygian beast*
> *He gathers the fruit of the gallows trees!*
> *Driving legions to victory*
> *The bringer of war walks tonight!"*

The kilted children poured up the sloping road to the dun in a chattering mass, eager for home and supper. It took a bit longer than usual for the wall to loom ahead of them out of the swirling white; the rough surface of the light-colored stucco was catching the snow now, obscuring the curving flower-patterns painted beneath the crenellations of the battlements. The great gates were three-quarters shut, and the snow had caught on their green-painted steel surfaces too, making little white teardrops where the patterns of copper rivets showed the Triple Moon above—waxing, full, and waning—and the wild bearded face of the Horned Man beneath.

One of the gate guards yelled down: "What were you trying to do, Chuck, feed the little twerps to the Wild Hunt? It's as dark as a yard up a hog's arse out there!"

Chuck Barstow put a hand on his hip and looked up as his horse's hooves struck sparks from the concrete and fieldstone of the square before the gate. "They're not going to catch their deaths from a wee bit of snow," he called back. "They might from missing when someone's coming at them with a blade."

The tunnel-like entrance was flanked on either side by god-posts of carved and painted wood hewn from whole Douglas fir trunks thicker than his body; the Lady as Brigid with her wheat sheaf and crown of flames on one side, and the Lord as Lugh of the Long Spear on the other. Rudi made a reverence

with palms pressed together and thumbs on his chin as he
passed, a gesture as automatic as breath, feeling the warm
comfort of their regard, like his mother's smile. Everyone else
made the gesture as well, except Mathilda and a few other
Christians, mostly the children of foreign guests. The school
room crowd broke up, waving and yelling and promising to
get up early to build snow forts on the open ground below the
north wall, where the wind usually piled deep drifts. As the
last of them passed, a dozen adults on guard duty hauled in
grunting unison, and the gates shut with a hollow boom and a
long rattling, thunking sound as the bars slid home. In the
same instant great Lambeg drums sounded from the tops of
the four towers of the gatehouse, a deep rumbling thunder;
the dunting of horns went through it, and the screech of
pipers hailing the departing Sun.

Then they were through into the familiar interior of Dun
Juniper, their hobnailed brogans crunching on the gravel
roadways. The walls enclosed a smooth oval of several acres,
originally a low plateau in the rolling benchland. Lanterns
shone from the towers along the wall, and from the windows
of the log-built homes that lined the inner surface of the fortification; their light gleamed on the carved and painted wood
of the little houses; most were done in themes from myth or
fancy, a few left defiantly plain as if to tell the neighbors *so
there*. Smoke rose from chimneys to mingle with the white
mist of the snow, as the resin scent of burning fir mixed with
the homey smells of cooking and livestock; the clachan had
six hundred souls within the walls, more than any other
Mackenzie settlement save Sutterdown.

Folk walked briskly about the final tasks of the day, from
penning the chickens to visiting the communal bathhouse.
Voices human and animal rang, and hooves, the buzz of a
woodworker's lathe, the last blows of a smith's hammer, the
hum of a treadle-driven sewing machine, the rhythmic tock ...
tock ... of an ax splitting wood.

It had all been the background of his life, as were the dogs
that came and butted their heads under his hands. The two
armed Mackenzies who unobtrusively followed weren't.

"Oh, Aoife, Dan, do you *have* to?" he asked; at least today it was friends of his. "Can't I even go pee by myself? It's like being a little kid again!"

"Yup, we do have to follow you around, sprout," Daniel said unsympathetically; he was tall and lean like his sister and only a year younger, with shaggy tow-colored hair and a mustache on his upper lip that stayed wispy despite cultivation and spells. "I've got better things to do myself, you know, and Aoife would *certainly* rather be somewhere else with someone else since she's in luuuuuuuuve *again*—"

His sister snorted and made as if to clout him with the buckler in her left hand; the movement was slow and symbolic. A real strike with a two-pound steel disk was no joke.

"—but it's Sam's orders, and Dad's, and Lady Juniper's. You and the princess here get a guard, every hour of the night and day."

Mathilda pouted a little at the title—she'd tried to insist on it when she first arrived at Dun Juniper after her capture last spring, and found that to be a mistake, like talking about the splendors of the palace in Portland or Castle Todenangst. That reminded him of how she'd arrived, and what had followed from that. His fingers rubbed at his side through his jacket, where the giant's sword had wounded him that August night. Mathilda's voice was small as she leaned close and said: "Does it still hurt?"

"Nah," he said, smiling, remembering how she'd sat by his bedside through the long days of pain, reading out loud or playing checkers or just being there. "I heal quick."

"I'm sorry, Rudi."

"Well, *you* didn't do it, Matti," he replied cheerfully.

"Eddie was always nice before . . . well, nice to me. And Mack, I thought he was just sort of big and, well, stupid. Dad just sent them to rescue me. He and Mom are scared for me. They didn't mean to hurt you."

"Mack was big and stupid," Rudi said. "And he was a bad man, Matti. He did mean to hurt me." He put an arm around her shoulders. "I know *you* didn't."

"You want to go and visit Epona?" Mathilda said hopefully.

He hesitated; Epona was the *good* thing that had happened last summer, the horse that nobody but he could ride . . . Rudi sighed. There wasn't time, and he didn't have the excuse any-more that the mare would only let him groom or feed her—she'd relaxed a bit about that.

"Oh, come on, let's go get dinner. I'm clemmed," he said instead.

The center of Dun Juniper held the larger, communal build-ings; school, bad-weather covenstead, bathhouse, armory, li-brary, stables and workshops, granaries and dairy, brew-house and storehouses. The heart of it was the great Hall. It loomed bright through the thick-falling snow, firelight and lantern light red and yellow through the windows and on the painted designs graven into the logs. The ends of the rafters that sup-ported the second-story galleries were carved into the heads of the Mackenzie totems, Wolf and Bear, Dragon and Tiger and Raven and more; their grinning mouths held chains that ended in lanterns of wrought brass and iron and glass. The high-peaked roof of moss-grown shingles reared above like the back of a green, scaly dragon, and the rafters at each end of it crossed like an X, carved into facing spirals, deasil and widdershins to balance the energies. The two children and their escorts paused on the veranda to stamp and kick the mud and sticky wet snow off their brogans and brush it off their plaids and jackets and caps.

Through the big double doors, and into a blast of light and sound, warmth and smells; woodsmoke, damp wool clothes dry-ing, leather, meat and cabbage cooking, fir and polish and soap, bright paint and carving seeming to move on the walls. The great stone hearth across the room on the north face of the Hall was booming and roaring, and a group around it were laughing and finishing a song as they threw in chunks of timber:

"Oak logs will warm you well, that are old and dry;
Logs of pine will sweetly smell, but the sparks will fly;
Surely you will find
There's none compare with the hardwood logs
That are cut in winter-time, sir!
Holly logs will burn like wax—you can burn them green
Elm logs burn like smoldering flax, with no flames to be seen
Beech logs for wintertime, and Yule logs as well, sir—"

He genuflected to the altar on the mantel and signed the air with the Horns for the Hall's tutelary guardians, and his body-guards did the same. The long tables were up as well, set in a T this day with the upper bar on the dais at the east end of the Hall, and people were bustling in and out of the doors on either side of the fireplace that led to the kitchens. The western end of the Hall held the great Yule Tree, not yet decorated, but fragrant with promise and Douglas fir sap. Rudi waved to friends as he took off his coat and flat Scots bonnet and plaid, hanging them on pegs; by now Mathilda attracted fewer glares and more smiles than she had right after he got hurt, but she was still a little subdued and stuck close to him. Few dared to be unfriendly when he was around, or when his mother was watching.

One of the glares was unfortunately from Aunt Judy, who hadn't forgotten how her fostern-son Sanjay died last summer.

Well, neither have I, Rudi thought. Everyone had liked Sanjay, who was smart and funny and brave. *But it wasn't Matti's fault! And that was a whole* year *ago, or nearly! Aoife and Dan aren't mean to her! And Uncle Chuck doesn't look at her like that either.*

They hung up their bows and quivers and knives in the children's section. Rudi sighed as he watched Dan and Aoife stow their weapons with those of the other grown warriors. Short-swords and dirks and bucklers swung on their belts from oak pegs; spears were racked in gleaming rows with their bright, rune-graven heads high. In pride of place were the great six-foot war bows of orange-hued yew, the terror of the Clan's enemies and the guardians of Mackenzie freedom and honor, each flanked by its well-filled quiver of shafts fletched with the gray goose feathers.

He knew that the time to wield one would come for him, just as his voice would break someday and he'd start being interested in girls as more than friends. But while that was just knowledge without much impact, the yearning for a war bow of his own was a burning need.

Lady of the Ravens, please don't make me wait forever! he thought.

There was some foreign gear there as well, from Lord Bear's territories on the western side of the Willamette Valley; long basket-hilted backswords and short, thick recurve horseman's bows hung up in harp-shaped saddle scabbards. Rudi looked up at the top table; yes, a big, blond young man in his late twenties and a woman a little younger, brown-skinned and frizzy-haired. There were others at the lower tables who must be their escorts, all in pants, and jackets with the red bear's head on the shoulder.

"Hi, Unc' Eric, Auntie Luanne!" he called to the pair, and they waved back over the gathering crowd.

His mother was talking with the Bearkiller couple when he hopped up on the dais and walked over to make his respects and greet her. She stopped to give him a grin and a hug, then pulled back a little.

"Well, it's sopping you are, *mo chroí*!" she said, green eyes twinkling.

"Just a little snow, Mom," he replied. He saw Mathilda out of the corner of his eye, a plaintive look on her face, and whispered in his mother's ear.

"And would you like a bit of a hug too, my fostern girl?" Juniper Mackenzie said.

"Ummm . . . yeah. Thanks."

She got one, and a kiss on the forehead; the Lady of the Mackenzies ruffled both their heads before she sent them off to their end of the high table. Nigel Loring was there at his mother's right hand; he nodded solemnly to Rudi as he passed, then winked. Rudi grinned back at the English guest; besides saving his life last year, and becoming his main tutor in the sword and horsemanship, Sir Nigel was just plain fun. He knew a lot of stories, too.

Those Hall-dwellers on kitchen duty brought out bowls and platters and set them out, then sat themselves. Most families in Dun Juniper had their own hearths, but there were always a fair number eating in the Hall, besides the Barstows, Trethars and others who lived there; guests like the Bearkillers, or people from elsewhere in the Clan's territories come to learn craft skills or to share the holy mysteries or do a hundred types of business. Even a wandering gangrel could find a meal in the Chief's Hall in return for a little wood-chopping or other chores; after all, any such could be the Lord or Lady in disguise. Though it was hard to believe a lot of the time, since they were always smelly and often mad.

"We start to decorate the tree tomorrow," Rudi said. "Nine more days of the Twelve, and then it's Yule."

"Christmas," Mathilda said, nodding. "But the twelve days come *after* Christmas."

Rudi grinned; he liked explaining things, and the grown-ups had been really careful not to say anything at all against Mathilda's religion, or even tell her much about the Craft. That didn't apply to him, of course; it was one of the few advantages of being a kid.

"No, this is *Yule,* Matti. That's the shortest day, the twenty-first this year. On the First Day we go out and find the tree and cut it, on the Second Day we bring it here, and Third Day we put it up; for the Maiden, the Mother and the Crone, you know? And the Tree is the Holly King's . . . well, you know. Then we've got nine days for the rest, cooking and making presents and getting ready for the Solstice Vigil. Mom says we stole the Twelve Days and changed them round 'cause the Christians stole Yule and messed it up."

"We did not!" Mathilda said, then hesitated. "At least, I don't think so. What do you decorate it with?"

"Oh, all sorts of things. Old-time stuff, and strings of popcorn, and little carved sprites, and, oh, lots of stuff. It's fun."

"We didn't decorate our own Christmas tree at home, but it was very pretty," Mathilda said. "We always had Christmas at Castle Todenangst. I'd come down in the morning, and open the presents with Mom and Dad."

Rudi frowned. "But decorating it yourself is half the fun!"

They loaded their plates from the platters and baskets as they spoke: corned beef, chunks of grilled venison with a sauce of garlic-laced yogurt, mashed potatoes with bits of onion, fresh steamed kale, boiled cabbage and glazed carrots and fresh brown bread and hot cheddar biscuits and butter. Mathilda slipped a sliver of the beef to a big black tomcat crouched under her chair; he bolted it and then went back to glaring around with mad yellow eyes. Saladin had come as part of the ill-fated diplomatic mission from Portland last Lughnasadh, and the other Hall cats hadn't accepted him yet . . . or vice versa.

Juniper Mackenzie stood, and the hum of conversation stilled. She raised both her hands in the gesture of power and blessing before she spoke, her strong soprano filling the Hall, half song and half chant:

> *"Harvest Lord who dies for the ripened grain—*
> *Corn Mother who births the fertile field—*
> *Blesséd be those who share this bounty;*
> *And blessed the mortals who toiled with You*
> *Their hands helping Earth to bring forth life."*

Most of the crowd joined in the final *Blesséd be;* then they waited politely while the Christians said their grace. The two Bearkillers at the top table crossed themselves and murmured words: *Bless us, O Lord . . .* So did Mathilda, in another fashion—Catholics who followed Abbot-Bishop Dmwoski at Mount Angel used a slightly different rite from the Orthodox Catholic Church of the Protectorate's Pope Leo.

Juniper went on: "And special thanks to Andy and Diana and everyone working the kitchens, who managed to produce what looks like a great dinner right in the middle of preparing for the Yule feast."

The Trethars stood and bowed as everyone clapped. Rudi's mother took from its rest a silver-rimmed horn of wine—that had started its life as one of a pair of longhorns over a Western-themed bar in Bend—and poured a small libation in a bowl. Then she raised the horn high over her head and cried:

"To the Lord, to the Lady, to the Luck of the Clan— *Wassail!*"

"Drink hail!" fifty voices replied, raising their cups and drinking with her.

Rudi dutifully sipped at a tiny glass of mead, watered for a youngster's strength; he preferred the cream-rich milk in the waiting jug, but the proprieties had to be observed. The hum of conversation began again, along with the clatter of cutlery.

Rudi poured himself milk and a glass for Mathilda, spread his napkin on his lap and ate with the thoughtless, innocent greed of a healthy nine-year-old after a day's hard work in cold weather and with a holiday in prospect.

"Blueberry tarts for dessert!" he said happily. "With whipped cream and honey."

"So that's Arminger's kid," Luanne Larsson said, meditatively mixing some melted butter into her mashed potatoes with her fork as she glanced down the table; one advantage of the white noise that filled the Hall was that conversations could be private, if you spoke softly and leaned a little close.

"No," Juniper Mackenzie said, using a spoon to put some horseradish beside her corned beef.

She did it cautiously; the crock was a gift from Sam's wife, and though nuclear weapons didn't work post-Change, Melissa Aylward's horseradish sauce was an acceptable substitute.

"No," she went on. "She's Mathilda, a girl whose parents are Norman and Sandra Arminger, through no fault of her own, so. And who for the now lives with me and my son."

Eric Larsson grinned in his dense, short-cropped yellow beard and raised a glass of red wine in salute. He was a broad-shouldered, long-limbed man who stood two inches over six feet; his features were sharply cut on a long, narrow head, eyes a bright blue, golden hair falling to his shoulders beneath a headband of leather tooled and stamped. The face it framed was a Viking skipper's born out of time and place, down to the kink a sword had put in his nose and thin white scars that made him look a little older than his twenty-eight years.

"Gotcha, honey," he said to his wife. "It's touchdown to Juney, point and match."

"OK, enough with the mixed metaphors," Luanne said. "OK, OK, I get it. No sins of the fathers and all that."

"And she's . . . what's the word, Juney?" Eric replied.

"My fostern," Juniper supplied. *He's grown into himself,* she thought to herself.

She'd met Eric Larsson in the fall of the first Change Year, and known him fairly well since as he developed into Mike Havel's right-hand man as well as just his brother-in-law.

Back then he was eighteen and just trying on a man's life, like someone with a new coat that's a little too big for him. Now he's like a big golden cat—good company to his friends, and very dangerous to something he decides might be good to eat. Vain as a cat, too, though with reason. And more at home in the Changed world than we who were full-grown can ever be, though not so much as his children will be.

He also added flamboyant touches to the long jacket and pants most Bearkillers wore: embroidered cuffs on a coat left open to show more embroidery on his linen shirt and neckerchief, a gold hoop earring, silver buttons on his jacket worked into wolf heads, rings on the fingers of his large but curiously graceful hands.

"Arminger's still going to come at us," Eric said. "Kid or no kid."

"Sure, and you're right about that," Juniper said. "He's a bastard of a man with the soul of a mad weasel, and no mistake. And that was obvious even before the Change."

The two Bearkillers looked at her. "You knew him then?" Eric said in astonishment.

"No, but I knew *of* him. Under his Society name—Blackthorn of Malmsey—so it was years after the Change before I realized who it was; I haven't *seen* him since, and knew nothing of him beyond his Society persona, you see. He was the one who brought an ox to a tournament. *That* I had from an eyewitness."

"He brought an *ox*? He's into bestiality, on top of everything else?" Eric laughed.

"Not as a date," Juniper said in quelling tones. "He had a taste for sweet young things even then. No, he wanted to demonstrate how out of touch with reality the Society fighters were, bashing each other with rattan blades and relying on the honor system."

She grinned and quoted: *"Come back here, you coward, and I'll* bite *you to death!"* At their blank looks she went on: "Classical reference. Anyway, he killed the ox with a real sword, the same one he carries now. With one blow, actually; it was supposedly impressive, in a sick sort of way."

Nigel Loring raised his brows; he knew how difficult it was to kill a large animal that quickly. "What did they do with the ox? The Society chappies, that is."

"Grilled it whole and ate it, but the other Society—the Humane Society—got on his case."

Luanne snorted laughter, and then returned to business. "Arminger knows you won't hurt his daughter, no matter what he does. And I'm not sure he'd care if you did. Not enough to stop him, anyway."

"Oh, I think he cares for the girl," Juniper said. "She wouldn't have been as . . . healthy as she was, otherwise. Even a bad man often loves his children, and he's invested a good deal of his ego in having one of his blood follow him, to be sure."

The scowl left Luanne's face, on which a smile looked more natural. She was a year or two younger than her husband, her skin coffee-dark, blunt features a comely full-lipped mélange of her Texan father's African-Anglo heritage and her Tejano mother's mestizo blood. Faded and dusky blue, a small scar between her brows marked her as one of the Brotherhood, the A-listers of the Bearkiller Outfit; her husband had an identical brand from the same red-hot iron. Mauve silk ribbons fluttered along the outer seams of her jacket, making her a little careful when she reached across one of the laden platters.

"It's just hard not to see Arminger, looking at his kid," she went on a little defensively.

"Well, it's important that we don't see only that," Juniper said, pouring her more dark, frothy beer from a pitcher. "Since the Lord and Lady saw fit to put her in our hands . . . wait a moment."

She thought, looking inside herself, and then she sighed. "There's something I should have done some time ago, but I hoped it wouldn't be necessary to get formal about it. I hate throwing my weight around . . . oh, well, if it has to be done, it has to be done."

She sighed again, then rose to her feet and waited until the buzz of conversation died. A little way to her left Chuck Barstow was looking at her quizzically; beside him was his wife Judy, with dawning understanding in her dark eyes and handsome proud-nosed face. They'd been friends since they were teenagers, and they'd discovered the Craft together.

Of course she'd know, Juniper thought. *Well, my old friend, that's why I'm doing it, you being so stubborn and all, and others taking their cue from you.*

Aloud, she said: "You all know we've had a guest among us, a girl by the name of Mathilda."

Rudi was staring at her, delight in his dancing blue-green eyes. Mathilda was too, puzzled and a little apprehensive.

"Mathilda was captured through no fault of her own, in fighting against her folk that we of the Clan took on ourselves for reasons we thought good, and still do. And later her folk tried to take her back, and in that fight some were killed, and some were hurt—my own son Rudi among them. Now, some here have held that against her, and I was waiting for that to vanish through its own lack of sense and unkindliness, but it hasn't altogether. And that diminishes my honor, and the honor of Clan Mackenzie. So here and now, I say that while this girl is with us, she is *fostern* of mine, and is to be treated as if she were a child of my blood, necessary precautions aside, until I unsay this word, or she leaves us and so breaks it."

Juniper took a deep breath, and raised her hands in the V of power, palms out, closing her eyes and feeling the current of it running through her, like a fire in the blood until the little hairs along her arms and up her spine struggled to rise. When her green gaze flared open again her voice rolled high and clear through the great space of the Hall, linking her to every soul like chains of fine silver light:

"And this I bind on every man and woman and child of this Clan, and I make it geasa *to break it. I bind you all, by the Dagda and Angus Og and Lugh of the Long Spear; by Macha and Edain and the Threefold Morrigú; by the Maiden, the Mother and the Hag, and if any break it by word or deed may the Mother's Earth open and swallow you . . . the Mother's*

*ocean rise up and drown you . . . and the heaven of stars which
are the dust of Her feet fall and crush you and all that is yours.
This is my geasa, which I, Juniper Mackenzie, Her priestess,
and Chief of the Clan by the Clan's choice, lay upon you! So
mote it be!"*

An echoing silence fell, and lasted until she put her hands
on her hips and spoke in a normal tone: "And that is that!"

She sat again and drank, conscious of eyes rolling white as
they looked at her, and mouths gaping. It took a moment for
the others to follow suit, but when the roar of conversation
started up it was louder than ever.

"Whoa," Luanne said quietly.

Her husband had blanched and was clutching at a crucifix
beneath his shirt; sweat darkened the fine linen a little, and
gleamed on his forehead.

"Remind me never to piss you off that much, Juney!"

"I doubt you'll ever do it, so," Juniper said. "Now, where
were we? Ah, yes, Mathilda, and her being Arminger's only
heir."

"Ah," Luanne said. "Yes, we've talked that over a bit at
Larsdalen, with Signe and Mike and Eric's dad and my folks."

"And what did Ken have to say about it? And Will?" Juniper asked; she had a lively respect for Kenneth Larsson's
brains, and for those of Luanne's father.

"That we shouldn't build too much on the foundation of
one little girl," Eric said. Then, elaborately casual: "You know,
this dried-tomato-and-onion thing in vinegar is *good.*"

"Ken has a good heart," Juniper said. *Although he and Will
have the advantage of being a ruler's advisors, not the ruler
himself.* "And a keen mind."

"Yup," Eric Larsson said, obviously glad to change the subject for a moment. "But Dad's also got a mind full of weird
shit. The latest—" He rolled his eyes.

"What is it?" Juniper asked with interest.

Kenneth Larsson had been in his fifties before the Change,
an engineer by training and an industrialist on a large scale
by avocation; both had proved surprisingly useful since. Mike
Havel did ordinary civil administration when he had to, but
he hated it and was self-confessedly not very good at it, ei-

ther. On the other hand, Ken was also given to what he called
long-term thinking and others dubbed eccentricity. In someone of lower rank, the word *cracked* would probably have
been used.

"Asteroids," Luanne said. "He's worrying about *asteroids*."

Juniper looked at her as blankly as the younger couple had
at the reference to *Monty Python and the Holy Grail*. Eric and
his wife both laughed, and he took up the tale.

"You know how an asteroid was supposed to have killed off
the dinosaurs?"

Juniper frowned. It had been so long . . .

"I think I read about it in a *National Geographic* once.
Wouldn't it be better to worry about Mount Saint Helens
blowing up? It started smoking again a few years ago, after all.
Does Ken have some reason to believe we'll be hit by a big
rock from above?"

Eric's grin grew wider. "No, but he says we're overdue for
one, give or take a few million years. He gets worried about it
because there's nothing we could do about it now."

Juniper blinked. *Even for Ken, that's a bit eccentric.* "Well,
what could we have done about it before the Change?"

Luanne crossed herself and put her hands together in the
gesture of prayer, before giggling. She was pious in her way,
but not too solemn about it.

"I know every coven in the world would have been on the
hilltops, spellcasting to beat the band," Juniper said. "But
apart from that . . ."

"Dad says they could at least have detected it," Eric explained. "And possibly have launched, ah, nuclear-tipped
missiles"—he spoke the phrase as if he was repeating it ver-
batim, almost from another language—"or something. With
another few decades or generations of technical progress, in-
tercepting 'em would have been easy, he says. But now that's
impossible."

Luanne giggled again. "Oh, I dunno. We could build some
really big catapults on top of really tall towers. Or we could
build, oh, some gigantic hot-air balloons and mount the catapults on top of them and float them up—"

"God, did Dad get furious when she sprang that one on

him," Eric chuckled. "On the one hand, I sympathize. On the other, it was sort of funny."

And here we have a whole slew of generational gaps, Juniper thought. *Not to mention social ones.*

Eric had been eighteen when the old world ended; and a rich man's son, attending high-priced private schools, interested in the sciences when he wasn't playing football or chasing girls or drinking beer with his friends and being resentfully angry at his father in the usual testosterone-poisoned head-butting of male adolescence.

But a third of his life—everything beyond that last tag end of childhood—had been spent in the Changed world. That was where he'd become a man and a lord of men, a husband and a father, not to mention a warrior of fearsome repute. Things like rockets, asteroids and nuclear weapons were real to him, in a detached and intellectual fashion, instead of not-particularly-interesting myths the way they were to those a bit younger, but they didn't really *matter.* Not the way a horse with splints did, or an attack of brucellosis in the cattle, or getting a good clear shot at a deer with his bow, or how well a line of pikemen kept alignment while advancing over rough ground. Luanne had the same detachment, only more so; she was a bit younger, and she'd been brought up deep-country-rural on her family's Texas horse ranch or traveling around the country to deliver stock. To both of them it was natural to exist in this world, where the Willamette Valley and a few days' travel about it were all that really counted.

The thought ran through her mind in an instant; she turned and met Nigel Loring's eyes, and knew that the thought was shared.

"We adapted," he murmured. Unspoken was: *Those who couldn't are dead.* "But never completely."

"No, never completely," she replied in the same undertone. "Although *déan crónán cupla barraí agus cuirfidh mé bréagri-ocht air . . .*"

His involuntary chuckle helped her shake the gloom off; in Erse, she'd just said *if you hum a few bars, I can fake it.* Looking into his eyes, she knew she'd lifted his mood as well, and that was a pleasure in itself.

Glancing around her Hall, she made it come real again with a mental effort. The younger Larssons had finished chuckling over their own joke.

"Well, whatever or Whoever caused the Change, I doubt they did it so we would be done in by celestial debris," Juniper said.

"They could certainly have finished us off without doing anything so elaborate," Nigel confirmed.

"Moving back to practicalities, what did your father say about our . . . guest, Luanne?" Juniper asked.

Will Hutton was at least as intelligent as Kenneth Larsson; he had much less formal education, but he made up for it with a good deal more focus.

"Pretty much the same thing as my honorable father-in-law, for once," Luanne said. "Not to sweat it, basically. And believe me, after Reuben got killed by the Protector's men last year"—that was her foster-brother, adopted after the Change—"Dad was as angry at Arminger as anyone."

"I don't know precisely what we can make of Matti's being here. Still, the Lord and Lady wouldn't send us an opportunity if there weren't some way to use it."

She reached for the horn again. The wine was made by Tom Brannigan over in Sutterdown, the Clan Mackenzie's only real town, farther west in the Valley; Tom owned a vineyard, and was a brewmaster and vintner besides being mayor and High Priest of the coven there. The drink had a pleasant scent like cherries and violets, and a smooth, earthy taste just tart enough to accompany the rich savor of the grilled venison. There was an art to drinking from a horn without spilling half the contents on your face, as well.

"But," she went on, after she'd rolled a sip around her mouth, "do consider what happens if he doesn't manage to beat us. Say that *we* beat *him*. Are we going to destroy the Portland Protective Association utterly, root and branch?"

"Nope," Luanne said. "Signe and Mike've thought about that. Even if we beat them in the field, we could only wreck ourselves trying to dig 'em out. Too many of those damn castles; too many knights and men-at-arms. And it's just too damned *big*. Portland rules more people than there are in all the rest of the northwest outfits put together."

From her other side Sir Nigel Loring nodded and spoke. "And while the man is a tyrant of tyrants, I saw last year that his obsession with feudalism means that you can't destroy that kingdom of his by chopping off the head. It's decentralized, and he built that into its bones. If it split up, the parts would be nearly as troublesome."

"Yeah," Luanne said. "Plus the way he recruited his lords. All those gangers; and the Society types who stuck with him may have been the roughnecks, but they're tough ones, not to mention the men who've worked their way up out of the ruck. Now they all have families and want to keep what they've gained for their children. Winkling every one of them out of his manor . . ."

"And there are limits to what we can do by encouraging the common folk to snipe at his barons," Juniper said regretfully. "Especially now that things there have had a chance to settle down. I have hopes for that, sure, and contacts there—but the farmers can't hope to rise up against his new-made knights unless they have more help than it seems likely we can offer. We have a network of informants and sympathizers there, but I can't ask them to take up arms if all it gets them is dead, so."

"Guns are great equalizers," Loring agreed. "Guerilla warfare isn't impossible without firearms and explosives, but it's . . . much harder to pull off."

"Not as many force multipliers, Mike says," Eric added. "Plus it's harder and takes longer to learn to use the weapons we've got."

"So," Juniper said. "Let's be optimistic. Say that Norman and Sandra Arminger are sent off to the Summerlands to make accounting for what they've done and select an appropriate reincarnation."

"I'd prefer a nice, fiery, eternal hell for 'em, Juney," Eric said, more than a trace of grimness in his voice.

"I confess the thought is tempting but that's not my mythos. So then, hypothetically speaking, they're off to choose their reward or punishment . . ."

They all shot a glance at Mathilda; she was laughing, with a forkful of beets halfway to her mouth, as one of the other children told a story; Chuck and Judy's Tamsin, born three years before the Change.

"I don't think they'll wait ten years, and then take back a Princess Mathilda who's a Mackenzie in all but name to rule them," Loring said. "The thought is tempting, my dear, but I fear it's not likely."

"Not exactly that, no," Juniper said. "And trying to deliberately shape her outright, that would be . . . futile, as well as unkind. She's a proud little thing, and no fool—I've known her for half a year, which is quite a while for a child that age. Best to just . . . leave her be, and treat her like any other, and wait to see what opportunity offers."

CHAPTER TWO

Portland, Oregon
December 12th, 2007/Change Year 9

The presence room had been built for intimate conferences when the library was remodeled into the Lord Protector's city palace. It was small and comfortable, with a new fireplace flickering, Oriental rugs glowing on the floor, and walls lined with well-filled bookshelves and good pictures—mostly old masters, including a couple of Maxfield Parrish originals scavenged from as far away as the ruins of San Francisco, plus a fine modern carving of *Christ Crucified* done half life-size. Rain beat against the night-dark windows, but within was warmth and the light of gasoline lanterns; those were a rarity these days, but brighter than the natural oils or alcohol that were the alternative. The maids in their uniforms—a white tabard over a black t-tunic and a long, loose undertunic down to the ankles, and silver-chain collars around their necks—set out trays of small pastries with the unthinkable luxury of real coffee as well, in a Sevres pot suspended over a spirit lantern on the mahogany table.

"Leave us," Arminger said, leaning back in the leather-upholstered chair.

They bobbed curtseys and scuttled out. The guards followed at his nod, with a stamp of boots and crash of metal.

Arminger grinned to himself as he watched the two Corvallans, a tall, horse-faced blond woman and a short, thickset brunet man, twitch their noses at the scent from the coffeepot.

Master Turner was a fixer and backer of budding enterprises, a sort of neo-medieval equivalent of a venture capitalist and the closest thing Corvallis had to a banker; closer every year as trade and handicraft flourished. Mistress Kowalski had made handlooms and spinning wheels before the Change for the handicraft market and still did—in a large workshop with dozens of employees—renting the equipment out to poor families, supplying the raw materials, and taking payment in thread and cloth. In Europe in the old days they'd called it the *putting-out system;* evidently she'd reinvented it on her own initiative. The two had joint interests in flocks of sheep out on shares with farmers, and in mills for breaking flax and finishing cloth.

Both had influence in the city's Faculty Senate through their clients and debtors, and through business connections with other budding magnates. Those still called their get-together and steering committee the Faculty of Economics, but it might as well have been the Guild Merchant.

"You've met Conrad Renfrew?" Arminger said to the two visitors from the city-state. "Grand Constable of the Portland Protective Association, Count of Odell, and Marchwarden of the East, as well."

They murmured *my lord Count* together. "Mistress Kowalski, Master Turner," the Constable replied in a voice like gravel and sand shaken together in a bucket.

Kowalski frowned suddenly, and looked at Arminger's commander more closely: "Lord Count, didn't we meet before the Change? At a tournament . . . Was Renfrew your Society name?"

The Grand Constable was a thickset man built like a barrel, with a shaved head and bright blue eyes in the midst of a face hideously scarred. The two from Corvallis looked at him a little uneasily, but they didn't show much fear despite his reputation. Arminger nodded to himself; they'd be useless to him if they did. Although if they were going to be afraid of anyone in the room it ought to be *him,* with Sandra a close second.

"No it wasn't, Mistress Kowalski," Renfrew rumbled. "Yes, I think I remember the occasion. But I've put all that behind me. The time for playing at things is past. We don't have the luxury of make-believe anymore."

Arminger cut in; pre-Change connections in the Society could be a sore issue these days, considering how badly its survivors had split between his followers and the rest. Not to mention that if he remembered correctly that particular tournament had been the Day of the Ox, about which memory he had mixed emotions himself.

"You know Lady Sandra, of course."

She gave each of them a nod as she sat, adjusting the skirts of her cotte-hardi and smoothing back her headdress. Both were in fabrics rich but subdued, in shades of dove gray and off-white, the jewels silver and diamond with a few opals.

"And this is Father McKinley."

McKinley was a lean young man in his early twenties in a coarse black Dominican robe with a steel crucifix and rosary at his belt. He also had a quill pen and blank paper, and took unobtrusive notes; the priest-monk was Pope Leo's man, of course, but he and the Holy Office of the Inquisition also reported directly to the Lord Protector.

It was best to remember that Leo's Dominicans took their nickname—the *Domini Canes,* the Hounds of God—quite seriously.

Sandra poured coffee with a smile of gracious hospitality. "Sugar? Cream?" she asked.

Arminger added a small dollop of brandy to his; it was the genuine product of Eauze, the crop of 1988, and aged in black oak, recovered from a warehouse in desolate Seattle by his salvagers in '05. From what he'd learned from the Englishmen who'd arrived last spring, and the crew of the Tasmanian ship that brought them, there wouldn't be any more even if traders crossed the waters again. France was a howling wilderness, without even the tiny band of survivors that King Charles the Mad and his junta of Guards colonels had brought through in the British Isles. The English and Irish would resettle France in due course and prune the abandoned vines, but he doubted they'd ever rival the French as vintners and distillers.

"There's more coffee where that came from; it's fresh-roasted bean imported by sea, not pre-Change leftovers," he went on. *And our own brandy's passable, and will get better as we master the knack. In the meantime . . .*

He poured small glasses of the amber liquor. "Do have some of this as well. Genuine Armagnac, Larressingle, nearly twenty years old and quite marvelous."

Carefully he did not sneer at the way the pair's ears pricked in trader's reflex when he mentioned the coffee. There was no more point in despising a merchant for being a merchant than a dog for being a dog.

Not that you don't kick a dog if it gets out of place, he thought. *How did the poem go? Ah, yes, something like:*

> *Gold for the merchant, silver for the maid;*
> *Copper for the craftsmen, cunning at their trade.*
> *Good! Laughed the baron, sitting in his hall;*
> *But iron—cold iron—shall be master of them all!*

"The coffee's from Hawaii," he amplified. "Kona Gold, and none better in all the world."

"Hawaii survived?" Turner said in amazement. Then, hastily: "Lord Protector."

"Not Oahu, that was toast, but the Big Island did; not too many people, a lot of farms and ranches, and they didn't get too chaotic so they made the best of what they had. And Ni'ihau."

Or so those Tasmanians told me, he thought. *I suspect their folk at home will be a bit peeved with me when they find out what happened to the* Pride of St. Helens; *and they and the Kiwis on South Island came through amazingly well. It's a good thing they haven't anything I want to trade for.*

Those Antipodean islands were among the few places where there hadn't been a collapse or mass dieback in the aftermath of the Change; he supposed it was having scores of sheep per person, and *not* having any unmanageably large cities.

Taking the ship was a just payment for them bringing the Lorings and their pet gorilla to Oregon, and the trouble they caused me.

"And the Hawaiians are ready to trade sugar and coffee and

citrus fruit and macadamias for . . . oh, any number of things. Wheat and wine, for instance. Dried fruit. And timber; they don't have much suitable for shipbuilding themselves. Smoked fish too, perhaps . . . but all that would be more your line of work than mine. We rulers keep things stable and safe for the traders and makers."

Or the smart ones do, he thought. *Some of my new-made nobility apparently can't grasp the parable of the goose that laid the golden eggs.*

He had the Tasmanian ship, the *Pride of St. Helens,* safely docked at Astoria, and he was training his own crew from fishermen and surviving yachtsmen. There were still enough people who remembered coffee fondly for it to be a valuable trade. The two merchants looked at each other; Corvallis had its own outlet on the sea at Newport, and a railroad and highway link across the Coast Range that the city-state had kept up. They were probably wondering if they could find a hull big enough for a Pacific voyage themselves.

"Salvage goods?" Turner asked hopefully. "Since there weren't any large cities on the Big Island."

"No, I don't think so. They have enough sailing craft of their own to mine the ruins of Honolulu and that had all the usual assets." Arminger stopped to consider. "On second thought, there might possibly be a few things; medical supplies, perhaps. Definitely cloth. It's getting hard to find any pre-Change cloth in useful condition here, and it would rot faster down there in the tropics."

"*That's* the sort of thing we should be exploring," Kowalski said. "Instead of wasting our slender substance on fighting each other."

"My sentiments exactly." Arminger beamed.

Everyone nodded and murmured agreement. Arminger grinned like a shark behind his smoothly noncommittal face. He'd spent the previous decade snapping up every surviving community too weak to stand him off, and claiming all the intervening wilderness.

Perhaps I was a little too enthusiastic reducing the surplus population back in the first Change Year, he thought. *More labor would be very handy now, and dead bones are useful only for glue and fertilizer. On the other hand, I needed to ride the wave of chaos.*

"Did you have anything more concrete to discuss, my lord?" Turner said.

"Oh, very much so," Arminger said. "As you know, I've been having ... difficulties ... with the cultists and bandits that lie between Portland and Corvallis. Why, they've even kidnapped my daughter!"

"Terrible," Kowalski said; she even seemed sincere. "I have children of my own, and I can imagine how you feel, my lord Protector, Lady Sandra. Those people been very uncooperative with us, as well."

Sandra smiled, very slightly, under an ironically crooked eyebrow. She'd found out the way the Mackenzies had forced the pair into something like a fair deal for mill work—waterpowered machinery to full and scutch and slub wool and flax—and markets for Mackenzie produce in their territory. The Clan and the Bearkillers had also gotten together to preserve the bridges in Salem, the old state capital, which gave a route across the Willamette that wasn't controlled by Corvallis.

"Ah ... my lord ... you do understand that there are plenty of people in Corvallis who feel that having, ah, buffers between us is a good idea. Particularly people on the Agriculture and Engineering Faculties."

"But of course," Arminger said.

That translated as *the farmers* and *the craftsmen,* more or less. Oregon State University had been the core that organized survival in the little city, and its Faculty Senate still governed the place—as much as anyone did. Everyone there affiliated with the Faculty closest to their daily occupation, though the town had gone to great lengths to keep the teaching functions active as well.

"Still," the lord of Portland went on, "I'm sure you can see that disunity—and especially the anarchy that bandit gangs like the Bearkillers and the so-called Clan Mackenzie spread—are bad for everyone. We're all Americans, after all! The Association has been the main core of survival and order on the West Coast—the only large one between Baja and

Alaska. Its expansion throughout the central and southern Willamette could only benefit everyone, and then it would soon include the Bend country as well."

He smiled slightly at their hunted expressions; that was more than they'd bargained for. And while they were influential in Corvallis, they didn't rule it. A rumor that they'd sold the city out to him would be disastrous for their reputations.

His wife took up the tale: "But of course the Association is a decentralized organization. We've incorporated a number of independent communities through agreements with their own leadership."

Which translates as made deals with *and* gave titles to *local warlords and strongmen, my love,* Arminger thought.

She went on: "We realize that Corvallis has developed its own system, and a very successful one too. We don't want to incorporate the city directly, or even the lands it holds beyond the city walls."

"You don't?" Kowalski blurted in surprise. Turner glared at her and made a placating gesture to his hosts.

"Not directly," the Grand Constable said. "No fiefs, no castles, no bond-tenants. Besides, frankly, your militia is too well equipped and too numerous for us to be comfortable about fighting it head-on. Not while the Free Cities League in the Yakima is hostile, and we have the Pendleton area to pacify."

"Plus," Arminger said, "and quite commendably, you in Corvallis came through the bad years with much less damage than most areas. That means, however, that, ummm, the old habits of mind are still entrenched in your city's territories. It would be difficult to introduce new ones as we did up here during the chaos."

He made a spare gesture with one long-fingered hand. "As you know, I've drawn a good many precedents from my pre-Change studies in medieval European history; they suit our times, and they've generally worked well. Let me explain another medieval idea, the concept of the autonomous, self-governing chartered *free city;* that was a way of accommodating urban life within a rural world. You'd have a, as it were, constitution, guaranteed by the Association, confirming your autonomy and your own laws, but—"

*   *   *

When the Corvallans had left, Renfrew poured himself more of the brandy. The three of them lifted glasses in salute.

"Do you think they'll buy it?" the commander of Portland's armies said.

"Why not, Conrad?" Sandra replied, nibbling a flaky pastry centered on hazelnuts and honey and sweetened cream. "We actually mean it, for a wonder, this once."

"More or less," Arminger said. "More or less."

A maid came in to clear the table; she smiled at their laughter, glad to find the overlords in so merry a mood.

Larsdalen, Willamette Valley, Oregon
December 12th, 2007/Change Year 9

"Hold them!" Michael Havel shouted. "Hold them!"

The long pikes bristled out, a sixteen-foot barrier in front of the line. Horses reared and bugled as the charge stalled before that hedgehog menace, giant shapes in the gray misty light of the winter afternoon. Breath snorted white into the fog from the great red pits of the destriers' nostrils, and eyes rolled wild in the faces concealed by the spiked steel chamfrons. Mud flew from under their hooves, and squelched beneath the infantry's boots. Pikes stabbed for the horses' unprotected bellies; the peytrals of their barding only shielded the chests. There was a hard, sharp crack as a hoof shattered the ashwood haft of a pike, and curses as splinters flew and the foot-long spearhead pinwheeled away. Clods of earth flew into the air; riders leaned far over in the saddles, hacking at the points or thrusting with the lance. Wet, oiled chain mail gleamed with a liquid ripple.

"Now forward!" Havel shouted, when he saw that the charge was thoroughly stalled, and the lancers at their most vulnerable, tangled and unable to maneuver. "Push of pike! *Hakkaa Paalle!*"

"*Hakkaa Paalle!*"

Trumpets blared and drums thuttered in the wake of that huge, crashing shout. The line of pikes advanced, jabbing with two-handed thrusts at the mounts and riders; the wielders' faces were set and grim under the wide brims of their kettle helmets. A horse slipped on the treacherous footing and crashed over as it tried to turn, adding its high, enormous scream to the racket of voices and the scrap-metal-on-concrete din. The formation grew uneven as it surged forward, leaving wedges of open space between the files; Havel cursed as two riders pushed their mounts through a gap in the wall of weapons, striking down left and right at helmets and shoulders.

The fifth and sixth ranks had glaives rather than pikes; seven-foot shafts topped with heavy, pointed blades for stabbing and chopping, and a cruel hook on the reverse. Havel held one himself. He dodged a slash, and his weapon darted out. The hook caught on mail beneath an armpit; he braced his feet and hauled, and the rider came off with something halfway between a screech and a squawk, and then an almighty thump as armored body met sodden, muddy turf.

He reversed the glaive with a quick, expert flick and drove the point down to menace the rider's face. The fallen lancer wheezed and raised one fist, middle finger extended.

"OK!" he shouted. *"Time out! Time out!"*

It took a minute or two for flags and trumpets to pass the message. The huge noise died down, leaving only the bellows panting of humans and horses, and a few moans or screams from the injured. Havel grounded his glaive and reached a hand down.

"You all right, honey?" he said as he hauled her erect.

Signe Havel grinned up at him, unbuckling her helmet and shaking back long, wheat-colored braids. Her cornflower blue eyes sparkled in a long, oval, straight-featured face; it would have been Nordic perfection except for the slight white line a sword had nicked across the bridge of her nose.

"You mean, apart from the bruises and contusions? You betcha." The last was in a parody of Havel's flat Upper Midwestern accent.

"Wimp," he said, deliberately exaggerating his U.P. rasp. "Real women wear contusions like they were a corsage." Then, louder: "All right, everyone gather 'round!"

The infantry company did, and the forty A-lister cavalry. Stretcher parties carried off half a dozen with injuries bad enough to need the medicos; that was a pity, but sweat shed in training saved blood, and to be useful it had to be at least a little dangerous. The occasional broken bone or concussion was well worth it. At that, it was easier to practice realistically with pre-gunpowder weapons than it had been with firearms, in his first incarnation as a fighting man, which had been as a Marine; Force Recon, to be precise . . .

Fortunately none of the valuable and exhaustively trained warhorses had been seriously hurt; destriers were *expensive,* harder to train than humans and a lot less likely to recover from a broken limb.

The hale survivors of the exercise gathered around— bloody noses, sprains, bruises and incipient shiners didn't count as serious these days—panting as they cooled off in the rain-swept pasture, legs and bodies thickly plastered with mud. It wasn't raining, not quite, but it had been fairly recently; what they were getting now was weather that couldn't quite make up its mind between fog and drizzle and a possibility of snow.

The infantry were farmers and artisans and laborers, militia who drilled in the slow parts of the agricultural year and fought when he called them out. Their equipment was a little varied and a lot of it homemade, though everyone had some sort of metal helmet, and at least a brigandine or chain-mail shirt for armor; some of the more affluent had breastplates hammered out of sheet steel, and plate protection on their shins and forearms, and long, metal-plated leather gauntlets. Good steel was abundant in the Changed world, salvaged from the ruins; it was the time of the scarce, skilled craftsmen that made armor expensive.

The cavalry were A-listers, full-time warriors and the elite of the Outfit, uniformly kitted out in knee-length chain hauberks, greaves and vambraces of plate or steel splints on leather, round helmets with nasal bars, hinged cheek-pieces and mail-covered neck-flaps, and two-foot circular shields. Their weapons were lances, recurved bows made of laminated horn and wood and sinew, and long, single-edged swords with basket hilts; the shields were dark brown, with the stylized outline of a bear's head in crimson. His own helmet had the tanned, snarling head of a bear mounted on it; he'd killed the beast himself, shortly after the Change, with an improvised spear. From that, a great deal had followed.

A great deal including the Outfit's name, though that was Astrid's idea, as usual. Aloud: "All right, Bearkillers. What would have been different if this was for real?"

"We'd have crossbows on our flanks, Lord Bear," one of the infantry said, a stocky, freckled young man with shoulders like a blacksmith—which was what he was—leaning on a glaive. "When the charge stalled in front of the pikes, we'd have shot the shit out of them, killed a bucketful and made the others easy meat. Armor's not much help at close range like that."

Havel nodded. A hard-driven arrow or crossbow bolt was just too damned dangerous to use in a practice match, even with a padded, blunt head, and having people standing around shouting *Twang! Twang!* as they pretended to shoot was sort of silly. Instead the referees had tapped on a certain percentage of the mounted troops with their batons, often starting furious arguments, while the missile troops were off shooting at targets.

"Hey," one of the A-listers said. "If this were for real, we'd have been using *our* bows and that line of pikes would have been a lot more ragged before we hit it."

Havel nodded again, but added: "Yeah, Astrid, that's true. But we're practicing to fight the Portland Protective Association, and the Protector's men-at-arms don't use saddle bows. Sword and lance only, and they rely on their own infantry for missile weapons. OK, we'll say that cancels out."

He didn't add: *And there aren't many who can use a horse-bow like you, either.* It was true—everyone on the A-list was a good, competent shot, but Astrid was a wonder. *Your ego doesn't need any stroking, however.*

Astrid Larsson pouted a little as she leaned her hands on the horn of her saddle. "I suppose so."

She was twenty-three to her sister Signe's twenty-eight, with white-blond hair and huge blue eyes rimmed and veined with silver. They gave her face an odd, nearly inhuman quality despite its fine-boned good looks. She was intensely capable when it came to anything involving horses or bows, a fine swordswoman and in Michael Havel's view just one hair short of utter-raving-loon status. Unlike many, she'd been that way at fourteen, *before* the Change and its aftermath.

"Lord Bear," she added, confirming his thought.

And she stuck me with that moniker and this damned taxidermist's nightmare on my helmet, he thought. *Plus that shield . . .*

Hers wasn't the standard outline of a snarling bear's head that was the blazon of the Outfit. It had a silver tree instead, and seven stars above it, around a crown. Her helmet was even stranger-looking, with a raven of black-lacquered aluminum on the steel, wings extending down the cheek-pieces and ruby-eyed head looking out over the nasal bar.

It's all those books she reads, those giant doorstopper things with dragons and quests and Magical Identity Bracelets of the Apocalypse.

She'd been obsessed with them when he first met her, and the ensuing decade had made her worse, if anything. He wished, very much, that she'd only been weird about archery and horses, but no such luck.

Not to mention she's become so popular and influential among the younger and loopier element. I can't really clamp down on it because that Ranger outfit she and Eilir put together are too fucking useful, dammit! OK, so she can be the Elf-Queen of the goddamned woods if that's the way she wants to play it.

Aloud he went on to the audience: "Here's the important thing. As long as that line of pikes stayed solid, the lancers couldn't get anywhere near you infantry types. And when they got crowded and stalled, they got tangled up bad. A lot of them would have died before they could disengage—which, incidentally, they'll have to practice more. Charging's easy; retreating without getting your ass reamed is a lot more difficult. So—it's official. The infantry wins today!"

Everyone cheered. The younger A-listers looked a bit sullen as they did, but *their* fighting morale didn't need bolstering; if anything, they tended to be a little reckless and cocky. It took serious effort and native talent to get onto the A-list, and the fact that their families were usually the ruling class of the Outfit, more or less, didn't hurt in the self-esteem sweepstakes either. An occasional ass-whupping by the horny-handed sons and daughters of toil did them good, in his opinion; that was one reason he'd been fighting on foot in today's match.

"Certainly, Lord Bear," Astrid said again. "But once some gaps opened up, we could get in past the pikepoints."

Havel nodded vigorously, then removed his helmet and handed it to a military apprentice—a teenaged aspirant to A-Lister status—and ran his hands over his bowl-cut hair. That was straight and coarse and still crow black in his late thirties, a legacy of his Anishinabe-Ojibwa grandmother. The high cheekbones and slanted set to his gray eyes might have been from her, or from the Karelian Finns who made up most of the rest of his ancestry; the sharp-cut features were startlingly handsome in a harsh, masculine way, emphasized by the long white scar that ran from the corner of his left eye and across his forehead. He stood just under six feet, and his lean frame moved with a leopard's easy grace under fifty pounds of armor and padding.

"Yeah, good point," he said to his sister-in-law.

He gave the militia a glare, and they shuffled uneasily—which produced an alarming volume of clanks and clinks among two hundred people in metal protective gear.

"This field's pretty level; if you can't advance over it without breaking front, what's going to happen on a battlefield, maybe with grapevines or fences, and people shooting at you? Or if you have to do something more complicated than pushing straight ahead? You let a pike wall get ragged, and the Protector's knights will be all over you like flies on cowshit. One-on-one, they'll slaughter you. Keep drilling until the formation's always tight, and you slaughter *them*. It's as simple as that. Understood?"

"Yes, Lord Bear!"

"I can't hear you."

"Yes, Lord Bear!"

"All right, that's enough for today. Fall in, and we'll see if the barbeque's ready."

That brought more cheers, and more cheerful ones; the padding around the blades of weapons was stripped off and tossed into a light cart, and everyone wiped their faces, scraped off the worst of the mud and straightened their gear. The apprentice brought him his horse, Gustav; he swung into the saddle easily enough, despite the weight of hauberk and weapons. The infantry company formed up on the roadway that led westward from this stretch of pasture; an officer gave a shouted *pikepoints . . . up!* and *fall in!* and the long shafts rose, like an ordered bare forest. The footmen went first, as the victors of the contest, swinging off with a good marching step; the A-listers followed along, looking fairly glum at first.

Except for Astrid, and the young man riding by her side. Alleyne Loring wore different gear, a complete set of jointed steel plate topped by a visored sallet helm, what Havel had thought of as King Arthur armor when he was a kid, the type beloved of Victorian illustrators. The Pre-Raphaelite look was emphasized by the fog that clung to hollows and treetops round about, making a fantasy of the rolling fields and wood-lots. The armor was actually late-medieval in inspiration, fifteenth-century or so, but manufactured post-Change out of high-strength alloy steel stock by jury-rigged hydraulic presses in southern England.

Havel grinned like a happy wolf. Alleyne was also young, only a few years older than Astrid, and six feet tall, blondly handsome, dashing, charming, from a far-off foreign place and in the process of saying—

"*Sinome maruvan ar Hildinyar, vanimálion noastari . . .*"

"*Onen i-Estel Edain—*" Astrid replied in the same liquidly pretty tongue, which sounded Celtic but wasn't; Havel understood not a word of it.

My languages being limited to English, a bit of Ojibwa, rudimentary Finnish and some Arabic cusswords I picked up in the Gulf, he thought. *None of the Tongues of Middle-earth included in the package.*

"You're looking like the coyote that met the rabbit coming 'round the rock," Signe said.

"Thanks to those Tasmanians—poor bastards—and their world survey voyage I think we may finally have gotten your little sister hooked up," Havel said. "And out of our hair."

"Hey!" She punched him on the shoulder. Since he was wearing a hauberk with padded gambeson beneath, that was mostly symbolic, but her voice was only a little defensive as she went on: "Astrid's been . . . useful."

"And a lot less trouble since she started up that Ranger outfit out in the woods. But she's still trying to trick us all out in costumes from those books she likes. She makes Norman Arminger sound as everyday as a dental hygienist."

"Granted she's a flapping wingnut, but a handy wingnut to have around. A lot of stuff we've done wouldn't have been nearly as popular if we hadn't had her to slap some cool, antique name on it and give it some style. It kept those Society types we recruited happy too, they love fancy titles and playing dress-up. Useful . . . and if they're here being useful to us they're not up north being useful to Lord Protector Arminger, who was one of their own after all. Besides, this lords-and-ladies stuff . . . once it stops sounding so silly it sort of grows on you."

"And fungus grows on your toenails if you aren't careful. Yeah, she's useful, and also a goddamned pain in the ass. For a while I thought she'd probably settle down with Eilir, who's sensible, sort of—"

His wife shot him a look; the sisters had quarreled all their lives, but he liked the way they closed ranks. "Astrid isn't gay."

"Nothing so convenient or conventional. She's an elf instead," he said dryly.

Signe grinned. "I think she's settled on being a, what's the word, *Numenorean* instead of an elf."

"I thought it was *Dunadan* . . . or is it *Dúnedain*? I forget which."

"*Dúnedain* is the plural. . . ." She smiled wickedly as he mimed clutching at his head. "*Dunadan* is the word for *Numenorean* . . . in another language."

"*Another* invented language? Christ Jesus, didn't the man

have anything else to do with his time? Trimming the shrubbery, visiting the pub? How many of them *are* there?"

"Let's see . . . the Common Speech, the Black Speech, the tongue of the Rohirrim, Halfling dialects, Quenya elvish, Sindarin elvish . . ."

"Stop! Stop! Anyway, why . . . whatever . . . instead of an elf! Hell, I've got to admit, she *looks* like one."

"But elves don't get cooties on campaign, or smell. Or have monthly cramps, which she does, bad. Anyway, Eilir's just her best friend."

"Alleyne there will do even better, nothing like kids to calm you down. Someone who shares her interests—"

"Is nutbar about the same stuff?" Signe clarified helpfully.

"Nah, he just likes the books; he's not goofy over living it all out. He's a pretty regular guy, once you get past that Jeeves-old-chap-fetch-me-a-biscuit accent. But liking the books'll help him keep her from doing a swan dive into the deep end. Christ Jesus knows nobody else ever had much luck at that! Foreign prince—well, son of a baronet—exotic, great warrior. It's a natural! And I get a first-rate fighting man on my side, too; he can king it off in the woods with her in between wars. Win-win situation."

"You haven't said anything about it to her."

"Christ, no! That'd be the best way to spoil things."

"Well, maybe you're learning after all," Signe said, and touched an ear when he started to reply.

They were leaning together and speaking quietly, and the rumbling clatter of hooves, the crash of boots and the *thrrrrip-thrrrrip-thrrrrip* of the marching drum covered it. Still, she was right. Another time would be better for chewing over family matters.

Not that there's much difference between family stuff and politics anymore, he thought. *Or between either and the military side of things.*

"Aaron wants to visit Corvallis and see if he can get more medical supplies," Signe went on.

"Aaron just wants to find a cute young thing," Havel answered. Aaron Rothman was chief physician of Larsdalen; he

was very competent, but had his quirks. "He's been itching for
some social life since his last boyfriend left him."

"That's because you're the unrequited love of his life, darling. You *did* save him from the cannibals."

Havel laughed. "Saved all of him but his left foot," he said,
which was literally true; that band of Eaters had gone in for
slow-motion butchery to keep the meat from spoiling.

The road curved westward towards the distant Coast
Range, dark green slopes whose tops were covered in gray
mist that merged into the low clouds. The broad, shallow valley on either side was a patchwork of dormant bare-fingered
orchards, peach and apple and cherry, with fleecy white sheep
grazing beneath the trees, grainfields showing wet red-brown
dirt between the blue-green shoots of the winter wheat, and
pasture dotted with Garry oaks and grazing cattle. Workers
and herdsmen waved at the troops as they passed, but this
close to Larsdalen there weren't any of the usual walled hamlets or fortified A-Lister steadings that dotted the other settled parts of the Outfit's lands; the folk who tilled these lands
dwelt inside the Bearkiller citadel. Horsemen and plodding
wagons and bicyclists swerved to the side of the road to let the
troops pass, and gave cheerful greetings to their friends and
relatives as they did.

He took a deep, satisfied breath; he was fairly happy with
the way the exercise had gone, and happier still with the
way the half-dormant farmlands promised good crops next
year. And the way that his folk all looked well fed and
warmly clad in new homespun, drab wadmal, or wool and
linen and linsey-woolsey colored in yellows and browns,
greens and blues, by the dyes they'd learned to make from
bark and herbs and leaves. The air was heavy with the musty
smell of damp earth and vegetable decay; this season in the
Willamette Valley was more like a prolonged autumn with
an occasional cold snap than the brutal Siberian winters of
the Lake Superior country where he'd been raised. He'd always liked autumn best of the four seasons, although he
missed the dry, cold, white snow-months that followed. Sometimes he'd gone on week-long trips then, cutting school and

setting off through the birch woods on skis, with a bedroll and rifle on his back . . .

The valley narrowed as it rose towards the crest of the Eola Hills, where they broke in a steep slope towards the lowlands around the little town of Rickreall. Orchards gave way to vineyards spindly and bare, with a few red-gold leaves still clinging, and more littering the ground. The vines had been there before the Change, when this area was the Larsson family's country estate; great-grandpa Larsson had bought it back a century ago, when he made his pile out of wheat and timber. The big pillared brick house beyond would have been visible then . . .

Now the narrowing V was blocked by a steep-sided earth-work bank covered in turf, with a moat at its base full of sharpened angle iron. They'd started on that late in the first Change Year, right after the core of the Bearkillers arrived on their long trek from Idaho; he'd been flying the Larssons to their ranch in Idaho on that memorable March seventeenth, and ended up crash-landing in a half-frozen mountain creek in the Selway-Bitterroot National Wilderness. Which had been a stroke of luck, nerve-wracking though it had been at the time to have the engine cut out over those granite steeps.

"What's that saying Juney uses?" Havel asked. With a grin: "Pardon me, Lady Juniper, herself herself."

"Something pretentiously Gaelic which boils down to saying a man's home is his castle," Signe said, a very slight waspish note in her voice.

"Yeah, but it's true in English too," Havel pointed out, looking pridefully ahead. "We've got a hell of a lot done in a decade, considering we can't use powered machinery."

A wall topped the mound, thirty feet high and built like a hydro dam; rocks the size of a man's head and bigger in a concrete matrix, around a hidden framework of welded steel I-beams salvaged from construction sites in Salem, the old state capital thirty miles northeastward. Round towers half as high again studded it at hundred-yard intervals as it curved away on either side to encompass the whole of the little plateau that held Larsdalen.

Gotta get the inner keep finished before spring, he reminded himself. Work on fortifications was another thing that they did in wintertime . . . *Although there's always fifteen different things we should be doing with every spare moment.* Everything done meant something else nearly as urgent sidelined; one thing that seemed universally true in the Changed world was that all work took a lot longer or cost more or both.

The gate where road met wall was four towers grouped together on the corners of a blockhouse, with his flag flying high above each. The drawbridge was down, but the outer gates were closed. They were steel as well, a solid mass of welded beams faced on either side with quarter-inch plate and probably impossible to duplicate now that the hoarded oxyacetylene tanks were empty. The surface was dark brown paint, but this year for swank they'd added a great snarling bear's head in ruddy copper covered in clear varnish, face-on to the roadway with half on either leaf. The Mackenzies had something similar on the gates of Dun Juniper, though they used the Triple Moon and the head of the Horned Man.

Trumpets blared from above. Astrid brought her Arab forward on dancing hooves, throwing up one hand in greeting.

"Who comes to Larsdalen gate?" the officer of the guard called down formally.

"The Bear Lord returns to the citadel of the Bearkillers! Open!"

"Open for Lord Bear!"

"Oh, Christ Jesus, how did we let her get away with this bad-movie crap?" Havel said—but under his breath. "And now everyone's used to it and they'd be upset if we insisted on a plain countersign."

"She's the only theatrical impresario in the family," Signe said, also sotto voce. "Every time we did something new, she was there to tell us how to manage the PR. Don't sweat it. After all, she's not home much anymore."

"Ah, well, names are funny things," he said with resignation. "Someone has an impulse and then you're stuck with them. That's why I've got a Karelian pedigree and a Bohunk moniker."

They both chuckled at the old family joke; back in the 1890s

one Arvo Myllyharju had arrived in Michigan's Upper Peninsula, fresh off an Aland Island square-rigger and looking for a
job in the Iron Range. The Czech pay-clerk at the mine had
taken one look at the string of Finnish consonants and said:
From now on, your name is Havel!

His great-grandson remembered. *Though will it make any
sense to our kids?* he wondered. *Finland might as well be Bar-
soom, to them, and Michigan about the same.*

There was a solid *chunk . . . chunk . . .* sound as the heavy
beams that secured the gates were pulled back, and a squeal
of steel on steel as the great metal portals swung out, salvaged
wheels from railcars running along track set into the concrete
of the roadway. Winches grated as the portcullis was raised,
and the dark tunnel behind suddenly showed gray light at the
other end as the identical inner portals went through the same
procedure, to reveal a cheering crowd lining the way. The
gates were normally kept open anyway in daylight, during
peacetime; this was for show. Signe and Havel reined in beside the gate, saluting as the infantry company went by, followed by the lancers. Feet and hooves boomed drumlike on
the boards of the drawbridge and echoed through the
passage.

Havel looked up as he followed; there were flickers of
lantern light through the gratings in the murder-holes above,
and a scent of hot oil bubbling in great pivot-mounted tubs.

"Always thought we could save some effort with those," he
said. "Sort of wasteful, all that cooking oil, and burning all
that fuel, when all it does is sit there and simmer."

"They've got to be kept hot," Signe said.

"Yeah, but we could do French-fries in 'em. Maybe onion
rings too . . ."

Dun Juniper, Willamette Valley, Oregon
December 15th, 2007/Change Year 9

There was a chorus of giggles from the sixteen-year-olds
preparing their choir at the other end of the great Hall. One
of them sang in a high, clear tenor:

"It's the end of the world as we know it!
"It's the end of the world as we know it and I feel fine!"

The rest of them took it up for a moment. Sir Nigel Loring put down his book and looked up with mild interest from his armchair beside the big fireplace on the north wall, sipping at the last of his honey-sweetened chamomile tea. It wasn't quite as vile when you got used to it, and the dried-blueberry muffins that stood on the side table were quite good. Flames played over the glowing coals, red and gold flickering in an endless dance.

I quite liked that little tune the first time around, for some reason, he thought, relaxing in the grateful warmth and the scent of burning fir as firelight and lamplight played on the colored, carven walls. *But that changed with the Change. And these . . .* infants! *They were six-year-olds then. All they know is that it scandalizes their elders.*

Juniper Mackenzie—since the Change the Lady Juniper, Chief of the Clan Mackenzie, which nowadays meant ruler secular and sacred through most of the southeastern Willamette—hopped up onto the dais to put her head above the youngsters. Loring smiled at the sight. There was a crackling energy to the slight figure; she was a short, slim woman just turned forty, with a little gray starting in her vivid fox red hair, pale-skinned and freckled with bright, leaf green eyes; the fine lines around them were mostly from laughter. Besides the tartan kilt and saffron-dyed shirt of homespun linsey-woolsey she wore a belted plaid pinned at the shoulder with a gilt knotwork brooch, a flat Scots bonnet with three raven feathers in the silver clasp, and a little *sgian dubh* knife tucked into one kneesock. She gave a mock-scowl as she stared at the youngsters with her hands on her hips, and they shuffled their feet and looked abashed.

Behind her loomed the Chief's chair, a thronelike affair carved from oak and maple and walnut, the pillars behind ending in stylized raven's heads for Thought and Memory, and arching to support a Triple Moon. Juniper went on to her crowd of kilted adolescents:

"Perhaps you'd rather not do a Choosing at all, then? Or is

it that you don't want it to go perfectly?" That got her ap-
palled looks and a babble of apologies. "*Maireann na daoine
ar scáil a chéile,* remember. People live in one another's shadows. This comes only once in your life; don't spoil it for your
sept-siblings or your friends. Now, we'll be starting with the
opening song."

The man in the chair beside Loring's chuckled quietly.
"That got their attention, the little bastards," Dennis Martin
Mackenzie said. "At sixteen you're wild to stop being a kid,
which is one thing that *hasn't* changed since the Change."

"This is practice for some rite of passage?" Loring guessed.

"Yeah, choosing a sept. We divvied up the Clan into septs
when it got too big for just a bunch of us hanging out at Dun
Juniper here, and it's become sort of important. You figure
out what your totem animal is, and that means you're in one
of the septs. Fox, Wolf, Raven, Tiger, Bear, Eagle, whatever."

He chuckled again. "We had this guy *insisted* his totem was
the Tyrannosaurus rex. Saw it in his dream-quest, he said.
Took quite a while to talk him out of it."

Nigel choked off a snort of laughter; he didn't want to be
caught mocking the customs or religion of his hosts. Dennis
cocked an eyebrow nonetheless, and there was a dry note to
his voice:

"Yeah, I thought the whole thing was sort of loopy myself.
It's not part of the Craft, strictly speaking. Andy Trethar came
up with the idea; he and Diana always did like that shamanis-
tic stuff and they were part of Juney's original Singing Moon
coven before the Change. The rest of us just went along,
mostly, but these days the youngsters . . . well, they take it real
serious."

"Far be it from me to object," Nigel said. "Just before I left
England—"

"Escaped from Mad King Charles, you mean," Dennis said.

Loring shrugged; that was a fair enough description. "By
then King Charles was doing some rather eccentric things . . .
making Morris dancing, thatched roofs and smock frocks
compulsory, for example."

Juniper signaled to the musicians; a bodhran and a flute, a
set of uilleann pipes and a fiddle. The tune began softly, a

rhythmic stutter with the wild sweetness of the pipes in the background. Then the music swelled and she raised her voice in an effortless soprano that filled the Hall without straining; she'd been a professional singer before the Change, of course. One hand went up as she sang, and the teenagers followed suit, first with the fingers spread and then held together.

> *"What is the difference 'tween feathers and hair?*
> *The handprint of a human or the paw of a bear?*
> *We all roar with laughter, we all howl with tears,*
> *Show our teeth if we're angry, and lay back our ears!"*

The youngsters came in on the chorus:

> *"A passion within you*
> *Whispering what you want to be*
> *Take a look in the mirror*
> *What animal do you wish to see?"*

Then louder, as they all joined in:

> *"We each meet our animal . . . in its time and place*
> *And gazing into those eyes . . . we see our own face*
> *It'll teach us and guide us if we but call its name*
> *For under the Lady's sky we're animals all the same—"*

"Here, try this instead of that lousy tea," Dennis went on, pouring from a pot that rested on a ledge in the hearth. "You were out in the cold and wet most of the day, and it's getting dark. And since I brew the stuff . . . What's that old saying about the time for the first drink?"

"*The sun's over the yardarm* is the phrase," Nigel said aside to Dennis, keeping his eyes on the Mackenzie chieftain as he sipped at the hot honey-wine.

The contents were mead, dry and smooth and fragrant with herbs. He worked the muscles of his left arm, his shield-arm, as he drank. The break where the greatsword had cracked the bone of his upper arm still hurt a little; he suspected it always would on damp winter days like this. It would take work to get full strength back, but the bone had knit and it could take the strain of a heavy shield and hard blows once more. He'd spent the morning sparring and beating at a pell-post with his practice sword along with some other adults in the open space under the northern wall. During occasional rests he'd watched while the children built their two snowmen and adorned them with antlers and feathers, and constructed two snow forts and named them *oak* and *holly* before fighting a ferocious snowball battle-to-the-death.

"And ... ah, yes, I remember now."

"Remember what?" Dennis asked.

He was a big man, probably fat before the Change and burly now. Hands showed the scars and callus of a woodcarver and leatherworker; besides that, he ran the Dun Juniper brewery and distillery. His face was wreathed in brown hair and beard, except for the bald spot on the crown of his head, and he was going gray in his late fifties. That made him half a decade older than the slight, trim figure of the Englishman sitting across from him, smoothing his silver-shot mustache and blinking blue eyes that were just a trifle watery from an old injury. They'd spent a fair amount of time talking since Loring had arrived at Dun Juniper seven months before.

"Why I liked that little ditty the youngsters were singing a moment ago," Nigel said. "About the end of the world. I was convalescing then, too. In a hospital ... a rather, ah, private one ... and someone kept playing that tune. It was the sort of place where you had armed guards outside the sickroom door."

"That made you like the song?"

"Well, I didn't die, you see," the Englishman said, with a charming smile. "And after having a Provo shoot me with an ArmaLite and blow me up to boot, that put me in rather a good mood. The tune brings back that feeling of sweet relief."

"What happened to the Provo?" Martin asked curiously.

"Nothing good, I'm afraid, poor fellow," Nigel replied.

His accent was English, in an old-fashioned upper-class manner shaped by Winchester College, the Blues and Royals, and the Edwardian-gentry tones of the grandmother who'd raised him. His mother had broken her neck when her horse balked at a hedge, not long after his father had vanished leading a jungle patrol against Communist guerillas in Malaya.

Just now the smooth, mellow voice had a sardonic note as well.

"You killed him, I suppose? Or what do the SAS call it, slotting?"

It wasn't a question Dennis Martin would have asked before the Change, when he was a pub manager in Corvallis and Juniper was a musician who sang Celtic and folk on gigs there, and on the RenFaire circuit and at Pagan gatherings. It seemed natural enough to Dennis Martin Mackenzie of Dun Juniper, a man who had survived the death of a world, and now lived in another where you took a bow or ax along whenever you went beyond the walls.

"Killed him? I wouldn't go that far. I simply stabbed him in the spine and kicked him out through the window. It was either the knife, the broken glass or the fifteen-foot fall headfirst onto concrete which actually *killed* him, I should think."

Most of the time Nigel Loring's face bore an expression of mild, polite amiability. Just then something different showed for an instant, in the closed curve of his slight smile. It reminded you that this was a good friend, but a very bad—as in "lethally dangerous"—enemy, who'd been a fighting man long before the world was broken and remade that March afternoon in 1998.

Since Dennis was a Mackenzie now, and hence a friend of the Lorings, he went on slyly: "Does Juney know you picked up Erse because it was so useful to the SAS in South Armagh?"

"*Nach breá an lá é?*" Nigel replied.

"I suppose that means 'I deny everything'?" Dennis said.

"More on the order of: *Isn't it a lovely day?*"

"And aren't the walls vertical," Dennis laughed. "Unless *snowy and cold* counts as lovely in the Emerald Isle."

Nigel chuckled. "Though in fact Ms. Mackenzie still despises the Provos with a passion, despite her Irish mother. Or because of her. It's Ireland's misfortune that the sensible people never quite manage to dispose of all the different varieties of lunatic. Even the Change hasn't changed that, I'm afraid; it must be something in the water, and it affects the English too, when they travel there. Celts do much better here—appearances sometimes to the contrary."

He touched his knee as he spoke. He'd arrived last spring as a refugee with the armor on his back and one change of clothing in his saddlebags. These days he dressed in a kilt like nearly everyone else in the Mackenzie territories—the knee-length pleated *féile-beag,* the Little Kilt, not the ancient wrap-around blanket style—and a homespun shirt of linsey-woolsey. The tartan was like nothing that the Highlands had ever seen, mostly dark green and brown with occasional slivers of a very dull orange. Handsome enough, if subdued, and excellent camouflage in this lush, wet land of forest and field; quite comfortable as well, but you had to remember to keep it arranged properly. His legs were well proportioned and muscled, particularly for a man his age, but he didn't think his graying shins were the most aesthetically pleasing part of him, not to mention the scars.

"You could at least have used the real Mackenzie tartan, if you were going to put everyone in pleated skirts," Nigel grumbled.

The other man grinned. "Hell, I only came up with the idea 'cause we'd found a warehouse load of these tartan blankets, and because I knew it would torque Juney off when she got back from the scouting thing she was doing, and found it was a done deal—pardon me, torque off Lady Juniper," he said, nodding towards the eastern end of the Hall where the dais stood. "I started the Lady Juniper bit, too, and it drove her crazy."

"Why would the kilts annoy her?" Nigel asked. "They're very easy to make, and quite practical in this climate, which I can assure you from much dismal training-maneuver experience is far milder than the Highlands of Scotland. She looks quite convincing in that getup as well, and she has a suitable accent, when she wishes—though Irish rather than Scots, to be sure. Still, the Scotti came from there, originally. And there's the religious aspect, of course."

"Yeah, but I was always teasing her about the Celtic stuff she put on to go with her music before the Change," Dennis said. "Sort of a running joke, you know? And the way her coveners—I was a cowan back then, didn't believe in anything much—were always making like Cuchulain or Deirdre of the Sorrows or whatever and raiding the Irish myths for symbols the way the old Erse stole each other's cows. So when the first bunch of us got here right after the Change, and she said we'd have to live like a clan to survive, I was the one who pushed for all this stuff 'cause I knew she hadn't meant that literally. There wasn't much to laugh at back then, and it was fun."

He looked around. "I didn't expect it to catch on this . . . emphatically."

"It certainly has," Nigel observed, matching his glance.

The Englishman had heard the building's story from Juniper. Her great-uncle the banker had been the single wealthy exception to the modest middle-class rule of the Mackenzies, and he'd bought the site of the ancestral homestead and the forest around it as a country hunting-lodge; her parents had visited every July as far back as she could remember and, later, more than once she'd spent a whole summer here, just she and the old man, walking the woods and learning the plants and the beasts. It had been the last of the childless bachelor's many eccentricities to leave the house and land to the teenage single mother she'd been, more than a decade before the Change.

The lodge had been built in the 1920s of immense Douglas fir logs on a knee-high foundation of mortared fieldstone; originally it had been plain on the interior, and divided into several rooms as well. The budding Clan Mackenzie had ripped out the partitions when they put on a second story late in the first Change Year, leaving a great wooden box a hundred feet by forty; on the north side a huge stone hearth was flanked by two doors leading to the new lean-to kitchens, and on the other three walls windows looked out onto verandas roofed by the second-story balconies.

And it certainly isn't plain *anymore,* he thought.

Over the years since, the great logs that made up the walls had been smoothed and carved, stained and inlaid and painted, until they were a sinuous riot of colored running knot-work that reminded him of the Book of Kells, crossed with Viking-era animal-style and a strong dash of Art Nouveau. Faces peered out of that foliage, the multitude of Aspects borne by the twin deities of Juniper Mackenzie's faith; the Green Man, stag-antlered Cernunnos, goat-horned Pan; flame-crowned Brigid with her sheaf of wheat and Lugh of the Long Hand with his spear, Cerridwen, Arianrhod and silver-tongued Ogma, Apollo and Athena, Zeus and Hera, Freya and one-eyed Odin, blond Sif and almighty red-bearded Thor.

Beneath the high ceiling were carved the symbols of the Quarters; over the hearth comfrey and ivy and sheaves of grain for North and the Earth; vervain and yarrow for Air and the East; red poppies and nettles for the South and Fire; ferns and rushes and water lilies for West and the Waters.

A few people were doing touch-up work on it all, on ladders propped against the wall. Winter was the slack season for farmers, and so time for maintenance work, and for leisure and crafts and ceremony. There were others here, reading or playing at board games, three in animated discussion over the plans for a new sawmill at another dun and a circle of younger children listening raptly to a storyteller in a corner.

"I'm off," Dennis said to the Englishman as the practice group around the dais broke up, rising and giving a nod to Juniper Mackenzie as she approached—and a wink to Nigel. "I've got apprentices doing practice-pieces to check on and then Sally'll have dinner ready. 'Night, Juney."

"Tell Sally we need to talk about the Moon School schedule tomorrow, Dennie," Juniper said, then: "And how are you today, Nigel?" She sat and stretched out in a leather armchair, feet towards the fire on a settee.

Sir Nigel Loring picked up his thick, white ceramic mug with his left hand. His fingers tightened on it until the knuckles whitened and cords stood out in his forearm, and then relaxed.

"Your healer seems to be correct," he said. "Full function is returning."

Slowly and painfully, he added silently to himself; he'd

never been a whiner. Old bones didn't mend as fast as young, and that was all there was to it. And he was fifty-three now, even if a very fit fifty-three.

"Judy Barstow knows her business," Juniper said, and nodded. Then she smiled: "Or Judy Barstow Mackenzie, to use the modern form."

He could see sympathy in the bright green eyes; her voice held a hint of her mother's birthplace, Achill Island off the west coast of Eire, running like a burbling stream beneath her usual General American. Her father's heritage had been mostly what Americans called Scots-Irish, and it showed in the straight nose, pointed chin and high cheekbones; so did the very slight trace of Cherokee that side of her family had picked up in the mountains of Carolina and Tennessee before they made the long trek over the Oregon Trail.

"And the headaches?" she went on.

"Fewer as the weeks go by, and not as bad; the herbal infusion works wonders. Ye gods, but that man was strong! What was his name?"

In two strokes the greatsword had buckled the tough alloy steel of his helm, ripped the chin-protecting bevoir right off his breastplate, and cut through the sheet metal and strong laminated wood of his shield to break his arm while he lay semiconscious on the ground, trying to protect Rudi Mackenzie from a death as unstoppable as a falling boulder.

"Mack," she said. "Although I've heard that was a nickname—for the truck."

Juniper Mackenzie's usual expression was friendly; more sincerely so than his own, he thought. Just then it changed for an instant, and you could see the fangs of the she-fox behind her smile. She glanced over to another corner, where a nine-year-old with copper-gold locks to his shoulders was playing chess with a black-haired young woman in her early twenties. They looked up for an instant from their game and waved at their mother and the Englishman. He felt himself give an answering grin; young Rudi was irresistible, and his sister Eilir charming in her slightly eerie way.

"Mack wasn't so strong as you and your son Alleyne and John Hordle put together," Juniper said. "Since he was trying to kill my son, I would consider that a fortunate thing, so. I won't forget whose shield it was covered Rudi."

Her hand tightened on his shoulder for an instant, and he covered it with his as briefly before she leaned back, arranging her kilt and plaid gracefully and then taking one of the muffins from the plate beside Nigel's chair. They were made from stone-ground flour, rich with eggs and thick with dried blueberries and hazelnuts; one steamed gently as she broke it open and buttered it.

"And if one has to convalesce from a broken arm and a cracked head, this is as good a spot as any," he went on with a smile, waving his mug. "And as good a season of the year."

With the summer's wealth stored and the next year's wheat and barley in the ground, supporting a guest too weak to work or fight was no hardship. The Great Hall of Dun Juniper was comfortably warm in the chill, rainy gloom of the west-Oregon winter, too, not something you could count on in a large building after the Change in a place like the Cascade foothills.

Or in a large British building even before *the Change,* he thought mordantly. But the Yanks always were better at heating. Snow beat at the windows with feathery paws amid December's early dark, but the great room was bright with firelight and the lanterns that hung from the carved rafters.

"The winters weren't the Willamette's strongest selling points," Juniper said. "Though with my complexion, I find them soothing. At least I don't turn into a giant freckle!"

"I like your climate. The tropics wear after a while"—she knew he'd had plenty of hot-country experience in his years with the 22nd Special Air Service Regiment before the Change—"but this is homelike enough for comfort and just the right bit milder."

Juniper laughed, and waved a hand around the great room and its flamboyant decoration. "Now, *this* I don't think you'll find homelike."

He found himself laughing with her, although he'd been a rather solemn person most of his life. "I grant it isn't what you'd find in Hampshire, even after the Change."

He recognized the symbolism of her faith and he could interpret most of it, partly from his readings in ancient history, partly from occasional contact with practitioners of the Craft—some had been on the Isle of Wight, the main enclave of British survivors, and a few had even managed to hide out in the New Forest to be discovered by his scouts in the second Change Year. And his son Alleyne had been a recreationist before the Change, one of those who played at medieval combat, and the odd Wiccan had overlapped with that set.

Extremely odd, some of them, he thought with a smile.

Then he raised his gaze to the brooding, feral face of Pan, and the smile died. The heavy-lidded eyes were shadowed as they stared into his, given life by the flickering firelight. They brought with them a hint of green growth and damp, moldering leaves; the dark scented breath of the wildwood, and the fear that waits to take the souls of men who wander too far beyond the edge of the tilled, tamed fields.

That isn't just good carving, he thought.

It reminded him of medieval art in ancient churches; not the style or the imagery, but the raw power of bone-deep belief. The Wiccans he'd known in England before the Change had mostly seemed at least slightly barmy to him, when they weren't playacting. He didn't know what Juniper and her friends had been like before the modern world perished, but they weren't putting it on now. Not in the slightest.

Juniper's green eyes twinkled, following his thoughts with disconcerting ease; she linked her fingers around one knee and considered him with her head tilted to one side.

"It wasn't like this when I inherited it from my great-uncle, that good gray Methodist," she said, her tone mock-defensive. "We didn't have much to do but carve, those first winters after the Change, and it was useful with so many new Dedicants, sort of a visual training aid. At first it was just me and my coveners and a few friends like Dennie. Then we had to help other people, get the farms started again and make tools and save the livestock, fight off the bandits and Eaters and . . . It all just sort of . . . snowballed."

"I had the same feeling of riding the tiger in directions unpredictable over in England, my dear," Nigel said. "I've seen it elsewhere. While things were in flux, one strong personality with luck and, hmmm, *baraka*, could set the tone for a whole region, like a seed-crystal in a saturated solution. As Charles and I did in England, until I fell out with His Majesty."

Juniper shivered very slightly as she looked around. "And as I appear to have done hereabouts."

"I should think you'd be glad to see more come around to your way of thinking?" he probed gently.

"The Craft never did hunt for converts the way the religions of the Book do; we waited for those who were interested to seek us out. When the student is ready, the teacher appears. Then suddenly there were so many . . ."

"Are you sorry?" Nigel asked.

She thought for a moment, then shook her head. "No . . . no, I'm not really sorry. The old world was dead the instant the machines stopped working. The new one needs a strong belief, a hearth-faith to strengthen folk through hard times. That's helped us make as good a life here as humankind can live nowadays, I think. Or it would be if there weren't robbers and hostile neighbors, sure."

"It's certainly taken on your, ah, coloration, your Clan Mackenzie." He nodded at her pleated kilt and the plaid pinned at her shoulder with a silver brooch. "Symbols become important at a time like that."

"That was Dennis!" Juniper protested, laughing; then she grew grave. "Do you remember that flash of light and the spike of pain, when the Change came?"

"Indeed I do," he said. "It was the middle of the night in England and I was asleep, but—"

Inwardly, he shivered a little at the memory. He'd woken shouting, with Maude's scream in his ears. The pain had been over in an instant, but it was as intense as anything he'd ever felt, even when the RPG drove grit into his eyes in the wadi back in Oman, and he'd thought he was blind for life.

Every human being on Earth—and every other creature with a spinal cord—had felt the pain and seen the wash of silver fire. Half London had been screaming. The sound had come clearly through the window, in a place where the throb of machines was absent for the first time in centuries. Then the beginning of the city-consuming fires had broken the utter darkness. . . . The failure of everything electrical and of all combustion motors had been obvious within an hour. It hadn't been until troops under his command tried to put down rioters and looters next day that it had become apparent that explosives didn't work either, starting with CS gas and baton rounds and moving up to live ammunition.

Juniper shook herself, casting off dark memories of her own; anyone who'd survived had them. "I've wondered whether that moment, the white light and the pain, didn't do something to us. To our minds, you see."

"Hmmm," he said. "That's an interesting thought, though. My wife—Maude—said something similar to me once . . ."

Her fingers touched the back of his hand, lightly, for an instant. "I wish I could have met her," Juniper said gently. "From the shape of her man and her son, she must have been a very special lady."

He drank the last of the mead to cover his flush. "She wouldn't want me to brood."

Juniper made a *tsk!* sound. "Nigel, grief's nothing to be ashamed of. It's the tribute we pay our dead, but they don't ask more than we can give."

He looked up and met her eyes, and felt an unwilling thaw at the concern he saw there. "That sounds . . . familiar somehow. Is it a quote?"

She smiled. "Something Mother said to me once." A shake of the head. "I do think that moment at the Change may have changed us, too, though. There was so much madness afterwards, and so swiftly."

"I'm afraid there's no way to test it. And while Johnson did say that the prospect of being hanged concentrates a man's mind, the prospect of imminent inescapable death can certainly drive people mad, especially if the laws of nature are mucked about with at the same time."

They were both somber for a moment; nine in ten of humankind had perished in the year that followed. Then they shook it off; those who couldn't had joined that majority long years ago. Despair could kill you just as surely as hunger or plague.

Instead they chatted of small, recent things, the new artificial-swamp waste system he'd help install here at Dun Juniper, Rudi's progress with the sword—which Nigel privately thought was alarmingly swift for a boy his age—and then fell into a companionable silence until the trestle tables were set up for dinner.

There aren't many women I've felt comfortable just sitting by, except Maude, of course, he thought; then he caught that disconcerting twinkle again. *Or ones who could read me that quickly.*

CHAPTER THREE

Dun Fairfax, Willamette Valley, Oregon
December 15th, 2007/Change Year 9

"There," Sam Aylward—Sam Aylward Mackenzie, these days—said, as he finished smoothing the spot where he'd tooled his maker's initials into the deerhide covering of the bow's riser.

He wiped down the length of the longbow with an oiled linen rag and held it up to the lantern slung from the roof of his workshop before tossing it to the man on the other stool.

"Ah, now there's a proper job of work," John Hordle said, putting down his beer mug to slide the weapon between great spade-shaped hands whose backs were dense with reddish furze. "You could do a bit of shooting with this!"

The workshop had been a two-car garage and storage area attached to the farmhouse of the Fairfax family before the Change; they hadn't survived it long, being elderly and extremely diabetic. Now Aylward's wife Melissa had her loom over by the rear wall with a big new window cut for light, and the forward end held a bowyer's needs. There was a pleasant smell of seasoning cut wood from the lengths of yew and Port Orford cedar lying on the roof-joists overhead, and of paint and glue, leather and varnish and oiled metal from the benches with their vises, clamps and rows of tools. Everything was painstakingly neat, even the shavings carefully swept up into a box—that chore was mostly done by his son Edain and stepdaughter Tamar, who accounted it a privilege to wield a broom after he let them watch and occasionally hand him a tool.

They weren't here at the moment, since their mother had them corralled to help with dinner; Aylward was alone with Hordle and Chuck Barstow. Aylward was a stocky man going on fifty, with thick, curly brown hair a little grizzled at the temples, no more than medium height but thick-armed and broad-shouldered and even stronger than he looked; Barstow was a decade younger, lean and wiry and near six feet, with a sandy beard trimmed to a point and thinning hair of the same color. Hordle was the youngest in his late twenties, towering over both the others at six-foot-seven, three hundred and ten pounds of bone and muscle with a ruddy face like a cured ham and a thatch of dark red-brown hair and little hazel eyes, built massively enough that you didn't realize his full height until he stood close. When he strung the heavy longbow, it was with an effortless flex of arm and hip.

Aylward and Hordle had the same accent, a slow thick south-English yokel drawl out of deepest rural Hampshire; Barstow's was General American, what you'd expect from someone born in Eugene in 1967 and raised there. But they all had something in common, something beyond the Mackenzie kilt and the weathered skin of men who spent much time out of doors in all weathers, an indefinable quality of coiled wariness even at rest, a readiness for sudden violent action that only another practitioner of their deadly trade might have caught.

"There's a few improvements over the old plain crooked stick, y'might say," Aylward said. "The reflex out at the tips makes it throw faster, and the deflex in on either side of the riser keeps it stable. More accurate, less hand-shock. A strip of raw deerhide glued on the back, to keep splinters from starting."

He grinned with mock modesty as his giant countryman examined the bow. It had a central grip of rigid black walnut root, carved to fit the hand and covered in suede-finished leather that would drink sweat and prevent slipping; just above that was a ledge for the arrow-rest, cut in so that it ran through the centerline of the bow and lined with two tufts of rabbit-skin. The tapering limbs with their subtle double curve were Pacific yew, mountain-grown for a dense hard grain, the orange heartwood on the belly of the bow and the paler sapwood on the back. He'd made it the traditional length, as tall as the user when unstrung plus a bit, and it took a hundred and fifty pounds to draw it the full thirty-two inches. Few men could manage a draw-weight that heavy; Aylward's own war bow took a hundred and ten, and Chuck's was a hundred. Hordle managed this one easily enough . . .

"What's this then?" Hordle said, flicking a sausage-thick finger at the inside of the stave just above the riser. "I thought you didn't hold wi' laminations?"

"I don't," Aylward said, using the rag to wipe his hands clean of the linseed oil he'd used on the yew; it rasped a little as threads caught on the heavy callus on his hands. "Those fillets of horn are pegged into the riser and working free against strips of hardwood glued on the stave, ten inches either way of the grip. It gives it just that extra bit of"—he snapped his fingers out and back—"flick."

Chuck Barstow grinned. "And you'll be the envy of the whole Willamette, with a bow from the hands of Aylward the Archer, himself himself," he said.

Aylward snorted. "Bollocks," he said. "There's many I've trained who make bows as good as mine, and plenty more who're good as needs be, and I weren't the only bowyer around here to start with. Bowmaking isn't a master-craftsman's trade, you can learn it well enough in a few months if you're handy and have the knack, and God knows we've plenty of good yew in this part of the world. For that matter there's better shots than me among the Mackenzies, and no doubt more elsewhere."

"You could still make a good living selling your bows," Barstow said. "Those two you taught do it in Sutterdown, full-time. They've had clients come from as far away as Idaho."

"I like getting my hands into the dirt, when I'm not off on Lady Juniper's business," Aylward said stoutly. "And growing what I eat. Reminds me of growing up on the farm with Mum and Dad back in the old country." He jerked a thumb at Hordle. "Not far from where this great gallybagger idled his youth away."

John Hordle gave a theatrical shudder. "Now, *my* dad owned a pub," he said to Chuck. "That's a man's life, I tell you. Chatting up the totty and tossing back the Real Ale, and none of that shoveling muck into the spreader on a cold winter's day."

"Then why didn't you stay on at the Pied Merlin instead of going for a soldier?" Aylward asked.

"Because of all the ruddy lies you told me about being in the SAS while I was still a nipper," Hordle said good-humoredly. "Ended up humping a full pack over every sodding mountain in Wales doing the regimental selection, I did. Which probably saved me life come the Change. Otherwise I'd have starved or got et, like most, instead of getting out to the Isle of Wight with the colonel."

"Oh, I don't know," Aylward replied. "Sir Nigel always looked after 'is own. You told me he got my sisters and their kids out, didn't you? And he'd not seen hair nor hide o' me in years. From what you said, he had them set up with their men on their own farms afterwards, too, when things settled down a bit. He'd have seen you right."

Hordle nodded. "Might be, though things were just a bit hairy right then. Want to go and have a try with this?" he asked, flourishing the bow.

"Always a pleasure to watch you overshoot and miss, mate. You still pluck on the release, after all these years."

The men already wore their homespun wool jackets; the workshop wasn't exactly cold, but it wasn't shirtsleeve-comfortable either. Over those the two clansmen draped and pinned their plaids, and they all put on hooded winter cloaks, woven of undyed gray wool with the grease still in it to shed water. They also slung quivers over their backs, took their own bows from where they hung on pegs, and buckled on sword belts; Barstow and Aylward wore Clan-style shortswords, twenty-inch cut-and-thrust blades modeled on the old Roman gladius, with bone-hilted dirks on the right for balance. Hordle's was more suited to his height, though not quite a full-fledged greatsword: a broad forty-two-inch blade with a long ring-and-bar crossguard and a hilt that could be used in one hand or both, what the Middle Ages had called a bastard longsword. Aylward whistled sharply as they left.

"Heel, Garm, Grip," he said, and two big shaggy dogs rose from curled-up sleep to follow them.

Dun Fairfax was busy outside, in a relaxed winter way. There were a dozen homes inside the earth berm and log palisade, besides the century-old original Fairfax farmhouse and barn, along with a fair collection of lesser buildings: henhouses and storage and pens. A chanting came from the Dun's covenstead, where the coven and the year's crop of Dedicants practiced a Yule ritual; a half dozen more stood and admired the big, carved wooden mask of the Green Man they'd just fastened over the doorway. From homes and sheds there was a clatter of tools: the rising-falling moan of spinning wheels, less commonly the rhythmic thump of a loom, a cracking as a sharp steel froe split cedar shingles from a log under the tapping of a wooden mallet. The air held farmyard smells, though nothing too rank, and woodsmoke, the smells of baking bread and cooking meat as kitchens prepared for the evening meal.

A hammer rang on steel as well in a brick-built smithy with the face of Goibniu painted on the door, and Sam Aylward grunted satisfaction.

"Glad we finally got our own smith," he said. "Pain in the arse, it was, always going up to Dun Juniper or sending for someone when something needed fixing. I tried me hand at it, but it's fair tricky."

Melissa Aylward stuck her head out of a second-story window before the three were out of hailing distance: "Sam!"

"Yes, love?" he said, pausing and looking upward.

Melissa was a comfortable-looking woman in her late thirties, with a frizz of yellow hair surrounding a round blue-eyed face; she held their youngest in the crook of one arm, and Fand kicked her arms and legs with a determination that had increased notably as she neared ten months. Her other hand held toddler Richard Aylward back from the windowsill with practiced ease. Melissa's first husband had been on the East Coast at the time of the Change, and Aylward had met her in the summer of the first Change Year.

"If you're off to shoot, remember the chicken stew will be ready by dark, and the dumplings won't keep," she warned. "If you want to eat them, not shoot them at a castle with a catapult."

"We'll be there," Sam said, waving.

"Not me, sorry, Melissa," Chuck called up. "Judy's expecting me back at Dun Juniper."

He waved northward up the slope of the low mountain that overhung Dun Fairfax; the Mackenzie headquarters was a mile in that direction, on a broad ledge that nature had cut back into the hillside.

"The two of you, then," she said. "Full dark and not later!"

"I should say we will be there," Hordle said, smacking his lips as they turned away. "Your missus can cook a treat, Samkin."

He winked at Barstow. "Sam, he could burn water, himself, unless he's changed over here."

Chuck shuddered. "Tell me. I've been on hunting trips with him these ten years past, not to mention campaigning. We learned to put him on woodchopping detail fast enough."

Hordle shook his head. "Hard to remember Sam's had a life since the Change. Back in England we thought he'd be dead somewhere, and then seeing him here, a father three times over no less—gave me a turn, it did."

"Which is why you've been hanging about down here at Dun Fairfax, catching up with your old mate," Aylward said with heavy sarcasm. "And not doing your best to chat up Lady Juniper's daughter, eh?"

"And studying Sign until the brains ran out of his ears to do it," Chuck Barstow added. "Eilir's charmed. Though not as charmed as she was with young Alleyne."

"Don't know what the 'ell you grizzled old farts are talking about," Hordle said. "I was just being friendly, like."

"Hullo, Sam." A woman nodded to the men as she drove half a dozen Jersey milkers towards the old Fairfax barn, which held the cream separator and barrel-churn and the precious galvanized milk-tins all the households used.

"Kate," he replied.

A man did likewise as he pushed a wheelbarrow of straw

and manure, steaming slightly in the damp chill, in the other direction. More greetings came from children who played whooping running games until their parents collared them for chores, and a couple called from where they made repairs to a roof, tapping home nails to hold on fresh shingles.

"Quite the squire, eh, Samkin?" Hordle asked, a teasing note in his voice, and Barstow laughed.

"No, I'm not," Aylward said shortly. "I've got a good farm and some help with it, like more than one here. If you want squires, you'll have to go and apply at the Bearkillers. Bad enough I ended up running the ruddy army, after swearing I'd die a sergeant."

"Running the ruddy war-levy of the Clan Mackenzie," Chuck said, and smiled at Sam's snort.

Men and dogs walked in companionable silence out through the blockhouse and narrow gate, waving answer to the sentry's hail, then down the farm road that ran southward from Dun Fairfax; Aylward and Chuck made a gesture of reverence at the grave of the Fairfaxes not far distant, and Hordle nodded respectfully. A pair of ravens flew up from the gravestone, probably attracted by the offerings of milk and bread that some left there—which was ironic, since the old farmer and his wife had been Mormons, who'd bought the farm not long before the Change as a retirement place.

The settlement was in a valley that thrust into the foothills of the mountains and opened out westward towards the plain of the southern Willamette. The snowpeaks of the High Cascades were hidden by cloud, but the lower slopes rose north and south and east, shaggy with Douglas fir and western hemlock and the odd broadleaf oak or maple; drifts of mist trailed from the tops of the tall trees. There was a scent of damp earth as they walked past rolling fields, plowland and pasture and orchard, until they reached the road that followed Artemis Creek west out towards the plain.

That was blocked by a flood of off-white sheep for a moment, parting around the men like river water around rocks; the heavy, slightly greasy scent of them was strong, and their breath steamed in the damp, chill air. The man who watched the combined flocks of the Dun Fairfax families waved to Aylward, who made an exasperated sound and then waited as he came up, his collie at his heels. He wore sword and dirk as well, had his bow in the loops beside his quiver and a heavy ashwood shepherd's crook in his hands.

"Anything, Larry?" Aylward said to the man who'd once owned a bookstore.

"Took a shot at a coyote skulking around, but I missed," he said. His face was irregular and shrewd, with a tuft of chin-beard, what people meant when they said *full of character*.

Then the crook darted out and fell around the neck of a ewe who'd decided to head down towards Artemis Creek.

"*Back* there, unless you want to hit the stewpot early, you brainless lump of fuzzy suet!" he said wearily, then went on to the men: "Otherwise, just another day with the damned sheep. Lord and Lady, but they're boring! It could be worse; I could be herding turkeys. Anyway, I wanted to talk about the Yule rites, if you had a minute, Sam."

"I'm a bit busy just now, Larry," Aylward said. "Later. And I'm only a Dedicant, any rate."

As they walked on past the sheep Chuck grinned. "And there's a sore point," he said to Hordle. Aylward snorted as the lean man went on: "Melissa's High Priestess of the coven here. She thinks Samkin should be an Initiate—High Priest eventually, too. Everyone else in the dun does, too; he's their landfather."

"Larry does a perfectly good job of it," Aylward said stolidly. "Better than I could, any rate."

"And you can't see yourself with antlers on your head dancing beneath the moon, eh, Samkin?" Hordle teased.

"Chuck's High Priest at Dun Juniper when he's not Lord of the Harvest and Second Armsman," Aylward pointed out with satisfaction. "Antlers, robe, dancing and all."

"Ooops! Sorry, mate, I forgot—no offense."

"None taken," Chuck Barstow said, laughing aloud. "I just like getting a rise out of Sam about it now and then."

"It's being raised Church of England," Hordle said, entering into the spirit. "Actually believing in anything isn't allowed."

Aylward chuckled himself, then shook his head. "When you're around Lady Juniper for a while, you can believe anything, straight up. I just embarrass easily . . . well, I'm still English, so it's only natural, innit? But when you think about it, how likely was it I'd be in the Cascades in March, back in ninety-eight? Or get trapped in a gully and have Herself find me before I died?"

Chuck Barstow nodded. "Juney's right about you being a gift from Cernunnos, Sam. Having you around may or may not have saved us; I think it did, starting with seeing off those foragers from Salem. We certainly wouldn't be nearly as strong without you."

He elbowed the tall form of John Hordle. "And figure the odds on you and Sir Nigel and Alleyne ending up here, too, nine years later, you scoffing cowan. The Lord and Lady look after Their own."

"He's got a point there, John," Aylward said. "It's turned into Old Boys Day here for the 'ampshire 'ogs. Must be the Gods, mucking about with the numbers."

Hordle snorted. "Mate, everyone still alive is lucky enough to have won the bloody National Lottery twice over back before the Change. For that matter, the sodding Change burned out my habit of asking why things turn out the way they do. If that can happen, what's impossible?"

They came to the pasture Dun Fairfax was using for target practice and vaulted the gate. It was ten acres, surrounded by decaying board and wire fences that were lined with young hawthorn plants in the process of becoming hedges, and studded with a dozen huge Oregon oaks. They checked carefully—they didn't want someone's cow, or worse still a child, wandering about—and threw back their cloaks to free their right arms.

"Dropping shots over the third oak suit you two for a start?" Aylward said, indicating a tree a hundred and fifty yards off.

When the others nodded he brought up his bow and shot three times in eight seconds, the flat snap of the string on his bracer like a crackle of fingers; two more shafts were in the air when the first one went *thunk* into the board outline of a man with a shield. All three struck; the first two within a handspan of each other in the target's chest, but the last was pushed a little aside and down at the last instant by a gust of wind.

"Well, even if you didn't kill him outright, *he's* not going to breed again," Hordle said, drawing the new bow to the ear and raising it at a fifty-degree angle towards the sky. Then: "Bugger!"

His shaft cleared the crown of the oak, and the target as well, by about twenty yards.

"Told you you'd overshoot with that, Little John," Aylward said smugly. "You're getting another dozen feet per second with the same draw."

"First try with a new bow," Hordle said defensively. "Only natural I'm off the once." The second landed a little short; the third . . .

"Did he miss?" Chuck Barstow asked, peering.

"Not from the sound," Aylward replied. "Punched right through. Extra point."

"It does have that little extra flick. I'll get used to it."

"Over by the tree, this time," Chuck said.

Those targets were rigged to resemble men leaning out from behind the trunk, and they were hung on hinges so that they swung in and out of sight when there was any wind. Barstow shot three times with the smooth action of a metronome, and the shafts flicked hissing through the gray gloaming to land with a hard, swift *tock-tock-tock* rhythm.

Hordle looked at the chewed-up surface of the targets. "Does everyone here practice like your kilties, Sam? It's the law back in Blighty these days everyone has to keep a bow and use it, but most just put in an hour or two on Sunday and take the odd rabbit."

Chuck Barstow grinned. "That's one of my jobs as Second Armsman, going around from dun to dun and checking that they do practice every day. I threaten them with Sam if I find out they've been goofing off. And testing to see who meets the levy standards, of course."

"Which are?"

"Fifty-pound draw at least, twelve aimed shafts a minute,

and able to hit a man-sized target at a hundred yards eight times in ten."

"Fifty's a bit light for a war bow," Hordle said.

Sam Aylward shrugged. "A heavier draw's a better draw, but fifty's useful enough—I've seen a bow that weight put an arrow all the way through a bull elk at a hundred paces, and break ribs going in and going out. Which wouldn't do a man any good, eh?"

Chuck nodded. "And that's the minimum, of course; the average is around eighty. Nearly everyone hunts for the pot these days, what with the way deer and wild pigs have gotten to be pests, and absolutely everyone knows there's times your life is going to depend on shooting fast and straight."

Hordle grunted, drawing and loosing. The arrow whacked home, and a chunk of the fir target weakened by multiple impacts broke off and went out of sight.

"Well, you've more fighting to do here than folk back in England," he said. "There's the Brushwood men, but they're not much more than a bloody nuisance unless you're up on the edge of cultivation north of London."

Aylward sighed and shook his head; he'd been here in Oregon at the time of the Change, and there hadn't been any news from the Old World until the Lorings and Hordle arrived on a Tasmanian ship before this last Beltane. It was still a wrench, visualizing southern England as a pioneer zone, a frontier wilderness where a bare six hundred thousand survivors fought encroaching brambles, hippo roamed the Fens, wolves howled in the streets of Manchester, and tigers gone feral from safari parks took sheep even on the outskirts of Winchester, the new capital.

"And of course there's the odd dust-up with the Moors, or the wild Irish when we have to help out Ian's Rump over in Ulster," Hordle said slyly, in the next interval in their shooting. "There's a joke for you—the Change and all, and we're *still* having problems with the Provos."

"Better not mention that too often among Mackenzies," Aylward said. "Half the folk in our territory here have hypnotized themselves into believing they're cousins of Finn Mac

Cool. For all that they're Ulstermen by descent as much as anything, a lot of them. Scots-Irish, they call it here."

"Not me," Chuck Barstow said. "English and German in my family tree, plus a couple of Bohunks, a trace of Canadian French and a little Indian way back. And Judy's Jewish—or Jewitch, as she likes to put it."

"At least you don't try putting on a brogue, Chuck. Every second kiltie these days does, or tries to rrrrrroll their r's as if they were from Ayrrrrshire."

He went on to Hordle: "We still get a fair count of plain old-fashioned bandits now and then, too, which keeps everyone on their toes. Plenty of places aren't doing as well as us, just scraping by, and east of the mountains there's always fighting, all of which gets us a yearly crop of broken men too angry to beg but hungry enough to steal."

"And you've got Arminger waiting up in Portland," Hordle said. "After Sir Nigel and I had the pleasure of his hospitality for weeks, I'd have to agree you've got a roit nasty old piece of work there."

Chuck Barstow nodded grimly. He'd lost an adopted son in a skirmish with the Protector's men only the summer past. Then his face lightened.

"Look!"

The dogs had strayed off a little while the men moved around the pasture shooting; the beasts were far too well trained to get in front of an archer without permission. Now the three archers could hear a frenzy of barking from across the road to the south, down in the alder and fir woods that lined Artemis Creek. An explosion of wings came seconds later, and a gabbling, honking sound as a quartet of Canada geese came out of the willows, thrashing themselves into the air on their broad wings with long necks stretched out in terror. The birds had bred beyond belief in recent years; they were a standing menace to the crops . . . and very tasty, done right.

"You first, Chuck!" Aylward called jovially.

The Armsman held the draw for an instant, still as a statue except for the minute movement of his left arm, then let the string roll off the gloved fingers of his right hand. *Snap* as it struck the bracer, and then one of the geese seemed to stagger in midair, folding around itself and dropping like a rock.

That only took an instant, but the birds were rising fast. Aylward shot twice, the arrows disappearing in the murk as they rose, and another two of the big birds fell as if the air beneath their wings had turned to vacuum.

"Too late, Little John," Aylward taunted; the last was nearly out of sight. "Too late!"

Hordle made a wordless sound, then shot. The dusk was falling, but they could see that the goose stumbled as if it had hit a bump in the air, before circling down with a broken-winged flutter.

"Not so late as all that, Samkin," Hordle said smugly.

"Tsk, Little John. Nobody taught you to finish 'em off?" He shot as he spoke, and the bird fell limp the last hundred feet to hit the grass with an audible thump.

"Aylward the Archer!" Chuck Barstow said with good-natured mockery. "Showoff!"

A dog ran up, wagging its tail and dropping a goose at Aylward's feet. Collecting the others took a few minutes, and finding all the arrows they could.

"Sorry, little brothers," Chuck said, making a sign over the birds when they had the bodies laid out in a row. "But we need to keep our gardens and grain safe, and we have to eat. Cernunnos, Lord of all wildwood dwellers, witness that we take in need, not wantonness, knowing that for us too the hour of the Hunter shall come. Guide them flying on winds of golden light to the Summerlands. Mother-of-All, let them be reborn through You."

Aylward murmured polite assent, and then they trimmed a sapling from the hedgerow and headed back towards the walls of Dun Fairfax with the stick thrust between the birds' trussed feet; four big geese came to a considerable weight.

"Good eating, these," Hordle said, smacking his lips. "Hang them for a bit, roast them with bread-and-nut stuffing, some mushrooms in it, and some bacon grease on the outside—"

"Andy and Diana would like a couple for the celebration dinner up at Dun Juniper," Chuck said. "We're having a competition next week—bagpipers from half a dozen duns."

At Aylward's shudder, he went on: "Come on, Sam, that many pipers . . . it'll be a sight and sound to behold!"

"So's a pig with its arse on fire," the older man said dourly, and Hordle's laughter boomed out like artillery.

♦

CHAPTER FOUR

Mithrilwood, Willamette Valley, Oregon
December 17th, 2007/Change Year 9

*P*erfect, Eilir Mackenzie said in Sign.

There were a dozen others here in the woods with Juniper Mackenzie's daughter; her *anamchara*—soul-sister—Astrid Larsson, and half a score of their Dúnedain Rangers. Those were youngsters who'd joined them in what was first more than half play, a chance to ramble and hunt, and then turned serious over the years. She and Astrid were the eldest of those at twenty-three; the youngest here was sixteen-year-old Crystal, a refugee from the Protectorate. They'd saved her and her family from a baron's hunters and hounds this last spring, just as their original oath demanded, the one they'd sworn back at the beginning, to protect the helpless and succor the weak. It had seemed like a great idea when they were fourteen; since then it had turned out to be a lot of work, though satisfying.

The other two with them were Alleyne Loring and Little John Hordle, both a few years older than the Dúnedain leaders, but still young men.

This will make a perfect Yule Log, Eilir went on. *If we can get it through the door.*

The log had been bigleaf maple, growing on the side of the canyon; it had fallen whole as it came down, pulled out of the rocky soil by its own weight and falling across a basalt boulder a few feet above the root-ball. Bigleaf maple was like stone itself, useful for furniture or tool handles or fancy carving and yielding a pleasant, sweet sap in spring. This one had fallen about a year ago, to judge by the state of the wood; it was grown with moss and shelflike fungi and the bark had peeled away, but the feel was still solid when she stamped her boot on it. That meant it would be hard to kindle but would burn long and slow, unlike the fierce, swift heat of Douglas fir or hemlock or the spark-spitting enthusiasm of Ponderosa pine.

Astrid nodded solemnly, setting her long white-blond braids bobbing in the shadowed gloom, the overcast winter sky shedding only a silvery-gray shadowed light through the branches and needles above them. Then she looked up at Eilir, a twinkle in her strange silver-shot eyes; not many could have seen it there, but they'd been inseparable since they'd met in the fall of the first Change Year, when the Bearkillers came west over the High Cascades. Eilir's hair was raven black and her eyes green, nose shorter and mouth fuller, cheekbones not so chiseled; apart from that they were similar in looks as well, both tall at five-eight or so, moving with whip-cord grace.

"It'd be hard work cutting this to a useful length," Lord Bear's sister-in-law said casually in the Sindarin her Dúnedain used among themselves, as if addressing the air. "We need about, oh, ten feet." The thick bottom section of the trunk was fifty feet long before it frayed out into a tangle of crown, lying half on the old state park trail and half off it. "We'll have to break out a whipsaw . . . too tough for ax-work."

"Hordle and I can handle it," Alleyne said. "Shouldn't take long if we spell each other."

Eilir cocked one leaf-colored eye at Hordle, whose great hamlike countenance assumed a woebegone grimace; that turned into a grin at her as she giggled silently.

I'm glad Astrid finally found a fellah, she thought, and pushed down wistful thoughts about Alleyne's handsome countenance. *Though it must be sort of frustrating for the poor guy, stuck on first base while he's courting a skittish virgin. I'm pretty sure she still is, too, from the signs. I love you dearly,* anamchara, *but that's sort of slow off the mark and he won't wait forever! Get your legs locked around him before he escapes!*

The two men stripped to the waist; it was cold, just around freezing with the ground a mixture of melting snow and mud, but working hard in jacket and shirt just got you sweaty and then chilled. They were down at the bottom of a cleft in the basalt rock, anyway, and well out of the wind; you could see the banded layers in the steep slope to the north, and the creek ran behind them with clumps of ice around the rocks in it. Streamside and slope and the rolling hills higher up were densely grown with big trees; fir and hemlock on the upland, maple and cottonwood and alder lower, yew and chinquapin, with the blackened stems of ferns sticking up out of the leaf litter and duff. The smell of decaying leaves and needles was pungent as boots disturbed them, suddenly intensely aromatic as someone crushed the branch of an incense-cedar sapling.

Eilir smiled at her friend as they moved the two-horse team they'd brought along and wrapped a chain around the thicker base of the tree.

Got Alleyne to show off, hey? she signed.

You betcha, Astrid replied, with a smile of smug satisfaction. *He's a wonderful guy, but he's still a guy, you know? Which means he's sort of stupid at times. Besides, he looks good with his shirt off.*

Little John's smarter, Eilir signed. He *saw through it.*

He is not! Astrid's hands moved emphatically. *Alleyne just has too noble a nature to suspect anyone!*

Yeah, blond, beautiful and dumb, like someone else I could name but won't—like for example you, Eilir taunted. Astrid stuck her tongue out in reply.

The friends finished their task, jumped free, checked that nobody else was in the way and waved to Crystal, who stood at the horses' heads. The girl urged them forward, and the beasts leaned into their harness. The big log swiveled across rocks, then came down onto the bike path with a thud that echoed up through the soles of her feet. It was far too heavy for the team to drag back while it remained whole, even though they had a two-wheeled lift to put under the forward end to ease the work. There was a good ton of weight involved.

We'll save the upper part, there's some useful wood there, Eilir signed.

The tree being dead already, they didn't have to do more than sketch a sign over it; you had to apologize and explain the need when you cut living wood, the way you did when you killed a beast. They were all children of the Mother and part of Lord Cernunnos' domain, after all.

The men got busy, standing on either side of the log and chopping, while a few of the Dúnedain trimmed the branches further up with hatchets and saws. Eilir cradled her longbow in her arms and watched appreciatively. Alleyne was a bit over six feet, and built like an Apollo in one of Mom's books, broad-shouldered and narrow in the waist, long in the arms and legs; the muscle moved like living metal under his winter-pale skin as he swung the felling ax and chips of the rock-hard maple flew, startling yellow-white against the dark ground. Beside him Hordle looked like a related but distinct species, arms like the tree trunk itself, and a thick pelt of dark auburn hair running down his chest onto a belly corded like ship's cable; the log shook under the impact of the heavy double-bitted ax he used.

It was still seasoned hardwood, and the work went slowly. Eilir grinned.

Ah, hard honest work, she signed. *It does me good just to watch it.*

Alleyne's ears burned a little redder. The wood yielded, but slowly; it took only a little more to finish trimming the branches and roll the upper section of the trunk off the path for later attention.

Eilir had been deaf from birth; before it, in fact, when a teenaged Juniper Mackenzie contracted German measles in the fourth month of her pregnancy. That didn't make her other senses more acute, the way many believed; what it did do was encourage her to use and pay attention to them. She'd also spent much of her life in the countryside and amongst its wildlife, around Dun Juniper when it was just her and her mother before the Change; and in mountains and woods, hills and fields all over western Oregon in the years since, hunting, Rangering, or wandering and observing for their own sake. And she had been trained by experts, Sam Aylward not least.

All that told her that *something* was not quite right. . . .

Mithrilwood had been a state park before the Change, and since then the area all about it had been mostly unpeopled, young forests and abandoned fields growing lush fodder for beast and bird. It normally swarmed with life, even in winter when many of the birds went south; upland game migrated down here from the High Cascades in this season, and everything from beaver and rabbits to deer, elk, coyote, wild boar, bear, cougar and feral tiger were common. The bigger animals would avoid the noise and clatter of humans, though not as widely as they did before the Change. The smaller would be cautious, but . . .

She turned and clicked her tongue at Astrid. The other woman was already frowning.

"Hsssst!" Astrid Larsson said as she turned, to attract everyone's eyes, and moved her hands in Sign as well: *Someone's near. Watching. Don't let them know they've been seen, but be ready.*

Nobody froze; the dozen Dúnedain continued to muscle the big log towards the waiting horses and the two-wheeled drag that would support its forward end. The forest floor was mostly clear of undergrowth, and the trees had closed their canopy long ago.

Then they casually reached for their bows; you had to know Sign as well as Sindarin to be a Ranger. Astrid's silver-veined eyes flicked about. They were in a canyon, one of the many that laced the old state park. Rock stretched up on either hand, layers of basalt cut through by millennia of rushing water. Much of that was frozen this day, on the stone and on the moss-grown limbs of the great trees. In the middle distance a waterfall toned, out of sight around the dogleg to the west, but rumbling through the cold, wet air. That white noise covered conversation, and many of the ordinary sounds of movement.

"Who?" Alleyne Loring said quietly as he donned his mail shirt and buttoned the jacket over it again.

Six heads were close together as they bent to lift the end of the long timber into the clamp and fasten the chain across it. Astrid spoke smiling, as if chatting casually among friends out to find a Yule Log.

"Yrch," she said; to the Dúnedain that meant *enemies.* "Could be bandits, could be servants of the Lidless Eye. I saw only two that I'm sure of, so they've got some woodcraft."

Eilir Mackenzie nodded and casually stretched with her arms above her head, which gave her an excuse to look about.

I spotted him—the fir over from the boulder with the point, snow knocked off the branch, she signed. *The other's behind the boulder?*

Astrid nodded as she mentally tallied their strength here. Herself and Eilir, her *anamchara.* Alleyne Loring and John Hordle; first-class warriors, though not exactly Dúnedain themselves, not quite. Young Crystal, but she didn't really count for a fight. Only sixteen, and not fully trained; brave, but the weak link, the more so as she was slight-built. Another ten Dúnedain, in their late teens or early twenties, six of them Mackenzies and the other four Bearkillers. Everyone had bow and quiver, sword and knife and targe or buckler; you didn't go outdoors without, any more than you'd walk out naked. The two Englishmen had light mail shirts under their jackets; under her own she wore a black leather tunic lined with mesh-mail and nylon; Eilir had on a Clan-style brigandine, a double-ply canvas affair with small metal plates riveted between the layers. Most of the others had something similar, but none was wearing a helmet.

"We don't know how many or why," Astrid said. "So we'll all just walk around the corner of the trail up ahead, and then wait for them—double linear ambush upslope. That way we can shoot without hitting each other. They won't follow close."

Send Crystal on to the Lodge with the horses from there? Eilir signed.

Crystal's face was a little pale, but she glared at Eilir; besides being offended at the implication that she couldn't hold her own with the rest, she also had a furious crush on Astrid at the moment . . . which was *so* embarrassing. Though she was beginning to show signs of transferring it to Alleyne, which would be *infuriating*.

Astrid signed back: *No. Too risky—they might have an ambush along the trail already. We'll go around the corner, drop the log, and . . . wait a minute!*

The word *drop* triggered something in her mind. "Here's what we'll do," she began. "Remember that trick we practiced? Like the old story about how the little furry Halfling men fought the wicked Emperor's troopers?"

Eilir's eyes went from the log to the coils of rope draped around it. Her smile grew, and the faces of her companions went from grave to grinning. They were all young.

We'll have to hurry, she signed.

Twenty minutes later Astrid waited behind a tree, wishing for a war cloak, what Sam Aylward called a ghillie suit, of camouflage cloth sewn all over with loops for twigs and leaves. The wool of her jacket would do, it was woven from natural beige fiber; she breathed shallowly and slowly, lest the puff of vapor give her away, and ignored the drip of melting snow from the branches of the big hemlock. She couldn't see any of her Dúnedain, though, except for Alleyne, and that was from the rear where he crouched behind a big basalt rock.

If I can't see them, when I know where they are, the yrch *certainly won't. Raven, totem of my sept, watch over us! Queen of Battles, Lady of the Crows, be with us now! To you, Dread Lord, we dedicate the harvest of this field!*

The canyon widened out a little here, the slopes not quite so steep until they ran into cliff-faces north and south. The old park trail was down fifteen yards below her hiding place, visible between the wide-spaced trunks of the great trees in a twisting line of trodden mud; the horses waited patiently a hundred yards farther east, nearer the waterfall—you could see the mist lifting above the icy curve of it from here. The noise would be good cover. . . .

There was an arrow on the shelf of her bow, cord to the knock, the whole held in her left hand, and forty-four more in her quiver. Her sword was leaned up against the deep-fissured trunk, a single-edged weapon with a basket hilt of brass and a yard-long blade, and her two-foot circular shield was slung over her back on its carrying strap. Everything ready . . .

A flight of birds rose from the eastward, spooked by movement: the yellow undersides showed clearly as they flitted overhead in long, swooping curves, and the buff-brown-black markings as they sped away. *Meadowlarks,* she thought; they were just getting to be common again. *Which was why*—

The distinctive fluting trill of the birds sounded from above her, close enough to the genuine article to fool most.

"—which is why we picked that call for signaling," she murmured to herself.

It was modulated, though, with stuttering intervals that the living bird wouldn't have used. They spoke to her: *they're coming,* and *thirty of them.*

"Thirty. Ouch. Still, nothing for it."

The first came into view, close enough for her to see the snarl of tension on his thin face. He was dressed in rags and patches, but he carried a good crossbow, and there was a sword worn slantwise across his back with the hilt jutting above his left shoulder, a heavy, single-edged chopping blade. The lone figure stood tense, looking about, then turned and beckoned the unseen band behind him.

Astrid's throat grew tight. She forced a deep breath down into her diaphragm, then let it out, with the tension following it, repeating until her body felt loose and ready. She hated bandits with a passion, even more than she loathed the Protector's men; outlaws had killed her mother, right after the Change, and she'd had to watch. The memory was like meat gone off on a hot summer's day.

Soon now. Don't be too eager. Love not the arrow for its swiftness, or the sword for its bright blade, but the things that these guard.

More men followed, until a dozen stood behind the scout, adding their eyes to his. They weren't in any hurry; they must mean to follow the Dúnedain back to the lodge and ring it in, probably for an attack under cover of darkness. More and more, until there were over a score of ragged-gaudy figures. She waited until one looked in precisely the right direction, and until the puzzled cock of his head showed that he'd seen something unnatural.

"Now!" she shouted, snatching up her sword in her right hand.

In the same instant she cut upward, where the stay-rope was secured around the stub of a thick branch. The keen steel went through the hemp and into the tree trunk with a solid thunk; she left the blade embedded in the living wood as she stepped around the trunk for a clear shot. The long arrow came back as she flung the strength of arms and shoulders and gut and hips against the tension of yew and horn and sinew. The double curve of the saddle-bow turned into a pure C as the kiss-ring clamped on the string touched the corner of her mouth.

Eye on the target, not the arrow. There!

Even in the diamond focus of concentration, she saw the mouths below gaping as the log swung down towards them, tumbling free of the loops halfway through its trajectory. The five-hundred-pound balk of maple did a slow spin around its own center before it struck. In a piece of cosmic injustice an end came down right on top of one of the few who'd had the presence of mind to drop to the earth, like a maul in the hands of an angry god or a hammer on a soft-boiled egg. Then the log bounced up and bowled over several more. She could hear the crackle of bone beneath the screams and the heavy, thick *boonnnnk-bonk-bonk* as the log hammered itself to a stop on the rocky ground.

Pick a target, track along until an uninjured man stood gaping with his spear wavering in his hand . . .

Snap.

The string of her recurved bow slapped against the bracer on her left wrist. The arrow flashed out in a smooth, shallow curve, the razor edges of the broadhead twirling as the fletching spun the shaft. It struck with a wet smacking sound audible even fifty yards away; the man goggled at the feathers that bloomed against his breastbone and collapsed, kicking and coughing out blood and probably pieces of lung. Out of the corner of her eye she could see Alleyne stand and draw his longbow to the ear, sighting as calmly as if this was a day's practice at the butts; he was a swordsman rather than an archer by avocation, but he was still a better-than-average shot. On both slopes the Dúnedain were up, and a shower of long cedarwood arrows rained down on the advance party of the enemy force, hissing as they flew, and another flight, and another.

Not all struck. The strangers looked like bandits, and they reacted with the feral swiftness needed to survive in that profession. All but the dead or wounded dove for cover, and a flurry of crossbow bolts and arrows came back at the ambushers; one bolt went by overhead with an unpleasant *vvvvwhh-ppt* sound of cloven air and hammered into a chinquapin to stand buzzing like an angry wasp. Astrid ignored it and shot again, again, then dropped her bow and reached up for the next rope as the remainder of the gang ran shouting around the curve and into sight. It wound tight around her left forearm, and a quick snatch and wrench of her right hand put the cord-wound hilt of her long sword in her grip.

"A Elbereth Gilthoniel!" she shouted, from the bottom of her lungs.

She took three steps forward and launched herself into the air. The weight wrenched at her left arm, and she felt the strong pull of the rope and the springy branch it was lashed to bending beneath her solid hundred and sixty pounds of body and gear. Momentum swept her forward with blurring speed, higher above the surface as she fell towards the trail, skimming in a great arch that left her barreling down the trail towards the enemy at head-height.

"A Elbereth Gilthoniel!" she shouted again, a great, high-soaring silver trumpet-call as she flew.

"Fuck me!" a snaggle-toothed man screamed, as much in astonishment as fear, just before her boot heels struck him in the face.

Crack.

The bandit was flung half a dozen feet backward at the collision, his face a red pulp of flesh and bone fragments. Something heavy and strong seemed to flow up from her feet through her body, cracking it like a whip and snapping her teeth together with a painful click, but she dropped to the ground and let the rope fall away, twitching her shoulder to slide the shield around to where she could run her forearms through the loop. Eilir dropped beside her, jackknifing in the air, her sword and buckler flicking into her hands even as she landed. A spearman gaped at her, then thrust overarm. Eilir ducked under it in a smooth continuation of her fall, whirling as she crouched to snap her shortsword at the back of his knee in a hocking stroke. There was a grisly popping sound like a taut cable parting and he went over backward, screaming and clutching at the injury as if he could squeeze the hamstring back to wholeness.

Astrid brought targe and blade up as another bandit ran at her *anamchara,* stepped forward with a raking stride of her long legs. Her backsword came up and around and down with a looping cut as her right foot squelched into the mud, flashing down in a blurring arc with the weight and the flexing snap of her whole body behind it.

Crack! as the edge cut, and a billman was left staring at the ashwood stub of his weapon's haft as the business end pinwheeled away; she recovered and killed him with a snapping lunge to the neck, fast as a frog's tongue. He dropped with blood spraying from his severed carotids, the red unearthly bright against the dun colors of winter. The enemy were trying to rally, but their heads whipped about as Dúnedain ran down the hills to either side, looking to be twice their actual numbers as they leapt and shouted, their blades out and bright. The outlaw gang froze for crucial seconds as the Dúnedain war cry rang out from a dozen throats:

"Lacho calad! Drego morn!"

Then the rest were beside the two leaders, Alleyne to her left with his heater-shaped shield blazoned with five roses up and his blade ready.

"St. George for England! *A Loring! A Loring!"* he called, handsome face set and grim.

Little John Hordle came thundering up beyond Eilir with his great sword gripped in the two-handed style.

"Sod this for a game of soldiers!" he shouted.

The great blade spun in a horizontal circle. It sliced through a wooden shield and gouged bone-deep into the arm beneath, and took off half the man's face on the upstroke, like a knife topping a boiled egg. A spray of droplets hung in the air for an instant, a red curve splaying out like a ripple in a pond.

"You bints are fucking mad!" he went on in a roar like a foghorn in a fit, as he kicked a spearman in the stomach and crushed his skull with the ball pommel of his heavy blade. *"Who do you think you are, Errol sodding Flynn?"*

The enemy wavered, then as one man turned and ran. A dozen paces were enough to put them around the bend in the trail, and the ground to its left was near-vertical cliff. Astrid swung sword and shield up.

"Hold!" she shouted. "Rally, Dúnedain! No pursuit, it could be a trick. Miniel, get back up the tree and tell me what's happening! Everyone else, get your bows and recover arrows."

Her head twisted back and forth, skimming, and she was suddenly conscious of the sweat running down her flanks. One of her own was down, a black-braided girl named Sadb, clutching at a crossbow bolt in her thigh and struggling not to scream; a boy knelt and vomited, a pressure-cut on his scalp showing where he'd been clouted with something hard; a few others had hurts that ranged from slight to one that would need a few stitches. There were none of the sucking chest-wounds or gut-stabs or pulped bones or depressed-fracture blows to the skull that meant a good chance of death.

About what you'd expect from a good ambush, she thought with relief. *Always a lot cheaper than a stand-up fight, and we caught them flat-footed. Not bad for something improvised on the spot!*

Eilir jerked her head, and red-headed Kevin sheathed his blade and ran to Sadb; he was their best medico. Astrid pulled a horn from a sling at her waist. It was ivory, cream-colored with age—originally part of a tusk at Larsdalen, brought back from a safari her great-grandfather had made with Teddy Roosevelt—and set with silver bands at the mouthpiece. She set it to her lips and blew, a long *huuuuuu,* then three shorter blasts. That would let the rest of the Dúnedain force at the lodge know what was going on; it meant *enemy* and *come quickly;* an answering call came echoing down the canyon walls almost immediately. That would give them enough blades to run the bandit gang to earth and wipe them out.

The rest of her band went about the after-battle chores, retrieving arrows and giving the enemy wounded the mercy-stroke. Whimpers and screams died away to silence.

"Astrid!" a voice called. "Astrid!"

That was Crystal, back with the horses. She had her bow in her hand, though it shook like an aspen leaf.

"I . . . I . . . he came at me and then turned back, and I . . ." she said, lapsing into English.

A bandit was on the trackway not far in front of her, trying to pull himself off it with his hands; an arrow stood jerking in his spine, and his legs were limp.

"Well done, Crystal!" Astrid called, pleased. A memory of some satisfaction teased at her for a moment. "That's good work for your first fight! *Algareb cú!* Now finish him."

The girl stared at her, eyes wide, her mouth opening and closing.

"Don't let him suffer, Crystal," she said impatiently; the bandit collapsed and lay motionless save for the heaving of his chest, eyes blank as his fingers scrabbled feebly in the mud. "Everyone's busy. Put your dirk in under the breastbone and push up and a little to the left, that will do it clean."

"Sloppy-looking lot," Alleyne went on thoughtfully as she turned back.

Astrid nodded agreement. The dead men were mostly skinny, scarred, hairy, and had stunk badly even before edged metal ripped into body cavities; lips drawn back in the death-grimace showed teeth as much yellow or brown as white, though none were older than herself and some as young as Crystal. They'd probably grown up half-feral in communities barely surviving without the tools or skills or stock to make a success of farming, or in bands that had been preying on passersby and neighbors since the dying times just after the Change, or some might be runaway peons from the Protectorate by origin. Lice danced in one sparse beard that jutted skyward from a body arched back in a semicircle; that made her itch by reflex, and make sure nobody was standing too long near a body while they yanked out arrows. Lice carried typhus; they'd have to leave the bodies a full ten days, or burn them, and scrub everyone and do a clothes wash.

The bandits were clad in a patchwork of pre-Change scraps, badly tanned leather, or the crudest and cheapest sort of modern homespun. One or two wore better clothes, doubtless taken from the body of some victim, though they were just as filthy and on their way to being ragged.

Banditry wasn't a very well-paying profession for most practitioners, particularly in winter.

"Well armed, though," she said thoughtfully.

Their crossbows were good, smoothly finished with rifle-style wood stocks and leaf-spring steel bows, and spanning cranks at their belts; the others had competently shaped yew bows; all of them had some sort of sword, most often the heavy machete-like choppers known as falchions . . . or as machetes, outside the Valley. Several had boiled-leather jerkins strapped with pieces of sheet metal, and a couple had bowl or kettle helmets.

"Yes, suspiciously well armed," Alleyne agreed. "And the weapons are far too uniform."

"Now that you mention it—" Astrid began, and then whirled at a sound of distress.

Crystal was kneeling beside the dead bandit, being noisily sick into a growing pool of blood. Eilir made a tsk sound with her lips.

Sometimes, soul-sister, you are sort of insensitive, she signed, and went over to put an arm around the girl's shoulders and urge her away from the body.

Astrid blinked. *Well, I* said *she'd done well,* she thought, then dismissed it.

The horses were restive, tossing their heads; then they pricked their ears and snorted. More hooves pounded on the trail, and then another dozen mounted Dúnedain came up, as many again running on foot beside them gripping the stirrup-leathers for support, all well spattered with muck and woods-duff thrown up by busy hooves. Astrid waved them forward, and turned back to Alleyne.

"—now that you mention it, yes, they are well armed," she

said. "Normally bandits just have odds and ends, no two alike. The ones we ran out of the lodge here a couple of years back, they were using it for a base, they were certainly like that . . . and these all have shoes, see? Fairly new shoes, too."

The robbers' footwear was modern, tanned leather uppers with laces, and either hobnail-studded alder wood or pieces of rubber tire for soles. Not expensive: village cobblers and workshops in a dozen towns from the Protectorate to Corvallis turned out the like. A Mackenzie crofter might have worn them, or a Bearkiller tenant-farmer. But oddly uniform, again; not identical, nothing was these days when handmade was the rule, but as if they'd all come from the same place. She frowned, absently taking her bow as someone handed it to her, and a handful of arrows with bloody points and shafts. Her hands moved automatically, wiping blood off the steel, checking the fletching and slipping them back into her quiver.

"Now, if I was trying to make a gang of bandits more effective, what would I give them?" she mused aloud.

Eilir was back. She and John Hordle began to speak simultaneously, in Sign and aloud, then looked at each other and grinned. Alleyne answered instead.

"Weapons, and in this season, shoes. A man with chilblains can't fight very well."

The lookout she'd posted called down from his perch high in a Douglas fir. "They're coming back! More of them!" Then, after an instant: "I think someone's after them. They look like they're running! Running hard!"

"Positions!" Astrid said. "Kevin, you stay with Sadb."

She joined Alleyne behind his boulder this time; there weren't as many good positions, with their numbers more than doubled. He was chuckling as she settled in. At her arched brow, he leaned his head towards the trail.

"Eilir is reusing the rope," he said. "I like that girl's spirit, damn me if I don't."

Astrid chuckled herself as she saw the trip-rope deployed; covered in mud, it would be nearly invisible while lying slack. There wasn't time for anything fancy, just a knot around one tree and a half hitch around another.

"Eilir's *láwar,*" she agreed happily.

The first of the bandits came around the bend again, running hard. The rope snapped up, and three went down like puppets with their strings cut. A clash of metal and war cries sounded from behind them; somebody *was* chasing them. And then she noticed another figure with the outlaws; this one had a white-and-brown camouflage surcoat over his mail hauberk; both were knee-length. Similar cloth masked his kite-shaped shield, and a conical nose-guarded helmet; his blade was a double-edged longsword.

The rest of the Dúnedain stood as she did, and the outlaws screamed in despair at the sight of better than thirty bows drawn to the ear. A few tried to run on; the Dúnedain bows snapped, and nearly every one of the slashing volley struck.

"Surrender!" Astrid called, carefully not adding any promise of quarter. "Throw down and kneel!"

Most of the survivors threw down their weapons and knelt in the mud, hands clasped on top of their heads, silent amid the moans and screams of the wounded.

The man in the knight's hauberk didn't; he just shouted wordlessly and charged, blade up and shield covering his body from knees to nose. Hordle's bow snapped; the bodkin point slammed into the shield and the shaft punched through the metal and wood, stripping its feathers to flutter to the ground as it did. The man pivoted as if he'd been hit in the shoulder with a sledgehammer, and it must have felt much like that. At close range, a heavy bow could smash a bodkin point right through even the best armor. This went through shield and arm and hauberk, snapping the links of the riveted mail like cloth, then through the shoulder bone and out the other side of the hauberk as well. He pitched over backwards and lay writhing.

The pursuers behind them came into view, and stumbled to a halt at the sight. There were two dozen of them, armed with broad-bladed spears and crossbows or pre-Change compound hunting bows, shortswords and daggers and bucklers. All were clad with rough practicality for a foray in the winter woods, but the leader drew her eye. He was a stocky man in a black robe over mail-and-lamellar armor, with a poleax in his hands and a heavy broadsword belted at his waist. He wore a helmet with a neck flare and an eyeslit visor, now pushed up; on the brow of it was a black cross in a white disk, and the face below it was covered in a close-cropped brown beard. When he handed the long-hafted ax-spear-warhammer to a follower and pulled off the helm, it showed bowl-cut hair and a tonsure in the center of it, the artificial bald spot gleaming with sweat. He passed a gauntleted hand over it.

"Bind them," he snapped to his followers, and then waved at the Dúnedain as the arrows were returned to their quivers.

"Hello, Lady Astrid," he went on genially, climbing towards her, puffing like someone who'd come hard and fast for miles with fifty pounds of steel strapped to his body.

The men behind him worked in pairs, one holding a spear-point to a bandit's neck, the other pulling cords from his belt to bind the robbers' arms behind them, tight-cinched at elbow and wrist. Those badly wounded were given the mercy-stroke. There was no point in letting them suffer until their inevitable execution.

"*Mae govannen,* Brother ... ?" Astrid said.

"Father Andrew," the man said, smiling broadly; he was about her own age. "Ordained priest, and also a humble brother monk of the Benedictine order. I don't think you noticed me, my child, but you were with Lord Bear when he visited the abbey two years ago, for the treaty talks."

That meant he was one of Abbot-Bishop Dmwoski's men, from Mount Angel. The abbey had organized survival around the town and governed its own small state there now; it was a thumb thrust into the Protectorate. There was absolutely no love lost between Dmwoski and the Protector, either, or between the abbot and what he called the blasphemous Antipope Leo, the prelate Arminger sponsored in Portland. Anathemas as well as arrows had flown over *that* border.

"I'm with the border guards," he went on. "We had a report of livestock missing from a farmer with an outlying steading, and tracked them well past our usual patrol range. We spotted these scum crossing the creek south of Scott's Mills."

Astrid's brows went up. That was about twenty miles north; deserted country, which made boundaries a bit theoretical.

"We thought they might be trying to slip down over the

Santiam and into the Mackenzie country," the soldier-monk said. "So I called out some militia and gave chase. We lost their tracks for a day. But when we found them again, they came straight south and into your territory. I hope you don't mind our pursuing onto your land, but it seemed a shame to give up. Particularly when they hadn't spotted us."

"Thank you very much, Father Andrew," she said. "We appreciate the help. They'd have scattered if you weren't behind to corral them. Chasing them down might have cost us lives—probably would have. An ambush is one thing, but a running fight is something else again."

He shrugged robed and armored shoulders. "Just doing our job, my daughter, looking after the flock. And there were a few too many for us to tackle comfortably ourselves. It's a comfort to have you Dúnedain taking up residence in this stretch of forest. They're too cursed convenient for woods-running swine like these otherwise."

Alleyne called to her. "This one's no bandit," he said, as he stripped off a man's sword belt and tossed it aside.

It was the man Hordle had shot. Blood welled out around the broken arrowshaft, but he clutched it and glared hatred at her. Another young face, a little younger than her own, but neatly shaved; when Alleyne pulled off the coif—a mail-covered, tight-fitting leather hood—his light-brown hair was moderately long in front, cropped like a crew cut behind the ears. A blunt face with an old scar on one cheek, and gray-blue eyes. Beneath the armor he was broad-shouldered and thick-armed, not skinny-scrawny like most of the outlaw gang. It was the body of a man who ate well but worked sweating-hard with sword and shield and lance while wearing full armor.

"False priest and devil-worshipping whore," he rasped, and tried to spit at her. "Kill me now!"

The sword that lay a little distance away was a broad double-edged slashing type, though with a respectable point, the classic Norman sword that most of the Portland Protective Association's men used. She looked down at his feet. Good boots, but no golden spurs. Still . . .

"Protectorate knight," she said. "A man-at-arms wouldn't be so bold."

She looked up at the priest. "Shall we dispose of them, or do you claim the privilege, Father Andrew? You saw them first, after all, and on abbey soil."

He shrugged. "The abbot and Lord Bear and the Lady Juniper all agreed this forest of Mithrilwood was Dúnedain land, and that you have the right to dispense justice here, my lady. High, middle and low."

"Only as custodian for the Dúnedain Rangers," she corrected, not wanting to claim more than her due.

Another shrug. John Hordle had been talking in Sign with Eilir. He nodded and went over to the fallen knight; a muffled scream broke past clenched teeth as Hordle gripped the stub of the arrow between thumb and forefinger and casually drew it out, then stripped off the mail hauberk. That was normally a complex business, but the big man handled the other as if he had been a doll, despite respectable height and solid weight. When the armor had been tossed aside he ripped open the man's gambeson and shirt over the uninjured right shoulder.

"Ahh," Astrid said.

There was a symbol tattooed there, a circle with a Chinese ideograph in it. She'd learned that Eddie Liu had adopted that as his blazon in mockery; it was the glyph for *Poland,* which was where his maternal ancestors had come from. Liu was very dead, Eilir had killed him last summer, but . . .

"You're a liege-man of his," she said grimly.

The captive spat at her again, making a worse job of it; his mouth must be dry with pain and shock. "I'm brother to Lady Mary, the dowager Baroness Gervais. My name is Sir Jason Mortimer of Loiston manor," he said. "Baron Gervais was my liege lord and my kin by marriage. His handfast men will never rest until we've avenged him!"

Eilir made a clicking sound with her tongue, and Astrid looked over at her. *He probably hired the bandits,* she signed. *What's the old phrase, plausible deniability?*

As if on cue, one of the bound men spoke: "You motherfucker!" he swore at the knight. "You said there'd be food and women and a place of our own for the winter!"

"We'll keep you for ransom, then, Sir Jason," Astrid said; nobody paid any attention to the outlaw's outburst. "And it'll be a heavy one." She grinned. "You can explain back home how a pair of girls captured you. The same ones who killed your liege-lord, by the way."

She turned to the priest and away from the knight's incoherent curses. "Why don't you and your patrol stay with us tonight at Mithrilwood Lodge, Father Andrew? It's no trouble, we've plenty of space, and it'll spare you a winter bivouac." At his slight hesitation and frown: "And not all of us are of the Old Religion. I'm sure there are some who'd be grateful to make confession, if you wished, and receive communion if you've the Bread and Wine with you."

That seemed to tip the balance. "Most generous of you, my child."

"We've some of Brannigan's Special Ale, too," Astrid said impishly, and just a bit louder. "We traded venison and boar for it, but that's not all gone either. Roast yearling boar tonight, and scalloped potatoes, and cauliflower with cheese, and dried-blueberry tarts with whipped cream to follow."

The warrior-monk's company of militiamen suppressed a cheer, and let grins run free. Mount Angel had a winery of note and fine maltsters, but Brannigan's brew was famous all over the Valley. Juniper Mackenzie had made a song about it years ago, and it was sung in taverns from Ashland to Boise. Hot food and dry beds were a great deal more attractive than damp sleeping bags and trail rations, as well.

"Let's finish up here, then," Astrid said.

The monk addressed the half-dozen other captives who waited on their knees. "Do any of you wish to confess your sins and save your miserable sin-stained souls from Hell? No?"

Astrid's face was calmly lovely as she looked at the row of men, kneeling in the mud with elbows and wrists lashed behind them. A few wept or babbled; most were silent and shocked, a few bleeding from wounds.

"Does anyone think there's any doubt these are outlaws, bandits and wolf-heads, the enemies general of humankind?" she said formally, looking from face to face of the Dúnedain, and then to Alleyne and Little John Hordle.

"That's buggering obvious, if you ask me," Hordle said.

Nobody else bothered to do more than nod assent. Hordle

hefted the long, heavy sword he carried, checking for nicks, and Father Andrew took back his poleax, running an experienced thumb down the edge. Two of his men unlimbered their axes. Eilir nodded herself, and then sighed in silent regret; Astrid smiled at her.

You always were tender-hearted, soul-sister, she signed. *Do you want to ask mercy for any of them?*

No, I'm afraid not. Though they might have been decent enough men, with different luck, Eilir replied.

"But they are as they are," Astrid said. Then she raised her voice slightly, in a tone of calm command: "Behead them every one, and that instantly."

CHAPTER FIVE

North Corvallis, Oregon
January 10th, 2008/Change Year 9

The lands claimed by the Faculty Senate of Oregon State University—in effect, by the city-state of Corvallis—began where the village of Adair had been, before the Change. The steep crest of Hospital Hill to the west overlooked Highway 99 from less than a quarter mile away; on it beetled a small but squat-strong fortress of stone and concrete and steel with a round tower rearing on its eastern edge. The snouts of engines showed, ready to throw yard-long darts, steel roundshot and glass globes of clinging fire four times that distance.

As Michael Havel watched a light blinked from it, as bright as burning lime and mirrors could make it, flashing on the news of their arrival southward to the posts that would relay the message to the city. Most of the village east of the highway was brush-grown rubble; a few houses had been linked by cinderblock and angle iron and barbed wire into an enclosed farmstead, with barns and outbuildings about, and a sign— "Lador's Fine Liquor and Provisions"— showing that it sold to passersby as well. The dwellers had heard the fort's bell and turned out from field and barn with bill and spear and crossbow, then relaxed when they saw it was friendly Bearkillers, remaining to stare and comment at the size of the party and its members.

He'd brought a dozen armored A-listers along for swank— he had to keep up the Outfit's credit with the Corvallans, who were overbearing enough as it was. Their lances swayed slightly as the standing horses shifted their weight from hoof to hoof, and the whetted steel of the heads glittered in the pale sun of a winter's noon. It was one of the rare clear January days, only a few high wisps of cloud in a sky pale blue from the Coast Range on his right—he could see the four-thousand-foot treeclad summit of Mary's Peak, a rarity in winter—to the High Cascades in the far distance on his left, hints of dreaming snowfields at the edge of sight. Overhead a red-tailed hawk floated, the spread feathers of its wings sculpting the air, then stooped on a rabbit. The air was crisp and colder than usual, cold enough that the frost still rimed grass and twig and brush with white even at noon; the breaths of men and horses steamed, a light fog strong with the mounts' grassy scent. A four-horse wagon brought up the rear with their gear, a few household staff walking beside it and the Bearkiller's chief physician riding atop; he'd lost a foot to some Eaters soon after the Change, and loathed riding as well.

Havel and Signe were mounted and armed but in civilian garb; tooled-leather boots, broad-brimmed hats, brown serge jackets and precious intact pre-Change bluejeans, almost new, and cunningly reinforced on the inner thighs with soft-tanned deerskin. Their eldest children were with them, eight-year-old twin girls identical down to the silver rings on the ends of their long, tow-colored braids and the slant to their cornflower-blue eyes; he'd left young Mike Jr. behind at Larsdalen, with the staff and nannies and indulgent grandfather and step-grandmother, since he was at the stage where he could move pretty quickly but still had a toddler's suicidal lack of common sense. Mary and Ritva were excited enough to bounce up and down in their silver-studded charro-style saddles, or would have been if they hadn't ridden nearly as long as they'd been walking. They pointed and exclaimed as the drawbridge on the fort came down and the gates swung open.

Eric Larsson commanded the Bearkiller escort; he had a crest of scarlet-dyed horsehair nodding from front to rear of his round bowl helm, gold on the rivets that held the nasal bar at the front of it and the mail aventail at the rear and the hinged cheek-pieces, and more on his belt buckle and the hilt of his backsword. The metalwork of his war-saddle was polished bright, and the animal he rode was eighteen hands at the shoulder and groomed to glossy black perfection, an agile giant of Hanoverian warmblood descent. The man made a hand signal to the rider beside him; Luanne took up the trumpet slung on a bandolier across her chest and blew a complex measure. The column of lancers reined their mounts about as one to face westward, turning their formation into a double line; then they brought their lances down in salute until the points almost touched the patched asphalt of the roadway, and back up again in a flutter of long, narrow pennants.

A small party came down from the fort, four mounted figures, the metal of their armor colored an inconspicuous greenish-brown that barely showed against the thick woods of the hills behind; the McDonald Forest had been University property even before the Change, and well cared for. Havel recognized the one who led them, a medium-tall man with brown hair and brown eyes behind the three-bar visor of his helmet and a pair of sports glasses.

"Major Jones," he said.

"Lord Bear," the other man replied; he was in his early thirties, of medium height but deep-chested and broad-armed; he'd been a Society fighter and teaching assistant in the Faculty of Agriculture before the Change.

He saluted; Havel returned the gesture, turning in the saddle to make it towards the banner one of the Corvallans carried, its pole resting in a ring on his right stirrup. The flag was orange, with the brown-and-black head of a beaver on it, attempting a ferocious rodentine scowl; privately Havel thought it was dorky beyond words, but it had been the University's symbol for a long time and they were devoted to it.

"Welcome, Lord Bear, in the name of the people and the Faculty Senate of Corvallis," Jones said formally.

Then he stripped off his metal-backed gauntlet and shook hands, a dry, firm grip: "Good to see you again, Mike. And you, Signe, Eric, Luanne."

Eric had been looking at the weapons his escort carried. "Finally got that quick-loading crossbow working, Pete?" he said.

"Yeah," the officer said. "Gear, ratchet and bicycle chain in the butt and forestock, crank inset underneath. Turn it six times, and the weapon's cocked and ready to go as soon as you pull the trigger. Double the rate of fire of the old type and you can do it lying down, or in the saddle."

Havel's crooked smile quirked. "Easy to build and repair?" he said.

"Well . . . we're still working on some problems with production and maintenance," Jones said reluctantly. "How's that car-jack thing your father-in-law is working on?"

"Classified," Havel said.

Jones smirked, which meant he thought *classified* translated as *haven't got it working yet.* Usually that was true, but in this case it was precisely the opposite. He wanted to spring it on the city-state as a done deal in a month or two when they reequipped everyone, to take their pretensions of technological superiority down a peg. Nobody denied they'd come through the Change unusually well, but the way they acted as if they were the last island of civilization in a world of bare-assed savages got a bit old after a while.

The Corvallan looked at their party. "Astrid and Eilir aren't along?"

"They're coming separately," Signe said. "They've got . . . a bit of a present to show around, you might say."

"And the Rangers are independents themselves, these days," Havel said. "Since we all agreed to give them that stretch of woods. Sort of prickly about it, too."

Damned if I'm going to call them the Dúnedain *Rangers,* he added to himself. *Bad enough I have to do the Mad Max on Horseback thing myself.*

One thing he *did* like about Corvallis was that it was a bit less given to weird names than the rest of the present-day Valley.

"Ken's not coming?" the Corvallan officer went on, looking surprised as Havel shook his head. "Your father-in-law usually doesn't pass up an opportunity to haunt our bookstores and the Library."

"Tell me," Havel said, thinking of the bills the Outfit had paid in grain and wool, tuns of wine and barrels of salt pork; they'd had words on the matter.

I'd have gotten even madder if the stuff he dug up weren't so helpful sometimes.

Books were expensive these days, unless you were talking salvaged paperback copies of Tom Clancy or the like, and even those were getting rare and fragile in this damp climate. Real books on something useful were pricey, either because they were irreplaceable—books made good kindling and a lot of libraries had burned after the Change—or because they'd been new-printed with hand-operated presses on dwindling stores of pre-Change paper. Or on the even more expensive rag-pulp type Corvallis had started making recently. The city-state had a biweekly newsletter, all of four pages, and copies cost more than a day's wages for a laboring man.

Luanne chuckled. "We unloaded the grandkids on Ken—Mike's youngest, and both of ours. And since he and honorable step-mom-in-law Pam had the bad taste to produce two more at their decrepit ages, he's up to his distinguished wizardly white beard in rugrats. Labor-intensive work."

Jones nodded. "Tell me," he said, and touched the rein to the neck of his horse to fall in beside them. "Between the kids and the farm and the weaving, I don't know how the hell Nancy stays sane when I'm out on patrol, even with Mom and the hired help."

"We do have our doc along," Signe said. "He needs some supplies."

Jones nodded proudly; Corvallis was the best place in Oregon to buy such. Havel shot a glance at his brother-in-law, and Eric's hand chopped forward. The column rumbled into motion southward.

> *"OSU our hats are off to you,*
> *Beavers, Beavers, fighters through and through*
> *We'll cheer thru-out the land,*

> *We'll root for every stand,*
> *That's made for old OSU!*
>
> *Watch our pikes go tearing down the field;*
> *Those of iron, their strength will never yield*
> *Hail! Hail! Hail! Hail!*
> *Hail to old OSU!"*

Christ Jesus, what an abortion of a national anthem! Mike Havel thought, behind a gravely respectful face. *Just as well we* don't *have one. Though we use "March of Cambreadth" a lot; at least the lyrics aren't outright stupid and it's got a great tune.*

Then again, at least the city-state wasn't pretending to be something it wasn't. There were half a dozen governments in this general part of the continent that claimed to be the United States, from single small towns to one that covered most of southwestern Idaho. All of them were rather nasty dictatorships. *They* used "The Star-Spangled Banner," which was not only presumptuous of them but to Mike Havel's way of thinking in extremely bad taste.

The Corvallans weren't just singing. Pompom-wielding cheerleaders led the crowd through the fight song, their short-skirted orange-and-black costumes swinging as they kicked and leapt. That was fairly ludicrous too, but then, he'd thought cheerleading was dumb even back in the eighties when he'd been on the bench and the local maidens were egging on the audience for the Hancock High Wolverines. As a teenager he'd considered football the chosen sport of idiots; track and field had been what he liked, and cross-country skiing, and by choice he'd hunt or ride his Harley or tinker with its engine or even work chores at home instead of doing head-butts with behemoths. The little Upper Peninsula high school hadn't had talent to waste, though, and he'd been effectively conscripted as the fastest running back they'd had for years.

And wasn't that a complete waste of time, he thought.

Which didn't prevent him observing with interest when a pretty girl shook it hard, then or now, and there was some

righteous booty here; he caught Signe raising an eyebrow at
him, and smiled back at her.

"Monogamous, alskling, not blind," he murmured.

The cheerleaders looked even odder doing their leaps and
pyramids in front of ranks of armored troops standing to attention. The sixteen-foot pikes made a steel-tipped forest
above them, points catching the red light of sundown in a
manifold glitter as the sun set over the low hills to the west;
the rest stood with crossbows held at present arms. He supposed the folk of the city had gotten used to it, cheerleaders
and all.

Corvallis proper had about eight or nine thousand people
inside its walls, and besides the militia battalion a quarter
of them were out to see the visitors, singing along heartily and
then cheering, plus people from the countryside round about.
They made a huge dun mass in the open space between Highway 99, the railway, and the old Hewlett-Packard plant to the
east and the Willamette River beyond, trampling up to the
edge of the mulched, harvested truck gardens. The low-slung
campus-style buildings of the high-tech factory had been
taken over for noxious trades not allowed in the city proper;
he could smell the whiff of leather curing in the tanning pits,
and see acrid charcoal smoke from the squat brick chimney of
a foundry.

Mary and Ritva were quiet behind him; they were well-
mannered kids. He'd been brought up that way himself, in a
straitlaced rural-Lutheran tradition enforced with love, discipline and an occasional swat on the butt when necessary. He
could sense their excitement at the huge crowd, though;
they'd never seen any place larger than Larsdalen. And their
awe at the city wall, a little to the south. It wasn't higher or
thicker than the one around their home; in fact, it was pretty
similar, down to the girder-reinforced boulder-and-concrete
construction.

But a hell of a lot longer, he thought.

Nearly eight miles in circuit, an immense feat of labor. Two
major bandit attacks and a large raid out of the Protectorate
had bounced off it like buckshot off a tank in years past, but

he thought the Corvallans tended to overestimate the security it gave them.

After the anthem, a delegation walked up to him. He swung down from the saddle and waited courteously; there were about two dozen of them, and they took a fair bit of hand-shaking and honored-to-see-you-sir-or-ma'ams. That was the problem: the President, the Provost, the representatives of the Faculty Senate . . . back right around the Change, they'd gotten a lot done here because it was obvious what needed doing, and they'd have died if they didn't do it. And the mechanisms they'd set up went on working well enough, as long as the rest of the world cooperated by not changing much either. But try to get a policy change . . . right now, just getting them all in the same spot at the same time was like pushing rocks uphill.

They're tired of fighting and want to relax and enjoy life, he thought. *Pity the world won't cooperate.*

When the formalities were over and the troops and spectators had marched off, the Bearkiller party and Major Jones walked their horses through the entry complex. That was a little more difficult than it would have been at Larsdalen; here they'd overlapped two sections of the city wall, so that the entrance was at right angles to it. You had to turn sharp left to get through the outer portal, go a hundred yards with walls on either side, then abruptly right again to enter the city through the inner gate. That meant that nothing longer than a wagon could come straight at the leaves of either entryway, even if someone filled in the perimeter ditch.

Eric looked up at the complex of tower and wall and sighed as the iron clatter of hoofbeats on pavement echoed back from the concrete and stone of their heights.

"Getting fortification envy?" Havel asked quietly. "Theirs is bigger and harder than ours?"

"Well . . . yeah, bossman. It'd be harder to get a shot at the weak point where the leaves of the gate meet with this setup."

"Nah, it wouldn't. 'Cause the gate ain't the weak spot back home. They made their gates of timber here, with sheet steel bolted onto the surface."

Eric thumped himself on the forehead, a fairly loud process

when you were wearing a metal-backed gauntlet and a helmet. "And ours are solid welded steel. Probably stronger than the wall."

"It'd be quicker to dig the concrete and stone out from around," Havel agreed. He made a gesture up and around. "What happened here is that someone got a bright idea out of a history book. Your esteemed father tends to do that too. Sometimes it's brilliant. Sometimes it's a waste of time."

Behind him Ritva giggled. "Dad's right, Uncle Eric, and you're wrong." Her sister chimed in, and they chanted: "*So he gets to sing the* I was right *song.*"

"Silence, peanut," Havel said affectionately, turning and winking at her.

There was one more formality as they came out of the gatehouse: having their swords peace-bonded, as all edged weapons over ten inches had to be within the wall. That meant a thin wrapper of copper wire, sealed with a lead disk crimped in something that looked like a heavy-duty paper punch; that stamped the beaver-head symbol of the University into the soft metal. The wire didn't make it impossible to draw the sword, or even difficult; it just meant that it was obvious if you'd done so, and so simplified police-work.

Law here said every family had to keep its militia weapons at home and always ready, but most people walking the streets didn't bother to carry a long blade, which looked a bit unnatural to him now. Back in Bearkiller territory, a farmer plowing did it with sword slung at the hip, and a spear or crossbow or whatever across the handles. These days you didn't need them all that often, but when you did you needed them very badly indeed, and the occasions came without warning. You put on your weapons when you went outdoors, like your hat.

They turned their horses right along Monroe at the redbrick Julian Hotel—now a barracks for militia doing their wall-duty—and continued west past the white-plastered Italianate pile of the old courthouse with its central clock-tower, which provoked more rubbernecking. Mary spoke up; he flattered himself he could tell her voice from Ritva's, and was right about three-quarters of the time. Except when they were trying to fool him, which happened every so often.

"Dad, how can they have all these people in one place? Thousands of them!"

"About eight thousand, punkin. Ten times what we have at Larsdalen and a little more."

"What do they all *eat*? They couldn't walk out to their fields! It's too far!"

He smiled; one thing he liked about the Changed world was that nobody assumed food and goods magically appeared in shops shrink-wrapped in plastic, not even kids, and not even the kids of the big boss. Not even the people who really *did* believe in magic; they were farmers too. He pointed to the railway that ran across their path, along NW Sixth Street.

"That runs along out into the farmlands south of here. Corvallan farmers don't make as much of their own tools and cloth as ours do—they buy it from the city-folk instead with the food they don't eat. And there's another railroad that goes west all the way to the ocean, at Newport, so they can bring in fish from there. The rails were laid before the Change, but the Corvallans keep them up. It's easy to haul wagons on rails, easier than on the roads; and they have boats on the river, and they buy from us and the Mackenzies and some of the people farther south—the McClintocks, a couple of others. And some things come from even farther away, like cattle from all the way over the Cascades."

And let's not go into taxes and such, he thought, as the two girls nodded gravely. *Sufficient unto the day. I didn't know shit about economics until experience and Ken Larsson showed me I had to.*

Just then the streetlamps began to go on. They were gaslights, fed by methane from the town's sewage works, sparse and not very bright to anyone who remembered electricity. The girls and a couple of the younger house-staff near the wagon still gasped in delight as the lamplighters held their long rods up, nudged open the glass shutters at the tops of the metal standards and snapped sparks that turned into yellow flame. Near the river the buildings they showed were mostly warehouses or small factories of frame and brick; fire had

gone through the riverfront on the night of the Change, when
an airliner out of Portland crashed, and more later in the riots
and fighting. The streets were clean, but there was a yeasty
smell in the air, the sort you got from bulk storage of farm
produce. Signs hung creaking above doors, advertising millers
and maltsters, dealers in hops and cloth and salvaged bulk
metals, leather and glassware, makers of disk-plows and
reapers and sewing machines, purveyors of fine sewing
thread—or as fine as you could get without cotton—and custom gear-trains, hydraulic power systems, livery stables that
rented the teams for railroads, blacksmiths . . .

"Did you see that?" Signe asked, turning her head so
abruptly that her tired horse tossed its own in protest at the
shift in balance.

"What?" he said abstractedly; one of the great things about
horses was that they had autopilots when it came to ambling
straight ahead, so you could think about something else.

"The graffiti," she replied.

"No," he answered, surprised. Corvallis was a very tightly
run ship these days; he supposed it came with all the civic
spirit. "What did it say?"

"Help, I've fallen into the RenFaire and I can't get out!"

She giggled and her brother and sister-in-law smiled; Mike
Havel gave a full-throated laugh. Mary and Ritva turned puzzled eyes on their elders.

"I bet that was written by someone over forty," Havel
chortled.

They turned right again and into a district where most
houses were a century old or more; this part of Corvallis was
laid out along a grid, and the streets were broad and tree-
lined. Traffic was thick as the sunlight died, another strange-
ness in a world that mostly went home with the sun. Bicycles
and pedicabs were numerous, and oxcarts and horse-drawn
wagons, people on foot still more so as men and women
walked home from work. The sound of human voices and
feet was louder than wheels or hooves; most ground floors
were workshops or small stores, with the proprietors living
over them. Street vendors pushed barrows and cried out their
toasted nuts and hot dogs in buns or toffee apples or hot

cider; children ran home from school with their slates slung over their shoulders, and housekeepers came back from daily markets in chattering clumps with their full baskets; once a splendid red fire engine pulled by six glossy Belgians trotted past. That looked like a museum piece and probably had been until ten years ago, and it was pursued by still more children.

Feels more crowded than American cities this size ever did before the Change, Havel thought. *Even in rush hour. They've built up most of the old open space and there are a lot more people per house. Well, you have to jam 'em in, when you've got a wall around them. Every extra foot of defensive perimeter means spreading your forces that bit thinner. But they aren't poor, crowded or no. Even the smelly types sweeping up the ox dung and horseshit into those little pushcarts look reasonably well fed.*

Lamplight from most windows shone on the sidewalks, adding to the streetlights to make the night nearly bright enough to read by. The Havel children goggled at cobblers, tailors, bakers and saddlers, shops selling books and bicycle repairs, lanterns and eggbeaters, swords and knives and crossbows, candles and vegetables, eggs and jams and hams and bacon, taverns lively with raucous singing or even more raucous student arguments that spilled noise out into the chilly air along with the odors of frying onions, French fries, hamburgers and wine and beer, at churches of half a dozen varieties besides the two styles of Catholic, a miniature Buddhist temple and a couple of covensteads. There were doctors' offices, architects' . . . and once even a law firm's shingle.

Civilization, Havel thought, grinning to himself and shaking his head. *Christ Jesus, we've got* lawyers *again. Ten years ago we were fighting off cannibals.*

"Penny for 'em, honey," his wife said.

"I was just thinking that I'm starting to gawk like a hayseed," he said. "And this place is smaller now than the town where I went to high school!"

"You *are* a hayseed, darling."

"I am?" he said, making his eyes go round in mock surprise. Signe laughed. "You were born on a farm and lived on it until you enlisted in the Marine Corps. You thought Parris Island was the big time."

"My dad worked the mines, mostly. We were close to town. The farm was just our homeplace."

"Where your family raised spuds and pigs and cooked on a woodstove. And your idea of a good time was hunting deer."

"Chasing girls and running my motorcycle were right up there. Besides, you like hunting deer too."

"I do *now*. Back then I was a vegetarian. And when you got out of the Corps, you went and became a bush pilot in *Idaho*. You, my darling, are a hayseed of hayseeds and a hick of hicks. It's why you've done so well!"

The smile died a little as she looked around at the busy brightness and rubbed an index finger on the little white scar that nicked the bridge of her straight nose. "You know, it's scary, but *I'm* sort of impressed myself, and I grew up in the big city."

"Portland's still bigger than this," he said grimly.

"Portland isn't a city anymore," she said shortly. "It's a labor camp and a mine. The city's dead. This is alive, at least."

He nodded, then cast off gloom as they turned into a residential street overshadowed by huge oriental sycamores and lined by old homes, on Harrison near Twenty-third; it was less crowded, and some of the traffic was closed carriages with glazed windows, the CY9 equivalent of a stretch limo. Most of the homes belonged to the well-to-do, merchants and high officials of the Faculty Senate, with a sprinkling of the sororities and fraternities where the scions of Corvallis' elite did their bonding. A pair of the big brick houses were owned by the Bearkillers, for times like this when a delegation was in town; the arrangement was more or less like an embassy, though less formal. It would be undignified for the Outfit's leaders to stay at an ordinary inn. Staying with friends in town would be an imposition, and besides that gave political ammunition to the friends' rivals.

Corvallis had what was officially described as "vigorous participatory democracy"; Havel tended to think of it as more along the lines of "backstabbing chaos."

Staff from Larsdalen had gone on several days ahead to

prepare the Bearkiller consulate for them, and the windows were bright and welcoming, with woodsmoke drifting pungent from the brick chimneys. Hugo Zeppelt crowded out onto the veranda and bellowed greetings as he windmilled his arms: "It's the tall poppies! G'day, sport—good to see yer! And the little sheilas; Uncle Hugo's got a lollie for the both of you."

He was the sort who could be a crowd all on his own, a short, stocky balding man with a glossy brown beard going gray. He'd been winery manager at Larsdalen from the mid-nineties until the fifth Change Year, and had taken over as steward of the Bearkiller properties here partly because it ministered to his second passion, food.

"It's the Unspeakable Antipodean," Signe said with a mixture of sarcasm and goodwill. Zeppelt's Australian drawl was as rasping as ever. "Hi, Zeppo."

"Still a bit of a figjam, eh?" he laughed back at her. "And grinning like a big blond shot fox, my Lady Signe is."

"Dinner's ready, I hope?"

"Fair dinkum, no fear," Zeppelt said. "On the bloody table, and it's grouse tucker."

"Did you ever talk like that in Oz?" Havel said curiously, dismounting and tossing the reins to a groom.

"Why, that would have been superfluous considering the cultural context, would it not?" Zeppelt answered in dulcet tones.

Bathed, fed and sitting around the table as the children were sent yawning to their bedroom, the adults relaxed over nuts, cheese, fruitcake and wine. A low blaze in the small fireplace made the room comfortable by Change Year nine standards, which meant in the mid-sixties.

"Great job, Hugo, but Christ Jesus, I may grow gills," Havel said. "I liked the smoked salmon cooked in cream and dill. And I always was partial to a good Dungeness crab. Can't get them in our territory; I wish *we* had a railway to the coast. Or a port at all."

"Why do you think I asked to get sent down here?" the Australian said, belching contentedly. "Chance to get a bog in with something besides roast and spuds. Those crabs're bonzer when you stir-fry them with scallions and ginger, aren't they? Got to get them fresh, though. They ship them in from Newport on the railway in saltwater tanks with little fans worked by the wheels to keep it circulating. The sea's full of them these days, so they're cheap even so."

"What about the rest of your job?" Signe asked, a little sharply; Havel could feel her putting on her CIA hat.

"Oh, everyone here thinks old Hugo's just a harmless larrikin who doesn't know Christmas from Bourke Street," Zeppelt said, giving her a thumbs-up. "They talk around me like I was cactus. I'll give you the drum, all right; the good oil, deadset."

"And?" she said.

"Someone's spreading money. Someone who doesn't like the Bearkillers, *or* our kiltie friends eastward," he said, his face going serious. "They're no galahs, either. Going at it subtle, about how we're blocking trade, that sort of thing. How much everyone would make, if they had the railway through to Portland back up and running."

Peter Jones grunted. "I didn't know that," he said. "I'm not surprised, though. You think it's Portland putting a spoon in our stewpot?"

"Nar," the Australian said. "I'd be gobsmacked if it were. Someone local, I'd say, but with an eye cocked north."

Signe nibbled at a cracker covered in blue-veined cheese, and sipped at a Rogue River zinfandel. "According to my sources—"

My spies, Havel thought affectionately.

"—Kowalski and Turner were in Portland last month. Officially they were looking into getting their wool shipments from Pendleton going again now that the war there's over. Which I'd be more ready to believe if half the sheep out that way weren't dead."

Havel grinned mirthlessly. That four-sided civil war had let the Protector's men in, which gave him the Columbia valley as far east as the old Idaho border and cut the remaining independents in eastern Washington off from the Association's enemies in Oregon unless they went around by way of Boise. It would take years for Arminger's people to get the area sub-dued and producing, not least because they were at daggers drawn—literally—over who would get what, but when he did it would be a nasty accession of strength. And in the short run, it gave the Protector some experienced light cavalry from the victorious faction he'd backed.

"But Turner and Kowalski had several meetings with Arminger," she went on. "And his wife, and Grand Constable Renfrew, and a couple of priestly bureaucratic types. From the Chancery, officially, but I smell Holy Office. Not exactly what you'd expect for trade talks. Arminger usually hands those off. This had the scent of something political."

She wrinkled her nose to show what sort of scent. Jones winced.

"Hell, that's a pretty serious accusation," he said. "I don't like either of them, but that doesn't make them traitors, nec-essarily."

Havel tossed a couple of nutmeats into his mouth. "It doesn't mean they aren't, either," he said. "Signe's reading of both of them is that they'd do anything for enough money. I trust her judgment; that type're a closed book to me. Arminger I can understand—he's sort of like me, only with megalomania and bloodlust where his ethics ought to be. Businessmen I never did grok, and that means I can't really tell a good one from a bad one."

"They wouldn't want Arminger taking over," Jones said. "In his territory he and his bullyboys squeeze people like them a lot harder than the Faculty Senate, with tolls and what-not. And I can't see either of them getting a title or setting up as barons."

"Yeah, that's bugging me, too," Havel said. "Money means more here than in Portland territory, the way the Association is set up. Land and castles and men-at-arms count for more up there, at seventh and last. So you'd expect your budding Rockefellers to keep arm's length from the Lord Protector. But something doesn't smell right. You know anything else they've been up to?"

When Jones hesitated, he went on: "Come on, Pete, this is Mike Havel talking. You know I've got nothing against Corvallis. You and I've worked together for years."

"Well . . . they've been active in this 'select militia' proposal," the Corvallan said slowly. "You heard about that?"

"Yup. Paying volunteers to drill more often and do things like garrison and patrol work. It makes a certain amount of sense, from Corvallis' point of view. Calling out *our* militia is a royal pain in the ass too, what with the lost work, but we need everyone who can walk and carry a crossbow. You've got what, thirty-two thousand people? To our twenty thousand. That gives you more of a margin. Especially since we and the Mackenzies are between you and the main threat."

"That's what they're saying," Jones agreed. "What I *hear* is that they'd like the select militia to *replace* the present setup eventually. And have individual Faculties sponsor battalions, or possibly individuals do it. It's got some appeal. Drill isn't popular; we've had peace—more or less—for the past couple of years. And there are people who'd like the extra money, too, particularly ones whose work isn't steady year-round, so they're selling it as a sort of income-spreading measure as well. I don't like it, though. It smells to me like those Economics Faculty types trying to put one over on the rest of us, somehow."

Havel grunted again, turning an eye on Signe. She shook her head. "This is where Dad would come in useful," she said. "There's probably some historical analogy . . . he and Arminger have read a lot of the same books, you know?"

Jones hesitated. "What exactly did you want to talk to the Senate about?" he said, and then went on: "And to quote you, this is Pete Jones, you know I've got nothing against the Bearkillers, and we've worked together for years."

"OK, couple of things. First, we want the informal alliance made formal—we want to be able to count on Corvallis when Arminger goes for us and the Mackenzies and Mount Angel. A straightforward promise to treat an attack on us as an attack on you, the way the three northern Outfits have agreed. That might actually scare him off and we could avoid the war altogether. I could use those seven thousand militia of yours *real* bad."

"Ouch," Jones said, shaking his head. "You know me, Mike, *I'm* all for it. But a lot of people would rather pretend it's your fight and not ours."

Havel's fist hit the table, and a bottle of Chardonnay wavered. "Well, Christ Jesus, that's the problem! For years now he's been needling and probing and pushing, and we've been bleeding to keep you guys safe!"

Jones spread his hands. "You don't have to convince *me*, Mike! He blames it all on his barons, or on bandits, or on you for fighting back when you get attacked." A hesitation. "You might have a better chance if you'd agree to let us refurbish the railway through your territory to McMinnville."

"Not a chance, in the present situation," Havel said.

"The trade would do the Bearkillers good, as well as Corvallis and Portland," Jones argued. "That's not a zero-sum game."

"It would strengthen him more than us. The bastard squeezes his farmers as hard as he can, and he uses it to keep what amounts to a standing army. If I call out every booger and ass-wipe, I can put twenty-five hundred in the field, but only three hundred and fifty of them are A-listers; the Mackenzies can raise about the same, all infantry, and Dmwoski has about fifteen hundred, a tenth of them mounted. Say five hundred more from here and there, and some people from the Bend country. Arminger can field *ten thousand* full-time fighting men, a quarter of them knights and men-at-arms, and he's had enough time and cadre to train them properly by now. That means he outnumbers all three of the northern outfits put together by three to two, and a *lot* more than that in cavalry, eight or nine to one. Those heavy lancers are hanging over us like a sledgehammer and his logistics problems are the only thing that's keeping us from being squashed—"

He picked up a walnut between the thumb and first two fingers of his right hand, his sword hand, and pressed. The shell cracked and fragments scattered across the white linen tablecloth.

"—like that. So no way am I going to give him a rail net to take over and support his men with when he invades us."

The Corvallan militia officer winced. "All right, that's the first item. What's the rest?"

"Different view of a similar problem. The Valley's getting to have bandits the way a dead rabbit has blowfly maggots. It's worse than it was a couple of years ago, if anything."

"More to steal," Eric put in, contemplating another slice of fruitcake; he'd been mostly silent until now. "Coyotes go up and down with the rabbits. Same-same with bandits and honest folk."

Havel nodded. "OK, the problem there is that they hang out in places where there aren't too many people, which these days is most places. We've got millions of acres of forest in the mountains on both sides of the Valley, and lots of swamp and new brush country right in it, not to mention places like the ruins of Salem or Eugene. The roads are still pretty good, so they can get around, hit and run and get away. And I'd swear Arminger's giving help to some of the gangs on the sly to keep us distracted, but leave that aside for now. The problem is catching them so we can hang or chop them."

Luanne nodded. "They keep running over a border when they're chased," she said. "We and the Mackenzies and Mount Angel, we're all pretty good about hot pursuit, but that's limited. And—no offense, Pete—Corvallis is almost as bad as the Protectorate about letting us follow up across your frontiers. By the time we've notified your people and waited for you to take over, the bad guys have disappeared."

Havel leaned forward. "Ideally, what we need is to all get together, burn out pestholes like the ruins of Eugene, and then sweep the whole Valley, every little island in every marsh, every patch of woods, and the Coast Range and the Cascades too, hang or gut every outlaw, and patrol to keep things clean."

Jones laughed unwillingly. "Good luck, Mike," he said. "You and a couple of divisions, hey?"

"Yeah, that's not going to happen anytime soon. So what we need is a force that can go anywhere—bandit chasers, caravan guards, road patrollers. And we've got one. The Rangers."

Jones laughed again, this time at the statement. "You mean Astrid and Eilir's little pointy-eared Elvish Scout troop?" he said. "I mean, Christ, Mike, I know Astrid's your sister-in-law, but have you ever *listened* to her? She makes the Mackenzie herself herself sound like the Spirit of Pure Reason."

"They're all grown up now, Pete. You know I don't bullshit about stuff like this. They're good, playing dress-up or not. They've already handled a couple of gangs that were giving us real trouble, and we—we and Juney Mackenzie and Dmwoski—have handed them that forest around the old Silver Falls State Park. What they've got in mind is places like that up and down the edges of the Valley; not good farmland, but livable, sort of a disconnected nation of, oh, call it crime-fighters and who-do-you-call types. And we've all three agreed to pay 'em, food and weapons and cloth and a little cash. You know I'm pretty tight with a dollar—or a sack of wheat. So's Dmwoski, and Juney's bunch don't like voting taxes on themselves any more than your Senate does."

Jones' eyebrows went up. "That's going to take some selling if you want Corvallis in on it," he said. "Extraterritoriality, didn't they call it? I can hear the lawyers now, screaming about how we've only just got the rule of law back and this would mean foreigners with the right of high justice on our own soil, and what if they decide some farmer out hunting is an outlaw and chop him? Hell, these days the goddamned shysters complain when *we* string a bandit up, out on patrol; I hoped they'd die out with the Change, but no luck, they're like cockroaches. And the Faculty Senate squeezes the pennies like they came out of their own pockets . . . which they do, a lot of the time."

Signe leaned forward. "Some traders from here are already hiring the Dúnedain," she said. "For escort work as far south as Reading, and east over the Cascades into the Bend country and as far as Boise, as escorts. They can be sure they won't get robbed by their own guards that way, and that the Rangers know their business, even if they keep name-dropping in Sindarin and striking poses like a Hildebrandt cover illustration. Being reliable means they get top dollar."

"Which merchants, exactly?" Jones asked.

She gave names; the Corvallan's eyebrows went higher still.

"Well," he said, "maybe we can do something along those lines. It might be a good idea to start with that. It's not likely to put backs up the way the railroad and Arminger will."

Havel rose and nodded. "Talk to you again later, then. Give our regards to Nancy and the kids."

One of the house staff they'd brought down from Larsdalen came in after the Corvallan had left. "Luanne, Signe, the rooms are ready. And the juniors are asleep." She smiled. "They claim they're keeping count of the stories they've missed and they'll want them all, with interest, when we're back home."

"Thanks, Jolene," Signe said, and patted her mouth to hide a delicate yawn. "I'm bushed. Time to turn in."

"I'm sure," Luanne said, and made a rude noise; her sister-in-law returned it with a gesture.

Mike Havel snaffled a three-quarters-full bottle of pinot gris and two glasses off the dinner table, getting a glare from a kitchen worker who didn't like the perquisites being infringed. Their bedroom was on the third floor; Signe went first, and Havel laughed softly as he admired the view. At twenty-eight and after two pregnancies she was a bit fuller-figured than she had been when they met the day of the Change, but it was just as firm in the skirt of fine dress wool.

Riding and sword work do wonders for a woman's figure, he mused happily. *Who'da thunk it?*

"What's that in aid of?" Signe asked, looking over her shoulder.

"I was remembering the first time I really noticed your ass," he said. "When you were climbing into my Piper Chieftain, Change Day, remember? Those hiphugger jeans you had on . . . man!"

She snorted in mock indignation, sky blue eyes alight. "I remember thinking you were a rude, crude jerk and were probably looking at my butt," she said. "And I was right, wasn't—hey!"

She yelped and jumped. Havel waggled eyebrows and fingers, leering. "I've got a license now, *alskling*. And the bedroom's that way."

"I *was* right!" she said, and put an arm around his waist as they came up to the landing. "On all three counts."

South Corvallis, Finney farm, Oregon
January 11th, 2008/Change Year 9

"I miss Luther," Juniper Mackenzie said quietly as she walked with the farm's master, looking to where her wagon stood beneath an oak.

It was nearly sunset under a sky the color of wet concrete, with spatters of rain now and then, feeling cold—as if it wanted to be snow, but didn't quite have the nerve. She wore a hooded gray winter cloak of wool woven with the grease still in, and her host had a rain-slicker over a homemade parka. The damp chill made her tuck her hands under her plaid; the air held the earthy smell of wet soil from a field of winter wheat beyond the pasture, and woodsmoke from the houses. Drops spattered on the puddles the wind ruffled, and gravel crunched under their shoes.

"Seeing it there takes me back. Before the Change I'd come every year just before the County Fair started up Corvallis way, and pick up the wagon and horses, and they were always spotless and shining. I think he kept Cagney and Lacey more for the fun of it than for what I could afford to pay to board them."

Her wagon was the classic barrel-shaped Gypsy home on wheels with two small windows in the sides and a stovepipe chimney through the curved roof, meant to be drawn by a pair of draught-beasts. It was still very useful for traveling, although the bright orange-red triangle for "slow vehicle" on the back was no longer very relevant. . . . Two big Percherons had hauled it here across the Valley from the Clan's territory to just south of Corvallis; they were the offspring of her old mares, and right now they were in one of the Finney barns, enjoying a well-earned oat-mash.

Edward Finney nodded. "I miss Dad too. He was one in a million."

And this was the first place Dennis and Eilir and I stopped after we got out of Corvallis, that terrible night, Juniper thought.

"He was a friend," she replied simply, remembering the weathered smiling face, tough as an old root. She brushed at an eye with the back of her hand; that might have been a drop from the slow, light drizzle, or it might not.

The approach to the Finney farm was much the same as she remembered from that night, even the tin mailbox on its post. Juniper nodded towards it.

"I remember when I showed up on Luther's doorstep the night of the Change. I was still trying to get my mind around the concept—I knew what had happened, but my gut didn't want to believe it, you see—and I wondered if anyone would ever deliver mail to that again," she said.

Edward Finney snorted. "Local delivery only, these days! And I was in Salem, wondering what the hell was going on and trying to keep the children from panicking," he replied. "I'd just begun to suspect the truth around dawn on the eighteenth, but I didn't want to believe it. I might not have if Dad hadn't shown up. Not really believed it, not in time to do any good."

He was in his early fifties now, a middle-sized man with iron gray hair and weathered skin and hazel eyes, his build a compromise between his father's lean height and his mother's stocky body; he'd left the farm out of high school, spent twenty years in the Air Force, and never wanted to go back except for visits. Old Luther had thought he'd be the last farmer in the Finney line . . . until the day when farming became the difference between starvation and life.

"The old man came in that very next day, wobbling along on some kid's bicycle, and got me and Gert and the kids, and Susan and her husband and her daughter, and herded us back out here, wouldn't take no for an answer and drove us until we nearly dropped. We'd all be dead if he hadn't."

Juniper nodded, shivering slightly. Salem had attracted refugees beyond count, certainly beyond the ability of the hapless state government to feed, and it was in those camps that unstoppable disease had broken out a few months after the Change—cholera, typhus and in the end plague, the Black Death itself. The swift oblivion brought by the pneumonic form had been a mercy for those doomed to starve, but then it had spread through all that remained of the Pacific Northwest, save for areas like hers where rigid quarantine, hoarded streptomycin and the Luck of the Lady had kept it out. Corvallis itself had suffered gruesomely despite its best efforts.

She shrugged. "I told him what I thought the Change was when we showed up that first night. He believed us, but he never said a word about me leaving with my wagon and horses, useful as they'd have been. Just gave me breakfast and Godspeed."

The avenue of big maples leading to the farmhouse was the same as well, though winter-bare now rather than budding into spring; Ted's great-great-great-grandfather had planted them in the 1850s, to remind him of New England, after coming in over the Oregon Trail. So was the big, rambling white-painted frame house that first pioneer Finney had built later to replace the initial log cabin, and the additions his son and grandson had made as they prospered, down to the wooden scrollwork over the veranda and the rosebushes and lilacs their womenfolk had tended around the big parlor bow window.

Much else had changed. A ditch and bank surrounded the steading, and on top of it was a fence of thick posts and barbed wire; not a real fortification like a Mackenzie dun, as this part of the Corvallis lands had been spared outright war, but it was enough to help deter hit-and-run bandits and sneak thieves who'd know there were ready weapons behind it. One of the silos had a watchpost on top, as well as fodder within. Off to one side rectangular beehives stood on little wheeled carts, dreaming the winter away in their coats of woven straw.

New barns and sheds had been built, and four smaller houses behind the main dwelling. Like most surviving farmers the Finneys had taken in town-dwellers without work or hope or food, to help do by hand the endless tasks machines could do no longer. Some had left to set up on their own once they learned the many skills needed; there was abandoned land in plenty, after the first terrible years were past. Seed and stock and tools weren't to be had for the asking, though. Encroaching brush made clearance more difficult every year; country life was hard for a family alone, full of deadly danger on the outlying fringes where land was open for homesteading. Some remained here and others joined them, working for food and clothes, a roof over their heads and a share in the profits that grew with more settled times and hard-won experience.

At last the Finney place could be called a thorp, its owner a wealthy yeoman who tilled several hundred acres of plowland and pasture, orchard and vineyard and woodlot, fed his folk well, paid his taxes without difficulty, and sold a healthy surplus in Corvallis. Smaller households for miles around looked to him and his like for leadership in the Popular Assembly and militia muster. He could well afford hospitality, even when the Chief of the Mackenzies arrived with a score of her clansfolk.

Tonight windows were bright with lamplight and voices spilled out of the farmhouse, and more showed where the eastern guests were bedded down in barns. One had been cleared for dancing. Corvallan country-folk weren't quite as isolated as rustics elsewhere, since they had a real city within a day's travel. Still, a visit on this scale was a welcome excuse for sociability, and the Mackenzies were old friends here. A violin tuning up made Juniper's fingers itch for the feel of her own fiddle, and a snatch of song came clear through the slow soughing of the wet wind, as a dozen voices joined in the chorus:

> *"—I'll ride all night and seek all day,*
> *till I catch the Black Jack Davy!"*

"I thought Dad would go on forever," Edward said. "He wouldn't take it easy, no matter how often Gert and I told him to."

"It happened during harvest, didn't it?" Juniper said.

"The tail of it, end of July, the last of the wheat. We were watering a team, and he scraped the sweat off his forehead with his thumb and said, *Got us a hot one this year,* then stopped and said *Oh, shit!* and dropped down dead. At least it was quick, not like Mom."

Juniper made a sign and smiled. "He was well over eighty this year, wasn't he? He told me once that after making it back alive from Frozen Chosin he swore he wanted to die on his own land, and on the hottest day of the year with sweat dripping into his eyes. There's always Someone listening when you make a wish, you know."

The farmer laughed ruefully. "Yeah, he told me that story too when I was a kid—showed me where he'd frozen a couple of his toes off, too. I think his Korea stories made me decide on the Air Force—anything but the Marines! 'Course, if I hadn't, I'd never have met Gert. Speaking of which, let's get back before she gets dinner on the table."

Juniper nodded and they turned to walk back down the row of maples; a pair of well-trained Alsatians fell in behind them. Gertrud Finney had been born Gertrud Feuchtwanger, in a small Bavarian town near a USAF base. She'd met a young airman there in 1975 . . .

"Reminds me of my own mother, a little, she does, but don't tell her that. I wouldn't risk that dinner for anything."

Edward Finney rolled his eyes. "We've earned every mouthful. The minute she heard you folks were coming Gert started working overtime, and conscripting everyone, worse than Christmas and New Year together. Pretzel soup with smoked pork and caramelized onions. Sauerbraten *Bofflamott*-style in red-wine-and-vinegar marinade with spices, over dumplings; spaetzle, kaiserschmarn—"

"Stop, stop, before I drool down my plaid, for Her sweet sake! I had waybread and hard cheese for lunch, eaten damp!"

"How come Eilir isn't with you?" Finney said. "Hans and Simon asked," he added, and grinned; those were his two sons, just turned twenty and eighteen, who had a lively and absolutely unrequited admiration for Juniper's daughter.

"She's with Astrid, on Dúnedain business." She winked at him. "To be sure, she's also with John Hordle."

"Little John Hordle? I've heard of him. He's the one put down Mack, Baron Liu's mad dog, isn't he?"

"With help. And with him is Alleyne Loring, who's a good friend of Astrid now."

Finney cocked an enquiring eye at her. "And where's Sir Nigel Loring? I've heard of him, too."

Juniper frowned for a second, then shrugged. "He stayed in Dun Juniper, said he had something to do there."

Then she shook off whatever was troubling her and went on: "And then tomorrow we can talk seriously about the Faculty Senate."

"Damn right," Edward Finney said, looking every inch his father's son, despite the stocky frame and the beginnings of a kettle belly. "*Damn* right. I really don't like that proposal they've got that the city should lease out the vacant lands in big lots to the highest bidder. Sure, it would cut taxes, and sure, it's just supposed to be for temporary grazing to keep the brush down, but—"

Mathilda Arminger bobbed her head enthusiastically with the beat and tapped her hands on her knees, perched on a truss of hay. The floor of the big barn had been cleared, except for the loose-boxes behind her that held the farm's draught-horses and some of the visitors' riding mounts; lanterns made it bright, in a flickery way that shifted as draughts swung them from the rafters. Juniper Mackenzie was perched on a bale she'd spread with her plaid not far away, her legs tucked beneath her, grinning and fiddling in perfect improvised accord with a scrawny middle-aged accordion player in bib overalls and a billowy young woman wielding a tuba. The *oom-pa-pa-oom-pa-pa* beat of the polka filled the big timber-frame building, and the feet of a dozen couples thumped on the boards of the floor; fragments of straw glistened gold as they floated around the dance floor amid the scuffing shoes, and she sneezed at the dusty smell.

Not much like home, Mathilda thought; neither the tinkle and buzz of Society-style music, nor the a capella rap and norteño which were the alternatives, nor the hoarded classical vinyl that her mother adored, even played on a wind-up gramophone. *But I like it. Makes you want to jump!* Home seemed more and more distant now anyway, most of the time. It had been a while since she cried quietly into her pillow for her mother.

The tune built to a conclusion and died away. The dance broke up in laughter and talk, and people headed over to the rough trestle table of planks spread with drinks and nibblements, with hot cider in a big, bubbling pot suspended over a metal brazier, and root beer and soda water as well. Edward Finney's sons Hans and Simon attended to the beer kegs they'd brought in on their shoulders a careful forty-eight hours before, and left in their U-shaped wooden rests to settle and chill; they were big young men, bullock-muscular from hard work, much alike except that one had dark brown curly hair and the other's was straw-colored and straight. They handled the beer barrels with casual expertise, adroitly whipping out the spile bungs on top, and knocking the taps into the corks with a few sharp blows.

Hans shouldered his slightly younger and slightly lighter brother aside and drew a frothing mug, holding it up to the light, sniffing it to make sure no secondary fermentation had spoiled it, and then taking a long draught.

Then he grinned broadly and shouted: *"Das Bier schmeckt gut!"* in German with an execrable American accent.

"Lots of practice there!" someone yelled, and there was more laughter as three sisters ranging in age from seventeen to six set out mugs.

Mathilda belched gently while she considered heading towards the table herself. There were some *very* good-looking things there, and good-smelling; *Honigkuchen* honey cakes, *Elisen* gingerbread made with powdered hazelnuts, *Pfefferkuchen* fragrant with a hoarded package of spices whose like nobody was likely to see for a long time, fluffy *Springerle* with anise . . .

No, she thought. *I'm real full from dinner. I'm really full. I'd better not.*

One thing she remembered well about her father was that he always looked down on people who couldn't discipline themselves. She clutched harder at memories as they faded.

Rudi came back with a slice of cake and sat and nibbled beside her. "This is great!" he said. "I always like visiting the Finneys."

Epona came over to the edge of the box behind them, drawn by the sound of his voice; the great wedge-shaped black head bent above the wooden railing, and started to gently lip his tumbled red-gold hair. Rudi laughed, and fed her a bit of the cake; she took it from his palm with a delicate twitch of her lips.

Mathilda nodded. "And . . . well, nobody's being mean to me anymore," she said.

The son of the Mackenzie chieftain looked at her as he rubbed a hand along the mare's jaw. "Well, yeah! Duh! It's *geasa*. Mom should have done that months ago, you ask me. But she doesn't like to *make* people do things, even when it's something good."

"Why not?" Mathilda asked.

Rudi frowned. "I think it's 'cause people aren't as happy or good when they think you're pushing them around," he said after a hesitation. "Nobody should be a bully. It comes back at you, Mom says, and always when it's the worst time. But sometimes you *have* to give them a push, if you're the Chief."

Juniper came back to her bale with a mug of the beer in her hand, and sat to drink and blow out a *wuff* of satisfaction. She caught the last of the words, and nodded.

"You do, sometimes. Just remember that the world has a way of pushing back." She took a long drink of beer the color of old honey and raised her voice: "Now, that's a noble brew, Ted. Wheat beer, isn't it, for all that it's dark?"

Gertrud Finney answered from over near the tables; she was a full-figured woman a few years older than Juniper, with dark blond braids wound around her head, wearing a blouse and dirndl that looked as if they spent most of their time in a chest. A slight guttural south-German accent still marked her English.

"It's *Hefe-weizenbock,* Juney, yes, half wheat, half barley. My father and brother worked in the *Aktienbrauerei Kaufbeuren,* and I remember a bit. We experiment, now that we have time for it. It is not perfect, not yet."

"Not far from it, though," Juniper said, smacking her lips slightly, with what Rudi called her Chief-face peering out for a moment. "Dennis Martin in Dun Juniper would be interested in the way of making it, and Brannigan over to Sutterdown."

"Not even Abbot Dmwoski gets this formula!" Gertrud said, with a mock-ferocious scowl, shaking a finger. "Much less you heathen witches!"

They made signs at each other—the Horns and the Cross—and then raised their mugs, laughing across the barn's floor. Aoife Barstow came up to Juniper as she finished and bent to murmur in her ear. The Mackenzie chieftain nodded, looked around and called a few names. A drummer with the bodhrans under her arms came to sit beside her, and a piper—the uilleann pipes, not the great war-drones—and a young man known for his voice stood smiling nearby.

Juniper exchanged a few words with the other musicians and then raised her voice; the buzz of talk instantly dropped away.

"We'll be doing a piece named 'Donnal MacGillavry,' and perhaps a final song or two, then allowing everyone to seek their beds, or their straw," she said, tucking the violin under her chin. "And if you'll clear a space for them, Aoife Barstow and Liath Dunling here will dance a bit."

The bodhran drum began, beaten slow but gradually speeding its tempo, and then the pipes behind it. The young man's clear tenor joined as Juniper's fiddle did:

> *"Donnal's come up the hill, hard and hungry*
> *Donnal's come doon the hill, wild he is and angry—"*

Mathilda leaned over, looking at the kilted dancers; Aoife was familiar, but the other woman was a little younger, just turned eighteen, with long brown hair in a single braid and an unremarkable round face made pretty by youth and health and happiness. She wore her shirt open a little to show a new tattoo at the base of her throat. That might have been a crescent moon, but it wasn't; it was a strung bow, the Warrior's Mark, a fashion among the younger Mackenzies when they passed the First Armsman's tests and became liable for the Clan's fighting levy, and for duties like this trip escorting the Chief. Sam Aylward himself disapproved of it, as he did painting faces before a fight, but both new customs had spread nonetheless.

Rudi thought it had come from one of the old songs or stories, but he wasn't sure; he *was* sure he intended to have it done himself, just as soon as he was old enough.

Mathilda whispered in Rudi's ear as the two Mackenzies unsheathed their dirks and held them overhead, the bright metal catching the lantern light; they stood side by side, left hand on hip, weight on that leg and right toe just touching the floor, and they'd put their flat bonnets back on, with the signs of their sept totems, Aoife's raven-feathers and Liath's tuft of wolf-fur.

"Liath . . . I thought her name was Jeanette?" she said. "Doesn't she live at Sam's place?"

"She's his wife's youngest aunt's daughter," Rudi said automatically, leaning forward as the dancers took their first step forward. "Changed her name when she was Initiated just a little while ago—you know, the way a lot of people do, if their birth-name's old-fashioned and silly. Aoife used to be called Mary, I think."

"Oh," Mathilda said. "I think some people do that up north, too. Different stories, though, so the names are different. Arthur and Roland and Ger and Lancelot and Verranger."

Liath and Aoife bowed and twirled and leapt, their feet flashing faster and faster, the sound of them on the worn oak boards of the barn's floor like the skittering throb of the bodhrans themselves, dancing side-by-side, then face-to-face, then back-to-back. The audience clapped to the rhythm and roared out the chorus:

> *"Come like the white wolf, Donnal MacGillavry!*
> *Here's tae the Chief and to Donnal MacGillavry!"*

"Oh, no!" Rudi said suddenly, slapping himself on the forehead.

"What?"

"That's what Dan meant about Aoife falling in love again! *He* was bummed about it too!"

"I thought her boyfriend's name was Connor?"

"Connor Ianatelli? He dumped her and got handfasted with someone over at Dun Carson and moved there just after Yule. Didn't you hear about it?"

"Who cared about that soppy stuff? I was sooooo excited when Sam gave me that bow. A new one! All my own!"

Rudi smiled. "Well, Mom *did* lay that *geasa* on all of us, you know. So Sam had to be as nice to you as he was to me. Besides, he likes you. It's hard to tell that with Sam if you don't know him."

"So Connor got married and left?" Mathilda said; she liked to keep things straight and orderly in her mind.

"Yup. To a cousin of Cynthia Carson, a girl named . . . named . . ." He slapped himself on the forehead again. "A girl named Airmed! Her family's got a part of the new vineyard there. I remember it all 'cause Mom yelled at Aoife about it."

"Yelled at Aoife because Connor dumped her for Airmed?"

"No, 'cause Aoife was so mad she tried to cast a spell to make Airmed's toenails split and her hair fall out and things."

"Can't you witches do that?"

"Well, of course we *can*, we're just not *supposed* to, it's against the rules. Besides, Airmed's a witch too. That's really really *really* not a good idea, putting a hex on another witch. They can tell."

"Oh. Well, so who's Aoife in love with now?"

"Liath, of course," he said impatiently, gesturing towards the dance, and rolled his eyes upward.

"But Liath's a girl too!"

"So?" Rudi said, puzzled. "Sometimes that's the way it happens."

Mathilda looked at him. "But *that's* against the rules. And it's . . . icky."

"Why?" Rudi asked, and then nodded as he remembered. "Oh, yeah, it's *geasa* for you Christians, isn't it?" he said tolerantly. "Like not eating meat in Lent? It's different for us witches."

"But then why was Dan bummed about it?"

" 'Cause Aoife's cool most of the time, but she's a complete *pain* when she falls for someone, everyone knows that. You weren't around the last time, with Connor. She gets real boring; all she wants to talk about is how wonderful whoever-it-is is; she won't do anything that's fun at all, it's all gooey eyes and mushy songs and stuff like it wasn't just the same way the *last* time. And we're gonna be stuck listening to her 'cause Uncle Chuck has her *guarding* us all the time . . . maybe it'll be better this time . . . Oh, Lord and Lady, Liath's in the First Levy now, she'll be on guard with us too! You're my best friend, Matti, but this guarding thing is a pain in the *arse*. Really. I wish your folks would . . . oh, never mind."

"Am I?" Mathilda asked, her voice quiet.

"Are you what?"

"Your best friend."

"Well, duh, why do you think I hang out with you all the time?" he said cheerfully, giving her a punch on the arm. "It's not so Uncle Chuck can have the same *bo*ring grown-ups following us around with spears, you know. *Or* because you're my fostern-sister. You're cool."

They leaned back against the hay bale, sharing their plaids as the night grew a little chilly, and passing the chunk of fruitcake back and forth for the sort of small bites you took when you were full and just eating for the taste. Mathilda felt her eyelids drooping as Juniper sang *"Odhche Mhath Leibh,"* slow and sad and sweet.

Then they came open with a snap, a wariness prickled by a change in the air. Not at anything that was said or done, or any sudden sound at first. Then she noticed a mud-splashed man in leather pants and jacket talking to Edward Finney; and the farmer's face changed. He came over to Juniper, bending to talk in whispers. Juniper's face changed as well, and she rose to walk over and crouch before the children. Rudi smiled sleepily at her, and she absently smoothed a lock of red-gold hair back from his forehead.

"Mathilda, my dear, I have news for you."

"What?" Mathilda said, feeling a sharp stab of fear draining away the good feelings.

"Your mother has come to Corvallis, child. You'll be seeing her tomorrow, or very soon."

CHAPTER SIX

The fort on the eastern bank of the Willamette guarded the twin bridges running into Corvallis town, but the ground around it was open save for a small lake and a few woodlots, cultivated fields that had been part of the University's experimental farm, and more that had once been a golf course. In midwinter all that was fallow ground, dusty green pasture, or the lumpy dark brown of plowed furrows, patches of it covered by a drifting ground-mist that turned distance to shadow and trees to looming shapes.

A small stone monument outside the gate listed the names of those who'd died defending the desperately needed crop in that first dreadful year. Lieutenant Sally Chen remembered those days, sometimes much better than she wanted to, late at night; remembered the cramping hunger in her belly as her bones poked through her skin, and the cry of *bring out your dead* . . . She'd been a first-year student then, and used a sharpened shovel in the scramble to keep refugees and foragers off the fields of grain and vegetables and the hoarded livestock; helped bring in the harvest too, often with her bare hands or a kitchen knife. She'd also fought in the internal battles, carefully not commemorated, with those who wanted to fall in with the state government in Salem and its insane plan to put all the food in one pot and try to carry everyone through. When that civil war was over—and the plague victims had been buried in mass graves north of the Hewlett-Packard plant—there had been food enough for the survivors in the city and its surrounding territory to keep eating until the next year's crop . . . just barely.

Beyond the river was a thin strip of settled land about two farms deep, with grainfields and orchards and defended homesteads, and then mostly vacant brush-country to the notional border with the Mackenzie territories along old Highway 99E; and more of that beyond, because the first Clan duns were well east, past the old I-5 interstate. In between were old ruins and new wilderness, growing up worse every year in bramble and weeds and sapling trees save where wildfire preserved grassland; the central core of the Valley had taken the worst damage in the aftermath of the Change, and what people remained still clung to the bordering mountains.

Chen spent much of her time under arms patrolling that budding jungle, keeping it a little less unsafe for traders and travelers, which was less boring than sitting here watching the road, but also less comfortable. Now she sat on a bench in the fort's courtyard across from the open east gate and took a bite of the sandwich her eight-year-old son had brought over from home; smoked pork and sharp-tasting cheese on black bread, with mayonnaise and chopped pickled onion . . .

Pweeeeet!

The whistle of the speaking tube brought her on her feet with a sigh; just standing around in armor all day was work, and unlike the shop you didn't have a pair of shoes or a set of harness to show for it afterwards. She looked up, then walked over to the stand and pulled the cork out of the funnel on the bottom end of the tube. The striped fabric of the hot-air balloon a thousand feet above was a looming shape in the fog, a gaudy black and orange against the pale gray of the sky when wisps of mist blew aside and gave her a view. The mooring-rope climbed in an ever-steeper curve from the heavy winch to the gondola, and a rubber hose ran beside it.

"What've you got, Hillary?" she shouted into it, then put her ear close to listen.

"Mounted party on the highway, armed—I can see some

lanceheads. About twenty riders, with two two-horse wagons. Coming at a walk."

Chen looked out the open gate: nothing there but roadway stretching out into the mist; then she scratched her head under the brim of the helmet with her free hand and took another bite out of the sandwich. Twenty armed riders with only two small vehicles didn't sound like merchants; you'd never make a profit on it. She knew that well, since in civilian life she ran a leatherworking business with her husband and brother and sister-in-law, as the marks of awl and thread and needle on her hands bore witness. They'd taken small shares in several caravans buying hides farther to the east, and checked on the costs to make sure the accounting was honest.

Chen looked around the small courtyard that held the winch. The fortress was a solid, square block of stone and concrete about the height of a two-story house, with round towers at the corners and a wet moat without; one of the minor hardships of being stationed here was the everlasting slight stagnant smell, except when the spring freshets from the Willamette changed the water.

"Keep an eye on them," she called into the tube, and then took another bite. Her next remark went to the courtyard in general: "Turn out, everyone: wall-stations. But not the gate, not yet."

Booted feet pounded up the steep staircases as someone beat on a triangle, and hastily donned helmets showed along the crenellations of the battlements. The drawbridge was worked by counterweighted steel levers, which made it easy to close quickly; they had to be cranked down, but that was usually less urgent.

"And load the engines," she went on, a little less distinctly as she finished the heel of the sandwich.

A series of deep *chrunk-tunng* sounds came from the catapults and bolt-throwers as valves were opened. Water from the reservoirs in the towers flowed into the hydraulic bottle-jacks built into the war machines, pushing back against the coil-springs and throwing arms until they were cocked and locked with the trigger mechanisms. Those engines could cover half a mile around the fort with showers of forged-steel darts and globes of homemade napalm. Or at least they could when visibility was good, which right now it wasn't.

"Now let's see what we've got," she said, wiping her mouth with a napkin and tossing it into the lunch-basket.

She dusted off her metal-backed steerhide gloves, settled her sword belt and picked up the glaive that leaned against the stone of the inner wall. That was much less cumbersome than a pike in the strait confines of a fortress interior; five feet of ashwood with a heavy pointed length of steel like a giant kitchen knife on it, and a hook welded to the base of the thick, straight back of the blade. Then she walked out onto the drawbridge over the moat, careful not to step beyond the edge of it. The counterweights could snatch it up quickly, and she'd slide down to the bottom on the inside with nothing lost but dignity. That would leave plenty of time to close the steel-shod gates and drop the portcullis.

Not that she expected trouble. Enemies or bandits would have to be insane to attack here; the fort was strong, and it had a garrison of thirty, and there was another just like it where the bridge met the city wall on the west bank of the river, and the city itself could muster near two thousand defenders almost at once if the call to turn out in arms came. It was probably just some Mackenzies, or possibly travelers from east over the Cascades . . . though the passes would be difficult, this time of year. Or it might be Bearkillers, though they'd be more likely to come from the north, past the border station at Adair.

She scowled slightly, and absently snapped down the triangular three-bar visor of her helmet and peered out into the fog. Mackenzies were all right, she supposed—sort of bizarre in varying degrees, but all right. Bearkillers . . . well, they weren't cutthroats and thugs like the Protector's men, but they were almighty hard-boiled, and their A-listers were often outright arrogant. They made her glad Corvallis had avoided developing a landed aristocracy of the type that seemed to be growing up like mushrooms on cowflops in most places.

Leaning on the shaft of the glaive, she waited. The lookout in the balloon didn't say anything more, so the riders were still coming on, and she hadn't recognized them. Her second-in-command came up, a long-hafted war-maul across one mail-clad shoulder as he stroked his square-cut brown-yellow beard with his free hand. He was also her next-door neighbor, a house carpenter, a member of their regular Friday-night bridge club and they'd been in several classes together back in 1998.

"What the hell do you think it is, Sally?"

"Jack, I keep telling you, it's Lieutenant, Lieutenant Chen or ma'am, when we're on duty!"

A grin. "OK, ma'am, what the hell do you think it is?"

"Damned if I know, Jack," she replied.

"Hey, when we're on duty that's *Sergeant* Jack to you, bitch," he said, and they both laughed.

A moment later Chen shoved her visor up for a better look at what came looming out of the fog. *"Mud lun yeh!"* she said, startled into swearing in Cantonese for the first time in many years. "What the *fuck*?"

"Erainnath Dúnedainon nelmet, Astrid a Eilir!" Astrid Larsson called, reining in where the roadway met the fort's drawbridge.

Her Arab mare Asfaloth tossed her wedge-shaped head, and her long mane flew silky, wound with bright ribbons as the slender legs did a little dance in place. Astrid raised her right hand high, palm-out in the gesture of peace.

"Ennyn edro hi ammen!" she cried.

"But darling, the gates *are* open," Alleyne Loring murmured.

"Greetings, Lady Astrid, in the name of the people and Faculty Senate of Corvallis," the militia officer said; or at least Eilir thought so, even though uncertainty made the movements of her lips less crisp than the deaf woman would have preferred.

That's irritating, she thought. *Lip-reading is hard enough even when people enunciate properly!*

There was wonder in the Corvallan's eyes as she looked down the row of mounted Dúnedain, with the brace of baggage-carts bringing up the rear. The column of twos had halted with a single surge and stamping, and the Rangers sat

their horses nearly motionless . . . except for wondering eyes
on the watch-balloon overhead.

"*Mae govannen,*" Astrid said graciously. "Or in the common tongue, well met."

Eilir smiled to herself at the way the militia soldiers' eyes
were bugging out; Astrid had laid herself out for Yule presents, and the entire column of Dúnedain was wearing the new
black tunic-vests with the silver tree, stars and crown, while
Eilir herself held the banner with its cross-staff. They'd also
agreed that if the Rangers were to be a thing they lived rather
than did in their spare time they should look more alike, and
not like Bearkillers or Mackenzies on holiday. The pants felt
strange on her legs, and she missed her kilt and plaid, but she
supposed she'd get used to it again . . . and they'd also agreed
they could wear what they liked when visiting their kinfolk.

I used to think this was goofy, she mused, rolling her eyes
down at the tunic for an instant. *Of course, I did always think
they were sort of cool as well, and it looks* less *goofy with us* all
dressed this way.

The Larsdalen artisans had done them well, and the mesh-
mail-and-nylon lining was very comforting, when you didn't
have time for real armor.

Dread Lord and merciful Mother-of-All, I don't even really
remember *what it was like when nobody was trying to kill me.*

There were three men with the column not in the new . . .
well, Alleyne had called it the *national costume.* Alleyne himself was in his suit of green-enameled plate armor, with his
visor up but the heater-shaped shield with its five roses on a
silver background on his left arm, and a long lance in his right,
the butt resting on a ring welded to his right stirrup-iron. John
Hordle wore a green mail shirt, and an open-faced sallet helmet pushed up until it rested on the back of his head, with his
bow and long sword worn crosswise across his back; the cob
he rode had a goodly share of Percheron in it, which was only
fair considering that he weighed more than Alleyne did riding
armored cap-a-pie in steel.

Sir Jason Mortimer was in the pants and quilted gambeson
he'd worn under his armor, complete with old bloodstains,
and cuffs that ran through a ring on the pommel of his saddle

securing his right hand; he looked frowsy and disheveled, even apart from the way his shield-arm was in a sling. Nobody had hurt him, and his wounded shoulder had been competently tended, but they hadn't been all that considerate either; he'd spent Yule locked up in a storage shed near Mithrilwood Lodge, with a lump of salt pork, waybread, water and a bucket for his necessities.

They'd made him empty the bucket himself, too.

"Ah . . . Lady Astrid . . ."

The militia lieutenant was floundering, but she knew who she was talking to. There weren't many in the Valley who'd fail to recognize Astrid and Eilir together. Then she visibly pulled herself together, shifting her glaive into the crook of her left arm.

"What's the purpose of your visit to Corvallis, Lady Astrid?" she said politely. "And who are those with you?"

"We come to speak the truth before the people and Faculty Senate; what other business we have in Corvallis is our own. And those with me are the *Ohtar* and *Roquen* of the Dúnedain Rangers," Astrid said loftily.

"Ah . . ."

Well, when you're with Astrid, things are never dull, Eilir thought, delighted. Then she signed to Little John: *Have pity on the nice lady with the glaive, excessively biggish boyfriend, and translate. I doubt she knows Sign or Sindarin.*

"That's *squires* and *knights*," the big man said in his bass voice. "I don't suppose you speak Elvish, ma'am?" he added, his little brown-amber eyes twinkling.

"Ah, where were you planning on staying?" the militia-woman said, blinking again. "You understand, such an, ummm, imposing force—"

All the riders had helms and some sort of body armor besides their swords and bows; four carried long horsemen's lances as well.

"We're staying with Master William Hatfield," Astrid replied, pulling a folded letter from her saddlebag and handing it down. "Or at least leaving our horses and gear with him; he stands surety for us. And our prisoner."

"Ummm," the lieutenant said, a variation on her previous

nonverbal placeholder as she read. The *You can't keep prisoners in Corvallis!* she obviously wanted to say died silent.

"Errrr . . . I know Bill Hatfield. OK, I suppose . . . Who *is* this man?"

Alleyne cut in. "He's Sir Jason Mortimer, from the Protectorate. He won't be hurt on Corvallan soil," he said. "Or at all, really. We captured him in company with bandits; *leading* bandits on a raid, in fact."

"You're going to accuse him before a court, or the Faculty Senate?" Chen said sharply.

"We're going to show him to the Senate, yes," Alleyne replied.

Everyone looked a little gloomy at that. Sir Jason had resolutely refused to cooperate, and the Dúnedain didn't go in for the toenails-and-burning-splints forms of persuasion. Which wouldn't work here anyway. If he kept his mouth shut, there went most of the public-relations effect of capturing him in the first place.

Maybe we should just have chopped his head off anyway, Eilir thought. *Though of course . . .*

"We're also going to arrange his, you might say, repatriation with the Association's consul here," Alleyne went on.

Meaning we're going to squeeze him until his eyes pop out, Eilir thought happily.

Running an embryo nation had turned out to be unexpectedly expensive, with endless things they needed to get; and besides, by rights they should have whacked the man's head off with the rest, who were only his tools after all.

Besides, the way the Association works, Liu's widow will have to cough up to help him.

In the end it would all come out of the people who worked Mortimer's lands, but he probably took as much as he could from them anyway. The payments on the ransom would have to be subtracted from his own income, unless he wanted his peasants to die, revolt or run away in despair. Bad as they were, the Protectorate's nobles had learned that you couldn't skin the sheep if you wanted to shear it next year, and there was more work than hands to do it everywhere these days.

The rest of the formalities took only a few minutes, not

much longer than required to peace-bond their swords. Few of the Rangers had visited Corvallis before; they stared about them in wonder as they crossed the northernmost bridge. Fog covered the water, but the current made odd swirling patterns in it, and Celebroch moved uneasily under her, feeling the toning of the swift water against the pilings through her hooves. Barges and boats and booms of logs for timber moved beneath, dim and half-seen; a few sported tubby masts and gaff sails, and more were tied up along the waterfront. Eilir ran a soothing hand down her mount's neck, and again when they passed through the inner gate and the city wall and the Arab mare shied at the bustle of the crowded street.

The Stone Houses, Astrid signed. *Fallen from their former greatness, aren't they?*

Eilir looked at her, slightly alarmed; it was possible—not likely, but possible—that her *anamchara* would decide that this decayed city needed a princess or two to lead it *back* to greatness, and you didn't need three guesses to know who'd be in that role. And she just might pull it off . . . she'd brought off crazy schemes before. Perhaps she could have brought off the ones Eilir had talked her out of, as well.

Or maybe they'd just have gotten us all killed, Eilir thought, searching for inspiration. *Help!*

"Little do they know our labors in the distant wilds, that keep them safe," Alleyne said before she could sign, and Astrid nodded.

Phew! Eilir thought. *She was always one for going off on tangents, but it was all a lot less scary and more fun when we were younger and less powerful.*

Their destination was just right of the gate to which the bridge led, tucked into the northeastern corner of the city wall and separated from it only by the paved strip around the base, the *pomeramium* kept clear for military use. Parts of the complex looked like they had been something on the order of a car dealership before the Change, and more timber-frame buildings had been run up on a parking lot to add space; a house had been tacked on as well, probably moved from somewhere outside the walls and rebuilt here.

A group of men waited under a sign that read "Hatfield & Hatfield." Will Hatfield was a wiry man in his forties; he smiled broadly and waved as the Dúnedain column drew up before his complex of warehouses, stables and workshops.

"All's ready," he said; his eyes narrowed as they saw the captive knight. "Including a nice tight room for your little pigeon there. Harry, Dave, see he's stowed away."

Eilir unlocked the handcuffs. Two tough-looking young men in rough clothes helped Sir Jason Mortimer off his horse, and then frog-marched him away. They didn't carry weapons, strictly speaking—their belt knives had blades under ten inches long. That was enough, and they also had ax handles thonged to their right wrists. The city bylaws said nothing about carrying a stick.

Hatfield was a wholesale merchant who dealt largely in hides and leather, a growing business as the pre-Change plastic equivalents finally wore out, with a sideline in tallow and wool and hemp and other goods. The actual tanning was done outside the walls, but the big shadowy spaces of his warehouse were still pungent with the smell of leather, the greasy lanolin scent of the wool, and the fatty-beefy smell of tallow, with beeswax and horses and half a dozen other goods beneath. Eilir took a deep breath; it was the smell of faraway places and happenings.

I wouldn't like to live in a city, she signed to Hordle. *But it's nice to visit once in a while.*

The woods can get quiet, he replied, then winked. *Although there are ways to make them lively, eh?*

Hatfield handed Astrid a key to the padlocks that secured the space he'd turned over to the Dúnedain. He waved aside her thanks. "You saved my life that day over in the mountains," he said. "Not to mention a wagon train full of goods I couldn't afford to lose."

Astrid smiled with regal courtesy, and greeted his family likewise; his wife was a competent-looking person with cropped black hair and ink-stained fingers, with a six-year-old girl clutching at her leg and peering out shyly from behind it. His son was just into his teens, and he looked at the Dúnedain with awe.

"Mae govannen sinome—" he began, and stumbled through a clumsy greeting in Sindarin.

From the stiff way he shaped the words he'd learned strictly from books; the Ranger version had become more like a living tongue, and they'd had to make up a good deal to fill in the irritating gaps—words for "sexual intercourse" and "to pee," for instance.

Astrid's face blossomed into a smile, and Eilir knew wryly that she'd made another slave for life; she answered in the same language, then shifted into English:

"I know your father to be a brave man and a good friend," she said to the boy. "It's good to know his son is a scholar of the ancient tongues as well!"

Much of the covered space was loose-boxes for horses, and there was enough room for their mounts and a little to spare. Hatfield and his staff helped with easy competence, and his son practically flew around running errands, but the Dúnedain saw to their own horses. Her Celebroch and Astrid's Asfaloth went into a stall on their own; they got along well, being sisters themselves, dappled-gray and beautiful, accepting the wedges of dried apple the two women fed them as only their due after the currying and rubdown.

Got that youngster under your spell, Alleyne signed a few minutes later, his blue eyes laughing, as they walked out into the street. *And really, you know, the languages aren't all that ancient.*

He might make a Ranger, someday, Astrid replied. *Or at least a Dúnedain-friend. And who's to say they're not really ancient? Are dragons and rings of power any stranger than the Change?*

She turned to the assembled Rangers. "All right, how many of you know how to handle money? Really, I mean."

About a third raised their hands, some uncertainly; the confident ones included all the few Dúnedain from the city and its lands. The Rangers had all been twelve or younger at the Change, and few of them remembered using currency at all well. Money had only come back into circulation in the last couple of years, starting with Corvallis and the Protectorate. The Bearkillers had their own mint, but the Mackenzies hadn't bothered; neither folk made much use of coin as yet.

"Everyone gets two silver dollars each," Astrid said. "You can get a room and your meals for longer than we'll be here on one, at a good tavern. Two is the price for a pretty good horse, or a sword. So be careful while you're shopping! You should have some left over when we leave. And remember, you're on best behavior. The honor of the Dúnedain Rangers is in your hands! Not to mention our secrets; use Sign or Sindarin if you have to discuss anything confidential."

One of the Dúnedain grinned; he was all of eighteen, and newly promoted to *ohtar*. "Besides, Sindarin's great for wowing the women. All you've got to do is look into their eyes and whisper something like *I lempë roccor caitaner nu I alta tasar* and the townie girls go all weak in the knees."

A girl about his own age thumped him on the top of the head. *"Talam e-gass,"* she said. "You're using *the five horses stand under the willow tree* as a *make-out line*?"

Talam e-gass was another compound of their own coinage, added to the Elvish stock. It translated roughly as *asshole*.

Astrid snorted. "What part of *best behavior* didn't you understand, Dathar? And nobody goes off on their own—pairs of *anamchara* together at least. We'll meet each morning at Hatfield's."

They nodded solemnly, and Eilir pulled the pouch out of her jerkin and handed over the dime-sized coins; about three-quarters bore the beaver head of Corvallis, and the rest a mix of the snarling bear mask of Mike's Outfit and Arminger's Lidless Eye. Those made her palm itch, but it was good silver and you couldn't avoid using it, since the Protectorate had been minting money the longest and made the most. Everyone coined to the same fineness and standard weight, anyway.

Eilir cocked an eye upward. Between the clouds, the fog and the short winter day, it took experience to estimate the time. Then she looked at the signs of the eating-houses that congregated along lower Monroe Street. The smells were appetizing, and included the scent of frying fish.

Anyone else feel like lunch first? she signed.

"A good idea," Alleyne said. "Never bargain on an empty stomach."

"That was a good bacon cheeseburger," Astrid said over her shoulder. "I hate to admit it, but sometimes I just get *tired* of roast venison."

Tired of food? Eilir signed ironically, making her eyes go round; she'd had pizza lavishly strewn with dried shrimp.

They all laughed as they headed up Fourteenth on their way to Polk; deer were abundant in Mithrilwood . . . sometimes *too* abundant. So much so that salt pork stewed with lentils and dried onion was a relief occasionally.

"Even the Fellowship got tired of *lembas,*" Alleyne said. "I liked the grilled chub with herbs, personally."

"At least in winter the deer lasts long enough you can trade for something else before it goes off," Hordle rumbled. "I take a good deal of fueling up, I do. It's not 'ealthy for me to go off me feed."

Since he'd just put away three platters of crab cakes, several pounds of what he insisted on calling chips rather than French fries, and vegetables on top of it, nobody argued. The four of them had also shared a green salad, a scandalous luxury in January, when the winter-gardens were giving out; some of it came from the old University greenhouses, and it had cost as much as the rest of the meal together.

Astrid and Alleyne went first down the crowded sidewalk. Eilir watched with tender amusement as Astrid's hand moved out towards Alleyne's, drew back, then darted out and gripped his fingers. Her own arm was tucked through John Hordle's—which took some arranging, even though she wasn't a short woman by any means. Their eyes met, and Hordle's rolled up. She knew exactly what he was thinking: *Seven months, and they're just up to holding hands in public?*

Eilir scowled at him and then gave her silent giggle; it *was* sort of funny, when you thought about it. *And sweet and sad at the same time.*

Amusement died when they came up to the old brick-built Victorian structure that housed the consulate of the Protectorate, and alertness replaced it. A banner hung from the eaves to just over the door, night black save for a flame-wreathed Lidless Eye in gold and crimson.

Something's up, she thought.

The building usually made do with the discreet plaque reading "Portland Protective Association" to keep from provoking the citizenry. The four-horse carriage that had just drawn up outside it was unusual as well, very like a Western stagecoach except much fancier and with pneumatic tires, with brass and lacquered leather and glazed windows with sashes drawn across them, and a different blazon on the doors—a blue-mantled Virgin Mary standing on a submissive-looking dragon.

Even after what must have been days of travel in the wintertime the vehicle still had a subdued dark gleam, and the horses looked reasonably fresh. The outriders were four men-at-arms in full fig: conical helmets with nasal bars that splayed out to cover the mouth over mail coifs, knee-length short-sleeved hauberks with the skirts split up the middle for riding, plate or splint protection on shins and forearms; the destriers had steel chamfrons on their heads and peytrals to protect their chests. They'd diplomatically left their lances somewhere else, their swords were peace-bonded, and their four-foot kite-shaped shields were slung diagonally across their backs from left shoulder to right hip by the *guige* straps, point-down like a country-singer's guitar in the old days. They swung down and let grooms lead their mounts away to the stables behind the house, taking position around the carriage facing out with their arms crossed over their chests, standing with a relaxed alertness like so many hunting dogs.

Two footmen had been riding on the back of the carriage, blue with the chill despite warm woolens. They leapt down and opened the door facing the sidewalk, and swung down the folding stair. A young maidservant in double t-tunic and long, embroidered tabard stepped down, a light suitcase in her hand, an elegant pre-Change French type surfaced with ostrich leather and closed with a built-in combination lock. Another woman followed her, dressed in Portland's idea of male civil garb and wearing a sword at her belt, which was more than a little odd in Association terms, and carrying a lute; she handed that to the servant when she saw the Dúnedain. The bundle slung over her back was probably a crossbow in a zippered nylon bag. Her plain, dark t-tunic had long sleeves that flared below the elbow; from the way it moved, Eilir suspected a mail lining, and a sheathed dagger strapped to her right forearm; she was in her early twenties, blond hair cut in a pageboy bob, with eyes the pale gray of the sea on an overcast winter's day, graceful features as hard and watchful as the guardian warriors'.

Look at her wrists and the backs of her hands, Eilir thought, conscious of a quick, professional appraisal directed at her. *Look at her* eyes, *look at the way she* moves. *That's a fighter and a very good one.*

Then a third passenger left the coach. . . .

Astrid forced her hand back from the hilt of her sword and rested both hands on the broad, heavy belt that cinched her waist; she stood there bristling quietly with her face a beautiful, calm mask, something that would make anyone who knew her well nervous. Alleyne raised an eyebrow, and John Hordle muttered an oath; the passenger was someone they'd both met, when they came into Portland on the *Pride of St. Helens* last spring.

Sandra Arminger! Eilir thought.

"Why, it's *Roquen* Astrid, *Hiril* of the Dúnedain!" Sandra Arminger said with a smile.

She stepped out of the carriage, bundled in a long, shimmering ermine traveling cloak and holding the skirts of a rich cotte-hardi aside; the woman with the sword handed her down.

Her voice was warm and pleasant as she went on: "And her *anamchara* the *Kel-Roquen* Eilir Mackenzie! We meet at last! *Mae govannen, ndek!*"

Astrid grew conscious that she was about to hiss in sheer fury, and made herself take a deep breath and let it out slowly. *It's just like her to know the Elven tongue,* she thought. *This means we'll have to be careful while she's around, because we can't tell how* much *of it she knows. Damn!*

"Lady Sandra," she forced herself to say. "We had business at the consulate here, but we'll come back later."

Sandra Arminger's eyes were a dark brown just short of black, steady and clever and watchful. Her smile seemed to reach them, but with a secret amusement, as if she was always laughing at some secret joke at everyone else's expense; she was a good deal shorter than Astrid or Eilir's five-eight, doll-like before Hordle's hulking mass, but not in the least intimidated as she went on: "Lord Carl is a very competent man, but if you wish to discuss the unfortunate Sir Jason Mortimer . . . yes, I've heard about that . . . it'll save you time to talk to *me*. And Sir Alleyne, Master Hordle, how nice to see you again, even if you were naughty the last time."

She shook a finger at them. "You took me in completely! Not many men can say that. I look forward to our conversation."

"You're doubtless tired from your journey," Alleyne demurred. "Tomorrow is also a day."

"Not in the least, Sir Alleyne—"

"That's plain Mr. Loring," he said. "My father's the baronet."

"As you will. The roads are still good, even the I-5, now that it's mostly been cleared of obstructions. I'm perfectly fresh."

So that's how she got here, Astrid thought.

"And I changed out of my traveling garb before we got here."

The old interstate wasn't much used, since the center of the Valley held few folk south of the Association's territory these days, but over the years the various communities had pushed the dead vehicles aside, often in the course of salvaging useful parts like the springs and tires. It would be a very bold bandit indeed who'd attack Sandra Arminger with her household knights around her.

She probably had more than that, Astrid guessed. *Another carriage, spare horses, more men-at-arms and some mounted crossbowmen. Left them at a hidden camp outside the settled zone before she came on to Corvallis.*

Two days would be ample to cover the eighty miles between here and Portland. It was a bold move, but not foolhardy, if she had important business here. Alleyne looked at her and raised a brow. Astrid glanced at Eilir, and got an almost imperceptible nod, and the same from John Hordle.

"Thank you," Astrid said. "There's no point in wasting time."

Sandra inclined her head. "Ivo, Ruffin, Joris, Enguerrand," she said, and the men-at-arms came to attention without moving. "See to things. Tiphaine, with me."

The consul was a lanky blond man in his thirties with a face that showed no expression at all and a knight's little golden spurs on his boots, who stood aside with a little bow as Sandra swept past, and nodded to the Dúnedain.

Funny names, Astrid said in Sign behind his back.

Mom said it's Court fashion in the Protectorate, Eilir replied. *Taking names out of old books.*

Silly, Astrid answered, and then blinked as John Hordle bit his lip and fought a laugh down into a wheeze. *What are* you *laughing at? Never mind.*

Lord Carl bowed them through into a conference room, and left silently at a slight movement of Sandra Arminger's fingers.

The room had been remade in Association style with a tapestry on either side of the fireplace, but there were bookshelves flanking the bow window that looked out over a winter-sere garden and a huge oak where a few dry yellow leaves yet clung; lilacs tapped their bare fingers on the glass. A long table of some polished reddish wood ran down the center of the room, with pens and ink, writing paper and blotting paper and little silver cups of fine sand to dust across a page when you were finished writing. Fire crackled in the hearth, shedding grateful warmth on the raw winter's day; the room held the scent of burning fir and of wax and polish and a sachet of dried roses on the mantel. Astrid was suddenly conscious that her boots might have been a little cleaner after tramping through the streets and mud earlier that day, and that it had been two days in the saddle since her last cold-water bath or change of underwear.

"Do be seated," Sandra said, stripping off her fur-lined gloves.

Astrid ground her teeth; she hadn't planned on asking for permission. The maidservant handed the gloves and heavy traveling cloak to another and then took three steps backward and stood waiting, with her hands folded in front of her with fingers linked, and her eyes cast down. Briefly, Astrid wondered why the girl didn't run for it; perhaps she had family back up in the Protectorate, or possibly Sandra Arminger was smart enough to treat her personal staff well.

Probably, not possibly. Don't underestimate an enemy!

The servant pulled humble obscurity over herself like a cloak of invisibility. The woman in the dark tunic and breeches didn't; behind her ruler's right shoulder she stood silent and immobile with her hands folded inside the wide sleeves of her black tunic, pale eyes looking nowhere in particular . . . and she was as easy to ignore as a spearpoint pointed at your nose. All four of them gave her a single long, considering glance and then stopped looking at her, but Astrid could tell everyone kept her location in mind.

Refreshments were offered and—politely—declined. Sandra Arminger warmed her hands on a goblet of mulled wine that smelled of expensive spices. She *did* look tired, and not only because she was fifteen years older than Astrid. There were dark circles under those piercing eyes, and she sighed in relief as she sank back in the comfortable cushioned chair; she wore no jewelry apart from the silver-link band around her linen headdress, and a simple chain bracelet bearing an odd-looking coin.

"I always enjoyed Society events before the Change," the consort of Portland's ruler said. "But there are times when I miss being able to slop around in sweats . . . not to mention just getting into a car and *going* somewhere, especially after a trip like this. God alone knows what it'll be like when the roads and bridges have washed and worn away. But I know you youngsters aren't interested in hearing us decrepit fogies talk about the good old days."

She held out a hand, palm-down over the table. The maidservant took a book from the shelves and slid it forward under her fingers. It had a black-leather binding, and gilt-stamp letters on the spine beneath the Lidless Eye. They read:

Fiefs of the Portland Protective Association: Tenants in Chief, Vassals, Vavasours and Fiefs-minor in Sergeantry. That meant among other things that the maidservant wasn't *just* a maidservant; she could read at least, which a lot of people her age in the Association's territories couldn't. Sandra flipped the book open, then turned two pages over to find precisely the entry she wanted.

"The mesne tithes from Sir Jason's manor of Loiston—"

She raised a brow at them, and they all nodded to show they were familiar with the Association's terminology. Mesne tithes were what a fief-holder paid his own overlord for seizin of the land, part of which would be passed on to the Lord Protector by the tenant-in-chief.

"—amount to eight hundred silver dollars yearly, or fifty-seven rose nobles in gold," she went on, running a finger down a list of figures. "That's notional, money of account. Most of it is paid in kind, and he's assessed to maintain three crossbowmen, three spearmen and two mounted men-at-arms for the war-levy of Barony Gervais. Besides his own service in arms and eighty days castle garrison duty for a man-at-arms and three footmen annually in time of peace, and the usual boon-work from his tenants for roads, bridges and fortifications."

She looked up at Astrid and raised a brow. The younger woman made herself refrain from licking her lips by an effort of will, feeling more than a little rushed. She'd expected to come into these talks with all the advantages. It wasn't working out quite like that, somehow.

"We'll turn him over when his steward sends us five years' yield," the Lady of the Dúnedain replied curtly. "In cash or equivalents in cloth, horses, tools and provisions of types and quantities to be agreed. We won't release him until the ransom is paid in full."

"Five years' mesne tithes?" Sandra said. "Oh, come now. The standard ransom in the Protectorate is *two*, for men captured in a private quarrel, and this *was* private war, not one between realms."

"I'm not interested in how you pay each other off," she replied firmly. "Five years."

Sandra put her elbows on the arms of her chair, steepling her fingers together and tapping them gently on her lips. That let the brow of her wimple shadow her face while she thought.

"How's this, then," she said after a moment. "Make it two and a half years, and I'll pay the entire sum to you in cash right away. That'll save you a good deal of trouble, and spare you Sir Jason's company, which frankly I always found tedious myself."

Silence ran heavy for a moment. Then Astrid went on: "We wanted to make the ransom heavy to send a message," she said. "We don't want your *yrch* trespassing on our land. Three and a half years."

Sandra laughed softly. "My dear girl—" At Astrid's expression, she modified that: "My dear *Roquen* Astrid, I don't intend to make him a *gift* of the money. Rest assured that he'll pay back every barley grain of it. If it's any comfort to you, the humiliation of paying *me* will be even greater. Shall we say three years?"

"We should have taken his head with the scum he hired," Alleyne said, his voice quiet and cold. "That would teach others not to attack us on our own ground."

Sandra sipped at her goblet. "You killed his brother-in-law and liege-lord," she pointed out. "It's only natural for him to be a bit ticked."

I *killed his brother-in-law and liege lord,* Eilir signed. *While he was trying to kidnap or kill my brother Rudi on* our *own land. Rising thrust that cut the femoral artery, not to mention the testicles. He should have worn a metal cup under the hauberk.*

Sandra's eyes flicked to Astrid and she made a questioning *hmmmm*? Astrid translated the Sign without being in the least convinced of the Portlander's ignorance. Sandra shrugged.

"Well, well, at that point you'd already kidnapped *my* daughter on *my* own land, and Eddie . . . Baron Liu . . . was trying to get her back, with your brother as a wergild," Sandra said, and for a moment something showed behind her eyes.

Then she smiled charmingly. "These chains of grievances go in both directions. For example, you also killed Katrina Georges, Mathilda's tutor who I sent along to be with her in her captivity."

"That was me, actually," Astrid said. "I shot her in the back with a broadhead after we Dúnedain disposed of your ambush party. She was killing a Mackenzie with a sword at the time, as I recall. Some *tutor*."

"She was Mathilda's physical-education tutor," Sandra chuckled, and the glacier eyes of the young woman behind her chair shifted to Astrid, going slightly wider and then narrowing. Arminger's wife went on: "And Tiphaine Rutherton here was a good friend of Katrina's; they were both members of my Household from shortly after the Change. I don't doubt she'd like to pay you back for killing her friend. Wouldn't you, Tiphaine?"

"Yes, my liege," Rutherton said, her voice as unemotional as water running over polished stones. Heat radiated from it. "Very much, in fact."

"So you see, there's a certain symmetry to all this. But back to practicalities. If you take my offer, you get the money immediately. Otherwise you'll be negotiating with dowager Baroness Liu, Sir Jason's sister. I don't think you'll do better, and things may well drag out. Lady Mary would have been pleased if Sir Jason had succeeded, but right now she's rather annoyed with him—for failing, and for embarrassing her politically in the process. *I'm* rather annoyed with him, which is why I'm making this offer. The debt will hold him like a choke chain on a disobedient hound. I'll even make him lease out the hunting rights on his woodland to help pay it, which will grieve him no end since he dearly loves to pursue the boar."

Her smile invited Astrid to share in the hapless Sir Jason's woe. The Dunadan had to make a conscious effort to reject that complicity and the momentary warmth it brought. She glanced around at the others instead, reading their expressions as her own qualified yes.

It really *would* be more convenient. They'd have the gold, the distilled yield of two hundred people working two square miles of good land for three years, and they'd have it right here, in the Valley's best-supplied marketplace, or at least the best for tools and clothing and weapons. And they needed more trained warhorses, which were hideously expensive whether you spent money or your own time. *Everyone* was buying them.

So why is she making things convenient for us? Astrid thought. *Perhaps she's afraid he'll talk . . . and there's no reason at all to relieve her anxiety.* Then, aloud: "I presume you're here for the meeting of the Faculty Senate or something like that?" she said.

Sandra nodded.

"So are we," Astrid went on. "So we'll hand him over on Sunday, when everything's finished. We have a use for him until then."

Sandra's expression remained the same, but Astrid didn't need the sudden pressure of Alleyne's foot on hers beneath the table to realize that the dart had hit.

"I'd really rather have him now," Sandra said. "If it's all the same to you."

"Is that a condition for paying the ransom?" Alleyne asked, a sharp note in his voice.

"No," she replied easily. "Not at all; if you want to keep seeing Sir Jason's scowling face that long, you may. As long as he's in reasonable health when you hand him over, you'll have the money—one hundred and sixty rose nobles in gold, or any mix of gold and silver you wish at the usual exchange ratios."

"Agreed," Astrid said promptly, and at Sandra Arminger's nod the four rose and left.

"That one is formidable," Sandra Arminger said softly, speaking to the snapping flames in the fireplace. "Quite mad, that's beyond doubt, but formidable. And she will grow more so. All of them will. If they live. This would be a great pity."

"My lady—" Tiphaine began, going to one knee, naked eagerness on her face.

"No," Sandra said, and there was iron in her voice. She turned in her chair so that she could see the younger woman. "If she, either of them, or the men, were to die just now . . .

You will do *nothing* that could link me to an assassination in Corvallis while the peace lasts, do you hear? *Do* you?"

Tiphaine bowed her head. Sandra went on in more friendly tones: "But there *is* the matter of the egregious Sir Jason. Something must definitely be done to ensure he isn't the star of their little PowerPoint presentation to the Faculty Senate."

The other woman nodded, though the computer reference went over her head, then froze as Sandra extended a finger almost to her nose.

"Listen to me, Tiphaine. I took you *and* Katrina in after the Change, trained you, and found you work you liked better than breeding heirs for some oaf in an iron shirt. I kept your little secret from the priests, or at least from official notice. His Holiness wouldn't approve of your . . . lifestyle choices, if he knew about them."

"I am my lady's grateful and faithful servant."

"Yes, you are," Sandra agreed aloud. To herself: *And the younger generation can say things like that and not seem silly at all. It's distinctly weird sometimes, like living in a dream . . . focus, woman, focus! This isn't a game and the stakes are very high. Mathilda—*

She leaned forward, gripping the arms of the chair. "But so was Katrina. Your dearly departed girlfriend *failed* me, Tiphaine. You'd better not."

"No, my lady." Tiphaine's tongue touched her lower lip briefly. "There will be nothing to link any . . . events to you. If necessary, I will retreat rather than risk exposure. I'll work alone. Or possibly with Joris . . . no, he's good, but he doesn't take orders well."

"I'm glad you noticed that; I think our good Joris Stein has a self-esteem problem." At Tiphaine's raised eyebrow: "Too much of it, and largely unjustified. And an excess of entrepreneurial spirit. As to the ladies of the Dúnedain . . . eventually, we may arrange for you to settle your scores."

She smiled to herself as a red flush chased pallor across the face of the young woman in black. When Tiphaine rose and bowed and withdrew, she turned to the maidservant.

"These people who bottle up their passions . . ." She made

a *tsk* sound between her teeth. "Now go and see if my bath's ready, would you, child? And tell Lord Carl that I require his attendance at dinner and conference with his intelligence officers afterwards. We're going to need something a bit more subtle than head-bashing for what I have in mind."

CHAPTER SEVEN

"Nigel!" Juniper Mackenzie said in glad surprise as the door opened.

"My dear," the Englishman said, blinking his slightly watery blue eyes and shedding his cloak and sword belt; he was dressed for travel in winter . . . and not in a kilt.

"I thought you had other business?" she went on. "And you didn't come all the way across the Valley by yourself?"

"I did have business," he said, smiling with a little constraint in it. "But it's finished . . . and that's what I'm here in Corvallis to talk about."

"But come in, and have something hot to drink!"

He did, putting a parcel on the mantelpiece and warming his hands before the fire, then taking the cup and draining it. The little sitting room in the Clan's Corvallan guest-house was warm and cozy enough, with a low blaze in the hearth, and windows closed against a cold slow rain.

"Mathilda's having a nap," Juniper said, nodding to the corridor. "She's overexcited, poor thing. You've heard—"

"Yes, I spoke with Eilir, and heard about Mistress Arminger," the Englishman said, smoothing down his mustache with a forefinger. "Ah . . . I was . . . that is, Eilir knew I was coming here to meet you, in any case. With a, um, present."

Well! Juniper thought. *He's nervous! That's not something I've seen often!*

He cleared his throat and took a deep breath. He also took the package down from the mantelpiece, unwrapping the scrap of cloth that enfolded it and silently handing it to Juniper. Within was a box of hardwood about the size and thickness of a hardcover book, seasoned amber-colored bigleaf maple streaked with darker color, the curling grain brought out by rubbing and polishing. A Triple Moon had been inlaid on the surface in ivory, waxing and full and waning—and She alone knew where the ivory had come from. The Chief of the Mackenzies turned it in her hands, and saw that on the other side the wood had been carved in the likeness of a wild, bearded face, a man with curling ram's-horns on his brow; the features were brought out by the carving alone, but the eyes were milky-white opals that seemed to shine with an inner light.

"Why, Nigel, it's beautiful!" she said. *But if a gift, why not at Yule?* Aloud she went on: "Dennie's work?"

"Eilir found the wood, Astrid the ivory and opals, and I did the basic shaping and metalwork, with some help from Sam Aylward. Dennis very kindly managed the inlay and carving."

He went down on one knee before her and took the box in his hands. "At first I thought I might use the traditional ring," he went on steadily, meeting her eyes. "But then I had a bit of an inspiration. At least I hope so, my dear!"

He held the box up for her, and she unhooked the little brazen latch and opened it. A soft *ah!* escaped her as she looked within. It *was* a ring, but of a size to fit around her neck rather than a finger, glowing against the dark velvet that lined the interior of the box; a torc, the ancient royal emblem of the Gael, the gold of it worked in a delicate tracery of leaf and vine. The open ends swelled into a lunar disk and a flame-wreathed sun opposite each other, carved of moonstone and amber.

"Nigel, it's beautiful!" she cried softly, and took it up. "You really *thought* about this, didn't you?"

His smile was shy, oddly charming on the weathered, middle-aged face. "I tried."

Juniper started to put it around her neck, spreading the soft metal a little, then hesitated. "This is meant as an *engagement* torc, isn't it, Nigel my heart?"

"Yes, my dear. I hope it'll do, until I have a wedding gift—besides myself, that is."

Her smile broadened. She settled it around her neck; it was snug when she let the circle close again with the Sun and Moon on her right and left collarbones. The metal was surprisingly heavy for all its delicacy, and a bit cold. It warmed quickly; she felt her breath grow a little short, and more so after she leaned forward and took his face between her hands and kissed him.

"Then I'll take it in the spirit it's given," she said after a moment. "Beauty, and love, and friendship."

They clasped hands and looked at each other, then laughed. Her smile grew impish for an instant. "The child will need a father, after all."

She laughed delightedly at his astonishment. "No, I'm not, not yet—that *would* be a miracle, and from the wrong mythos! But I'm still under the Moon, and I always wanted three, you know! For the symbolism? And this time I get to keep the man to help with the chores, which will be a nice change."

"My dear . . . darling Juniper . . . you've made me a very happy man, and I hadn't expected to be happy again, you know."

"Not nearly as happy as I intend to make you!" she went on, standing and taking him by the hand. "I've waited long enough."

"And so have I," Nigel said.

He moved with a lithe suddenness and she was swept up in his arms; she could feel the compact strength in his chest and arms.

"First door on the right," she murmured.

Second roof to the right, Tiphaine thought.

The Hatfields had built their business up gradually, and the result was a complex of boxlike buildings joined to each other higgledy-piggeldy, each with its own tin roof, or covering of salvaged asphalt roofing tile. She avoided the metal as much as possible; even in her soft-soled climbing boots, it was hard to avoid making noise on it, and it was dangerously slippery when wet—and during a Willamette Valley winter, it would be wet about ninety-nine percent of the time. Luckily the Hatfields hadn't skimped, and the roofs had solid, heavy-duty plywood or planks nailed to the stringers beneath the waterproofing layer, so they didn't creak much. The sky was overcast, and the streetlights were turned down with dawn near. That made it near enough to pitch-dark up here as no matter, and in her matte-black outfit she was effectively invisible. Everything was covered save for a slit in the tight hood that let her see, and the skin around her eyes was blackened with charcoal.

Katrina had said once that made her look like a raccoon. She stopped for an instant; let the fury wash through her and over her without tensing her muscles or disturbing the even tenor of her breathing. Then she went on, walking step by step, careful to keep below the ridgeline. She crossed it flat on her belly, moving with cautious speed. Sir Jason Mortimer was in a second-story storeroom on this side, with only two guards, according to what the consulate knew. Nobody in Corvallis knew how to keep their mouths shut, evidently.

Yes.

Everything looked the same as it had through binoculars from a taller building not far away. Her chamois-gloved fingers went to her belt. The sling was of leather like her gloves, equally butter-soft, yearling doe hide tanned with brains. The cup at the bottom was just the right size for the projectile, an egg-shaped thing of sand molded with wax. Lead or stone were too likely to kill . . .

I miss my crossbow, she thought, as she systematically tightened and relaxed muscles to keep them limber while she crouched in the near-freezing dampness.

She had a little beauty, a pre-Change model with a 7x scope and a built-in crank for reloading, its skeleton body all synthetics and carbon composites, half the weight of a standard modern wood-and-steel military model and just as powerful. Out of the question to use it here and now. This was taking a long time, but it all depended on how big the guards' bladders were. Hopefully they wouldn't come down to pee in chorus, but that wasn't likely. One would stay by the door at all times;

from the files, Hatfield didn't hire incompetents. Right now that would help her. They were concentrating on keeping Mortimer prisoner, not on protecting him.

Ah. Her mind slipped effortlessly back into full alertness. A door swung open, then banged shut again as a spring took it. She looked away to make sure the momentary glow of lamp-light through it didn't lessen her night vision, then back. *I was right.* The man unbuttoned and let loose on a heap of straw and manure near the center of the L formed by the two build-ings, with his back to her. There really wasn't much point in staying inside and using a pot, when there was a dungheap so close, and only the house here had a connection to the city sewer system. It was another two hours before either man was due to be relieved.

The stream of urine smoked in the cold, wet air. Tiphaine took the ends of the sling in her right hand and the cup in her left, holding it taut but not tight. She kept the position while the man shook off and buttoned back up; it would look suspi-cious if he wet himself. Then . . .

Up from the crouch, smooth and steady. A single sweep around her head, and *release.* Cloven air hummed, a subdued whirr and swish. Then a dull, wet thump.

Bull's-eye, the huntress thought.

The man fell limp as a half-full sack of grain. Behind the mask the Association warrior's lips skinned back from white teeth. She waited nonetheless, counting the seconds against her heartbeat—which was a useful technique for keeping calm in itself. A half minute passed, and another. The quiet re-mained absolute, the loudest sound a dog barking for a few moments. She started to move, then froze: footsteps on the street outside, beyond the fence to her right, loud and care-less. Her head turned; just a flicker of motion through the boards of the fence, a rhythmic tapping—

Watchman on patrol, she thought; that was a nightstick. *No, they call them police officers here.* He didn't call the hour, or that all was well, either, as he would have in Portland, or check non-nobles for their night-pass. *Sloppy.*

The steps faded off into the distance. She waited only a few seconds beyond that; much longer and the guard's partner would come to see what was going on. A rope and grapnel were looped around her shoulder like a bandolier, and she set the two rubber-sheathed hooks on the guttering, over a bracket where the thin metal would be strong enough to bear her weight. The rope dropped twenty feet to the brick pavement of the yard, and she slid down it with the cord locked between her shins. A flick, and the grapnel came loose and fell into her hands.

Half a dozen strides took her to the fallen man. She checked his breathing; it was slow and natural, and the shot had only broken in three pieces when it flattened against his skull, which made it easy to pick up. He hadn't injured himself falling, which was to be expected—most people fell much more skillfully if they were completely limp. Then she peeled back the eyelids to confirm that she hadn't scrambled his brains either; knocking someone out and not doing lasting harm was a lot more difficult than you might think, hard enough with a cosh, requiring real skill with a sling.

Moving with careful speed she opened a leather case on her belt and took out a small hypodermic, pinching a fold of flesh on the inner thigh before she injected him. Working the limp form over her shoulders in a fireman's lift took only an instant. A slight grunt escaped her as she rose; the merchant's man weighed at least a hundred and eighty, better than forty pounds more than she did. It was all solid muscle, too . . . but then, so was she, if built along more graceful lines. Her nostrils twitched slightly in distaste at the beer-sweat-and-horses scent of him. From the downy blond beard, this was Harry Simmons; the other guard was Dave Trevor, black-haired and clean-shaven, probably because he couldn't raise serious face-fuzz yet. They were both young.

And up *we go. You're the luckiest man in Corvallis tonight, did you know that, Harry? Although you and Dave may not think so in the morning. But if I'd been planning this op, I'd have killed you both and set a fire to cover it.*

Walking in a crouch she moved crabwise to the door under the heavy weight. This was the tight part of the operation. It was a simple frame door with a knob, salvaged from some house in the suburbs, and it swung open soundlessly. The light within seemed bright to her night-adjusted eyes, but it was dim enough, a trickle from the lantern at the top of the stairs. That was turned down low, but she could see that this end of the big open space of the warehouse first floor was nearly filled with burlap sacks holding something—oats, from the slightly sweetish smell, and a pile of empty sacks as well. That would do nicely.

Tiphaine let the man slide to the ground at the foot of the stairs, face-up; the construction was open, simple two-by-fours and planks, honest carpentry but nothing fancy. Then she slid the haversack off her back for an instant. Inside the black-leather sack were a number of padded compartments, and some held bottles—the label read Vat 69, though it was actually an ordinary brand of Corvallan rotgut made from potatoes. A *real* bottle with the original contents would buy you the price of a plow team.

A little of the liquid went into his mouth; then she recorked the bottle and put it into Harry's hand. Then she reached out and stepped on the bottom stair, hard. It creaked with a satisfying loudness, and she made a single silent bound into the pile of empty sacking. That gave her an excellent view of the stairs from behind.

Light flared as the wick in the lantern was turned up. It didn't move, though, which meant that the excellent Dave wasn't bringing it with him to the stairs. Stringers and plywood creaked over her head as he came to the head of the stairs, looking down.

"Harry? What the fuck's taking you so long? Are you taking a piss, or a vacation? Harry?" He paused at the sight of the limp body sprawled below. "Harry? You all right, man?"

There was a very slight sound, one she recognized without effort. Steel on leather, a knife coming out of a sheath. It went back in when the booted feet and shapeless wool trousers were halfway down the stairs.

"Have you been *drinking*? And on the *job,* you stupid bastard? The boss will have your *balls* for this!"

Another deep breath. The man bent to examine his friend, grunting in puzzlement as he saw the stopper was still in the neck of the liquor bottle, and presenting her with a perfect target. She opened another case on her belt, took the pad of damp cloth in her hand.

Be quick, now. He'll smell it, otherwise.

She leapt. Dave was bigger than she, and strong as an ox, but she had surprise on her side . . . and the pad clamped tight over his mouth and nose. He staggered and thrashed, fell to the earth, tried to crawl. For a moment she thought she would have to resort to an old-fashioned thump on the head, and then Dave sprawled beside his friend. A second hypodermic made sure he wouldn't wake up prematurely; the cocktail contained scopolamine for amnesia, and something else that produced a splitting steel-band-around-the-brow headache. The overall effect was very much like going on a bender and being very, very sorry that you had when you woke up.

Then she moved, and quickly, dragging them both back into the darkness beneath the stairs one after the other. She opened the Vat 69 again, sniffed with a wince—wine was her drink of choice, and she had a weakness for cherry brandy, but couldn't stomach even the better brands of whiskey. And this stuff was vile even by whiskey standards. She poured a little onto their clothes and, taking care to raise his head so he wouldn't choke, into Dave's mouth. That and the empties she left scattered around would make it *very* hard for them to deny in the morning that they'd drunk themselves into insensibility.

She looked at the label, then giggled silently and spent a few extra seconds rearranging the unconscious bodies and re-moving clothing. Let them try to explain *that* to whoever found them! A few empty but still-fragrant bottles scattered around added detail.

Maybe this way is better after all. Never a dull moment in Lady Sandra's service!

Then she took the keys and Dave's belt-knife and headed up the stairs, automatically placing her weight to one side to minimize creaking. The floor above was mostly open storage areas as well, holding bundles of redolent tanned hides, but across one end of the building was a set of three small, heav-ily timbered rooms with metal doors, used for light, high-value goods. There were two stools and a basket that had held a meal near the one farthest from the stairs; the lamp stood on a barrel. A grille was set in the door. She looked through; Sir Jason was on a cot, the room otherwise bare.

"Hissst!"

The sleeping man was snoring slightly, flat on his back; that was doubtless because of the wounded shoulder. Pain had grooved lines in the young knight's face as well, and there was a thick, fair stubble on it.

"Hissst!"

This time he woke, rubbing at his face with his good hand. *Good. He has to see and recognize me, or this could get awkward.* She knew him fairly well, and while his impulse control was poor, his reflexes and muscles weren't. Amateurs also tended to underestimate the difficulties of a resisting subject . . .

"Quiet, Sir Jason! It's me, Tiphaine Rutherton, of Lady Sandra's Household."

She pitched her voice to a low, conversational tone, less likely to carry or be noticed than a whisper. Sleep struggled with comprehension on the knight's face. His notorious bad temper won out as he came to the grille and she pulled back the mask for an instant so that he could see her.

"Yes, I recognize you. Little Tiphaine, the tomboy lady-in-waiting. Perhaps you've decided you like me after all? Get me loose and I'll forgo the dowry."

Mother of God, not now! she thought; that had been two years ago. Aloud: "I'm here on my liege-lady's orders, Sir Jason."

"Dyke!" he spat with sudden fury—more than a casual insult, where the writ of the Holy Office ran; a cold shudder of rage and fear went over her skin.

Then he went on more calmly: "Well, get me out of here, woman! Those maniacs weren't just going to bankrupt me, they were planning on dragging me through Corvallis like a dancing bear."

"Just a second, Sir Jason," she said, putting the key in the lock.

The man tried to push past her as the door swung open; that gave her the perfect position to stamp on his instep, a thrust-kick with the heel of her left foot. He jackknifed forward with a slight, shrill squeal of pain as the small bones there cracked like twigs breaking, and then the knife in her hand came down—the pommel, not the blade. It smacked into his right collarbone with a muffled wet snap that left the man with two crippled arms; she followed it up with a swift whipping blow to the larynx, then pushed him back into the little windowless room. He fell backward across the cot, turning as he tried to scrabble away from her. That let her pounce again, one knee in the pit of his stomach and her left hand gripping the longer hair at the front of his head, jerking it to one side to press his face into the bedding.

"Lady Sandra didn't send me here to get you out," she said. "She sent me here to shut you up, you loud-mouthed moron."

He was still conscious enough to feel the cold kiss of steel; then she rammed the blade up under his breastbone, angling slightly to the left. It was an ordinary single-edged belt-knife, more tool than weapon, but eight inches of sharp steel would do the job anyway.

"And you know," she went on to the still-twitching corpse, "I *really* don't like it when anyone except another dyke calls me a dyke."

Tiphaine left the knife where it was; if there were any useable prints on the horn of the hilt, they'd be the unconscious Dave's. Now, to get out, she should be able to use the courtyard door . . .

"Hold it! We don't want to harm you!"

A head rose, a man standing on the stairs. Blond, sharp-featured; enough like her to be her brother, ironically enough. No way back. Decision and action followed together; she closed her eyes to get the advantage of a crucial second's adjustment, whirled, kicked over the lamp and leapt forward over his head as it winked out. Darkness descended, not absolute but shocking to anyone expecting the light to continue. In midair she twisted and drew her legs up, and landed in a crouch behind him; wood rapped painfully against her shin, but she didn't fall. Instead she was in a perfect three-point stance, two feet and left hand supporting her, the right fist curled back to her ear.

The narrow confines of the stairwell trapped the man above her for an instant. In that instant she struck, hammering a knuckle into the inside of his thigh where it would paralyze the muscle. The leg buckled under him. Tiphaine slapped both her hands down on the wood of the stair as he fell and struck out behind her with both feet, a mule-kick at the shadowy figure behind her at the bottom of the stairs, lashing out with all the strength of her long, hard-muscled legs.

Thump.

Surprise almost slowed her as the half-seen opponent managed to get forearms up for a cross-block, riding the bone-shattering force of the blow backward, falling to the asphalt floor of the warehouse.

Fast, that one. Be careful!

Tiphaine let her feet fall back just in time for the man she'd leg-punched to topple back on top of her. The weight drove an *ufffff!* from between her teeth, but she made her arms and legs springs to push back at him, tossing him head-foremost with his spine to the stairs. With a strangled yell he went hurtling down the stairs behind her, even as she turned and crouched and leapt again; he landed hard, and yelled again, this time in pain.

The ground floor of the warehouse gave her space to move. The man was tangled up with the one she'd kicked. A corner of her mind registered moon-pale hair: Astrid Larsson. The door was temptingly open . . .

Instead she turned and ran down an alleyway between towering piles of full, sixty-pound sacks of oats, the layout flashing through her mind as she moved. A deep bass voice swore outside the doorway, and the floor thudded as a man came through; he'd been waiting outside. *John Hordle.* Every bit as big as she remembered him but astonishingly quick, right on her heels. If *those* hands closed on her, she was doomed. It would be like trying to fight a grizzly.

No choice.

She sprang again, landed halfway up a fourteen-foot stack of bagged grain and scrambled to the top like a squirrel running up a tree. Across the top of it, slippery burlap moving beneath the soft gripping soles of her boots. The whole stack thudded and shivered under her as Hordle's massive weight slammed into it without slowing, then started to topple towards the wall in an avalanche that could shatter bones and kill. Desperate, Tiphaine let that fling her towards the window there, launching herself out with her arms crossed before her face.

Crash.

Glass shattered, and the thin laths broke and twisted. Tiphaine's belly drew up of itself—she had a fifty-fifty chance of carving her own guts out and spilling them on the ground, with a crazy stunt like this. At least she wouldn't have to try and explain to Lady Sandra how she'd missed four people lying in wait—

Then she was rolling on the asphalt in the cold darkness; only superficial cuts. They stung, but no tendons were severed, no muscle deeply gashed. Rolling, up on her feet again, and another figure was coming around the corner of the warehouse, clearing a stack of boxes with a raking stride and landing smoothly, beautifully fluent. A woman, as tall as she, black hair—Eilir Mackenzie. The others would be seconds behind her.

Tiphaine turned and leapt again, her foot hitting the top of a wheelbarrow leaned against the cinderblock outer wall of the Hatfield property and giving her a brace for another scrabbling jump. The top of the wall had a coil of barbed wire on it, bad but better than spikes or broken glass. She grabbed, heedless of the sharp iron punching into her palms, wrenched, pulled, flung her body up sideways and rolled across it, pulling with desperate strength as cloth and skin tore.

Whump. The sidewalk outside struck her, nearly knocking out her wind. That wouldn't do.

She was up and running down the street, pulling the rope and grapnel slung over her shoulder loose. As she did she filled her lungs and screamed:

"Help! Police! Murder! Help!" and for good measure added a scream pure and simple, a shriek of fear and pain. Summoning one wasn't all that difficult.

There weren't many houses in this neighborhood, but there

were some, and night-watchmen as well. Lights flared, and doors opened, spilling yellow flame-light onto the pavement. A whistle sounded sharply not far away, and a clatter of hooves. The grapnel buzzed over her head and flew out, and the thin, strong rope snaked behind it. The tines came down on the peak of a roof, and she hit the side of the building running, swarming up the knotted rope with the strength of her arms alone and fending off with her feet; for a heart-stopping instant she thought the blood on her palms had made them too slick, but the chamois leather gave her enough traction.

No time to stop on the roof, though her lungs burned and the cold air was like some hot, thin gas rasping her lungs. She snatched up the rope behind her as she ran, heedless of the risk of tripping, gathered it into a rough bundle and jerked the grapnel free as she passed. An alleyway beyond, another roof past it; she pumped arms and legs to gather momentum, leapt outward—

Behind her a great bass voice shouted: *"What a sodding balls-up!"*

Corvallis, Oregon
January 12th, 2008/Change Year 9

Michael Havel stirred the body with a boot, carefully avoiding the tacky red-brown trickle of blood from the death-wound and the corpse's mouth and nose, still congealing in the cold air of a winter dawn. He was thankful there weren't any flies; a few tiny footprints indicated that the rats had been nosing around, though they hadn't had peace enough to settle in for a snack.

"Three guesses as to the cause of death," he said dryly, touching a toe to the staghorn hilt of the knife whose blade had been driven up under the ribs.

"Gee, that's a toughie," Signe said, her tone as pawky as his.

We've been married going on ten years and we're starting to think alike, Havel thought. *Apparently that old saying is true.*

Signe wrinkled her nose at the smell, but stooped over the tumbled corpse, which lay in a tangle of limbs and the collapsed cot. The others were out in the open space that made up most of the upper story of the warehouse, apart from Bill Hatfield, who was apparently still reaming out his unfortunate guards down below, near where they'd been found. In between times, he yelled at the police, who were shouting back. The gray light was gradually swelling, as the sun rose behind the clouds.

And am I glad I'm not those guards! the lord of the Bear-killers thought. *Assuming it* wasn't *what it looked like, they're still* never *going to live it down.*

"Look," his wife said, and pulled back the padded gambeson the dead man wore—they made passable winter coats—and the shirt beneath. "Someone broke his collarbone before they killed him. I thought the way his arm was lying was a bit strange."

Havel grunted and leaned over, his hands on his knees. There was a little blood where the skin had been broken, and the bone gave under his probing fingertip. Someone had done exactly that—good sharp fracture, but not enough damage to have been done by a blade. At a guess, something metal and with an edge, but a blunt one.

"Whoever it was did it quick," Signe went on. "One thrust and they left the knife in to cork him."

Havel nodded agreement. Killing with a knife was messy unless carefully managed; but then, anyone who'd butchered pigs or sheep knew that.

"Get Aaron—" he began, when someone cleared his throat behind him. "Oh, hi, Aaron. We need your expertise here."

"My expertise as a theatre critic?" Aaron Rothman said.

Havel straightened and courteously stepped aside as the physician limped into the room; he had a pair of rubber gloves still on, and they went rather oddly with the rumpled elegance of his jacket and turtleneck and trench coat. Wherever he'd slept, the slim Jewish doctor hadn't been at the Bearkiller consulate houses last night, and the circles under his eyes beneath the glasses suggested he'd been burning the candle at both ends. He was all professionalism now, his intelligent brown eyes narrowed in a pleasantly ugly fortysomething face shadowed with heavy morning stubble.

"Theatre critic?" Havel asked.

"Well, that was an inspired little piece of bitchery with the guards, but it was all put on, you know," Rothman said, a little New York still detectable in his voice though he'd been living in Lewiston, Idaho, at the time of the Change.

At their enquiring expressions he went on: "Whoever did it should have just left them with the bottles; a murderous drunken frenzy followed by swinish collapse. Making it look as if they'd been doing the nasty as well was a bit much. And Vat 69—I ask you! Catty, very catty."

"You're sure?" Signe said, her glance keen. "They were supposedly drunk."

"O delightfully strong-jawed Amazonian queen of Castle Rustic, mother of my honorary nieces and nephew . . . radar may not work anymore, but my gaydar is, I *assure* you, fully functional. You could draw the shortest line between any two points with either Harry or Dave. Pity. Dave's a bit dishy, in a rough-trade Tom of Finland sort of way."

He struck a pose, and Havel snorted laughter. Aaron wasn't only gay, but outrageously swish—two characteristics which Havel had learned in the Corps didn't necessarily go together. He suspected the doctor enjoyed shocking the rather insular rural community he'd ended up in, as well.

"Gosh, you're making me feel so *butch* again, Aaron," Signe said.

"Oh, just let me do the makeover! A nice James Dean cut for the hair, the right plaid shirt, that brutally handsome little scar on your nose . . . OK, OK, let's get back to business."

He stooped over the body, manipulated wrist and limbs, rubbed a little of the blood between rubber-clad finger and thumb to test how much it had thickened, then moved clothing aside to check on the lividity. There was an impersonal gentleness in the way he moved the corpse.

"Someone crushed his foot, too," he said. "That would be quite, quite agonizing. Not as bad as having it cut off and eaten in front of your eyes"—he tapped his own artificial foot against the floor, encased in a trim Oxford loafer with a tassel—"but sufficiently painful. And there was a blow to the larynx; that would have kept him quiet."

Havel grunted again, and looked at the door. "He came over to the door. Someone unlocked and opened it, and then maybe he started out. Whoever was outside stamp-kicked him on the instep, broke his collarbone, hit him in the throat and pushed him in. Jumped on him as he tried to get away and killed him with a single thrust to the heart."

"Which means the late unlamented probably knew whoever it was and let them get close, not expecting to be attacked," Signe said, with a low whistle. "Slick!"

"Yeah," Havel said. "Real pro job. Time of death?" he went on to Rothman.

"Sometime within the last few hours. And the esteemed Mr. Hatfield checked on them before he went to bed, so that narrows it down. The police doctor was right about that at least."

"Right about *that at least*?" Havel asked.

Rothman nodded, taking off the rubber gloves with slow care—they were hard to replace, and had to be reused after a spell in an autoclave.

"She thought they really had passed out after three bottles of eighty-proof local 'whiskey,' pseudo, so-called. I can't absolutely prove it but I'm pretty certain one was slugged behind the ear with something heavy but malleable, and the other was chloroformed. Then they were tranked, at a guess with a cocktail including scopolamine. My colleague is competent but she's young, trained here post-Change—not as familiar with the concept of exotic drugs as a big-city boy like *moi*. Whatever it is, it mimics an alcohol-induced stupor and the aftereffects quite convincingly, including some retrograde amnesia. Scopolamine wipes your short-term memory, so you don't recall what happened before you went bye-bye. Anywhere from a few minutes to an hour or so is blanked."

"But if they don't have anything like that here in Corvallis, where—" Havel began.

Signe and Rothman were both staring at him, a slight look of exasperation in their eyes. "Portland," he said.

Rothman nodded. "I've talked with doctors who work there, a few times. They have quite a pharmacopoeia. Less new production than here in Corvallis, but the Lord Protector's had a scavenging operation of quite remarkable scope going since the first Change Year, stockpiling everything his men could find. No dust from a saint's tomb for *him* when he's feeling a bit peaked, I assure you."

"Sir Jason here would have made the Association look bad if he talked when the Rangers showed him off," Havel said thoughtfully.

"Astrid says he *wasn't* going to talk, which cut his value. But having him dead will make the Dúnedain and Bill Hatfield look *very* bad," Signe said. "Those rumors that we're all fanatics, barbarians and nutcases? What better proof than our dragging a man in and him ending up knifed and dead here in law-abiding Corvallis?"

"*We're* supposed to have killed him?" Havel asked. "Or at least, Astrid and Eilir are supposed to have brought him into town, and *then* killed him? Or the Bobbsey Twins out there did it?"

"Honey, betcha the rumors are spreading right now. Rumors don't have to be credible, just juicy."

Havel looked at the doctor, who threw up his hands in a theatrical shrug. "No, I *can't* prove what we all know to be true. Not enough to satisfy a court."

"Not a court here in Corvallis," Havel said grimly.

"Oh, this is bad," Juniper Mackenzie said sorrowfully, as a stretcher team brought the body down the stairs. "This is very bad indeed."

The policeman turned on Hatfield. "Bill, what the hell were you thinking, keeping someone locked up on your lonesome, in the *first* place? You may have noticed we don't have slavery in this town, unlike some people I could name, and kidnapping's still a crime last time I looked."

Detective Simon Terwen was a man in his early thirties with rather shaggy brown hair and a gold wedding band on his left hand, in civilian clothes, denim jacket and pants and tire-soled leather boots, unremarkable except for the badge on one breast pocket and the shortsword, handcuffs and nightstick at his belt. The constables behind him were in blue uniforms with the same equipment, except that one—the tall man standing next to the close-coupled stocky woman—had a catchpole as well, a shaft with a Y-shaped, spring-loaded fork at the end. All three of them looked disturbed; violent crime within the city wall was rare, with no more than one or two murders annually since the chaos of the first Change Year. Most of the small police force's time was taken up with traffic control, enforcing the health and safety bylaws, and settling the odd family dispute.

"Lady Astrid, Lady Eilir, Mister Hordle, you all say a figure in black came out of the room where the deceased was held, eluded you and ran away? After calling for the police."

"That's right," Astrid said stolidly. "She was very fast."

"She?" Terwen asked.

Alleyne nodded stiffly, his right hand kneading his neck; there were fresh bruises on his face as well. "From the sound of her voice when she called for the police—which meant that we couldn't chase her, since we were too busy explaining things to your people, Detective."

"Things were completely shambolic," Hordle said. "Like chasing a bloody rubber ball, it was." He turned to Eilir, who spoke to him in Sign, then turned back. "Eilir says she was about her size and build, but that she couldn't get close enough to see anything else."

"Well, there is blood on the ground outside the window," Terwen said. "And on the barbed wire, and on the rooftop across the alley. That does tend to corroborate your story . . . which doesn't mean it's very convincing. I still have a dead body with a knife in it, and it's *your* employee's knife, Mr. Hatfield, and you were imprisoning the victim without legal authority. You may have noticed judges are getting more sensitive about stuff like that this last little while, Bill."

"That bastard was from the Protectorate, not a Corvallan citizen," Hatfield said stolidly.

"Well, why were *you* dragging him around?" Terwen asked, turning on the Dúnedain leaders.

"He led a bandit attack on our territory," Astrid said, making a dismissive gesture. "We brought him here to explain that to your Faculty Senate, with the rest of the evidence."

"Evidence?"

"There," she said, pointing.

One of the younger Dúnedain helpfully stepped over to a leather trunk stacked against the wall, one of a set designed to go on either side of a packsaddle, and flipped it open. A few of the spectators stepped back at the spoiled-meat smell, not overwhelming in the cold weather, but fairly strong. The glassy stares of the dead bandits stared out into the room, bloated, smiling with the rictus that draws back the drying lips.

"Oh, Astrid, Eilir," Juniper murmured under her breath. "You girls just cannot resist a dramatic gesture, can you?"

She put her hand in Nigel Loring's. Even then, and despite what must be a chorus of devils beating out a tune on the inside of his skull, Alleyne Loring noticed and smiled.

"Thirty-two dead bandits, and we didn't lose one of our own," Astrid said proudly. "And this *orch* from the Protectorate was leading them against us."

Terwen sighed himself. "You know, Lady Astrid, I actually believe every word you've said. The problem is there's no *proof* of anything, including who those heads belonged to."

Astrid looked at him, her silver-veined blue eyes puzzled. "But we wouldn't have killed them if they weren't bandits and evildoers," she pointed out.

Eilir made a clicking sound with her tongue. Astrid looked over at her, and the other signed: *There's that paper that the monk gave us.*

"Ah!" Astrid said. "I'd forgotten that . . ."

It was in another box, a smaller steel one they used for money and documents. Terwen looked it over; the writing was a fine copperplate, but a little unsteady due to internal application of Brannigan's Special. He held it up to the gray winter daylight from outside, checking that it had the Abbey's watermark—Mount Angel made its own paper too, at least for official documents.

"Well, this corroborates your story," he said. "Mind if I show this to the chief of police? Thanks. OK, you two"—he pointed a finger at Harry and Dave, sitting with numb expressions on overturned buckets—"don't try leaving town, or I will *definitely* bring charges and you go to the lockup pending trial. There'll have to be a judicial hearing, as it is."

He turned to the Mackenzies and Bearkillers. "You folks know what I did before the Change?"

"No," Mike Havel said. "You weren't a student, like everybody else in this town?"

"Nah, I was a cop. Sometimes I think that's a disadvantage. I may . . . will need to talk to you all again. Please notify me if you're leaving town before this is settled."

"This is bad," Juniper said again, as he left.

"It was bad when we arrived, Juney. This just makes it worse," Havel said, and looked at his sister-in-law and her companions. "You couldn't, just maybe, have told the rest of us what was going on?"

"We didn't expect Lady Sandra to have Sir Jason *killed*," Astrid said, a slightly defensive note in her voice. "He was her own liege man . . . well, her husband's baron's liege man. We thought she'd try to *rescue* him. All she'd have to do would be to get him out on the street and we couldn't take him back."

Signe snorted. "Anyone who underestimates Sandra Arminger's . . . focus . . . is going to be sorry and sore," she said. "She's just as smart as the bastard she married, and a lot more clear-headed."

"And sir . . ." Alleyne said. "Perhaps we were being a trifle vain, but we thought the four of us could intercept whoever she sent and Sir Jason as they left. We also felt that a larger party would have been too likely to be detected. We *wanted* to catch someone, after all, not deter them from trying at all."

"Yeah." Havel nodded. "That's the way I'd have bet, too. Sandra's got a real pro working for her. Pity you didn't kill her."

"Wait a minute," Signe said. They all glanced over at her. "I've got an idea."

She spoke for five minutes. When she finished, Astrid frowned and spoke. "But what if Lady Sandra doesn't buy it?"

"Then at least we'll be able to see who she uses to contact them. She'll have to investigate."

Astrid smiled sweetly. "Oh, I think I have an idea about

that too. A fail-safe. We have to be careful. But I think I know the right bait, if it was Tiphaine Rutherton."

Mike Havel glanced back and forth between them. After a moment, he began to laugh. "I see why the Larssons stayed on top of the heap all those generations."

CHAPTER EIGHT

Corvallis and area, Oregon
January 12th, 2008/Change Year 9

"Matti!" Sandra Arminger said, holding out her arms.

"Oh, *puh*-leeze," Astrid muttered under her breath. "*Raica pedeth!*"

No, Rudi Mackenzie thought. *She really means it. Yeah, she's showing it off, too, for those guys*—his eyes went to the Corvallan officials, who were looking uneasy—*but she's really sad and upset too.*

It was odd, the way other people had trouble telling each other's feelings. They were pretty obvious to him, most of the time.

Mathilda ran to her mother. They were in a seldom-used public room, some sort of meeting place in one of the town government's buildings, empty except for windows and chairs and a table, gloomy, dead light fixtures still in the particle-tile ceiling, with a bare, fusty smell of stale linoleum and dead insects. Rudi didn't like it; he'd grown up in buildings made of honest logs and planks, and preferred the feel of wood. He stood a little closer to his own mother.

This old stuff is creepy, he thought, shivering slightly, and focused on the people instead.

Sandra Arminger's cotte-hardi and headdress made a splash of silver and pearl gray and white, the silk and linen and wool warm despite the restrained colors. Mathilda's sumac red jacket and plain kilt were a contrast to it as she hugged her mother. For a long moment they embraced, and then they spoke together in low tones. When the girl turned to beckon him, her face was wet with tears.

"Hello, young lord," Mathilda's mother said, after he'd walked over and bowed.

She extended a hand, and he took it and kissed it courteously, bending a knee slightly; it was polite of her to treat him like a grown-up. When he looked up their eyes met; hers were dark and deep, like wells full of cleverness and hidden thought; Rudi could feel them probing at him, as if she could see inside him, or was trying to. He smiled, and saw her mouth quirk up at one corner in response.

"Lady Sandra," he said formally. "I'm happy to meet you."

"My daughter tells me you've been a good friend to her," the woman said.

Rudi's smile grew into a grin, and he put an arm around Mathilda's shoulders for a momentary squeeze. "Sure!" he said. "Matti's cool. We're best friends."

"Ah!" her mother said, and her eyes warmed, losing a little of that knife-keen look. "Now isn't that nice? She needs a friend, being so far from home. Could we talk a little more?"

He bowed again and withdrew; Astrid and Eilir and Juniper stayed by the door, well out of earshot; his mother gave him a little nod at his enquiring look, and he went out through the door into the corridor. That was a little better, even if it was dark except for one smelly lantern. Aoife and Liath were there, leaning on their bows.

"Can I go outside?"

The two young warriors of the Clan looked at each other; Sandra Arminger had come with only her one bodyguard, and Astrid and Eilir were in there with her, and it was all very official and aboveboard, with the Corvallans ready to be *very* angry at anyone who broke the peace. The meeting had been set up on the sixth floor, just to make any dirty business impossible, with a sheer drop smoother than the city wall, and taller. Nobody was going to be jumping out of windows.

"Yeah, I guess so," Aoife said.

"These big old buildings give me the creeps," Liath said. "I feel like I'm smothering. I wish the townies would tear them all down."

Rudi cocked his head, distracted for a moment. "That's what I was thinking," he said. "But isn't your house an old building? Sam's place."

"Not like this," Liath said, and shivered slightly as she looked around.

"Yeah, it never feels bad there when I'm visiting," Rudi acknowledged.

"It's an *old* old building, if you know what I mean. It was always a farmhouse, and that means it belongs to the Mother."

He nodded; that made sense. Aoife went on: "Let's go outside, then. We can wait in the court."

She stuck her head through the door and spoke something quietly. Then they went down the dark echoing metal stairwell; on the lower floors they passed a few Corvallans, busy about the town's business—the more easily accessible parts of the building were still in use, and they had a more living smell as well, wool and the hot metal of stoves and candle tallow. At the bottom of the stairs was a swinging metal door with Exit painted on it in flaking red paint.

Silly, Rudi thought. *What else would it be? Did people in the old times have to* read *before they knew what a door was?*

They might have, at that. From the stories, they'd been very very odd back then, in the old times. The sign also said an alarm would go off; he chuckled at an image of someone standing there blowing a trumpet or a horn every time the door was opened, or a big brass bell ringing. That probably wasn't what the sign meant, but then the old stuff was often incomprehensible or dumb or both.

I'm glad I live now and not then, he thought, taking a deep breath of the fresher air outside. It still had more smoke and the smell of more people than he was accustomed to. Even Dun Juniper could get stuffy and give him a closed-in feeling, but you could always run out into the meadows. *And I'm glad I don't live in a big city like this, either. You'd have to* walk *and* walk *to get to the fields and woods!*

There were new watering troughs and hitching posts around the asphalt square that filled the hollow of the L-shaped building. Horses were tethered there, and Lady Sandra's carriage—and enough City guards to outnumber her escort of men-at-arms very thoroughly, just in case. The Association warriors stood in a group, with their shields slung over their backs and their hands resting casually on the peace-bonded hilts of their swords. They carefully didn't look at the Corvallan crossbowmen standing behind them, and the crossbowmen carefully didn't point their weapons anywhere near them—but they were spanned and had quarrels in the grooves. Rudi grinned to himself; it was like two groups of big, unfriendly dogs watching each other from opposite ends of a lane; most times they'd just run up and down barking at each other, and then go back and flop down and pant as if they'd done something important.

The rest of the guards were leaning on their glaives and talking with each other—he could hear a couple complaining how this special call-up was cutting into their regular, everyday jobs and hoping it would all be over soon. Now and then their armor would rustle or clank; most of them were wearing brigandines or chain shirts, but a couple had sheet-steel breastplates and tassets.

A pair in lighter gear were grooming their horses and tending their tack. They looked up and brightened as Rudi walked over towards them. People usually smiled back at him—that was only natural, since he liked most people he met, so why shouldn't they like him? His own smile had a little extra calculation; the two were looking at Aoife and Liath, and hoping to strike up a conversation. Witch-girls had a reputation for being friendly, and this raw windy day was beyond boring. Rudi didn't intend to be bored; he seldom was, and never when there was a horse to investigate.

"That's a good horse," Rudi said, after everyone had exchanged names. "Is it yours?"

He had some dried fruit in his pouch; he offered it carefully in his palm, and the big bay gelding bent its head to eat, the hairs on its lips tickling his hand.

"Yup, Blockhead here's mine. The city rents him from me when we're called up together. My folks have a farm outside the Westgate, and I think he's glad to get a change from pulling a cart."

"Can I help you curry him, Walter?" Rudi asked.

"You know how?" the young man said.

Aoife and Liath laughed. "Oh, brother, you put your foot in there," Aoife said. "This is *Rudi Mackenzie* you're talking to."

"Aren't all you guys called Mackenzie?" he replied.

His partner winced and tried to whisper something to him as Aoife snorted and looked down her nose. Liath cut in: "I'm Liath *Dunling* Mackenzie," the younger woman said patiently. "My friend here's Aoife *Barstow* Mackenzie. The little goblin here is Rudi *just-plain-and-simple* Mackenzie—the Chief's son. Like the Chief is Juniper Mackenzie full stop herself herself."

"Well, excuse me!" the guard said, smiling and making an elaborate bow. He offered the currycomb. "Go right ahead!"

"I can't handle the top parts without something to stand on," Rudi said. "I bet this fellah here really can canter for miles—look at those legs and the chest."

Walter looked at him, pale brows rising. "Blockhead's not the fastest horse in town, but he's a stayer," he said respectfully.

They all talked horses and tack while the work went on. It was nice to talk with the Corvallans, and in a way it was a relief nobody was older than Aoife—even his own mother tended to go on about the old days far too much. Someone bought a jug of sweet, heated clover tea from a passing street vendor, and they passed it around in mannerly fashion, pouring from spout to mouth without touching lips to the tin and giving it back to the seller's little wheeled cart when they were finished. Then the door opened again.

It was Mathilda, by herself; she looked up and waved at a window before walking out with her hands tucked in her armpits. Rudi went over to her.

"You OK?" he said.

"Sure," she replied with patent falseness. "They said I could come out here while the grown-ups talked. I didn't like the way their voices sounded."

"Were they yelling?" Rudi asked, frowning. *Mom doesn't yell very often, but it's scary when she does.*

Her lip quivered again, but she mastered it. "No. It was all quiet, but I was frightened."

Oh, that's worse than yelling, he thought. "I feel bad about it too," he went on aloud, blinking his own eyes and rubbing at them with the back of his hand. "I wish our folks weren't all mad at each other. It makes me feel rotten, like I'd eaten something bad. If we can be friends, why can't they?"

Mathilda nodded. "Me too. I mean, *we're* never going to be enemies, are we, Rudi?"

"Never! Not for anything, Matti."

"But if I go back home, we'll never get to see each other again," she pointed out. "Not for years and years and years, until we're grown-ups ourselves. And there may be a war."

They stood and looked at each other for a moment, knowing that the quarrels of the adults could do that. Then Mathilda's face lightened.

"We could be *anamchara.* Then we'd never be enemies, not all our lives."

"Yeah!" Rudi said enthusiastically. Then more seriously: "It's a big deal, being soul-friends, though, Matti. We'd have to share all our secrets, all our lives long, and fight for each other, and all that stuff. If you die in a foreign land, I have to give you your rites, and you for me. Even if our clans are at feud, we have to help each other. It's serious."

Mathilda nodded. "That's why we should do it. Then nobody could ever make us fight." Then she hesitated and a tiny frown appeared. "I don't know . . . my confessor wouldn't yell at me, would he? Mom just now said I shouldn't do anything that would make the Virgin cry."

Rudi didn't say that no Aspect of the Lady would cry about people swearing friendship; it wouldn't be tactful. But . . . *Mom says you've always got to be careful when you ask the Mighty Ones for something. They may give it to you.* Decision: *This is a good idea. Really.*

"Nah, it's not a witches-and-Christians thing, not really. Not *rún,* not a whadyacallit, a sacred mystery. Mom says that over in Ireland they used to swear the oath of *anamchara* even after they became Christians themselves. You wanna?"

"Then let's do it!"

"You *sure*?"

She nodded vigorously. "We'll have to get away from all these people . . . how long? Mom said it'd be half an hour until she was through talking."

"That's plenty of time. And we'll need some stuff. I know!"

He strolled over towards his bodyguards again. "Liath," he said quietly.

Aoife and the two Corvallans were looking at a hoof and discussing the shoeing; the horse snorted and swished its tail, but it was a good-hearted beast and stood patiently on three legs. Liath stood back a little; she was less outgoing than Aoife, who had enough self-confidence for three ordinary people and always had.

"Yeah, sprout?" she said, then bent down when he beckoned.

Rudi could smell the herbal wash on her braided brown hair, and the linseed oil on the chain-mail collar of her arming doublet; her smile was open and friendly. They got along well, and he'd known her off and on for most of his life, she having been part of Sam Aylward's household until just lately; she and Aoife were talking about handfasting, though most thought them too young. He didn't know her quite as well as he did Aoife, who'd lived in the Hall at Dun Juniper all his life. . . .

But Aoife is a lot more strict about things. Better not to ask her; she'd be all questions.

He spoke quietly, not quite whispering: "Liath, could you get us some stuff? This is real important to Matti and me."

"Sure. What?"

"Oh . . . ummm . . . a couple of candles, three cups, and could we borrow your war-paint kit? I know you've got it along. And two blessed wands."

Liath's brown eyes went wide. She darted a look at Aoife and licked her lips. "Are you sure about that, Rudi?" she said seriously.

She's thinking she should tell Aoife, Rudi thought, and pushed at her with his will. "Well, duh, would I be asking if I wasn't? C'mon, Liath, this is *real* important."

She looked at Mathilda then; the girl nodded, her lips compressed into a line of determination, dark circles of worry and stress under her eyes. Rudi shifted from foot to foot.

"*Please,* Liath. We've gotta do it now, before the grown-ups get everything messed up."

"OK. But if you get me in trouble—"

"Don't worry. Mom'll understand."

Liath sighed. "OK. But keep it quiet, sprout."

She strolled over to her own mount and made a show of checking its feedbag. Then she took a few small cloth-wrapped parcels from her saddlebags. Most Initiates on a long trip would have the basics for casting a Circle or spellwork with them. They sidled to the edge of the paved strip and waited until no eyes were on them; Liath leaned casually against the wall with her bow in her crossed arms, one boot heel up against the stucco, whistling as the wind scuffed dried leaves across the asphalt, and then Rudi vaulted into the open window.

Mathilda followed with something of the same eel-quick efficiency. The room within was empty and looked as if it had been deserted all their lives; the window on the other side was lodged open, and there was a rain-stain and a scattering of old leaves across the floor.

"What do we do?" Mathilda asked, a little breathless.

Rudi had the words memorized; such things came easily to him. Mathilda knew a lot less than most Mackenzies would, of course, though it wasn't a secret rite reserved for Initiates.

"Do we have to mix our blood in the cup and stuff like that?"

"Yeah," Rudi said absently. "Sorta. We've got to mix our blood, but we mix the *drink* in the cups . . ." He closed his eyes and breathed out, feeling for what was *right* in this time and place. *OK, this will have to be a little different 'cause Matti's a Christian . . .* "OK . . . you've got your crucifix with you, right?"

Mathilda pulled the silver-and-diamond amulet from under her shirt and jacket. "Now, here's how we'll do it—"

Twenty minutes later they knelt facing each other. Matti lifted the cup to his lips; it was cold tea from Liath's canteen, acrid and pleasant.

"I drink deep from the cup that the Goddess offers to the Lord," he said, then took the cup from her and held it for her.

"I drink deep from the cup that Mary held for her son," Mathilda replied, her eyes solemn in the candlelight; the early winter night was coming.

They lit the candle between them from the other two, each holding one flame to the wick, and spoke the words together. Then they picked up their knives and each nicked the back of the other's right wrist; the touch of the steel was a gentle sting, and Mathilda concentrated with squint-eyed care as she made the tiny wound. His own hand moved in a single small, swift flick. They pressed the cuts against each other, the thin hot trickle of blood mingling as their wrists locked in the chilly, damp air of the room as the chant went on: ". . . I am your brother"—he paused a little so Mathilda could say *sister*— ". . . your parent and your child. I will teach you and from you I will learn. I am the shield on your shoulder, the sword in your hand, the lamp that lights your feet. By earth and air, by fire and water, by the blood we share and the steel that shed it, we are one soul! All my wisdom and all my secrets I will share with you, as long as this life endures. Until we meet in the world beyond the world, *so mote it be!*"

"Amen," Mathilda added and signed herself, kissing the crucifix before she dropped it back around her neck.

"Oh, dear," his mother's voice said. "Oh, dear. Oh, *dear*."

Both of the children looked up, shocked from exultation back into the dying light of common day. Juniper Mackenzie and Sandra Arminger stood in the doorway, with Liath and Aoife and the dark-clad blond bodyguard in the background. The bodyguard looked amused; Liath looked as if she wanted her vital functions to stop right then and there; Aoife was scowling like a summer thunderhead.

"Oh, dear," Juniper said again.

The two mothers shared a look. When the Lady of Portland spoke, it was with crisp assurance.

"Oh, shit."

"What's *their* problem?" Tiphaine asked the barkeeper casually.

The Suds and Spuds was a respectable tavern near the riverside part of the city wall, but not fancy. A long room held tables and booths, a bar, a kitchen in the back and rooms upstairs; blackboards listed prices. And rather astonishingly there had been a four-piece chamber ensemble playing until a moment ago, students performing for food, beer and what tips the audience could afford. She herself was dressed like a local, of the same class as the laborers and roustabouts and carters who made up the clientele, or like a farmworker in town for a day—there were plenty of such, with a meeting of the Faculty Senate due soon, which was the story she'd given when she rented a room.

An equivalent riverfront place in a Protectorate town would probably be named the Slut and Brew—there was a well-known dive in Portland called exactly that—and conducted accordingly, with more noise and worse smells and without the clean sheets.

"Them?" the barkeeper said, polishing a glass and looking at the two men. "They got fired, and they're not happy about it. Wouldn't have pegged them for whiners, but you never know." He set the glass down and wiped the bar down with the rag. "Didn't you hear about the murder at Hatfield's? Man got his throat cut while those two were supposed to be guarding him. It's a three-day wonder. You want a beer, or what?"

Tiphaine nodded, and the man took a mug down and filled it from the wooden barrel as she grabbed a handful of pretzels from an orange plastic bowl on the bar. He slid the chipped mug over to her and she sipped; it was passable, and coolish if not cold. The two men were definitely Harry and Dave, looking sullen. There was a fair crowd in, and some of them were listening to the two of them holding forth.

"—not even any severance pay, and our rent due next week. And Dave here is getting married this spring. It wasn't *our* fault. How are we supposed to keep a roof over our heads?"

"There's this thing called *saving,* and some of us do it every payday," a stevedore said, getting a general laugh. "Anyway, even this time of year you can get something, work on a salvage crew in Albany, whatever. It may not pay as well as what you had, but you blew that off, didn't you?"

Tiphaine leaned an elbow on the bar, standing with one foot on the brass rail. Her hair was up under a woolen cap, which was believable enough, since even with a woodstove the place wasn't what you'd call hot. Lady Sandra's traveling gear had included a selection of contacts to turn her eyes an unremarkable brown. With a little artfully applied padding under her clothing and subtle differences in stance and walk it was unlikely anyone would connect her with the Association's consulate.

"I heard those loonies who live in the woods and think they're some sort of fairies cut that guy's throat," she said aloud. "The hired swords, the Rangers. Knocked you guys out and just killed him, like that—" She snapped her fingers. "Hell of a thing you should get the boot because Hatfield's weirdo friends like killing people. And collecting their *heads*. I heard they've got boxes full of heads, right here in town."

That got the conversation going again; of course, unless you were on the road, the main reason for coming to a tavern rather than staying at home of an evening was to schmooze and gossip. The noise level went up as the pro-Dúnedain, anti-Dúnedain and the more numerous who-the-hell-are-they-anyway factions started exchanging ill-informed opinions, louder and louder. More people were coming in, too, as the sun went down.

Eventually she used the noise and crowding to sidle over to where Harry and Dave were sitting in a booth along the back wall. They were still nursing their first beers, and the waitress had been giving them the hairy eyeball as space got more scarce and time passed.

"Mind if I join you?" she said. "Wendy Madigan's my name."

They looked at her, surprised, but shook her hand and gave their names. When the waitress came around again she looked at Tiphaine with raised brows. "Another for me," she said. "And get my friends here a shot of vodka each, with beer chasers. What've you got to eat?"

"Fish stew, or mutton and barley," she said. "Bread and fixings come with it. Five cents all up. Or you can have a side of French fries for an extra penny."

"I'll have the fish stew," Tiphaine said; it smelled all right, and the price was modest enough to suit her cover. "You guys? It's on me."

"Sure," Dave said; he looked to be the brighter of the two. "And you're doing this 'cause you like our faces or something?"

"Nah, I need the town news," she said easily. "My folks and I work in a dairy, a little place near Philomath, up Woods Creek, and they sent me in with a wagonload of butter on the railway. Everyone'll want the latest when I get home."

The two men looked at each other. Then they began to talk.

This could be an opportunity, she thought, as they took turns to pour out their grievances while she spooned up the fish stew . . . which wasn't bad, with chunks of white chum salmon, onions, carrots and potato; the bread was good, if a little rougher than the white variety the Lord Protector's court ate.

Trouble is, I'm not entirely convinced. Something not quite right. A little too smooth.

These two were too coherent and sure of what they were about. Most people told a story with a lot of umms and aaahs and disagreements, even if they'd seen the same thing—especially if they had. Nothing was more unreliable than human memory, and when she went in after Sir Jason she'd shot these two full of enough babble-juice to confuse a Dominican.

Their story is too much like a story. They're not bewildered enough at what happened to them. Smells wrong.

"You guys going to testify at the hearings?" she asked, when they'd run down.

"Ummm . . . I don't know," Dave said. "Hatfield's got a lot of pull with the Economics Faculty. Might screw up our chances of getting another job."

Hmmm. A perfect opportunity to bribe them to badmouth Hatfield and the Dúnedain, possibly too *perfect.* Decision firmed. *They're bait. Someone's keeping an eye on them, most likely, which means they're keeping an eye on* me.

"Well, I hope things turn out all right for you two," Tiphaine said. "I hate to see the high-and-mighties putting the boot into a couple of working men."

She left an extravagant nickel tip for the waitress and went back to the washrooms, sitting in a stall thinking hard until the room was empty save for her. Then she opened the window at the rear; it was a tight fit, being small and high up on the wall, but she hopped up on a sink, wiggled through and came to her feet in the alley. Something scuttled away from her . . .

"Ms. Rutherton," a voice said.

Eilir watched the Association warrior come out of her crouch after a quick, flickering examination of her surroundings. High, blank walls on two sides; Alleyne and Astrid at one end of the alley, John Hordle and her at the other.

Tiphaine smiled and pulled off her knit cap. "You can't possibly hold me prisoner," she pointed out. "And disposing of my body in a walled city . . . not easy. So I'll walk out to the street now, and if you try to stop me . . . why, I'll start to scream. People are odd in Corvallis; if you scream, they run towards you instead of away."

"We don't plan to kill or capture you," Alleyne said. His mouth was slightly pinched—he didn't like this part. "We're here to offer you something you want very badly, in return for telling the truth to the Faculty Senate."

She laughed at him. "What exactly do you have that I could want?"

Eilir felt John Hordle shift beside her. She took time out to nudge his ankle; this was no time to improvise.

"Me," Astrid said, standing forward a little. "My oath to meet you with any weapon you choose, in the wilderness, right after the Faculty Senate finishes its meeting."

Eilir could see a flush wash up Rutherton's neck and face, and her nostrils flared. "You mean that?" she said, tilting her head to one side. Then: "Yes, you do. And I suppose your boyfriend there would be waiting to kill me, after I won?"

"No," Alleyne said. "The deal includes two horses, a hundred and sixty rose nobles, and free passage to wherever you please, so long as it isn't Bearkiller or Mackenzie land."

"Corvallis," she said. "Or there's always the Yakima towns, or Boise . . ."

Astrid shook her head. "That's all moot, because *I'll* kill *you*," she said. "But you'd have the satisfaction of trying."

Tiphaine Rutherton closed her eyes for a moment, then opened them and smiled a hungry smile. "Agreed. Knives, fought *estrappado*," she said, and turned on her heel. Astrid and Alleyne had to turn sharply as she pushed between them without another word.

I have a bad feeling about this, Eilir thought. And not just because the Association fighter had specified a knife duel with left wrists tied together. *Quite bad.*

Sandra Arminger dusted the surface of the letter with sand and waved it gently back and forth to dry for an instant. "My compliments to the noble Faculty Senate, and this is my reply," she said. "I'm most pleased to comply with their request."

The messenger bowed his head and took the page from her hand, then carefully slid it into a leather-bound folder. When he had left Sandra sat toying with the lower edge of the peplum pinned atop her wimple, twisting the sheer fabric around a finger where it fell over her shoulder. The flames burned blue and red and gold over the coals in the fireplace, and one of the consulate cats brushed around her skirts before jumping to her lap and curling up for a nap; papers and books littered the table.

Tiphaine Rutherton stood by the side of the fireplace, as relaxed as the cat, with her hands in her sleeves.

"I find this rather odd," Sandra said carefully. "You don't think anything can be made of the men this merchant Hatfield had guarding Sir Jason, now that they've been dismissed?"

"No, my lady," Tiphaine said. "I don't think they *were* really dismissed. They were bait. The other side is trying to turn the situation to their advantage."

"Ah, that would be young Signe," Sandra said. "Clever girl! She's been quite annoying."

"And that's why I slipped away after sounding the two laborers out. You did emphasize that discretion was of the essence."

Sandra's eyes narrowed as she lifted the letter the messenger had brought.

"Yes, I did, didn't I?" she said. "But now the Dúnedain have requested that you be there when the Foreign Relations Committee meets. Some of the Corvallans are *very* annoyed at all this commotion in their orderly little city. The political situation is quite delicately balanced . . . and it is *very* important that Corvallis stay neutral when we move against the Bearkillers and the Mackenzies and those annoying schismatic monks at Mount Angel. Which will happen soon; the Lord Protector would prefer it be after the next harvest at the latest."

"My lady, they were expecting something to happen, but not the way I approached. None of them saw my face, when I . . . attended . . . to Sir Jason. They *did* hear my voice, so they know it was a woman. I'm the obvious suspect, but they have no proof. All they can do is swear that a dark-clad, masked woman trounced the four of them and fled . . . and that sounds pretty unlikely."

"Did you, by the way? Trounce them, that is. I know you're very capable, but . . ."

"Well . . . no. I managed to get away from them, though, which wasn't easy. Told secondhand, it sounds pretty much the same thing, and that's useful."

"It does, and it is," Sandra said. "I'm not annoyed with you, child. Simply a little puzzled. At least we've taken Sir Jason off the board. He was deplorably impulsive."

Tiphaine's calm face snarled for an instant. "He was a *pig*!"

Sandra chuckled. "Well, yes, but if we were to stick knives in all the pigs on the Association's rolls, we'd have a lot of pork and very few living noblemen," she pointed out. "At any rate, at worst we can convince the noble Senate and public opinion here that getting mixed up in a messy business like this is bad; at best, we can shift the blame onto our enemies. Well done."

She extended a hand, palm-down. Tiphaine went to one knee and took it, kissing the knuckles formally and then rising to leave with a bow. Of course, in strict form she ought to have curtsied, but unless you were wearing a skirt that wasn't really practical.

Odd, Sandra Arminger thought idly. *I spent most of my youth in jeans, but even to me a woman in pants is starting to look vaguely indecent. Habit is lord of us all, I suppose.*

She picked up the quill pen—she found them more aesthetically satisfying than the surviving reservoir types—and brushed the swan feather meditatively across her lips. The cat on her lap blinked its eyes open and rolled on its back, reaching for the feather with both paws; she teased it until it decided to jump down and groom.

Ordinarily she didn't like improvising on this scale, but Jason Mortimer's ill-timed raid had left her with no alternative, and the damage control had worked. Granted, there was that absurd ritual the children had gone through . . .

Which seems to have been their own idea, unless that Mackenzie woman is much better at deception than I am at penetrating same, she thought. *Still, it may be inconvenient. Matti doesn't seem to have changed much in one way; she's still very self-willed . . . well, not surprising considering her parentage. I'm not surprised she's fallen under the boy's spell; he's quite charming. Now, something could be made of that, perhaps?*

Schemes spun their way through her mind; it was dangerous to have a rigid plan for an unpredictable future, that made you too like to try and force events back onto a track rather than adapt to them, but you did need to prepare for contingencies. Yes . . . that might be quite useful.

"But why do I have this sense that something is eluding me?" she asked herself softly. "It all seems to be proceeding as well as could be expected, yet . . ."

Bowers Rock State Park had lain on the south bank of the Willamette north of Corvallis, where the river turned in an S-curve to avoid low hills; now it was just another piece of uninhabited riverbank, and upstream were islands and more serpentine reaches. It had been swampy even before the Change; since then entropy had undone the works of men far faster than they'd been built, as floods burst levees and dams, silt and leaves and slumping lands clogged drains and culverts. Sloughs and disused gravel pits dotted the area; dead reeds rustled in the cold wind from the north, and tossed the branches of fir and alder, cottonwood and oak, a long creaking groan beneath the whistle of the air. The natural levee along the river was densely grown with tall trees and brush; elsewhere many trees were dead as encroaching wetland killed their roots, with fresh saplings growing on spots of slightly higher ground and tangled brush nearly everywhere. The air was heavy with the chill, silty smell of standing water and vegetable decay, and the air was thick with moisture turning bit by bit into ground fog, kept to tatters and patches by the stiff breeze.

Sam Aylward grinned to himself as he knelt behind a bush. He was cold, and one thigh ached a bit where an Argentine bullet had broken it in '82, and his shoulder would stiffen up if he didn't watch it, and he could have been home playing with Fand and Edain while dinner cooked. He *should* be leaving this sort of thing to the youngsters he'd spent the last decade training, too. Yet this was a chance to use a hugely difficult set of skills that he didn't want to rust; everything hurt more, but he could still do it. Nobody had seen the small party of Mackenzies as they filtered slowly in from the east, not unless you counted deer and feral cattle.

Although this is just the roit bit of bush for one of those sodding tigers to den up, he thought; they bred fast, and a lot of the older ones were still maneaters when they got the chance. Even then a corner of his mind had time to curse the sentimental idiots who'd turned so many loose from safari parks and zoos after the Change. *Haven't seen any pugmarks yet though ...*

His eyes scanned the ground ahead, where a clump of oaks and Douglas firs occupied a higher hummock. That's where the idle bastards should have put a sentry, up one of the trees in a blind, with a pair of binoculars. They hadn't, he was pretty sure of that, and there weren't any lookouts covering it either. He was close now, close enough to smell the woodsmoke, though he couldn't see a plume.

He made a soft clicking sound with his tongue, impossible to filter out of the background unless you knew what you were listening for. Then he moved forward from clump to clump, pausing every fifty paces with the ghillie cloak around him like a shaggy, twig-sewn blanket. A crackling branch off to the left made him halt motionless, even as he winced inwardly. That was the price you paid for working with strangers . . . but the man had done the right thing by stopping.

After a moment he moved forward again. Stories to the contrary, you couldn't move through brush or forest without making noise. The saving grace was that the forest made noise of its own all the time, and if you froze when you put a foot wrong the sound would vanish into the background, especially when there was a nice lively wind like this. A head might come around when they heard a crackle, but if they didn't see movement or hear anything else right away, they tended to let it go. You *couldn't* investigate every noise that *might* be someone.

Slow and careful, that's the ticket.

He made another careful sound as he eeled into the slightly higher ground that bore the trees, one that would announce that he was where he'd intended to go. The surface here wasn't exactly dry, but at least it wasn't outright bog. A fallen alder gave shelter to the west, thick with young seedlings growing about the nurse-tree's rotting trunk.

Well, well, he thought as he slowly raised the binoculars to his eyes and moved his thumb on the focusing screw. *Isn't that interesting? The colonel was right.*

A half-dozen large canoes were drawn up in a slough that gave off the Willamette. Willows trailed drooping branches on them, but the camouflage netting on the frames that spanned their hulls would have made them hard to see in any case; otherwise they were *voyageur*-style boats, aluminum versions of the type Canadian fur traders had used in the old days. He'd used similar craft on wilderness trips before the

Change, and in training with the SAS—though apart from the Falklands and a spell in Ulster his active service had mostly involved extremely dry deserts full of homicidal lunatics.

Still, you never know when training will come in handy. You can get better than a ton in one of those things. Paddle slow and at night, lie up by day and you could get from here to Portland without anyone the wiser, or at least to the falls at Oregon City, which is much of a muchness. Not many folk living right by the river these days.

Ragged men unloaded wicker baskets and poplar-wood boxes from the canoes. Others loaded cargo, mostly in sacks; part of it was prisoners, bound and with bags over their heads, which was an excellent way of keeping captives disoriented and passive. Aylward whistled silently through his teeth, then handed the binoculars to the man who'd crawled up beside him.

As he did so he kept counting the number of fighting men down there. *Two dozen at least, all up,* he decided regretfully. *Not a chance.*

It was with even more regret that he grabbed Major Peter Jones by the collar of his camouflage jacket and touched the point of a dirk to the inner angle of his jaw when he showed signs of leaping up and advancing on the canoes with drawn sword. The Corvallan wasn't *quite* angry enough to try and fight him, and they moved backward with commendable stealth.

"Those were Protectorate soldiers!" Jones snarled quietly, when they were back where they'd left the horses.

Aylward nodded as he tightened a girth and bundled up his ghillie cloak to strap behind the saddle. "Right you are, mate," he said. "Some of them. The rest were your common-or-garden bandit shites."

"And you've *known* about this?" Jones said.

"More or less suspected," Aylward said.

"We've got to do something!"

"We're not going to go charging in with four archers and you against that lot," Aylward said, jerking a thumb over his shoulder. "They've got six to our one, *and* about half of them looked like they had hauberks on. Mother Aylward didn't raise any of her kids to be bloody fools."

"Why didn't you tell us before?"

"We tried to, didn't we? It was always 'no proof, no proof, no bloody proof, you kilties are just trying to get us fighting Portland, oh dear, oh dear.' Colonel Loring was the one suggested we stake out this location—he's had the time to think about it, you see, and he always did have a fine eye for ground, and for putting bits of this and that together to get a picture."

"They're stealing *people*," Jones said, incandescent with anger.

Aylward nodded. "Stands to reason, short of labor as everyone is, and the Protectorate's not going to get many volunteers. At a guess, the border barons started hiring bandits to catch runaway peons and bond-tenants. Not a big step from there to buying replacements, and who's going to listen to one more poor, unfortunate bugger in a labor gang?"

"The Faculty Senate is going to hear about this!"

A grin split Aylward's square Saxon face. "That's the point of this little walk in the woods, innit? Hopefully they'll listen to *you*."

Corvallis, Willamette Valley, Oregon
January 14th, 2008/Change Year 9

"It's indecent," Juniper said.

"What, the kilt?" Nigel Loring asked, glancing down as they strolled arm-in-arm between the booths. "I admit that my knobby knees aren't much to look at, but I wouldn't say they were actually *obscene*—"

"That so much is going wrong, and I'm still so *happy*," Juniper replied, prodding him in the ribs with a finger.

He laughed. "My dear, if I were any happier, I'd be dead and in heaven—and on a related topic, I soon may be, at this rate. I'm not a young man any more."

"*Dá mbeadh cuinneog ag an gcat, ba mhinic a pus féin inti,*" Juniper said with a wicked grin. "If the cat had a churn, it's often her own face would be in it. And you know what they say about Witch girls . . ."

Eilir snorted and freed her arm from John Hordle's for a moment to sign: *Oh, get a room, you two! It is indecent, at your age!*

Juniper stuck her tongue out at her daughter. "*Ní bean níos sine ná airíonn sí.* A woman's no older than she feels. I'm feeling sixteen again, so why shouldn't I act it? *Or* Nigel, who can put many a sixteen-year-old boy to shame, let me tell you."

Nigel flushed and grinned at the same time. Astrid, Alleyne and John Hordle developed an intense interest in the plank-and-plywood booths that filled what had once been a parking lot, beneath old broadleaf trees. With so many in town for the meeting of the Faculty Senate business was brisk; the sheds sold winter crops in this season—kale, Asian greens, turnips, endives, chicories, dried beans, fennel, carrots, parsnips, strings of garlic and onions. And plucked and gutted chickens, eggs, tubs of butter, big round cheeses . . .

"Hi, Juney!"

"Bob!" Juniper said to the stall-keeper, where he stood amid his produce. "Merry met! In from the farm, I see. Where are Karen and Danny and Karl?"

"The family's all hard at work, since we got a dairy herd and a barrel churn," the man said; he was middle-aged, with a graying beard. "You don't own cows, cows own you. Here, try this."

He smeared butter from an opened bucket on a heel of bread before handing it to her. Before the Change she'd have been astonished at the rich, intense taste of it; now that was normal, and she mostly noted that it was perfectly fresh and only lightly salted.

"That's good, as good as any we make at Dun Juniper. If I lived here and didn't have cows of my own, I'd certainly buy from you."

He looked at the golden torc around her neck. "New Mackenzie fashion . . . or just ring around the collar?"

"I'll have you know this torc is an *engagement* torc! Meet Nigel Loring, my fiancé."

"Congratulations!" Bob said, enthusiastically pumping

their hands. "I heard about Sir Nigel getting in . . . when's the happy day?"

"Beltane's best for a handfasting, but we may not be able to wait past Imbolc."

"Here, all of you have one of Karen's rolls, and a slice of ham to go with it. Mr. Pig smoked up pretty well this year, if I do say so myself."

Juniper savored a bite; the salty brown taste of the cured meat complemented the crusty bread and fresh butter wonderfully, and somehow it was even better on a raw January day with rain threatening from a low iron sky.

"Nigel, this is Bob Norton. He and his family actually moved back from Silicon Valley and started a little farm up in the Coast Range foothills southwest of here two years *before* the Change. I used to buy eggs from him at the old Farmer's Market when I passed through Corvallis." With a sly smile: "Back then, they were something special."

The farmer grinned and nodded towards the well-worn pile of cardboard egg cartons as he shook hands with the Englishman: "All free-range, grass-fed, with those nice orange yolks . . . just like everyone else, nowadays. I thought the farm would be a nice hobby place for the kids to grow up on while I did technical writing to pay the bills. Then—wham! I've been a cautious man ever since."

The *because I used up a lifetime's luck right there* didn't have to be spoken. Juniper went on: "I hope you can come to the handfasting. It's open-house."

After a moment's wait while a woman bought two broilers and half a large, round cheese, Bob replied, "If we're not all dead by then, of course. I'll be voting, though . . . what was all that about a murder?"

"Knife work in the dark by the Protector's people," Juniper said grimly. "To shut their own man's mouth, whatever else you may have heard."

"About what I figured," Bob said. "Bastards. Good luck! I'll be voting for you, no doubt about that!"

Eilir stopped to order a dozen of the hams sent to the Mackenzie guesthouse for the Dúnedain to take with them when they left town; Bob's knowledge of Sign was rudimentary, but enough for bargaining, which she did with cheerful ruthlessness. Then they bought mugs of mutton soup rich with barley and dried mushrooms at a stand by the road; Juniper looked up in surprise at a deep, accented voice ordering another.

"Not 'alf bad," Sam Aylward said, raising the steaming mug to his lips. He winked at her. "Congratulations, Lady, Sir Nigel."

Juniper touched her torc, then threw her arms around the stocky Englishman and hugged him hard—more symbolic than anything else, since he was wearing his brigandine.

"Thank you, my old friend!" she said. "Thank you, thank you for helping! It's the loveliest surprise present I've ever had."

A flush went up the thick, corded neck and square face. "Well, I hope I can do more than a little carpenter's work for you two," he said gruffly.

A bell rang, a slow, steady tolling. The crowds around the booths began to thin as people streamed westward, across Twenty-sixth Street and up the stairs to Gill Coliseum, where Corvallis held its public assemblies; many of the stallholders closed up and headed that way themselves. Juniper felt her stomach tighten, then forced it to relax as she drew a deep breath down to her diaphragm. There was no hurry; foreign dignitaries didn't have to hustle in, or elbow for a seat in the bleachers, either, though she remembered doing just that at basketball games before the Change. Instead she made herself drain the mug, and then use the spoon to hunt down the last barley around its bottom.

"Let's go," she said at last, after she set it down on the counter.

She looked across the street, where two lines of armored troops with glaives waited, making a line up the stairs and under the columned entrance.

It's just another entrance and just another stage, she told herself, taking another deep breath. *And it's a performer you've always been.*

*   *   *

Mike Havel sat. "Here we go," he muttered, the sound lost
under the shuffle and rustle and whisper of the crowd seating
itself likewise.

The interior of the coliseum was huge—it had been proudly
hailed as the biggest basketball stadium west of the Rockies
at its opening in 1949; when the seats were full they held over
nine thousand, half of the adults in the whole territory of the
city-state. Today there were less than half that, but the delegates voting proxies represented everyone. The western wall
was mostly glass, letting in pale, cold light tinged with gray;
concrete arches spanned the roof high above. More of the
militia ringed the inside of the basketball court, which had
been covered in rolls of broadloom; at the eastern end was a
dais with tables and chairs. The four foreign delegations were
grouped before it, with the Bearkillers on the right, the
Mackenzies on the left, and the Dúnedain and Sandra
Arminger's party between.

He looked over at the Rangers and nodded in friendly fashion. Eilir grinned back at him, with an urchin cockiness he'd
always liked. Astrid, as usual, looked smoothly regal and not
quite human in her black-and-silver outfit. Beyond them at
the Mackenzie table, Juney appeared relaxed and confident . . . well, she always did, when the pressure was on; she'd
gotten over stage fright a long time ago. Sir Nigel Loring was
beside her, doing his Imperturbable Englishman.

*But I think I catch a bit of a glint in his eye. He likes people
to underestimate him, that one.*

A herald—or whatever they called them here—came out
on the dais. Silence fell, and then she shouted: *"All rise for the
noble Faculty Senate!"*

They all filed in, wearing their mortarboard hats and aca-
demic robes—the latter were fur-trimmed, and probably
fairly comfortable in the vast unheated space that smelled of
chill concrete and, very faintly, of locker room and disinfectant. Everyone did stand, including the foreign delegations.
Havel looked casually over to the Portland Protective Association's envoys before they all sat down again. A couple of
clerical nonentities in robes and tonsures with their pens and

briefcases, plus the consul—Lord Carl Wythman, Baron Kramer, a dangerously smooth hard case whom he hoped to have the pleasure of hanging someday. And Sandra Arminger, looking as I-picked-your-pocket-and-you-never-knew-it satisfied with herself as she had when he saw her in April of the first Change Year, with her bodyguard Tiphaine Rutherton standing behind her.

And preparing a nasty surprise.

Signe opened her folder and smiled, very slightly, a closed curve of the lips. *She* was looking forward to this, and had a nasty surprise of her own in store. Calm-faced, Havel made a *tsk* sound within. His wife was an excellent fencer, but if she had a fault with the sword, it was relying too much on outsmarting her opponent. That worked . . . sometimes. Sometimes you had to remind her that the object was to ram a yard of sharpened leaf spring through someone, not leaving them blinking and rubbing their heads in amazement as you turned a double somersault in midair with a fiendish laugh and came down on both sides of them simultaneously.

I've got great confidence in her, he thought. *The problem is, I've also got great confidence in Sandra over there . . . and she's years older and miles more experienced than my beloved better half. I'd never try to match wits with her. Smash her skull like a pumpkin, yes: get all subtle and wheels-within-wheels, no.*

The President stood. "We are met to consider troubling matters relating to our relationships with our neighbors," he said. "Therefore—"

Havel let the words flow over him; mostly politician's chatter. His mouth quirked: his sister-in-law Astrid hadn't talked to him for a week when he'd told her why he stopped reading *The Fellowship of the Ring.*

She just hadn't wanted to hear that the Council of Elrond was a classic committee meeting, and a badly managed one at that.

Signe was taking in every word. When she tensed he stopped thinking about modifications he'd like to make in the Outfit's logistics train in the event of a full mobilization and focused once more.

The President of the Faculty Senate was looking at him; as

far as appearances went Thomas Franks was a pleasant, balding old buffer in late middle age, and plump in a way you rarely saw anymore, but his eyes were extremely shrewd. Nobody who'd brought so many people alive through the Change and its aftermath could be stupid, to begin with, and he'd been uncomfortably sharp in any number of negotiations since.

"—and lay the foundations for a lasting peace," Franks finished. "Lady Sandra, you may speak."

"Let it please the noble Faculty Senate," she said. "The Portland Protective Association wishes for nothing but peace."

"Yeah," someone shouted from the audience. "A piece of this, a piece of that—"

"Silence there!" the Senate's presiding officer shouted. "Silence, or I'll have the Provost clear the room! We have free speech here!"

"Thank you, Mr. President. We've been beset by lawless attacks and raids from the so-called Clan Mackenzie and the groups in the Eola Hills known as the Bearkillers. They've even kidnapped my daughter, and held her a prisoner—yes, even here, in your city, a city ruled by law. And they've done murder here, taken a distinguished Associate of Portland and murdered him on your own soil!"

A murmur went through the crowd. Juniper Mackenzie raised her hand: "Point of order, Mr. President. Mathilda Arminger isn't being held prisoner. She's being treated exactly as my own son; in fact, I laid a *geasa* to that effect on the whole Clan, which means—"

"I studied anthropology, Lady Juniper," Franks said, dryly. "Nevertheless, you *are* preventing her from going home, are you not? And you did seize her by force? In the course of a raid on Association territory?"

"We did that, and set free over a hundred folk who fled under our protection," Juniper said stoutly. "Some of them have settled here. The raid was launched in retaliation for *repeated* violations of the truce between the Clan and the Portland Protective Association. The sworn testimonials are before you, Mr. President. Mathilda fell into our hands by accident, if you believe in accidents. She's a lovely child and it has been a pleasure to guest her."

Franks turned his eyes on Sandra Arminger. She rose to reply. "We categorically deny any intentional violations. There may have been criminals using our territory—are there no bandits based on yours? In fact, many of the alleged 'violations' of Mackenzie territory were in fact cases where our forces tried to pursue criminals—"

"Escaping serfs, you mean!"

"Lady Juniper, please let Lady Sandra finish."

"—pursue criminals over *very* nebulous borders in uninhabited territory. Only to be viciously set upon!"

Thomas raised a hand. "I don't think that in particular is any business of ours," he said. "Nor is this the place to hash out your differences. Lord Bear?"

Havel rose. "Short form, we agree with Juney ... Lady Juniper. The Protector's men probe and snip at us whenever they get the chance and they do it with his knowledge and encouragement. As for criminals, we're perfectly ready to cooperate with anyone to put them down. We just don't include poor bastards with iron collars on their necks in the deal. Any of them who make it onto our land are free men and women and they're going to stay that way."

Another murmur went through the great hall. Franks sighed and nodded to Sandra Arminger. "Mr. President, as you said there's no point in hashing over these stale allegations. More to the point, I wish to make a personal appeal: I want my daughter back."

The President winced slightly, and then glared at Juniper Mackenzie. He couldn't afford to alienate the Clan; too much Corvallan trade went that way, both with the Mackenzies and over the mountains via Route 20 through their land. On the other hand, that put him in a cleft stick; if he pleaded diplomatic immunity for Juniper and her party, he risked Portland's anger.

"Mr. President, we're perfectly willing to return Mathilda to her parents," Juniper said. "As part of a general peace, to be sure."

"We're already at peace!" Sandra snapped.

"You had an odd way of showing it, sending assassins to Sutterdown Horse Fair and attacking my camp in the night, killing my people and wounding *my* own son near to death!"

"Parents are entitled to rescue their children from kidnappers—"

"Ladies!" Franks said; that had the advantage of fitting both the old etiquette and the new. "Lady Juniper, what do you mean by a general peace? Don't you have a treaty with the Association? We do, and we've been reasonably satisfied with it."

"With all respect, Mr. President, you don't have a frontier with the Protectorate. We do, and we've not had six months without an incident—which is one way of describing some lad down with a crossbow bolt through his belly, or houses burned or stock stolen. What we want is an agreement that doesn't depend on Norman Arminger's word or the goodwill of his barons, the which are worthless and nonexistent respectively."

"I protest!" That was Lord Carl. "Mr. President, is a friendly power to be insulted before you?"

Havel stood again. "Norman Arminger is no man's friend," he said; the Protectorate baron flushed. "So what we're proposing—and Abbot Dmwoski concurs—is that we need a general agreement on collective security. Everyone agrees to treat any attack on any one of the Willamette Valley outfits as an attack on all and to send their forces to repel it."

He grinned. "We're perfectly willing to have everyone gang up on us if we invade the Protectorate. It would help if some of the rulers around here weren't murderous warlord bastards—"

Lord Carl shot to his feet. "And the Bearkillers are a democracy, *Lord Bear*?" He bore down on the title with sardonic relish.

"Hey, we're ready to elect a House of Commons if you do," Havel said. "In fact, we're thinking of doing it anyway."

"Thoughts are worth their weight in gold," the Protectorate noble said.

"OK, how's this: we'll let anyone in Bearkiller territory who wants to move to the Protectorate do it—they can if they want

to, *we* don't go around sticking iron dog-collars on people—
and you do the same on your own side of the border. We'll call
it 'voting with their feet.' Let's see who's got how many people after a couple of years. Hell, a fifth of our farmers are
refugees from that shitheap that you guys run."

The baron flushed; the penalties for a peon or bond-tenant
trying to leave an Association fief were fairly gruesome, assuming they survived recapture.

Sandra Arminger intervened, her voice full of sorrow:
"Then you're holding my child to political ransom?" she said.

Juniper's eyes narrowed. "I prefer to think of it as rescuing
her from an unwholesome environment," she snapped.

Sandra's lips tightened, the more so as laughter rose in the
background. She turned to the dais. "Mr. President, I appeal
to Corvallan law."

"Yes, there are matters of law involved," Franks said.
"Now . . . Lady Astrid? You represent an independent state
now, I understand?"

"*Mae govannen,* lords of the city. I speak for the Dúnedain
Rangers. We hold Mithrilwood in trust for all honest folk; we
fight evildoers and dangerous beasts, and we guard caravans,
and we fight the minions of the Lidless Eye. Who are in league
with bandits and evildoers."

Sandra rose, swift and graceful. "Mr. President, do we have
to listen to someone who's so obviously mentally . . . chal-
lenged? This isn't the Third Age of Middle-earth, after all."

That got a laugh too. Mike Havel cocked his head at the
sound; judging by that, he thought there was probably a
claque at the heart of it, paid to guffaw at the crucial places.
Not that it wasn't funny, when you thought about it.

"No," Astrid said calmly. "This isn't the Third Age."

*Hmmm. I notice she's not denying it's Middle-earth. Still, I
suppose in a sense it* is.

"But," she went on, smiling very slightly, "good and ill have
not changed since then, and it is the part of every one of us to
discern them, whether in the Silver Wood or here in your city,
Mr. President."

Beside him Havel heard his wife choke slightly, and whisper: "*Oh, Jesus, you . . . you little dork!*"

"Then you might explain the boxes full of heads," Sandra Arminger said dryly.

"Those were bandits," Astrid said simply. "They attacked us in Mithrilwood; they were led and guided by Sir Jason Mortimer. Unfortunately, he's dead now too."

"Very unfortunately," Sandra said, her voice pawky. "Or fortunately, if he had a different story to tell. The severed heads aren't inclined to speak much either. This is hearsay—"

Franks cut in. "And this isn't a court, Lady Sandra."

"He's dead, all right," Astrid said. "We were keeping him to speak here, and an assassin came in the night, over the roof; clad all in black, so we didn't see her face, but she was very quick, and we did hear her voice." Her eyes went to the relaxed shape behind the Protectorate's table. "The voice of that woman there. Where were you on the night Jason Mortimer died, Tiphaine Rutherton?"

The blond woman smiled. "Me? I was curled up with a good book at the consulate, Lady Astrid," she said. "Isn't it enough you see elves, without adding ninjas?"

That got a laugh that was mostly genuine; for the first time, Astrid looked startled and worried. *Right,* Havel thought. *That was too convenient to be real. Damn, but it would have been nice to do a Perry Mason!*

Sandra Arminger caught the byplay, and smiled a small, secret smile. Franks rapped sharply on the wood of his lectern. "I repeat, this is not a criminal court, or a court of any sort," he said shortly. "I have to say, Lady Astrid, that you're not helping your cause by bringing these feuds into Corvallis."

"It's not we who are doing that," Juniper said. "Mr. President, I draw your attention to the codebook we captured this spring from the late Baron Liu, the Association's Marchwarden of the South. We've decoded it—"

"Made it up?" Sandra Arminger murmured, loud enough to be audible on the dais; her skeptical expression could be seen from much farther away.

"—and it shows plans to attack Corvallis and Newport. Sir Nigel Loring here can tell you how the Protector tried to force him to salvage nerve gas from the old Army storage dump at Umatilla to support this attack. We've had copies of the coded plans and their plain intent printed up and distributed."

"This entirely *fictional* attack," Sandra Arminger said, raising a hand in a brushing-away gesture. "Really, Mr. President! Secret codes, ninjas, weapons of mass destruction . . . need we take any of this seriously? We could instead focus on *facts*. It is a *fact* that the Bearkillers and Mackenzies are deliberately blocking the trade routes between Corvallis and Portland, despite the natural unity of the Willamette Valley. It is a *fact* that . . . Ms. Larsson and her friends . . . have graduated from playing harmless games in the woods to chopping heads off wholesale, and dragging people in chains into your city. And it is a *fact* that the Association wishes to end this anarchy and open the railway between Corvallis and Portland once more, to our mutual benefit."

Franks knocked on the podium before him again to still the murmurs that swept through the bleachers. Havel scanned them; then his head snapped to the entrance. Another Mackenzie . . .

Sam Aylward Mackenzie, he thought. *Looking like a fox in a henhouse. And the good Major Jones, as well. Kreegah, tarmangani!*

Jones curtly ordered the guards to stand aside; he and Aylward walked forward to stand before the dais.

"I hope there's some good reason for this interruption," Franks said sharply as the militia officer saluted, with his helmet held under his left arm.

"Mr. President, members of the noble Faculty Senate and the Popular Assembly, there is," he said grimly.

Havel grinned like a shark as the Corvallan began to speak, an expression Signe echoed. Sandra Arminger rested easily in her chair, elbows on the armrests and steepled fingers under her chin. When Jones was finished, the rumble of the crowd had taken on a distinctly hostile air. . . .

"Lady Sandra, do you have any explanation for this?"

"Several, Mr. President," she said easily. "Starting with the *fact* that anyone can wear a blazon or a surcoat or a helmet of a particular type. Major Jones doesn't have any of these supposed Protectorate men-at-arms with him, does he? Any documentary proof? It's scarcely our responsibility if bandits are operating on Corvallan territory; we of the Association have our problems with the scum as well."

Jones scowled and clenched the hand that rested on his sword hilt into a fist, but Aylward tapped him on the shoulder and whispered in his ear.

"I can only report what I saw, Mr. President. But as a citizen, I do say that this—combined with the affidavit of Brother Andrew of the Mount Angel border patrol—strongly supports Lady Astrid's argument that the Portland Protective Association, or elements in it, are acting in cooperation with the bandit gangs. In this case, I saw Corvallan citizens being kidnapped as slaves with my own eyes."

"But apparently did nothing about it," Sandra Arminger put in.

Ah, that was a mistake, Havel thought. This time the growl from the audience was ugly; Jones was a popular man, and too many people knew him personally for a slander to have much effect.

Astrid rose, and spoke in that beautiful, cool voice: "We Dúnedain Rangers spend our time in the wilderness, fighting bandits and maneaters. Some of us have died fighting them."

And she didn't mention the orcs of the Dark Lord. That must have taken real discipline!

"We guard caravans"—she named a few Corvallan merchants who'd hired them—"and nobody has complained that we didn't do the job properly. Our work benefits everyone in the Valley, and beyond."

Havel came to his own feet. "Mr. President, I and my Outfit have always been friendly to this city. We and the Mackenzies and Mount Angel have all found it worthwhile to help the Rangers, the Dúnedain Rangers, in their work. They're doing things we don't have the time for. Leaving aside the bigger issues, we'd like Corvallis to do likewise. It's only fair to chip in, since you're getting the benefits."

Several of the guards around the rim of the old basketball court began to thump the butts of their glaives on the floor. Someone shouted *Vote!* and others took it up, until the great building echoed and rang with the thunder of the chant: *"Vote! Vote! Vote!"*

"Well, we didn't get the alliance we hoped for," Juniper said.

"No," Mike Havel replied. "But we will. Not right away, but we will. Ms. Arminger played a weak hand pretty good, but I think she knows it too. Astrid and Eilir got their bunch recognized in Corvallis, and that's a start. Plus I think that codebook made a lot of people real thoughtful. Every bit of weight on our side of the balance counts. And the Protector took a heavy public-relations hit."

"Not so bad a one as I'd have liked," Juniper observed. "Alas, would that it were like a story, where you capture the enemy's secret plan and they're undone at a stroke."

"No, Arminger's bitch played defense very well," Signe said. "And you saw that bit at the end of the coded sequence—he's read the list."

Juniper chuckled unkindly; then her voice grew sober. "There's one thing that's bothering me, then, Mike, Signe. If Sandra knows the Corvallans will ally with us eventually . . . what will her husband do when she tells him?"

Mike Havel looked at his wife. He could tell the same thought was running through both their minds.

Well, shit. He'll strike before that can happen, is what.

Signe scowled over at the Protectorate party; an attendant was draping a spectacular ermine cloak around Sandra's shoulders, a waterfall of shining black-streaked white fur that swung to her ankles. It must be heavy, but there was a coach drawn up to spare her the effort of walking in it; the space immediately outside the entrance was kept clear for the VIPs.

"I wonder what went on there—" Havel began, and then stopped as Tiphaine walked towards the Dúnedain party. "And wouldn't I like to be a fly on someone's head *there*!"

"So," Astrid said, sneering slightly. *"Bauglannen i gos?"* Which meant "you chickened out, neener neener," more or less. "Didn't like the thought of that knife duel?"

"Not at all," Tiphaine said, with a smile of amusement

copied from Sandra Arminger, and none the worse for that. "I'm going to kill you, all right. But you haven't *suffered* enough yet."

She turned on her heel, throwing a final word over her shoulder: "I don't know if I'll be able to bring myself to kill you, in the end—because by then, it's going to be a *relief.*"

CHAPTER NINE

Dun Fairfax, Willamette Valley, Oregon
March 5th, 2008/Change Year 9

"Whoa, there," Sam Aylward said; he could see his step-daughter Tamar heading his way down the lane from the Dun, with her pair of little red-and-white oxen following behind pulling a two-wheeled cart. "Dinner's on its way. Steady, steady. Whoa, boys."

This would be the last furrow; the field was a little under five acres, gently rolling land near the southwest part of his farm and on the boundary line between Dun Fairfax and Dun Carson; he could see plow teams at work over there too, now and then. Four miles to an acre, back and forth with a double-bottom riding plow that left a yard-wide swath of turned earth; they'd started on this field when the sky was just turning gray with dawn. It was an hour past noon now, and he'd driven the two-horse team back and forth the full twenty miles at about the speed of a man walking briskly, with ten-minute rests every hour. The disks ahead of the plow-blades cut into the sod of the lea-pasture with a long *shhhhsshsh,* and then the shares made a multiple crinkling *tink* sound beneath it as the thicker roots of the sainfoin parted before the steel.

There was a sweet, sappy smell to the cut ryegrass and clover, beneath the rich earthy-mealy scent of the wet earth turning away from the moldboards in twin curves; the soil was just damp enough to make for easy plowing, without being wet enough to puddle and damage the tilth under hoof and share. Earthworms and grubs moved in the furrows of dark brown dirt, and white-winged birds swooped down to feed with shrill cries. His dogs Garm and Grip were over by the fencerow, watching him work—they'd lost interest in leaping and snapping at the flock some time ago.

I daresay they'd rather be out hunting, he thought with a tired grin. *Me too, you idle furry bastards!*

He reached down and worked the lever that raised the business part of the sulky plow out of contact with the soil, then guided the big blocky-headed roan draught-horses onto the narrow strip of grass beside the fence and the young hawthorn hedge growing up through it, a few yards from the field-gate on the northern side. Then he slid down to the ground with a grunt, worked his shoulders and rubbed at the small of his back; riding the machine was a lot easier than holding the handles of a single-furrow walking plow, but it still wasn't anything like sitting in an armchair, either.

Not to mention the pleat-marks in the skin of your arse from sitting on a kilt, he thought, rubbing those affected parts too.

His first care was for the horses; he freed them from the traces and let them bend their heads to crop at the grass of the verge. They'd been working since dawn's first red tinge showed over the Cascades, but they weren't sweating much, just enough to make the musky, homey scent strong in his nostrils as he stroked their thick necks, a familiar counterpoint to the cake-rich smell of turned earth. It was a clear midday after several weeks' gentle off-and-on rain, sunny with a high white haze and a few clouds, but the temperature was just on the right side of brisk and perfect for outdoor work. He was glad it wasn't any warmer. You had to be careful not to overheat big horses like these Suffolks; they could keel over on you if you did, and they were still fantastically scarce and valuable. And they were good-hearted beasts, who deserved fair treatment.

Then he turned and called into the field: "Oi, there! Time for dinner! Harry! Miguel!"

The other two men were harrowing the ground he'd plowed, getting the tilth ready; this field was going into oats, and the dark brown soil had a rippled smoothness after the disks had chopped apart the clods and mixed in the last of the grass and clover. They hadn't knocked off just because they saw him finish, which pleased him—doing the work yourself wasn't half as tiring as trying to keep a slacker's nose to it. Neither of these had that problem.

This was getting into the busy part of the year again, after the lull of midwinter. It was time to plow and plant the spring-sown crops, the barley and oats, hops and roots and truck, time for the sheep and cattle to drop their young, time for wool-shearing and time to heat up the long battle with the weeds.

"Oi! Miguel!" Aylward called again. " 'arry!"

Miguel Lopez halted the two yoked oxen he'd been leading and unhitched them from the harrow, leaving it where it could take up the work again immediately; he was a dark, stocky man of about thirty who'd arrived last spring as a refugee from the Protectorate, along with his wife and two children. A refugee from the Barony of Gervais in particular, though he'd been born in Jalisco and come north with his parents years before the Change. The younger man out there was Aylward's cousin-by-marriage, son of his wife's youngest aunt.

He kept on, seemingly deaf. . . .

Aylward sighed. "Oh, bugger." Louder: "All right then, it's time for dinner, *Húrin!*"

Many younger Mackenzies took new names out of the old Celtic myths when they came of age and were sworn as Dedicants of the Old Religion—Harry's sister Jeanette was now named Liath. Harry himself had been hanging around Astrid and Eilir and their gang, so he'd gone the whole hog and picked a label out of the books that lot were crazy for; he waved back at Aylward when he heard the name he'd chosen, and not before. He was a little past eighteen, lanky and strong, with longish hair of a color between light brown and dark yellow, and stubborn enough to make a piece of black walnut root look flexible. He'd probably go off with the Rangers full-time soon, which was a pity since he was a good, solid worker around the farm and handy with tools, but the Dúnedain did valuable scouting and bandit suppression. He'd earned it; he was a fine shot, better than average at fieldcraft and useful with a blade as well.

And Samkin Aylward isn't going to cark at a country lad who wants to go for a soldier. At least Húrin *wasn't supposed to be some poncing* elf's *name . . .*

"Hi, Dad!" Tamar called as she got closer, waving; she was fourteen just now, a gangly tow-haired girl with a round face much like her stepfather's.

Aylward waved back. Tamar opened the gate and brought her cart through; the red-coated, white-faced oxen were yearlings she'd hand-raised and almost as obedient as dogs, following her without needing to be led. The cart held two big plastic bins of water, a light-metal trough, a couple of bales of fodder for the oxen, and buckets of oat-mash with beans for the horses; the big beasts couldn't live on grass alone when they were doing hard graft like this.

The men and girl occupied themselves watering and feeding the stock. When his team had their muzzles in the buckets and were eating with sloppy, slobbering enthusiasm, the humans washed up themselves and unpacked the lunch baskets: crusty rolls sliced and stuffed with ham and sharp-tasting cheese, pickles, covered bowls of potato salad, sweet nut-bread and a bucket of Dennis Martin Mackenzie's homebrew, which the Aylward household got in trade for their hops and barley. Aylward scooped the thick-walled glass mug full twice with water before he filled it with beer; ale quenched thirst and tasted a hell of a lot better, but the alcohol made it go through you fast. Early training had made him careful about maintaining hydration, and it stuck even in this mild, wet climate.

He never discarded a good habit. They tended to prolong your life.

Tamar ate with the casual voracity of youth; the men with the solid appetite of those who burned six or seven thousand calories a day every day of the year except for the high holidays; Miguel Lopez added the reverence towards food of someone who'd worked nearly as hard and been kept hungry most days to boot since the Change.

Aylward grinned to himself. Miguel had nearly wept when Melissa took the trouble to do up a dinner in the style of his homeland, not just Mexican but specifically Jaliscan, from *tor-*

tas ahogadas to sweet *jericalla* custard. It had been a long time for him; Mrs. Lopez was what the Yanks called an Anglo, in a fit of mislabeling that never failed to amuse the man from Hampshire. Which in this case meant mainly Irish and German, and they'd met after the Change, so she'd never had a chance to learn that style of cooking. A Protectorate peon got enough to keep going, but not much more, and the quality was even lower than the quantity.

"Where's Edain?" he asked Tamar, when the first draught of the dark brew had gone down his throat; school was only four days a week this time of year, with the farming calendar starting to creak into motion. His eldest son wouldn't be willingly inside.

Tamar gave an evil chuckle. "Helping Mom. She roped him into minding Fand and Dick and Mrs. Smith's kids while they turn the cheeses," she said.

Aylward smiled back, and the other two men laughed; for an active seven-year-old boy on a fine spring day child-minding would be purgatorial.

Miguel looked out over the field as he stretched and worked his shoulders. "Not so bad," he said with satisfaction in his voice.

"Not 'alf bad," Aylward agreed.

Nothing skimped or shirked, he thought to himself, nodding. They'd put honest sweat into the effort, and hard-won skill, and it showed. The disked field looked as smooth and rich as a cup of chocolate.

"You know what I like about farming?" Miguel went on.

"The lying about late in the morning?" Aylward asked, mock-solemn. "The freedom from worry and care?"

All three men and the girl laughed, but Miguel went on: "It is, what's the word, *straightforward.* My children, I will never have to explain to them what it is their father does far away in some office. With the help of God"—he crossed himself—"we grow the food we eat. This is simple."

Then he shrugged a little self-consciously, though nobody was disagreeing, and scooped up a mug of the beer. "So, *patrón,* what do we do next?"

Aylward wiped his mouth with the napkin and tossed it

back into the basket. "I'll take the team over to the Oak Field and give it a going-over with the spring-tooth cultivator while you two are finishing up the harrowing 'ere," he said. "Folding the sheep on it last autumn was an easy way to dung the land, but there were too many weed seeds in it for comfort. That's the price of keeping them on rough grazing."

"Didn't we do that field already?" Miguel asked.

"I want to make certain and sure. It'll be a right cockup if that couch grass comes back on us. Then tomorrow we can get the compost out on the rest of the truck plot and disk it in, and some muck from that old stack by the field-byres. The root-stock on the new cherry orchard looks good, so we can start grafting on the scions in a week or—"

The dark man nodded, listening carefully, frowning in concentration. *Good,* Aylward thought. Miguel wasn't just hard-working and willing; he was an eager learner on the *thinking* part of running a farm, the way you had to juggle time and effort and risk. He was getting ready for the time when he had land of his own. That was why Aylward always explained what had to be done, rather than just giving directions; Tamar was bending an ear as well.

His voice cut off abruptly at the sound of galloping hooves, and everyone reached for the weapons that were always within reach, buckling on their sword belts. He and Húrin strung their longbows and slung their quivers over their backs; Miguel picked up the spear he carried instead, since he had trouble hitting a barn as yet unless he was inside it and the doors were closed. Tamar looked startled, but she readied her own light child's bow and drifted backward a little, ready to jump to any direction her stepfather might give.

"One rider," Húrin said, cocking his head and using his keen youngster's hearing.

Despite the sobering bite of caution, Aylward grinned at the thought. He'd once caught the lad standing in front of a mirror and pulling his ears up into points with thumb and forefinger.

Harry-Húrin had blushed every time he saw Sam for weeks after.

Not that I'm one to point a finger, he thought generously.

Back when he was Húrin's age he'd dyed his hair blond because a girl told him it would make him look like Michael Caine, who he'd admired tremendously anyway, having seen the film *Zulu*—often—at an impressionable age. The color had come out more like a bright carrot orange, the girl had dropped him like a hot brick, which was more than she'd ever done with her knickers, and his father had hooted himself redfaced every breakfast for months as the botched mop grew out. Eighteen was the right age to make a proper burke of yourself, and there were worse ways than playing make-believe with your friends.

"Coming fast up the main road from the west," Húrin went on; there was no nonsense in him when serious matters were at stake.

The rider trotted into view, reined in and around when he saw them in the field, backing up a few yards and then putting his mount at the fence. It cleared ditch and boards and spreading, white-flowered hawthorn and landed with a spurt of damp clods under ironshod hooves, a goodish jump and fine riding. In the saddle was a nondescript young man with long, dark brown hair done in a queue through a silver ring, not a Mackenzie or at least not wearing a kilt; he was dressed instead in jacket and pants of plain green homespun linseywoolsey, mottled with streaks of brown. A horn-and-sinew horseman's recurve bow rode in a case at his left knee with a round shield slung over it, a quiver over his back was stuffed with gray-fletched arrows, and a good, practical straight sword hung at his broad, brass-studded belt.

"Mae govannen," he said, which cleared up which lot he ran with, if the white tree and seven stars and crown on the shield hadn't been enough. It made young Húrin prick up his nonpointed ears. "I'm looking for the First Armsman of Clan Mackenzie. Aylward the Archer."

"That's me," Sam Aylward said, and got the *expecting someone taller* look he often did from those who knew him by reputation only. "Sorry if I don't live up to the stories. And who are you?"

"I'm called Pilimór, sir."

Or Pillock for short, Aylward didn't say aloud. The young

man didn't smile as he leaned over and took Aylward's hand; he looked tired and a little frightened.

"I've got a message for the First Armsman from the *Hiril Astrid.*"

He pulled an envelope out of one saddlebag. It was a brown office type, with the little folding split tin thing for closing it through a hole in the flap, in this case covered with a blob of off-white candle-wax stamped with the Dúnedain seal. That was a starry thing of ancient majesty dreamed up by Eilir about six months ago and set in rings for her and Astrid by a metalworker in Corvallis.

He flicked the wax off with his thumb and carefully bent back the metal wings rather than ripping the paper; nobody was going to make any more of these anytime soon. Inside was a hand-drawn map of the Waldo Hills just east and north of the ruins of Salem; he recognized it at once, mainly because he'd been studying the Willamette Valley with professional thoroughness since that vacation in the Cascades just before the Change, and also because he'd taught Astrid and Eilir and many another how to sketch a field map. Arrows and notes were drawn across it in a close, neat hand. The message with it was short and to the point, despite the opening flourishes:

From Astrid Hiril *Dúnedain, suilannad mehellyn în and well-met to Aylward the Archer, Aran Gweth Nô Mackenzie: Given by my hand at Mithrilwood, 4th March in the Ninth Year of the Fifth Age, in the Old Reckoning 2008 AD.*

Three columns of Protectorate troops have crossed the border into the Waldo Hills. Troops crossing border observed number approximately two thousand five hundred of which three hundred and fifty are light cavalry, scouts and mercenary horse-archers from the Pendleton area, and the remainder regulars, one-quarter knights and men-at-arms, the remainder bicycle- and horse-mounted infantry spearmen and crossbowmen, with heavy wagon trains including siege machinery and field engineering supplies following. Another force of roughly equal size is investing Mount Angel and its outposts. Labor gangs numbering at least five hundred accompany the supply trains, under guard, but we have made contact with anti-Protectorate elements among them and they inform me further

*force of indeterminate size is preparing to embark river trans-
ports escorted by turtle boats Oregon City last night, intended
to seize the bridges at Salem. Locations, composition and directions of travel of all identified enemy forces marked on attached map. The Dúnedain Rangers have kept contact with the
enemy forces and will endeavor to slow them as much as possible while interdicting their supplies. A copy of this message
has been dispatched to the Bear Lord at Larsdalen.*

Aylward stood thinking for a moment, lips tight, looked at
the state of the messenger's horse—tired but not blown—and
nodded.

"Get this to Dun Juniper," he said, slipping message and
map back into the envelope. "Tell the Chief and Chuck
Barstow I'll be by directly, and that I advise calling up the
First Levy immediately by mirror and smoke signal, with Sutterdown as the rally-point. Evacuation as per the war plan."

The First Levy was the younger and better-trained portion
of the Clan's militia, and the town of Sutterdown was the
most convenient place near the border.

"Roit, Tamar. Get up behind the gentleman, drop off home,
and tell your mum to have my kit and 'enry ready."

Henry was his best riding horse; he could pick up a couple
of remounts elsewhere. She looked at him with a worry-frown
between her brows and then made it go away, and gave him a
grin and a thumbs-up as she vaulted easily up behind the
Dunadan.

Good girl! he thought, with a momentary flash of warmth
through chill focus as the horse went out the gate and down
the laneway at a trot. This wasn't the first time he'd ridden
away quickly, and she was getting old enough to know the
possible consequences, but she didn't let it daunt her.

"Miguel, you see to the beasts," he went on.

Harry-no-I'm-Húrin was already following the messenger's
horse at a tireless loping trot, the kilt swirling around his
knees; he was in the First Levy, of course, and was off to get
his gear and bicycle.

"*Patrón—*" Miguel began.

Aylward sighed and clapped him on the shoulder. "Nobody
doubts your guts, Miguel. But you're not a good enough bow-

man yet for the levy, and that's a fact. If worst comes to worst, you'll be on the walls with an ax. In the meantime . . . look after the beasts and the home-place for me, would you, mate?"

Miguel put his own hand on Aylward's shoulder, to match the Englishman's gesture; the First Armsman of the Mackenzies reflected that, training or no, this was a man Arminger would find it expensive to kill.

"*Sí,*" he said. "I do not forget how you rescue us from the baron's dogs, take us into your house, treat us like your own. I won't let any harm come to your home or wife or little ones while I live, Sam. I swear it by God and the Virgin."

Larsdalen, Willamette Valley, Oregon
March 4th, 2008/Change Year 9

"Yeah, the letter said potatoes. Yeah, everyone's supposed to plant an extra fifth of an acre per adult. And yeah, I *know* it'll screw up the rotations. It's insurance because potatoes are a lot harder to burn in the field than ripe wheat. With the spuds, we can count on not starving this coming winter, at least. You *do* remember what it's like to starve, don't you?"

The delegate from the town of Rickreall looked at the Bear Lord with horror in his eyes. "You mean . . . there's really going to be war, my lord?"

Havel curbed his impatience. "Yeah, just like I've been warning everyone for months," he said.

The Bearkiller ruler was dressed in a loose white linen shirt and the closest approach the handlooms could come to blue jeans and he had his two-year-old son on his lap. He looked almost as intimidating as he did in armor, with the bear's head on his helmet . . .

"I'm sorry, Lord Bear, we just didn't understand—"

"It's OK. My fault. I've got to learn to explain things more when I'm not giving orders on a battlefield. In the meantime, why don't you go around to the kitchens and get something to eat before you head home? Or you can bunk here for the night."

When the farmer had gone, Mike Havel stretched back in his recliner. His son sighed and stretched out on top of him, tucked his yellow-thatched head under his father's chin and went to sleep with the limp finality small children shared with kittens and puppies. Havel put an arm around him, enjoying the solidity of the small body, the sense of absolute trust, even the smell of cut grass and clean hair.

He'd never felt much urge to be a father before the Change . . . in fact, he'd been a loner to the core, happiest in the air flying, or in the wilderness. He hadn't even been able to keep a long-term girlfriend, despite being extremely handsome in a rugged Scandinavian-Indian fashion—as more than one *ex*-girlfriend had informed him, often popping it in the middle of a long list of his personality faults expressed at the top of their lungs, things like "cold" and "not giving." Now he was not only married, but the father of three . . . well, four if you counted Rudi Mackenzie, which around Signe was best left unspoken even if she'd come to terms with it last year after that monumental cluster-fuck at the Sutterdown Horse Fair. Remembering that small figure standing before the killer horse still gave him the willies, too, so he banished it by hugging his son.

Got to admit, family life has its points. Hope I can do as good a job of being a father as my dad did.

He smiled his crooked smile. Their sole dinner guest tonight was Peter Jones of Corvallis. The rest of the extended family was gathered on the veranda of the pillared yellow-brick except for the kids. *They* were all out there on the lawn, running and shouting as they threw Frisbees for dogs that leapt like furry porpoises breaching for a fish at vanished Marine World. Or in the case of the younger children, just tumbling like puppies themselves. It was a fine spring afternoon, the first three-day stretch of clear weather they'd had since last October, and the grass had just been cut; the sweet, strong scent gave promise to the swelling buds of the lilacs and ornamental cherries.

Good-looking bunch of kids, he thought with pride.

There were his own twin girls, with their long golden braids swinging as they tried to bodycheck their cousin Billy, Eric and Luanne's eldest, from either side. The boy was a few months younger than them; he had the same hair color, but his skin was a sort of warm wheat-toast shade, which made his yellow thatch and turquoise eyes look brighter. His reflexes were something unusual too; that wicked double play generally worked for the twins, but he dropped flat and rolled away with the Frisbee in his hand, laughing as they cannoned into each other and collapsed in a squalling tangle. Not far away, his younger brother Ken was grimly trying to climb a tree, with a nurse looking a little anxious underneath—four was a bit young to get that high. Pamela's eldest played hopscotch. . . .

No more of that oh-dear-beanbag-is-too-aggressive-for-kids horseshit, at least, he thought, holding back the belly laugh to avoid waking the child sleeping against him.

Out beyond the gardens columns of smoke rose from the buildings along the road to the gate, people getting ready for supper, finishing up work in the smithies and the forge, kids coming home from chores or school; sound came faint, metal on metal, a long dragonish hiss of something hot going into the quenching bath, the bugling call of a startled horse, a faint rumble from the overshot waterwheel he could see turning in a white torrent. The sun was heading for the horizon, and the crenellations of the gate-towers showed like black square teeth bared at heaven. Soon they'd be playing taps and lowering the Outfit's flag for the night, and it would be time for the family to go in and eat as well—eight adults counting the Huttons, and twelve kids counting their adoptees.

He made a beckoning gesture with his free hand. The nanny came forward smiling and lifted Mike Jr. off his chest; she was a comfortable-looking middle-aged person with short, graying hair. They'd found her living in a culvert on the trip west from Idaho; she'd been caught on the road by the Change, miles from the arse-end of nowhere in the desert, and managed to keep her own two kids alive on what she could scavenge, mostly rabbits but at least one dog. Both her boys worked in the machine shop here.

"I'll get him cleaned up and ready for supper, Mike," she said.

"Let him sleep for an hour or so, Lucy," Havel said. "Little fellah was going at it hard today."

I'm finally getting used to having all this household help, he thought. *It does simplify things considerably.*

It was no novelty for the Larssons, of course; they'd been richer than God for three long generations before the Change, and Ken's first wife had been a Boston Brahmin who looked down on them—and the Rockefellers—as parvenus. She'd probably looked on Mike Havel as a monkey from the outback. Even when he was busting his ass trying to get her badly injured self back to a civilization neither of them knew had crashed and sunk like that Piper Chieftain he'd piloted over the Selway-Bitterroot. Though even when dying she'd been too genteel to show it.

OK, gentility not my strong point, he thought. *I'll leave that for my descendants. They'll* have *ancestors. I* am *an ancestor.*

When the nanny had gone he turned his head in the lounger and sighed. "OK, Ken, you're goddamned right. We've got to get that House of Commons thing we talked about going. As soon as this war's over—"

His father-in-law snorted and turned his single bright blue eye on him, across the table with its plate of cookies. He was a big man in his early sixties with a short-cropped white beard, a patch over his left eye and a hook in place of the hand on that side, both the fruit of an encounter between the Bearkillers and a would-be warlord and friend of Arminger's in the first Change Year, out east up the Snake River. The kettle belly he'd had before the Change was gone, and he looked tougher and fitter than he had when he climbed into the Piper Chieftain in Boise, but he'd never pretended to be a fighting man. His mind made him far more valuable; an experienced administrator and engineer had been beyond price a dozen times. Plus he asked disturbing questions . . .

"When did I hear that tune before?" he said. "There's never going to be a convenient time, Mike. Not unless we make it. There isn't going to be a time when there's no emergency, either."

"OK, I said it, and I mean it. January. The Association's going for us soon, and it'll all be over one way or another by

Christmas. I swear to God we'll elect . . . OK, call it two from every A-lister steading and strategic hamlet. On that Australian ballot thing you're fond of. Christ Jesus, it'll be a relief to have some single group I can go talk to and bargain with and settle things with! Plus it'll help put a leash on some of our A-listers who've got delusions of baron-hood."

"Give the man a cookie!"

He offered one. Havel shook his head. "Nah, don't want to spoil supper. They butchered a nice plump steer a couple-three days ago, and Talli down in the kitchens says the steaks look great."

Ken's wife—second wife—Pamela snorted; she had a plate of carrot sticks beside her chair. That wasn't what kept her lean, though; partially genes, and partially the fact that she'd been a hobbyist who studied Renaissance sword techniques before the Change, and the Bearkiller's primary blade trainer since. She'd taught *him* the backsword, and a good many others, and her pupils had passed it on. Quite a stroke of luck to stumble onto her, that day in Idaho when they took in their first recruits, and not just for then-widowed Ken because they'd ended up married.

But then, if I wasn't very lucky, I'd be dead about one hundred and thirty-eight times, he thought. *Don't let that make you overconfident, Marine. The dice have no memory.*

"And not a word about the first early greens of the year," Pam went on, rolling her eyes and shrugging expressively, then asked rhetorically: "How do you make a Finnish salad?"

Havel grinned. "Yeah, yeah, I know—first you fry sausages in bacon grease. Then you add a dozen potatoes . . ."

The laugh died as trumpets screamed from the gate-towers. All the adults' heads came up; those three rising notes meant *attention*! And after that came the signal for *urgent courier.*

Havel swung erect, his hand automatically picking up the basket-hilted sword that leaned against the recliner, with the belt wound around it. They waited, watching two riders trot up the roadway and draw rein before the veranda, tumbling down out of the saddle while the guards grounded their polearms and took the reins. One of the riders had a black jerkin with Astrid's tree-stars-crown thing on it, a young woman in her late teens with reddish-brown hair plastered to her face by sweat and wind; she raked it free and bowed. The man beside her was a Bearkiller scout wearing a mail vest and a helmet, more practical for quick work than a full hauberk. An A-lister, though, a lieutenant commanding a unit of couriers who doubled as scouts and light cavalry.

His name's Smythe, memory prompted. The A-list wasn't yet so big that he couldn't remember every Brother and Sister. His eyes flicked to the horses. The one the Bearkiller scout rode was breathing hard though not blown, but the Ranger's looked as if it might drop dead any minute: head drooping, panting like a bellows, its neck and forequarters streaked with dried foam.

The Dúnedain Ranger was reeling with fatigue too as she scrabbled in her saddlebags and handed him an envelope; he didn't need to ask if it was urgent.

"I had to go far out of the way and dodge Protectorate scouts, Lord Bear," she said. "I'm sorry it delayed me."

She inclined her head towards her horse. Behind him Eric Larsson whistled softly; there was a broken-off stub of arrow standing in the cantle of her saddle. Three inches forward and it would have gone into her pelvis.

"You got it here, which is what counts," Havel said, taking the envelope. "If there's no verbal addition, why don't you get the horse seen to and get something for yourself?"

She stumbled away, leading the horse; its dragging hooves made a counterpoint to her boots. Havel ripped the letter open and read on aloud: "Elvish, Elvish, Elvish—meaning *it's me, Astrid*; Elvish, Elvish, Elvish—meaning *Hi, Mike;* Elvish . . . OK, here's the meat of it: *Three columns of Protectorate troops . . .*"

He went on to the end. "Right," he said, passing it to Will Hutton.

The black Texan's graying eyebrows shot up as he looked over the map. "Some motherfucker up north has decided it's a beautiful spring day, so let's have a war. Three guesses who."

The children sensed the adults' tension and fell silent. Mike took an instant to wave them into the house; the older ones shooed the protesting youngest along with them, or dragged them by the wrist. That gave time for the message to be passed around from hand to hand as well, and for him to call up the maps in his head. The river and the ruins of Salem, with the bridges; then open country north and south, the Eola Hills to the west, then more open country with the odd hill, then the Coast Range if you went far enough . . .

"OK," he said, his voice flat and cold. "This is the opening move. He's investing Mount Angel, pushing through the Waldos to the edge of Mackenzie country, and to back it all up, he's going to try and rush the Salem bridges to cut the opposition in half. If he can hold them, he'll cut us off from each other. Anyone got any ideas on why the ones going south out of Molalla are carrying all that heavy gear and taking labor gangs with them?"

"Going to put up a forward base, if they can punch through to the open country north of Lebanon," Eric Larsson said. "Prefab castle, or maybe more than one, base for a campaign south of the Santiam and protection for their supply route."

"Right, that's what I thought."

He paused, weighing options. Silence lengthened as everyone looked at him.

And it's all up to me, he thought.

When he'd been a Marine in the Gulf it had been just him. Well, a Force Recon corporal had a fire team, but his biggest worry had been what was in the wadi and where to put the SAW. *Semper Fi,* slip in, find the position, report, maybe do some demolition, GOPLAT, VBBS, playing a deadly game with the ragheads, sometimes down to knives in the dark. Sure, they'd cut your balls off with a *blunt* knife if they caught you, but that went with the territory, and anyway they were such total half-hards and dipshits it was usually just dangerous enough to let you show your *sisu.* And let them go to Allah and the seventy-two virgin white raisins.

Fight for the Corps, yeah, fight for your buddies. For the goddamn country, too, show them nobody fucks with the US of A without ending up sorry and sore, all right and proper. But nobody was going to invade Michigan, burn down the Havel home-place and kill my family if I screwed up. Shit, I'm scared. I don't want to fight. I'm thirty-eight and a father, not nineteen and a killing-mean dick-on-legs the way I was then. I want to stay home and watch my kids play and enjoy a steak dinner and screw Signe silly tonight and go hunting tomorrow.

He smiled, hard and confident. "Arminger's an armchair general," he said. "He likes to draw pretty lines on maps and think he's Bobbie Lee. Actually it's my guess he's more on the order of John Pope. You know, the guy who said 'my headquarters are in the saddle'?"

"Headquarters in his hindquarters," Ken said, and his laugh boomed out. He'd gotten them all interested in the Civil War over the past decade; it was one of his hobbies, and damned useful.

Grant, though. Grant was always my favorite general. Havel turned his head. "OK, Will. That force they've got up around McMinnville, my guess is that they're a distraction, but they'll raid if we let them. Get over the hills, call up—"

He looked at Signe, who kept track of the intel. She answered without hesitation. "A hundred A-listers ready for duty in the steadings there."

That was the point of having an A-list; they were fully trained and always ready to muster. The militia took longer, and they couldn't be kept away from the fields forever, and the spring planting was under way . . . *Christ Jesus, thank You this isn't harvesttime!*

"Collect up fifty lances from the A-list, and say two hundred infantry from the strategic hamlets, and screen the area between the Coast Range and the Amity Hills with 'em, send the rest east to me. Make it obvious you're there, and if you can make them think there are more of you than there really are, all the better."

Damn, that's not much of a force for the job, Havel thought, as the weathered brown face of the ex-cowboy nodded, hard and grim. He fought back the temptation to send more. *I've got four drains in this bathtub and only one plug. Gotta remember to keep focused and put the troops at the point of maximum effort.*

"You don't think they'll make a serious attack thataway, son?" Hutton asked.

"No. Not if they're trying to do everything else at once. Like

I said, armchair general." His grin grew wolfish. "Now, if *I* had his ten thousand men, you'd bet I'd throw every one of them in, and all on the same front. Finish up one of us, then concentrate on the others. We couldn't move around as freely to match him, bridges or no, we're all defending our homes, but he's trying to do it all at the same time. The result is he's not overwhelmingly strong in any one place."

Ken Larsson nodded. *"If you try to be strong everywhere, you are weak everywhere,"* he quoted. "Frederick the Great."

"I'll snort and paw the ground up there some, like a mean bull out to hook you." Hutton nodded, satisfied. "I'll keep 'em occupied. Maybe raid a bit, get 'em hot and bothered."

Havel nodded back. *And I can rely on you to do* just *that, thank God, and not get a hair up your ass and decide you're going to win the whole damned war,* he thought. *Which is why your mad Swedish bull of a son-in-law is going to be kept right under my eye. He's a wonder when you can point him right at something that needs smashing, but a bit short on the self-restraint thing.*

"Just so you don't try to fight any big engagements," he said. He looked at his mental map again. "Damn, but I wish we could have put a garrison in on those bridges at Salem. It's going to be close even if we leave tonight."

"We didn't have enough troops," Signe said. "Not in the spring planting season."

Havel nodded. *Well, shit. Four drains, one plug.* That was Arminger's advantage; his troops were full-timers, paid men or landholders with bond-tenants and peons working their fiefs and fiefs-in-sergeantry. The Association's leadership wasn't getting as much out of it as he would have in the Protector's position, but the advantage hadn't gone away, either.

"Right, everything's ready to roll at Rickreall?" he asked his father-in-law.

Ken nodded. "I'll leave right away, and get the stuff started by midnight. We got that whole section of the old Southern Pacific line reconditioned last year when we cleared the bridge piers at Salem. I checked it over a little after Christmas and nothing's washed out since then. Shouldn't be any problem to get to Salem by dawn if we push the horses, and once

I get those beauties on the railroad bridge, I defy anything built since the Change to sail past."

"Whoa, Ken. You personally?"

"I bossed the shops that made the damn things, didn't I? For exactly this contingency. Damned if I'm not going to boss them when they're going into action."

Havel pursed his lips. *Yeah, he did. And the crews did the work with him. They're not A-listers. They'll do better with him there to steady them. He's not much with a sword and he's too old for a forced march, but he's got guts to spare and he's smart.*

"OK, but Pam, you take ten lances and go with him. Your job is to see he's not distracted by nasty men killing him while he's doing his job. They may try to slip some commando types past us to the bridges."

"Will do, bossman," she said, grinning the way a wolf did at a rabbit.

"Ken, tell your guy Sarducci to get the field artillery here ready to go—"

"It's ready to go on one hour's notice anyway. All we need to do is get the horses and crews together. He's the most punctual Italian I ever met. Glad we got him to move up from Corvallis; he was wasted as a university professor."

"Good; tell him to fall the engines in outside the gate. When you get to Rickreall, commandeer anything you need in the way of horses to pull the trains with the heavy stuff for the bridge, and get the militia mobilizing and following you as fast as they can, Rickreall and Dallas both."

"What about me?" Eric Larsson said plaintively.

"Oh, you and Luanne're going with me," Havel said easily. He leaned over and punched the big man's shoulder. "I'm gonna need someone to take care of the cavalry."

Eric grinned, his eyes lighting dangerously. Beside him Luanne looked dourly determined, like her father.

"We'll take the two Field Force companies of infantry from here at Larsdalen," Havel went on.

That was everyone fit to march and fight; pretty much everyone who wasn't lactating, pregnant, too old, too young, or not big enough to carry a crossbow or strong enough to work the lever that spanned it. He hated mobilizing that completely, but if he lost this fight then they were all dog-meat anyway. The tests for the militia were simple and set to take in everyone capable of being useful.

"Plus all the A-listers here, and all the ones we can sweep up on the way. We'll muster by Walker Creek. Lieutenant Smythe!"

The scout had been waiting by the head of his horse; he looked tired, but not knocked out the way the Ranger—*oh, hell, if they want to be the* Dúnedain, *they're the* Dúnedain, *and I'll buy 'em their rubber ears*—was. He would be just that tired before long, though.

"Turn out your scouts. Sweep every Spring Valley steading and west to the Eola crest. Give them the rally-point and tell everyone to turn out their A-listers and first Field Force company. We'll be moving southeast from there down the Bethal Heights and Brush College roads towards Salem. Rations for three days and basic medical supplies only, keep it light, but plenty of arrows and bolts."

"Lord Bear!" the man said, snapping a salute and vaulting back into the saddle; he reined around and took off in a spurt of gravel.

Havel looked over at Angelica Hutton. She'd been camp boss in the wandering days right after the Change, when they were heading west from Idaho, and still handled the Outfit's logistics. It was a much bigger job, but the middle-aged *Tejano* woman handled it with matter-of-fact competence. She'd already pulled a pad out of a pocket in her long black skirt.

"Supplies?" he asked.

"We have ample in reserve," she said, her voice warm and husky and soft with the Texas-Hispanic accent; she'd been born in the brush country between the Rio Grande and San Antonio.

Angelica was still a handsome woman, but you only had to close your eyes and listen to that voice to see the fiery young girl who'd eloped with the reckless roughstock-riding rodeo cowboy Will had been back then, with death threats from her father and brothers raining about their ears.

Briskly, she went on: "It is not fancy, but nobody will starve on the beans, cheese, dried fruit and smoked sausage. Remounts, they are sufficient also."

Havel nodded. Will had quit the rodeo when his first child was born, reconciled with Angelica's family, and he'd put his considerable winnings into a little ranch in the Hill Country and a horse-wrangling business. Angelica had been his partner in that, too. Today they ran the Outfit's horse herds, breeding program, and training program for both mounts and riders.

One thing's not so different from the Corps. I've got good people backing me up, folks I'm tight with.

"OK," he said, slapping his palms together. "First things first. Let's eat; we can finalize the operations orders while we do, then we'll get going."

Peter Jones spoke for the first time. "Not me, Mike. I'm going back to Corvallis and see if I can kick enough ass to get *them* doing something."

"Thanks, Pete," Havel said, leaving silent: *For what it's worth.*

As they went in under the high fanlights of the front doors, Havel was whistling under his breath. The tune was one he'd learned from a buddy in the Corps, a guy named Thibodeau who'd come from a parish west of New Orleans:

> *"People still talks about Cajun Joe*
> *Cajun Joe was the Bully of the Bayou—"*

Waldo Hills, Willamette Valley, Oregon.
March 5th, 2008/Change Year 9

Astrid Larsson hissed slightly between her teeth. This was going to be very tricky....

"Like Faramir and the Rangers of Ithilien, when they ambushed the Haradrim on the way to the Black Gate," Alleyne whispered.

His teeth showed white in the shadow cast by his war cloak's hood, dim through the gauze mask that covered all but his gray-blue eyes. It was a cool gray morning, but last night's rain was over and the clouds were breaking up, letting long beams of sunlight spear through, turning the early spring grass bright green. His visored helm rested on the grass beside him, and as they watched the road he plucked a stem of the candy-sweet new growth and chewed on it meditatively.

Astrid nodded, returning the smile with a brief grin of her own, then turning again to the steep slope before them. *It is like that, actually*, she thought. *Except they don't have any oliphants. Or even elephants.*

She'd heard there *were* a couple of old zoo elephants in Portland, but they were kept for ceremonial occasions.

The Waldo Hills weren't very high; more of a rolling table-land split by abrupt gullies. Most of it had been grassland with scattered oak groves before the pioneers came west on the Oregon Trail. By the Change it had been cleared and culti-vated, with patches of forest on the higher parts, and fir and willow and alder along the small streams. Mount Angel was on their northern fringe, and it had preserved an island of survival during the first Change Year; the rest had gone under in the tidal waves of refugees and Eaters. You still found human bones here and there, sometimes burnt and split in token of dreadful feasting. Nobody had returned since except occa-sional hunters and the odd bandit, and brush and bramble grew thick on the old fields, checked only by summer blazes set by lightning or campfires or branches rubbing. The field edge they occupied now had been planted in oaks; they'd grown taller, and seeded saplings amongst the thick, spiny Oregon grape and thornbush that had grown up around them. Pink flowers clustered on the grape-stems; the hedge-nettle wasn't flowering yet, but the stalks were already a yard high.

The horses were back a bit, under spreading trees that hid them from above, grazing hobbled among chest-high grass and brush starred with scarlet fritillary. John Hordle came that way; Astrid was amazed again at how quietly the big man could move. Then he dropped prone and crawled up beside the leaders, in a sweet-pungent cloud of crushed herbs. He might be stealthy, but he wasn't light.

"They're coming," he said softly. "Eilir says she recognized the contact with the labor gang and passed the signal—got too close for comfort to do it, too. Their cavalry screen should be here any moment."

Astrid nodded, looking downward. "Regular scouts?" she asked.

Hordle shook his head. "Pendleton levies, it looked like; hired light cavalry. Horse-archers. Saw the buggers myself last year, when Sir Nigel and I were east up the Columbia with the Protector's men. Fair enough riders and good men of their hands. Always ready to mix it up, but not what you'd call long on discipline."

"And they're not used to this country," Alleyne said thoughtfully. "That may be rather helpful."

Poor melindo nin, she thought, sensing the strain beneath his hard calm. *He's not used to campaigning with his beloved.*

Even as she pushed the glow of that word out of her consciousness, Astrid smiled. *This was* my *idea,* she thought. *I know Alleyne loves me, but sometimes I think he doesn't think I'm very practical. This will convince him . . . if it works.*

There was a short, steep slope below them, falling two hundred feet to the marshy banks of Puddle Creek a few hundred yards southeast; the road came looping down from her left and ran south towards the Mackenzie territories. Ten years of neglect hadn't been kind to it. Subsidence and rushing water had cut half-moon bites out of it where culverts had been blocked and ditches overflowed; vines covered it in places; silt had drifted over in others, and young saplings were sprouting in potholes and cracks, their roots working at the foundations with the endless patience of growing things. In a few lifetimes of Men water and trees would have made it a memory and a faint trace through forest, but for now it was still passable for wheeled traffic, with a little effort. The bridge over the little stream still looked solid, though streaks of rust marked the concrete where cracks exposed the rebar within.

A clatter of hooves came from the north. Slowly, cautiously she raised the binoculars to her eyes. A dozen men rode into view, and the glasses brought them close. They rode mounts of range-quarterhorse breed, which were familiar enough. Their clothes were rough leather and homespun wool, with here and there a patched pair of pre-Change jeans, the same outfits you might have seen on the cowboy-retainers of a rancher from the CORA—Central Oregon Ranchers' Association— country around Bend and Sisters, but a little more ragged. All of them had plain, round bowl helmets of steel; one of them had a horse's tail mounted as a crest in the center of his headpiece. That man also had a sleeveless chain-mail vest; the rest had cured-leather breastplates, usually strapped with chevron-shaped patterns of metal strips. Most of them carried short saddle-bows, some pre-Change compound types, more modern copies of hunting recurves; their small round shields bore the Lidless Eye newly painted. Their swords were strange, looking like a machete lengthened into a point-heavy slashing saber . . . which was probably exactly what the design came from.

She froze as the leader with the crested helmet stood in the stirrups and scanned around carefully. The binoculars brought his face close, broad and flattish-looking because his nose had been squashed and healed that way, with a dark beard trimmed into a fork shape and a terrible scar that curled one lip up in a permanent sneer. He shielded his eyes with a hand as he peered eastward, then turned again to look up at her. She knew that he couldn't see her—they were too far away, and in scrub like this a war cloak made you nearly invisible even at arm's length—but it was still a little daunting.

"Tough-looking chaps," Alleyne said softly. Speech vanished into the background noise as well.

He hadn't been out east last year; the Protector had kept him hostage while his father and John Hordle were searching the old poison-gas dump at Umatilla. They'd fooled that hard and wary man into thinking they'd found what he wanted and would work for him, and then run for it . . . Nigel Loring's cunning had seen that the poison gas didn't fall into Arminger's hands, but the stretch of country around Pendleton had. The Lord Protector had the whole of the Columbia's south bank now, as far east as the old Idaho border.

"There's been war in the Pendleton country almost since the Change, and a cruel war at that," she said. "They've grown up fighting, even more than we have here. That's how

Arminger got them to join him, backing some of them against the rest."

"Bad bargain," Alleyne said.

"By then they hated their neighbors so much they'd take any help against them," Astrid said, between pity and disgust.

At a guess, none of the men down there were older than she or Eilir, and the time before the Change had grown dreamlike to her. War to the knife would have been all they knew, that and hunger and fear and hate.

The leader with the crested helmet called an order, swinging up a hand.

"In yrch derir," one of the Dúnedain whispered: *The enemy stop.*

The mercenary light horse shook themselves out on either side of the road, combing the bush and checking any patch of trees that might shelter a watcher. The leader and three others rode on towards the bridge, arrows ready on their bows. Just then two figures burst out from underneath it, leapt on horses tethered and hidden among brushes and galloped away southwestward. The mercenaries pursued, rising in the stirrups to shoot, arrows flicking out. Astrid caught her lip in her teeth as she watched; those were her folk, her friends . . .

They passed out of sight around a bend in the road. The leader of the Pendleton scouts threw up his arm again, sensibly calling off the pursuit, since the fleeing men might be leading his into an ambush; he had to shout to make one man stop, and clouted him across the helmet when he returned. The rider extended a fist with one finger raised, and they both laughed. Then they dismounted and looked at the support pillars, one of them climbing awkwardly down a little and pointing, holding something up for his leader to see. The figures were tiny in the distance, their voices insect-small as they argued and shouted. After a moment one of the easterners turned his horse and cantered back northward towards the main body of the Protectorate's column.

"They found the cut marks and the tools, then," Alleyne said. Astrid felt a warm glow below her breastbone as he went on: "That was a remarkably clever idea, letting them find *incomplete* sabotage. Well worth all that night work."

A curled trumpet spoke, and the rest of the Protectorate force came around the curve of the northward road. A score of crossbowmen on bicycles came first, weaving among the obstacles on the road; they dismounted and set their machines on their kickstands, fanning out to either side of the road. That freed the mercenary horse who'd been guarding the crossing, and most of them trotted southward over the bridge to scout farther on. Next came gangs of laborers in metal collars and rags, carrying mattocks and picks and shovels, some pushing wheelbarrows, all guarded by infantry equipped with shields and spears, conical helms and mail hauberks. The peons set to work on the roadway, shoving aside the rusting hulks of cars, chopping back the vegetation and filling holes with earth and rock. After that the wagons came, huge things with steel frames and twin four-wheel bogies from heavy trucks, drawn by sixteen span of oxen each and loaded high with shapes of metal and timber—a prefabricated fort, with the hundreds-strong labor force that would build it trudging in coffles beside the roadway and carrying their tools. Then there were several dozen ordinary baggage wagons loaded with food and supplies, and last of all a dozen mounted men-at-arms around a rider in a knight's plumed helmet, the lanceheads swaying bright above their heads. The horseman beside the knight carried a banner that hung from a crossbar—the Portland Protective Association's Lidless Eye, not quartered with a baron's blazon; that meant the commander must be of the Protector's own household troops.

"Didn't expect the lancers," Alleyne said, as the mercenary with the horse-tail crest cantered back to report. "Now let's see . . ."

Astrid felt the tension rise, and trained reflex take control of her breathing, making the diaphragm pull air down to the bottom of her lungs and release it slowly. That slowed the beating of her heart, and kept her hands steady. Words and images flitted through her mind: fire and arrows and a white tower like a spike of pearl and silver, tall gray-eyed men riding through wilderness and by tumbled ruins, a host of horsemen charging across a plain wracked by battle, while winged shapes hovered overhead . . .

"*Nazgûl!*"

Everyone froze. Astrid let her head drift up. The slim shape of the glider slid through the sky above, toy-tiny at about two thousand feet. None of her Rangers should be visible from there . . . but it turned on a wing and dove, coming down the road at a third that height. *Which will be a real test of our field-craft,* she thought.

Fingers moved in gestures of aversion among the Dúnedain, with here and there a sign of the Cross. John Hordle raised one massive fist, with the middle finger extended, but kept it below head height.

Then it was past; it flashed across Puddle Creek, swift and graceful, and soared on an updraft that rose from the slope opposite, wheeling skyward like a falcon in a gyre until it was high above. Then it waggled its wings and turned southward once again, scouting the road the column would take.

"He didn't see a thing," Alleyne chuckled. "Victory through Air Power, what?"

They all nodded, though they also knew it would be a hideous handicap to have the Protector's gliders overhead when they were trying to move larger forces than this raiding party, spying and dropping messages to his troops.

The knight commanding the column nodded and waved his men forward. Half of them went over the bridge, and the forward labor gangs to clear the way, while the first of the huge freight wagons inched into movement. That took a minute or two. Whips cracked as the long line of paired oxen leaned into the traces with their heads down and shoulders straining at the yokes, nostrils flaring wide and mouths open with the effort. Here and there one slipped a little on the asphalt, lurching and scrabbling and bawling in alarm. A man-at-arms barked a command, and several score of the laborers added their shoulders to the effort, and the wheels began to turn slowly. The humans fell away gasping as the big vehicle moved, building up to a steady walking pace.

Astrid felt her smile waver as the first team put its hooves on the bridge. *Wait for it, wait for it, the bulk of the weight's in the wagon—*

It rolled across. The next two wagons followed, each occupying one lane, and she felt sweat trickling down her flanks. They'd had to calculate the stresses roughly—

"What's plan B?" Alleyne whispered.

"Tail, caro!"

Her beloved wasn't the first to chuckle; his Sindarin was still improving, and he took a moment to realize that she'd just said, *Feet, do your stuff.* Because if the trap failed, running away was all they could do. . . .

The paired wagons rolled onto the bridge; she could see the man leading the first ox-team suddenly stop and look around him in puzzlement, then stare down at his feet in horror before running screaming for solid ground. The first lurch came soundlessly; they'd labored all night on the bridge pillars just below the water level, miserable work in relays as hands grew too numb to grip the saw handles. They'd gone through an implausible number of the blades, too, which could never be replaced. But it was worth it; and if the scouts detected a little incomplete sabotage they'd stop looking before they found the real thing.

We hoped, she thought, with an enormous relief that left her stomach feeling oddly liquid for an instant. *And it worked, it worked . . .*

The scream of tortured metal was joined by the screams of the rest of the wagon crews as they pelted either way off the lurching length of the bridge, arms and legs pumping in panic flight. The next jolt was even louder, with a popping, crackling sound beneath it as the leverage of the severed uprights ripped welds and rivets loose. The bridge swayed right, hesitated for a moment and then collapsed to the left. The bellows of the oxen did tear at her heart, but there was no way to spare the innocent beasts.

Chaos boiled among the hundreds of men below as two of the giant wagons slid into the water. Astrid hit the toggle that released her war cloak and rose to her feet with a slight grunt—she was wearing a full hauberk and gear. She filled her lungs as she rose, drew her bow and shouted: *"Lacho calad! Drego morn!"* The same Dúnedain war cry broke out from two-score throats: *Flame Light! Flee Night!*

Arrows followed. By prearrangement, everyone was aiming

at the crossbowmen at first. There were a dozen of them left by
the side of the road. As many again had crossed to the other
side of the bridge, but they were out of range and the swift-
moving water was as deep as a tall man's chest. That cut them
off from the action here. And most of the ones within range of
the Dúnedain had turned to gape at the disaster unfolding as
ten tons of metal and wood and two score of oxen slid inexorably into the river. The first forty shafts struck before they
could do more than begin to turn back. Two more volleys were
in the air before the first hit; the Dúnedain were all *good* with
the bow, and the range was nowhere more than two hundred
yards, mostly less. The light mail shirts the crossbowmen wore
were no more protection than their woolen jackets.

"Yes!" Alleyne shouted as he drew and shot, using a longbow as skillfully as any Mackenzie. *"Yes!"*

There were sixty Association troops with the convoy. There
were more than seven times that number of laborers . . . and
as the crossbowmen fell beneath the arrowstorm, the workers
turned on the soldiers guarding them in a screaming mass of
fury, swinging shovels and mattocks and dragging men down
with their bare hands to be beaten and stomped to death. A
dozen swirls of vicious combat broke out all at once, arms and
armor and skill against numbers and surprise and hate; the
soldiers fought their way towards each other, the laborers
hanging on their flanks like wolves. Here and there a knot
stood back-to-back and beat off their assailants. More went
down before they could reach help. . . .

The Protectorate lancers had their destriers as well as their
weapons, rearing and lashing out with steel-shod hooves; only
two of the men-at-arms were pulled out of the saddle and
pounded into bags of shattered bone and pulped meat inside
their harness. The others cut their way free, with short-gripped
lances stabbing and swords casting arcs of red into the morning air. One laborer died as a warhorse sank its great yellow
teeth into his shoulder and shook him like a terrier with a rat.
Ten men-at-arms and the knight who commanded them
spurred into the open, drawing together, getting ready to
charge to the aid of the footmen in a wedge of armored muscle. That couldn't be allowed.

"To horse!" Astrid shouted with a voice like a silver trumpet, then whistled sharply. *"Tolo, Asfaloth!"* she called to her own mount.

Her gray Arab mare came, cantering, moving so lightly her feet barely seemed to touch the ground. Astrid caught the saddlebow and used the momentum and a skipping spring to vault into the saddle, her feet catching the stirrups easily. The raven-topped helmet hung by her bow-case. She slipped it on. The cheek-pieces that clipped beneath her chin were covered with wings, their pinions blackened aluminum; the tail feathers that made up the aventail protecting her neck were steel of the same color, on a mail backing, and the eyes that looked out over hers were rubies. One of the Dúnedain offered her a long ash lance, but she shook her head.

"Lacho calad! Drego morn!" she called again, and then to the horse that trembled with eagerness beneath her, tossing its head and snorting. *"Noro lim, Asfaloth, noro lim!"*

A dozen of the Rangers were in the saddle, Alleyne beside her. They put their horses recklessly at the steep slope ahead; her Asfaloth plunged down it agile as a cat, sometimes resting her weight on her haunches for an instant and sliding, sometimes twisting to avoid a sapling or tangle of thorny brush. When she hit the level ground it was with a long bound that landed her in a hand gallop. Alleyne's heavier mount reached the flats almost as quickly; the big gelding had a steel barding plate on his chest and simply smashed through much that Asfaloth had dodged. The other mounted Dúnedain all made the passage, though two had to struggle back into the saddle after losing a stirrup.

Behind them the rest of the Rangers were leaping down the slope in turn, shouting their war cry. Ahead the Protectorate men-at-arms were turning to meet the menace of their mounted foes; they had no choice, if they weren't to be taken in the rear. The laborers took heart and threw themselves on the spears that faced them in a screaming swarm, led by men willing to hold the steel in their own dying flesh while their comrades beat at heads and shoulders beyond. A helm and mail coat and the padding beneath were good protection, but there was a limit.

Time to look to her own fight. Alleyne was coming up on her left, the long steel of his lancehead ready. Ahead the knight in the plumed helmet was coming for her; some hidden sense told her that she was the target of his lance; all she could see of his face were the eyes glaring at her from over the curved rim of his big kite-shaped shield, its black surface marked with the Lidless Eye. She shot once; the arrow struck the surface of the knight's conical Norman helmet and flipped off into the air. Divots of grass and dark, moist earth shot skyward as well, as the destrier's hooves pounded at the turf and brush. The lancehead pointed at her midriff, directed over the neck of the knight's horse with unerring skill, and her smaller round shield was slung at her knee—you needed both hands for a bow.

Her right hand whipped back for another arrow and she put shaft to string in a single smooth motion; there would be time for just one more shot, and the knight was well protected, the horse a small target with a steel chamfron covering its head and a peytral on its chest.

Two seconds, one . . .

The Protectorate lancer was expecting her to duck, or swerve her more maneuverable mount. He wasn't expecting her to throw herself to the right with her left knee over the bow of her saddle, hanging off the side of the horse Commanche-style. The lancehead flashed through the space where her breast had been a moment before with the driving power of an armored man and tall horse behind it, yet cutting only air.

It was a risky thing to do even for a rider of her skill, especially in armor, and for an instant she felt herself begin to slip towards the earth dashing by at thirty miles an hour beneath her before a desperate wrench of straining thigh muscles brought her back upright. The horses flashed past each other as her left foot found the stirrup again; as it did she turned in the saddle, the cord coming to the angle of her jaw as she drew against the heavy resistance of wood and horn and sinew. The lancer was pulling up, screaming a curse as he tried to get his mount around and to turn the long point of his shield behind him to cover his back, but the same weight and momentum that put terrible power behind a lancehead made a galloping destrier hard to turn. Shield and weapon, mount and rider were locked into a drive forward behind the narrow steel point.

Even with the combined velocities of the two horses she was less than twenty yards behind him when she shot. *Snap* of the string on the bracer, a flash of fletching and pile-shaped bodkin head, and the arrow struck the knight's hauberk over the kidney. It broke the links of the riveted mail and sank three-quarters of its thirty-inch length into his body with a solid, punching impact, a dull thudding sound audible even over the thunder of scores of hooves and the screaming of men, the shrill calls of horses, the low, deep bellowing of oxen. He shrieked again, wordlessly this time, dropping his lance in reflex and then toppled leftward to the ground, dragging with one foot tangled in the stirrup until his warhorse came to a halt, looking back to see what it was that tugged so at its harness. Asfaloth braked to a halt, rearing and turning in her own length.

"Lacho calad! Drego morn!"

That was Eilir's party, dashing in at the gallop from northward along the road. Eilir herself was silent of course, but she was the first to throw her Molotov cocktail on a load of massive timbers; it was a quart glass bottle with its neck wrapped in oily cloth that gave off a long, thin line of black smoke as it smoldered. Glass shattered, and the sticky fluid within spurted out, caught fire and burned as it dripped and spattered over the dry Douglas fir wood. The flames were a fierce red-orange; the stuff was made of gasoline and laundry soap and rubber dissolved in alcohol and turpentine, until it had the consistency and stickiness of thin honey. More arched out as her team of six dashed down the line of wagons. By the time they'd pulled up near the wrecked bridge, pillars of smoke and fire were beginning to rise from the wagons. Better still, burning the heavy loads of timber would turn the steel members and fasteners into twisted, useless scrap, and those were a whole lot harder to replace than the shaped wood.

All that came out of the corner of her eye in an instant. If there was one thing in all the world she was certain of, it was that she didn't need to check on Eilir doing her part.

Astrid's eyes flicked over the action nearer her as Asfaloth's forehooves touched down again. Alleyne's man was down with a stub of broken lance-shaft sticking from his chest. Two of her Dúnedain riders were down likewise, dead or crippled, with their horses running free. The rest were in a melee with the Protectorate men-at-arms, horses circling and snapping as blades swung in bright, glittering arcs. As she turned she saw the tall figure in the green plate armor use the stump of his lance to break a swordsman's arm, and then cast it aside and sweep out his own long blade, bringing up the shield with its blazon of five roses. Astrid set another arrow on her string, rode close and ended a duel with a shaft between the shoulderblades, neatly cutting the shield strap that ran diagonally across the back. At that range the bodkin came out the front of the man's hauberk and went *thunk* into the inside of his shield.

She'd learned combat from Sam Aylward and Mike Havel. The rest of the Dúnedain running up had graduated from those same hard schools. Or something similar for John Hordle; he ran straight into the mass of enraged horses and bright steel with a wicked grin on his red ham of a face and the bastard sword in both hands. His first stroke took a man's leg off at the knee, just in the gap between the mail of his hauberk and the steel-splint shin protector . . .

The fighting was over in moments, with only a whimpering left that ended as steel was carefully driven home. A dozen or so of the laborers ran up to her, brandishing their bloodied tools or weapons snatched from the fallen Protectorate troopers. She stood in the saddle and held a hand up; beside her Alleyne raised his visor with a red-splashed steel gauntlet.

"*Silence!*" he shouted. Quiet fell. "Listen to the Lady of the Dúnedain."

"Or listen to this," John Hordle said, hefting his great sword.

The workers were rebels, but they'd lived in the Protectorate for a long time—half their lives for most of them, from their looks. They were used to obeying armored men.

Astrid went on quickly, with the growing crackle and roar of the burning timbers in the background: "There will be soldiers here soon. We have to get you to safety. Cut the oxen loose from the harness, take as much food as you can carry, and weapons, and nothing else and follow."

They scrambled to obey, pulling sacks of hardtack and beans and flitches of bacon and strings of dried sausage and blocks of cheese off the supply wagons, loading them onto their own backs or the bicycles of dead crossbowmen; the more alert stripped the weapons and gear from the enemy fallen, and drove the oxen into wild, stampeding flight with shouts and spear-prods. Dúnedain guides divided the labor gangs into parties of twenty or thirty and led them away quickly, up into the trackless hills. Her riders went after the enemy horses with their lariats.

And we must give the mercy stroke to any of the workers who are badly wounded, she thought; there were enough horses to get the hurt Dúnedain out, but that was all. *It would be no kindness to let them fall into the hands of the* yrch *again.*

Astrid herself rode down to the edge of Puddle Creek, reining in beside Eilir.

They didn't seem inclined to shoot at us, Eilir signed, resting her bow across the saddle in front of her and nodding across the creek and the wrecked bridge. *So I didn't see much point in provoking them.*

"Right," Astrid said.

The Pendleton mercenaries were back, but the swift water was too deep on this spring day to cross easily, and the bridge was a tangle of twisted metal like some monstrous dish of ferrous pasta littered with whole dead oxen. They might try to get the two wagons on the far side away, but Eilir's group had carefully shot a couple of draught-beasts in each team. John Hordle came up with a dozen arrows clutched in his great right hand; each of them had a wad of napalm-soaked cloth just behind the head, the scent sharp and mineral under the fug of blood and smoke.

"Thought you'd want to do the honors, luv," he said, offering one to Eilir.

The mercenaries' scar-faced leader reined in on the other

side of the river, within easy bowshot, but with a white rag
tied to a light spear.

"Neat job," he called, laughing. "You're that Astrid they
told us about, aren't you? Or are you the deaf one? I'm Hank
Bauer, Sheriff of Lonerock."

"I am Astrid, *Hiril Dúnedain*," she called coldly. "Lady of
the Rangers. This is Lady Eilir."

Sheriff was equivalent to *baron*, in the country east of the
mountains. And Rancher usually meant *lord* or *knight*, pretty
well, with cowboy filling in for *man-at-arms*.

He chuckled. "You are one mean pair of killin' bitches, I've
got to give you that. The big fellah there's no slouch either, I'd
guess, or the guy in the fancy armor. Pleasure to meet y'all."

"Leave this country, Sheriff Bauer, you and all your men, or
you will leave your bones here. Go home to your own land and
your families."

"Shit, it's better grazin' land than anything to home, just
like the man said," he replied; the scar made his smile gruesome. "And we left to get away from our families, anyhow. If
you're such a great fighter, girlie, why don't you come over
here and *make* me leave? I'll give you a kiss if you do."

The men around him laughed and hee-hawed at her, calling
comments they doubtless thought very funny.

"If you're such a great warrior, why don't you come over
here and make me fight you?" she called sweetly. "Or send
your sister, if you're scared."

"Watch out!" Alleyne said, snapping his visor down and
drawing his sword again.

One of the mercenaries had pulled a light, yard-long javelin
out of the hide bucket slung over his back in place of a quiver.
It was a long throw . . .

But the horseman didn't cast the weapon he brandished
over his head. Instead he gave a high, warbling shriek like an
Indian war cry and put his horse at the water, shrugging off
the surprised snatch his leader made for the bridle. The horse
hesitated for only an instant and then slid in; the gray-blue
surge came to its chest, and then it was picking its way across
just upstream and west of the fallen bridge.

Alleyne shouted furiously: "This violates the flag of truce!"

Hank Bauer shrugged, looked up at the white rag, then pulled it free and tossed it aside. He laughed and called through cupped hands: "Hell, you can kill the little fuck for all I care. The dumb bastard's always pulling shit like this! I'd have killed him myself weeks ago except he's my wife's cousin."

The man charging across the creekbed was young, younger than her, with only a fuzz of yellow beard on a face that also bore a set of black painted chevrons; long blond braids swung from under his steel cap as he howled and brandished the javelin. Alleyne began to wheel his destrier, but Astrid smiled and put out a hand.

"*Bar melindo*," she said: *My beloved.* "Better I do this."

"Why?" he said.

"Because . . ." She frowned, not quite certain of what her intuition told her. "I think it may be useful. These men aren't lieges of Portland. They're fighting for money and plunder. And I think that all they respect is success in battle. If they respect us more than the Association . . . something might come of that."

His mouth quirked. "And it'll be more spectacular if you do it. You've got a damnable habit of making sense, darling. By all means—he's yours."

She suppressed an impulse to kiss him—that would not go over well with the target audience just now—and leaned down for an instant, running her left arm through the loops of the shield hanging over the bow-case at her knee. The young easterner brought his horse surging up the shallow bank of the creek and charged her, shrieking; Asfaloth turned beneath her in response to leg and balance, going from a standing start to a gallop in seconds. The distance closed with dreamlike speed, and she let him turn his horse to come in on her unshielded right side. Ten yards away he twisted back and uncoiled in the saddle, throwing the javelin hard and fast.

It seemed to float towards her. Javelins weren't much used here in the Valley . . . but there was a game she'd played for years . . .

Her backsword came free of the sheath and flicked from left to right in a long curve, the arc of its flight perfect as a song in the mind of the gods. With a hard *crack* the metal-tipped wooden rod flew by in two pieces, just as the dragonflies she usually practiced on did. A cheer went up from the Dúnedain still watching and another from the mercenaries on the other bank of the creek. The young man's astonishment made his voice break in midshriek; he was goggling at her as they passed in a blur of speed, and she could have killed him with a single sweep of the steel. Instead she wheeled Asfaloth and waited while he drew the heavy blade at his saddlebow.

" *'Chete! Give her the 'chete!"* voices called from across the river, among other things, including advice on where to put it.

The man was a wild chopper; he almost killed her in the first exchange because her swordswoman's reflexes couldn't believe someone would just barrel in like that. He also nicked Asfaloth on the neck, and she felt her lips go tight in genuine anger.

Their blades struck, slid down until guard locked with guard in a skirl of steel on steel; the horses shocked shoulder-to-shoulder in the same instant. The easterner rose in the stirrups, throwing the weight of his heavier shoulders against her arm. Astrid smiled sweetly as she twisted her foot, got her toe under his stirrup-iron and heaved her knee upward sharply. The young mercenary's eyes went wide in panic; he yelled as he pitched up and to one side. Then he did something sensible, kicking his feet free of the stirrups and rolling over the crupper of his horse, dropping to the earth on the other side in a back-somersault. He landed stumbling, and Asfaloth was on him before he could set himself; the Arab mare was trained to ride men down. He dodged enough that the impact wasn't bone-crushing, but that sent him tumbling over the ground. He was sensible again, letting the sword go; you could get a nasty cut that way, particularly if only your torso was protected.

When he rose again he was weeping with rage and mortification, tears cutting streaks through the dirt and paint on his face, and losing themselves in the blood that poured from his bruised nose. He drew a bowie knife and waited.

Astrid laughed, and held up her sword, looking from the

yard-long blade to the knife. "Do you want to die of stupidity?" she said, and flourished the weapon towards the stream.

The youth screamed a curse at her and hurled the knife, turning and running for the water. Astrid shifted her balance and Asfaloth gave one of her astonishing leaps, landing nearly at the edge of the creek. That let her deliver a ringing slap with the flat to the seat of his buckskin pants as he dove into the water and struck out for the other side; when he rose above the surface his face was as red as his buttocks probably were.

"Here's your wife's cousin, Sheriff," she called as she sheathed her unblooded sword and caught the reins of the mercenary's mount when it looked like following him. "Tell him thank you for the horse. It's a fine one."

The scar-faced man was laughing as she turned; some of his companions toppled from the saddle, wheezing and holding their sides and drumming their heels on the ground in mirth. My-wife's-cousin would probably never live this down.

"He won't thank you for it, Lady," the mercenary leader said, confirming her guess, and then touched the hilt of his blade. "See you another time, without a creek in between."

"We'll let you get out of bowshot," Astrid replied.

The mercenary looked at the riverbank on her side; better than thirty archers lined it, and they could swamp his men even discounting the three who had swatches of burning oil-soaked tow tied to their arrows. He shrugged and neck-reined his horse about, calling to his men to take the Protector's crossbowmen up pillion. Then he shouted and leaned forward, and his horse leapt into a gallop southward. The others followed him around the curve in the road in a hooting, whooping mass, bent on only the Gods knew what deadly mischief.

Eilir raised her longbow—she was one of the few who could shoot the unwieldy weapon from horseback. Her shaft made a long curve in the air, trailing black smoke, and went *thunk* into a balk of timber on one of the wagons; more followed it, until the air over the river looked as if vanished fireworks had spanned it. The Dúnedain cheered and waved their weapons in the air as those wagons began to burn as well, adding their bitter plumes to the smoke that was making the air hot and tight in her chest.

Alleyne reined in next to her. "They're happy," he said.

"Good," Astrid replied. "We've stung the *yrch*, at least."

"A bit more than that," the young Englishman said judiciously. "Still, there's no denying they can shrug off a loss like this more easily than we."

Astrid flung him a smile; the way he took everything so equably was one of the wonderful things about him. She knew her own nature was more changeable.

"Not much more. Even if Lady Juniper brings off what she's planning, that would only be a start: It *is* like trying to shoot an elephant!"

Aha, Eilir signed, after she'd pushed her bow back through the loops on her quiver. *You should remember that my most magical Mom's plans usually have a couple of little hidden wheels within the big obvious one.*

CHAPTER TEN

Waldo Hills, Willamette Valley, Oregon
March 5th, 2008/Change Year 9

The Grand Constable of the Portland Protective Association looked back at the tumbled wreckage of the bridge, and coughed slightly at the wafts of bitter smoke from the wagons that had borne the framework of his portable castle. The bodies lay about it; he gritted his teeth at the tumbled, naked corpses of his men-at-arms. Their commander still looked comically surprised as he sprawled on his side in a pool of congealed blood swarming with flies. The stump of the arrow that had killed him had broken off short when someone pulled the hauberk and gambeson off over his head; that someone now had a fine suit of mail, with only one small hole in it.

Conrad Renfrew repressed an urge to dismount and kick him in the face. It wouldn't do any good; it wasn't as if the idiot was still alive and able to feel it. Besides, right now his boots were full of water from fording the stream. The engineers were getting a temporary wooden bridge ready, but that would take at least eighteen hours, short as they were of grunt labor.

And I'm short a dozen men-at-arms and a knight, he thought sourly. The infantry weren't that much of a much, but losing skilled lancers *hurt.* Men-at-arms had scarcity value, and knights also had relatives and comrades who mattered at court.

"So I reckoned the only thing I could do was get the word to you," the mercenary said, tugging at his forked beard. "There were a few too many of 'em for my boys to tackle. They didn't lose more 'n four, five all up when they ambushed your folks.

" 'Course, a lot of them peons got it where the chicken got the ax while they was swarmin' over your boys. We had a ringside seat over there on the other side of the water."

He jerked a thumb at a file of nearly fifty bodies laid out in a row, all of them with the iron collars still on their necks.

"You're not here just to drink and screw the peon girls, Sheriff Bauer," Renfrew rumbled.

He knew his face intimidated most men, which was some compensation for the memory of pain. The fact that they were surrounded by the household knights of the Constable's personal guard shouldn't have hurt either, but Bauer was smiling slightly . . . or that might just be his own scar, which was as spectacular as any of the Constable's, and stood out more for being alone. Renfrew tapped the serrated steel head of his mace on his stirrup-iron with a *chink . . . chink . . .* sound and stared at him; the other's green eyes blinked innocently.

Aloud the Portland commander went on: "Or to sit in the saddle across a chest-deep creek and watch my men getting massacred while you pick lice out of your beards."

Bauer shrugged. "We ain't here to get kilt for no reason, neither. Your men weren't outnumbered much but they managed to lose that fight good and proper, the way them Rangers outsmarted 'em and took 'em by surprise; the only ones got out was the ones we took with us. Then I lost three good men chasin' the Rangers into the woods when they pulled out afterwards. You got too many woods around here for comfort. But that was fair business; like you say, we're here to fight, and I'm a man of my word. We're not here to get our asses kicked certain-sure."

Renfrew shrugged massive shoulders made more so by armor and padding. It was a fair point. The Pendleton area was theoretically under the Association now, but they couldn't afford to lean too hard on the men from there yet. They were volunteers from the winning faction the Protector had backed, and from a mercenary's point of view, Bauer had been making a perfectly valid argument. You couldn't expect hired men to throw themselves away on a forlorn hope just to do the enemy some damage, and you couldn't punish them if you wanted them to stick around. A mercenary leader's men were his capital assets, and if he lost too many of them then he had nothing to sell. This particular band were the Sheriff's friends and kinfolk and neighbors, as well.

In fact, that little pursuit was well handled. At least thanks to Bauer I've got some idea which way they went, and he did save a dozen crossbowmen.

"OK," he said, turning and looking at the wagons again. "We'll salvage the metal; they can rework it at the foundries up in Oregon City. And get someone to pull those oxen out of the river and hang them up to drain. No sense in letting good meat spoil."

"My boys already got one ready to barbeque," Bauer said. "We can handle the rest iff'n you want us to."

He gave a vague, sketchy salute and wandered off. Renfrew looked over at his clerk. "Do up a report and have it ready for dispatch to the Lord Protector inside twenty minutes," he said.

That got the man out of earshot. He was probably reporting to the Church and certainly to the Chancellery as well; it was amazing how a country with fewer people than a medium-sized city in the old days could develop layers of competing institutions and factions. Then he turned to the young knight beside him who commanded his guards.

"Buzz, get that idiot Melford's body packed up and send it on back to his kin with the usual nonsense about how bravely he died."

"Why not leave it for the buzzards and the coyotes?" Sir Buzz Akers said.

He was one of the Constable's own vassals, whose father had seizin of a manor near the castle at Odell; Renfrew had known the family in the Society before the Change, and arranged to get them the estate when he led the conquest of the Hood Valley for the Association, back in the second Change Year. The father stayed home these days and did his military service as castle garrison commander, since he had a leg that would never work very well again; that happened when they were smoking a lunatic archer in green out of the ruins of Seattle on a salvage mission five years ago. The son was here to learn, as well as serve.

And because my *family will need loyal, able vassals if I kick off too early.* He hadn't married until after the Change; his countess was a gentle soul and his children were all young.

"I won't leave the carrion where it belongs because it would piss off his family," Renfrew said. "Otherwise that's just what I'd do. Who cares if the coyotes choke on it?" He looked up at the sky; three hours to sunset. "That fool didn't scout carefully enough, and it's cost us a day and that fort, God damn it!"

Akers nodded. "Are we going to bring up more timber?"

"Not in time enough to do much good. Without the steel cladding and braces it's too vulnerable; we'll do what we can with earthworks for now and get fancy later. You take over here, Buzz; I've got to get back and make sure that Piotr doesn't screw things while I'm gone. Though how he could foul up a straight advance to the Santiam with three hundred troops, God only knows."

"Sir Ernaldo's a good man," the knight observed.

"And if Piotr would listen to him, I wouldn't worry so much. I wish he was over fighting the Bearkillers. He hates them but he doesn't underestimate them. I've tried to hammer into his head how dangerous the kilties can be if you let them call the tune for the dance, but it won't sink in. Sometimes—"

He made a gesture with the steel mace to show how he'd *like* to hammer some sense into the younger nobleman. Akers laughed.

"It's a pity Old Man Stavarov's too important to diss," he said, shaking his head regretfully.

Renfrew nodded. That was one of the drawbacks of the Association's setup. His aide went on: "I think Piotr may underestimate the kilties because they look so fucking weird—all those kilts and plaids and bagpipes, and that dumb face-

painting thing they do. And that screwy religion of theirs. All
that makes it hard to take them seriously, unless you know
what's under the make-believe."

Renfrew started to nod, and then looked around at his host
of spearmen and crossbowmen, the armored knights with the
plumes fluttering from their helmets and the pennants from
their lances, the golden spurs on their heels and the quartered blazons on their shields, the peasant laborers in their
tabards by the oxcarts and the monk-doctors seeing to the
wounded . . .

Akers glanced at him oddly as he started to laugh. "What's
so funny?" he enquired.

"How old were you at the Change, Buzz?"

"I'd just turned twelve . . . well, hell, you'd been giving me
sword lessons for a year already then, my lord Count. Why do
you ask?"

"If you have to ask why it's funny to say the Mackenzies
look weird, you're too young to ever understand," the thickset, scar-faced man said. Then he looked southward and
scowled.

"This whole plan is too fucking complicated," he muttered.
"Not enough allowance for screwups and accidents, too many
separate things we're trying to do all at once."

"My lord? If you think it's too complicated, why didn't you
advise the Lord Protector and the Council of War?"

"Why do you think it isn't even *more* complicated, Buzz?"
Renfrew grunted.

"This ambush couldn't have been anticipated," his aide remarked, obviously trying to be fair.

"Not exactly. Not the details. But Sir Buzz, when you're up
against anyone good enough to give you a run for their
money, you *can* be pretty damned sure that they're going to
fuck you *somehow* at *some* point and the first you'll know
about it is when the bunny dies. That's why you build in a
margin of error; every added bit of fancy footwork means
another opportunity for the other side. We're not fighting
some pissant village militia in Lower Butt-Scratch, equipped
with baseball bats and kitchen knives tied on broomsticks
and old traffic signs for shields. Not this time. I get this feel-

ing I'm trying to juggle too many balls with not enough hands."

"Not to mention the kilties are tricky," Akers said. "Christ, how I wish we'd managed to wipe them out when they were small, back in the first Change Year. Now those bastards have plans of their own."

Renfrew forbore to mention that Akers had been a page then, and just getting used to the idea that all this wasn't a tournament or a trip to the Pennsic War with his folks, and that he'd never be going on to high school.

Instead he shrugged. "Right. The enemy, that dirty dog, usually does have a plan of his own. That's why we call him the *enemy*. It's a mistake to think *your* plan isn't going to trip over *their* plan."

Such frankness was slightly risky, since it was the Lord Protector's orders they were critiquing, but Sir Buzz and his family were the Count of Odell's own sworn vassals, not the Lord Protector's. The Grand Constable *was* Arminger's own vassal himself, but Norman needed him nearly as much as vice versa.

And if he wanted to avoid his noblemen saying what they thought sometimes, he should have based this setup on Byzantium or the Chin Legalists, not William the Bastard's Normandy.

He slapped his gauntlets into the palm of his left hand, then began to pull them on. "All right, let's get to work. Keep a sharp eye out and don't let your lancers get in bowshot of any cover without beating it clear first. Those damned Rangers are too tricky for comfort and the kilties aren't much better."

Dun Juniper, Willamette Valley, Oregon
March 5th, 2008/Change Year 9

Epona turned her head and butted Rudi Mackenzie affectionately in the chest. He laughed and shooed a horsefly away from her nostril; it was starting to get warm enough for them. Then he hugged her neck as she tried to nibble at his hair, the warm scent of horse all around him. The long dark stable smelled of horses in general, manure-musk, the sweet hay stored above their heads, the dry sneeze-scent of straw and sawdust on the ground, of liniment and leather. Light came through the big double doors down at the other end, or through knotholes that had fallen out of the fir boards, spearing into the dimness in shafts of yellow swimming with dust motes. Now and then a horse would shift a foot with a soft, hollow *clop* of horn and steel on the dirt floor, or make wet tearing and crunching sounds as it stripped grass-and-clover fodder through the wooden bars of a crib and ate.

We did a lot of shoveling out, Rudi thought virtuously. *And we oiled all that tack and pitched the hay down and groomed all the horses that're left.* And *got all that schoolwork done this morning. I deserve some time for myself. 'Sides, Epona'll get antsy if she doesn't get a run. She* needs *to run.*

Besides, it would help him forget that his mother and so many of his friends were away at war.

Mathilda's big black tomcat Saladin looked at him with bored yellow eyes; the feline didn't think it was warm enough on the ground, and was curled up on the withers of the black mare. The two animals had become friends, which was strange, since Epona still wasn't friendly much with anyone but him, and usually responded to small annoying things with an uncomplicated stomp. But then, she and Saladin had come to Dun Juniper about the same time, last Lughnasadh, and they'd both lived in the stables; Saladin ran the gauntlet every evening so he could cadge stuff at dinner and sleep on Mathilda's bed, but the Hall cats were still hissing and spitting and generally making him unwelcome every chance they got.

Mathilda was off in one corner of the loose-box, sitting cross-legged on a bale of hay and watching him currycomb his horse, with a book open on her lap—he could see an archer in a helmet and jack drawing a longbow on the cover. He recognized his own copy of *The Free Companions* with the Wyeth illustrations, a gift from his great-great-uncle to Juniper before he was born, and from her to him; he'd read it with Matti while he was in the tail end of his convalescence, restless with the orders that kept him quiet and in bed so much.

It was a great story, and the people and everything in it

were a lot more understandable than most books from before the Change. Sir Nigel had told him more stories about the people in it, too; he'd had more books by the same writer when he was a kid, a man named Donan Coyle.

Two big, shaggy, brown dogs named Ulf and Fenra were curled up with her, siblings from a litter old Cuchulain had sired with a mastiff bitch three years ago. Ulf had his head on her feet, thumping his tail absently when she patted him now and then, and Fenra was pretending to be asleep, but occasionally sneaking a mock-casual peek at Saladin and heaving a wistful sigh. She was far too respectful of Epona's hooves and probably of the cat's claws to do anything about it, though.

"She needs a run," Rudi said to the air, clearing his throat to add emphasis. "Epona needs a run."

Aoife and Liath were on guard, which for the past half hour had meant sitting in the *next* loose-box; they'd been talking softly until a few moments ago.

He cleared his throat again and spoke more loudly: "I *said,* Epona needs a *run*! I'm gonna take her out."

A giggle came from the loose-box beyond this one, hidden by the barrier between, planks as tall as a grown man's chest. Then Aoife cleared her throat in turn and said from there, a bit breathless: "Didn't Sally say something about an arithmetic assignment your crop of little goblins had to have ready by Monday?"

"Aoife, I haven't told *anyone* about that poem you wrote about Liath. And it was *really* soppy. I bet everyone would laugh and laugh and laugh when they heard you said her eyes were like two pools of—"

"Poem?" Mathilda said, looking up with interest from the book.

He felt a little guilty about blackmailing Aoife—she'd been using scraps of smooth bark for practice and probably hadn't thought anyone would go to the trouble of picking them out of the Hall's kitchen-kindling box. On the other hand, he was a ten-year-old kid . . . nearly ten . . . and she was twenty-one, so it was only fair that he was sneaky now and then. Aoife had been so caught up in composing it, she barely complained when Uncle Chuck—her father—made her and her friend stay here on guard duty rather than ride with the First Levy.

"Poem?" another voice from the other loose-box said, even more breathless. "You wrote a *poem* for me?"

"Hey, I'll tell you about it later, all right, honeybunch?" Silence, and then Aoife rose and came around to the door of the stall, brushing straw out of her dark red hair and off her kilt. "OK, sprout. Just on the meadow, though. It's a couple of hours till dinner, anyway."

Epona tossed her head as if she knew what was happening, and tossed it again and stamped a foot eagerly as Rudi and Mathilda started to get the tack ready. The big black mare had the loose-box all to herself, and did even when the stables were full; there were three horses in the next, though. The girl's favorite horse was out with the levy, who had first call, but a good solid cob was available from the remains of the common pool kept for Clan business; it crunched a carrot enthusiastically, and then sighed as the saddle blanket was tossed over its back. They led it ambling over to a mounting block so that they could saddle it.

"Lazy old thing!" Mathilda said, shaking a finger at the bay gelding. "See if I give you any more carrots!"

"Well, how would you feel if someone put an iron bar in your mouth and made you run around carrying them on your back?" Rudi said reasonably.

"But that's a horse's *job*," Mathilda said. "Look at Epona—she'd put on her own tack if she could."

"That's Epona," Rudi pointed out.

"Yeah," Mathilda agreed. "I think she could talk, if she wanted to."

"She *does* talk, to me. But for most of them, it's just what they have to do 'cause we tell 'em to," Rudi said. "What they really like is hanging out with their herd, and eating."

He lifted his own saddle—both the children were using a light pad type—off its rest and carried it over to Epona; she stood patiently while he clambered up on a box and laid it carefully on her back over the saddle blanket. The tall mare seemed to be on the brink of a run even standing still; she was glossy black, her mane combed to a silky fall; she was also sixteen hands, and better than a thousand pounds, for all that she was as agile as the sulky Saladin, now looking down at them resentfully from a cross-timber where he'd jumped when pushed off his equine heating pad. Aoife leaned against a wooden pillar with her arms crossed, chewing on a straw and offering comments as he arranged the straps and buckles.

Epona stood still for it, though, with no more movement than shifting weight from foot to foot, not even swelling her belly out when the girth was buckled on. He didn't use a bit, just a hackamore bridle; Epona needed no compulsion to go the way she should.

Liath appeared a few seconds later, blushing furiously when Rudi made a languishing kissy-face at her behind Aoife's back. The two adults carefully checked the harness on both horses, then nodded before picking out mounts and getting started on their own heavier war-saddles, what the oldsters called a Western type. When the horses were ready they pulled on their own harness; padded jackets with elbow-length mail sleeves and leather-lined mail collars and the brigandines that went over that. The torso armors had a heavy, smooth, liquid motion as the warriors swung them on and buckled the straps on their left flanks, making a subdued chinking sound as the small rectangular plates shifted between the inner and outer layers of green-dyed leather.

"Good job, sprout," Aoife said, running her fingers over Epona's harness without quite touching it—the tall warm-blood mare still didn't like anyone but Rudi laying a hand on her. "You've got a natural talent for horses. Yours is pretty good too, Matti. You're really picking it up."

"I'm glad I've learned how to do it for myself," Matti said. "Now I'll always know how."

Unexpectedly, shy Liath spoke up with a grin and a joke as she strung her long yew bow: "What *don't* you have a natural talent for, Rudi?"

"Arithmetic," he said, making his face serious. "I really have to *work* at that."

The warriors buckled on the broad metal-studded leather belts that held their shortswords and dirks and bucklers, then slung their quivers and longbows over their shoulders; Liath took a battle spear from where she'd leaned it beside the big doors, the edges glinting coldly in the stuffy dimness of the stables.

"Don't forget your plaid, sprout," Aoife said. "And your jacket, Matti. Still pretty brisk out there."

"You're worse than Mom," Rudi said.

"You betcha I am! The Chief lets you get away with anything. Put it on. It's a lot chillier out there."

Rudi rolled his eyes, shrugged, then wrapped and belted the blanketlike tartan garment, pinning it at his shoulder with a brooch of silver-and-niello knotwork; he didn't feel the cold as much as most people, but Aoife was always at him like a mother duck with one duckling. Aoife's foster-mother Judy had always fussed at her children, and she'd picked it up.

I feel sorry for her *kids, when she has them,* he thought, then shrugged ruefully. *She just doesn't want me to catch a chill 'cause she likes me.*

Mathilda put on her red woolen jacket and buttoned it; that was a gift from her mother in Portland, and a really nice piece of weaving—Juniper Mackenzie said so, and she was an excellent judge, being the best loomster the Clan had. Then she proudly added a belt with a dirk.

They all led their horses out of the warm, dim stables; the dogs followed along with their tongues lolling and tails wagging, glad to be moving too. The way to the gate turned right from there, past the hot clamor of the smith's shop with its open front and bearded mask of Goibniu Lord of Iron done in wrought metal and fixed to the smoke hood over the forge-hearth, flanked by the Hammer and the great twisted horn that held the Mead of Life. Rudi's feet slowed for a moment. The master smith was sitting at a bench with drill and punch and file, putting the finishing touches on a helmet shaped from a sheet of steel plate, keeping an eye on his apprentices at the same time. One pumped her turn at the bellows with weary resignation. Another at the square stone hearth took an odd-looking thing like a cross between a spearhead and a spade out of the white-glowing charcoal in his tongs and held it on the anvil as he shaped the crimson metal with his hammer, *clang!* and a shower of sparks and *clang!* again and then swiftly *clang-clang-clang-clang,* muscle moving under the sweat-slick skin of his thick arms, face sharply intent on the task.

Then he plunged it in the quenching bath with a seething bubble and hiss of oily steam, held it up for the master to see and got a nod of approval before he returned to the finicky task of putting in the hinge for one of the helm's cheek-pieces. Another apprentice was doing farrier-work, shoeing a horse—one of the big Suffolks—and looked up from the hoof to wave her hammer, smiling around a mouthful of long horseshoe nails. A wave of heat and the smell of charcoal and scorched hoof and hot iron came out of the smithy, and soap and boiling water and wet cloth from the laundry behind it.

Gotta go, Rudi thought reluctantly, though he wouldn't have minded lingering a bit; smithing fascinated him, and the making of weapons in particular. *But someday I'm going to learn that stuff.*

He couldn't do it as a living—Mom had other plans, and people would disapprove, and what he really wanted was to be First Armsman of the Clan someday—but there wasn't any reason he couldn't help out the master smith when he was a bit older and big enough to be useful. Everyone said he had clever hands, and he was already good at making little things, harness straps and carvings and pottery.

In the open roadway between the stables and the infirmary the air was sharper, with the cool, damp bite of early spring, though the day was fair. Rudi felt his blood flow faster as he took a deep breath, and when the prickle of sweat on his skin went chill he was glad of the plaid.

Aoife still fusses, he grumbled to himself.

Under the usual smells was a spicy-sharp one from a two-wheeled cart near the infirmary doors, drawn by a pair of oxen; Aunt Judy was there, wearing a long, stained bib-apron and inspecting bundles of dried herbs and bark, and talking with a man he recognized as a healer from a dun down on the southern border of the Clan's lands.

"Hi, Mom!" Aoife called; the situation was too casual for *merry met.* "How's it going?"

"Hello, Aoife. Hi to you too, Liath—still keeping bad company, I see," Judy Barstow Mackenzie said. "I'm just checking the willow bark and tansy Frank brought in. If you two don't have anything to do, we'll be chopping and steeping and distilling, the children could watch . . ."

Aoife grinned. "I'm a warrior on Clan business, Mom, orders from Dad-the-Second-Armsman no less," she said. "Taking the sprouts out for some exercise counts as part of the job, since they can't go alone."

"Clan business," Judy sniffed, and put her hands on her hips. Rudi smiled to see it; his mom used exactly the same gesture. She and Judy had been friends forever. "Meaning you get to laze about snogging with your girlfriend while everyone else works."

It was strange to think of them as young like him and Matti, running around and playing.

"Snogging?" Mathilda said, sotto voce.

"Snogging. Liplocking," Rudi answered with an innocent look, and somewhat louder, watching the tips of Liath's ears turn red—she hadn't taken off her flat bonnet and put the helmet on yet. "Smooching."

Then Aunt Judy grinned, even at Matti. She wasn't what you could call easy with the girl yet, but she was trying.

"I'd like to help you with the herbs again," Matti said. "Could I do that later?"

"Sure," Judy said. "I think you've got a talent for the healing arts. Drop by after dinner, and I'll show you how we make the willow-bark extract."

Rudi gave his mother's best friend a big grin. She *was* trying. She snorted at him, then winked and pushed Epona's head away when the mare came up and nuzzled at the herbs on the cart—or rather began to; that way the horse knew enough not to try a nibble, and she saved her fingers. Then they led their horses out onto the graveled roadway that ran all around the oval interior of Dun Juniper, in front of the log cottages and workshops built up against the inside of the wall, turning right towards the gate and the tall green roof of the Hall. Cold wind ruffled the puddles from yesterday's rain; they were gray with rock-dust from the pavement. They walked through snatches of conversation, the thump of looms and the hammering of a gang doing repairs on one of the heavy ladders that ran up between the cottages to the fighting platform, the *tippty-tap-tap* ching!-*tappy-tap*-tap of a typewriter, through gaggles of younger children running and yelling and playing, and faintly the sound of a work-song from a group kneading bread in the Hall kitchens. A sharp scent of fennel and sausage and garlic meant someone was making pizza.

Smells good, Rudi thought, and took a handful of dried plums from his pouch, offering them to the others. Mathilda took one; the two warriors shook their heads.

Early flowers bloomed in the narrow strip of garden that each house had on either side of the path leading up to the doorways, mostly crocus in lavender-blue and gold. Many householders were touching up the paint on the carvings that rioted over the little houses as well, making them bright for Ostara with proud defiance. The northern foe might be at the doorstep, their sons and daughters and brothers out with the First Levy, but he wasn't going to stop anyone from showing their best for the Lord and Lady!

Rudi waved at friends as they went by. You didn't ride inside the walls without good reason, since anything from a chicken to a toddler might dart mindlessly under the hooves, even now with Dun Juniper a lot less busy than usual; nearly a hundred people had gone with the levy, and there was a subdued, waiting feel to the rest, even as they went about the day's work. He could hear a ritual going on in the covenstead, even though it was still only a few hours past noon, and feel the pulse of power in the air as folk called on the Mighty Ones to aid their kin.

"Just going out for some exercise," Aoife called up to the guards on the gate-tower; Uncle Dennis was in charge there today, one of the older folk filling in with so many of the youngest and strongest gone.

"Well, that should be OK," he said, leaning on his great ax. "Be careful, though. We don't have as many scouts out as usual. Don't go past the lookout station."

The tunnel through the gatehouse was dark; that made Rudi blink as they came through into sunlight once more.

Dun Juniper faced southward, and lay at the midpoint of a sloping ledge that ran east and west on the mountainside, an island of rolling meadow amid the steep forests; it was half a mile wide here in the middle, and tapered in either direction to make a rough lens shape. The little plateau that held the dun gave him a view of it, the rolling green and the occasional warm brown of plowed earth, the fences and hedges and the white dots of sheep, the red-coated white-faced cattle, then the tips of the fir trees downslope, and the hills in the blue distance beyond. You couldn't see the valley below that held Dun Fairfax, or the road leading out westward into the Willamette. North and east peaks floated white and perfect against the dusky blue of the sky; it was full of birds as the spring migration got under way, great white pelicans, ducks, geese, snow swans . . . and then a burst of panic sent wings in every direction as a bald eagle wheeled above.

The day was mild for March—just warm enough to sweat if you were working yourself hard, just on the cool side of comfortable if you were standing still. The sky was canyons of blue and white as they halted on the small paved square outside the gate, broken, fluffy white shapes hanging like cloud castles in the infinite blue over the low green mountains southward. The first camas were out in the meadows, small blue eyes blinking at him from among the fresh green, and the first tiny white blossoms of the hawthorn on the young hedges; the cool, sweet scent was in the spring air, along with new grass and the intense fir sap of the stirring trees in the woods around. Rudi waved back at the gate guards, and called out another greeting to some clansfolk planting gladiolas and dahlias in the flower-gardens down at the base of the plateau. More were pruning and grafting in the orchards that would soon froth in pink and white billows.

They mounted and walked their horses down the slope to the level, then cantered eastward; Epona whickered, and a stallion paced along beside them behind a board fence for a while. Cattle and sheep in the next paddock raised incurious heads for an instant, then went back to cropping at the fresh grass. They drew rein at the eastern head of the benchland meadow, by the pool and waterfall. The graveled, graded dirt road stretched west behind them the full mile of open country; ahead of them it turned sharply right—southward—running down through the woods with the flow of Artemis Creek. That was the main wagon road to Dun Fairfax, turning in a U to head west again on the lower level, and out into the Willamette Valley proper.

Liath and Aoife were singing as they rode. He recognized the tune, a hymn to the Goddess in Her Aspect as the Lady of the Blossom-time:

> *"Laydies bring your flowers fair*
> *Fresh as the morning dew—*
> *Virgin white and through the night*
> *I will make sweet love to you.*
> *The petals soon grow soft and fall*
> *Upon which we may rest*
> *With gentle sigh, I'll softly lie*
> *My head upon your breast—"*

The four of them drew rein where the road entered the streamside trees, then turned to face the sun sinking ahead of them.

> *"And dreams like many wondrous flowers*
> *Will blossom from our sleep;*
> *With steady arm, from any harm*
> *My lady I will keep!*
> *Through soft spring days*
> *And summer's haze—"*

People were working in the gardens to their left, an acre for each household and everyone taking turns on the extra Chief's Fifth, mostly plowing and disking in rotted manure and last year's old mulch and compost and fermented waste from the sewage pits, turning the soil to a smooth, even brown surface ready for planting. Others were marking beds with string and stakes, and getting in the first cold-season vegetables: peas, lettuce, chard, onions and cabbage. Tomorrow was a school day; he might help with the gardens after class. It was fun, getting your hands into the dirt and making things grow. Up by the waterfall others spread sawdust and wood chips from the sawmill around the berry bushes.

But today ... Rudi could feel the mare's great muscles quivering between his legs, and she tossed her head, begging for the run. Nobody was ahead of them right now on the long white ribbon of road—

"Go!" he cried, and leaned forward, tightening the grip of his thighs.

The horse exploded into motion beneath him, launching herself forward off her haunches and leaving the mounts of the other three behind as if their hooves had been sunk in concrete. The clansfolk working in the gardens laughed as he went past, Epona's great legs throwing gravel head-high. He laughed himself as his bonnet flew off and his red-gold hair streamed out behind him in the cool spring wind, fluttering like the edge of his plaid. Behind him the song cut off as the others followed.

I don't want to get too far ahead, he thought. *This isn't any sort of real work for Epona, either.*

He turned left—all he had to do was think about it and shift a little, and Epona swerved and then they were airborne as she cleared the roadside ditch and fence. Rudi shouted in delight, and then the horse touched down and pivoted to the right in the same motion, seeming to land lightly as dandelion fluff but scoring the thick turf and sending a spatter of it flying leftward. Mathilda and the two warriors kept to the road, galloping up on his right as horse and boy thundered across the meadow in a scatter of sheep and took the next hedge in another soaring leap, landing without breaking stride.

Matti grinned at him across the rushing distance, hunched forward on her cob—and that stolid gelding looked as if it was starting to enjoy itself too. They passed the Dun again with faint cheers ringing from the gate-towers. Now the two children had drawn ahead, Epona's sheer speed as she took one hedge after another and the girl's lighter seat on her gelding leaving Liath and Aoife trailing; the women had their wargear on too, of course, adding thirty pounds or better to their riding weight. Ulf and Fenra were between the guards and the children, dashing at their best pace and sparing a little breath for a bark now and then. A big lean dog—or a wolf—could keep up with a horse in a short sprint, if not longer.

The meadows narrowed around them as they thundered westward, trees drawing in on either side and the ground getting steeper. They went past the tannery with its smelly vats and the bark-mill, where an ox walked in a circle pulling a great, toothed wheel that crushed tanbark from hemlocks; soap was made there too, an equally stinky trade. Now Dun Juniper was tiny in the distance, walls bright as the afternoon sun tinted the stucco that coated the walls. Epona cleared a last hedge, but Mathilda's cob was ahead of them—even Epona couldn't travel as fast jumping fences as the other horse could gallop down a nice straight road. The roadway didn't end, not right away; it went on through the forest for a couple of miles to the lookout station at the westernmost tip of this ridge of hill, where it gave a wonderful view over the valley below. That had been just a foot trail in the old days, but since then it had been widened and leveled to take carts.

"Catch me if you can!" she taunted, and vanished under the trees.

Rudi grinned and followed, ducking his head reflexively as the first of the branches flashed by overhead, even though it was far too high to hit him. There were big Douglas firs on either side, and Garry oak, silver fir, and hemlocks. They kept the undergrowth down, save for some thickets of berry bushes, so he could see the hoof-churned surface of the dirt track as it twisted this way and that ahead, and the ruts of the oxcart that took supplies out to the lookout station. He was gaining on Mathilda; the girl was very nearly as good a rider as he was and a bit lighter, but Epona wasn't just faster, she was more surefooted and confident on the narrow, winding path, and he leaned into the turns as effortlessly as the mare made them. The trees flashing by made the speed even more fun than it had been in the open meadow; glimpses through the forest like a world of green-brown pillars with sunlight filtered through the canopy into a soft translucent glow, but touched by beams of fire where there were breaks in the roof of boughs. The air was full of the deep, cool scent of fir sap and moist earth, the first yellow blossoms of twinberry catching the light and the green tips of the new ferns pushing up through last year's litter. They'd made more than a mile since they entered the woods, and soon they'd come out together on the little clearing there at the end; there they could lead the horses back and forth to cool them, and give them a drink from the spring.

Then something pricked at him. *Matti's stopped,* he thought, feeling an interior sensation like an ear cocking. Epona's hooves made a muffled drumbeat in the cathedral silence, and the two warriors were coming up fast behind him, but . . . *I can't hear her horse at all.*

"Whoa," he said, and shifted his weight back in the light saddle. "We don't want to run into her."

Epona slowed as they approached the next twist in the road, but the dogs belted on past, tongues lolling out of their smiling jaws. There was a huge black walnut there, planted by his mother's great-uncle all those years ago and with a spreading crown a hundred feet high, just leafing out now for the new year; it had rolled its nuts downhill through lifetimes, and there was a teardrop of smaller trees and then saplings down the slope. A little shrine to Herne stood near its man-thick trunk.

An explosion of birds went up from the huge hardwood's branches as he turned the corner, and Ulf and Fenra were barking furiously. Then they fell silent—not before he heard one of the dogs give a howling whine of pain, and he heard Mathilda's voice shouting protest.

"Wait—" he began, alarmed now, and tried to halt the horse.

It was too late. Around the tree he had just time enough to see Mathilda sitting her horse, white-faced and shaking with armed strangers in mottled green-brown clothes about her, before a rope snapped up in front of the mare's feet. Even Epona couldn't stop *that* quickly, but she managed to leap it, with a hopping crow-jump nothing like her usual grace. Rudi lost a stirrup, and then a branch hit him painfully in the chest just as Epona hopped again, half in protest and half to get her feet back under her.

He felt himself toppling, knew he couldn't recover in time, and kicked his other foot out of the stirrup as he came off, tucking himself into a ball as he flew, landing loose and rolling. His brooch burst; his plaid came loose and wrapped itself around his legs, and his bow flipped him onto his face. Something rapped him painfully as he slid to a stop in the wet, loose leaves and fir needles, knocking the wind out of him. He smelled blood as he landed, the thick copper-iron scent of it heavy and rank like butchering-time, when a carcass was hung up to drain into the oatmeal-filled tubs below.

And as he fell, a crossbow bolt whined through the space he'd occupied an instant before, hammering into the hard, dense wood of the walnut with a sharp crisp *tock!* sound.

Just beyond him, behind a bush, Fenra lay dead with a great slash in her neck and the red still ebbing out of it, her lips curled back from her fangs in a last snarl. The shaggy leaf-strewn shape beyond with the stiff plastic flight feathers of a crossbow bolt showing against its flank must be Ulf. Epona reared and bugled as she stood over him, milling her forefeet in the air like steel war-hammers, her nostrils flaring as she took in the scents of death. And men in camouflage clothing were running towards them. One stopped and bent to span his crossbow so that he could reload; others were raising theirs.

"Epona!" he shouted, trying to make his will into a dart, the way his mother had taught him. "Home, Epona. *Home! Go home!*"

The horse came down and turned in the same motion, bounding forward with that astonishing jackrabbit leap she had, going from a standstill to a gallop in less time than it took to draw a breath. Four of the men shot at her; three missed, and one bolt scored across her withers just as she turned the corner and vanished back eastward on the road to Dun Juniper. Hands grabbed at his hair. Rudi drew his dirk and slashed back and up. The keen edge hit flesh; he could feel it part under the steel, and a man swore: "Jesus, the little bastard cut me!"

Christians, Rudi thought, rolling erect and kicking his feet free of his loosened plaid. He felt calm somehow, and everything was very slow, like swimming underwater in the pool by the mill. More closed in on him, grown men, with hoods and masks of the same mottled cloth as their jackets and pants. The others laughed at the man clutching a slashed arm, with blood leaking from between his fingers. *Not bandits. From the Protectorate.*

"Watch out, the little fuck's quick as a snake!" the wounded man growled; he was thickset and bearlike, with a fringe of reddish hair over hazel eyes.

"Don't you hurt him!" Mathilda screamed, and a woman's voice answered:

"Take him alive if you can."

"Aoife! Liath! *Danger!*" he shouted—once, and darted a thrust at a slim olive-skinned man advancing with his arms spread wide to grab.

The man-at-arms grunted as the point took him in the belly, but there was mail under the jacket, and the hand that closed on his wrist was quick and troll-strong, twisting the knife out of his grasp. Rudi kicked—neatly, the way he'd been taught— but his toe hit a box protector and produced only a pained grunt, not a scream. Then a hard hand clouted him on the side of the head, and everything went gray and remote as he slid to the ground, not quite unconscious but not connected to the world. A pad of cloth went over his mouth, fastened with a strip of priceless duct tape, and another twist pinned his wrists in front of him.

"Gutsy little prick," someone muttered. Then a woman's voice: "Joris! Enguerrand! Two horses coming!"

Aoife and Liath came around the corner; they'd slowed back a little way as they saw Epona dashing by riderless, but they were galloping now, screaming war cries. Liath was two horse lengths ahead, with her battle spear held overarm; she threw it just before three crossbow bolts hit her mount in the chest. The heavy stabbing weapon wasn't designed to be used that way, but the range was short, and it had the momentum of a galloping horse behind it as well as the strength of her arm.

A dark-skinned man jerked his left arm up diagonally across his breast, as if he was used to having a knight's long kite-shaped shield on it. The solid length of ashwood and metal struck him in the chest, the twelve-inch steel head punching in with an ugly dull, wet thudding *smack* sound, through cloth and mail, flesh and bone. He flew back and landed, kicking, blood spraying red from his mouth and nose but already dead. The young woman's horse fell in the next instant, screaming itself. That gave her just time enough to slide her feet out of the stirrups, hitting and rolling in a tumble of spilled arrows; her bowstring parted too as the six-foot yew stave slung diagonally across her back caught violently on a root with a strong, unmusical *snap*. Her horse came down with its neck outstretched, and the greenstick sound of its neck breaking cut the huge scream of bewildered terror off with the abruptness of a knife slicing a taut rope.

Aoife managed to get her horse to jump before it ran into the rope, but the rest of the raiders were too close for her to use her bow, and the animal was crow-hopping in near panic. She drew her sword instead, her left hand stripping the buckler off the sheath, slugged her mount's head around until it pointed directly at Rudi and the man standing over him, and booted the horse into motion. The man dodged aside, not quite quickly enough, and drew his own blade; there was a flash and a rasp of steel, and he staggered back with his hands clapped to his face as one of his comrades closed in on the mounted warrior. Liath had shaken off her fall in seconds and was on her feet as well, fighting the other two men left, a skirling crash of steel on steel and desperate gasps of effort as she backed and they tried to get behind her.

"Oh, by the saints!" the woman's voice he'd heard before snapped. "Will you clowns just *kill* them? Do I have to do *everything* myself?"

Rudi felt as if his eyes weren't under his control; as if he was watching everything on *teevee,* like the old stories, small and distant and not quite real. Even his feelings seemed distant. All that was left was facts. The woman who'd spoken stepped into view; she was dressed like the men, with her sword slung across her back, and she held a crossbow—an odd-looking one, like the black skeleton of the weapon he was used to, and with a telescopic sight mounted on it.

She shot once, and Aoife's horse stopped in the middle of a

bugling neigh, with the dark fletchings of the crossbow bolt
standing right behind one ear. The Mackenzie warrior managed to kick her feet free and land standing as the horse collapsed like a puppet with cut strings, but the northerner stood
unconcerned, turning a crank handle built into the crossbow
and slipping another silvery bolt into it, then aiming with
quick grace.

Tung!

The bolt took Liath squarely in the back, punching through
the brigandine and the spine beneath. She collapsed backward beneath the arc of a sword's blade that would have
taken off half her face, landing limp and wide-eyed. Blood
bubbled out of her mouth when she tried to scream.

"Go watch the pathway," her killer said, and set the crossbow down, drawing her sword instead, and a long knife with a
basket hilt in her left hand, smiling faintly. "All of you! Shoot
anyone who comes down it, but be *quiet*."

And as she saw Liath fall, Aoife gave a high, wailing screech
and charged the woman who'd shot her friend. The Protectorate fighter met her with sword held high and knife low, and
then they were whirling in a rage of flickering steel, cut and
thrust with the lengths of razor-edged metal sparking in the
forest gloom as they met and clashed and sparked. Aoife's
face was bone white, her eyes gone dark as the pupils ex-
panded to swallow the iris, and her teeth showed in a rictus-
grin of frenzy.

"Morrigú!" she screamed, transported and possessed, face
twisted into a Gorgon mask. *"Morrigú!"*

The Black-Winged One *was* with her. Aoife wouldn't have
been assigned to guard him if she wasn't good, but now sword
and buckler moved with a speed and power beyond anything
she'd shown before. The woman from the Protectorate gave
ground smoothly before the frenzied attack, moving with a
fluid dancer's grace that reminded Rudi of something—

Astrid, he realized, his thoughts still muzzy and slow and
distant. *She moves like Aunt Astrid.*

Fine swordswoman that she was, Aoife couldn't have
stood for more than a few moments before Astrid Larsson,
Hiril Dúnedain. The Crow Goddess gave her strength and

speed to drive the stranger back for a dozen paces. Then a root caught at her foot, the winter-softened moss on it coming loose beneath the hobnails, leaving streaks of raw white sapwood amid the black. The stranger struck like sudden summer lightning, as if she'd known and planned for the misstep. The long knife in her left hand blocked Aoife's shortsword and locked at the guard; she ducked her shoulder into a blow with the buckler aimed at shattering her jaw, and stabbed downward neatly with the sharp point of her sword. It sliced into the clanswoman's inner thigh below the edge of her brigandine, through the wool of the kilt and deep into the flesh. She twisted it, withdrew and cut backhand with the knife at Aoife's neck in the same motion, scoring her savagely just above the mail collar, below the angle of the jaw.

Aoife staggered forward two more paces and collapsed; the blood flowed with a bright arterial pumping that showed the wounds were mortal.

"Joris, Ivo, get the horses, all of them!" the victor snapped, and men dashed off. "Ruffin, can you ride?"

The man whose arm Rudi had cut looked up, his teeth clenched on a bandage he was tightening around his forearm. The slash had bled spectacularly, but the canvas sleeve of his jacket had taken most of what force Rudi could put into the blow, and the wound wasn't serious. He nodded, making an inarticulate grunt, then managing:

" 's not deep. Just bleeding like a stuck hog."

The woman nodded back, and stepped over to the man whose slashed face bore the mark of Aoife's sword. He was on the ground, one eye sliced open and blood leaking between the palms he had pressed to the side of his face.

"You *can't* ride, Enguerrand," she said. "Do you want to be left for the kilties, or—" And she showed him the sword.

He started to shake his head, gave an awful bubbling moan, and then tilted his head back and to one side. One hand scrabbled in the dirt, and he brought a clod to his lips; Rudi recognized the rite, a symbol of his desire to receive communion and his unworthiness to do so.

"God witness it's his wish and none of mine," the woman

said formally, looking at her men; there were three left on their feet, two holding leading-reins with four horses on each.

"You're free of blood-guilt, Rutherton," the man she'd called Joris said formally; his mask was down and revealed a pointed yellow beard and heavy-lidded blue eyes. "Any one of us would ask the same, or do it if they were commander."

The others nodded. She set the point of the sword behind the crippled man's ear and pushed with a hard lunge of arm and shoulder; the man's body flexed once in a galvanic shudder and went limp. A flap of cheek peeled back when his hand fell away, showing a grin red and white. Then the woman stood and turned and looked at Rudi. Her eyes were gray, pale and cold as glass.

Mathilda was off her horse and in front of Rudi in a single scrambling rush. "No!" she said shrilly, spreading her arms. "You can't hurt him, Tiphaine! We're *anamchara*! Blood-brothers. I'll have right of vengeance against anyone who hurts him, all my life! I'm gonna be Protector someday and I'll remember!"

Tiphaine Rutherton seemed to sense the men behind her looking at each other in doubt—that was a credible threat to anyone who knew how stubborn Mathilda could be—and made an exasperated sound between her teeth. Before she could move, Mathilda's knife was out, and she pressed it to her own throat—hard enough that a trickle of red blood started down the white skin as she swallowed convulsively.

"If you hurt him, I'll *kill* myself! I swear it by God and the Virgin, and then you'll have to explain to Mom and Dad and His Holiness how come I'm dead and in Hell for suicide!" Mathilda said with desperate earnestness. "Not just now! If you hurt him later, I'll do it!"

Rutherton stopped as if she'd run into a stone wall; she stared into the girl's eyes for an instant, saw a bright focus of intent.

"Princess, I'm not planning on hurting him," she said gently. "My orders from your mother are to take him alive if possible. But to do that I have to restrain him, because now we have to run for our lives and we can't have him slowing us down. You understand?"

Mathilda swallowed, nodded and brought the knife down. Tiphaine turned her head.

"Well, what are you all waiting for, the kilties to arrive? Ivo, get the brat over a horse." To Mathilda: "This is just to keep him quiet, Princess. I won't hurt him now; on my honor as a warrior of the Association."

Something stung Rudi in the cheek of one buttock as hands heaved him over a saddle and lashed him to it with leather thongs. His head felt as if it were spinning down a whirlpool, with the world upside-down. He saw Aoife twitch as she tried to crawl; the blond woman who'd killed her bent for a moment, grabbing her by the collar of her brigandine and dragging her closer to Liath's body. Then everything contracted to a point of light and went out.

CHAPTER ELEVEN

Waldo Hills, Willamette Valley, Oregon
March 5th, 2008/Change Year 9

Lord Piotr Stavarov lowered his binoculars and scowled. "Are those scouts back yet?" he asked.

"Yes, my lord," Sir Ernaldo Machado said. "They report no enemy presence on the right. There are light screening forces in the woods to the left, although not all the scouts are back from that area yet. The glider couldn't see any of them except *those*."

He pointed to the band that blocked the road ahead. Stavarov gritted his teeth; they were excellent teeth, white and even, in a handsome, regular young snub-nosed, high-cheeked face. He knew he was young for this post . . . but the Stavarovs and their followers had backed Norman Arminger in his initial grab for power in Portland, less than ten days after the Change. He'd been sixteen then, and he could remember his father's relief and excitement that *someone* offered a way out. And now he was out from under the thumb of that scar-faced lout Renfrew.

Though, to be fair, at least he isn't as much of a pussy as most of those Society retreads.

He raised the field glasses. The Protectorate force was halted in column on the road, blocks of bicycle-mounted spearmen and crossbowmen and supply wagons, the two hundred infantry sitting motionless on their cycles, flanked by two mounted columns with fifty knights and men-at-arms each.

The pennants on their lances snapped in the morning breeze, and the same wind poked trickles of grateful cool through the mail of his hauberk and the padded gambeson beneath.

There aren't enough of them to hold us, he thought, looking at the Mackenzie force.

There were a hundred of them, barely enough of them to block the road between the hills on either side; fifty with spears or polearms—what the kilties called Lochaber axes, broad arm-long slashing blades that tapered to a point and had a hook on the reverse. Swung two-handed, the six-foot weapons could cut right through mail just as well as a glaive or halberd; best to remember that. Another fifty of their archers to the west of that, thrown forward along the edge of the low scrub-grown hills that had been pasture once and were head-high brushwood and thorn now. It was a good position, but they didn't have the numbers to stop his men, and if they broke his lancers would hunt them like game. Odd, you'd usually expect a lot more longbows in a Mackenzie formation, from what the briefing papers said. . . .

And under the banner, there was a figure in plate armor enameled green, not the brigandine and kilt the Mackenzies usually wore. Piotr's lips skinned back from his teeth.

The Lord Protector has a serious hard-on for Sir Nigel Loring after the way he betrayed him last year. It won't do me or the family any harm at all at court, if I bring him the Englishman's head. Maybe another fief? There's good wheatland out by Pendleton, or perhaps around here after the war . . .

"Nothing much on the left?" he said, swinging his glasses eastward.

The hills there were higher and steeper than the low, rolling ground on the westward side of the road, the crests better than a hundred and fifty feet above him. The rising face on their north slope was also heavily wooded with oaks and alders, Douglas fir and western hemlocks, all big trees planted long before the Change. The edge where the patch of forest met the abandoned fields was thick with saplings and bramble and thorn and Oregon grape. It was like a wall along the edge of the forest, and he couldn't see far into the depths beneath the big trees. Presumably there was a lot less undergrowth in their shade; farther out towards him the open ground was covered with nothing more than green grass knee-high on a horse, kept free of brushwood by a fire last summer. Good open ground where his troops could use their superior discipline and formation.

I wish they'd put some of their bare-ass miniskirt militia there, he thought. *Still, I can't expect them to be* that *stupid.*

"Nothing on the left as yet, my lord. As I said, not all the scouts have returned from that direction."

"Probably still sniffing around the road on the other side," Piotr said. "Let's get going. All three columns are supposed to be over the Santiam by nightfall. Speed is why we're traveling in separate bodies."

A hesitation. "My lord, shouldn't we wait for the Grand Constable and his escort to get back?"

Piotr felt himself flush, hot blood darkening his skin from the mail collar of his coif upward. "Count Odell is in overall command, but I'm in charge of this column!" he snapped. "Do you dispute that, Sir Ernaldo?"

"No, my lord," he said dutifully. "We can make them scatter from beyond bowshot, if we set up a couple of the catapults."

Piotr shook his head. "That would delay the march for hours. We should be able to reach the Santiam today, that's the objective."

"My lord, their archers are good. And a solid line of spearmen and halberdiers is no joke. We only outnumber them by three to one on this field, and we'll be the ones attacking. It will cost us."

Piotr made an impatient gesture. "Yes, yes. But there aren't enough of the rabble to hold us up, and we can afford the losses more than they. Spearmen are easy enough to replace."

"Still, we could work men over the hills to either side. Then they'd either have to withdraw or be surrounded."

Piotr considered, then shook his head. "We'll have to fight them sooner or later anyway. They're obviously here to delay us while their militia gets mobilized. I won't risk a destrier's legs on them, though. Send in the foot. Spearmen on the left, centered on the roadway. Crossbows on the right; they should be able to drive off half their number of bowmen. Lancers to hold themselves ready for pursuit."

Piotr smiled at the thought. Once they turned their backs on mounted lancers, foot soldiers were so much meat to be shishkebabbed. Some of them might get away if they ran up into the forested hills, but most would probably just panic and try to escape and bolt down the road leading southward. His knights and their *menie* of men-at-arms would spear them from the saddle as if they were wild boar. He reached back to pull the padded weight of his mail coif over his head, fastening the lower part across his chin, then snapped his fingers. His squire rode forward to be ready with helm and shield and lance.

Juniper Mackenzie hugged the tree and peered around its trunk; the dark furrowed bark of the Douglas fir was rough under her free hand. The branches were thick with blunt, thin-stalked needles an inch long, green and whitish on the underside. Twigs of the same breed had been thrust through the loops that made her war cloak shaggy, turning her into a part of the forest; the strong resin smell of the sap was heavy in her nostrils, and it made sticky spots on her gloves. More needles obscured her vision when she leveled the binoculars, for the branch she stood on was fifty feet up on the pillar-shaped trunk. The column of Protectorate troops shifted as she watched, the spearmen and crossbowmen dismounting from their cycles and quick-stepping forward, spreading out from a thick marching column to a four-deep line as they moved. The black-and-scarlet banner of the Lidless Eye swayed from the crossbar as the line came on down the road to her left, edging out into the fields to overlap the knot of Mackenzies waiting where the road ran between the two hills. That would put them in a broad, shallow V, this forest on the east, the western flank low hills covered in thick scrub you couldn't move through without hacking a pathway.

Her stomach knotted. Those were her friends and neighbors and clansfolk waiting on the road to lure the Protector's men forward. And leading them was Nigel Loring. It made sense—he had his suit of plate armor, and he was an experienced commander—but she still didn't like any of it.

On the other side of the tree, Sam Aylward was watching as well. "Taking the bait," he said quietly, his deep, slow voice calm. "At least the first bite of it. Impatient bugger, 'ooever's in charge—good thing Eilir and Astrid drew Renfrew off. Now things get lively."

That was a curiously antiseptic way of talking about people dying, but every trade had its jargon. *And it's a business I'm in, like it or not,* she reminded herself.

"I'd better get down and help things along," Aylward said stolidly. "Remember, Lady—only if they send in the lancers. Otherwise, we all just sod off on our bicycles."

"Yes, teacher," Juniper said, and gave the older man a smile. Then more seriously: "Merry meet, and merry part—"

"And merry meet again," he replied, giving her a thumbs-up.

Then he reached out for the rope that was fastened to a branch above their heads, took an expert half hitch around his blocky armored torso and slid swiftly downward, landing as lightly as a man stepping out of his own home. Even knowing who was where, she was a little surprised when three figures rose and followed him, trotting silently between the great trees. That was reassuring. If *she* couldn't see them, it was unlikely their foemen could.

She looked back out over the open field. The lancers were in a single block a hundred strong now, waiting, a flashing ripple above their heads as the honed steel moved and caught the sun. The Protectorate foot soldiers double-timed forward.

The spearmen broke into a trot as they approached, their booted feet hitting the broken asphalt in a uniform pounding thump that Nigel Loring could feel through the soles of his steel shoes, their mail coats jingling and clashing as the skirts swirled around their legs. The enemy crossbowmen were fanning out west of the road; they and the archers would be occupied with each other. This would be edged metal at arm's length. Not everyone had the eyesight or inclination to make a good archer, even among Mackenzies.

"Haro!" the enemy shouted. *"Haro! Portland! Molalla!* Haro!"

They came with their big kite-shaped shields up under the eyes that glared from either side of the helmet nasal bars, the front rank holding their spears underarm, the second and third raised in an overarm stabbing grip, the ones behind slanting theirs upward; they'd add weight to the attack with their shields pressed against the backs of the men in front.

"Ready!" Nigel called to the men around him.

It was mostly men, in the front rank, you needed a fair bit of weight and heft to swing a Lochaber ax, or the war-hammers or broadaxes some of the others carried. He swung his visor down with the edge of his shield, and the day dark-ened to a single slit of light through the bucketlike steel dome of his sallet.

"On the mark . . . *now!"*

They surged forward with a shriek, whirling their huge polearms up to the ready position. Nigel strode forward with them, his own shield up and his longsword held over his right shoulder with the hilt forward and the point back. Others fol-lowed behind them with spears ready to stab over their shoul-ders or around them. It was best not to let the enemy charge strike home while you stood still.

Closer, closer, oiled mail and black shields and whetted iron reaching for his life—

A spearpoint flashed towards his eyes. Sir Nigel Loring caught the ugly glint of sunlight on honed steel as it drove at the narrow slit of his visor and ducked his head; the twelve-inch blade scored a groove across the smooth enameled metal of his sallet helm, a painful thumping blow even with the steel and padding, but then the dangerous point was past. He snarled behind the face-covering combination of visor and bevoir and cut over the top of his shield, aiming at the man's neck. The spearman's eyes went wide with alarm, and he raised his own shield and ducked, slapping sideways with the shaft of his spear. The ashwood bounced off the side of Nigel's helmet, staggering him; his own sword struck wood and metal, not vulnerable flesh. Then the hook on the reverse of one of the Lochaber axes snagged the enemy's shield and yanked him forward. He came with it, attached by his left arm in the loops and by the leather *guige* attached to the shield that ran over one shoulder like a bandolier. A spearpoint eeled past Nigel and stabbed the Protectorate soldier in the face, not a killing blow but enough to break teeth and bone and make him stagger back, shrieking.

Nigel recovered, catching a spearpoint on his shield and then throwing the man behind it back by tucking his shoulder into the curve of it and pushing with all his weight. An ax flashed past him and broke a man's shoulder; he stabbed at another's face and gashed open a cheek. He panted to draw air into lungs that seemed stiff and dry and reluctant to move. The clamor around him was enormous, a white-noise cataract of screams and shouts, trampling, weapons beating dully on shields and with a harsh scrap-metal clangor on the steel bucklers of the Mackenzies, and now and then the dull thudding of edged metal ramming home in meat and bone.

He slid forward, hooked his heater-shaped shield inside a spearman's bigger kite-shaped one and heaved it aside with a twisting wrench of body and shoulder and arm. The man's eyes went wide with fear as he was dragged off-balance, and the spear in his right hand was far too long to strike at close quarters like this. The Englishman's longsword punched up under the Protectorate soldier's chin; the man convulsed as the long point rammed through his mouth and brainpan. Nigel grimaced as he yanked it free and bowled the man over, sending him backward to disrupt the others. Three more spearheads probed for him; he caught one on his shield, but the other two glanced off his breastplate and the fauld that protected his right thigh. The suit of plate wasn't invulnerable, but it gave him a terrible advantage.

The triple impact staggered him back; a spearman who tried to pursue lost the top right quarter of his shield to a two-handed swing from a Lochaber ax that sliced it the way a knife would a hard-boiled egg, and ducked back cursing.

And here we are, back where we started, he thought.

The noise of combat died down for an instant, as warriors stood and panted and glared at each other in one of those odd little momentary truces that broke out spontaneously in this kind of fighting; perhaps it was because nobody could keep up the effort needed for hand-to-hand combat for long without rest. Wounded on both sides crawled back behind the front lines, or hobbled or were dragged or carried by their comrades. Dead men lay sprawled, their blood making the asphalt slick underfoot. Nigel Loring controlled his breathing with an effort, dragging air down into the bottom of his lungs, holding it for an instant until they'd had a chance to get all the oxygen out of it. He didn't let himself bend over and wheeze—that was less efficient, and besides, it showed weakness. He'd been in his early forties when the Change occurred, and he was fifty-three now; most of the men facing him were two decades younger or more. No matter how fit you kept yourself, a little endurance drained away every year.

But age and treachery beat youth and strength, he told himself, snatching a mouthful of water from a canteen someone was passing around. *Until they don't, at least.*

He could hear officers and noncoms among the Protectorate spearmen shouting at them to get back at it, see them rearranging their lines and occasionally shoving men into place, or holding a spearshaft horizontally and straightening a line by pushing it against men's backs. That was another difference from war before the Change. Then battlefields had been empty, lonely places swept by fire. You were alone, or with a small knot of your comrades; usually the fallen didn't see the man who killed them, and you rarely had more than a fleeting glimpse of the target.

Now when you fought you did it shoulder-to-shoulder with your comrades, under your leaders' eyes, and close enough to see who you were killing—with spear and sword, close enough to look him in the eyes and smell his sweat and the garlic on his breath and see that flare of disbelief when he felt the bite of the steel.

Changes the whole mental dynamic, he thought with professional interest. *Though some things—*

The spearmen had been spitting on their hands and hefting their weapons, while the Mackenzies around him growled or cursed and tightened their grips on their own polearms. Then they froze, their heads turning to the east, Nigel's right and their left. Eyes went wide in shock, and the next yells were alarm and dismay, not war shouts.

—stay the same. Surprise, for instance, is a wonderful thing if you're not on the receiving end. Bless you, my fiancée!

Piotr Stavarov could hear his men shouting *Haro! Haro, Portland!* as they walked towards the Mackenzies and their green horn-and-moons banner; and cries of *Molalla!* as well—most of the levy for this central column came from that barony.

This won't be too difficult. The Bearkiller A-listers are real fighters, but these kilties are just peasants in fancy dress.

The spearmen were in a compact block facing their Mackenzie equivalents; as he watched their weapons came down with a uniform snap and the big shields came up, the men crouching slightly. The rear ranks brought their own up, to present an overlapping surface like a snake's scales. To their right the crossbowmen spread out, their weapons spanned and ready . . .

He heard Sir Ernaldo take a sharp breath as the fifty Mackenzie archers on the far right stood and raised their bows. He gave the man a sharp glance, but the flat, narrow-eyed olive face was impassive.

"That's long range," Piotr said. "Just a little under three hundred yards, I'd say."

"About that, my lord," Ernaldo said.

The front rank of his crossbowmen stopped and knelt just then; the second rank stood behind them. Both leveled their weapons just as the kilted warriors loosed their arrows. Faint and far he could hear the rushing sleet sound of the shafts, and then the deeper *tunnggg* sound of the crossbows firing back. The arrowheads twinkled as they paused at the top of their arc and plunged downward. Longbowmen threw up their arms and collapsed as the short, heavy bolts thrown by the spring-steel bows struck—and a few got up again, their brigandines proof against glancing hits at extreme range. More of those struck stayed down, still or screaming and thrashing. Half a second later the first arrow-fall hit his men, slowing the rhythm of their reloading—you had to drop the front of the crossbow to the ground, put your foot in the stirrup bolted to the forestock, and fix the crank's hook to the string and its mount over the butt before you could spin the handle and pull the heavy draw back to catch in the trigger mechanism.

Three more sleeting ripples fell on the crossbowmen before they were ready to fire again; they took their losses stolidly, closed ranks and kept shooting while the spearmen tramped forward. The archers had to keep their aim on the force that could hurt them from a distance, leaving no spare shafts to slow the advance to contact of the spearmen.

"Yes," Piotr murmured. "Excellent. Most excellent."

"My lord!" Ernaldo said sharply, grabbing at his armored arm and pointing.

Piotr bit back a curse as his head pivoted left; you had little peripheral vision with your helmet and mail coif on. More archers were appearing from the woods to the left of the road, seeming to spring from nowhere. One minute a fringe of brush and saplings stood still and empty; the next it writhed and sprouted armed Mackenzies, along with birds and a deer fleeing the sudden movement. His heart lurched, and then steadied as he studied the saw-toothed line the kilted warriors made.

"How many? A hundred? That many could have fooled the scouts; they're good at camouflage, from all I hear."

"Yes, my lord; about a hundred. Probably ninety-nine, they use a nine-man squad. Shall I sound the retreat? Our foot are going to be in range soon and the numbers are nearly equal now. We don't have any missile infantry on that side of the action, either. They can take the spearmen in defilade."

Piotr stared at him incredulously. "Retreat from a force smaller than our own? Knights and men-at-arms of the Association retreat from half-trained peons? And retreat when better than a third of them are *women*? Of course not! They think they can shoot at the spearmen in safety . . . but I have more than enough lancers to overrun them. Sound the advance."

The knight sighed and crossed himself, and spoke to the trumpeter. Piotr grinned at the scene bisected by the nasal bar of his helmet.

The kilties got overconfident, he thought. *I have them pinned here out in the open, and without protection they're easy meat for a charge. Father will be pleased—and more pleased that the credit goes to the Stavarovs of Barony Chehalis, not to my lord Renfrew, Count of Odell.*

Juniper Mackenzie gripped the rope between locked boots and in her gloved hands and stepped off the branch of the tree, letting Earth pull her homeward. The downward swoop took seconds, leaving her palms tingling-warm beneath the leather when she landed. Cynthia Carson was steadying the rope and waited tensely for the word; her face was a Gorgon mask of black and gold and scarlet behind the gauze mask of the war cloak, painted with the wolf-head emblem of her totem. Most of the younger Clan warriors painted their faces before a fight these days, despite Sam's grumbles that it reminded him too much of football hooligans back home. . . .

"They're moving," Juniper said grimly. "Pass the word to be ready."

"We're ready, Lady of the Clan," Cynthia Carson. "Ready and eager."

She looked it; Cynthia was a tall, fair woman of twenty-eight who'd lost father and brother to the Protector's men in skirmish and raid over the years since the Change, and her blue eyes were as cold and grim as any wolf's. She followed Juniper forward, with the signaler and banner-bearer. All around them the First Levy were rising and shedding their war cloaks, taking their bows in their hands but waiting on one knee until the signal came. Juniper pressed forward to the edge of the woods, using her own bow to press brush aside, ignoring the body of the Protectorate scout who lay with his horse, both bristling with feathered shafts.

There they are . . .

A hundred lancers were a terrifying sight, and they looked a lot more imposing from ground level than from fifty feet up. Big men on big horses, steel and tossing plumes and blazons and the twinkling sharp-honed menace of the lanceheads above the colorful flutter of pennants. The long block of horsemen walked out from the roadway and aimed itself at the hundred bowman who'd come out of the woods to lure them. Then the curled brass trumpets screamed and a long ripple went through the men-at-arms as they lifted the butts of their lances free of the scabbards and brought them to rest on the toes of their right boots, slanting slightly forward. In the same instant the horses took their first pace, stepping high, heads tossing beneath the spiked steel chamfrons. The big kite-shaped shields came to the front as the riders pulled on the leather *guige* straps that hung around their necks and slid their left arms into the loops.

All the shields carried the Lidless Eye; most also had their own or their liege-lords' blazons quartered with it, the heraldry of knight and baron and their vassals and paid men. There was an arrogant splendor to the sight, one that roused hate and grudging respect at the same time. There was no fear in those young men, even though they knew they might be going to the Dread Lord in the next handful of minutes. They'd been told they were the lords of human kind, and they believed it.

Well, like them I might be heading for the Summerlands today, she told herself. *And I've got less to worry about when I set to discussing my deeds with the Guides. Wait. Breathe in, breathe out. Ground and center, ground and center.*

Even across double bowshot the beginnings of a trot from four hundred hooves could be felt through the earth, a thuttering through the soles of her feet. The lancers would try to hit a hand gallop just at extreme bowshot, to get them through the killing ground as fast as possible. Against a hundred archers, it would work. Against eight hundred . . .

She filled her lungs and then shouted, her singer's voice filling the tense, waiting stillness of the woods: "At them, Mackenzies!"

With the word she dashed forward, the banner-bearer and signaler beside her. The Horns-and-Moon flag of the Clan went up, a breeze from the south streaming the green-and-silver silk out ahead of her, and the horn made its dunting *huuuu-huuuu-huuuu*. Seven hundred archers followed her, sprinting forward into their three-deep harrow formation, a staggered row that left each a clear shot to the front. As they halted a shaft went to the cord of every bow, and every cord was drawn to the ear. Behind them the bagpipers set up their catamount screeching, and the Lambeg drums sounded with a *boom-boom-boom* that rumbled like thunder through the trees.

The lancers were at full gallop now, but their line checked and wavered as they saw the trap sprung. Beside her she could hear Cynthia chanting under her breath.

> *"We are the point—we are the edge—*
> *We are the wolves that Hecate fed!"*

And the words ran up and down the line, louder and louder:

> *"We are the point—we are the edge—*
> *We are the wolves that Hecate fed!"*

"On! On!" Piotr shouted, and thumped the trumpeter riding beside him with the flat of his shield to get the man's attention. They were at the point of a blunt wedge now, centered on the flag. "On! *Charge!*"

The trumpet sounded, without even a preliminary blat or squeak despite the ghastly surprise ahead. The lancers booted their horses back into a full gallop after that moment's involuntary check, realizing from years in the saddle that no matter how deadly the peril ahead was, stopping would be worse.

You *couldn't* stop a charging destrier quickly.

Doubly so with another man-at-arms galloping boot-to-boot on either side and another right behind you; there was just too much mass and momentum involved. Trying to do a full-stop in a tight formation of a hundred lances was asking for a disaster of collisions and fallen mounts and men crushed under ton-weights of rolling barded horse. It would take the better part of a hundred yards to halt the formation safely, and more time to turn around without blocking and fouling each other; at best they'd be stalled for a full minute under the deadly steel-and-cedarwood hail of the arrows. If they could just cover that two hundred yards ahead, the lightly armed archers would be helpless before their ironclad violence at close range. Piotr braced his feet in the stirrups and brought his shield up, covering the whole left side of his body between neck and knee; his lance jutted out over the chamfron spike that pounded up and down with the destrier's speed. Clods of earth flew head-high as the steel-shod hooves tore open the damp sod, the pennants fluttered with a snapping crackle, and a great shout went up:

"*Haro!*"

The air whistled—

> "*We are the point—we are the edge—*
> *We are the wolves that Hecate fed!*"

The foremost knight passed the split wand planted at precisely two hundred and fifty yards—planted with the inner white side towards the woods and the dark, concealing bark towards the enemy. Up and down the line the bow-captains' voices broke into the chant, and it turned into a wordless shrieking snarl of fury as they shouted: "Let the gray geese fly! Wholly together—*loose!*"

Juniper let the string roll off the three gloved drawing fingers of her right hand. Eight hundred bowstrings struck the smooth hard leather of the bracers in a simultaneous crackle like some monstrous whip falling on rock. Over it rose the high, keening whistle of eight hundred shafts as they rose at a forty-five degree angle into the air, paused for an instant, then turned and plunged downward nearly as fast as they'd left the bows. Her hand was by her ear as she released; it went back to the quiver and snatched out a shaft, her movements smooth and economical with long practice. Even so several of the First Levy were ahead of her; sixteen hundred more of the bodkin-pointed lengths of cedar were in the air before the first struck, and more followed at a rate of two hundred each second. It would take the Protector's men-at-arms less than a minute to cross the beaten ground between them and the Mackenzie archers, but in that time ten *thousand* arrows would be aimed at one hundred men and horses.

She let her eyes blur a little out of focus then; you didn't need to see every detail when you were shooting at a massed target. The screams were bad enough, and the horses more pitiable than the men, for they were brought unwilling to the field of war without understanding why their flesh must be torn and pierced.

"Heads up!" Cynthia shouted in her ear.

A lancer had broken through the hideous tangle of thrashing horses and dying men. An arrow dangled from the nostril of his horse, and it was wild with terror, running blind as only a frightened horse could do. Unfortunately it was running right at *her*.

The bannerman and the horn-caller threw themselves aside with a yell. Juniper dropped flat under the point of the lance, rolling frantically; one hoof landed close enough to take a sliver of skin from the tip of her nose, and another struck her in the stomach as she threw herself across the grass. The metal plates of her brigandine and the padding of the arming doublet beneath kept it from rupturing organs or splintering bone, but the shock was like being hit in the gut by a swinging battering ram, and all the breath came out of her in a single agonized *whoosh*.

She lay paralyzed, struggling to draw in another breath. Cynthia Carson had been behind her; she spun aside from the lance-point and smashed the boss of her buckler into the horse's injured nose with dreadful precision. The same motion brought her around again and she plunged twelve inches of her shortsword into the horse's belly just behind the saddle at the junction of body and haunch, where no bone protected the body cavity. The animal screamed like a woman in childbirth, stunningly loud even on a battlefield. It went over with a crash of metal, landing on the knight's shield-side leg; he screamed himself, at the pain and as Cynthia launched herself snarling over the horse's body and onto his, red blade raised to kill.

Juniper forced her lungs to work, drawing in a shaky, shallow first breath, and then another. The spike of pain in her stomach was almost welcome, after the first numbness. She blinked her eyes clear, and saw that the remnants of the men-at-arms were in full retreat, some on foot, more falling with shafts in their backs as she watched. The arrowstorm ceased as the last of them moved out of range; the spearmen had retreated in a solid phalanx, covered by their overlapping shields. Here and there along the Mackenzie line at the edge of the forest a scrimmage rippled where a lancer had reached the Clan's position. Dozens swarmed each one under, working together like wolves pulling down an elk. From the rest came a cry directed at the Protector's men, high and mocking and shrill.

Juniper wheezed and forced herself to her knees, groping for her bow and then leaning on it as she came to her feet. A clanking sounded as Nigel Loring ran up, moving as lightly as a man in running gear despite the steel on his back, his mild eyes blinking anxiously, his face red and streaming with sweat under the raised visor.

"Are you all right, my dear?" he asked.

Juniper nodded. "Just . . . winded . . ." she managed to gasp.

"You're wounded!" he said.

A knot of men followed him, the broad blades of the Lochaber axes glistening-wet and slinging sprays of red drops as they dipped and jostled above the heads of the running warriors. She wiped her face and looked in surprise at the blood on her palm; more dripped from her nose onto her upper lip, hot and salt and tasting of copper and iron.

"Just a scratch," she said. "We'd better—"

She looked around for her signaler. Sam Aylward came trotting up, mounted and leading their horses. She caught his eye.

"Sound the *retreat*," she called.

The boy with the ox-horn trumpet put it to his lips and blew, a droning and snarling combination of rising and falling notes. The Mackenzies turned in their tracks and trotted away, eeling back through the dense brush and into the woods, scrambling upward; their bicycles were on the other side of the ridge. Juniper gratefully accepted Nigel's helpful lift into the saddle.

"Now let's see what they do next," she said.

Nigel Loring nodded, smiling. The warmth of his regard melted a little of the cold control she must keep; it was good to feel his straightforward happiness at seeing her whole, and to know her own matched it.

"It's a judgment on them," he said.

"Judgment, Nigel?" Juniper asked, neck-reining her horse about.

"A judgment for their choice in historical models," Nigel went on, waving northward across the grassy field. "When a man establishes a military force, and then decides to base it not just on the medieval nobility, but on the medieval *French* nobility . . . well, really, now . . ."

Unwillingly, Juniper's mouth quirked. Aylward's laughter sounded like sword on shield as they spurred their mounts into motion.

Conrad Renfrew's horse was panting beneath him like a great bellows between his knees as he reined in; he'd ridden it hard and fast up the road, only to arrive when the battle was over. Gray-faced with pain, Lord Piotr lay propped against a saddle while a surgeon worked on the arrow that transfixed his sword-side shoulder. The wound was a simple in-and-out with a narrow bodkin point, though serious enough; it bled when the shaft was withdrawn, but with none of the arterial pumping that told of death, and from the way he worked his hand it hadn't even crippled him by cutting tendons or nerves.

Unfortunately, Renfrew thought, grimly silent for a moment as the man bit back a shriek as the disinfectant was poured in.

Then he dismounted and knelt beside a man far more gravely wounded. There was a froth of blood on Sir Ernaldo's lips as he gave the Protector's commander an account.

When he stood again, his experienced eyes confirmed what the dying man had said. There was a fringe of bodies along the road and up to the point where it ran between the two hills, but the infantry had come off fairly lightly—no more than a score of dead, and twice that seriously injured. It was the great mass of dead horseflesh and armored bodies lying like a windrow across the meadow to the west of the road that made him breathe quick and hard, panting like his horse as soldiers and laborers dragged men free, laying out the dead and bringing the wounded back on stretchers to where the doctors worked beside the supply wagons.

Spearmen and crossbowmen could be recruited easily enough, there were always more volunteers from the ranks of the tenant farmers than they could use. You could train a spearman in a few months, if he had guts and strong arms; it took only a little more to turn out a decent crossbowman. Skilled men-at-arms took *years,* and their mounts almost as long, years of effort and sweat and expense . . .

He walked to his horse and hung the serrated mace thonged from his wrist on his saddlebow, to put temptation beyond reach. Then he looked down at Lord Piotr Stavarov and ground out: "You fool. You cretin. You complete fuckup. You shit-for-brains. You—"

"My lord!" The young nobleman struggled to his feet, ignoring the clucking of the medic. "My lord Count, you cannot address me so!"

"You . . . no, shit has some use. You're worthless even as fertilizer!"

The bystanders were backing away; the Grand Constable of the Association had a reputation for icy control, and his flushed face and snarling voice were shocking.

"My lord," Stavarov said, drawing himself up. "I . . . I admit we've suffered heavy losses, but we can inform the Lord Protector that we did drive the enemy from the field. What would you have me do?"

Renfrew struck with the leather-covered palm of his hand, not his ironclad fist, but the blow still sent Piotr spinning to the ground; the doctor cried out in alarm for his patient as fresh blood broke through the bandage.

"Give me back my knights!" the Grand Constable roared. "That's what I'd *have you do,* you Mafiya moron! *Give me back my knights!*"

CHAPTER TWELVE

Near West Salem, Willamette Valley, Oregon
March 5th, 2008/Change Year 9

"Hell, I didn't like cities even before the Change. Always made me feel cramped," Mike Havel said, reining in his horse and flinging up his clenched right fist for *halt*. "Now they give me the willies," he went on.

The Bearkiller column clattered to a stop, without the bunching or collisions you might expect from over a thousand tight-packed humans on horseback and on bicycles and driving wagons. A few horses snorted, and one bugled in protest, but the only voices raised were a few sharp commands. There was a massed scuffing as the infantry squeezed their brakes and each put a foot down to bring themselves to a halt. Most of them were red-faced and puffing; cycling in armor was a little less strenuous than marching, and a *lot* faster, but that didn't make it easy. The majority of the bicycles had solid rubber on their wheel rims, built up of strips salvaged from car and truck tires, which made for a rougher ride.

Havel squinted eastward, where the sun was just over the Cascades on the farthest edge of sight. It was going to be a bright day with scattered white clouds, mild and cool and damp with yesterday's drizzle—the sort of day you could have anytime but high summer here.

What did the Sioux call it? "A good day to die"? Hell with that, but it's a good day to fight, if you have to.

"Graveyards give me the willies too," Signe Larsson replied grimly, looking south and then east.

They were just outside the brush and incipient forest that covered the wasteland that had been West Salem; wind soughed through spiky brush and tall grass, through fir needles and leaves just beginning to bud out. There was a little noise from the troops behind, bike wheels and hobnailed feet and steel horseshoes clopping on pavement or crunching in gravel, the voice of a noncom here and there blistering someone's ear about a loose strap, the flutter of a pennon crackling in the wind from the north. Below that was a deep silence, where the *gruck-gruck* of ravens was the loudest sound—they always seemed to know when a fight was in the offing, and a flock of them was gliding down from the hills.

To his left the old Salemtown Golf Course had hugged the northern edge of Wallace Road. The river was about a mile eastward, hidden from here by scrub and feral orchards and wet grassland that had once been fields. To his right were rolling hills, upscale horse farms and more orchard and woodlot before the Change; he had a lookout on Chapman Hill, the highest ground nearby at a little over four hundred feet. Beyond that were the old suburbs proper, where the bigger pre-Change trees towered over scrub and saplings where they hadn't been killed out by the fires, and an occasional chimney or snag of wall reared out of a green jungle. The treacherous net of bramble, vine, car-wrecks, twisted metal, scattered brick and glass shards made it nowhere he'd take troops willingly, but if he had to retreat the narrow cleared zone along the railroad tracks would do nicely. A few taller buildings still stood by the river, showing black trails of scorch-mark above the empty windows.

More and taller ones reared on the eastern shore, where the bulk of the old city had lain; three spans crossed over, a railroad bridge on the north and two road crossings just a little south. The Mackenzies and Bearkillers had spent considerable effort last autumn, clearing the piers of wrecked cars and logs and accumulated rubbish that were acting like giant beaver-dams and threatening to bring the bridges down. All that might be wasted effort now . . .

The roads were fairly clear of dead cars and trucks; the state government had managed to get that much done before it collapsed, but tendrils of vine thick as his arm crossed them except on the main thoroughfares, and sprays of brick and rubble stretched out where buildings had collapsed. The bridges were still in use for trade across the valley, and the ruins were mined for metals and useful parts. Nothing human had lived there since the last cannibal bands self-destructed late in the first Change Year, Kilkenny-cat fashion, although he supposed there might be a few lunatics hiding in cellars and living on rats and rabbits. Otherwise there were only occasional bandit gangs looking for hideouts and vantage points. The mass graves didn't stink anymore, not physically, and they'd been on the east side of the river anyway.

It still creeped him out. A world had died here in a convulsion of agony and bewildered terror, and its remains haunted the new one that he and his like were building on the bones.

And will until the last of us dies who remember the Change, he thought. *Then this'll just be ruins, like the Pyramids to me.*

A rider came up the road from the bridges, riding on the graveled verge to spare his horse's hooves at the trot. He was a Bearkiller scout, with an A-lister's mark between his brows but lightly equipped with sword, bow, helmet and a short mail shirt. His name was Bert, and he'd been a Marine before the Change, on leave and visiting family in Idaho.

"The bridges are still clear," he said. "The nearest boats are still two miles downstream and coming on slow; the current's strong."

"Good!" Havel said. "That confirms what the lookouts said. Signe, let them know it's OK for Ken to bring his toys up. Time for my esteemed father-in-law to strut his stuff."

His wife took a convex mirror out of her saddlebag and angled it to the sun, blinking light across the mile to the hilltop south of them. A half minute later the reply came through: *Message relayed* and then *Confirmed. Kenneth Larsson out.*

"Take care, Daddy!" Signe called softly.

"Heads up!" her brother Eric said.

Havel looked up into the sky, following his gauntleted finger. "Well, shit!" he said. "Crap and double-damn and hell. I expected this, but not so soon."

The winged shape of a glider turned in the air a thousand feet above them—it was riding the thermal thrown up by the concrete mass of the ruins, spiraling in a widening gyre. He unlimbered his binoculars; the aircraft was a pre-Change sporting model, shaped like an elongated tadpole with long, slender wings, but those had the Protector's Lidless Eye on them, and a mirror rigged for heliograph signals stood outside the cockpit. That worked as the glider banked, the bright light a flicker of dots and dashes meaningless to him. Signe sighed regretfully—they hadn't broken the Association Air Force's latest field code yet, but there wasn't much doubt what it was telling the boats and barges coming southward on the Willamette. Starting with his numbers and dispositions.

"OK, they'll disembark their force well north of the bridges—north of here," he said.

"You sure?" Signe asked.

"Yeah. They're not going to get them tangled up in the ruins while they disembark. And they probably want a fight here—they can't chase us, they don't have enough bikes with them. They'll try to come ashore close to here and march down River Bend Road till it joins this one, then south on that past the old radio tower. We'll move a little north—see where River Bend makes that elbow and heads more north of east? We'll anchor our line there."

The others nodded. Havel went on: "Eric, you take the lancers and move a little north, couple of hundred yards. See those old gravel pits?"

He pointed with his right hand, a little south of east. "About a mile thataway? The ground's too soft for movement past there so I'll anchor my right on it, and straddle the roadway with the pikes and glaives, more crossbows on the west. But that leaves my far left swinging in the breeze. You cover it, be ready to move forward or back to hold 'em off if we have to pull out through the ruins—we'll use the railway line if we have to do that, and you can either follow or pull out west according to circumstances. We've got good coverage from Chapman Hill so keep your scouts just far enough forward to make theirs stay out of direct sight of the main body."

"Right, bossman," the big blond man said, fastening the cheek-pieces of his crested helmet under his chin.

He nodded to Luanne, and she blew a complex series of notes on the trumpet slung across her mailed torso. The banner-bearer on the other side moved with them as they kneed their horses forward over the roadside ditch with a scramble and surge. The two hundred A-lister cavalry followed by squads and sections and troops, the long lances swaying in their scabbards as they deployed onto an overgrown putting green. Havel nodded gravely to them as they passed. Some were grinning in excitement, with the older ones mostly flatly calm, although few enough here were much over thirty.

I'm starting to feel like an old man at thirty-seven, he thought, smiling like a shark himself as he turned away. *Old enough to know how easy it is to die, at least. Old enough to know how much turns on this fight. It's amazing how much more serious you feel when you've got kids.*

He turned his horse with a shift of balance and leg-pressure; Gustav was feeling the tension himself, and stamped a forefoot as he moved. The foot soldiers were the home-levy of Larsdalen, and the companies from the hamlets and steadings north and east of it in the Eola Hills and along their foot, the Field Force units he'd had time to collect on the way here—every Bearkiller adult would go to war at need, but the Outfit was a bit more selective about who went into an open-field fight. There were just under a thousand, half with polearms—glaives or the two eight-foot staves of a take-down pike—in scabbards riveted to the frames of their bicycles. The rest had crossbows, all of them the new fast-loading type, thank God. A lot of the crossbowmen were actually crossbow-women. Any sturdy farm-girl used to working in the fields could handle one, and the pointy end of the bolts hit just as hard whoever pulled the trigger; the Outfit certainly couldn't afford to leave anyone useful home just because of their plumbing. Pikes and glaives took more mass to use properly, and two-thirds of the troops holding them were men, about the same proportion as the A-list.

Many of the foot soldiers' faces were tight with conscious self-control as they stood in their ranks. The A-listers might do other things in their spare time, but fighting was their life-work. The infantry were precisely the other way 'round. On the other hand . . .

"Right, Bearkillers," he said, rising in the stirrups and throwing his voice to carry. He pointed northeast. "The Protector's men are coming up the river to try and take away our homes and kill our families. We're going to fight them." He grinned. "Any questions?"

A rippling growl went through the formation. Someone shouted *Hakkaa Paalle!* and the rest took it up, a deep, roaring chant, each stamping a foot in time to it, beating their gloved hands on the bucklers slung at their belts. Havel felt himself flush with pride; he'd brought them through the terrible years after the Change, and from starving refugees made a nation of them. Now they trusted him . . . The sound cut off when he raised one gauntleted hand.

"Now get ready and wait for the word," he said into the silence that followed.

For a wonder, he and Signe had a moment to themselves. The troops put their bikes on the kickstands, then got to work—for the pikemen, that meant unslinging their weapons and fitting the two halves together with a snap and rattle as the spring-locks clicked home. A leafless forest sixteen feet high rose as they fell in four-deep along the road, facing north and east, the long steel heads of the pikes above them; the glaives waited to the rear.

"What do you think?" she said.

"Depends on how many of them get off the boats, *alskling,*" he said. "If there's more than we can handle, we pull back sharpish and wait for the rest of our call-up companies to arrive. They'll be gathering fast."

"Why not do that now?" she asked.

"I *really* don't want to lose the bridges," Havel said, nodding in the direction her father had gone. "If Arminger takes those, or breaks them down, he can operate on both sides of the river, and we can't help each other. And if he fortifies the crossing, it's a major blow. Worth risking a battle for, even against odds, as long as it isn't totally impossible."

"Aren't we risking defeat in detail?"

Havel grinned at his wife, who'd been an occasional vegetarian and quasi-pacifist before the Change. "Learning the family business, eh? Nah, there can't be all that many of them, not if they're besieging Mount Angel and pushing into Mackenzie territory at the same time. Armchair generalship, like I said—he likes drawing arrows on maps. He's trying to get fancy and I'm betting he doesn't have enough men to do everything at once."

"We're all betting that," she said gravely, and he nodded. "Do you think it's Arminger in person? Here?"

"Nope," Havel said. "At a guess, it's Stavarov or Renfrew. Hopefully Renfrew."

"But Renfrew's his best commander!" Signe said.

"Exactly," Havel said, licking a forefinger and marking the air with it. "Plus he's the only one Arminger really trusts. This would be a *good* day for the bastard to die."

He'd been keeping an eye on the Chapman Hill lookout. Now a mirror blinked from there; he read the code as easily as he would have print.

"Barges holding back," he said. "Turtle boats coming forward. Now it's up to your dad."

"We should have set the engines on the bridge up earlier," she fretted.

"Nah, that wouldn't work," Havel pointed out. "They would have twigged to that, even if Arminger's troops aren't long on individual initiative. But *if* you don't give them too much time to think and consult higher echelons they'll try to go through with a plan even when things have changed."

They both looked to the river, a mile and better northward. The low, beetling shapes of the armored riverboats were hard to see at first, marked more by the white froth curving away from their bows and sloping forecastles than by the hulls themselves. The sight was a little eerie—you could believe that motors drove them, rather than dozens of dozens of bicycle cranks geared to a propeller shaft. That smooth mechanical motion without sails or oars looked unnatural, in this ninth year of the Change.

"I just hope Daddy can deal with it," Signe said as they slid silently by and headed for the bridges. "He's not a hands-on fighter."

"Yeah, but he's got Pam to look after that," Havel said reassuringly. Then, harshly, as the barges and transports showed at the edge of sight: "Trumpeter! Sound *fall in*!"

Kenneth Larsson shifted under the uncomfortable, unaccustomed weight of the mail hauberk as he sat his horse beside the railcar, waiting for the signal from Chapman Hill. The armor he wore was strictly for protection-just-in-case, like the blade at his side. He'd put a lot of effort into the various weird-looking contraptions on salvaged rail-wheels that followed him, and was metaphorically rubbing his hands at the chance to use them. Right now that wouldn't be too advisable, because the leather and steel cup that covered the stump on his left wrist held a simple hook . . . a very *sharp* hook . . . rather than any of the various tools he found useful in the labs and workshops back at Larsdalen.

The heliograph on the hilltop a mile and a half north blinked at him. He nodded and waved to his own signaler to respond, then looked back along the wagon train—a phrase literally true, since the dozen flatcars were each drawn by four horses. Rail made a smooth surface, and the beasts could pull five or six times as much as they could on even the best roads, and do it faster. Here they pulled flat surfaces that bore a weight of gears and ratchets, frames and tanks and tubing; the hard angular shapes and smooth mathematically precise curves made him nostalgic for the lost world. . . .

"Move out!" he called, waving his hook forward, neck-reining his horse to the side of the railroad tracks and bringing it up to a canter.

His personal guard followed—commanded by his wife Pamela—and the crews of the war-engines rode their charges like grinning, hunched baboons, cheering him as they went by amid a clattering rumble of hooves and whine of steel on steel. The rail line lay along the riverbank farther south, but here it turned inland through the ruins of West Salem, running five or six hundred feet from the water, amid buildings whose smoke-stained windows peered out from shattered glass and rampant vines . . .

"What's chuckle-worthy at this point?" Pamela asked him from his blind side.

She didn't find scorched, overgrown ruins any more cheerful than most people did. These had the further distinction of having been flooded out a couple of times. He turned his head to grin at her; the helmet and nasal bar framed her narrow, beak-nosed, brown-eyed face, and the armor added bulk to her whipcord figure. They'd met in Idaho not long after the death of his first wife and married late that year. A decade—and two kids—later, he still thought he'd gotten the better of the deal. Somehow the throttled fear that made his stomach churn with acid brought that home still more strongly. He kept his voice light as he answered: "I was just thinking that anyone else here would have said it's half a long bowshot to the river, instead of estimating it in feet," he said, waving his right hand across the brush-grown rubble towards the blue-gray water.

"Except possibly me," she said. "I'm an old fart too."

"No, you were the one who belonged to the Association for Hitting Things with Sharp Pointy Things," he pointed out.

"Hey, I wasn't one of those Society get-a-lifes," she said, aggrieved. "I practiced the real thing in ARMA. The Association for Renaissance Martial Arts didn't spend time playing at the kings-queens-damsels-and-minstrels stuff."

"Prancing around with swords . . ." he teased. "Well, it turned out to be a good career move."

She shuddered a little. "And there was the hiking. I owe my *life* to that."

Which was true; it had been that hobby that had taken her from San Diego to Idaho just under ten years ago. Southern California had been the worst of all the death-zones, twenty million people trapped instantly in a desert without even drinking water. Not one in a thousand had escaped; explorers who'd been there since told of drifts of desiccated corpses lining the roads for a hundred miles out into the Mojave, preserved by alkaline sand and savage heat.

Then: "Here we go."

The railway broke out into open fields; the brush had been cleared from hereabouts last year, during the joint project with the Mackenzies to unblock the wreckage and drift-logs piled around the bridges. That had given them a good reason to do maintenance work on the permanent way, as well. The rails turned rightward, east over the water, with the tall ruins of Salem proper ahead of them on the eastern side of the fast-running spring water.

"Here comes the kimchee," Kenneth Larsson said. His assistants looked at him curiously. "Classical reference."

He didn't actually think that the low, beetling shapes moving upriver towards him were modeled on the Korean turtle ships that had turned back a Japanese invasion in the sixteenth century. The similarities were functional; when you covered a boat with a low sloped carapace of metal armor, it had to have a certain shape, just as a wheel had to be round. Evolution and design turned up similarities all the time, which had befuddled generations of the wishfully superstitious before the Change shot scientistic rationalism through the head.

His wife knew that bit of Asian history too. Pam grinned back at him over her shoulder, before turning to oversee the gangs fitting steel shields along the northern edge of the railroad bridge. Ken walked down the line of engines, keeping a critical eye as the crews unfolded and bolted and braced, and tested that the water-lines that carried power to the heavy hydraulic cocking-jacks were securely screwed home. Everything looked ready . . .

"Looks like Arminger's men can't make up their minds," Pam said as the horses were led back westward out of harm's way, riders guiding long leading-reins of the precious beasts.

Either we win and they can come back . . . or we don't, and we won't need horses. They did have some handcars for escape if worst came to worst without time to get the engines clear; those were the fastest way available to travel by land.

Ken grunted and leveled his binoculars, adjusting them

one-handed. The six low, dark shapes of the armored craft *had* slowed, barely keeping station a thousand yards north against the current that curled green waves over their bows. In the center of each was a hexagonal turret with eye-slits on all sides, probably the bridge the craft was conned from. He tried to imagine the sweltering closeness within, lit only by dim lamps, the long rows of bicycle cranks geared to the propeller shafts and the near-naked, sweating human engines . . .

"Watch it!"

A hatch opened on the foremost turtle boat. Something within went *snap,* then *snap-snap-snap* about as fast as a man could click his fingers.

"They're ashore north of here at Rice Rocks," Mike Havel said, looking over his shoulder at the hilltop observation post. "Deploying from the barges; horse, foot and catapults. Let's go. Signaler: *Advance by company columns, at the double.*"

The militia responded to the trumpet-calls, turning left from Brush College Road and going northeast at a pounding trot, seven columns of a hundred and fifty each; the tall grass and brush swayed and went down before their trampling boots as they moved off the roadway. Each had a mounted A-lister officer, usually an older member of the Brotherhood or one some injury had left fit enough for command but no longer quite up to the brutal demands of front-line cavalry combat.

Light war-engines went with them on two-wheeled carts, each pulled by a four-horse team, bouncing and swaying as they trotted along; the sloping shields that fronted them had words painted on them—jocular graffiti, *Hi there!* and *Knock-knock, guess who!, Many Happy Returns!* and *Eat This!*

He turned Gustav eastward, cantering along with the column on the far right. Wet, brushy grassland stretched ahead, bugs springing up where the hooves passed, and occasionally a bird. A mile to the north he could just see the first little dots that were the enemy scouts meeting his light cavalry. As he watched, arrows flew between the scattered riders, and there were little flickers of pale spring sunshine off steel as the swords came out. He glanced west, and saw Eric and the bulk of the A-listers waiting ready just this side of Glen Creek, their lances a leafless forest above their heads. East, and the ground ran out in sloughs with the rank, green look of bog, patches of reeds among the tall grass and dead trees killed by the post-Change floods. The blue eyes of old, flooded gravel pits blocked the way, and beyond that the ground was even worse.

North, angling gradually east towards the Willamette, stretched the old River Bend Road, its thin pavement buckled and pitted by ten years of weather and several high floods that had left drifts of silt across it for grass and brush to root in. He spoke to the easternmost column's commander: "Captain Dinsel, get your people set up. Shuffle east until your boots start sinking in. You're the far anchor of the line; don't let them get around you. Refuse the flank if you have to."

Her face split in a grin. "They're not likely to get any closer to the river than this, Lord Bear. Not unless they can walk on liquid mud. Another ten yards and it's too thin to plow and too thick to drink. This is a *good* position."

"Keep an eye on it anyway," he said.

Then he turned back towards the central column, the one advancing up River Bend Road, the pathway the enemy would use. The artillery was following it, sparing horses and wheels as long as possible.

"Sarducci," he said.

The man in charge of the war-engines looked up; he was one of Ken Larsson's buddies, recruited from the Corvallis university faculty where he'd been teaching engineering at the time of the Change, tall with a dark, narrow, big-nosed face and a walrus mustache. Not an A-lister, but keen enough for all that, and with a very useful hobby in Renaissance history. Havel pointed westward to where the lancers waited.

"Put them about there. A little to the left of the cavalry and advance 'em say a hundred yards beyond our stopline. Dig in; they've got to come to us. I want you able to rake their flank."

"Won't we be masking the A-listers there, Lord Bear?" the Tuscan asked.

Havel nodded; not agreeing, but acknowledging it was a fair question. "Nah. They can go in on your right, or stop a flanking attack—and they can support you if the Protector's people get too close. Go for it!"

He followed them westward down the formation, shouting: "Deploy! Deploy into line and halt!"

The columns opened like fans, with only a little cursing and adjustment as the militia infantry shouldered into position. The center was the pikes, a block eighty across and four ranks deep, with two files of glaives behind them. On either side the crossbows spread in a looser double line.

Most of them had fought before . . . *But nothing like this. Nothing on this scale.*

"Captain!" This time to the westernmost end of the line. "Help the artillery dig in. Do it fast, then get back here."

The company commander nodded and turned, barking the order; his unit was crossbows, and they stacked their weapons and broke open their folding entrenching tools, trotting forward to help the artillery crews. With nearly two hundred strong arms, the job went quickly; they laid out semicircular trenches, using the blades of their shovels to cut the turf in rectangular blocks, then set it aside while they piled up the soft, damp earth on the inner side, shovelfuls flying as they labored with panting, grunting intensity. When that was high enough to leave only the business end of the engine behind it exposed they laid the turf back on the surfaces of the mounds and pounded it down with the flat, folded their spades again and trotted back to their own weapons. The twelve engines settled in, each behind a chest-high horseshoe mound, each ten yards from its neighbor, each showing only the top of its metal shield split by the slot for the casting trough, what would have been the muzzle back in the days of guns.

Havel nodded at the beginning of the process and turned back to his own station, in the center where his line crossed the River Bend Road at right angles; he didn't have to hand-hold his people for something elementary like that.

"Big fight," he said cheerfully to Signe; the gallopers and staff here had to see the bossman confident. "Biggest we've had so far." Then, to the trumpeters: "Sound *stand easy*."

The brass throats of the instruments screamed. The block of pikes and glaives in the center let the butts of their polearms rest on the dirt and leaned on them; those with crossbows checked their weapons once again. Light wagons advanced until they were a suitable distance behind the line; ambulances, medics—including Aaron Rothman, despite loudly voiced claims that violence made him queasy and faint—vehicles with bundles of crossbow bolts, ammunition for the artillery, bandages and disinfectants. A little forward of that and just behind the main line was the clump of his headquarters staff; the brown-and-crimson bear's-head banner, mounted messengers, signalers and a block of seventy picked infantry with glaives. The messengers were mostly teenage military apprentices, which was a measure of just how desperately thin they were stretched.

I'd like to have a bigger reserve, he thought; it was amazing the number of things a CO could find to worry about, which was one reason he felt nostalgic about the days the Outfit was smaller, or even the time . . .

Christ Jesus, is it nearly twenty years since I was a corporal in the Gulf? Going on eighteen years, at least. Another world, and probably everyone there's dead, and who cares about the fucking oil now? Nowadays people fight over horses and cows and wheat. And people . . . so that hasn't changed.

He shook his head and went back to wishing he had more troops waiting behind the line to patch holes if—when—the enemy punched through.

But I just don't have enough on hand. This line's nearly a mile long as it is and it's too damned thin for comfort, but the Protector's men will overlap it. On the west, at least. The only good thing about it is that they have to get by me to get at the bridges and support their gunboats . . . they have to go through *me. If they tried to loop around I could punch the A-listers at their flank while they were in column. It'd take days for them to do it safely and by then the rest of my militia would be here for sure.*

Commanding a battle like this was uncomfortably like a knife duel . . . and he'd always despised those, because they guaranteed even the victor got cut up pretty badly.

More signals flickered in from the hilltop to his rear; the Protector's glider went by again, its heliograph stuttering.

And beyond the skirmishing scouts came a long flashing, twinkling ripple across the fields to the north; a ripple of sunlight on thousands of steel points and edges, like summer at the lake when he was a kid, and light flickering off a wave. But this wave was human, an army's worth of men walking shoulder-to-shoulder, riding boot to boot. With it came a hammer of drums, the shriller scream of the long, curled trumpets the Association used, and the endless grumbling, rumbling sound of hooves and booted feet striking the soft earth. Havel leveled his binoculars.

"Well, shit," he muttered to himself, doing a quick count. *Let's see, a yard per man, formation's four ranks deep . . .* "You were right, honey. Two thousand men, or a bit more. That's bad odds. Four, five hundred knights and men-at-arms. That's *real* bad odds. He's got as many lancers on this field as we've got pikemen."

"Told ya, told ya," Signe said, without taking her own eyes from her field glasses. "Did you ever hear of that study they did before the Change, when they found out that only the clinically depressed had a realistic view of the world?"

Havel looked over his left shoulder at the depressingly empty roads from the south and west. The rest of the Bear-killer militia would be on the road to him here . . . which did him very little good right now. Then Signe hissed.

"Look," she said. "Look at the banner in the middle of their line."

Many fluttered there; the Protector's force was moving with its heavy horse in the center, and every tenant-in-chief and baron had his own flag. One drew his eye, on a tall crossbar next to the Lidless Eye, its white background conspicuous in that company.

"Argent, double-headed eagle sable," he said. "No cadet baton. It's Alexi Stavarov."

"Alexi Stavarov, Baron Chehalis, Marchwarden of the North. Even Arminger isn't crazy enough to send little Piotr out with a force that size," Signe said absently, still counting banners and reading their blazons. "I see a lot of his vassals, and some from the other baronies over the Columbia—Pomeroy, Alequa, Vader. More tenants-in-chief and their followings from up in the northwest part of the Valley, the Yamhill country, and the Tualatin valley. None of the Protector's household troops, I suppose they're with Renfrew. It's a baron's army with a baron in charge."

"Refresh my memory," Havel said. "Alexi's the Protector's point man north of the Columbia. He was in command in that last brush with the Free Cities of the Yakima, wasn't he?"

"Yeah," Signe said. "Last year, while Arminger and Renfrew were taking over the Pendleton area. He beat the League's muster in an open-field battle just north of the Horse Heaven Hills, then stalled in front of the walls of Zilla—you know, they're on the edge of that bluff—and spent a fair amount of time devastating the countryside and breaking down the irrigation ditches to soothe his frustrations. That *really* hurt them. The Protector wasn't serious about taking any territory there yet; it was more like a warning to the Yakima League not to push at Walla Walla or Burbank or Richmond while he was busy getting a hold on Pendleton. It'll probably keep them out of *this* fight, though."

"OK, so Alexi's not as hot on the throttle as his kid. Let's see what sort of a general he thinks he is," Havel said.

He'd have to be a pretty piss-poor one to lose a battle where he outnumbers the other side three to two or better, he thought. *He's got a good five, six hundred knights and men-at-arms there, too. I've got a bad feeling about this.*

He looked aside at a sudden deep *tung* sound and a chorus of startled obscenities as a crossbow bolt whistled up from the second rank of the company to his left. The careless militia soldier stood at rigid attention, a red flush gradually filling in the space between her freckles. A noncom's snarl—he was probably a well-to-do tenant farmer or bailiff or craftsman back home—followed the accidental discharge:

"Angie, you dim, thick bitch, what the fuck do you think that is you're holding? It's a fucking crossbow trigger, not a cow's tit or your boyfriend's dick! Do us all a favor and point it up your *own* ass next time, not at Wendy's! Christ crucified, if the Protector's men don't kill you I'll have you digging latrines from now until the last gray hair falls out of your crabcrawling—"

Well, you can tell our original noncoms were Marines like me, Havel thought, suppressing a grin at the corporal's inventive vocabulary.

The glares and mutters of her neighbors, who *were* her neighbors and relations back home in the village, probably hurt just as much; and the knowledge that the reaming was abundantly deserved—the bolt could just as easily have hit someone in the back of the head. Silently, she reloaded: gripping a pivoted lever set into the forestock of her weapon and pumping it six times. There was a ratcheting sound as she did, and the string drew back and the heavy steel bow made from a car's leaf spring bent, until the trigger mechanism engaged with a *click*. Still red-faced, she pressed the quarrel into the groove and stood with the weapon at port arms, point skyward and finger carefully *outside* the trigger guard this time.

That new crossbow is really going to help, and with a little luck it'll be a nasty surprise to the Protector's men. Bless you, esteemed father-in-law.

The cocking mechanism built into the forestock was made from cut-down car jacks salvaged from the trunks of abandoned vehicles and auto-supply stores, and it shortened the reloading time from just over twenty-five seconds to around eight or nine; still not as fast as a good archer, but a lot closer. *And* you didn't have to practice incessantly with a crossbow the way an archer did; you could learn to use it well in a couple of months, and keep it up practicing once a week. Plus this model could be loaded easily lying down . . .

All in all it's a lot better than the Rube Goldberg thing with chains and cranks the Corvallis people keep working at; simple and sturdy is better when it comes to things that get you killed if they break down. On the other hand, better is better too. I think the Protector hasn't pushed his R&D types for an equivalent because he doesn't want a weapon that gives a footman too much of a chance against a lancer. That'll teach him to be such a snob.

"Messenger," he said, giving another close look at how the enemy was advancing. "Polearms rest in place, missile troops on the left swing in about ten degrees."

The youngster galloped off. A few moments later the long

double line of crossbows on the left began to move—those closest to him marching in place, those out at the end of the line double-timing until the whole formation slanted forward a little. It looked as if the enemy were going do it *hey diddle diddle, straight up the middle,* and that would give his people enfilade fire.

The barons' men were closer now, barely a half mile, well within catapult range; the light horse on both sides scurried off to the flanks. Before he could signal Sarducci to begin the curled trumpets screamed again, and the Protectorate's force came to a halt in three well-drilled paces. Silence fell, or what felt like it without the ground-shaking thudding of men and horses moving in mass. He looked over; Sarducci's crews had their catapults cocked and armed, and behind each a pumping apparatus on a wheeled cart with two men on each end of the lever and an armored pipe running to clip under the carriage of the split-trail fieldpiece. Relays were running light horse-carts back to the main supply wagons and piling up extra ammunition—four-foot javelin-arrows, six-pound iron roundshot like smallish cannonballs and larger glass globes full of napalm with gasoline-soaked fuses of twisted cloth wrapped around them.

The artillery chief evidently thought he'd get a chance to do some serious reach-out-and-touch-someone, and he was grinning like a devil Satan had assigned to stoke the furnace holding Arminger's soul. Havel cantered his horse up and down behind the line one last time, checking and finding nothing to quarrel with. As he passed the artillery their commander stood on one of the berms, waving his arms and making taunting gestures at the enemy and singing exuberantly:

> *"Quant' è bella giovinezza*
> *Che si fugge tuttavia!*
> *Chi vuol esse lieto, sia!*
> *Di doman' non c' è certezza."*

Havel grinned at the sound; the war-engine crews were laughing, but with their commander and not at him, which was a good sign. A leader had to show the troops he knew his business, but after that the odd larger-than-life gesture didn't hurt at all.

A glance at his watch when he reined in beside Signe and the banner again . . .

Ten o'clock. This is all taking longer than I expected. OK, they want to wait, we'll wait. This is a delaying action, after all. If I had the rest of our Field Force here, I wouldn't be worried—not at even odds. Of course, that's only about a fifth of their army there, and what I've got here now is half of mine. Where are the other eight thousand men Arminger can field? Are they all over on the east side of the river, taking on Mount Angel and the Mackenzies and my wife's lunatic little sister? Or are they going to send another couple of thousand down between the Eola Hills and the Coast Range, swarm Will Hutton under and bugger us for fair, as Sam would put it? That's what I'd do in his shoes . . .

He still kept an eye on the Chapman Hill lookout post now and then; they could tell him if Stavarov was trying to get fancy, working a force west around his flank through the hills, or if his own reinforcements were in sight. Instead the next move from the Protector's ranks came as a surprise.

"What's *he* doing?" Signe asked.

A knight had spurred out from the block of men-at-arms, his plumed helmet and the forked pennant on his lance fluttering in the wind. He tossed the lance over his head, whirling the eleven-foot weapon like a baton, shouting something not quite understandable at this distance and putting his horse through fancy footwork. His kite-shaped shield was divided into wedges of gold and black with their points meeting in the center, and a purple motorcycle wreathed in flames painted over it.

"Gyronny or and sable, a Harley purpure," Signe said, reading the blazonry.

"At a guess, that guy's folks were gangers, not Society types," Havel said, grinning despite himself. "It has a certain style. I used to *really* like my Harley in high school."

"That's the Wereton family," Signe said in a quelling tone. "Of Laurelwood Manor, up near Chehalem Mountain; they hold it by knight-service from the Barony of Forestgrove.

Lord Harrison Decard's their liege. And Mr. Motorcycle out there is challenging all and sundry to single combat. Stavarov's going to let his hotheads work off some steam. Idiots."

Havel felt his grin spread wider; here was something besides the tangled complexities and haunting fears of high command. . . .

Speaking of gestures . . . and I'm not forty yet, he thought. *Besides which, this* is *a delaying action. Playing at El Cid is delay, all right.*

He ignored Signe's horrified yelp and brought Gustav up in a rear that turned into a gallop as he shot ahead, north down River Bend Road. A roar went up from the assembled Bearkillers, turning into a rhythmic chant from a thousand throats as they punched their weapons in the air:

"Lord Bear! *Lord* Bear! *Lord* Bear!"

A swift glance showed his wife's mouth moving too, but he suspected she wasn't cheering. Her brother would be cursing enviously over there on the right, but he was too well disciplined to try anything on his own.

There's method in my madness, alskling, he thought, and then: *I hope.*

The Protectorate knight drew up, raising his lance and letting the butt rest on the toes of his right boot, and trotted towards the Bearkiller leader. Havel slowed down likewise, turning left off the treacherous surface of the road's broken asphalt. As they drew closer . . .

Aha, he thought, looking at the painfully young face behind the helmet's nasal bar, and the way his eyes went wide as they darted to the snarling bear's head on Havel's helmet. *Thought so. That's a young guy's stunt, and for more reasons than what my charming wife calls testosterone poisoning.*

The man was at least as tall as Havel and broader built even allowing for the effect of the hauberk and gambeson, but his light brown beard was scarce and tufty. The hazel eyes were fearless and delighted; this boy would have been a year shy of ten when the Change happened, and those golden spurs on his boots were a very recent acquisition. The horses halted, mouthing their bits and tossing their heads and making the spikes of their chamfrons glitter, pawing at the turf of knee-high grass and glaring at each other. Wet, dark soil showed where the steel-shod hooves broke through the sod, the rich, meaty green smell blending with horse sweat and leather, the old-locker-and-dirty-socks scent of gambeson padding and the slightly rancid canola oil that glistened on the mail and metal gear of the two warriors. The challenger undid the mouth-covering flap of his mail coif and let it hang free while he spoke.

"You do me great honor by meeting me lance to lance, Lord Bear!" the young knight said, grinning from ear to ear.

"Damn right I do, boy," Havel replied. "But hell, it's a nice day for a spanking and I always did believe in corporal punishment for delinquent youth."

The youngster looked a little affronted and more than a little bewildered. "My lord, I am Sir Jeff Wereton of Laurelwood, by rank a knight, and the son of a knight."

"I'm the son of a hard-rock miner, myself. And your dad was a Hell's Angel," Havel observed dryly.

Wereton nodded proudly. "A band of fearless warriors in an age of city-dwelling cowards!" he said. "Knights of the roads! I remember their great roaring steeds of steel, and everyone fleeing in fear before them—once my father bore me before him on his *Harley,* though I was only a child at the time."

"Well, that's one way to look at it," Havel said, letting his crooked smile show.

Let's not get into the drug-dealing, extortion and such. Nowadays they just collect a third of the crops, and labor-service and heriot fines . . .

"The Angels rallied to the Protector first of all, and stood like solid rock amid chaos."

Yeah, that's the problem with bringing kids up on legends. They really believe *them, no matter how much of a crock of horseshit they are.*

"Two hundred yards suit you, boy?" he drawled, letting his tone say the *get on with it, dickweed* part.

"Yes, my lord," Wereton snapped.

Good, got him mad. That'll make him careless, Havel thought, reining Gustav around. *Lot of testosterone running*

*loose there. Arminger would make him a duke with his own
castle and estates to the horizon if he killed me, but he couldn't
have known it would be me coming out. He's probably even
more over the moon at the thought of the* glory *he'd get if he
beats me in public.*

The Portland Protective Association was a protection
racket, and a rather nasty one. But when the kids asked what
the family did for a living, even your average thug didn't like
having nothing to say but: *Well, son, we're thugs, oppressors,
vicious parasites and members of the Brute Squad in good
standing.*

Without Arminger and his re-creationist cronies and
hangers-on the roughnecks and gangbangers who made up
the rest of his following would have gradually invented an
ethos justifying their rule and stories telling why they were
the bee's knees. But the Society had provided a ready-made
mythos to feed the younger generation. God alone knew
what the *third* generation would be like . . . probably they'd
wait at crossroads to joust all comers with a lady's glove
tucked under their helmets, or make goofy vows to liberate
the Holy Sepulcher and set sail for the walls of Jerusalem
with Crusader crosses on their surcoats.

From what Pam and Ken had told him the whole thing
wasn't more than loosely connected to real medieval
chivalry; say, about the way *Treasure Island* was to real pi-
rates. Mostly it was drawn from stories and make-believe,
starting with the ones Cervantes had laughed his compatri-
ots out of by mocking them in *Don Quixote,* and going on
from there to *Ivanhoe* and *The Cid* and finishing with *Brave-
heart* and Disney's Magic Kingdom. But it worked as a
morale booster just as well for all that. Which was mostly a
plus for the people running the Portland Protective Association, but the downside was that they had to play along with
it themselves, including things like letting this valiant young
idiot play at knight-errantry with real blood and real bones
at stake.

Although . . . he thought, as he turned the big gelding and
reached back to lift the bottom four feet of his eleven-foot
lance out of the tubular scabbard, *at what point does make-*

believe become real? When it's the way you live every day of your life? When you're prepared to die for it?

He reached down and ran his arm through the loops of his shield, lifting it off the hook on his bow-case as he let his knotted reins fall on the saddlebow. Doll-tiny, the figure of Sir Jeff dipped his lance in acknowledgment. Havel did the same with his own, then couched it loosely. Ten feet of tapering ashwood, thick as his wrist at the steel-capped butt, just wide enough to be gripped comfortably in the hand at the balance-point a third of the way up from there, a little over thumb-thick where the socket of the narrow twelve-inch knife head was heat-shrunk onto the wood. The two men's armor differed only in detail, except for the Bearkiller's shield; that was a convex circle about two feet in diameter, rimmed and bossed with metal, and made of a layer of thick leather over stout plywood.

The Protectorate knight's was of similar construction, but much larger, a curved top a yard across tapering to a rounded point four feet below. It covered most of his body now as he brought it up under his eyes and crouched forward, his feet braced in the stirrups.

"Let's go, Gustav," Havel said to his horse, and shifted his weight.

The big gelding tossed his head again and paced forward, building to a trot and then a canter and then a controlled hand gallop; he knew this game as well as his master. Havel kept the lance loose in his gauntleted hand, trained across the horse's head so that it jutted over the spike in the middle of the chamfron's forehead. The figure of the knight grew with sudden, startling speed; he could see the divots flying from under his mount's hooves and the unwavering spike of the lancehead aimed at his throat, the skillfully sloped shield, the high metal-shod saddlebow . . .

Havel's knees clamped home on Gustav's barrel, bringing the last plunging bit of speed out of the great muscles flexing beneath him. His hand clamped as well on the shaft of the lance as he trained it over the horse's head, and his body tensed . . .

And the very last instant his left arm whipped up the shield, sweeping it out. The lighter, more mobile, round Bearkiller shield that could be used as easily as a sword, not a twenty-pound kite-shaped weight that stayed in one place.

Crack-crack!

The curved surface and the artful sideways blow flung the knight's lancehead out of line; the impact was brutal and rammed Havel back against the high cantle of his war-saddle, but not nearly so much so as the strike of his own lance. That punched the gaudily painted kite-shaped shield neatly at its midpoint, and the lancehead pierced the facing and gouged deep into the tough alder-plywood, driven by the huge momentum of a pair of armored horses and armored men. For one stomach-clenching instant Havel thought it would lever him into the air like a fly on the end of a fishing line, but then the ashwood broke across with a gunshot snap.

Sir Jeff slammed back into the cantle of his own saddle and over it, turning a complete somersault in the air and landing flat on his face as Havel galloped by and his own horse went off like a shooting star. The Bearkiller lord reined in as quickly as he could—you couldn't stop a ton of man and horse and metal on a dime—and looked around.

Wereton's conical helmet had burst free from the straps that held it and rolled away, and the mail coif beneath had come off too; the shield-strap looped diagonally across his back still held, hindering him as he rolled over faceup. Mouth and nose and ears dribbled blood and he twitched like a pithed frog, but Havel judged he'd probably recover—though not in time for the rest of this campaigning season. Not with a squashed nose, concussion, whiplash, head-to-toe bruises and probably half a dozen sprung ribs. His body would probably heal faster than his bruised ego, at that.

"Thought so," he panted, spitting to clear his mouth of thick saliva mixed with blood where the shock had cut the inside against his own teeth. "Never jousted with anyone who wasn't using Association gear before, did you, sonny-boy?"

He gestured with the stump of his lance for Sir Jeff's friends or attendants to come and get him; a boy in his early teens galloped out with an older man in servant's clothing, and between them they caught the fallen knight's destrier, levered him over it and headed back for the shelter of the Protectorate army's lines. As the defeated champion returned draped across his saddle a long, low, disconsolate muttering came from there, plus curses and shaken fists. The Bearkiller force roared Havel's name as he cantered down the line, tossing the six-foot stave that was all that remained of his lance in good-natured mockery of the knight's flamboyant gesture before the fight. When he drew in before the A-lister cavalry the cheers grew even louder, and the horses neighed and snorted in protest.

Eric Larsson spoke: Havel couldn't hear it under the pulsing beat of the sound, but he was pretty sure it was *you selfish glory-hound son of a bitch!* shouted in tones of deepest sea green envy.

Havel grinned at his brother-in-law and tossed him the stump of the lance. Eric caught it, then reached behind, pulled his own free of the scabbard and tossed it to his commander in a casual display of strength—it took a lot of muscle to treat one of these barge poles as if it was a garden rake. Havel caught it neatly, hiding the grunt of effort under the smack of leather on wood, and slid it into the tubular socket.

Beside Eric, Luanne rolled her eyes and made a remark of her own; probably *You idiot!* Or *Men! Why does everything have to be a pissing match?*

"Because in this life everything, absolutely everything, is either a challenge or a reward," he said to himself, and turned his horse and cantered back to the Outfit's banner.

"Don't say it," he said, as he reined in and most of the staff crowded around to pound him on the back.

One handed him a canteen of water cut with a little wine that was more like vinegar; he took a mouthful, swilled it around his mouth and winced as it hit the cuts, then drank down a dozen long swallows. Sweat was running down his face in rivulets, and the padding of his mail collar was already chafing a little under his chin, despite the coolness of the day and the silk neckerchief tucked inside it.

"Why shouldn't I say it, when we both know it's true?" Signe snapped. "Dammit, Mike, this business is dangerous enough without—"

"That wasn't showing off," he said, and at her glare added: "All right, it wasn't *just* showing off. I knew whoever it was, it was probably some dick-with-legs first-timer type I could take without breaking a sweat."

"And if it had been Stavarov sending out his best lancer to mousetrap *you*?" she hissed, when they were close enough for the remark to be less than totally public. "You know, I'd like my children to have a living father—and not grow up hiding from the Protector in a cave in California, either!"

I'd have beaten his best lancer, too, Mike didn't say aloud. Instead he went on reasonably: "But he didn't. It was like stealing candy from a baby. We won some time, our troops' peck—ah, tails are up, and the enemy's men are feeling half beaten already. Stavarov must be chewing on the rim of his shield. I wouldn't like to be Sir Jeff when the lord baron gets around to him!"

Signe snorted, but changed the subject. "I wonder how Dad's doing over at the bridges?" she said. "At least he's old enough not to try the Achilles-before-the-walls-of-Troy stuff."

"That's geek to me," Havel replied, grinning like a wolf.

And yeah, I am *feeling pretty pleased with myself,* he added silently. *So it's atavistic. Whoopee-shit.*

Then he looked south again, and worry returned with a rush, like cold water trickling up his spine. That was the problem with losing yourself in action; like booze, the oblivion was temporary and the troubles came right back, often worse than before.

And where are the rest of my troops, goddammit? He tried not to wonder if they'd be enough when they *did* get here.

Snap. Snap. Snap.

Ken Larsson ducked involuntarily as the metal bolts from the war-boat flicked towards him, mere blurred streaks at better than four hundred feet a second. They struck the row of heavy sheet-metal-and-timber shields his crew had rigged along the northern edge of the railway bridge. The sloping surface shed the impact with a tooth-gritting sound halfway between a bang and a squeal; the bolts flickered and tumbled upward, still moving so quickly they were barely visible, leaving an elongated, dimpled dent in the quarter-inch steel.

Ouch, Larsson thought. *Glad I thought of the shields and didn't just rely on the ones on the engines themselves.*

The nearest of the turtle boats was well under a thousand yards away now; they were coming on in a blunt wedge, slowly, no more than walking pace—probably because they'd diverted the power of the pedals to the weapons rather than the propellers. The open hatch snapped down again as he watched, and he turned to one of the engines mounted on the railway cars.

"They're probably too far away for our bolts to penetrate yet," he said. "Let's see how good their sealing is. Number Three, let 'em have it."

The catapult crew nodded, and two of them used a scissors-like clamp to raise a big ceramic sphere into the metal throwing cup. Its coarse clay surface had an oily, glistening sheen to it, and the sharp petroleum stink of the gooey stuff oozing through the thick pottery was pungent enough to carry several yards. Firebombs of this size were kept empty, and filled from steel barrels only a few minutes before action. Ken repressed an impulse to step back; there were fifteen gallons of the stuff in there, and sometimes—not often, but every once in a while—the container shattered when the machine cut loose, with very nasty consequences. If you made the pottery thick enough that that never happened, you cut down on the payload too much and sometimes it didn't break at all when it struck at the other end, if it hit a soft target like dirt or brush.

The aimer sat in a chair behind the sloping shield of the war-engine, peering through a telescopic sight and working traverse and elevation wheels with her hands. The aimer's chair and the throwing-groove and arms rose and turned smoothly, with a sound of oiled metal moving on metal.

"Range five hundred," she said crisply. "Ready—"

One of the crew lit a wad of tow on the end of a stick and touched it to the napalm bomb. Blue-and-yellow flames licked over the surface of the porous clay, and wisps of black smoke began to rise. The rest jumped down, and a hose team stood by.

"Ready!"

"*Shoot!*"

The aimer squeezed a trigger. The machine's throwing arms snapped forward with a hard, flat *brack!* sound and thudded into the rubber-padded stop plates. The clay globe snapped out, trailing more smoke as the wind of its passage fanned the flames. Ken leveled his binoculars eagerly; the shot had the indefinable sweet feeling of a mechanism working perfectly. . . .

Crack!

The sound came sharp and clear despite the distance; a gout of flame enveloped the turtle-boat, the tulip-shaped orange blossom rising from its curved steel deck. A cheer went up from the crews on the railroad bridge. It died to a grumbling, cursing mutter as the war-boat slid forward through the smoke, the fire running down its sloping carapace to burn on the surface of the water, hurried along by water gushing from a valve near the view-slits of the bridge.

Ken tried again to imagine what it had been like inside, in the dim hot sweat-and-oil stench of the interior, the slamming impact making the frame groan, the sudden roaring through the thin plates, the heat and the sharp acrid stink sucked in through the ventilators—and all the while having nothing to see but the back of the man ahead of you, knowing you could burn and drown at the same time at any instant.

Serves 'em right, he thought grimly. *If they want to be safe, let them stay home.*

Which wasn't quite fair—probably most of them had no say in the matter, unless they wanted to face the Lord Protector's men who wore black hoods, or provide the tiger-and-bear-feeding halftime spectacle at the next tournament.

On the other hand, I'm not feeling like being fair right now. Aloud: "Three, Five, Seven—rapid fire, and concentrate on the lead boat! Fry the fascist sons of bitches!"

As a student rebel in the sixties, he'd made Molotov cocktails.

"OK, now we get serious," Havel said, as the Protectorate's host began its advance.

Lessee. Spearmen on the far west wing, call it three hundred of 'em, opposite our A-listers; then crossbows, more spears,

*more crossbows, and so forth, until they end up with spearmen
again on the far east end next to the river. The heavy horse behind the center, but not far enough behind. They'll overlap us
on the west unless we do something. So . . .*

"Signal, *artillery open fire, priority target enemy cavalry,*"
Havel said. It was long range, but when you hit someone, you
hit them where it hurt.

The trumpets called. Seconds later a ripple of *tunngg . . .
tunnggg . . . tunnggg* repeated four times over sounded from
his left as the batteries fired. The basic principles were those
of Roman or Greek ballistae, but the throwing arms of the
catapults were carefully shaped steel forgings rather than
wood, and the power was provided by the suspensions of
eighteen-wheeler trucks, not twisted skeins of ox sinew. The
javelin-sized arrows they threw were visible, but only just—
they traveled at half the speed of a musket ball. The six-
pound spheres of cast iron that followed were almost as
swift.

Havel tracked them with his field glasses. One ball struck
short, bounced and slammed rolling into a file of spearmen.
The first three went down in a whiplash tangle as the high-
velocity iron snapped their legs out from beneath them; then
it bounced high again and came down on an upraised shield.
He couldn't hear the shield's frame and the arm beneath it
crack, but he could imagine it. The screaming mouths were
just open circles through the binoculars, but he could imagine
that as well. Two more struck at waist height; a broken spear
flipped fifteen feet into the air, pinwheeling and flashing sunlight as the edges twirled.

The big darts lofted entirely over the block of infantry—
heads twisted to follow them as they flashed by about ten feet
up. The cavalry formation behind them exploded outward as
four of the heavy javelins came slanting in, punching through
armor as if it were cloth, pinning men to horses and horses to
the ground.

"Good work, Sarducci!" Havel called, and waved at the
man. At the enemy he muttered the names of the engines as
they fired:

"*Hi there,* you bastards! *Knock-knock, guess who!* you sons of bitches! *Eat this!* motherfuckers! And *Many Happy Returns,* Alexi!" he said, pounding his right fist into the palm of his left hand with every greeting.

He got a thumbs up from Sarducci; seconds later the *tunnngg . . . tunnngg . . .* began again. The teams behind the fieldpieces were pumping like madmen, sending water through the armored hoses to the cylinders under the firing grooves—compressed gases didn't work the way they had before the Change, but hydraulics still functioned the way the textbooks said they should. Water filled the cylinders and pushed out the pistons; the piston rods rammed at the steel cables that linked the throwing arms, bending them back against the ton-weights of resistance in the springs until they engaged the trigger mechanisms. The crew chiefs snapped their lanyards to the release levers, and the aimers on seats on the left trail spun the elevation and traverse wheels, while the loaders slapped fresh darts and roundshot home, ready for launching.

Havel turned the field glasses back to the enemy lancers. They were trotting back out of range, some of them shaking their fists at him as they went. He laughed aloud, and Signe gave him a quizzical look.

"I can tell what they're saying," he said. "Something like *no fair throwing things!* And then *why don't you fight like a gentleman, you peasant!*"

His laughter grew louder, and her corn-colored eyebrows rose farther over the sky blue eyes as the troops took it up and it spread down the line, a torrent of jeering mockery directed at the backs of the Protectorate's lancers. He shook his head and went on: "What's *really* funny is that some of them actually *mean* it!"

After a moment she chuckled as well. Then: "Oh-oh," she said. "Here comes *their* artillery."

Havel nodded. "Yup, right on schedule. That's heavy stuff for mobile field use—looks like light siege pieces, really. Six horse teams; six, eight, ten of them all up. Tsk—they should have more and it should be as easy to move as ours. They've certainly got the engineers and the materials. Arminger's a . . . what did the Society people call guys who had a hair up their ass about getting historical details just right instead of mixing and matching?"

"Period Nazi," Signe supplied.

"Yeah, his fixations are getting the better of him again. William the Conqueror of Normandy didn't use field artillery, so Norman the Magnifolent of Portland doesn't like doing it either. Signaler—*cavalry engage enemy engines with firing circle.*"

Off to the west, he saw Eric Larsson nod and wave acknowledgment. Ahead the enemy formation parted to let the heavy throwing engines through, and then the infantry lay down in their formations; which was sensible of Stavarov, though not as sensible as pulling back out of catapult range and waiting for his engines to silence their opposite numbers.

Of course, that would take all day, Havel thought. *And without infantry support . . . well, what a frustrating dilemma for Alexi Stavarov, you Slavo-Sicilian wannabe, you!*

The A-listers were moving, but their lances stayed in the rests, and their shields stayed slung. Instead, two hundred horn-and-sinew recurve bows were pulled from the saddle-scabbards by their left knees, and two hundred hands went over their shoulders for an arrow. The long column of horse-archers moved in a staggered two-deep row, rocking forward from a canter into a gallop. The thunder of hooves built, until it was a drumroll over the half-mile distance. Near as loud came the crashing bark:

"*Hakkaa Paalle!* Hakkaa Paalle!" And from the watching Bearkiller foot: "*Hakkaa Paalle!*"

"This is where it pays off," Havel muttered as he adjusted the focus of his field glasses. "Hack them down!"

Bearkiller A-listers could play armored lancer just as well as the Protectorate's knights . . . but they could also shoot as well as Mackenzies, and do it from a fast-moving horse, twelve times a minute, and actually *hit* what they were aiming at half the time—more, if it was a big target. Six heavy horses pulling a large-ish catapult with a twenty-man crew running beside the team qualified as a very big target indeed, and there were ten of them moving out into the open beyond the Protector's infantry. They'd just begun to turn, swinging the business-ends of their massive weapons towards the Bearkiller fieldpieces, when the charge of the A-listers brought them into range. Havel's cavalry masked the fire of their own catapults now, but they didn't need it.

Eric's scarlet crest showed as he stood in the stirrups and drew his bow to the ear. Havel's fingers tingled in sympathy, and his shoulders remembered the heavy, soft resistance. The arrow flickered out from his bow, covering the two hundred yards in a count of one . . . two . . . three . . .

The first of the draught-horses reared and screamed, immobilizing a team; the catapult's crew killed the thrashing animal with a poleax, cut it loose and dragged the rest of the team into motion again, ducking their heads and holding up shields as they pushed forward. Commendable courage; so was that of the crossbowmen off to their right, who stood and volleyed at the riders. An A-lister fell, and another collapsed limply across the withers of his horse. But arrows were falling in a continuous sleet on the catapults now as the A-listers dashed across their front from right to left, and the infantry right behind them were spearmen; the Bearkiller formation bent back into a moving oval of galloping horses, each horse-archer turning right to come around for another firing pass at the target.

"And Stavarov pulled his cavalry too far back to counter-charge us," Signe said.

Havel noticed that the military apprentices—A-list under-studies—were leaning forward, their ears practically flapping as they heard the leaders talking. Well, they were *supposed* to be learning . . .

"Yeah, it's paper-scissors-rock," he said, making the three gestures with his right hand. "Now, young Piotr, from what the spies say and what Will Hutton did to him last year up by the Crossing Tavern, he would have just barreled straight up the road at us, taking the losses to get stuck in. The catapults couldn't have killed enough to stop them."

"But charging straight in is *all* Piotr ever does," Signe pointed out.

"Even a stopped clock is right twice a day," Havel pointed out. "Whereas Alexi thinks things through . . . yup!"

Trumpets brayed among the Protector's forces. With a deep, uniform shout the block of spearmen rushed forward to shelter the catapults, shields up to form an overlapping shell. Arrows slammed into them, some standing quivering in the metal-faced plywood, *tock-tock-tock*; others punched through, wounding men even through their armor. But behind the shelter the crews of the catapults began to manhandle them around, frantically dragging away dead horses, driving the survivors out, wrestling the heavy steel frames and four-wheel bogies into position by sheer desperate effort.

The Bearkillers' own horns sounded. The A-listers reined around; suddenly they were all galloping *away* from the shield-wall protecting the enemy catapults, turning in the saddle to shoot behind Parthian-style while they were in range. The spearmen kept their shields up; as soon as the cavalry had galloped out of archery distance the Bearkiller fieldpieces started lofting roundshot and javelins over their heads—now at the conveniently massed spearmen protecting the catapults and their crews . . .

Metal smashed into metal. Some of the shot flew trailing smoke, and splashed into carpets of inextinguishable fire when they broke on shields. Men ran screaming when gobbets of the sticky flaming liquid ran under their armor, rolling and clawing at themselves as they burned to death; the rest of the spearmen gave back rapidly, not running but wanting to get out from under. Signe turned her head aside slightly, her lips tightening. She'd toughened up a great deal since the Change, but her husband had walked through the results of cluster-bomb strikes before his nineteenth birthday.

Havel gave a long look and a nod, before he turned his head towards the center of the enemy formation. *OK, our catapults cancel their catapults,* he thought, as bolts and round-shot and fire began to fall around the Protector's machines.

Their crews were struggling to respond, and as he watched, the first ragged volley came back at the weapons that were punishing them so. The Protector's artillerymen could throw heavier weights, but Havel's fieldpieces were protected by the earth berms. All that was to his advantage; shot could break up the infantry and open the way for lancers, and subtracting it from the overall mix favored the Bearkiller defense.

Besides which, when didn't infantry wish the artillery would shoot at each other and leave everyone else alone? Now, what'll Alexi try next?

Around the enemy center files of horsemen were coming forward, walking their mounts through the paths between blocks of infantry. The footmen cheered the knights and men-at-arms, beating spear on shield and fist on buckler, a harsh drumming, booming roar. The horsemen tossed their lances in the air, some of them making their mounts rear and caracole, but that didn't stop them from forming up in a four-deep formation a hundred lances wide. The double-headed eagle and the Lidless Eye came to the front, and the lancers shook their weapons and shouted to see it.

"OK, now Alexi's getting impatient too," he said. "Messenger: to Captain Sarducci. Concentrate on keeping the enemy catapults suppressed. Ignore the lancers unless they go for you, or you've got spare firepower or I command otherwise. Trumpets: *formation stand to,* and *prepare to receive cavalry!*"

The brass instruments screeched. The Bearkiller foot responded as if the notes were playing directly on their nervous systems, the front rank of the missile troops lying down and bringing crossbows to the ready, the second rank kneeling and aiming over their heads. And in the center, the sixteen-foot shafts of the pikes bristled skyward with a massed, grunting *huah!* as they were taken in both hands and raised to present-arms height. Ahead the destriers took a single step forward almost in unison. The riders' lances dipped, the barded horses tossing their heads and the curled trumpets toning and dunting.

Then an officer's voice among the Bearkiller infantry barked: "Pikepoints . . . *down!*"

A quick bristling ripple as the long poles dropped, presenting a row of knife-edged blades four deep.

"Prepare to receive cavalry!"

The front rank went down on one knee, jamming the butts of their pikes into the sod and bracing their left boots against them to make them even steadier, slanting the great spears out into a savage line of steel at precisely chest-high on a horse. The two ranks behind them held theirs with both hands at waist height; the fourth held theirs overarm, head-high. Behind them the two ranks of glaives stood ready. . . .

Havel's head swiveled left and right. *Gonna have to risk it,* he thought unhappily.

"Captain Stevenson," he called to the commander of the block of polearms. "Countermarch your glaives out to either side. Back up the missile troops. I think their men-at-arms are going to overlap our pikes."

The rearmost file of glaives hefted their weapons, faced left and trotted out to stand behind the crossbowmen there. The next did exactly the same, but to the right. Havel could see a few helmets turn and show faces among the pikemen, visibly unhappy at having the backing of those two extra ranks taken away.

"Eyes front, Matthews!" one of the file-closers snarled. "If you want to look at something scary, watch the fucking horses coming at you, you quivering daisy!"

"Steady, Bearkillers, steady," their officer said, his voice commendably calm.

A messenger came galloping up behind the line, drawing up beside the bear's-head banners with a spurt of dirt from under her mount's hooves, teenage face alight with excitement as she saluted.

"Lord Bear! Lord Eric requests permission to hit the enemy horse in the flank as they charge."

"Not this time," Havel said, smiling grimly. *What was it that Israeli general said? "It is better when you have to restrain the noble steed than prod the reluctant mule"?* "The A-listers are to support the artillery and wait for the command."

The Protector's trumpets screamed again, massed, like a chorus of metallic insects worshipping some alien god of war. The horsemen lowered their lances and began to advance at a walk, then a trot, then a canter. The thunder of the hooves grew, shaking the earth beneath their feet, the snap of pennants beneath it, shouted war cries, the glitter of steel and painted shields and plumes. Havel glanced along his lines, saw everything from bored calm to lips gripped tightly between teeth. He swung down from his horse and handed it to an aide, taking a glaive from another.

"Sure look pretty, don't they?" he asked, his voice calm and amused, but pitched to carry. "They'll look even better going away. *Hakkaa Paalle!*"

"*Hakkaa Paalle! Hakkaa Paalle!* Hakkaa Paalle!"

The chant grew until it was a hoarse, crashing screech; the Bearkiller pikemen began to sway ever so slightly as they chanted, faces flushed and lips peeled back over teeth. Havel grinned to himself as he shouted with them. That was the purpose of battle cries; they drove out thought. The same thing happened in the audience at games back before the Change, but this deliberately induced hysteria had a lot more purpose behind it.

Four hundred yards, he estimated. *Three fifty. Three hundred—*

He raised the glaive and caught the trumpeters' eyes: that took a second, lost as they were in the roaring chorus.

CHAPTER THIRTEEN

Sutterdown, Willamette Valley, Oregon
March 5th, 2008/Change Year 9

"Well, there it is, my lords," Conrad Renfrew said.

He accepted a cup of hot coffee from a servant and inhaled the welcome scent that had been a haunting memory for so many years. Coffee was unimaginable luxury, available only to the Protector and a few great nobles even now that a square-rigger from Astoria was on the run to Hawaii.

The command pavilion stood about a mile north of the Mackenzie town called Sutterdown, in open country out of catapult range, with good water from a creek running westward out of the hills. The cloth walls drawn up on the southern side gave the assembled officers a good view; the noise of two thousand troops pitching camp around the great tent came clear, the clink of shovels, hammers driving in pegs, the bawling of livestock and from the other chambers of the command tent the rattle of an abacus and the *ca-ching!* of a manual adding machine. They'd finally managed to duplicate those, and very useful they were—he didn't know how medieval commanders had managed, since most of them probably couldn't have counted past ten without taking off their hose and looking at their feet.

The big table in the center held maps and papers; there was a buffet along one side laden with lunch, and some of the commanders were holding chicken legs or cheeseburgers or roast-beef sandwiches as they looked at the maps, or at their target.

"And here we are," Renfrew went on after a sip of the coffee and a sigh of pleasure. "Anyone got any brilliant ideas?"

Sutterdown was the closest thing the Mackenzies had to a city. Even by CY9 standards it wasn't much, less than two thousand people in normal times; there were a dozen towns in the Association's territory as big or bigger already. The walls were impressive, though, better than thirty feet high and, by report, nearly twenty thick, and the circuit was big enough to hold a lot more people in an emergency. They were studded at hundred-yard intervals with round towers half again as tall topped by conical roofs sheathed in green copper and shaped much like—appropriately—a witch's hat. A four-tower minifort guarded the gates at the quarters; the one on the south gave directly onto a bridge over the Sutter River, and the town as a whole was nearly contained within a U-shaped bend, giving the south and east and west a natural moat. A ditch across the north side completed the protection.

The crenellations along the top of the walls had been covered over the last few days by prefabricated metal-faced hoardings of thick timber, like a continuous wooden shed with the roof sloping out; that protected the fighting platform atop the wall from missiles, and gave an overhang so that the defenders could drop things straight down on anyone climbing a scaling-ladder. Association forts had the same provision; he'd practiced assembling the hoardings during emergency drills at his own Castle Odell, the Renfrew stronghold in the Hood Valley. Evidently the architects here had been reading the same books the Portland engineers studied—*Castle* by Macaulay for starters.

It looked more formidable to the naked eyeball than he'd thought it would be from the reports and sketches, and he was surprised the near anarchy of the Clan Mackenzie had managed to put so much labor into something with a long-term payoff. The bright white stucco on the town wall was different from anything he'd seen before, and so were the odd, curving designs of flowers and leaves painted on them. If you looked at them long enough you started to see faces peering out . . .

It's not altogether *like one of our castles, or one of our towns, though: there's no inner keep,* he thought, freeing his eyes with a wrench. *Though those two hills on the west side of town might serve the purpose . . .*

They were about a hundred feet above the general level of the town, or of the Sutter River that flowed along its southern edge. One of them was topped by some sort of temple or church or whatever the kilties called it, according to the intelligence briefings. He could see a bit of it, a round open structure with Douglas fir trunks smoothed and carved as pillars all around. A drift of smoke came from the center of the conical roof.

Unfortunately the dark-robed Bishop Mateo could see it too, and it had set him off again. Nobody dared interrupt him. "There is the altar of Satan!" he said, pointing; the cleric was a slender brown-skinned man with burning black eyes. "It is a stink in the nostrils of God! You must destroy it!"

There were nods all around the table. "Well, that's exactly what I'm going to try and do, Your Grace," Renfrew said politely.

Does he talk like that all the time? he wondered. Then: *I'm not afraid of Leo's men,* he thought, slightly defensive. *Then again, I'm not anxious to butt heads with them, either.*

He'd been an agnostic before the Change. Now he was an ostentatiously dutiful son of Mother Church, like anyone in the Protectorate's territories who wasn't a complete idiot, since the Lord Protector was too.

Does Norman really mean it? some fraction of his mind wondered. *Or is it just part of the pageantry to him? Or was his mother scared by a copy of* King Arthur and the Round Table *while she was pregnant? Well, I'm not going to kick. I couldn't have put this show together myself.*

A fragment of poetry went through his mind, pseudo-Shakespeare:

> Lay on, MacDuff
> Lay on with the soup, and the Haggis and stuff;
> For though 'tis said you are our foe
> What side my bread's buttered on you bet I know!

Sometimes he wondered how many were trimmers like himself, and how many had come to genuinely believe. More

of the latter than the former, he suspected, and his own un-
belief got sort of shaky sometimes these days. When people
heard the same story all the time and had to act as if they accepted it, most just *did* accept it; maintaining private reservations was too much like hard mental work. And it did help the
Protectorate run smoothly, and would be even more helpful in
another generation, when his children were growing up to in-
herit what he'd built.

*But, oh, how I wish the damned priests would stick to their
churches!*

The bishop fingered the steel crucifix that hung around his
neck; His Holiness Leo disapproved of ostentation, save
where ritual demanded it. Fortunately Mateo's gaze stayed
locked on the Mackenzie settlement. As they watched, something flashed out from one of the towers, trailing smoke. It
landed a quarter mile closer to them, near a knot of patrolling
horsemen, and splashed flame near enough to make the cavalry scatter. When they rallied, it was farther out.

"Sir Richard?" Conrad asked calmly.

Dick Furness had been a combat engineer in the National
Guard before the Change and was in charge of the Association's siege train now; he was forty-two, the only other man in
the tent besides Renfrew to have seen his fourth decade, with
a sharp-nosed face and brown hair and glasses. He shrugged,
making his mail hauberk rustle and clink, and pointed. Another globe of napalm followed the first just as he began to
speak, and then two four-foot bolts like giant arrows. They
went over the cavalry's heads, and made them canter off
again, which was sensible. Those things could go through
three horses in a row . . . lengthwise.

"Well, as you can see, my lord Count, they've got lots of artillery, and it's well protected. Good reloading speed, too—
must have hydraulic reservoirs in the towers. I'd say they
probably bought the whole system from Corvallis, or the
Bearkillers. Probably the Bearkillers, I recognize Ken Larsson's style . . . anyway, the wall's that Gallic construction, a
frame of heavy timbers with rubble and concrete infill, and a
layer of mortared stone on the outside and inside to cover the
ends. Not as good as our ferroconcrete, but nearly."

"Couldn't you burn it?" someone said. "I was reading in one of the Osprey books"—that illustrated series on the history of warfare was important in the Association's military education system—"that the Romans used to burn 'em when they were fighting the Celts."

Good question, the Grand Constable thought. *That's Sir Malcolm, Baron Timmins' son. Have to keep an eye on him. For promotion, he's too young to be angling for my job. Yet.*

The engineer answered: "Sure thing, my lord, if you can figure out a way to make wood burn without oxygen."

Furness spoke more politely than he probably wanted to—he was a mere knight among tenants-in-chief and their sons, and most of the troops under his command were townsmen, although he hoped for ennoblement and a barony himself if this campaign succeeded. There was still a trace of irony in his voice. "I said rubble *and concrete* fill. And they used rebar. You'd have to knock the aggregate open before you could burn the frame. It's pretty good protection against battering, too. The timber lattice makes it more resilient than simple masonry; plus there's an earth berm on the inside. We can't undermine, either; the foundations are below the water table. Good luck on draining that with hand pumps."

Renfrew tapped his fingers on the map, where higher land rose just to the eastward of the town. "Emplacements here?"

Furness shook his head again. "That's extreme range for our engines—even trebuchets, even with the height advantage, my lord Count," he said. "And we'd have to build roads and clear timber to get the heavy stuff up there. Not worth the trouble. When we get the battering pieces here, we'll have to work them in by stages—build bastions for our siege engines, then zigzag approach trenches, then more bastions closer in. Hammer at the walls until we dismount enough of their machines, and then more pounding until we bring down a section and get a breech, and then assault parties with scaling ladders going in from the trenches under cover of the catapults and massed crossbowmen behind earthworks."

"That isn't how the books say they handled siegework the first time 'round," Sir Malcolm observed. "Sounds more like the way they did it with cannon."

Interesting, Renfrew thought. *He didn't stop reading at the end of the pre-gunpowder period the way most people do.*

Furness spread his hands. "Steel-frame engines with truck springs for power and hydraulic cocking systems can throw things *hard,* nearly as hard as black-powder cannon did, they're a *lot* better than that wood-and-sinew crap those dimwits used back in the Middle Ages, and they scale up easier too."

There was a slight bristling, mostly from families who'd been Society before the Change, or ones who'd caught the bug since. *Medieval* was a word to conjure with, these days.

Oblivious, Furness went on: "So's modern design better, if you've got a good engineer; we know more about using mechanical advantage. Ken Larsson *is* good."

"Siege towers?" young Timmins said. "If we can get men on top of the wall, it's all over but the rape and pillage."

"Nope. Their engines'd smash a wheeled siege tower into scrap before it gets to the wall, or burn it; anything that could stand up to the stuff they've got would be too heavy to move. We'd have to knock the wall down anyway to silence them. I'd say use the northern approach; that moat will be a problem, but less so than the whole damned river. The town'll be pretty roughed up by then, I'm afraid."

The commanders looked at each other. The Protectorate hadn't fought anyone before who had defenses this formidable, or skill with war-engines to match their own. It had mostly been improvised earthworks they faced, if it was anything beyond barricades of dead cars and shopping-carts full of rocks.

"That'll cost, working trenches up to the walls and then going right into a breech like that," someone said. "That'll cost *bad.*"

Everyone looked as if they'd sucked on a lemon . . . *Or on vinegar, to stick to things still available.* A nobleman's status depended on how many men he could put into the field. They couldn't just send the infantry in, either—honor meant a lot of the leaders had to *lead,* and from the front; otherwise the men wouldn't press an attack in the face of heavy casualties. Training replacements for lost knights and men-at-arms would be slow and expensive, particularly since the knights' families had a claim on their manors even when the heirs were too young to fight. Not to mention making vassals' allegiance shaky.

Renfrew grunted and looked at Sheriff Bauer, who'd been promoted to second-in-command of the scouting forces; as the Constable had expected, the Protectorate's forces were critically short of light cavalry, and the man seemed to know his work. The easterner shrugged as well.

"Them walled villages of theirs, duns they call 'em, the ones close to here are all empty and scraped bare-assed. A round dozen we checked are empty as an Injun's head."

They all looked at Sutterdown; that probably meant that the inhabitants and their supplies were within the town walls. Or possibly just the ones who could fight, with the others up in the eastern hills. Or possibly a mixture. That meant there could be as many as fifteen hundred of their damned archers in there, as well as the artillery, ready to deluge a storming party with arrows that went through chain mail as if it wasn't there.

Which is why they kept taking risks to delay us on the way south, Renfrew knew. *They had plans for this and they needed time to implement them. Probably those SAS bastards are the ones who set it up. I don't think it's a folk musician's approach to the Art of War, somehow. Damn her and her fucking luck, anyway.*

Then again, all the leaders who'd risen to power since the Change had a reputation for being lucky. If they hadn't been lucky, they wouldn't have been leaders, or alive at all. *Everyone* still around on the eve of CY10 was lucky . . . lucky so far, at least.

"Some of the ones farther south are still being held," Baron Timmins' son said. "They're just villages with an earth bank and log palisade. We could take them one by one without much trouble, burn them out if nothing else. That would hurt them badly. And we could interfere with the spring planting, to demoralize them without hurting the long-term productivity."

Renfrew grunted acknowledgment of the suggestion; it was a good thing for young men to be aggressive, within limits.

"But to do that, Sir Malcolm, we'd have to divide our forces *again*," he said. "And there are still at least eight hundred of the kilties at large, maybe a thousand by now—the ones who, ah, put up such stout resistance to Lord Stavarov before he drove them off."

Everyone nodded gravely, and all of them knew he meant *the ones who beat Piotr's ass like it was a drum*. Publicly slapping Alexi's son around might have been bad politics . . . *but it felt so good!* Still, he'd better be polite now.

"And there are as many again in there," he went on, pointing at the town while he sketched the air over the map with his other hand. "If we left a small screening force here, the enemy bands still at large could attack and catch the screening force between themselves and the garrison of the town. We don't have enough men to circumvallate."

That meant build a double wall around the besieged town; he checked that everyone caught the reference. There was a list of suggested reading, but some of the Association's baronage were what the charitable might call print-impaired.

"If we left a *large* screening force here, then they could follow any *small* force we sent against the duns and overrun them as soon as they were out of supporting range of us here. The duns aren't much as forts but they can't just be taken on the fly. Remember what happened to the dog with the bone who saw his reflection in the water. We can't afford to invite defeat in detail. Two thousand men is the minimum we need to be sure of beating off an attack by the Mackenzie forces not yet accounted for."

"Will the Lord Protector send us more troops?" young Timmins asked. "My lord Count, from what you say we need more men to deal with the enemy here."

"There aren't many to spare, Sir Malcolm," Renfrew said—carefully. "Twenty-five hundred are besieging Mount Angel and the town there."

Everyone nodded soberly. The *town* of Mount Angel was a lot like Sutterdown. The fortified monastery of the same name on its hill above made either look like a boy's toy castle made of pasteboard. Nobody had even suggested doing anything but starving it out; a siege train built in Heaven and twenty thousand men with the Archangel Michael for commander couldn't take it by storm.

"Another thousand are securing our communications all the way back to Molalla"—which the damned Rangers and stray kilties were doing their best to chop into salami—"and two thousand are facing the Bearkillers—and possibly the Corvallans—around West Salem. Another five hundred are screening the area between the Amity Hills and the Coast Range against Bearkiller raiding parties. That leaves very few back home. With essential garrisons—"

Everyone nodded again; stripping the fiefs and castles bare of armed men would invite peasant rebellion, not to mention attack from other enemies like New Deseret or the United States of Boise or the Free Cities of the Yakima League. Nobody much liked the Portland Protective Association, and that emphatically included a lot of its own subjects.

"—that means we have only about two thousand men as a mobile central reserve. If we commit our last reserve in one place and something goes wrong somewhere else, this whole war's fucked. The Lord Protector feels he should reinforce success. Hence, my lords, if we wish reinforcements, we must *succeed*."

Bishop Mateo spoke again; some of the warrior nobles started slightly. "You have yet to *punish* the Satan-worshippers," he said suddenly. "Let fire and sword teach humility, and show them the strength of Mother Church and Her loyal son and champion the Protector! If their walls are too stout to attack now, let them watch their lands burn!"

God, give me strength, Renfrew thought. *He* does *talk like that all the time! I always enjoyed the tournaments and meetings before the Change, but you got to go back to the real world afterwards.*

But now this *was* the real world; a reality that could be deadly. Aloud he went on:

"Your Grace, once the Mackenzies are conquered, you can lead them to the Truth, and punish any who persist in error. But my orders from the Lord Protector are to *conquer* these lands, not devastate them. The Lord Protector wants productive farmers and living towns to support fighting men and pay taxes. We already have more useless wilderness and ruins than we need."

Despite the churchman's glare, that brought yet another chorus of nods and even a few mutters of *fucking right we do*. They'd all been impressed by the well-cultivated Mackenzie farms, and the families represented around the table were all ready to jostle for a share after the war was over. And every nobleman in the Protectorate was acutely aware of the labor shortage. The territories the Association held could easily support ten times the numbers they had now, probably twenty or fifty. Their manors were all islands in a sea of resurgent brush and forest.

Mateo pointed eastward. "You could break down the aqueduct there," he said, waving towards the big water-furrow that directed water from the Sutter River south of town into Sutterdown, turning a number of mill wheels on the way. The mills were deserted—they were in the no-man's-land between the invader's pickets and the town walls, ground commanded by the catapults in the towers. "Let their bodies know thirst, even if their souls do not thirst for the Spirit."

And he wasn't even in *the Society. He was a junior social worker, for Christ's sake!*

Looking into the bishop's eyes, he knew that the cleric meant every word of it, too; you could feel it, coming off of him like the heat from a banked fire.

Oh, well, half of us survivors are a few cans short. I've done plenty of things I couldn't have imagined *before the Change, God knows. The bishop's particular breed of crazy is what Pope Leo looks for. He's that variety of lunatic himself. Smart, very smart, but the wing flew off his nut when the Eaters captured him right after the Change.*

"Sir Richard?" he said neutrally.

"Easy enough," the engineer said, tracing the way the canal took off from the river, several miles upstream to the east. "Wouldn't even have to wreck it, just block the intake here. Problem is, they've got a reservoir and deep tube wells inside the walls. I mean, they're not idiots, they wouldn't put up that wall with no interior water source and besides our spies got the plans."

He tapped a folder. "They'll have enough drinking water, though not much extra."

"But not enough for baths. The girls might be a bit smelly by the time we get to them," Sir Malcolm Timmins said, and there was a general laugh until the bishop glared around at them, whereupon a few muttered apologies and the rest made their faces grave.

Furness hadn't laughed; he had an old-fashioned squeamishness in many respects. Instead he went on: "It might screw up the sanitation system, yes. Risk of an epidemic if we do that, and it might spread."

"God and the Saints!" someone blurted.

This time everyone crossed themselves as well as nodding. Even those who'd been in their early teens during the aftermath of the Change remembered the plagues; they'd only burned themselves out when people grew scarce. Mateo took a look around and smiled sourly.

"I should not seek to advise you on your specialty, Grand Constable," he said. "You are the man of war here; I serve the Prince of Peace."

You are so *right you shouldn't try to advise me, you fucking ecclesiastical commissar,* Renfrew thought, but he bent his head with the others as Mateo signed the air in blessing. *That hasn't stopped you yet, though. And you serve a fucking lunatic, if we're talking about Leo.*

The bishop bowed slightly. "If you will excuse me, there is much work to be done arranging the infirmary with Sister Agatha and seeing to the army's spiritual welfare."

Everyone relaxed slightly when the cleric left. Renfrew spoke formally: "My lords, I suggest you all get your liegemen and contingents settled in according to the plan in the briefing papers, and we'll invest the city and see what we shall see. The patrol schedule is included in the folders. Sheriff Bauer, please remain for a moment."

When he and the Pendleton man were alone—except for Renfrew's personal guard—he raised an eyebrow.

"Well, I got all my boys answering to my orders," Bauer said.

I hope so, Renfrew thought.

"Only had to kill a couple-three of 'em, too." He worked his left arm as if the shoulder were sore. "I'll be good as new in a couple of days my own self."

The Pendleton area's spontaneous, homegrown version of neo-feudalism made the variety the Association had built out of books and Society make-believe look like Prussian centralization. The light horse from east of the mountains had come in the train of several sheriffs and half a dozen ranchers, and though they'd all theoretically been on the same side in the last civil war there, and all—equally theoretically—now accepted the Protector's overlordship, half of them had blood feuds born of previous abrupt switches of allegiances or just from the general bloody-mindedness produced by a decade of mutual slaughter.

The easterner went on: "Still, my 'chete-swingers ain't too happy. Nothing useful or pretty to pick up for the home folks, no girls to screw, not even much fightin'."

"They're getting paid regularly, aren't they?" Renfrew said impatiently. "The usual camp followers and sutlers will arrive soon enough and they can buy amusement. Or presents for their families. We've even got the postal service working as far as Pendleton; they can mail packages home."

"Yeah, but what's the point of a fight if you don't get to cut no throats or lift no cattle?" Bauer said.

Talk about rapid reversion to savagery! Renfrew thought. *He's too young to have been more than a high school student, but I wonder what this back-country clod's father did before the Change?*

Conrad Renfrew had been an accountant, himself, when he wasn't playing at knights.

"Where *are* the Mackenzies' cattle and sheep, then?" he asked aloud. *If anyone can follow a cow, these bastards can. Particularly if they're feeling sexual frustration.*

"Near as we can tell, they drove some into town—probably salting those down to eat later—and sent some of the rest south, and quite a few head up into the mountains," Bauer said. "Lot of their folks went up into the high country too, judgin' from the tracks. Woods're heavy up there. Bad country for riders, just right for hiding if they got supplies stockpiled."

And our gliders are nearly useless there too, Renfrew thought. He waved a hand; southward, east to the vast mountain forests that stretched up into the High Cascades, and then west towards the Willamette with its brush and swamp and prairie.

"They're out there somewhere, Bauer. Eight hundred to a thousand kilties, and too mobile by half. They showed that when they corncobbed Lord Piotr."

With bicycles, they could be anywhere in the Willamette Valley south of here in a day or two; they might be hiding in the brush-grown lands between here and Corvallis, for that matter. The only good thing was that they couldn't get past him, not in any numbers, although that would be a reckless move even if they could. The mountain tracks to the east were too narrow and rough. He'd know it if they tried to go north in open country to the westward, and then he could move quickly to force battle on his own terms. Also, they didn't have any cavalry to speak of. Those were the only consolations he had, and he clung to them hard.

"*Find* them for me, Sheriff. I don't like sitting here with my thumb up my ass and a blindfold on."

"Will do, boss," Bauer said cheerfully, and left in his turn.

Renfrew stood for long moments looking at his map, and then traced a thick finger down from Mount Angel, through the Waldo Hills and over the Santiam, past the ruins of Lebanon and down to Sutterdown and past it to the Mackenzie clachan at Dun Juniper. Somewhere out there the First Levy of Clan Mackenzie were hovering. Somehow he didn't think they were just waiting to react to what *he* did. Which meant they were planning something themselves, the dirty dogs . . .

"Not thinking of going farther south, my lord?" Sir Buzz Akers asked him, handing him a blue plastic plate heaped from the buffet. "Heading for Dun Juniper, on the hope that they'd come out and fight us if we attacked their holy place?"

Renfrew started slightly. "With an open left flank all the way from Molalla to here, sixty miles as the crow flies and half again as much on foot? *Christ*, no!" he said.

Then he smiled unwillingly as he realized his younger vassal was teasing him out of his brooding mood, took the plate,

ate a spring roll and forked up a mouthful of potato salad. When he'd swallowed, he said: "We should be back up around Mount Angel, doing one thing at a time. It'd take a while, but we could do it, nice and safe, and our good Pope Leo could send the wicked abbot to the stake, he does love a nice cheerful blaze at an auto-da-fé. Then we could move on the Mackenzies with Mount Angel as a base of operations, not a hoe handle stuck up our collective assholes."

Sir Buzz looked at him oddly. "Do you think this campaign is in danger of failure, my lord?" he asked.

"Hmm? Oh, no, we'll *win* all right, there's not much doubt of that. We outnumber them so heavily we can afford to make mistakes, and they can't. I just don't want it to cost us more than it has to. That's why we should have taken Mount Angel first. Then I'd have four thousand men here, and we'd be able to leave plenty west of the river to make sure the Bearkillers didn't interfere, as well. Alexi uses his brains instead of just his balls and his fists like that idiot son of his, but I'd be happier if *he* had more troops, too."

He pointed his white plastic fork at the symbol on the map that represented Dun Juniper, less than a day's march away to the southeast, even going around the spurs of hill which thrust out into the flat valley; that would be even nastier to take than Sutterdown, although not as bad as Mount Angel. From the descriptions the terrain would be a nightmare for a large force, and ideal for the sort of sneaking-through-the-trees business the kilties delighted in.

"Besides," he went on thoughtfully, prodding at the map, "I don't think Juniper Mackenzie is home right now."

Near Dun Juniper, Willamette Valley, Oregon
March 5th, 2008/Change Year 9

Dennis Martin Mackenzie stopped with a wheezing groan and shouldered his way through the circle of watchers, his long war ax in his hand. The three-mile run from Dun Juniper had left him purple-faced; he was a heavy-built man, and his usual trades of brewing and carpentry and leatherworking didn't do much for his cross-country ability. But that wasn't what made him feel as if his heart was squeezing itself up through his lungs. He recognized the smell of blood—a great deal of it, like iron and salt and copper, and the other unpleasant scents of death. Two horses down, and—

"Oh, Hell," he said, falling into old habits. Then: "Lords of the Watchtowers of the West."

Aoife lay with her head on Liath's chest; from the blood trail, she'd crawled there, though it was hard to imagine anyone having the strength to do so, with those wounds. A man lay not far away with his face cut open, and another with a spear standing up from his chest. The pale features of the dead looked very white in the dusk, but the blood was nearly black.

Poor kids. Too damn young— He'd seen a world die in the Change and its aftermath, but this was far too personal—he'd watched these two grow from childhood. A rising babble of talk cut across his thoughts.

"Quiet!" he said. "In fact, why don't the rest of you folks get back to the Dun? We're going to need some space here and we don't want the traces all trampled over. Jack, Burach, stay up at the edge of the woods and turn people back, would you? And send for a cart."

Most of the bystanders left. His eyes took in the scene and he stooped to examine the bodies; someone handed him a lantern, and he turned up the flame. That gave brighter light, but it made the space under the tall black walnut into a cave of light in a great, dim reach. Leaves rustled above him, turned ruddy by the flame.

The crossbow bolt that had killed Liath was pre-Change, the shaft made of some light metal; so was the one sunk behind the ear of Aoife's horse, lodged immovably in bone. There were three more bolts in the other horse's chest and throat, and another standing three inches deep in the dense hardwood of the walnut tree, at about head height. There was no sense in trying to get *that* out; instead he gripped one that was sunk in the horse's breast by the inch of wood still showing and withdrew it, the pinch of his powerful hand and thick-muscled arm pulling inexorably. It was modern, lathe-turned from dense ashwood, the head a simple four-sided steel pyramid designed to pierce armor, and the vanes cut from salvaged plastic—credit cards, Visa, to be precise.

"Protectorate issue," he said, swallowing a curse.

So were the mail-lined camouflage jackets on the two dead men; that was what a forester wore in the Association's territory—foresters being a sort of rural police-cum-forest warden. These, however . . .

He picked up one of the dead men's hands, ignoring the unpleasant limpness, and the little chill that always ran up his neck at the thought that his own hands—those marvelously precise and responsive instruments—could be so easily rendered futile and lax, already blotched purple beneath the skin with settling blood no longer kept in motion by the heart. There was a thick curd of callus on the inner web of the man's right hand, extending up the inside of the index finger and thumb, and more on the heel of his hand. Swordsman's callus, exceptionally well developed. Scars showed white on the thick right forearm; there weren't any scars on the left arm, but it had another band of callus just inside the elbow, where the inner strap of a horseman's kite-shaped shield ran. The man was young, although the great slash across his face made it hard to be sure; he was broad in the shoulders and long in the legs, well fed but without an ounce of excess flesh, and his hair was cut longer at the front, cropped close behind the ears.

"Knight or man-at-arms," Dennis said grimly. "Probably a knight." He looked around. "OK, they took off with Rudi and the girl. We and the Dúnedain aren't the only people who can do commando raids. Laegh."

A young man who'd stayed when the crowd left looked up from quartering around the trampled ground. His sister Devorgill had stayed as well. They were both noted hunters, only two years apart in age, tall and lean and with brown hair drawn back into a queue; the quickest way to tell them apart was by Laegh's mustaches.

"How many of them?" Dennis said.

"Six came here, Uncle Dennis. Four left—with eight horses, and the one the little princess was riding. First one came up here and climbed the tree—climbed it with irons on the feet, look, you can see where it scarred the bark. The others waited in the thickets lower down. Then they came up to wait in ambush, leaving the horses there with one to hold them, and I think the first, the scout who called them, was a woman. A large woman, or a boy nearly grown. Walking light, not digging her heels in like the others. She watched the Dun for hours from a high branch; it wouldn't carry *my* weight well. Then she slid down quickly—when she saw the riders headed this way, I guess. First the princess came, galloping fast, and on her heels the Chief's son—he fell from his horse—and then Aoife and Liath. After the fight the strangers went down the north slope, riding hard, taking both children with them."

"How long ago?"

"Half an hour or a bit less. The trails there are good. They could be ten miles away by now if they headed west into the Valley."

Devorgill touched the blood and smeared it between the fingers of her left hand, sniffing it and then offering him the evidence. "Twenty minutes or a little more," she said.

Laegh's sister was the one who'd ridden out to find what was delaying the children and their escorts; right now she was gripping her horse's reins right under the bit to control its rolling-eyed fear as it pivoted its rear end about that fixed point with nervous side steps, and she was looking pretty spooked herself. Dennis glanced up at the sky and cursed to himself; the sun was already on the western horizon, and it was a wonder even a tracker of Laegh's skill had been able to see anything with the gloom growing beneath the trees.

"Laegh, can you follow them in the dark?"

"Not quickly, Uncle," he said, using the usual term to address someone a generation older. "My dogs can follow the trail if they don't break it in water, though. Worth trying, they'd get too far ahead if we just wait for dawn. And they might split up."

"Devorgill," he told the man's sister. "Get back to Dun Juniper, *fast*. Get the hounds, get four or five people, you pick them, the gear, weapons, spare horses and get back here *fast*. You—" He picked out another. "Get down to Dun Fairfax and tell them what's up and that we need another six who're good in the woods, and some more horses."

The woman vaulted into the saddle, reined her restive, snorting horse around, and switched its rump with the long end of the reins. It neighed and reared and broke into a gallop; the messenger ran in its wake, his bow pumping back and forth in his left hand. Dennis grinned mirthlessly at Laegh's unspoken protest at waiting for a war party.

"Not much use finding them if you can't fight 'em when you do, eh?" he said. The young man hesitated. "And don't worry; I know I'm about as much use on a hunt as a hog at a hand-fasting. You're in charge. *I've* gotta stay here and see to things and figure out what to tell Juney."

There was a rustle through the watchers, and Dennis felt his stomach clench again. *And I'm really not looking forward to that. Poor little kid . . . no, Rudi won't be scared, not Rudi. But he should be.*

Someone else was coming down the trail, someone on a bicycle. Dennis swore again under his breath, feeling harassed; there were still five hundred people in Dun Juniper, and he didn't want any of them here right now. Then the bicycle came to a halt, and Judy Barstow let it fall and ran forward.

Oh, shit. Sanjay last year, Aoife this time. The dice are being really hard on her and Chuck. Thank Everyone that all my kids are still too young to fight.

She halted when she saw her foster-daughter's body. For a moment her strong-featured face was blank, and then she sank to her knees. There was no sound save the soughing of the evening wind in the trees, and the rustling flicker of the lantern flame.

"My little girl," she whispered, touching the dead face, and then holding the eyelids closed and doing the same for her child's lover; tears dripped from her own eyes, runnels along the weathered olive skin of her cheeks. "My little red-haired girl. You were so brave and so scared that day on the bus when we found you, and I loved you then. You grew so fast—"

Her hand shook as she touched fingers to the blood and marked her cheeks and forehead, and then fumbled with the knot that held her hair. It fell loose around her face and shoulders, grizzled and black, as she raised her hands northward.

"I am the mother and I call the Mother's curse on you who did this, by the power of the blood of my child spilled on Her earth! I curse you with cold heart and hearth and loins and colder death! Curse you—"

Her voice broke into a low moan, then rose into a keening shriek—literally keening. Then it sank again, then rose; she rocked back and forth on knees and heels, her hands tearing at her hair as the wailing scream sounded long and lonely in the darkened woods. Dennis stood back from it, shivering slightly under the thick wool of his plaid; so did Laegh, looking more frightened still as his hand moved in a protective gesture—a High Priestess so lost to herself *was* frightening. Curses tended to spill over and bounce back.

Then the young hunter's sister rode up, a dozen others with her and each leading a spare horse; four big flop-eared hunting hounds trotted along with them, curious and alert but too well trained to break free. One of the riders tossed a spear to Laegh. He caught it with a smack of palm on ashwood, whistled the dogs in sharply, dipped spearhead and head and knee to Judy, and led his hunting-party into the darkness. Before the hooves had faded from hearing the belling of the hounds sounded, echoing through the nighted hills, a hunter's salute to the rising moon.

Others came up the pathway with a cart, and torches trailing sparks. Hands lifted the bodies of the Clan's warriors and laid them on the straw in the cart's bed, folding their hands over their breasts and pulling their plaids across their faces. Others helped Judy to her feet, supporting her as she stumbled blind with tears behind the slow pace of the oxen. Dennis sighed, shouldered his ax and fell in with the rest of the party. Her kin and friends would spend the night at the wake, talking of the dead and keening them . . . but he intended to break into his own brewer's stock-in-trade more privately, with his family, and then sleep as long as he could.

As he walked, a voice began to sing; one at first, haltingly, and then with more and more joining in to the hypnotic rhythm of the chant:

"We all come from the Mother
And to Her we shall return
Like a stalk of grain,
Falling to the reaper's scythe
We all come from the Wise One;
And to Her we shall return
Like a waning moon,
Shining on the winter's snow
We all come from the Maiden—"

Near Appletree, Willamette Valley, Oregon
March 6th, 2008/Change Year 9

Tiphaine Rutherton looked at her watch. It was a sign of Lady Sandra's favor, a self-winding Swiss beauty made forty years ago, just before electrics became common, with a heavy tempered-glass cover and secondary dials showing the day and month. The glider pilot's timepiece was probably a good deal less fancy, but it would be functional.

In which case, where is *the moron?* she thought impatiently, scanning the sky above.

They were in the shelter of a patch of Garry oak, not far from a ruined farmstead whose chimney poked up among vegetation gone wild, and well beyond the settled part of the Mackenzie territories, just south of a height called Famine Hill. They were still well within the notional border, and hunters and traders used these lands—they'd seen a small shrine to Cernnunos not far back, an elk's skull and antlers fastened to a tree with the hooves below and signs of small parties camping repeatedly not far away. That made signal fires far too dangerous, or any fires at all for that matter. The men were caring for the horses, feeding them rolled oat pellets from the saddlebags because they couldn't let them out in the open to graze.

She looked over to where the children were seated side by side beneath a tree. The Mackenzie brat had a light chain hobble on, and gave her a steady, defiant glare when he felt her gaze. Princess Mathilda Arminger looked almost as hostile; if

Tiphaine had dared, she'd have handcuffed them together. The glare grew narrow as she walked over and went down on one knee.

"Young lord," she said. "I'm truly sorry about chaining your legs, but unless you give me your oath not to try to escape—"

"No," he said shortly.

"And I can't have my men shoot at you if you *do* try to run away," Tiphaine went on. "Not with the princess so . . . loyal a friend."

Actually I will, and keep the princess sedated until we get back if I have to, she thought. *Once I hand her over to Lady Sandra alive,* my *job's done. But I can't* say *that where she's listening. Mary Mother, what a situation!*

Aloud she said: "So I have to be very sure you don't try to escape. Please forgive me, but this is war, and I am the faithful vassal of Lady Sandra—the princess' mother. I did what was necessary."

The chiseled features softened very slightly, and the big blue-green eyes grew a little less chilly.

"I understand that, my lady," he said, with self-possession beyond his years, a voice like a well-tuned harpstring, giving promise of a chest-filling resonance when he came to a man's years.

Mathilda looked at him in surprise as he went on: "I don't hate you. You're a warrior doing your duty to your folk and chief, like Liath and Aoife did. I know people die in wars. But . . . remember it's *my* duty to stop you doing yours."

He smiled then, and shook back his mane of curling Titian hair, glorious even in the forest's shadow and tangled with twigs and leaves.

Mary Mother, she thought, slightly dazed. *What's he going to be like when he grows up? No wonder the little princess was taken with him!*

Normally she just wasn't affected by male looks one way or another, adult or child, but she had to grant Rudi Mackenzie was beautiful by any standard, like a cougar or an otter; and she could see the thoughts moving behind the blue-green eyes. He wasn't exactly precocious, but he was disconcertingly sharp for someone his age.

And at nine years old he gave Ruffin all he could handle with a knife right after being thrown from a horse ... Well, he's half the Witch Queen, and half Lord Bear ... I wish we could have kept that horse. It was beautiful too, and it would be a hold on him.

The wounded man came up with the rations—waybread, cheese, smoked dried salmon, raisins—and handed the children theirs with a smile, despite the pain he must be feeling from the cut arm and the dozen hasty stitches they'd had to put in at the first stop to keep him from leaking all over the backtrail. He said something to the boy; Rudi laughed and made a gesture as if holding a knife, and Ruffin grinned and slapped the hilt of his sword with his good hand.

I hope to hell Lady Sandra knows what to do with him, if she doesn't just have him thrown back at the kilties out of a catapult. Though it'll probably be a lot more subtle than that.

The raisins were lousy, particularly if you could remember what Sun-Maid tasted like, sticky and a little mushy; Oregon didn't have the right sort of climate for drying grapes, and she swallowed them as quickly as she could. The double-baked waybread looked like crackers, and had the consistency and taste of salty, sun-dried wooden slats from a fruit crate; she gnawed at hers cautiously as she ate the perfectly acceptable crumbly yellow cheese and deep pink salmon.

"The kilties are probably still on our trail," Joris observed.

"I think we shook them—" she began. Then: "There it is!"

Bird-tiny, the shape of the glider showed against a cloud. Tiphaine pulled the wigwags out of her saddlebags and stood in the open, signaling Girl-Scout fashion. She'd met Katrina in the Scouts, just before the Change. . . .

After a frustratingly long wait the glider turned and banked lower. Tiphaine repeated the signals patiently, amusing herself thinking how the so-called Lady of the Dúnedain was going to react when she heard about Mathilda's rescue—and the capture of Rudi Mackenzie, and that Tiphaine Rutherton had done both, and brought the children through what the murderous bitch called *her* territory.

And I did it, Katrina, she thought. *No,* we *did it, together.*

The glider circled three times as she repeated the message;

she could imagine the pilot with one hand on the control yoke and the other holding his binoculars. Then he waggled his wings and banked again, turning north. The glider mounted skyward in a smooth, arcing rush as it hit the updraft on Famine Hill, turning on one wingtip in a narrow circle as the sheet of rising air flung it skyward. When it was insect-tiny it banked again, heading north. The Willamette Valley was good sailplaning country, and it ought to have no trouble making the thirty miles to the launching field near the castle at Gervais.

She was grinning to herself at the thought when one of the men started up with a curse.

"It's those fucking dogs again!" he said. "Hell, don't the kilties ever get tired?"

"Get mounted, everyone!" she snapped, cocking an ear.

Sure enough, a faint belling sound was coming from the southeast, harsh and musical at the same time. It took only moments to get the tack back on the horses; the beasts were looking weary, but with remounts they hadn't come anywhere close to foundering them. Ivo unshackled the Mackenzie boy and then cuffed his ankles to the stirrups, and passed a chain on his wrists through the loop on the saddlebow. That was mildly dangerous, but the knight would be taking his horse on a leading-rein as well, so it was unlikely to bolt, and the boy rode as if he'd grown out of the horse's spine anyway. Mathilda had been good in the saddle before she was kidnapped and was even better now; evidently the Clan hadn't been neglecting her education in the equestrian arts over the past year. She'd pitched in with the camp chores without complaint as well, which was a bit surprising.

The sprayer was a simple thing like an old-time Flit gun. Tiphaine checked the direction of the wind—out of the north—and began methodically pumping a mixture of gasoline and skunk oil over their campsite in a fine mist. Rudi wrinkled his face, and so did Mathilda; it smelled awful to a human, but it would stun the sensitive nose of a tracking hound for hours.

"Out of the way, Ruffin, unless you want to smell so bad your leman sends you to sleep in the outhouse when we get back. What are you looking at, anyway?"

The young knight chuckled as he moved aside to avoid getting any of it on his clothes, and held up a ring. "The kid tried to drop this!" he said. "I like the little bastard, dip me in shit if I don't."

Tiphaine nodded; Rudi grinned impudently back at her. She checked the ground; sure enough, he'd moved leaves aside, drawn an arrow with his heel and then covered it again without anyone noticing. She looked back at him impassively as she scrubbed it out with her foot. Mathilda looked unhappy again; she must be feeling very torn.

"We'll go up the old railroad line until we hit Apple Creek," she said to the others as she swung into the saddle. "Then we'll wade up the creekbed half a mile."

"Then?" Joris said. "We should know, in case we're separated."

Tiphaine met his heavy-lidded eyes. He was a vassal of Lady Sandra's Household like her, and he'd obey whoever the Lady told him to, even an untitled woman. That didn't prevent him from resenting it, and needling her subtly.

"No we shouldn't, Joris, in case the kilties catch one of us," she replied. *So you don't have to know we'll head for Sucker Slough, cross the North Santiam there and make for Miller Butte, where there ought to be a couple of troops of men-at-arms to escort us home.*

"Yeah," Ivo said. "That might be the Witch Queen after us." He crossed himself. "Maybe that's *how* they're following us— magic."

"Sounds awful like a bunch of plain old hound dogs to me," Tiphaine said dryly, and reined her horse around. "Let's go!"

Missouri Ridge, Willamette Valley, Oregon
March 5th, 2008/Change Year 9

Juniper Mackenzie felt slightly guilty that she wasn't pushing one of the mountain bikes as she leaned into the welcome warmth of her horse's flank. It was cold and wet here in the foothills near Trout Creek, and the old gravel cutting was chilly under a slow morning drizzle and a low, gray sky; fifteen hundred feet was high enough up to be a bit colder than the Valley proper, and they were a thousand feet higher than Dun Juniper as well as sixty miles north and east. Fog drifted over the hills about them, hiding the tops of the trees and drifting down the slopes in tatters and streamers, dull gray against the second-growth Douglas fir; everything smelled of wet; the wet wool of her jacket and plaid, wet leather and horse from her mount, wet earth and brush from the ground. There was little sound, save for the slow sough of wind, the occasional stamp of a horse's foot, and the *gruk-gruk-gruk* of ravens that were the first birds she'd seen in hours.

Her thoughts went homeward, and she imagined Rudi and Mathilda reading by the hearth with old Cuchulain wheezing in sleep on the rag rug, cider mulling in thick mugs . . .

And oh, Mother-of-All witness, I'd rather be there than here! she thought ruefully, taking another bite from a dried, salted sausage.

It wasn't exactly eating in the usual sense: more like worrying a bit off an old tire, and then chewing until your jaws were tired and you gave up and swallowed the whole barely touched lump the way a snake did a dead rat. She gave journeybread to her horse, and the animal gratefully crunched the hard biscuit in sideways-moving jaws.

"And you don't have to worry about the sorry state of our dentistry, sure," she said. Then when it lipped at her fingers for more, smearing them with slobber: *"Niorbh a fhiú a dhath ariamh a bhfuarthas in aisgidh!"*

A hundred or so of the First Levy were in the cutting too; most were squatting by their bicycles, eating or looking to their gear or just patiently waiting despite the general, damp misery. Two near her were even chuckling softly about something. Ten times that number were scattered through the woods within a quarter mile of her, but they made little noise and gave less sight of their location. That and the wretched weather ought to hide them from the Protector's aerial scouts, even though they were far north, near his bases.

A clop of hooves brought her head up. Sam Aylward was riding towards her from the path to the east, his horse's hooves throwing up spatters of mud as it came. That coated his boots and stockings and kilt with gray-brown muck. The man with him had started out that way, clothed in leather pants and jacket of similar hue, his round helmet and steel breastplate painted dull brown, and his face and hair and eyes were all shades of the same color as well; he wore a long, hooded duster over the armor and carried a short pre-Change compound bow in a case at his left knee, with a long, slightly curved saber at his waist. Juniper grinned and moved away from her horse, extending a hand as the two men pulled up and swung down from the saddle; two young Mackenzies took their mounts.

"Sam!" she said happily. "And John!"

John Brown was most of a decade older than her; it had been a year or so since she saw him, and she was slightly shocked at how much more gray there was in his close-trimmed beard. As usual, he looked worried, the deep squint lines of a plainsman graven farther into the skin at the corners of his eyes.

But perhaps with more reason than usual, she thought.

"Well, we're here, Juney," he said, and she sighed slightly with relief. "All of us as could make it. Less than I hoped, more than it might have been."

"Four hundred twenty-five combatants," Aylward amplified. "Plus twenty-five youngsters along to help with the horses and gear. That's all they could spare. Raids from the Pendleton country on the CORA territories are keeping them hopping."

"Bastards," Brown said. He'd been one of the movers of CORA since the Change, and they'd fought the Protector's men together more than once. "They've been goin' downhill these whole ten years. Bunch of murderin' hillbilly bastards, the ones that came out on top there, and then they got into bed with Arminger. Might have been as bad with us, if we hadn't had that help from you the first couple of years."

Juniper nodded, smiling and acknowledging the compliment; the help had been mutual. Even then her fine ear noticed that his accent sounded a little stronger; speech was changing faster than it had in the old days, without national media or recorded sound to stabilize it. Highway 20 connected the Mackenzie territories with the CORA lands around Bend and Sisters, and the two communities were friendly and traded a good deal, but by pre-Change standards they had less contact than America had had with Bolivia back then.

"Four hundred riders's about all we could bring anyways," Brown went on. "Sneakin' over the mountains, that is. Not much fodder. Still snow lying up there. As it is, we don't have near as many remounts as I'd like."

He jerked a thumb behind him, at the invisible peaks of the Cascades. She nodded again, respecting his reticence. One of her Mackenzies would likely be boasting of the feat, unless it was Sam; the Clan was a talkative bunch. To get here from Bend you'd have to leave the route of old US 26 in the Warm Springs reservation—tribal country once more, but friendly to the Clan and CORA—and use old logging trails through the mountains. Hard work with hundreds of horses, and with the season too early for much grass. If they didn't get the mounts down into the low country soon, they'd start to take sick and die.

She said so, and added: "The which would apply to the people as well, so."

That included her folk as well. Most Mackenzies had *some* woodcraft but only a few from each dun were real hunters who spent much time away from the tilled lands; the rest were crofters and craftsfolk, used to sleeping under their own good roofs within tight log walls every night. Plus they were traveling light in a season still cold and wet—no tents, not much gear and most of what they had brought was extra arrows. In summer these cutover hills growing back towards forest were rich in game—deer, elk, rabbit, birds, boar and feral cattle—but it was early in the season for foraging, and there were far too many of them to live off the land without scattering recklessly. She'd been getting anxious about supplies.

"Where are your folks?" Brown asked. "You got more than this out before they reached Sutterdown, didn't you?"

Behind his back, Sam Aylward grinned. Juniper did too, and waved a hand around. "All within horn call. Just over a thousand, my friend."

"One thousand ninety-seven as of this morning's call," Aylward said. "Got a few more in from the southern duns day before yesterday."

Brown's eyes went a little wider; he'd ridden through their position. "Sneaky," he said. "They won't be expectin' this at all, hey?"

"Hopefully," Juniper said, not joining in the smiles of the men this time.

She'd taken nearly half the Clan's fighting strength right out of their territory while the Protector was invading it, and the best half at that, leaving only enough to hold the walls of Sutterdown and Dun Juniper and the southern steadings. It was a calculated risk, but her stomach still clenched and pained her at the thought of the enemy loose among her folk and their fields.

"I see your people all have those funny-looking shovel things," the rancher went on. "Somethin' new?"

"Eilir's idea," she said, turning to her First Armsman.

"Eilir's idea, and I hope they work," Aylward said, shaking his head. "Otherwise I'm the latest in a long line of inventive buggers who dreamed up something extra for the poor bloody infantry to lug about."

"Any word from the south?"

"Last news from the Rangers is that the enemy 'ave crossed the North Santiam, united their columns and invested Sutterdown. The Rangers slowed them down, though."

Brown slapped his hands together; there was a jingling from the stainless-steel washers riveted to the backs of his steerhide gloves, and water dripped off the hood of his oiled-linen duster.

"You mentioned a plan," he said. "What sort?"

"Well," Juniper Mackenzie said, "first my fiancé is paying a social call. There are advantages to marrying into the SAS . . ."

Sam Aylward's chuckle matched her own, but he shook his head as he spoke: "Well, strictly speaking, Lady Juniper, Eilir gets the SAS, and you'll be marrying into the Blues and Royals. Officers don't make a career of the regiment. Didn't, you know what I mean."

Brown looked between the two of them; it started to rain

again, making small *tink* sounds on his helmet and breast-plate. "You guys are crazy," he said with conviction.

"Sure, and that's what's brought us as far as we've come," Juniper said. "But *ná comhair do chuid sicini sula dtagann siad amach,* and the bird's still very much on the nest."

Then her head came up, and Sam's with it. A cry like a wild swan's echoed through the drizzle; that was the signal for *courier.* Moments later a man on a lathered horse came up. Juniper stiffened at the look on his face: whatever it was, the news was not good.

"Lady," he said, dipping head and knee. "It's about your son—"

Near Sucker Slough, Willamette Valley, Oregon
March 6th, 2008/Change Year 9

"Get the kids ahead, Ruffin," Tiphaine said.

Her voice was dragging with weariness, and she blinked against what felt like grit rubbed under her eyelids. The impulse to simply topple out of the saddle and sleep was overwhelming. They all looked weary, even the horses, though they'd been changing off every couple of hours. The children sagged in their saddles, eyes dull.

"Hey—"

"Your shield-arm's hurt and you can't fight well," she said bluntly. "We may have to delay them. Now get going!"

The wounded man-at-arms nodded grimly, and turned his horse up the far bank of the little creek. The strong legs of the warmblood took it in three surging heaves; Rudi's horse was on a long lead-rein, and even half-conscious Mathilda followed with the effortless ease of someone who'd been riding cross-country as long as she could walk.

The little guy keeps his seat well too, she thought. *Tough kids, those two.*

"Joris, get your crossbow. Ivo, have the horses standing by, and get the decoys ready."

She led the blond warrior back to the edge of the brush. He moved fairly well in the brush; she'd picked experienced hunters for this trip, and the chuckling of water in the brook behind them covered most noise. Tiphaine slung her crossbow, took three deep, quick breaths to force her blood to start moving again, aimed herself at the big white-barked alder that grew from the top of the bank and hit it running. She climbed it with the scampering speed of a squirrel despite the way the papery surface crumbled under her hands. Twenty feet up she hugged the trunk with one arm, reached down to slip the irons into place on her feet and felt them sink into the soft wood of the streamside tree. That gave her a secure stance once her elbow was over a branch.

A flick of her fingers opened the quiver of bolts on her belt, and then she unslung the crossbow and brought the telescopic sight to her eye. The magnification was three times; she could see things more closely, at the cost of losing a wider scan. But there was only one convenient way past the hulk of that over-grown tractor . . .

There. The whiplike tails of four dogs showed above tall grass that was mingled dead stalks and new growth. Occasionally a questing head came up, black nose leading in a tan-black-and-white face, trying to catch her scent on the air, but the wind was from the west right now, and the overcast sky promised rain. Even to her human nose the air felt wet and muffled. Long range, very, a good two hundred and seventy yards, but with this height . . .

Her hand curled around the pistol grip of the weapon, the checked metal surface rough and firm through the thin chamois leather of her glove. One finger stroked the hair trigger, light and delicate. *Tung!* The kick was solid, always a surprise if you aimed well.

The quarrel flew in a long, shallow curve, dipping down towards the leading hound, the one with its nose back down on their trail. A sharp, yelping cry of pain, and the big brown-and-white dog leapt into the air, biting frantically at the light-alloy shaft in its side. She'd never be able to recover that one, which was a pity. The dog disappeared again as she turned the crank built into the high-tech crossbow, but the grass thrashed where it lay. That was also a pity—she'd never have shot at an animal so far away if she were hunting. A kill should be clean and quick.

The animals were disturbed; the scent of blood and their pack-mate's pain would do that, and cover the trail a bit. Their belling sounded louder through the afternoon air, *arrooo, arrooo,* calling for their master's help. She slipped another quarrel into the groove, and brought the crosshairs on a white-furred throat.

Tung. Her fingers were reloading as the dog collapsed; quickly this time, simply falling down. If only there was time for one more—

The third dog turned, yelping. Riders came around the big tractor just as it would have fled; it stopped in glad surprise, and her bolt went home between its shoulder blades. The hindquarters collapsed, but before the dog died four of the riders were sliding out of the saddle, bringing up their bows and reaching over their shoulders for arrows even as they swung down. She kicked her feet clear of the climbing irons and abandoned them, sliding down the sloping trunk of the alder in a flurry of papery bark and taking a nasty whack on one elbow from an iron even as she did. She'd seen Mackenzie archers in action before.

"That leaves just one dog," she said to herself with satisfaction.

And before she'd slid ten feet, three thirty-inch arrows went *wheet-wheet-wheet* through the air on either side of the branch she'd used to rest her elbow. The fourth went *crack* into the base of the branch itself, and punched through it with brutal force. After an instant the limb ripped free as its weight levered against the strip of bark still holding it, hitting her on the head as her boots struck the ground. It was only a slight, muffled impact through the mail-lined hood she was wearing, but enough to make her blood race uncomfortably even so. If she'd stayed and tried for one more shot . . .

"Christ!" she said. Then: "Go, go, go!" to Joris, turning and racing back for the horses.

He paused for an instant to aim, and the heavier *tunnnngg* of his military crossbow sounded under his chuckle before he turned and followed.

"Got one, or at least a horse," he said as they all vaulted into the saddles and spurred their mounts up in Ivo's tracks.

"Let the spares with the drag go free," Tiphaine said curtly, and the leading-reins were dropped. *Dickhead. We didn't have time for a fight.*

One of the spare horses had a ball of cloth dangling from its harness on a line; that was Rudi Mackenzie's bundled kilt and plaid. As long as the horse dragged it, it would lay a scent trail for the last hound to follow. The horse curved away to the east across the open country, panicked by her slash at its rump with the loose end of her reins. Two more followed it, with the natural impulse of horses; their saddles bore crude child-sized dummies of grass and twigs stuffed inside spare clothing they'd brought along for the princess. They wouldn't fool anyone for long, but they might at a distance, for a little while.

"Boot it!" Tiphaine cried.

They spurred their mounts in the children's wake, and overtook them faster than she'd expected. Ruffin's haggard face turned towards her, grinning despite fatigue and pain.

"The little chief there managed to get away—tangled his lead-rein on a stump and made the horse snap it. I had to chase him down."

Tiphaine looked at the small jewel-cut face; it had dark smudges under the eyes now, and lack of sleep had stripped away the jaunty humor. What was left was pure determination. She bowed her head in respect, and then spurred her horse back into a gallop.

The three knights matched it, but Joris looked a little worried as he glanced over his shoulder. "We could founder the beasts in a couple of miles at this pace," he said. "We don't have remounts any more and the kilties probably still do."

"All we need is a couple of miles," she said. "You wanted to know? We're heading for Miller Butte. There's a *conroi* of men-at-arms there and a company of mounted crossbowmen, hiding and waiting for us."

Joris' heavy-lidded eyes narrowed. *And I'm not going to let you behind me until we get there,* she thought grimly. *I'm collecting the reward for this, and I'll see Ivo and Ruffin right. Lady Sandra will give you something, but as for me, you can piss up a rope for it.*

Then his head jerked back. The belling of the last hound had faded; now it was louder again. The Mackenzies must have found the decoy, backtracked and gotten onto the real trace. Tiphaine hunched in the saddle and headed her horse straight for the river ahead; it was the North Santiam, and she recognized the old transmission line to their left from maps and their trip south.

"Wait a minute!" Joris said. "We'll have better cover if we veer past those old poles. There's woodland there, they can't shoot at us."

Tiphaine jerked her head up, fighting the hypnotic rhythm of the hand gallop; the horse was beginning to labor, wheezing between her knees, foam spattering back on its neck and onto her.

"They'd shoot at us, Joris," she said. "They might even shoot at the princess. But sure as Christ died for your sins, they're not going to shoot when they might hit their Chief's son." She looked ahead. "Four more miles. Go for it!"

CHAPTER FOURTEEN

The thunder of the knights filled the world as they charged, four hundred strong; Mike Havel could feel it through the soles of his boots, a shaking that quivered through soil and leather into his skin. The great hooves of the destriers pounded the soft turf into a chopped surface like a rough-plowed field, flinging clods and tufts of grass higher than the riders' helmets. Their eyes rolled behind the spiked steel chamfrons that covered their faces, and their nostrils were great red pits above the square yellow teeth that mouthed the bits and dripped foam. The lanceheads caught the noon sun with a quivering glitter, and the pennants snapped behind them—and every one looked as if it were heading for *him*.

He spat to clear his mouth of gummy saliva and the trace of blood still leaking from the inside of his cheek; the salt-iron taste of it was still on his lips. Facing a single lancer was one thing. Facing this avalanche of steel and flesh was entirely another. Around him the militia were still shrieking the war cry, or in some cases just plain shrieking. He knew some would be pissing or shitting themselves . . . and that some of those would fight no worse for it. This was the moment when pride and fear of shame before your neighbors and fear for your home warred with the elemental terror of torn flesh and cracked bone and ultimate, unendurable pain and the final blackness.

Closer. Closer. The pikepoints waited, wavering only as much as the tension of the muscles that held the long shafts could account for. Closer, and the enemy were up to a full, all-out gallop, which meant they were about to enter the killing ground. Watch for that piece of cracked asphalt that marked the three-hundred-yard mark—

"Shoot!" Mike Havel shouted.

Trumpets relayed the order—one low blat and a sustained high note. The great *tunng* of the steel bows releasing sounded an instant later, six hundred missiles lashing out on either side of the great block of pikes. The bolts flickered in swift, flat arcs. Noncoms screamed *rapid fire, rapid fire, pour it on!* as they reloaded themselves; a heavy clicking, ratcheting sound ran along the line as the militia pumped the levers of their crossbows. Some bolts missed. Many struck, the hard smacking sound of their impacts lost in the huge noise of the onset.

Men pitched back off their horses; horses fell, screaming and thrashing or sometimes limply silent, or ran out of control, bucking and lashing out at whatever had hurt them. The men-at-arms weren't tightly packed enough to pile into a mass of collisions, or there weren't enough horses down to produce one; a few mounts jumped over the fallen ahead of them, and more swerved skillfully under their riders' guidance, but that made the whole charging mass falter. More fell, and more; the bolts were a steady drumroll flicker, fast and hard . . .

"They're going to hit!" Signe called; she was still mounted, and had a better view. *"Not enough down to stop them!"*

The knights loomed above the infantry, looking as if they could ride down mountains. Glaring eyes stared at him on either side of the nasal bars of the conical Norman helmets . . .

"Hakkaa Paalle!"

"Haro, Portland!"

The onrush of the knights hesitated . . . and then began to slow, or split to either side. Havel let out a gasp he hadn't been aware of holding; horses *wouldn't* impale themselves on sharp pointy things, not if they could avoid it. They had more sense than human beings.

Some destriers skidded into the line of pikepoints, unable to stop in time or bolder than most or just fleeing the roweling spurs. The foot-long heads of the pikes sank deep, punching through hide and bone and even the steel peytral plates the destriers wore on their chests. A few ashwood shafts burst under the massive impact, sending splinters and whirling batons flying in all directions, or cracked as flailing hooves milled in the air. More horses reared and stalled in front of the unbroken line, and the pikemen thrust in two-handed jabs at their bellies and heads, making the riders curse and wrench at the reins to keep them facing the foe. Knights tried to push their lances past the pikepoints, but infantry in the second and third ranks thrust at *them*. Men-at-arms dismounted when their mounts fell or fled, shoved and heaved forward, catching the points on their shields and cutting at the pike shafts with their swords, trying to push their way into the formation. But long lappets of steel stretched down the sides of the pikes below the heads to prevent precisely that, and showers of sparks showed where metal belled on metal.

Pikemen in the second and third and fourth ranks thrust at chests and faces, the polearms slamming back and forward like pistons. Bearkillers and Association men shoved and heaved and stabbed and hit, cursing and shouting or in sweat-dripping, gasping silence, or screamed in the sudden shock of pain beyond anything they had thought possible. The wounded crawled away, or lay moaning and crying for water or help or their mothers, until hooves or boots trampled across them and bone broke in a stamping urgency that saw bodies underfoot as only a menace to footing.

"Mike, left!" Signe called; her clear soprano cut through the white-noise rush of battle.

Havel looked, cursed and shouted: "Follow me!"

The knights had overlapped the block of pikemen there, some of them ramming into the crossbows. As he watched they spurred their mounts over the bodies of dead Bearkillers and turned to kill from behind, ready to burst the formation open. The seventy glaivesmen rushed after him, swinging like a great door, weapons extended—but a glaive was only six feet long.

"Hakkaa Paalle!"

A man-at-arms stabbed down at him, lance held overarm. Havel ducked, and felt the ugly wind of the steel head punching by his face. He spun the glaive like a quarterstaff and it slammed into the lance, throwing the lighter weapon high, vibrating in the lancer's hands. Before he could recover, the Bearkiller leader stepped forward, swinging the glaive again, this time in a circle like a horizontal propeller, letting his hands slide down to the end. The broad, curved cutting edge of the head hit the horse's leg just above the knee. Edged metal went into muscle and then bone with an ugly, wet *slap-crack,* and a jolt that ran painfully up into his arms and shoulders.

The horse screamed, a deafening sound, rearing and falling in a kicking heap. The rider kicked his feet out of the stirrups, riding the fall down and landing on his feet with astonishing skill, shouting: "Runner! Runner!"

Probably the horse's name, Havel thought in a moment's astonishment.

Then the man was rushing at him, screeching: *"Bastard!"*

The Norman broadsword swung down at his head. Havel caught it on the thick hook welded to the back of the glaive's blade, and let the impact pivot the heavy shaft around so that the metal-clad butt whipped at the man's face. He raised his shield and stopped it with a thud and hollow boom, but at the cost of blinding himself for a crucial instant. Havel kicked at the inside of his leg, just where hauberk and steel-splint shin-guard met, and the joint went sideways in a manner not suited to the construction or nature of knees. The Association soldier shrieked between clenched teeth as he toppled over backward, and then nearly killed Havel with a hocking stroke as he fell. The Bearkiller managed to hop over it, testicles pulling up at the lethal hiss of steel just under his boot-soles; then he snapped the business end of the glaive down, and thrust with a grunt of effort and all the power of shoulders and torso behind it. The heavy point split the mail and gambeson and the breastbone beneath; a crunching and breaking and popping sensation ran back up the ashwood beneath his palms. Blood burst out of the dying man's mouth and nose, spraying Havel from the thighs down.

He planted a boot on the corpse and wrenched the weapon free. Not five yards from him a lancer killed a Bearkiller with a thrust to the throat, then went down with his hamstrung horse. Another was lashing around him with his sword, until two glaives darted in and caught their hooks in the chain mail of his hauberk and yanked him out of the saddle as if he'd run into bungee cords. The destrier ran free to the south, stirrups flopping and reins loose . . .

Havel skipped backward a half-dozen paces, his head whipping back and forth to try to gain some picture of what was happening. The block of glaivesmen was stepping in, mingling with the other infantry as the last knights who'd gotten through the line died. On the right a hundred of the crossbows had pulled back into the soft ground, to where they sank ankle-deep; the lancers there had unwisely tried to follow them, and two score or better were in over their fetlocks, heaving and scrambling as the crossbow bolts flickered out at them at point-blank range. To his left the surviving missile troops were swinging farther forward, shooting into the stalled mass of horses and men in front of the line of pikes . . .

"Stevenson!" he shouted, trotting behind their backs, judging what he could see over their heads; the knights and men-at-arms were still trying to move forward, but they'd gotten tangled up good and proper. "Push of pike!"

The commander of the phalanx nodded, and shouted orders of his own.

The file-closers took it up: "Push of pike! One . . . two . . . three . . . *step*!"

The bristling mass of pikes took a uniform step forward, jabbing. "And *step*. And *step*!"

Then the curled trumpets wailed. A few of the horsemen were too transported to listen; they stayed, and died. The rest reined in, turning their destriers and spurring back towards the Association lines, with the deadly flicker of crossbow bolts pursuing them. The noise of battle faded with the drumroll of their hoofbeats, until individual shouts and screams could be heard;

Havel cursed mildly to himself as he saw Alexi Stavarov's banner going back as it had come forward.

"Halt!" the pike commander cried.

In a story, Alexi and I would have ended up squaring off sword-to-sword, the Bear Lord thought, pausing to pant some air back into lungs that seemed too dry and tight, against the constriction of armor and padding. Suddenly he was aware that he'd picked up a cut on his left arm just below the sleeve of his hauberk, and that it stung like hell and was dribbling blood to join the sweat soaking his sleeve. *Pity it doesn't usually work like that.*

Signe led his horse over. He grounded the glaive point-down in the earth and mounted, grateful for the extra height. Stretcher parties and friends were helping the wounded back towards the ambulances and the aid station; he saw Aaron Rothman glare at him for a moment as he knelt beside one that couldn't be taken that far, then go back to his work.

"Casualties," he rasped, reaching for the canteen at his saddlebow.

"Eighty dead or as good as," Signe said. "One hundred thirty too badly wounded to fight. Let me see your arm."

"Well, *shit,*" Havel said.

Christ Jesus, we lost over a fifth of our effectives in fifteen minutes— He checked his watch; it had actually been more like an hour. *All right, an hour. It's barely noon. And we barely killed more of them than they did of us; we lost a lot of crossbows when they made that breakthrough. I can't afford to trade at that ratio.*

"Messengers," he said. "To company commanders: consolidate to the right."

Which would leave a great big gap between the far left of his line and the artillery and the A-listers, but they had to do it; one in five of the people he'd had standing in the line to begin with were gone now. The line had to be shorter if it wasn't to be thinner, and it had been too thin to start with.

"To Lord Eric, close in on the infantry's left. Prisoners—I want prisoners, the men-at-arms as well as the knights. And to Dr. Rothman, get all the wounded who can be moved onto the railway and out of here."

Because we may not have time later, he thought grimly.

Squads ran out onto the field, checking for living enemies. Where they found them, they began dragging them back, in a few cases subduing those still showing fight with a flurry of well-placed kicks first.

"See that they get care," he said, looking back at the aid station.

"What's next?" Signe said, as they watched the formation shift rightward.

Havel pulled his binoculars out of their leather-lined steel case. Left, two of the catapults were out of commission, smashed, smoldering wreckage in their pits. Three of the enemy's were destroyed likewise, which meant they'd suffered proportionately more, and their unprotected crews had taken heavy losses. And Alexi Stavarov's banner was going along the front of the enemy formation; as he passed a cheer went up, guttural and savage. The cavalry were reforming behind the footmen. *They* looked as if they would be glad to try where their betters had failed . . . and they hadn't suffered much at all, yet.

"To Captain Sarducci, concentrate on the infantry as they advance—raking fire from the center of the enemy formation to the left. To Lord Eric, don't charge until you get the signal. Their cavalry is still in the game."

"What next?" Signe said, her horse stepping sideways as an auxiliary leading a mule loaded with panniers of crossbow bolts went by.

Havel kept his voice soft. "Next they send in their foot, and we see how good we are at a fighting retreat. We can't take another attack like that, and we didn't kill enough of them to rock them back on their heels. We'd have done better if they hadn't pulled back in time, but Alexi was too smart to keep them face-first in the meat grinder after we didn't break."

Signe nodded soberly, her eyes worried. Her voice was calm as she went on: "Report from the bridge—"

"They're burning!" Ken Larsson shouted.

"Keep *down,*" his wife screamed in his ear.

She grabbed him by the collar of his hauberk and hauled

him bodily from the box he'd been standing on for a better
view. He staggered, windmilling his arms and trying to keep
erect on the rough footing of the railroad track, then went to
one knee. Bolts went *snap-snap-snap* through the air above.
They might have missed, but then again, they might not. And
hurled by the flywheel-powered throwers of the turtle
boats . . .

As if to underline the point, a bolt flashing through the
space above an engine on one of the railroad cars *didn't* miss.
Larsson swallowed thickly as a loader's head disappeared in a
spray of red mist, and the body toppled backward to land
bonelessly limp. The helmet he'd been wearing spun away
with a painful *bwannggg* harmonic, and landed like a flung
Frisbee in the river a hundred yards south of the bridge.

But that one is burning, he thought, ducking for a better
look through the slit between two of the metal shields.

The lead boat that had taken three of the napalm canisters
at once had smoke pouring out of the ventilators and the eye-
slits of the bridge. Suddenly hatches popped open and smoke
billowed up in earnest, along with yellow-orange flames. A
half-dozen men jumped out and threw themselves into the
blue-gray water of the Willamette. The last two were burning;
one more tried to crawl out and then fell back, and the boat
drifted away northward in a fog of sooty smoke.

The war-engine crews along the railroad bridge gave a
brief, savage cheer. A replacement for the luckless loader
stepped up and grabbed the forged-steel bolt he had dropped.
She slapped the giant metal arrow into the machine's trough;
it was four feet of hard alloy, tipped with copper and with
metal vanes like a real arrow's fletchings at the rear, as much
like a tank's long-rod penetrator as he'd been able to manu-
facture with the machine tools he could salvage and rig to run
by waterpower.

The engine traversed a little on its turntable, and then shot
with a huge, almost musical crinkling. The bolt flashed out
and struck almost before the thud of the throwing arms hitting rubber-sheathed metal sounded; the range was close
now, no more than thirty yards. The *ptink* of its impact was
so much like a BB hitting a soda can that it made him feel a

little nostalgic, until he remembered what it must be like inside, with that fragment of high-velocity metal bouncing around in the dark. Two more struck, and one skidded off the curved plates but the other punched through as well. The turtle boat lost way and began to slip back northward, downstream, turning slowly as it drifted. When it came back under control it continued to retreat, moving slowly to avoid taking on water; those holes would let liquid fire in as easily as the river.

That left the rest. "Pour it on!" Ken shouted. "Let them have it!"

"Easier said than done," Pam noted grimly.

The boats were closer now. The *snap-snap-snap* of their dart throwers sounded again and again, and the dents they made in the shields were deeper; then one punched through in a shower of sparks and went *ktinnng* off a wheel of one of the railroad cars. Smoke-trails cut through the air north of the bridge, drifting backward along with the fumes from napalm burning on the water to make the air hot and acridly choking. Ken turned angrily when one of his engines paused overlong before firing. His mouth closed when it *did* fire, the canister catching a turtle boat just as the hatch was raised for a volley of bolts, cracking on the edge and sending its load of burning jellied gasoline shooting through the entrance with hideous perfection. Something inside caught as well, and in an instant flame shot out of every opening in the hull in white-hot jets.

Then the three remaining warcraft were too close to shoot at; the engines on the railcars could not depress far enough to bear on them. Ken and his escorts jumped up on the railcars themselves. A moment later a three-round volley of the darts came up from below, one of them smashing its way through the railway ties. The crews of the engines looked at each other . . .

"OK," Pamela shouted. "You two pump!"

She picked up what looked like a gun, connected to a metal tank by a hose. Two of the crew sprang to a plunger-pump and began to rock it back and forth.

Ken bit back: *What do you think you're doing?* His wife

knew exactly what she was doing, and she was far more of a warrior than he.

His teeth were still on edge when she hopped casually off the railcar and looked down through the ties and the open framework of the railway bridge at the boats maneuvering below. Another *snap-snap-snap* came loud; Ken felt something hard smash into the floor of the car beneath his feet. Pamela's teeth showed in her lean face as she jammed the muzzle of the weapon down through the decking of the bridge and pulled the triggers set into the handgrips. One opened the valve, and a stream of amber-colored fluid as thick as a man's thumb began to jet down into the girders and open space below, scattering into a mist of droplets. A second later the other worked a spark-wheel set at the end of the long metal tube.

Whooosh!

The liquid stream turned into a banner of fire; smoke and hot air shot upward around the woman's feet. Ken blinked and rubbed his single eye, then peered over the edge of the car. One of the remaining turtle boats was burning itself, held by the current against a bridge pier. The others turned and started northward, white foam showing at their sterns where the propellers churned at maximum power.

"Many good-byes, you sons of bitches!" he roared after them.

Exultation brought a flush to his face as Pamela carefully raised the flamethrower and plunged the muzzle into a big metal tub of water lashed to the side of the railcar. The crews broke into cheering as well, hopping up and down and hammering each other on the back.

"Well, what are you waiting for?" Ken said. "You going to let them *get away*?"

They dove back to the throwing engines. Ken hopped back to the deck of the bridge. Two of Pamela's A-lister guards saluted him; he eyed them with some surprise. Not that the Outfit's elite had ever treated him with anything but respect; he was the bossman's father-in-law, and Eric's father, and Pamela's husband, for that matter. He'd been there from the beginning, when Mike Havel's Piper Chieftain crashed into a river in Idaho's Selway-Bitterroot National Wilderness, and the long trek back to Oregon started. That was myth and legend now, and equivalent to having relatives on the Mayflower.

But those salutes were a little different. . . .

"What?" he said to them. "It was Pamela who toasted that boat."

They grinned back at him; both were young men. "But you designed the stuff and built it and commanded this action, Lord Ken," one of them said.

"So . . ." the other continued, and they both saluted again.

He shook his head in wonderment, then looked up sharply at a hammer of hooves on the westward end of the bridge. A military apprentice was there; the youngster's horse didn't want to come onto the bridge, with its uncertain footing and stink of chemicals and hot metal and burning, for which he didn't blame it. Instead Larsson walked over, noticing that the hauberk was starting to get seriously unpleasant.

"Yes?" he said. *Uh-oh. That's a serious-news face, if I've ever seen one.*

"My lord, the Lord Bear's compliments, and get your teams hitched."

"We lost?" Ken said sharply, looking over to his right. The battlefield wasn't visible from here, but they'd heard some noise.

"No, my lord. We beat off their attack and sent them running. Lord Bear says that you should remember the words of . . ." She hesitated, frowning over the unfamiliar syllables. "Phyross of Ipi-something?"

"Pyrrhos of Epiros," he said. "Thank you: message acknowledged, will prepare for departure."

He turned, thinking through the orders necessary to get his railcars headed south once more; he might not be a soldier, but scheduling was something he was good at.

One of the A-listers who'd saluted him said: "Pyrrhos? Who's that, Lord Ken?"

"A Greek general who fought the Romans," he said, which apparently satisfied the man's curiosity.

And who's most famous for beating a Roman army at

hideous cost and then exclaiming: "Another victory like this, and we're ruined!"

His eyes went east over the river. His daughter Astrid was there, and good friends, and they were fighting the Protector's men too.

There are just too damned many of them! Damn Corvallis anyway. Can't they see that if we go down, they're next?

CHAPTER FIFTEEN

Near Mount Angel, Willamette Valley, Oregon
March 6th, 2008/Change Year 9

Sir Nigel Loring whistled silently to himself as he looked up at the walls of Mount Angel through the binoculars. Even with his slightly damaged eyes and by moonlight, even to someone who'd seen castles throughout Europe and helped rebuild more than one in England, they looked daunting. And in this light it seemed otherworldly as well, the pale white-wash shining as if carved from a single opal and lit by some internal glow.

The hill that held the monastery rose steeply half a mile northward from this patch of woods, nearly five hundred feet at its ridgelike top above the flat farmland that surrounded it; the whole mass of earth and rock was shaped like an almond, running from northwest to southeast, about a mile and a half long and half a mile wide at its widest point. The greatly shrunken town stood at its northern end, surrounded by a wall much like that he'd seen around Dun Juniper or Larsdalen. A road zigzagged up the north slope through a series of sentry towers; trying to fight your way up it would be a nightmare. But what awaited at the top . . .

Someone was very ingenious, he thought. *But then, I'm told that they have an excellent library.*

The walls were curved in a smooth oval, following the four-hundred-foot contour around the hillside, leaning back with a very slight camber. Building them must have been fairly sim-

ple; cut back into the hillside until the earth behind was a vertical bank as high as you wanted, and then build the wall up
against it; the construction method looked like mass-concrete,
big rocks set in a matrix of cement. The walls were not only
thick in themselves; they were backed up by the whole intervening mass of the hill, millions of tons of solid earth and
rock.

You *couldn't* knock them down, not without functioning
pre-Change artillery or explosives. Even if there was no opposition, he doubted present-day technology could *tear* them
down without thousands of laborers and years of effort. The
towers that studded the circuit of the curtain were built out
from the wall itself, starting about thirty feet up and swelling
out from the surface; they were probably steel-framed. He
could see the roofs of some of the buildings inside the curtain
over the crenellations and hoardings, but that wouldn't matter much—with that height advantage, throwing engines inside could dominate everything for a mile around, smashing
enemy catapults like matchboxes, and they'd be nearly impossible to knock out by anything trying to loft missiles back at
them.

There was little or no cover on the slopes below, either;
everything had been trimmed back to knee-height or less, the
dirt from the excavations used to make the slopes smoothly
uniform and nowhere less than forty degrees from the vertical, and some tough, low-growing vine planted to hold the surface. If things were arranged anything near to the way he'd do
it, the defenders could toss heavy stone shot or pump flaming
oil at any spot. The skin at the back of his neck crawled at the
thought of trying to lead a storming party to the base of the
walls.

*And if you did get there, what on earth could you do? Raise
scaling ladders eighty feet tall? Hit the wall with a sledgehammer? Jump up and down and wave your arms and shout, "I'm
tired of it all, drop bally great rocks on my head?"*

The light died as clouds hid the moon. A moment later it
began to rain, a fine silvery drizzle, and the fortress-
monastery vanished like a castle in a dream. The soldier-monk

beside him looked at his watch, hiding the luminous dial with his other hand, and murmured: "Wait. Very soon now . . ."

Nigel waited with an endless fund of patience, despite the damp chill that worked inward, making him conscious of his joints and the places where his bones had been broken—not more times than he could count, but more than you could tally on the fingers of one hand, too. He and the others around him were dressed in dark woolens, and armed with sword and bow, but they wore no armor, and only knitted balaclava pullover masks on their heads. This was a mission where only stealth could hope to succeed; leaving a trail of dead enemy sentries would be failure even if they made it through, since they had to be able to get out as well.

Although he strained his ears he could hear nothing; the besiegers' camp was on the northwest side of the hill, two miles distant from the crest and better than three from here, just this side of Zollner Creek along the line of the old Southern Pacific railway. They were relying on mobile patrols to keep the rest of the circuit secure, but they had to send those well out to keep beyond catapult range.

"The diversion will start now," the monk said. Grimly: "Men are dying as we speak to distract the Protector's troops. Let's go."

The party went forward into the rainy night; the monk in the lead, as the native guide; then Alleyne Loring and his father; then Eilir Mackenzie and Astrid Larsson and John Hordle spread out in a fan as rear guard. They moved with cautious speed, across a meadow where no cattle grazed in this time of war, past a small farmstead equally empty and silent, and through a bare-branched orchard of peach trees just past bud-break. At the northern edge of it Nigel caught a flash of movement, more sensed than seen or heard; he patted the air with one hand, and they all sank down behind the weeds that flanked the fence and the laneway behind it.

Good, the Englishman thought. *Not a sound.*

He wasn't surprised at either Alleyne or Hordle; he'd helped train them himself, and knew their capacities. Astrid wasn't that much of a surprise either; Sam Aylward had taught her, and Michael Havel, and he knew the one and had a lively respect for the other. The movement had probably been nothing more than a fox or rabbit.

But Eilir is *a bit of a startling phenomenon. I wouldn't have expected someone who couldn't hear to be able to be so quiet. She must have natural talent. I should have taken Hordle's word on it. He's not a man to let personal attachments cloud his judgment, not at all.*

Lying by the fenceline, he put his ear to the muddy ground; even under the patter of the rain he could hear hooves approaching, many of them; at least a dozen riders, possibly twice that. Moments later a clot of horsemen followed the sound that heralded them, shambling along in no particular order, but with arrows on the strings of their short recurved saddle-bows or heavy machete-like sabers in their hands; one rose in the stirrups as he watched and slashed at an overhanging oak bough, bringing it down with casual ease though the wood was wrist-thick. He recognized the type; eastern mercenaries, plainsmen, the same folk he'd seen in action out near Pendleton last year, and which reports had placed in the Protector's service in this war. One had a light lance across his saddlebow and prodded at the roadside vegetation now and then.

Twenty of them, more or less, he thought; it was hard to be certain, with the light of the moon gone and the rain getting heavier.

They halted uncomfortably near, although there was a strip of meadow between the fence and the dirt road. One dismounted to piss into the roadway, holding the skirts of his long oiled-linen duster aside; a few of the others spoke, though most kept a keen eye out. Their ponchos and slickers made them look top-heavy and somehow inhuman through the murk and drizzle as they hunched in their saddles, and their heads swept back and forth.

I suppose they're nervous in close country like this, he thought; it was all small farms and fields here now, with new fences and hedges splitting up bigger pre-Change holdings. Not much like the great sagebrush plains and canyonlands of their homes, and doubly so in the wet darkness.

"What's got the Portland pussies all het up?" one asked. "They all tore over to the north there like it was a pretty girl spreading wide and yellin' *first man here gets a piece!*"

"Or like it was free beer on tap," someone else said.

"Oh, it's some raid or other, the monks kicking up their heels, I expect," a slightly older man replied; none of them sounded as old as his son Alleyne's twenty-eight. "Y'all know what the Portland pussies are like, hup-one-two-I-gotta-pike-up-my-ass. They spook easy, you ask me."

"Goddamn cold here," another said, wiping at the water on a face that was a blob of slightly lighter darkness. He looked up, which would only get him another face-full.

"Hey, who's the pussy now?" the older voice scoffed. "Been a lot colder, riding herd in winter."

"Yeah, but it's usually a *dry* cold. This country's too wet soon as you get west of the mountains. A man could get mushrooms growing on his balls around here."

"*You* could, Al, considering where you've been known to stick your dick. Rain's good for the grass, anyways," the leader's voice said. "Hey, Frank, you finished pissing or you got an irrigation system going there?"

"That was good beer we found," the one named Frank said, buttoning up his leather trousers. "*Damn* good. Better than any to home. I liked them little spicy sausages too, and the sweet cake with the nuts, but the beer was *fine,* with a real bite to it and a good head. Hope the monks got more for us to take."

"You want to take it, go up and knock that hard head of yours on them walls," the leader said, and there was a soft chorus of chuckles. "Anyway, saddle up. We got to patrol twice as much ground while the Portland pussies are away."

"Excuse me, while the *noble knights* and their *vassals* are off there chasin' noises in the dark," Frank said as he vaulted easily back into the saddle of his quarter horse, landing with a wet smack of leather on leather. "Christ, what a bunch of play-acting put-ons."

"They're payin' the bills. Mebbe we should dismount and scout some more. There's a farmhouse over to there, about a quarter mile. It'd get us out of the wet, at least."

Nigel's hand made a slight, almost infinitesimal movement towards the sword slung over his back. That farmhouse was directly in back of them; if the patrol leapt the fence, or came to tear it down—

"They ain't payin' me enough to get off my horse all the time," Frank said. "Considering we checked that house yesterday and there's no beer *there*. If I'm going to be cold and wet, I'd rather do it moving."

The mercenaries laughed again; then their horses rocked into motion in unison. The party waited silently until the patrol's hooves had faded into the rain; Nigel held out a hand and made them wait a moment more while he pressed his ear to the ground again. The muffled thump continued, fading steadily; they hadn't stopped to come dashing back.

"Go!" he said softly.

They crossed the road in pairs; he mentally blessed the overconfidence that had made the Protector leave only a bit over two thousand men here—enough to invest the town and the splendid fort, to be sure, but not nearly enough to encircle it, or keep small groups from infiltrating under cover of darkness. If they'd spread all their men in a thin ring around it out of supporting range of each other, they'd have been horribly vulnerable to counterattack and sally if the garrison was in any strength. Instead they'd sensibly kept most together in a single body big enough to defend.

Although in their commander's shoes I'd be screaming for another two or three thousand men, enough to put a fortified camp at each point of the compass and drive a ditch and trench all the way around. Interesting. There haven't been many sieges since the Change; nobody's quite sure of how to go about it, or how different it will be from the books.

A pruned vineyard covered the slight upward slope on the other side, the vines catching at their legs like twisted fingers in the dark. Then they went through a field, half plowed and half still in crimson clover; the disk-plow itself stood forlorn in the center of the field, abandoned when the word of war came, marking the spot where the sucking, gluey mud gave way to wet pasture. Nigel blessed the rain even as he cursed the squelching sounds their boots made and the way the ground clung to them; still, it was getting as dark as a wardrobe, and the hissing, drumming sound made a blanket of white noise around them. They were safe unless they blundered directly into another patrol; he could see less of the hill and fortress than he'd been able to half a mile back. It was fortunate the monk knew his way, because this was exactly the sort of situation that could get even experts thoroughly lost.

Ground lifted under their feet; they met a stone retaining wall about waist-high, and then scrambled up the steep slope. Whatever it was that grew there was tough, only giving a little under their boots with a ripping sound and a sharp green smell, but it was slick with rain and liquid mud from the soil below, and they had to bend double and pull themselves up with their hands as well. It was a relief to stop when they ran into the stone and concrete of the wall, to rest against the rough surface and let their hearts slow; the bad part of that was that it made him feel how the rain sucked heat out of his body. Even with the rain and the dead blackness of an overcast night, he still felt conspicuous in his black outfit against the whitewashed wall; a little light leaked out from the arrow-slits in the towers above, enough to make out his hand in front of his face.

Of course, my eyesight isn't of the best. Thank God for hard contacts, what?

John Hordle muttered something about hoping the monks could haul them up, but the expected knotted rope or Jacob's Ladder didn't appear. Instead their guide drew his dagger and pounded sharply on the wall in some sort of signal, with a dull *clunk* sound that made him think the pommel was made of lead. And there was something a little wrong about it even so . . .

"Be ready," the Mount Angel warrior said as he stepped aside.

A chunk of wall about four feet tall and three wide slid up soundlessly, with a smoothness that argued for counterweighted levers. The five of them went through into the gaping maw behind, Hordle swearing mildly at the way it cramped his huge form; as they passed the door, Nigel saw that it was stone and concrete covering a plate of steel. When the last of them passed, it sank back into place with a sough of displaced air, arguing for a nearly hermetic seal; more steel sounded on steel as bars went home with a *chunk* sound. Then a lantern was unshuttered. It was dim enough, but almost painfully bright to eyes so long in the darkness, showing a short arched tunnel leading to a tubelike spiral staircase rising upward. Two men in mail shirts with shortswords on their belts stood by a spoked wheel set into the side of the tunnel; they nodded in friendly fashion.

The round, unremarkable face of the third figure, carrying the lantern, was framed in a visored sallet helm much like the one Nigel Loring ordinarily wore himself, but he could have sworn . . .

"I am Sister Antonia."

Well, well. It is *a woman. I wouldn't have expected it of Catholics, and rather old-fashioned ones, from what I've heard.*

"Do you wish to see the abbot at once? You must have all had a very hard day."

"Thank you, Sister," Nigel said politely, smoothing his mustache with one finger.

The young woman's smile was charming and showed dimples; she wore a dark robe over what looked like three-quarter armor: breast-and-back, vambraces, tassets, mail sleeves.

"But if he's available—" the Englishman went on.

"Certainly, Sir Nigel. And to answer your question, I'm a Sister of the Queen of Angels Monastery, which has always been closely associated with Mount Angel. Please follow me, sirs, ladies."

Nigel shrugged, slightly embarrassed—assuming something that looked odd was odd had become a habit since the Change—and did so. Sister Antonia picked up a poleax in her other hand and trotted tirelessly upward despite the weight of her gear, which the Englishman knew from long personal experience would be considerable. Motion made the lantern sway, casting huge moving shadows in the tall stairwell, and the echoes of their rubber-soled shoes and the nun's hobnails provided a background of squeak and clatter. The effort of his own seven-story climb was welcome, warming him a little in his sodden clothes and squelching shoes. The concrete walls themselves were dry and smooth, and the soil around them probably well drained; this was obviously recent work, not more than a few years old. He wondered how the hilltop community managed for water.

Cisterns, I suppose, he thought. *And possibly deep wells with wind pumps; boreholes would do if they had to go down four hundred feet or better from the hilltop. They certainly have some good engineers.*

After an interminable time they came out into large dim cellars used as storerooms, stretching off into the distance. They were piled with sacks of grain and dried peas and beans, barrels of beer and wine and salt pork and beef, plastic trash containers recycled to hold sharp-smelling sauerkraut, flitches of bacon and hams hanging from racks, and great banks of metal office shelving supporting glass Mason jars of preserved fruits and vegetables and meats. Then they went up a much shorter flight of metal stairs and through an iron grillwork door and into a ready room-cum-armory, with pole-axes and crossbows racked around the walls. A sparse four armed men and two women sat at a table that could have seated twenty; Nigel smiled to himself at the sight of their stifled yawns. Military boredom seemed to be a universal characteristic, although most soldiers he knew wouldn't have a breviary open to pass the time. The guards nodded silently, gravely polite.

"You must be cold and hungry," Sister Antonia said. It was the first time she'd spoken since greeting them, but it had been a calm, friendly silence. "Please, this way."

Another flight of stairs and they were in what he suspected had been the Abbey before the Change, rooms modern-seeming but plain, dim except for the one lantern and occasional gas night-lights burning on wall brackets, turned down low behind their glass shields. Unlike the guardroom they were far from empty, but the people in them looked to be ordinary civilians, not monastics, many children and young mothers among them, asleep—not surprising given the late hour—on improvised pallets. There was a surprising absence of clutter or mess or smell, and Nigel knew from bitter expe-

rience how hard that was to avoid when you crammed displaced people into unfamiliar surroundings.

"This was our guesthouse," Sister Antonia said. "These folk
are refugees from our outlying villages and farms."

*Which confirms my guess . . . probably the town itself is full
to the gills, if the surplus is here.*

"Baths here, Sir Nigel, for you and your men. And in the
next room for you, Lady Astrid, Lady Eilir. Then something to
eat, and Abbot Dmwoski will be pleased to speak with you."

The bathrooms were literally that, with a row of big tin tubs,
and all the plumbing post-Change, with pipes running from
methane-fired boilers. Water steamed, and Nigel sank into it
gratefully, flogging himself with raw willpower to keep from
letting the infinitely welcome warmth soothe him into sleepi-
ness. Alleyne and Hordle were much more cheerful, but then
they were still a few years short of thirty. Hordle gave a snort
of laughter when water splashed onto the tiled floor as he
lowered his huge, hairy, muscular bulk into the largest tub and
found it a very tight fit.

"Never 'ad much to do with monks," he said meditatively.
"Even the Crowley Dads." That Anglican order had grown
spectacularly in England since the Change—several hundred
times, relative to the surviving total population. "Eilir says this
lot have a good reputation. Certainly the one who showed up
when we had the brush with the bandits and Sir Jason . . ."

"Father Andrew," Alleyne put in.

"He was a good sort. Tough as nails, mind you, but not
mean with it. And the militiamen with him, they were just
farmers and cobblers or what-'ave-you, but they liked him—
couple of them knocked back enough to let their secrets out,
if you know what I mean. They had nothing but good to say of
Abbot Dmwoski."

Alleyne nodded thoughtfully. "They must be fairly formidable to have lasted this long, though, Father. They're right between Molalla and Gervais. This fort would be invulnerable to
anything but paratroopers, but they had to survive long
enough to build it, and hold onto the lands around it."

Nigel called up the map in his mind; Gervais to the west,
Molalla to the east, both slightly north of the monastery and

its lands, both the seats of Association barons from the second Change Year. This place *had* been in the pincers, since the Protectorate first organized itself.

"And they've been very cooperative so far," he said. "But the proof of the pudding, and all that."

"Speaking of which, I could do with some pudding," Hordle said. "Or a crust, come to that."

Nigel had been conscious of hunger; that brought it home, a sharp, twisting pain in his gut. They stayed in the hot water just long enough to soak out the bone-chill of a long, hard day spent wet and cold; he suspected that the two young men lingered a little for his sake. Robes and sandals were offered as their clothes were taken away to be cleaned and dried; the light gear in their packs was stowed in another set of plain rooms, these with beds and woolen blankets, jug and table, and a crucifix on the wall of each; then they were led to a refectory.

That was a long, dimly lit room with trestle tables and benches and a reader's lectern. Nobody was there but themselves and an exhausted-looking squad who were probably the night watch, and a teenage boy minding the hearth; a big pot simmered quietly in the fireplace over a low bed of coals, and everyone ladled themselves bowls of thick lentil stew with chunks of salt pork and onion in it, and took fresh brown bread and butter and cups of some hot herbal infusion that tasted acridly pleasant. Nigel smiled quietly to himself as he spooned up the stew; hunger really *was* the best sauce, something he'd learned a very long time ago. That was the only thing that made much of what a soldier had to eat tolerable, and this was far, far better than a good deal of what he'd choked down in various bivouacs.

When they'd finished an older monk came to their table, a man with swept-back silver hair that still had a few blond streaks in it, round glasses, a square chin and an elaborate pectoral cross on the breast of his black robe.

"Abbot Dmwoski?" Nigel asked, though he'd expected someone younger from the descriptions.

Behind him Astrid coughed tactfully. The monk gave her a nod and smile, and then shook his head.

"I'm Father Plank, Sir Nigel, the prior here. I was in fact the abbot, but I resigned a week after the Change, since the office obviously required a younger and more vigorous man with different skills—this way, if you please."

He had the same soothing air of trained calm as Sister Antonia, and he led them through the guesthouse, through new-looking cloisters, and into an older building with a red-tiled roof in the same comfortable silence. There was a smell of clean soap and incense and candle-wax, and once in the distance a musical chanting—Gregorian, perhaps *Verbum caro factum est,* though it was hard to tell precisely. The office at the end of their travels showed gaslight under the door; within it were plain whitewashed walls, bookshelves, filing cabinets, a desk, chairs, and an angular painting of the Madonna and Child before which another man in a black robe knelt, his eyes closed, rosary beads moving through his fingers as his lips moved. The Englishman noticed that a bedroom let off this office, visible through a half-open door; small, not much bigger than a walk-in closet, and starkly furnished with an iron cot and a small chest of drawers. The only other furniture in it was an armor-stand and a rack for sword, helmet, poleax and metal gauntlets.

Eilir and Astrid made a silent gesture of reverence towards the icon; so, to his surprise, did John Hordle. He was a little less astonished when the big man gave him a wink, and Eilir tucked her hand through the crook of his arm. Dmwoski rose gracefully, despite his stocky build; that was apparently all muscle.

"Forgive me," he said when the introductions had been made; his hand was as sword-calloused as Nigel's own, and possibly stronger. The accent was General American, with a slight hint of something rougher beneath it. "Time for private prayer has been scarce lately."

He indicated the chairs with a wave of the hand, nodding in friendly fashion to the two young women who'd been here before, and the older monk sat quietly beside his desk.

"Father," Nigel said, a little awkwardly, and uncertain how to begin.

He'd been a courteously indifferent member of the Church of England like most men of his class, profession and generation, but despite the religious revival that had swept the survivors in his homeland during the terrible years, he'd never become comfortable with men of faith.

Even my darling Juniper makes me a little uneasy at times. But they were here to sound the ruler of Mount Angel out, to evaluate him as well as to make an offer of joint action.

The abbot's eyes were blue like those of his guest, but paler. They had a net of fine lines by their corners, and suddenly he was convinced that the man had come late to a cleric's calling; those were marksman's eyes. Nigel judged him to be around forty, or perhaps a little older if the tonsure in his coal-black hair was part-natural. A strong, close-shaved jowl was turned blue by a dense beard of the same color.

"A pleasure to meet you, Sir Nigel. I hope your needs were seen to?"

"Very well indeed, Father," Nigel said. "In fact, better than at many a five-star hotel I've checked into after a hard trip—less fuss, less babble and more real comfort."

The abbot's square, pug-nosed face split in a chuckle. "Ah, Sir Nigel, there you hit upon one of the worst temptations of the monastic life."

"Temptations?" Nigel said, surprised and interested.

"To men of discernment, my son, a mild and disciplined asceticism is far more comfortable than a surfeit of luxuries, which are a mere vexation to the spirit," he said. "As a soldier, I expect you understand; a monastic order and a military unit have that in common."

Nigel's eyebrows rose. "I do indeed, Father Dmwoski. And you seem to have combined the two rather effectively here."

This time the smile was a little grim. "Needs must. The Rule of St. Benedict and of course ordinary duty both enjoin us to take extraordinary measures for our flock in times of trouble. We had this position—secure even before the walls—nearly two hundred strong young men at our seminary here, the good Sisters in town, everything was falling apart and what needed to be done to preserve something from the wreck was obvious, if terrible . . . And there are precedents—the Templars and Hospitalers, the orders that ruled Rhodes and Malta, the Teutonic Knights . . ."

"No criticism implied!" Nigel said, recognizing a defensive tone when he heard it, and a little surprised to hear it from a man who struck him on short acquaintance as stolidly self-sufficient.

But at least he isn't a burning-eyed fanatic for the Church Militant. I don't know what sort of commander he makes, but I think I like him as a man.

"Your pardon," the abbot said, with a self-deprecating gesture. "I'm afraid it's a slightly sensitive subject. I was a soldier myself, before I made my profession as a monk here. Not that long before the Change, as it happens."

Nigel grinned. "I suspected as much. But after all . . . Think of Bishop Odo on the field of Hastings—as it happens, some of my ancestors were there with him. And doesn't the Bible say: *Benedictus dominus deus meus qui docet manus meas ad proelium et digitos meos ad bellum!*"

The abbot laughed wholeheartedly, yet with a rueful note below it. "Be careful, Sir Nigel, or I'll start suspecting you're the devil who can quote Scripture! Yet I became a monk and a priest to pray, and to seek God, to find forgiveness for my sins, and to serve His servants, not to wage war, and certainly not to exercise secular authority. Priests advising and criticizing politicians is one thing, priests becoming rulers themselves is altogether another. There may be a worse form of government than theocracy in the long run, but offhand I can't think of any. Even the greatest popes of the Middle Ages weren't up to governing laymen with any credit to themselves or the Church, and I most certainly am not."

The older monk shook his head at his superior. "*I'm* afraid our holy abbot is still a little resentful that we propelled him into that chair after the Change; and he bellowed like a bull when we insisted on his elevation to a bishopric. We had to nearly *drag* him to his consecration as bishop."

"There's the example of St. Martin of Tours," Dmwoski said dryly.

"And as his spiritual counselor I've told him several times not to confuse the virtue of humility with a sinful reluctance to take up one's cross. God obviously sent him to us just before the Change for a reason."

The abbot shrugged. "Hopefully someday we can return to a life of prayer and labor . . . ordinary labor, that is. Now, with regard to your plan, Sir Nigel, we have the general outline—"

"It's actually the Clan Mackenzie's plan, Father," Nigel corrected politely. "I'm one of the Chief's military advisors, no more. And of course the CORA contingent has agreed as well, and the Dúnedain Rangers."

The abbot nodded. "I have every confidence in Lady Juniper's abilities . . . and in her advisors, and in Lady Astrid and in . . . what do they call them these days? The CORA-boys?" A broader smile. "Sam Aylward and I have gotten on very well over the years. We have some things in common."

Nigel felt a small knot of tension relax in his chest; this was a man he could talk to, and probably persuade. "I realize this is a great risk to ask of you."

Dmwoski spread his hands. "Much must be risked in war. Yes, we have an impregnable fortress here, but if the Protector's men conquer everything outside, we will eventually starve. Not soon, we've been storing up supplies since we started building the walls, but eventually. And precisely because these walls *are* impregnable, they can be held by a small force. Allowing all our troops to be pinned down here waiting would be foolish . . . *if* there are allies sufficient to give us some chance of using them decisively outside."

"And if the Protector is very foolish, Father," Astrid Larsson said unexpectedly.

The abbot's slightly shaggy eyebrows rose. "You think he will be, my child?"

"He's a wicked man, and an arrogant one," Astrid said. "The two often make a smart man do stupid things. Oft evil will will evil mar."

"True." Dmwoski sighed. "But I have my flock to think of, their children, their lives, their homes and farms, all of which I risk by defying the Protectorate. For that reason, I considered taking his offer of full internal autonomy under his suzerainty, with only a modest tribute to pay—a generous offer, on the face of it."

The outsiders tensed slightly. Dmwoski's lips quirked. "But only *considered,* and not very seriously. I decided to decline it for two reasons: first, the man's word is not good. Even if I could stomach sending back runaways from his justice, so-called, once he was supreme in these territories, how could I hold him to any of it? Second, I have the souls as well as the bodies of my people to consider; the offer included recognizing his puppet Pope. Bishop Rule was once a good man, and I would have sworn a holy one—"

Father Plank cut in, seeing Nigel's question: "Arminger's antipope. Bishop Landon Rule. Quite legitimately a bishop, and since he collected two more, some of their acts are canonically valid, even legal—bishops can ordain priests, and three bishops can licitly consecrate another, particularly in emergencies and *in partibus infidelorum* when contact with the larger Church is cut off. Claiming the Throne of St. Peter is of course vain and blasphemous presumption, not to mention the atrocities of his Inquisitors and his support of a brutal secular tyranny."

Dmwoski nodded. "And to think that twelve years ago he ordained *me* . . . The most charitable interpretation of his actions over the last decade is that he was driven mad by what he suffered after the Change. So many were, of course . . . I understand that he was captured by Eaters, and freed by Protectorate soldiers. Norman Arminger is deeply wicked, a monster of lust and cruelty and power-hunger, yet his own selfishness and corruption put limits to the damage he can do. But when a good man turns with all his heart to evil, that is truly the nightmare of God. Rule has led many others astray, others who wished sincerely to return to the Faith, by falling in with Arminger's medievalist fantasies and resurrecting the worst evils to which the Church was prey before the modern era."

Nigel kept his face carefully neutral, a mask of polite interest. He felt an impulse to kick his son in the shin when he heard a slight muffled snort from the younger man's chair.

The abbot shrugged. "Yes, I see your point, Mr. Loring, though your father is too polite to speak. There is an element of the kettle calling the pot black there. We have been deprived of certain things by what I believe to be veritable divine intervention, like that which halted the sun over Joshua or sent the Flood in Noah's time; accordingly we must conclude that those things were vanities, leading us astray, or that they threatened worse consequences than the Change itself."

Alleyne made a skeptical sound. "Your pardon, Father, but *divine intervention* is a bit of an antiseptic term to describe the worst disaster in human history. And I fail to see how anything could be worse."

Dmwoski smiled, invincibly courteous. "God's lessons sometimes appear harsh, to our fallible perspective; consider Noah. Or consider what our Lord himself suffered at Gethsemane; without shedding of blood, there is no remission of sin. I always thought that the Flood was a metaphor, but after the Change, who knows? Without the Change, we might have destroyed ourselves altogether, or used genetic engineering and other forms of meddling to abolish genuine humanity from within, perhaps removing death itself, until there was no limit to the cruel empires of pride and lust that we could erect. God knows; I do not. And how will the Change be seen many generations hence? This particular space of years does not gain any special significance because our lives happen to occupy it, remember."

"That's more or less what many another preacher you hear these days says, some of them—no offense—quite cracked. It's also what Pope Leo proclaims," Nigel observed.

Dmwoski nodded. "However, Martin Luther—an intemperate and hasty man, but far from a fool—once remarked that humanity is like a drunken peasant trying to ride a horse. We mount, fall off on one side, remount, and fall off on the other. God was undoubtedly telling us something when He sent the Change, but I doubt that His intent was that Holy Church should repeat all the many sins and errors we so painfully repented. We are called, I think, to revive the *best* of our long tradition."

Alleyne spoke up again, a smile in his voice: "I gather you

won't be telling anyone *Slay them all, God will know his own,* then, Father. That's reassuring."

The churchman raised a hand, acknowledging the point with a rueful lift of an eyebrow. "The Albigensian Crusade was, I will admit, not the Church's high point."

"Or burning any witches," Astrid added dryly.

Dmwoski pointed an admonishing finger at her. "No. Mind you, my daughter, your remarkably young Old Religion is patently false, erroneous, conducive to sin in some respects, and—frankly—rather childish."

Eilir stuck out her tongue, put her thumb to her nose and waggled her fingers defiantly: the two monks chuckled. Plank spoke:

"Yet if mistaken and childish, not altogether evil or utterly damnable . . . as Rule's twisting of holy things is. A truth perverted is more terrible than any simple mistake, for such evil draws power from the good it warps, and discredits it by association."

"Exactly," Dmwoski said grimly. He hesitated, then went on: "I gather you can tell us definitely that the Holy Father did not survive? Rule has been spreading various tales purportedly from the Tasmanian ship that brought you here from England."

"No, I'm afraid he died in the Vatican, when it was overrun and burned about a month after the Change," Nigel said. "I led a mission to Italy four years ago on King Charles' orders, primarily to remove works of art or store them safely—a gesture, and a frustrating gesture, since there was so much . . . In any event, there are groups of civilized survivors in Italy, not just the scattering of neo-savages you find in France or Spain. Some small enclaves in the Alps, a clump of towns and villages in Umbria, and a somewhat bigger clump in Sicily around Enna. Several hundred thousand altogether. They all agree that Pope John Paul refused to leave Rome himself, although he ordered some others out of the city just before the final collapse; the Swiss Guard escorted them. Cut their way to safety, rather."

The clerics sighed and crossed themselves. "He is with the saints now. There is still some organized presence of the Church there in Italy, then?"

"Yes; at least one cardinal . . . what was his name, Alleyne? We met him briefly in Magione."

"A German name, Father Dmwoski . . . Yes, Cardinal Ratzinger; he was in charge, and had regular links with the other parts of Italy and southern Switzerland."

"Cardinal Joseph Ratzinger?" Father Plank said, giving Alleyne a keen look as the younger Loring nodded.

Nigel went on: "There was talk of a general Council once regular sea-travel resumes farther afield, to discuss the implications of the Change. Talk of reunion with the Church of England, too. And about eighteen months before we left, we heard that the College had been summoned, though it was expected to take some time—the largest surviving group of Catholics is in South America, of course, and conditions there are chaotic at best and a nightmare at worst. So you gentlemen should have a new pope by now, probably the cardinal we met, though God alone knows when we here will have regular communications with Europe again. I'm sorry we can't give you more details, but we had other priorities."

Both the clerics looked pleased; the abbot nearly rubbed his hands, and Plank went on:

"Cardinal Ratzinger is an extremely sound man, a theologian of note, with a special devotion to our own St. Benedict. Mother Church is in good hands, then. That's very good news indeed, Sir Nigel, and we thank you from the bottom of our hearts."

My oath, though, that was a strange visit, Nigel thought as he inclined his head in polite acknowledgment.

He'd always liked Italy before the Change; friends of his had lived in Tuscany, or Chiantishire as it was sometimes called, although he'd found their playing at peasants in the over-restored farmhouses that had once housed real ones rather tiresome. And after the Change, the empty parts of the peninsula were simply more of the all-too-familiar dangerous wilderness, the ruined cities an old story by then. The living Umbrian towns, though . . .

It was very strange to see the Switzer pikemen under the walls of the Badia . . . that gave me a bit of a chill. I half expected Sir John Hawkwood and the White Company to come over the hill next, or at least Sigismondo Malatesta and a troop of condottieri.

"The Church spanned the world before air travel," Dmwoski said stoutly. "Before telegraphs and steamships, for that matter. We have free bishoprics in Corvallis and Ashland and here at Mount Angel, and others within reach—Boise, and the Free Cities in the Yakima country. We Benedictines have carried the torch through a Dark Age before. *Succisa Virescit*—'pruned, it grows again.' We will knit the threads once more, here and all over the world; the more reason to resist the damnable pretensions of the antipope in Portland."

He shook back his shoulders. "And so, back to the immediate problem."

"If you could tell me exactly what forces you have available, then?"

"We can commit twelve hundred troops; all our knight-brethren, four hundred heavy infantry and the best of the town and country militia," Dmwoski said decisively. "That will leave enough over to hold these walls, at a pinch. And I will lead the force we commit, of course. But we cannot sally effectively unless the enemy can be drawn off from their investment of the town, most particularly their heavy lancers. We do not have the numbers to fight them in the open field by ourselves, and we have no cavalry to speak of. And whatever we do must be done before they bring in more men from elsewhere."

Nigel fought down a yawn and shook his head. "Drawing them out of their camp and into the field we can manage," he said. "This will require careful coordination, though. We have to draw them off, but not so far that we're out of supporting range of your force, or we risk being defeated separately."

"Very careful coordination." Dmwoski smiled. "And clear heads. I suggest we begin tomorrow with my staff, after Lauds."

The older monk rose to lead them to their beds. Dmwoski's hand rose to sign the Cross.

"Pax Vobiscum."

Castle Todenangst, Willamette Valley, Oregon
March 6th, 2008/Change Year 9

Rudi Mackenzie looked up at walls and turrets and banners, gleaming in the morning sun; the castle reared higher and higher as they rode eastward from Newberg. Rolling fields passed by on either side, where ox-teams drew plows that turned sod into dark rows of damp earth, and green quilted tree-studded pasture, acres of blue-green wheat rippling in the breeze, orderly vineyards and orchards of plums and hazelnuts, with forested hills behind—the Parrett Mountains, and behind them the tiny white cone of Mount Hood in the far distance. It reminded him of a picture he'd seen in a book . . . something with a French name that sounded like 'rich hours,' about the Duke of Berry.

The fortress-palace had been built on an old butte just south of the road; carved out of it by brute force, and then the remains bound in ferroconcrete, but despite its massiveness there was a curious grace to the great complex. A curtain wall with towers and gates surrounded it; the skyward-thrusting bulk of the keep rose above where the hill had been planed away to make its base; the high walls of the donjon were covered in granite of a pale pearl color, and towers higher yet were spaced around its oval length, with banners flaunting from the spiked peaks of their green-copper roofs.

A single tower taller than all the rest shone on the southernmost height, its conical roof gilded, but the circular shaft of the tower sheathed in some smooth black stone whose crystal inclusions glittered almost painfully bright.

A large village stood just on the northern side of the road half a mile short of the turnoff to the castle, unwalled but all looking new-built as well, houses in brick with tile roofs, a gray church with a square steeple, and a hall. He got a whiff of manure and pigsties from it, but the stock was neatly penned, and nothing but dogs and children and chickens scrambled in the street. A mass of people had turned out, five or six hundred, waving little black flags with the Eye on them; he could hear them cheering, or calling out Matti's name and title. It seemed a little odd to see all the men in trousers, and all the women in double tunics; apart from the occasional longer *airsaid,* men and women in the Clan wore kilts or robes or nothing much as the occasion indicated, and in Corvallis and the Bearkiller territories nearly everyone wore pants anyway.

It wasn't the first time he'd heard cheers since they'd entered the Protector's lands, but . . .

They sound a lot more like they mean it this time, he thought. *I guess they like her more here. Or maybe they like her mom and dad more here. None of them look hungry, at least, not in this place.*

The men-at-arms looking on from behind the crowd still gave him a bit of a chill, though. He didn't like the way the villagers moved aside when one walked close. And it was odd to have people pointing and murmuring at him, fright on their faces, as if he was some sort of exotic, dangerous wild beast.

"Wow, Matti," he said, waving at the castle. "That's something! You told me about it but it looks . . . like it's really something. Yeah."

He didn't say what that something was, but Mathilda Arminger beamed proudly.

"Yup," she said, and chattered on: "Dad built it for Mom, really. When I was just a baby. I don't remember it when it wasn't finished, though. There's this book on it the chief engineer did up when it was finished, it's pretty interesting, with drawings and everything—I liked it even when I was just a kid, before last year, there are a lot of pictures they took."

"It's real big to build so quick. I mean, it's as big as a lot of the old buildings from before the Change!"

Mathilda nodded proudly. "Dad says that castles were quick to build in the old days too—a couple of years. And it's easier the way we did it, with the concrete and the steel rods and stuff. We live here a lot, when we're not in Portland or visiting around with the counts and barons and Marchwardens. It's real quick, we ride over to Newberg and then get on the railway with guys pedaling, and we're at the city palace in Portland just like that."

She snapped her fingers, and Tiphaine Rutherton looked

over at them, then nodded and smiled when she realized the gesture wasn't meant to get her attention.

She's *been smiling a lot,* Rudi thought. *I mean, smiling a lot for her. I bet she's counting up what she's going to get for bringing Matti back. And for getting me.*

She was also wearing the war harness of a man-at-arms now, rather than her camouflage outfit, though with the helmet slung at her saddlebow; so were the rest of her party, and the children had acquired clothes rushed south to the border station where they'd paused for baths and food and a good night's sleep. They'd also picked up a four-horse carriage and servants, but Mathilda preferred to leave them inside and ride with him—the riding horses were splendid, not as magnificent as Epona of course, but better than any others he'd ever seen. Rudi had been given well-made boots that fit him, and trousers and t-tunic of fine green cloth. A loose linen shirt went under it and a leather belt tooled and studded with silver was cinched around his waist; on his head he wore a flat cloth hat with a roll around the edge and a tail hanging down the side, and a silver badge and peacock feather at the front.

Mathilda was wearing a similar set of clothes in brown, though with jeweled embroidery and a golden clasp on a hat whose tail was of red silk; that was a boy's gear by northern reckoning, but evidently Princess Mathilda was an exception to the usual rules. She'd also left off the dagger when she saw he wasn't allowed to have his dirk back. She said her mother had probably thought to have the clothes ready, and from his one meeting with her she probably had indeed.

Matti's mother is real smart, Rudi thought. *I don't think she's real nice, though.* He licked his lips slightly, then stiffened his back; he was about to meet the Lord Protector. *I'm not scared. And if I am, I won't let anyone see!*

His mother had said something about Castle Todenangst once, when she'd seen a picture of it: *Sure, and the man must have been Walt Disney in a previous life.* He wasn't sure precisely what that meant, but all the grown-ups had laughed, and the memory of it heartened him now.

It's no use saying anything to Matti. I mean, if I say, your dad's going to have them cut off my head, *she'd just get scared and mad and couldn't do anything. She loves her dad.*

An escort of the Protector's household knights flanked them on either side, the black-and-crimson pennants of their lances snapping in the mild southerly breeze. There were more soldiers about, on either side of the roadway; tented camps stretched there, set up in pastures and fallow fields, from little pup tents to big pavilions with the banners of knight or baron flaunting from their peaks. Crossbowmen shot at targets, footmen and men-at-arms hacked at pells; mounted men practiced spearing the ring or tilting at each other with practice lances topped with padded leather balls; Pendleton mercenaries galloped about firing arrows into hay bales, or slicing lumps of thrown horse dung in midair with their heavy, curved sabers. Some of the easterners broke off to ride over and stare at the procession; many were bare to the waist, with feathers stuck in horse-tail braids down their backs and patterns of black and red bars and dots painted on their faces and chests, or shaggy beards. Troops of all varieties crowded to the edge of the road, and began cheering themselves when they saw who it was, throwing caps and even weapons in the air. Mathilda stood in the stirrups and bowed to both sides of the road, waving and blowing kisses.

Then they turned right and the way rose south towards the castle's outer gates; spearmen lined the road on either side, but more people stood on the battlements above the gate and cheered as well; those had servants' tabards on over their clothes. The gates were of black steel with the Lidless Eye wreathed in flames on them in some red-gold alloy; when the great portals swung open it was eerily like riding into the empty pupil, like a window into nothing. Little flowers rained down as they went on over the drawbridge with a booming of hooves on thick planks, and under the fangs of the portcullis; there was a wet moat, smelling fairly fresh, and thick with water lilies. The tunnel-like passage beyond had a steep rise to it, and must have cut through a fair bit of the former hillside, not just the curtain wall.

"Do you like it?" Mathilda asked as they came back into the sunlight.

"It's really something," Rudi repeated sincerely.

Inwardly, he shivered slightly, feeling something of the demonic, driving will that had reared these stony heights amid the death of a world. Mathilda leaned over and gave his hand a squeeze; he returned it gratefully for an instant.

On the inside the wall was about half the forty-foot height it had been at the moat's edge, which meant that the lower half backed against the cut-away hill. They'd done the same at Dun Juniper and other places; he knew that was sound technique.

The outer wall isn't as high as Mount Angel, but it goes farther around . . . he thought. *It's pretty big, bigger than home or Larsdalen. Not nearly as big as Corvallis, though.*

He remembered to look for the things Sam Aylward and Nigel Loring had taught him.

Good location. This is the high ground for long catapult range all around. Probably lots of water inside—the mountains over there to dawn-ward would mean powerful springs and good wells. Good communications. And it dominates the passage between the Parrett Mountains and the Dundee Hills, and the bridge where we came across the Willamette.

Houses and sheds, workshops and barracks and stables and shops lined the inside of the wall's circuit. At their doorsteps was a broad asphalt-paved street lined with trees, and on the inner edge of that was another row of buildings built into the hill so that the rear windows of the two-story buildings were at ground level. Above rose steep hillside, terraced with smooth stonework retaining walls, scattered with flower-banks—a few already in bloom, crocus and narcissus—lawns and trimmed bushes, fountains shooting water high and white above carved stone salvaged from dead mansions—

I was right about the water. They must have plenty.

—and benches and pergolas. Nothing was substantial enough to give anyone on the slope much cover; every inch of it and the inner side of the walls and the ground outside could be swept from the battlements above.

A single road switchbacked up the northern face to the keep's entrance. Trumpets brayed triumphantly as they rode through; this time the roadway turned right in a deep cutting inside the gate-towers, and then left again before it reached the surface; that meant the walls must have the hill backing them for fifty feet up or better; the hooves of their party clattered in a din of harsh echoes until they came to the light once more.

The courtyard within was huge, better than an acre, but the walls and the towers at the corners still placed much of it in shadow this early in the morning. It was paved with patterns of colored brick, scattered with planters, and buildings were set against the walls around all sides of it; towers rose at the four corners, seeming to reach for the scattered clouds above. One flank was a great church covered in white marble, with stained-glass windows; the central rose showed the stern, bearded face of Christ Pantocrator sitting in judgment. The right seemed to be living quarters; along the south was a great feasting hall with strips of window alternating with tile-sheathed concrete piers in its wall. And there must be another courtyard beyond, with the great black tower on its southern edge.

More knights stood with their lances before them on either side, to make a passage through the crowds from the gateway to the stepped terrace at the hall's flank. Rudi firmed his mouth and dismounted; grooms hurried to take the horses.

Two thrones stood before the doors of the hall, under a striped awning. To either side was a crowd brilliant with dyed and embroidered cloth, jewels on fingers and around necks and on the hilts of daggers, wrapped headdresses ... most of them women in cotte-hardis, or priests in robes, and one standing beside the larger throne in a gorgeous outfit of gold and white, with a tall mitre on his head and a crook in his hands. Some noblemen were there too, in civilian garb or the mail and leather of war, but ...

Yeah, Rudi thought, taking a deep breath. *But most of the men are off fighting against us. That camp outside is just part of them.*

Two figures sat on the thrones. Sandra, Mathilda's mother, in pearl and dove gray and silver. And her father, warlike in black save for the gold headband, his harsh face unreadable.

He was a big man; a bit bigger than Mike Havel, a little smaller than Uncle Eric, but built like either of them—strong hands, thick wrists, broad shoulders, long legs. A swordsman's build.

Rudi lifted his chin and met the man's eyes as the party tramped forward, ignoring the murmurs from the nobles on either side. The air was still; he tossed back his hair; there was a chilly feeling in his stomach, like he'd drunk too much cold water right after exercising, and the vague sensation of needing to pee. Some of the women were cooing as he passed; more called greetings to Mathilda, who smiled and waved . . . though not as enthusiastically as she had outside.

They halted ten paces from the dais, at the line of knights who rested unsheathed swords on their shoulders and stood like iron statues between the ruling pair and the world. At a gesture from the man they moved aside, and Mathilda suddenly gave a squeal and dashed forward.

"Daddy! Daddy!" she caroled, and burst into tears as he rose and swept her into his arms, whirling her around and holding her high, then kissing the top of her head as she gripped him like a fireman's pole.

The crowd burst into cheers, many of them waving handkerchiefs in the air. The trumpets at the gates sounded again, and even a few of the guardian knights smiled for a moment; the noise was a deafening thunder of echoes in the great stone space. When her father put her down at last, Mathilda self-consciously drew herself together.

"I'm so glad to be home, Mom, Dad," she said, wiping her eyes, and went to stand beside her mother.

Sandra Arminger smiled as well when she embraced her daughter, and sat holding the girl's hand, but there was an enigmatic calm in her eyes as they flickered coolly over Rudi's face.

Norman Arminger turned back, and Tiphaine went to one knee in a rustling clash of chain-mail armor, bowing her head. So did the rest of the party; Rudi knelt as well, taking off his new hat. It was only polite.

"Tiphaine Rutherton, for this rescue of my daughter and heir—"

There was a slight ripple through the crowd, a murmur like a sigh. Mathilda's eyes went a little wider. *Yeah, he hadn't said she was his heir, not out loud,* Rudi remembered.

"—there would be few rewards too great."

For the first time Sandra spoke aloud, her voice cool and amused. "I suspect rank, gold and land would be a good start, Norman," she said. "Don't stint."

Arminger threw back his head and laughed. "Indeed, and I won't. Approach," he went on, drawing his sword. "Rank first."

Sandra Arminger rose as well as the woman in armor ascended the steps to the dais and knelt again on the last of them. The Lord Protector bowed slightly to his consort and offered her the weapon, holding it across one forearm hilt foremost—carefully. Rudi could tell it was a real sword, with an edge that would slice open your hand like a butcher knife if you pressed your flesh against it. The guard was a simple crossbar of scarred steel, the pommel a brass ball and the long hilt was wound with braided leather cord.

It wobbled ever so slightly as Sandra took the grip in one small hand. She added the other, turning and raising the blade, only a slight tightening of her mouth showing the strain. A ray of sunlight broke through cloud and made the steel shimmer; Rudi felt a prickling even then.

Something brushed the back of my neck, he thought. *Or Someone.*

It also gilded the kneeling woman's pale hair. The flat of the blade descended in a slap on Tiphaine's mail-clad right shoulder, hard enough to make the sword vibrate in a slight *nnnngggg* harmonic.

"I dub you knight," Sandra said, her voice carrying over the hush of the crowd. Another slap on the left. "I dub you knight." Then she handed the sword back to her husband. "Receive the *collée.*"

That was a light hand-buffet on both cheeks; Tiphaine stayed on her knee, raising her face to make it easier to strike. "I dub you knight, Lady Tiphaine," Sandra concluded. "And bid you welcome to that worshipful company."

Tiphaine drew her own sword and presented it across the palms of her gauntleted hands. Sandra took it, raised the blade before her, kissed the cross it made and returned it. "Take this sword, Tiphaine, knight of the Association, to draw it in defense of the realm and of Holy Church, or when your liege-lord and your own honor call."

"I will, my lady and liege," the new-made knight said, sliding the sword home; the guard made a slight *tinngg* sound as it went home against the metal plate round the mouth of the scabbard. Then she crossed herself. "Before God and the Virgin, I swear it."

Norman Arminger smiled again. "The vigil before the altar and other ceremonial can follow."

He took a gold chain from around his neck; there was a gasp from the audience as he dropped it over Tiphaine's bowed neck.

"This for a keepsake and mark of my lasting favor. With it I make you hereditary baronet. And now, since we can't eat rank—though sometimes I think we lords of the Association breathe it, like the Society in the old days—"

A gust of laughter went through the crowd.

"—I grant this newest fief-holder of the Association one thousand rose nobles, that she may meet the immediate needs of her new state and rank, starting with a pair of golden spurs. In addition to this, as head of the Portland Protective Association, I grant to her seizin of the castle, estate and domain of Ath, previously held in demesne as my own direct possession. This grant to include the manor of Montinore, and the two knight's fees attached thereunto, with mill and press, heriot and fine and forest-right, and power of the High Justice, the Middle and the Low over all below the rank of Associate. It shall be held by her as tenant-in-chief and free vavasour, on service of three knights and their menie, and mesne tithes."

Wow, Rudi thought; a clerk was scribbling frantically at the paper on his clipboard with a quill pen. *She's really getting the goods. I remember Sir Nigel saying that was the land the Pro-*

tector tried to buy him *with. Tenant-in-chief, too. And baronet—that's almost like being a baron.*

Arminger turned to his wife again. "Shall you do the honors, my love?"

Sandra nodded, and took Tiphaine's hands between hers, for the oath of vassalage. The younger woman's voice rang out clearly as she promised arms, life and faith; the voice of the Protector's consort was softer, but carried as well.

"Rise, Tiphaine, Lady of Ath!"

She did, then bowed as she kissed the hands of both rulers. When she spoke, it was in the same formal, quasi-hieratic tones:

"My lord Protector, I would petition you, of your favor, that my comrades on this mission also receive the accolade; Ivo Marks, and Ruffin Velin . . . and Joris Stein, men-at-arms of the Lady Sandra's Household. Without their courage and skill and good sword arms I could not have accomplished what I did. Also their comrades Raoul Carranza and Herulin Smith fell in battle aiding the rescue of the princess, and I would that you grant their lemans and families aid, for they were poor men."

"A pleasure," Arminger said. "And a hundred rose nobles each to the living; clerk, see to the pensions for those left bereft. You three, approach the Presence!"

The men-at-arms came forward eagerly and knelt in a row, stifling their grins into appropriate solemnity as they laid their swords at the Lord Protector's feet; this was the big step that made them eligible for all further promotion and, most importantly, for a fief. A hundred rose nobles was better than three years' pay for a man-at-arms, as well, or one for a household knight. The Protector drew his blade again and performed the ceremony; he handled the heavy weapon with casual authority, flipping it from the wrist to make a hard smack on each shoulder with blurring speed. None of the men blinked as the knife-edged steel skimmed over their bare heads. The *collée* was more than a gesture from his calloused hand as well, but they didn't seem to mind the ear-ringing buffet.

Before the men could rise, Tiphaine went on: "My lord Pro-

tector, my liege-lady Sandra, I beg leave to enfeoff part of the
lands which it has pleased you to grant me to worthy knights,
that I may bring a proper *menie* when the muster is called and
the banner of the Lidless Eye unfurled."

Norman Arminger's eyebrows went up. "You're a tenant-
in-chief now," he said. "You don't need permission to assem-
ble your *menie,* your fighting tail, as long as they're capable. I
think we're all agreed that *you* are, so that leaves you two
knights to find, or experienced men-at-arms would do at a
pinch."

"My lord Protector, I do need permission if they are vassals
of another. My lady, I beg that you release from their oaths Sir
Ruffin Velin and Sir Ivo Marks, landless knights of your
Household, that they may swear themselves to me."

Even then, Rudi smiled slightly at the way Joris Stein stiffened and glared, pressing his lips together against an outburst
that would ruin him. *I never liked him. Ruffin and Ivo are sort
of rough, but they were OK to me. I think Joris would have hurt
me if he could have gotten away with it. He's nasty.* Being left
out like this was a public slap in the face. Juniper's son knew
how much it meant to a northern knight to get a manor of his
own; they couldn't really marry or anything until they did, although being in the Lady Sandra's Household meant they
must be good fighters.

Sandra Arminger caught the eye of the knight with the
pointed yellow beard and shook her head very slightly, warning and promising at the same time. Then she smiled at
Tiphaine. "Certainly. They will serve me just as well by serving you, my loyal vassal."

Tiphaine bowed again and backed down the stairs, then
jerked her head at the three knights. They followed her into
the crowd; Tiphaine received a good many discreet smiles and
nods, as someone suddenly necessary to take into account
rather than just the bizarre hatchet-woman that the consort's
whim had raised up.

The smile on Norman Arminger's face went glacial as he
turned to look at Rudi, now standing alone before the dais.
Now it looked like the expression a deer beheld on the very

last cougar it ever saw. The boy crossed his arms across his chest and smiled defiantly.

I can be afraid of dying, he thought. *We're* supposed *to be. But I can't let anyone see. Liath and Aoife died for me. I've got to do this right. If I have to go to the Summerlands now, Dread Lord, Dark Lady, let my mom not be too sad until we meet again. Let me be brave, please, so the Clan will be proud of me, and Lord Bear too. But I wish I could have grown up, and ridden Epona more . . . can I tell Matti it's not her fault?*

The man's voice had a deadly purr in it now. "There remains the matter of the prisoner," he said, and paused.

His wife's voice fell into it with smooth naturalness, as she set an affectionate hand on his shoulder.

"Yes, there does. Come here, young lord."

Rudi started slightly, shocked out of his concentration. He looked at her doubtfully, then strode up the steps and knelt before her, taking the hat off again as he bowed his head. Her fingers brushed through the red-gold curls of his mane.

"We have heard of how you stood as friend to our daughter while she was held prisoner," Sandra said. "The Lord Protector and I can in honor do no less. Let all at this court know that Rudi Mackenzie is to be treated with the respect due a sovereign's child, until his fate is settled, on pain of Our most severe displeasure."

"Oh, *thank* you, Daddy!" Mathilda said, and clutched his hand in both of hers. "I knew it, I knew it! Thanks, Mom!"

There was only the slightest instant when it looked as if Norman Arminger would shake her off and draw his sword; Rudi didn't think anyone else would see it, except maybe Mathilda's mother. His smile even looked genuine, if saturnine.

"Such is our will," he said, and the strong voice boomed out over the courtyard. There were more cheers, and he raised a hand for silence. "My lords, my ladies, noble knights, faithful retainers—you are all bidden to our feast of celebration tonight. My daughter is returned! Let meat and wine be given to the commoners in bailey and village that they may celebrate as well, and to all the soldiers and men-at-arms in the camp. Only the fact that we are at war makes me hesitate to declare holiday across the Association's territories. When victory is won, we will mark both triumphs with banquets, tournaments and of course masses of thanksgiving."

With that, the master of Portland bowed himself, towards the man with the crosier. The cleric acknowledged the gesture with an inclination of his head, and then turned his eyes on Rudi. He met them, and a distinct jolt ran through him—almost the way it did when he met his mother's eyes after she'd Called the Lady, but without the warm comfort of it.

Uh-oh, the boy thought. *There's Someone there. And that One is no friend to us, or to anyone.*

"Our Lord Protector is both just and merciful," the former Bishop Landon Rule said. "Yet there is also the matter of the boy's spiritual welfare. Surely the hand of God is seen here, that he has been delivered from the Satan-worshippers on the same day as our own lord's daughter, and in despite of the evil will of the Queen of Witches. I myself will see to his instruction, and in time his baptism."

Mathilda began to speak. "But—"

Her mother silenced her with a touch on the lips that anyone more than a pace away would have thought a caress. "Of course, Your Holiness," she said. "Eventually, that must be done, as all must be brought to the comfort of Holy Church."

The churchman hesitated, then inclined his head in turn and raised a hand in blessing. The sonorous Latin sounded over the crowd and the thrones before he turned to go.

Oh, Rudi thought, relaxing and noticing sweat under his armpits and on his face. *That was scary. More scary than the Protector.*

"What the *fuck* were you thinking of, Sandra?" Arminger barked, striding back and forth. "Now I'm publicly committed!"

"For the present, my love, for the present," Sandra said soothingly. "Have some wine."

"It's a bit early," he snarled again. "And don't try to distract me, Sandra. You know I don't like to be upstaged like that without warning. I *am* the Lord Protector, by God!"

"Some coffee, then?"

They were in one of the small presence rooms of his own

chambers, high in the Tower of the Eye that rose from the southern face of the keep's wall; this was the last chamber the elevator reached, and the stairs above led to one more and then the rooftop. With the shape of the hill and the rise of the tower, that put them three hundred and fifty feet above the floor of the valley, looking down on the tree-bordered blue of the Willamette and the meadows between. That made the tall window and small balcony outside possible without compromising the castle's defenses; it was open, and impatiens fluttered in the boxes around the balcony, gold and purple and blue, adding their mite to the scents of spring and the river and the incense that burned in a holder in a wall niche.

Within, the chamber was floored in hardwood parquet, graced with Persian rugs; the walls held tapestries and bookshelves, and pictures—a Rubens and a Monet. The table at which Sandra sat was genuine Renaissance work, Venetian, with inlays in exotic woods and lapis; it had belonged to Bill Gates once, and Arminger's salvage team had found what were probably the computer magnate's bones not far away from it when they were combing likely locations in Seattle. His agents had plundered mansions and museums from San Simeon to Vancouver for treasures, and as far east as Denver; the best for him, the rest for gifts to his new baronage and the Church.

Usually that gave him a glow of satisfaction. Not today . . .

"Do stop pacing, darling. You're making me think of those panthers in the menagerie."

He turned and planted his hands on the table. "What *happened*? Did your better nature get the best of you, or what?"

Sandra laughed, a relaxed trill. "My love, you know me better than that. I don't *have* a better nature. And in the unlikely event that I ever did, it certainly didn't survive the Change. Remember who told you to . . . and I quote . . . *go for it* exactly ten years ago, minus fourteen days?"

He relaxed and threw himself into a chair, running the thumb of his sword hand along the ivory panels in the armrest; it has been William Randolph Hearst's once.

"Then why?" he said, in a tone that wasn't mild, but lacked

the rasp of a minute before. "What did you have in mind? And why the hell didn't you ask me first?"

"Darling, I don't have a better nature, but I *do* have a lively sense of our own interests. And of how you can forget them in the heat of the moment sometimes."

One brow went up. "I want that witch-bitch to *suffer*. She's been a pain in our arse since a couple of months after the Change. I want her to suffer, then I want to watch her die by inches."

"Oh, granted. Remember how you felt when Mathilda was kidnapped? She's feeling all that now, and more. As to dying, that can always be arranged."

Grudgingly, he nodded. "OK, and your people pulled it off—that was initiative. But I had something more in mind for Rudi; involving an iron cage and some cosmetic surgery."

She held up a finger to forestall him. "You're a brilliant man, my love, but you tend to forget something—you can only kill someone *once*. Likewise with cutting off their nose. And as for revenge, it's a dish better eaten cold. I think knowing she's been defeated and lost everything and we have her son and *then* killing her would be sufficient for the Witch Queen. And then young Rudi could be *very useful* to us. Do we really want to have our men potshotted by Mackenzies behind trees for the next twenty years, after we've taken the rest of the Valley?"

His eyes narrowed. "I can soon put a stop to *that* sort of thing. Guerilla wars don't happen if you don't care how many you kill."

"Yes, Norman, I realize that," she said, and her voice hardened slightly. "And then we'd have more empty fields, wouldn't we? Instead of farms that can pay us taxes . . . not to mention furnish very useful fighting men when the time comes to put the so-called Free Cities League of the Yakima in their place. Or even the United States of Boise and New Deseret."

"Ah," he said, taken aback. "You think that's possible? A tributary enclave? Perhaps along the lines of the Highlands and the Scots kings in the times of Wallace and Bruce . . . But young Rudi might not cooperate . . . on short acquaintance he strikes me as a stubborn sort. Giving his mommy-bitch the chop would likely put him off."

"Children forget—that was why I decided to risk everything to get Mathilda back now. We can do a great deal with Rudi *if* we play things carefully, and with the Mackenzies," Sandra said. "After all, there's the example of their little golden-haired prince to follow, isn't there? Into the arms of Mother Church, into loyalty to the Lord Protector, into pointing those distressingly effective bows the right way . . ."

Arminger felt the anger leave him. "Now that *is* something to consider." He felt thought replace the rage. "He does seem to be a charismatic little bastard, doesn't he? He had Ruffin and Ivo eating out of his hand, if you noticed—"

"I did."

"—and I think he even got your Tiphaine warmed up a bit, which is a miracle His Holiness Leo ought to canonize him for. He's got nerve, too, I'll grant him that."

"Very charismatic. Very intelligent too, from what the reports say. And a very good friend of Mathilda's."

Arminger's hand halted as he lifted the coffeepot from the spirit-stove on the tray. "You're not serious?"

"Well, you might give it a thought. That's rather speculative, but . . ."

"But any noble family Mathilda married into would be uncomfortably powerful, yes," he said. "Two sugars?"

He added the lumps and slid the coffee over the table, smiling as she sipped delicately. He'd always thought of himself as something of a wolf, or perhaps a tiger. By way of contrast his wife reminded him of something small and deadly and precise; a viper, for instance, or a stiletto, or some exotic highly evolved wasp.

"Ah, where would I be without you, my love?" he said affectionately.

"In very much the same place, but with only half the taxpayers," she said, smiling at him. "Once more we play bad cop—"

"—and worse cop," Arminger said, and laughed. "By God, now I'm looking forward to dinner!"

"And in the meantime . . ." She grinned at him, stretching in the chair and linking her hands behind her head. "I've always found this *quattrocento* furniture a turn-on. It's naughty, like fornication in a museum."

He smiled and unbuckled his sword belt, moving forward. Just then a bell by the door to the suite rang; it was controlled by a cable from the guardroom two stories below. The rulers looked at each other; only a *real* emergency would make the officer of the day interrupt a private conference.

"What now?" Norman Arminger said, striding over to the speaking tube. "This had better be *important,* and not just more excuses from Alexi."

CHAPTER SIXTEEN

"Now this is going to be awkward," Mike Havel said grimly, looking up at the sun.

It was late afternoon now. Out on the field before them the A-listers charged again; enemy infantry stopped in a sudden bristle of spears. Once more the flicker of arrows showed as the Bearkiller cavalry reversed and rode away shooting. Once more crossbow bolts harvested some of them.

More bright, eager young kids who half killed themselves to get that scar between the eyebrows, Havel thought. *Cost of doing business. Christ, I decided I didn't like being a soldier before the Change, then I had to go and become King afterwards.*

The northern men-at-arms waited behind their footmen. Out on the right, towards the river, the Protectorate's crossbowmen were slugging it out with their Bearkiller equivalents, and not enjoying it; there were twice as many of them, but the Outfit's shooters were firing three or four times as fast, and didn't have to stand up to do it. The spearmen there edged closer under the cover of that exchange, but they were leaving a trail of dead and writhing wounded to do it. Stretcher parties moved behind their line as they did behind his. Right now they were paying higher than he was, but the tables would be turned when they came to within arm's reach.

"Trumpeters, signal *cavalry withdraw left,*" Havel said. *Wish it would rain,* he thought; but the weather stayed obstinately nice, mixed sun and cloud.

The A-listers obeyed the trumpet signal, breaking off and returning to their position beside and a little behind the artillery. The six pieces still in operation opened up again. Three roundshot smashed into the upraised shields of the spearmen on the enemy's west flank, but the infantry ignored their losses and kept coming. They were only five hundred yards from his own front now; Havel could hear the shouting of officers keeping them under control, keeping them to a steady marching pace against the impulse to run forward. The whole formation edged towards the river to get away from the throwing engines, though, which put them in the path of more crossbow bolts.

"All right," he said to the commanders of his militia. "Our job now is to get out of here without turning a setback into a disaster. We back up to Brush College Road. The crossbow companies get on their bikes and belt out of here, west, and make for Larsdalen. The pikes will retreat through the ruins—the cleared road's narrow enough we can't be flanked. The A-listers will hang on their flank so their lancers can't pursue."

Bicycles could outrun horses, but only if they got a bit of a start, say a mile or two.

"Ah . . . Lord Bear, that leaves all of *them* and just four hundred of *us,*" the commander of the pike phalanx said. "What do we do then?"

"That's going to be the awkward bit," Havel said. "Signe, you oversee the withdrawal of the crossbows."

She was white about the lips, but she nodded.

"I'll stay with the pikes, of course. We'll back up Glenn Creek Road, and then the creek itself, moving west. We'll have to abandon the artillery, but it can't be helped. Their cavalry won't be able to get at us there."

But their crossbowmen will shoot us to shit, he didn't say aloud. *With a little luck, we might be able to get half of the pike companies away. We can turn on them a couple of times, make them use mainly spearmen to follow us up. Those crossbows of theirs can't stop a charge by firepower alone.*

"Ready?" he said, and saw grim nods. "Then—"

Signe waved to get his attention, and then pointed to Chapman Hill. He looked south to the lookout station, and managed to keep his face calm while he read:

Two thousand repeat two thousand bicycle-borne troops approaching from the southwest along Doaks Ferry Road. Forward scouts on Glen Creek Road.

It couldn't be his reinforcements. They wouldn't be anything near two thousand strong. The blinking heliograph continued; it was as unemotional as ever, of course, but somehow it seemed to have a tone to match the clamping feeling in his lower belly.

Force does not properly reply to my request for code of the day. Will continue to signal as long as possible.

"Serious pucker time," he murmured to himself.

Some of the militia captains were gaping at him; he relayed the message. "Signe," he went on. "Inform Eric of this, will you? And tell him you're in command."

So he won't do something nobly suicidal, he thought. *The kids need a mother and an uncle, because they're not going to have a dad, not after this. Maybe California is a good idea. Be a while before the Protector gets down there.*

He had the enemy to the front, what could only be more enemy behind him, and the river to the east. If he tried to run west they'd be all over him like ugly on an ape.

"You all know what this means," he said quietly, as his wife spurred her horse westward towards the only force mobile enough to break out of the trap. "The only thing we can do for our families now is kill as many of the enemy as possible before we go down. I take full responsibility. We'll form a half circle with our backs to the river—the swamp will cover us. Any questions?"

A few hasty swallows. Someone raised a hand.

"Yeah?"

"I'm not limber enough to kiss my own ass good-bye, especially wearing this fucking breastplate. Anyone care to do it for me?"

"By rights, that ought to be my job," Havel said, feeling a flush of pride as a grim chuckle ran around the half circle facing him. "But you can ask Lord Alexi to do the honors. Let's get going. *Hakkaa Paalle!*"

"*Hakkaa Paalle!*"

Near Castle Todenangst, Willamette Valley, Oregon
March 6th, 2008/Change Year 9

"Whoa, girl. Whoa, pretty lady! Where did *you* come from?"

Sir James Wickham raised his eyebrows at the mare that had jumped the fence to join the herd. He'd cursed the roll of the dice that gave him this duty—looking after the reserve destriers was important work, but deadly dull, and there was a girl among the castle staff who'd given him a sidelong look. Here he was stuck with the smell of horseshit, keeping strange horses trained for aggression from fighting for dominance when they were penned too close, and to top it all off he had to do it in full war harness. Because there was a war on, as if anyone was going to raid within a mile of Castle Todenangst!

Now he forgot the serving-girl and his own annoyance; the black mare was a lot more interesting than anything else out here at the edge of the war-camp.

Big 'un, he thought as she cantered around the edge of the crowded meadow. A few of the other horses nickered challenge at her, but she ignored them with lofty disdain. *Big and beautiful. Christ and the Saints, that one's fit for the Protector's stud! She took a seven-board fence as if she were stepping over a dead man. And wouldn't I love to have her myself!*

Sixteen hands and a bit, warmblood with a strong dash of Arab, and young—four or maybe even a little less, early teens in horse years. Enough muscle and bone to carry a man in full armor, but a floating gait like thistledown. Spring sunlight brought out the gloss of her black coat and mane, where mud hadn't spattered up her legs and onto her belly and chest. Some idiot had left her saddled for far too long, and it was an odd-looking saddle as well, a tiny thing.

"Any of you recognize her?" he asked sharply.

"No, my lord," the head groom said respectfully, shaking his head. "Never seen her before in my life, and I think I'd re-member; that's a fine horse. But there's a lot of bloodstock here with the army."

Wickham nodded in turn. The groom was a decade and change older than the knight, nearly forty, and very good at his job—otherwise he wouldn't be working at the Protector's principal country residence. Instead of replying the younger man walked farther on the dung-littered, close-cropped grass of the paddock, extending a hand and talking soothingly.

"Whoa, girl. Steady there . . ." In a slightly different tone: "By God, someone was riding her without a bit! That's just a hackamore! And that's a kid's saddle, look at the stirrup-leathers."

The horse snorted and tossed its head as he approached, turning three-quarters on and looking at him out of one eye. It tossed its head again as he ran a hand down its arched neck, and stamped one foot on the ground. That made a faint ringing sound, like a muted, far-off cymbal.

This is the first horse I've ever seen in all my life without a single fault I could find, he thought. *What a pity if nobody could claim her!*

"You're a good-natured lady too, I bet," he said. *You'd have to be, if a kid was riding you. Even so, what a stupid risk—this is a warhorse if I've ever seen one. What the hell . . .*

He eased the bridle off and gave it a look. It was a perfectly standard piece of harness, new-made but from well-tanned leather kept supple with neat's-foot oil and hard work, per-haps a little simpler and lighter than most; the metalwork was plain brass and stainless steel and someone had cleaned it carefully not too long ago. The saddle was elementary, a mere pad, even lighter than an English hunting saddle, and secured by a single girth. He unbuckled that as well, lifting it off her back, and then the saddle blanket, marveling at the condition of the muscles of her back and barrel. Leaving a saddle on a horse for days was a crime, although possibly she'd just run off. But whoever owned her had cared for her very well in-deed before that. He cast a quick look at her hooves, which was easier when she picked one up and pawed at the turf.

They were sound, and the shoes looked fairly new, and as if the farrier knew his business.

"Get me a hobble," he snapped over his shoulder, offering a piece of dried apple in one palm.

The horse took it, then turned away again; it twitched its skin when he tried to stroke its neck again. The head groom picked up the light pad saddle and turned it over in work-hardened hands.

"Sir James," he said suddenly. "Look at this!"

The knight drew himself out of a dream. It had been a very pleasant dream; nobody claimed the mare, he performed some heroic deed right where the right person could see it in the battles to come . . . title on the estate near Walla Walla he'd been half promised . . . the Protector gave him the stud services of his Salafin, and he bred him to this proud beauty to produce the perfect destrier . . .

"What is it?" he asked sharply.

"Look," the groom said simply, holding up the saddle.

There was a design on the flap, tooled into the fine-grained brown leather with an awl. A circle flanked by two crescents pointing out to left and right. . . .

"Jesus!" he said, crossing himself and taking half a step back, scrubbing his hand against his side. "Hecate's moon. The Witch-mark!"

"Should I get a priest, my lord?" the groom said expressionlessly.

"Yes. And get the officer of the day—Lord Burton. And *get me that hobble.*"

An under-groom came running with it an instant later. He took it in his own hands and advanced again, stooping.

"So, so, so, quietly there, girl—"

"Watch out!"

Sir James managed to get an arm up before the hoof hit his face. It was a forward flick with the forehoof, not a milling downward strike, and only the bone of his arm broke midway between elbow and wrist as the sheet steel of the vambrace bent. His breath hissed out at the spike of shrill, cold agony up the nerves of his arm, and he curled around it. More pain as a stamp cracked ribs through mail and padding, and then the mare was away and took the fence in a floating leap that brought a gasp of wonder to him, even through the agony in arm and chest.

Hands lifted him a little, and he cursed breathlessly. "Carefully, oaf! It's a sprung rib and a broken arm. Get a doctor."

So much for my visible heroism, he thought. *I'm not going anywhere except very carefully to the toilet for the rest of* this *campaigning season.*

"That was one beautiful horse, though."

Tail and mane like flags, it paced away northward.

Near Mount Angel, Willamette Valley, Oregon
March 6th, 2008/Change Year 9

"Nigel!" Juniper said, and seized him for a quick, fierce hug before stepping back.

"My dear," Nigel Loring said, slightly shocked at how haggard Juniper's face had grown. "I heard. I seriously don't think they'll hurt him, though. They'll want to make use of him."

Juniper nodded. "They'll expect fear for him to wear me down, the which I will not allow," she said stoutly. "And since there's nothing we can do about it now, let's attend to what we *can* do."

He nodded, keeping the admiration off his face. *I worry enough about Alleyne now, and he's a man grown,* he thought. *I can't begin to imagine what it would have been like to have him carried off at nine. And I know full well she's thinking* But I wasn't there! *Over and over again.*

Instead, he looked up at the sky. It wasn't raining anymore, this cold and windy afternoon, but it was wet enough, with wisps of fog drifting from the tops of the trees on the ridges about them. That would neutralize the enemy's air scouts, at least for a while.

Juniper took a deep breath and ducked back under the awning set up under an overhang of the gravel pit's wall. There was very little there, besides the shelter itself; a bedroll covered in hard-woven greased wool, and a small chest that mostly contained maps now spread out on a folding table. Sam Aylward was looking at one as they entered, standing side-by-side with John Brown; he dipped his head to Juniper, and then nodded to his old commander.

"Lady," he said. "Sir Nigel."

"What's the word?" the CORA leader said eagerly. "My guys' horses are gettin' hungry. They can't eat fir needles."

"I had a very productive conversation with Abbot Dmwoski and his staff," Nigel said. "A most remarkable man. We all left safely—they have a remarkable collection of secret passages and posterns, too. And now we should really begin."

The rancher nodded. "Glad to get on with it," he said. "Our fodder's just about gone and there isn't enough grass up here. Wouldn't want to try this if my remuda lost its edge."

"Very well," Nigel said. He bent over the map, and everyone else followed suit. "The encampment is here, with ditch, bank and barbed wire on top, and a surveillance tower at each corner."

Juniper nodded, blinking her leaf green eyes. He admired the way she could put aside grief; even more, he admired the way she'd picked up the tricks of the fighter's trade without any formal training, simply by experience and by being around experts.

"First, let's poke them with a stick," she said.

Lord Emiliano Gutierrez, Baron Dayton, Marchwarden of the South, looked down at the commander of the eastern mercenaries attached to his force.

"Sumbitch shot me a clear two hundred yards away. Wouldn't a thought any of those Sisters from Sisters could do it," the man said. "Musta been usin' one of those fancy bows from before the Change, with the wheels at the ends. That's not fair nor right." Then: "Shitfire!"

Words came to Emiliano's mind, but it was a bit awkward to curse a man who was having an arrow extracted from his thigh and who'd refused painkillers so he could report clear-headedly, or to tell him he was being an idiot—the only reason compound bows weren't used more widely was that so many of their parts couldn't be duplicated without computer-controlled machine tools and synthetics. Instead he rubbed a hand across his beardless brown face and rose slightly on the balls of his feet; he was a short stocky man in his midthirties, but quick-moving, full of bouncy muscle. He glanced at the medic.

The doctor wasn't a cleric, but an older man who'd been trained before the Change. His voice was crisp: "He will recover, my lord. It isn't a complex wound and the bone was not split. It will keep him immobile for a number of weeks."

The doctor's hands had learned their skill in an era of MRI scans and laser scalpels, but they were still nimble on the spoonlike instrument that had been invented several thousand years ago to deal with wounds of exactly this sort. The hospital tent smelled of blood and bedpans and antiseptic, but not too badly; they hadn't had many casualties yet, or much sickness—and most of that was among the plainsman mercenaries, who were careless about sanitation. They'd had time to lay the prefab timber and plywood floors, as well; the war against Mount Angel had been a nice leisurely siege, with nothing beyond a little skirmishing now and then, and nuisance raids on their supply lines. That pleased the baron well enough. Less was likely to go wrong with this than with the jobs Alexi Stavarov or Conrad Renfrew had gotten.

And the monks had it coming. They'd been a pain in the arse to all the southern baronies for years, giving refuge to runaways and sticking their oars in half a dozen other rackets, not to mention letting that *puta* Astrid Larsson and her gang of lunatics set up in the woods just south of here. And those Rangers so-called and the kilties had been spreading subversion with the monks' help. That was the only reason he was backing this war, that and fear of the Lord Protector. Arminger was right about getting rid of the disturbing influences.

Nice and quiet suits me fine, he thought. *I've got everything I want, or I will when we hang Dmwoski . . . no, the pope wants to burn him. I've got my good land and my castle and I just want the rest of the world to go away so my kids, they can have it too.*

The man on the table gave an animal grunt and sighed as

the arrow came out. It was a simple broadhead, hammered and filed down from a stainless-steel spoon into a razor-edged triangle; the doctor flipped it and a three-inch stub of the wooden shaft into a pan one of the nurses held.

"Wait a bit," the mercenary said as the doctor's assistants came forward with bottles and tools and a curved needle and thread.

This is one hard man, Emiliano thought with reluctant respect, as the mercenary went on.

"OK, they jumped us out of the woods. Looked like they was movin' north of us. We tried to hit 'em right away, but there was more of the bastards than we thought at first—two hundred, two-fifty, to our one-twenty, that I saw. Maybe a bit more. That's all I know."

"Good work, Sheriff Simmons," Emiliano said, and nodded to the doctor.

The wounded man relaxed as the nurse ran a hypodermic of morphine into the tube that was dripping saline solution into his arm; the doctor waited, then began to irrigate and close the deep fissure. Outside in the gray, damp not-quite-rain Emiliano's own guards fell in behind him as he walked to the commander's pavilion, hobnailed boots crunching and grating on wet stone; there had even been time to scrape up gravel from the monks' roads—which were very well kept, like the farms around here—and lay it down so that the laneways inside the big square camp didn't turn to bottomless mud. The guards wheeled into place at the entrance to his own pavilion, and he nodded to them as he passed.

Emiliano had learned a long time ago—in the Lords, before the Change—that you needed to keep tight with the men who had your back. The Lord Protector had run what he called a *diversity program* to make sure none of the greater lords had a following exclusively drawn from their pre-Change backers, so only a couple of the guards *were* from the Lords, or their younger brothers; a few more were Society types, or *their* younger brothers; and half were just ordinary survivors who'd worked their way up. But he still made sure that his guards were *his* men, men he could trust, and once he was sure, he *did* trust them. He'd also learned long ago that trusting nobody was just as deadly as trusting the wrong people.

He'd never trusted Norman Arminger, for example.

Lord Jabar Jones of Molalla waited for him in the outer room of the command pavilion. The big black man was brooding over the map boards, but he looked up and nodded at the Marchwarden. They were social equals—both barons, both tenants-in-chief—and the other man was his second-in-command in military rank for this expedition.

"He have much to say, Lord Emiliano?"

The former Blood's voice was deep and rich, and a lot smoother than it had been in the early days. They all were, come to that. Emiliano grinned to himself.

Dolores especially, he thought, thinking of how his wife did the Great Lady thing these days. *Hey, pardon me, that's* Lady *Dolores of Dayton. Mother of God, but you look at her in those cotte-hardi things and nobody would suspect she used to spray the jeans on her ass out of a can they were so tight. Nobody sees the ring in her navel anymore, either, except me.*

She'd learned to play the game with the Society bitches, and went at it with a convert's zeal. Sometimes he thought she worked as hard memorizing the Table of Rank and Precedence as he did with the sword, and she was already planning the marriages of their kids to link them to the other great houses.

Aloud, the Marchwarden said: "Yes, he did. Short and to the point, my lord Molalla."

You had to observe the courtesies; it wasn't too different from the way things had been with his *pandilleros* in the old days; you didn't diss a man unless you were prepared to meet him face-to-face and kill him. The names were fancier, but he'd gotten used to it, and there was a ring to being called "lord"; he supposed that was why they'd called the gang that back when. A servant slid forward and put a mug of hot coffee in his hands, then retired to invisibility in a corner of the big canvas room. He blew on the steaming surface and took a sip before he went on: "It's the CORA-boy types; we knew they and the kilties were tight, just didn't expect to see them this far north. Light cavalry like the ones we get from Pendleton, except not such balls-on-fire types, from what I hear. Better than two hundred of them, maybe more, and they're loose north of us."

Jabar shut one enormous fist. "Motherfuckers."

"*Sí,*" Emiliano said. "This trouble we don't need."

"How'd they get over the mountains without our knowing it?"

"How they got here, I don't know. Maybe over Route 20 and then the old logging trails, maybe through the reservation—we should teach the goddamned *indios* a lesson someday. Anyway, we got a problem. Plus the air cover ain't worth *mierda* right now."

"Bet your ass we got a problem, my lord," Jabar said. "We can guard our supply trains from small bunches of Rangers or kilties or any of that good shit. We can't guard it against no three, four hundred men on ponies. No how, no way, not without we jam everything into great big convoys with a couple hundred guards. 'Specially with God pissing on us this way."

They looked out at the gray spring day. The sky was the color of a wet iron manhole cover, with patches like a concrete sidewalk in the rain. This time of year it could stay like that for weeks, or break up into sunshine overnight; it wasn't as if they had weather forecasts any more.

Until I got to fighting out in the campo, *I never realized weather was so important,* he thought; he'd always been a child of cities and pavements, although his grandparents had been farmers in Jalisco and he was a lord of farmers now.

Along one edge of the camp was a long prefabricated ramp like a ski jump, with a hydraulic catapult that could throw a glider into the air. The problem was, cloud was at barely a thousand feet, with patches of mist and fog below that. Or to put it another way, the problem was Oregon.

"I got couriers out by a couple different routes," Emiliano said, looking at the map.

It was a modern one, showing wilderness and populated zones, ruins, living towns, which roads were passable and which weren't, and right now it had colored pins showing the locations of the Association's forces, and conjectured enemy ones.

"To Count Conrad and to the Protector. But neither of them's going to be what you'd call real happy with us if we don't handle this on our own."

Jabar grunted; he was still uncertain of his standing at court after the fiasco with Princess Mathilda. That might be forgotten now that the astonishing news about her rescue had come through; on the other hand, it might not. Nobody in their right mind expected Norman Arminger to forget a grudge, and Lady Sandra . . .

Emiliano hid a slight shudder with another sip of coffee. "OK, what we got to be careful of is getting mousetrapped the way that *hijo* Piotr was."

Jabar traced lines on the map with a thick finger. "He tried stomping eight hundred Mackenzies with a hundred lancers," he said. "Even if there's four hundred of those light horse, they're not going to ass-fuck four hundred knights. Not if we can pin them against something for a charge so they can't run away and shoot us up as they go. Those sheep-fuckers can't stand up to us hand-to-hand."

"Yeah, but there's a chance—just an off chance—that the Mackenzies might be up *here,* too."

The cannonball head came up, his eyes narrowing until they were white slits in the eggplant face. "You think so? The Grand Constable don't."

"Think? Bro, I *know* Renfrew doesn't have his dick on the chopping block here, whatever the hell he *thinks.*"

Jabar rubbed his jaw; his coif rested loose over his bullock-broad shoulders and down his back. "Eight hundred archers . . . even with, say, four hundred CORA riders, that's still not enough to take us on. Not even close. Yeah, their bowmen are good, but there's a difference between charging eight hundred with one hundred and charging eight hundred with four hundred. Without they got some spears or pikes or something, we could smash their ass, open-field. And that's just the lancers. We got the infantry, two thousand men, and the Pendleton scouts."

He was starting to look enthusiastic; Emiliano raised a cautionary hand. "My lord, let's not get a hard-on so all the blood runs out of our heads, like that little white-ass Mafiya cocksucker Piotr. We got the monks to think about too, you know."

Jabar's brows knitted. Emiliano had worked with him a number of times over the years, and knew the brutish appearance was a false front. Nobody had stayed on top through the turbulent early years of the Association without plenty of smarts, and not just the street variety.

"We got more men than we need to keep them bottled up," Jabar said at last. "There's no quick way to get out of the Abbey. They got to send men down the switchbacks on the north side of the hill into the town before they can sally. That takes time."

"So let's *find* the motherfuckers, my lord."

The round head nodded. "And then, if we can kill them before they get away, the war is over."

Near West Salem, Willamette Valley, Oregon
March 5th, 2008/Change Year 9

Ooof, Michael Havel thought, closing a jaw gone slack. *It's a pleasant surprise, but it's still a hell of a surprise.* He felt disoriented for a moment, with a whirling vertigo, as if his whole body had been prepared for a step at the bottom of a ladder and had instead run into a hard floor. *Actually, I was prepared for death.* A momentary surge of nausea surprised him, and he spat to clear his mouth.

The Bear Lord recognized the first pair of the men pulling up their lathered horses before him. Behind them troops were pouring down out of the ruins of West Salem onto Brush College Road, moving at the double-quick and making the earth shake with the uniform pounding of their boots. Pikes bristled above them, waving like ripe wheat in July, light glistening on the steel.

"Major Jones," he said, returning the man's salute. "Let's be understated and say it's good to see you."

"Edward Finney," the other man said, offering a hand in a metal gauntlet.

He was in his late forties, stocky and weathered, wearing

first-class armor—breast-and-back of overlapping articulated plates, lobster-style, mail-and-plate leggings and arm-guards, a visored helmet on his head—with a sword at his hip and a long war-hammer slung over one shoulder. It wasn't gear Havel would have cared to wear on horseback, but from the weapon that wasn't the way he fought, either, and the horse was for mobility. Two much younger men with a strong family resemblance and similarly armed rode behind him, probably his sons. An even younger woman followed—barely old enough to take the field—in lighter gear, with a trumpet and a crossbow slung over her back.

"Ah, you're a friend of Juney's," Havel said. A mental file clicked: *Big yeoman farmer down south of Corvallis city, the son of old Luther. Influential guy.* "So, the Faculty Senate finally got its collective thumb out?"

"Nope," Finney and Jones said together. The farmer shrugged and signed the soldier to go on. He jerked his thumb over his shoulder in turn.

"That back there is the First Corvallis Volunteers; two thousand of them, half crossbows, half pikes and heavy infantry, a couple dozen mounted scouts. Could have had more, but we didn't want to wait, since that message you read on your veranda the other day sounded pretty time-constrained. It was obvious Turner and Kowalski would keep the Senate chasing round in circles and biting its own ass with amendments to secondary clauses to reports of special committees on the Whichness of the Wherefore, so *we* convened an overnight emergency session of the Popular Assembly—your man Hugo helped a lot getting the word around quick. That man's got contacts!"

"The Assembly can't declare war or order mobilization," Havel said, surprised. *At least, if I know as much about the way Corvallis is set up as I think I do.*

"But it *can* authorize people to go off as volunteers *without* a declaration of war."

"It can?"

"It can now, because we just did exactly that, and it hadn't occurred to the Economics Faculty that we *could*. We rammed through a vote, and most of the people voting showed up with their armor already on, which was sort of a hint—Ed here turned out a good five hundred from south of town, and another farmer friend of Lady Juniper's did the same out around Philomath, and Bill Hatfield and I have some pull in town. Somehow nobody wanted to get in our way when we pushed our bikes up to the Northgate."

Havel grinned, imagining the scene. "I bet they didn't!"

"Yeah. We geared up, got in the saddle before dawn this morning and started pedaling like mad while the Bobbsey Twins of the Faculty of Economics waved their arms and screeched about unconstitutional actions and threatened us with paper-armored lawyers. Christ, watching their faces was worth it all by itself! Not as much fun as smashing the butt end of a glaive there, but still worth it."

"You didn't happen to run into *my* reinforcements on the way here, did you?"

Jones nodded. "The guy in charge there decided to go up and reinforce Will Hutton instead, since he hadn't got the last of his people in, and we were going to get to you first."

Havel fought down a surge of irritation; he *wanted* his subordinates to exercise initiative, and it was a perfectly reasonable thing to do.

"Where do you want us, O Lord Bear?" Jones went on.

Havel shook his head again, looking westward along his line and then north at the enemy. *No time to be flabbergasted.* The enemy had frozen in place when they saw the reinforcements coming up behind him; there was a lot of trumpeting and flag-waving and messengers riding back and forth.

"You're already up there, so form up on my western flank."

He put out his left arm, pointing it at the Corvallans as they poured out onto the road, then swung it around to his front. "We'll come in on them like this, and see if we can catch Alexi's nose in the door."

"Or his thieving fingers," Edward Finney said.

"Or his dick," Jones added, and the younger Finneys laughed. "Let's go!"

They turned their horses around and cantered west to direct their soldiers. Havel looked around at his company commanders, who were either standing slack-faced . . .

. . . or grinning like red-arsed baboons who've just stumbled across a stash of bananas.

"Gentlemen, ladies, let's get to work." He shrugged his shoulders as they scattered for their commands, settling himself as if preparing for a hard task. "Messengers: to Lord Eric, fall in on the extreme left flank of our friends from Corvallis, and try and get around the enemy and keep them from pulling back. To Captain Sarducci, limber up and hitch your teams. Trumpeters, sound *general advance!*"

Three-quarters of a mile westward other trumpets blew, their timbre and the sequence of notes they used different from the Bearkillers'. He understood them, though: *Pike-points down,* and *Prepare for push of pike!*

The sixteen-foot shafts came level in a quick, disciplined bristle of points. Flanked by the crossbows, the hedgehog shape of the phalanx began to walk.

Two hours later Mike Havel sat his horse and watched the Protector's men digging in. They were about two miles north of the battlefield, near Rice Rocks, where the Willamette turned north again after an east-west stretch. That was where the northern troops had disembarked that dawn. The Bear-killers and Corvallans observed from a safe distance westward. The falling sun at their backs threw their shadows before them, like goblin mockeries of men and horses; the air didn't have the stink of blood and shit that went with battle here, but it already smelled of turned earth and sweat.

"I take it back," Havel said sourly.

"Take what back?" Major Jones said.

"I told Signe earlier today that Arminger is too much of a Period Nazi"—he looked at the Corvallan and the younger man nodded to show he grasped the phrase; he'd been a Society fighter before the Change—"to use artillery properly. I take it back."

The barges that had landed the Association's men were still there, drawn up on the sandy-muddy beach that marked the south side of the river at the point of the curve. Their crews and the rowers who'd tugboated them south and upstream hadn't been idle. The square shape of an earthwork fort al-

ready showed on some low heights near the river, with workers and wheelbarrows and crank-powered lifts swarming over
it like ants. Skeletal gantries with huge lanterns at the tops
showed how they were planning on keeping going when the
sun finished setting, though there would be plenty of
moonlight.

Havel looked aside at Sarducci. The chief of his field artillery shook his head regretfully. "They outrange me by too
much, Lord Bear," he said. "The stuff mounted on the barges
in the river is bad enough, but they've been moving some of it
ashore, too. Couple of heavy, turntable-mounted trebuchets,
I'd say—"

As if to draw a line under his words, there was a monumental soft *whoosh* sound from within the budding earthwork
fort. The darkening twilight made the fireball that arced up
from inside the walls look enormous, trailing a mane of red-
orange flames. It landed and spread flame over a field already
marked by circular scorches; turf smoldered as the napalm
burnt itself out. The bitter reek drifted faintly to them. Steel
darts glittered in the same area, half buried; the barges had
some sort of machine that threw bundles of them, which came
apart in midair and landed traveling almost straight down,
dozens at a time.

"OK, I think everyone's agreed we can't rush them?"

The men and women around him nodded; Eric Larsson last
and most reluctantly of all. "They couldn't kill all of us before
we got to the berm," he said.

The others stared at him. "Yeah," his sister said. "They
could only kill five or six hundred of us. And then we'd have
a thousand crossbowmen shooting at us from behind cover.
And then we'd have a thousand spearmen and, say, four hundred knights and men-at-arms standing on the fighting platform they're building waiting to boogie on us. Do you think
they'd bother chasing whoever was left when they ran away?"

"All right, all right, Sis, I didn't say we *should* attack them,"
the big young man said, raising a placating hand. "But we
can't let them set up a base here. They could raid all along the
eastern flank of the Eolas and up into Spring Valley. A lot of
our farms are there."

Sarducci pointed to higher ground a half mile westward from the Protectorate position. "We could build a fort there and keep a watch on them," he said.

Signe made a hissing sound between her teeth. "What are we supposed to garrison this fort *with,* half the A-list? It's spring planting season. The militia have to go *home,* or even if the wheat harvest this summer is the best we've ever had it'll be a hungry winter. Unless we eat too much of our stock, and where would that leave us the year after?"

She gestured at the Corvallans; Edward Finney rubbed at his jaw—gingerly, since it had a bandaged slash on it now. One of his sons, the dark-haired one, had a bandage wrapped turban-style around his head, and was sneaking looks at himself in the still-polished inner surface of his vambrace, doubtless thinking how heroic he'd look back to home. The other was praying silently, his rosary moving through gloved fingers sticky with congealing blood, eyes still wide with what he'd seen on his first battlefield.

"And our friends here can't stay forever—most of them are farmers too, and they all have a living to earn."

"Hey, people," Havel said. They all looked at him. "A couple of hours ago we thought we were all going to die. This is an improvement."

He glanced at the fort, lacing the fingers of his hands together and tapping one thumb on the other. In his mind he called up maps, and memories of riding this ground before. Few Bearkillers lived on the actual banks of the river; it was too dangerous, from floods and half a dozen other menaces. But the drier ground just to the west was cultivated for miles north of here, and strategic hamlets and A-lister steadings were plentiful; it was part of the Outfit's heartland. Eric was right; they couldn't leave an enemy base here—their own people would rightly withdraw allegiance if they weren't protected. Signe was right, too; they couldn't afford to just stick a big garrison here to *watch* the Protector's new fort. Besides the fact that they just didn't have that many full-time soldiers, if they did that the Association would turn it into a castle over the next couple of months, and that would be completely intolerable.

"But two can play at the fort game," he said. "It's no use if they can't supply it, and that means riverboats. Hey, Ken."

The older man looked up with a start; he'd been lost in an engineer's reverie as he stared at the earthworks, making notes on a pad now and then.

"Ken, you said you punctured those turtle boats of theirs?"

"Some of them," he said. "Burned a couple more."

"Think they could make the armor much thicker?"

"Not much, not and keep them mobile. The reason we beat them was that they didn't have much room inside for weapons, with all the men on cut-down bicycles pedaling away in there. If you made the boats bigger, the armor problem would get worse—the inverse square law is still working fine! So if you increase the volume to fit in more men pedaling . . . well, human beings just aren't very efficient engines."

He shook a fist skyward. "And we're not *allowed* to have efficient engines! God damn you, Alien Space Bats!"

"Maybe God did it," someone said quietly.

"In that case, may God damn God!"

"Hey, gently, gently. Let's not discuss the Change, hey?" Havel said.

He got a quiet chuckle from most of those within earshot: that was a proverb for "utter waste of time."

"You know that bit where there's a bluff near the west bank of the river, maybe a mile and a half north of here, maybe a little less?"

Ken nodded; so did Signe and a few of the other Bear-killers, and Major Jones; a good eye for terrain was an officer's trait.

"We put in a fort there—doesn't have to be too big, just big enough to hold out against a storming party until help arrives from the Spring Valley settlements, and we can tie it into the message relays easily enough. And in that fort we put in some of those big-ass throwing machines you built, with a nice view of the river and good thick earth berms in front, and overhead cover. With that, we can interdict the Willamette even at night; it's less than a tenth of a mile across there, even counting that big sandbar, the Darrow bar. We can put obstacles in the riverbed under cover from the engines; come to that, you can rig us up a diving suit, right?"

Smiles broke out around the circle. They became a little strained when Havel turned to the Corvallans. "And I'm sure our friends here would be glad to help with building the fort before they go home, eh?"

Edward Finney winced. "Well . . . look, I've got enough hands back home to get by at a pinch, but a lot of our people are smaller operators—"

"Won't take all that long, not with three thousand strong backs. We may not even have to finish it. I expect that when we show we can cut them off, Alexi will haul everyone back north; we can work some sort of truce-and-ransom thing, which is why I made sure to get some prisoners he'll value. He's probably just hoping we don't have the equipment or the smarts to block the river, and hoping to show the Lord Protector *something* besides a bloody nose and Corvallis involved on our side. We only need to keep a lid on this bunch here until they realize they can't stay."

Jones cleared his throat. "Ed, we can do that. And if we have to keep people here more than a week, we can call for volunteers again and have a whip-round from the ones who *have* to go home to get the spring crop in. Everyone can chip in, oh, a couple of sacks of potatoes and some flour, or bacon or whatever. That way the weavers and blacksmiths and factory workers won't be out of pocket for their lost time."

"Yeah, we can do that." He looked at Havel, obviously thinking of asking the Bearkillers to chip in, then reconsidered.

Which is good. Because we just paid in blood. I lost two in every hundred of our militia today, and worse than that for the A-listers.

"And while we're digging, let's figure out how to make the *Protectorate* pay," Havel said. "I am"—he paused to consider—"a bit peeved."

The Corvallans blinked a bit at the ripple of wolfish laughter that went through the Bearkiller leaders.

♦

CHAPTER SEVENTEEN

Near Mount Angel, Willamette Valley, Oregon
March 7th, 2008/Change Year 9

Eilir Mackenzie flattened as the patrol rode nearer, peering *under* the branch of a bush with her bow across the crook
of her elbows to keep it and the waxed string out of the damp.
The damp, bedraggled mixture of twigs and grass in her war
cloak's loops would hide her well on this gray spring day. Wet-
ness soaked up into her brigandine and wicked into the
padding underneath it, bringing chill and a stale-sweat smell
to mingle with the damp earth and oiled metal. The patrol was
more of the easterners, strung out along a road that ran between new hedges and old rows of beech trees planted by
some nostalgic Swabian a long time ago—many Germans had
settled around here, a century and a half past.

The sun was just up over the Cascades behind the ambushers, but that was merely a spot of brighter gray in the overcast
sky; they were about a mile from the Abbey, as close in as the
Protectorate forces and their hirelings patrolled in daytime
for fear of the catapults. The huge white bulk of the fortified
monastery and the red roofs above it seemed like a dream in
the gloaming, like an illustration in one of Mom's books . . .

*The books that Rudi loved to read. Stop that, girl! We're
going to get him back, by the Dark Lady and the Dread Lord!
Get your mind on business!*

Her eyes flicked down the line of enemy horsemen; six of
them, riding down towards the southern edge of Mount

Angel's hill, before turning back around the other side towards the enemy camp north of Mount Angel town. She couldn't see fine detail, since they were a hundred yards away or better, but it was definitely easterners, not the Protector's own scouts. That was good—they'd let a patrol of those go by. The mercenaries were skilled at their trade, but they tended to be a bit more impulsive than the men who served the Protector and his barons. Plus they were all close relations, which made them hot for revenge when a man was hurt.

Closer, closer, and then they were in easy range.

This has to look good, she thought, then fought down a sneeze as a grass stem tickled her nose, smelling spicy-sweet with new growth. Then: *Now!*

She hit the quick-release toggle at her throat and shed the war cloak as she leapt to her feet. That was the signal, and the patrol's heads whipped around in horrified disbelief as a dozen archers appeared from the overgrown verge of the road by the orchard.

The last one was hers, by prearrangement. Tricky shooting at this range, but the air was millpond-still . . .

She let the breath go out between her teeth as she drew the eighty-pound longbow to the ear, pushing out with the left arm and twisting her body into the pull. It wouldn't be too hard to *kill* at this range, but precision was much more difficult. The broadhead came to the edge of the arrow-rest, and the bow moved up in a single curve as she exhaled. Watch the target, and let thousands of hours of practice tell you where the arrow would go, and hope no twitch of the man or the air threw it off. Let the string roll off the gloved draw-fingers, and you *were* the bow and the arrow and the target all in the same instant, driving it with your will like a spell.

The cord slapped at her bracer with a sharp impact felt up her left arm even through the metal and tough leather. The release felt *right,* smooth and sweet, the surge of recoil like a dance. She was so caught up in the moment that she almost ignored the arrows coming back towards *her;* then she ducked at the unpleasantly familiar feel of cloven air moving on her face. Then she drew and loosed again, and again, using bodkins designed to punch armor now. That startled volley was the only one the riders could fire, though, and that only because they'd been moving with their bows in hand and a shaft on each string. Five of the enemy were down almost at once; most of the Rangers loosed only two or three shafts.

Among the other qualifications, you had to be a *good* shot to be a Ranger.

Eilir grinned silently as the last enemy trooper galloped off northward, bent over his horse's neck with an arrow in his shoulder; from the look of it the broadhead had just barely punched through the stiff leather of his cuirass, enough to wound but not knock him off his horse. A bodkin would have sunk deeper and done more damage . . .

But that's the point, she thought with a silent giggle. Then she thrust the bow back through its carrying loops. *And thank Luck that nobody got carried away and shot him for real.*

Get the horses! she signed. They had to make this look like an ordinary nuisance raid, and they *wanted* to be chased. No real raiders would pass up the opportunity to snaffle off three good quarter horses and their gear.

The Dúnedain ran onto the road, one or two grim but the rest grinning like children pulling off a prank. *Sometimes they all make me feel very old,* Eilir thought; she and Astrid were the senior Rangers in years as well as rank. *Except for Alleyne and John, of course. And John can be like a kid sometimes, too. Alleyne's too serious for my taste. Lovely package, but he and Astrid were meant for each other.*

She could feel the wet gravel scrunch under their feet and see little milky spurts of mud come up under the horses' hooves; this was a road built after the Change. One of the enemy mounts had galloped away north after the wounded scout; another was down with an arrow through its ribs, breathing like a bellows and rolling an eye at her in piteous entreaty: *make it better.* She signed the air to ask its forgiveness and used her dirk to give it peace; Pilimór did likewise with a wounded mercenary with three shafts through his body who lay arching his back in a bow and spitting out wet bits of lung as he clawed at the stone with bloody fingers. Then they led the horses east at a trot through the orchard. Their own mounts and a dozen more Dúnedain waited there. Astrid slid down from the crown of a tall Douglas fir and dashed across the open ground. Alleyne was leading Asfaloth, with the mare's head already in the right direction, and the Dúnedain leader vaulted laughing into the Arab's saddle.

"Go!" she shouted. "They're coming! They had a force ready; two hundred riders or better. They probably think we're the ones who shot their chief yesterday, and they want vengeance."

The score of Dúnedain turned their horses' noses towards the east and a little north and the band surged into motion. John Hordle wasn't with them; it wouldn't have been sensible, when a pursuit on horseback was in order. The half-Percheron they'd found for him could bear his weight easily enough, and it was even fairly fast given time to work up a gallop, but it couldn't keep the pace they expected for long. The ground ahead was open farmland with plank or wire fences, a few with new, low hedges, mostly wheatfields or pasture, or half-readied for the spring planting and abandoned when the northern foe arrived. They fell into a long lope, the sort of gait used when they expected to be running for a while, turning a little aside now and then to avoid plowed ground where the mud would suck speed and strength out of the hooves and legs of their mounts.

Eilir looked over her shoulder. Horses didn't raise dust this time of year in the Willamette and the easterners' gear was mostly dull-colored, hard to spot against the brown of plowland and the green of pasture. Another fence came up, and Celebroch took it without needing directions . . . yes, she could see a mass of horsemen boiling down from the northward, angling out from the enemy camp, with one in the lead carrying a banner with a mountain lion worked on the cloth, and another beside him wearing the tanned head of one on his helmet. Perhaps they'd copied that from descriptions of the Bear Lord's headgear.

How Mike would scowl! she thought.

The Dúnedain slanted more directly east to avoid them,

making a great show of urging their horses on without adding much speed.

Celebroch tossed her head, as if to say: *Don't you know what you're doing? Am I supposed to run all out, or not? Make up your mind, woman!*

There were two hundred in the band that pursued them. She could make out the numbers clearly enough once they'd fallen in behind the Rangers, despite their having no more order than a swarm of attacking bees. Arrows began to flick out from them, falling well short—two hundred yards was about the maximum you could really expect to hit someone when both were moving fast. Their mouths were all open too, probably howling curses—or just howling. Eilir left the knotted reins on Celebroch's neck and stood in the stirrups, slanting her longbow across the mare's rump as she turned and drew. A six-foot bow was awkward on horseback, but not impossible if you practiced enough. Aim high—

There.

The arrow plunged down among the very first of the mercenaries; two of them surged away from each other a bit as they galloped. It must have come down between them. Both of them shot back at her; one had a pre-Change compound bow, and the arrow came uncomfortably close to Celebroch's heels.

Astrid fell back beside her and drew her recurve. The arrow struck. Eilir couldn't see exactly where but a horse went over as if it had been poleaxed, and the rider hit the ground rolling. He gathered himself into a ball and put his arms over his head; one of his friends jumped his mount right over him, and others swerved, with a couple of near collisions corrected with impressive skill. Then the Rangers were plunging down a bank into the shallow, gravelly expanse of Zollner Creek; they surged through in exploding sheets of cold spray, holding their bows high overhead to avoid wetting them, and then galloped in earnest. Something hit her between the shoulder blades— hard—and she gasped and lurched forward in the saddle for an instant, making her mount check its stride. Astrid reached over and pulled something free of her brigandine, showing it to her before tossing it aside; it was an arrow with a barbed head. There would be a spot on her back where the leather was scraped free of the little steel plates.

Wow. Too close for comfort—maybe we left it a little too long! They didn't have to shoot *her* to kill her, just cripple Celebroch. *Probably they don't shoot at horses much 'cause they want to steal them.* But sooner or later they'd get mad enough to ignore the niceties.

The Dúnedain were thundering over a stretch of rolling meadow now, towards an old country road and then a big orchard about a mile long and a quarter wide, the riders ahead throwing divots of turf and dirt at her. The trees were neatly tended, and the buds were just about to break, but she could only see the top halves though they were twenty feet tall or better. The northeast-southwest line of the road ran along a low ridge; the cherry trees were on the other side, and sloped down a little to a creek. Closer and closer, the white-painted fence along the roadway looming up and the first of the Dúnedain taking it in flying leaps. One had his horse refuse and fought it to a standstill, forcing its head around until it went in a circle for a moment, then riding off southward along the line of the fence, probably hideously embarrassed.

Asfaloth and Celebroch soared over it. She could see John Hordle there just beyond the other side of the road, lying flat as she had only a few moments before, grinning the way a Lughnasadh baked ham would if it had teeth. The twin Arab mares halted in a few strides; the rest of the Rangers continued for a few more paces, under the cherry trees, and among the CORA ranchers and their retainers waiting there. Those were all standing by their horses to keep out of sight from the meadow on the west side of the road; they grinned and gave her thumbs-up and worked their mouths.

Astrid drew up beside Alleyne. Eilir kicked her feet out of the stirrups, vaulted to the ground, dropped the reins—that meant Celebroch would stay, unless her mistress blew the high-frequency whistle that dangled around her neck—and ran a dozen paces to kneel beside John Hordle.

The big Englishman was lying on his back with his hands

behind his head, helmet pushed forward over his eyes, chewing a grass stem and smiling around it at her. She scowled and thumped him on the top of his headpiece with the flat of her hand, driving it down until it covered everything above his nose. Since it was a good, solid steel sallet with a padded lining, his grimace and wince was undoubtedly put on.

Get ready! she signed as he pushed it back and winked.

"I *am* ready," he said, turning his head towards her.

One of the many things she liked about him was that he always remembered to face her when he spoke; lip-reading was half guesswork at the best of times, though she was very good at it.

"I'm just not rushing about getting hysterical, like some people I could name," he went on.

Eilir would have thumped him again, except that he was rising to one knee and turning with a smooth ease astonishing in a man who stood six-foot-seven in his stocking feet. Then he took up his bow, and they raised their heads until they were looking head and shoulders over the much-patched asphalt of the roadway.

The Pendleton men were reckless fighters, but not fools: they'd reined in at long bowshot rather than ride straight into territory they couldn't see, even in hot pursuit. Where they came from war was largely a matter of raid and skirmish; feigned retreats to draw pursuers into an ambush were standard operating procedure. Half a dozen came whooping forward to the road, where they could see into the orchard and warn the others if it was a trap.

Eilir and Hordle came to their feet along with the rest of the Rangers. She drew again, sensibly aiming at one of the men in the vanguard only twenty yards away, and drove a bodkin point through his leather cuirass and chest and out the spine in a shower of blood and chipped bone. Hordle was grinning and he had a heavy four-ounce arrow to his bow, the type of four-to-a-pound shaft that his seven-foot stave with its hundred-and-fifty-pound draw-weight could throw. The muscles knotted in his arm as he pulled the shaft to the ear and loosed upward at a forty-five degree angle.

Two hundred and fifty yards away the doll-tiny figure of the enemy standard-bearer looked up sharply. Then he dropped the flag and fell off his horse, scrabbling at the arrow that had slammed through his face from right cheek to left jaw.

She gave him a glance that said as plainly as Sign: *Showoff!*

"They always look up," he said, and fell into a steady rhythm of draw-aim-loose, once every four or five seconds. "Bloody odd, if you ask me. I mean, here you are, bits of pointed iron flying about in a roit frightening way, you 'ear this *sssssss* noise, like an arrow coming down at you, so what do you do . . . look *up*?"

Eilir waggled her ears. *Wouldn't happen to me,* the gesture said.

The loss of their standard-bearer enraged the mercenaries, and so did the sight of the same dozen enemies they'd been chasing making a stand and inflicting yet more losses. They surged forward in a mass; Eilir could feel the growing drum-roll of their horses' hooves through the soles of her feet. Arrows flicked out, and heavy, curved slashing blades were swung in menacing circles.

"Time to scarper," Hordle said cheerfully.

They all turned and dashed back—which meant that the men from the eastern plains would see their prey escaping *again*, after killing yet more of their kinfolk.

They must be frothing and drooling, she thought. *From what I've been told and seen, they're very sensitive about being made to look foolish.*

Ahead in the orchard the CORA riders were swinging into the saddle. They rode the same type of ranch-country quarter horse that the Pendleton men did and were likewise lightly armed, although there were more with short mail shirts rather than boiled-leather cuirasses; a few had brigandines and their leader was resplendent in a steel breastplate painted brown. They all had bows and a long blade or light ax; most swords were stirrup-hilted sabers whose first models were the blades of the US cavalry of Old West times, salvaged from museums and antique stores after the Change; a few bore light lances, shorter and slimmer than those of Protectorate knights or Bearkiller A-listers. Rancher John

Brown did, and he waved it at her before he slapped his horse on the rump with the shaft. His followers moved forward in a rough double line, not a rigid formation but a lot more orderly than their enemies'.

Quarter horses had good acceleration. The four hundred riders went from a stop to a walk to a canter in half a dozen paces. The board fence along the road went over with a thud she felt even through the hoofbeats, its uprights cut through and smeared with mud in the night—that had been her idea, and she felt a flush of pride as she swung around and led Celebroch forward. Astrid and Alleyne had snatched up lances left leaning against cherry trees and were off with the rest. Astrid held back a little; with a six-foot man clothed from head to toe in jointed alloy steel on its back, the big gelding her lover rode took a little longer to hit a hand gallop. When it did it was as fast as any of the horses there; Asfaloth had no trouble accelerating with Astrid wearing a Bearkiller-style hauberk and her raven helm.

The mercenaries had checked only an instant when they saw the CORA force coming at them; more a matter of men leaning back in the saddle than of the horses actually slowing. Then they came on faster than ever; there wasn't room to switch and make a chase of it. A fast horse could make thirty miles an hour for short distances, and with their combined speeds the two groups were approaching each other at better than sixty. Arrows flew between them, but only for a few seconds. That was enough to empty a dozen saddles, but nobody wanted to be left with a bow when his enemy came within saber range. Then the two formations passed through each other in a mutual blur of speed and slashing steel, bright blades sparking on metal, or leaving trails of red through the damp air to glisten on the dew-wet grass. Astrid and Alleyne lifted their targets out of the saddle and discarded the lances, sweeping out their long swords as the battle turned into a wheeling melee. Eilir's eyebrows went up as she saw the swath the steel-clad figures cut through the plainsmen. She knew that Astrid was cold death with any weapon, but Alleyne was such a gentleman—

He dodged the sweep of an eastern slashing sword, broke

the man's jaw with the edge of his heater-shaped shield. In the same instant a backhand cut across the eyes left another mercenary lurching back with his hands pressed to his face, mouth an O beneath them ...

—that she sometimes forgot what he was like in a fight.

"Seems like a shame to disturb them," John Hordle said calmly, reaching over his shoulder for an arrow. "Still one always 'as to do one's bit, as Sir Nigel used to say."

Hordle was no more than passable at mounted combat. Eilir was far better than that, but she'd decided without thought to stand by him ... and now she felt a sudden slight pang, as if she'd abandoned her *anamchara*

Don't be ridiculous, she thought stoutly. *Didn't we swear to be goddess-mother to each other's children, all those years ago?*

Also she and Hordle were among the few present who could shoot into that whirling, slashing, hoof-milling chaos without much risk of friendly-fire accidents.

"I'll take the one with the steel cap and feathers," the big man said, lifting his seven-foot bow. "You want the one with the fringed ... what are those things called?"

Chaps, Eilir signed shortly, and drew her own bow.

"Got two chaps on 'is legs," Hordle chuckled, and let the string roll off his fingers.

I don't like killing people, she thought, and shot. *John doesn't either but he does like to fight—there's a difference. Me, I'd rather not do either. Odd. Alleyne's more like me that way, and John's more like Astrid—she doesn't like killing either but it's all the old stories to her while she's fighting, so she glories in* that. *I think she really* means *it when she says* yrch.

An arrow—almost certainly hers—nailed the man's thigh to his saddle through his fringed chaps. The horse must have been wounded too, for it suddenly went berserk, bucking and plunging while the man screamed and clawed at the steel and cedarwood that held him fast. A sweep from someone's sword put an end to that, and the body flopped and dangled and then fell as the horse bolted.

I don't want to fight them, but if they take the Protector's silver and come here to fight, they have to expect what happens, she thought, arrow on string and looking for another target. *May the Guardians help them choose a better way next time 'round. In the meantime, I'm not ready for the Summerlands yet!*

Outnumbered two to one, the mercenaries could not take the punishment for more than a few seconds. Then they broke like quicksilver and scattered, the largest clump of them running north, back towards the enemy camp. The CORA fighters hung on that group's flanks and rear, shooting and hacking with a ferocity born of feuds as old as the Change, which was either ten years or since the beginning of time, depending on how you wanted to look at it.

Alleyne and Astrid cantered back, talking to each other in Sindarin; Eilir thought he was using it to bring her down from that scary-exalted place she went when she fought, and humanness was returning bit by bit to the blue-silver eyes. She and John Hordle swung into their saddles along with the rest of the Dúnedain. They turned and trotted eastward, cross-country; that was the other big advantage of horses over most bicycles—you didn't need to stick to a road, or even a track. The gray clouds overhead had lightened a bit, but didn't look like either going away or raining. Ahead eastward the land rose, growing more rolling as it did; another ten miles and they'd be into the mountain foothills, trackless and densely forested.

They weren't going quite that far.

Now we find out whether that idea of yours works, me girl, Hordle signed.

Don't remind me, Eilir replied with a shudder. *I'll be so embarrassed if it doesn't.*

No, love, you won't be embarrassed, not likely, Hordle answered, his usually good-natured face gone more sober.

She nodded unwillingly. The chances were that if it didn't work, she'd be too dead to be embarrassed, along with her kinfolk and friends and all their hopes.

Boom.

"Sound *halt*," Baron Emiliano said.

The curled trumpets screamed. The long column of men on bicycles clamped on their brakes, skidding to a halt and resting on one booted foot; they'd just turned east at what the old maps said was a Lutheran church and what looks said was a Catholic one now. The long, crunching rumble of the cavalry moving up on the graveled verges stopped a little more slowly. For a moment, the Marchwarden of the South idly thanked the monks for keeping the roadways in their territories so well; the surface was smooth, the potholes patched not just with gravel but fresh melted asphalt, and the fields on either side were neatly trimmed.

Silence fell, or as much silence as a force of twelve hundred men could maintain; even their breathing was a susurrus under the sough of the wind, shifting of horse hooves, snap of banners, chink and jingle of chain mail and bridle-fittings, the occasional thud of a noncom's fist and *silence in the ranks!* The air was wet and close otherwise, leaving the sweat undried on his face despite its coolness. He sniffed at the breeze as if it could tell him what he wanted to know, and peered eastward down the road, at the empty fields on either side where only the distant cantering dots of his scouts and the odd drift of wildfowl feasting undisturbed on new-sown grain showed movement.

Boom.

The sound was deep and resonant, even in the muffling dankness, traveling as if it would echo across miles.

Boom. Boom. Boom . . . boom-boom-boom—

The thudding continued, building to a continuous thudding crash. Beside him, Lord Jabar stirred in the saddle. "Drums," he said unnecessarily, and then more precisely: "Lambegs. Mackenzies."

As to confirm his guess a raw, squealing drone started underneath the deep hammering, weaving around it with a sound at once jaunty and menacing; the war-pipes of the Clan.

"That's Mackenzies all right," Emiliano said with a grin. "But not close. From the sound, say two, three miles."

He started to raise his hand to shade his eyes, then stopped, feeling faintly foolish for a moment. For one thing it was very cloudy; for another he was wearing a new type of helmet, with a hinged visor like a pierced mask of flat steel. It was swung up at the moment, sticking out like the bill of a cap. Instead he glanced skyward, cocking his head as he judged where the bright patch was.

"Not ten o'clock yet," he said happily. "We got time."

Hails came from ahead, and he watched a figure approach at a canter. When he drew rein, it was one of Emiliano's own mounted scouts; the Pendleton cowboys weren't what you could call organized right now, though they were mad enough to get into a chewing match with a bear.

"Hey, my lord," the Association commander said to Jabar. "Remind me, next time we see the Grand Constable, if we hire any of those cow-country clowns next time, we put them under our officers. They make my old gangers look like fucking Marines."

The scout saluted. "My lord Marchwarden," he said. "We've located the enemy."

"How many, and where?" Emiliano asked, unfolding a map glued on stiff leather from his saddlebag; it was pleated accordion-style, and he held it open across the saddlebow.

The scout brought his horse close and sketched with a fingertip. "This road we're on, South Drake, it goes right east past the orchard where the cowboys got suckered this morning, till it hits Cascade Highway about three miles from here at this little town—town called Marquam. The town's empty, looks like the people ran for Mount Angel. Cascade Highway runs south from there, angling back west a bit too, down to Butte Creek, about a mile and a quarter. The Mackenzies and the CORA-boys are there at the southern end—they've got their left anchored on the bridge there where Cascade Highway crosses the creek, Jacks Bridge, and then up the road north and east."

"How many? How close you get?"

"I got within long bowshot for better than ten minutes, and I had some of my boys over the road on the north for a while until the CORA-boys ran them out. Nine hundred kilties more or less, my lord—that's the archers, and they're right along the road here, past these old school buildings. Another hundred, hundred and fifty with axes and spears in back of them, east of the road. Then the CORA-boys on their right, north, about four hundred or maybe a little less now."

Emiliano looked at the map, then up to turn it into real fields and trees, then down again. "OK, I think they made a mistake," he said. "They get their peckers up after they take Piotr and underestimate us."

Jabar rumbled deep in his massive chest. "They got hills back of them."

"Yeah, but they're low and open. You gotta go, *por Dios,* ten miles east of there before you hit heavy forest. That right?"

The scout nodded. "I've ridden all the way to Missouri Ridge and beyond since we got here, my lord. It's five miles to the edge of cultivation and then another four, five to what I'd call real cover that would stop cavalry."

"There's no fucking road heading right back east from there, either," Emiliano said. "So they can't bike away from us. They fight us straight up, they got nowhere to run."

"Could be more of them," Jabar said. "That's how they got Piotr's ass in a crack, my lord. Suckered him into thinking they weren't as many as they really were."

"No, a thousand, maybe a little less or more, is all they got. My lord the Count, he's seen at least that many in Sutterdown and they only got two thousand five hundred total when they call out everyone for field service, tops. A thousand here, a thousand there, that just don't leave no more. These *pandilleros,* they're the First Levy, their best, but it's all they got."

Jabar looked over his shoulder, westward towards Mount Angel. "We don't have enough back at the base camp to stop a breakout."

"Yeah, but we can see troops coming down that switchback into town. We can't stop them, but we can sure see them. That'll take a while and we'd get the message. The monks aren't going to come out in the open where our cavalry can get at them."

Emiliano's own finger moved on the map. "We'll keep going east until we're just north of them, here." That was about another three miles. "Then we deploy facing south, cavalry on the left, stickers and shooters on the right, and move straight down at them." His finger slashed across the page.

"That means we've got this big orchard on our right and this other one on our left, with those woods along the creek," Jabar said. "Like a funnel pouring us at them."

Emiliano shrugged. "If we try to get fancy, they'll just fuck off again and leave us holding our dicks, maybe get behind us and get on our supply lines, maybe even raid our manors—they've done that before. We got the numbers, and we got the lancers, and even with those orchards and shit we got enough room there to get everyone into the fight. If they had a line of spearmen to hold off the knights, it'd be different, but they don't. We got eight hundred foot and five hundred heavy horse with us here. Let's use 'em."

Boom. Boom. Boom-boom-boom-boom . . .

The hammer of the huge Lambegs massed behind them was soul-shattering, which had been precisely the intent of her ancestors, when they made them echo over moors and down the glens; to break the heart of an enemy and then charge home with claymore and Lochaber ax to break his head. Juniper Mackenzie let them echo in hers, until they were like the beating of her own heart; even the green-and-silver silk fabric of the Clan's flag shivered in rhythm with the sound, like the tympanum of an ear.

The bagpipes skirled beneath and around the huge sound, "MacNeil's Kin," jaunty and jeering and full of a swaggering threat as the pipers paced and turned along the road before the line of the Clan's warriors. Here and there a few of the younger fighters couldn't wait standing still, and began to do an impromptu war dance of their own, left hands on hips and bows aloft as their feet stamped and flashed, screeching out the ritual cries of their totems, hawk screech, dragon roar, wolf howl. The music spoke to something in her as well, something that bristled the fur along her spine and the fox red mane on her head, and peeled lips back from teeth.

Nigel Loring chuckled, squinting beneath the raised visor of his sallet; she laughed at the same instant.

"What's the joke, my love?" Juniper asked; you could speak privately in this din.

He leaned over. "That this must have been what Scotland sounded like to a great many of my ancestors, riding north to Bannockburn or Dupplin Moss or Flodden," Nigel said.

"You're such a fine human being that sometimes I forget you're a *Sassenach,* sure," Juniper replied, restraining a nervous impulse to check the arrows in her quiver one more time.

"You're only half Irish, and no more Scottish than I am."

"Scots on my father's side."

"And German, French-Canadian, Swiss, Cherokee . . . even English, from what you've said."

"I try to remember that they're human beings too, sure."

"And what was our good Chief laughing at?"

She nodded towards the leaping figures and their painted, snarling faces. "That if the Change hadn't happened, they'd be thinking about the senior prom, or what courses to take next semester, or a new fad diet to shed a few pounds, and watching TV ads for mouthwash and personal computers. That they'd be entirely different people, not even looking very similar." A deep breath. "Will you stand with the axmen and spears again this time?"

"I'll stay with you, if you please, my . . . Lady Juniper."

"You're a romantic at heart, my darling Englishman," she said softly.

"I'm repellently practical," he said stoutly. "It's just that my exiled existence would have little point without you, my dear."

She smiled and touched the cool braided gold and silver of the torque, now stretched a little to fit around the chain-mail collar of her arming doublet. The silver moon on the brow of her helmet reflected the gray of the sky as she turned to look northeast. Open fields stretched beyond the four-lane highway up to the road where the enemy would come. Off to their right were a few of the CORA riders, with the whole of their reserve horse-herd.

"Nonsense," she said crisply, with a twinkle in her green eyes. "We're not a boy and girl, Nigel. We're middle-aged, and we have grown sons and daughters and soon we'll have grandchildren to see to as well. I love you well and I'd grieve all my

life if you died, but I would go on living, and do my best to
find joy and work in it. So would you."

He blinked at her, then reached up a steel-clad finger to
brush his mustache, laughing softly. "Perhaps I *am* an incorri-
gible romantic. My dear, you never cease to amaze me. And
that, I think, will make life together very enjoyable indeed."

She nodded; the little exchange had helped her disperse the
last knot in her stomach, leaving her grounded and centered
for what must come. They stood by the banner, at the center
of the Mackenzie formation. That stood along the southeast
side of the old Cascade Highway, strung out behind the shallow roadside ditch and a post-and-board fence in a field of
rippling blue-green winter wheat, waiting patiently in their
three-deep staggered harrow formation. Even then she felt a
pang of regret at trampling someone's crop; it would have
been a good one, the stems thick and stiff and close-placed, already well over ankle-high four months before the harvest.
Trampled, it smelled sweet, like grass cut for haying, but with
a strong mealy undertone, mixing with the damp earth
beneath.

A gesture to the signaler, and the wild music died away into
a ringing silence. She took a deep breath and shouted: "Plant
the swine-feathers!"

She turned to look as the order was relayed to either side
of her. There were a few whoops and yips from the grinning,
gaudy-painted faces of her clansfolk; these of the First Levy
were mostly young men and women, few past their mid-
twenties, and they could appreciate Eilir's idea—the more
so since they were her generation, and eager to show what
they could do. Each reached back into a leather bag slung
beside their quiver, on the opposite side from the loops that
held their bows. Each brought out two poles bound together
with twine; one was like a shovel with a narrow, flat blade
and a yard-long handle, the other like a short spear of the
same length. Each stubby pole had a steel collar and locking device on its rear, where the handle or butt-cap would
usually be.

Shovel and spear fitted together with a push and twist, a

click and *snick!* and suddenly every archer held a seven-foot length of ashwood with a spade on one end and a knife-edged spearhead on the other. They turned in place and rammed the shovel blades into the dirt, stamping them home with the heels of their boots as if they were digging a ditch. Then each turned back, but now they stood amid a forest of long spears, pointing forward in a bristling block a thousand yards long and three deep, and each was slanted forward with the point a bit above chest-high on a man . . . or precisely chest-high on a horse. The whole process had taken barely twenty seconds.

Sam Aylward came trotting up the road, inspecting it from the front. "Lady," he said, with a quick nod. "It certainly *looks* bloody frightening."

"We already knew that, Sam," she said. "We'll just have to see if it works, won't we?"

The swine-feathers weren't a line of spearmen or a pike-hedge. They weren't much impediment at all to men on foot. Experiment had shown that a horse could get through them too . . . *if* it slowed down, and chose its way at a careful walk-ing pace, and didn't have anything to spook or frighten it out of what limited concentration the little herbivore minds could muster.

Aylward looked at her. She nodded, and he signed to the signaler. The low dunting snarl of the cow-horn trumpet—*huu, huu, huuuuuu*. Helpers were running forward, setting out bundles of spare arrows in the ground behind the swine-feathers, pushing them down until the points stood in the dirt deep enough to support the shafts, then undoing the slipknots. The archers trotted forward, vaulting the board fence, then across the pavement and over the fence on the other side and into the pasture there. On their left was a school—built before the Change, but still in use, though she could see from the signs that it had a different name from the one on the maps, Queen of Angels rather than Butte Creek.

Huuuuuuu—hu-hu!

The horn droned and blatted, and they halted as one, still in the harrow formation; the helpers rushed forward behind them, hurrying to get three or four bundles of arrows within reach of every string hand.

She looked northward. A column appeared on the road there; not the enemy, but two-score riders led by the tree-and-stars banner of the Dúnedain. They peeled off and galloped over the half mile of open pasture towards the Mackenzies and their friends; midway Astrid and Alleyne turned towards the CORA position with most of the Rangers, and Eilir and John Hordle led the rest to the Clan's banner. Juniper checked anxiously; neither was hurt, though both were splashed with mud. Her daughter gave her a wink and a thumbs-up gesture.

"Brown's following fast," Hordle said, and Eilir nodded. "The enemy's behind them."

"How many?" Juniper said.

"Twelve, thirteen 'undred, Lady."

About our numbers, she thought.

The big man went on: "Eight hundred foot, five hundred lancers, and some odds-and-sods of scouts. Not many of the mercenaries; they had a bellyful from Brown and his CORA cowboys."

Her daughter and her daughter's lover dismounted, handing their reins to a teenage helper who led their mounts to the rear. Both drew their bows from the loops with matter-of-fact readiness, looking around for spare shafts to fill their quivers and helping each other with the chore—Hordle had to bend for Eilir, a tall woman, to slide handfuls into his. Juniper sipped a little from her canteen—not much, she wasn't shy but peeing on a battlefield was still awkward—as she watched Rancher Brown and his men come galloping down the road, frantic to get to their remounts—the horses looked blown. And that meant . . .

Terrible as an army with banners, she thought, as the enemy followed them into sight. *Christian, but a telling phrase nonetheless.*

The Protectorate force was only equal to her own, but it seemed like an endless snake of dull-gleaming metal and spearpoints as it came eastward along the road, the men and beasts and bicycles toy-tiny with distance. When she focused her binoculars on them they leapt closer—dark eyes in a dark face above a mouth-covering mail coif, vanishing for a second as the helmet was brought up in both mail-gauntleted hands and adjusted. Banners and pennants, and a priest and acolytes pacing before men who knelt and crossed themselves, while incense and holy water went forth.

She could not hear the words under the distant grumble of feet and hooves, but she knew them: *Fight the Holy War . . . Heaven awaits warriors who fall in His service . . . smite the Satan-worshippers . . .*

Her people had had their own rituals. Juniper's lips tightened as she lowered the glasses; war of any sort was bad enough, but Holy War wasn't something she liked at all. Sir Nigel and Aylward were talking in low tones—probably nobody else but the banner-bearer could hear them under the racket as the pipes and drums greeted the enemy.

"They should have sent more infantry," her First Armsman said. "If they had enough bicycles for them. Got a fair well-balanced force but they're not what you'd call smooth at using it proper. Another couple of hundred infantry and they could pin us for a flank attack by the cavalry. As it is, I'd say they'll have to come straight at us."

"They'll not have met much serious opposition until now," Nigel said judiciously. "Learning by doing. Better next time, I would expect."

Does there have to be a next time? some part of Juniper's heart cried with anguish.

She said nothing aloud; the polite looks from the two life-long warriors would be too hard to bear, especially when she knew they were right.

I love Nigel like my life, and Sam like a brother, but the way they discuss chopping people up as if it was turnips still makes me feel . . . odd.

"Surprised they've managed to train so many men-at-arms," Nigel went on. "That takes serious application."

"That's those Society buggers, sir. They were odd before the Change and afterwards the ones who stayed with Arminger were bloody barking mad."

"A functional madness . . . Ah, they're shifting . . . cavalry forward to cover the infantry deployment, then to their left opposite our friends from the CORA on our right. Crossbows and spears in mixed blocks . . . underestimating how badly we can outshoot them, I daresay. They'll send the infantry forward to develop our position, and punch their lancers at Rancher Brown and his fellows to try and uncover our right. A good thing they didn't bring any of their field artillery."

"They keep that for siege operations when they can, sir."

The CORA leaders and their retainer-cowboys had finished slapping their gear on fresh mounts; they crowded forward over the road northward, except for a trickle of wounded from the earlier action who moved to the rear, towards the healers.

Juniper took three deep breaths, letting each out with a long, slow hiss, feeling the strength of Earth flow up her lungs to calm her heart with its unmoved solidity, feeling Air add its light quickness to the surging strength of Water in her sea-salt veins, and the thought of Fire reaching out across the field.

Sam Aylward rinsed out his mouth, spat, returned his canteen to his waist and put an arrow to his bow. "Sir Nigel, Lady, we've a roit proper job of work to do 'ere today."

Despite the gathering tension she smiled to herself. *Sam might be Earth itself. And Nigel is Fire . . . does that make me an airy wet blanket?*

Curled trumpets screamed in the enemy ranks.

Lord Emiliano scanned the field ahead. Suddenly he noticed small enemy parties setting out several strings of six-foot posts, planted in staggered rows out from where the banner of moon and horns stood in the field this side of the road. They were hard to see, because the side turned towards him was painted green-brown, and far too fragile to be any hindrance to men on foot or horseback. They puzzled him for a moment, until he realized they were ranging-marks, planted precisely fifty yards apart, probably with the other side whitewashed for better visibility. His lips tightened; it was a gesture of methodical, thoughtful ferocity more frightening than the screaming painted faces and the inhuman throbbing of the drums or the snarling drone of the pipes. And he would have to send his men into that killing field.

Sí, it will cost us, he thought. *Worth it. We break this force, they're finished; we get the land, and nobody bothers us no more. If I capture their witch-bitch alive, the Lord Protector will make me a duke, maybe marry his daughter to my Gustavo!*

"Let the foot advance!" he shouted. "Lord Jabar, take half the lancer *conrois* at the CORA-boys."

Juniper Mackenzie drew and loosed, drew and loosed, despite the burning pain in hands and arms and shoulders. The enemy spearmen were only thirty yards away now and coming on crabwise, crouched behind their big shields until only their feet and the narrowest slit under the helmet brim showed; the men behind them held their shields overhead. Arrows flickered out in waves over the distance between them and the Mackenzies; nine hundred bows, three hundred arrows a second, turning the shields into bristling porcupine shapes and the ground into a pelt like some gigantic stiff-haired, gray-furred dog. The sound of the bodkins striking was like surf on a gravel beach, or heavy hail on a tin roof, a hard, endless *tocktocktocktocktock,* louder than the shouts and screams. Many bounced off helmets with a ringing sound like a ball-peen hammer; many others rattled off chain mail and flipped away.

Others bit, and more and more, opening gaps in the wall of shields as men fell, shrieking and tearing at the iron in their flesh, or moaning and twitching, or dropping limp. The spearmen closed the holes, stepping in from the next ranks. As the distance closed, many shafts punched right through the tough leather and plywood of the shields, stripping their feathers off as they drilled into arms and faces. The air stank of damp sweat, and the iron-sea-salt odor of blood, turning soil to mud as hundreds of men bled out their lives. And still the wall walked, like a wounded bear lumbering forward with blood and slaver dripping from its teeth . . .

Juniper started to duck at a sinister hiss. The crossbow bolt struck her on the collarbone, and she nearly dropped her bow at the sharp stabbing pain; but the short, thick shaft bounced back, turned by the riveted plates within the brigandine and the distance from which it had been sent. Lightly armored and without shields, outnumbered two to one by the Clan's bowmen and carrying weapons that shot far less quickly, few of the Protectorate army's crossbowmen had lived to come within a hundred yards of the Mackenzie archers. Survivors formed a ragged line behind the blocks of spears, lofting their bolts at the archers on high arcing trajectories, but the stubby darts lacked the aerodynamic efficiency of a thirty-inch arrow.

She reached behind her shoulder for another arrow. Her hand froze. Trumpets wailed behind the Protectorate line. The blocks of spearmen halted; then they began to walk backward; she could hear file-closers and sergeants counting cadence, their voices harsh and loud enough to carry through distance and racket, keeping the ranks solid and the shields up for their lives' sake. For the arrows did not stop, and the trail of bodies they'd left coming south was added to as they went north.

Juniper lowered her bow, panting; her shooting was more of a symbol than anything else, to show her clansfolk the Chief was with them. She was as accurate as most, and quick. But the heaviest weapon she could draw was barely within the minimum set for marching with the levy, a good deal lighter than Eilir's eighty-pound mankiller, and nothing like the smashing power of Sam Aylward's war bow, much less the monster stave John Hordle could pull to the ear. Instead she stepped back to turn her head either way, caught the eye of bow-captains, grabbed the signaler by the mail collar and shouted in his ear: "Sound the first halt!"

He put the horn to his mouth: *"Huu-huu-huu-huuuuuuu!"*

Every third archer stopped shooting. Some of them busied themselves helping the wounded to the rear; one passed her with another man's arm held around his shoulder, the hurt Mackenzie swearing luridly every time his right leg touched the ground and the plastic vanes of the bolt in his shin waggled. Others dashed forward recklessly to pull arrows from the ground, from abandoned shields, even from the bodies of the dead.

"Ooooh, look 'ow short we are," Aylward said—*he* was still shooting, choosing every target with a second's care. "Bloody sad, isn't it, how we're running short. Eat this, you evil sodding shite!"

The enemy crossbowmen were backing up too, but stopping to shoot as they went as long as they were in range, not running away. She noted distantly how Nigel had quietly stepped between her and the enemy as soon as she lowered her bow, raising his heater-shaped shield; a last bolt hit it, and sank an inch deep into the tough bullhide and wood, quivering like a malignant wasp. If that had hit her in the eye . . . a body lay on its back nearby, a young woman with hair as red as Juniper's own and a bolt sunk halfway to its vanes in one eye, the other open and blue and staring. There was a surprised expression on her face beneath the raven painted on it, and only the slightest trickle of blood down the black design; she had the same totem, then . . .

The Hunter comes for us all in our appointed hour, she reminded herself, letting sights, sounds, stenches flow over and through her without giving them purchase to linger and leave horror behind.

Ravens and crows of the flesh hovered overhead, riding the slow, chill, wet wind, and eagles, falcons . . . all waiting. They had learned quickly what such doings as this meant, after the Change.

Ground and center, she told herself. Then she raised her bow and waved it to either side again. The silver mouthpiece of the long ox-horn went to the signaler's lips, and he blew round-cheeked.

This time the arrowstorm slackened to nearly nothing; that was the signal for only the chosen marksmen, the ones with the best scores and the heaviest draw-weights, to shoot. More went out collecting shafts, rushing desperately from one to the next in a great show of haste.

See, Juniper thought, looking to where the Marchwarden's banner hung beside the Lidless Eye and driving her will behind the glance like an arrow in itself.

Her hand moved in a gesture. *See and believe, Emiliano Gutierrez. By the keen sight of Brigid and the long hand of Lugh, by the silver tongue of Ogma, by the power of the blood shed this day upon the Mother's earth, by every soul*

*here sent untimely to the Lord of the Western Gate, by the
grief of children orphaned and the sorrow of lovers' tears, I
bind your thought, your hand, your loins, your eyes, blinding
the inward sight of your mind with the lust of your heart! So
mote it be!*

It would be easy enough for an outsider to believe that
they'd run short of arrows. Few who hadn't been under a
Mackenzie arrowstorm before could believe just how *many*
shafts they could lay down. The Protector's men had crossed
the three-hundred-yard mark only ten minutes ago; in that
time nine hundred archers had sent a hundred and thirty
thousand arrows onto the killing ground. And when near a
thousand men came marching at you shoulder-to-shoulder, it
was hard to miss . . .

*Let them think we're spent, easy meat for the men-at-arms.
We've fought the Protector's men often enough, but mostly in
skirmish and raid and ambush rather than pitched battles. Sam
is right—massed shooting like this is . . . different. And they
won't know we brought bundles of arrows in plenty.*

Hooves clattered behind her on the roadway. She looked
around, walked back; it was John Brown, his helmet knocked
awry, long dents—swordstrokes—in his breastplate, his left
hand a blob of bandages where spots showed sopping-red. His
face was red-brown now, drenched with sweat; a younger
kinsman rode by his side, looking ready to catch him if he
started to slide out of the saddle.

"We can't hold the knights," he said. "Sorry, Juney. Not any
longer, not hand-to-hand. We'll hang on their flank, use our
bows, try to keep 'em from getting around, that's all we can
do. Lost better'n a hundred riders trying. They've got too
much weight for us."

"The Mother-of-All bless you, John, you've done splen-
didly. Now it's with the Luck of the Clan."

Emiliano Gutierrez stood in the stirrups and focused his
binoculars. The infantry were coming back faster than they'd
gone forward, even walking in reverse, and a lot less of them
than had started out. They were shot for now . . .

Sí, shot up good, he thought with grim indifference, listening with half an ear to the screams as monk-surgeons and ordinary medics operated on the tables set up behind his position, cutting steel and cedarwood out of flesh—morphine took time to work, and seconds could mean the difference between life and death. Horse-drawn ambulances trotted westward, taking those who could endure it to the field hospital.

Lord Jabar rode up; he had his sword across his saddlebow, running red, and the shield hung from his shoulder was battered and hacked, with a broken-off arrow standing in the spear-wielding lion there and splinters showing white-brown through the facing. He'd hung his helmet by the saddlebow and pushed back his coif, panting as sweat rolled down his shaven head in rivulets.

"Got the CORA-boys to pull back," he panted. A squire handed him a canvas waterskin; he gulped, and then squirted water on his face, washing a thin reddish film from the ebony skin as the blood spattered there sluiced off. "Couldn't make them stand long enough to finish them, they kept pulling away and shooting, but we hurt them bad. Lost about twenty men, twice that wounded too bad to fight; I think we killed three, four times that many of them—they couldn't get their wounded away from us, either. Should I try to swing in behind the kilties, my lord?"

Emiliano shook his head and handed over the glasses, indicating the Mackenzie line. "Take a look."

White teeth showed in the brutally handsome, full-lipped face. "Sheee-it! They lookin' raggedy-ass fo' sure."

"*Sí.* I think they're short of ammunition."

Jabar grunted and nodded, returning the field glasses; Emiliano pulled a handkerchief out of a saddlebag and wiped the surface. It was hell getting blood out of the fine machining there if you let it dry and set. The black nobleman wiped his sword so he could sheathe it; getting blood inside the scabbard was an even worse pain.

"We better hit them fast, then, before they get more," he said. "I can't see any coming up behind them, though. Hard to miss that many arrows . . . sheee-it, they shot enough!"

The pasture for three hundred yards in front of the Clansfolk bristled with goose feathers at the ends of cedarwood shafts, enough to give a silvery-gray sheen to the whole patch of land—save where bodies lay, or twitched and writhed, or tried to crawl back.

"Yeah, that was why I sent the infantry in first," Emiliano said. "They'll do to soak up arrows."

Jabar pulled his coif back up, fasting the mouth-protecting flap by the thongs to the brass studs riveted through the mail on the right side. His squire came up with a fresh lance as he lifted his helm and set it on his head.

Emiliano nodded and waved to the trumpeters; the long, curled instruments sang and screamed. His banner moved forward, and the Lidless Eye with it. The reserve *conrois* of lancers came up to fall in behind it, along with those Jabar had led against the CORA riders; hooves rang as they stamped, and horses snorted. The men were silent behind coif and nasal bar this time, eyes hard and set.

Emiliano slapped down his visor. *Hey, I wonder if I can get Mount Angel tacked on to Barony Dayton? Or at least a couple-dozen manors here. Young Julio is going to need an inheritance too.*

The world turned into gray shadow, the eyeholes windows into a place narrowed to little more than the chamfron of his destrier. The big horse moved beneath him as he turned and reached out his hand for the lance that his squire thrust into his gauntlet. It had taken him years of practice before he could do anything more than knock himself out of the saddle with these things, and then more years to stay level with the young dickheads coming up who started with their first pimples . . . and it was time to mix it in.

Two days after the Change someone in the Lords had tried to move in on him with a fire-ax, figuring there weren't any rules anymore because guns didn't work. Emiliano had used a shovel on *him,* then cut his head off with the ax and hung it in a hairnet over the door. Guns, knives, chains, swords, lances . . . it was all a matter of your 'tude, how much of a pair you had.

He swung the point down. *"Haro!"* he shouted. *"Haro, Dayton! Haro, Portland! Holy Mary for Portland!"*

The answering roar of the men-at-arms came in like surf on a windy day.

Juniper licked dry lips. The earth shook beneath her as five hundred leveled lances came across the meadows, and the rain of arrows hadn't done more than slow it a little . . . *two hundred yards . . . a hundred and seventy-five . . .*

"Now!" she shouted, and the horns coughed and blatted.

Juniper turned and ran, the flag beside her. That was the easiest hard decision she'd ever made; when you saw that mass of armored men and barded horses coming at you behind the cruel spikes of the lanceheads, and thought what they and the pounding hooves could do to your own precious, irreplaceable self, you *wanted* to run away. Never mind that running away from a galloping horse was like running in a bad dream, where you pumped your legs and stayed nailed in one spot.

Every Mackenzie did the same. A long surge of them swarmed over the fence, over the road, over the second fence and dashed past the swine-feathers, panting. And then they stopped and turned, each with bundles of arrows ready to their hands, most working their drawing-arms and shaking out the wrist for an instant before they reached down and picked up a shaft.

"That's a relief," she gasped, reaching for a shaft herself. "I was a bit worried they'd keep going."

The earth trembled, and the knights came up the slight rise on the other side of the road. Their plumes and lanceheads were bright against the thinning pearl gray clouds.

"Haro! Portland!"

"On, brothers, on!" Abbot Dmwoski said.

He stood at the exit of the tunnel, and the column of armed monks poured past him and up the staircase into Mount Angel town. Some had thought him paranoid for wasting labor on a vertical stairway and sloping tunnel from the heights that bore the Abbey to a spot inside the walls of the town at its feet. He'd nonetheless insisted, and now men in armor with black robes kirted above it rushed by. When the last had passed him he followed, out into the gray light of an overcast spring day, wet air damping the scent of fear-sweat and the sour smell of oiled metal.

An aide held the reins of his horse, though almost all Mount Angel's host would be on bicycles, save for a few messengers. And the banner-bearer, with the flag that carried the image of Virgin and Child and was topped with the Cross.

"Good boy, Sobieski, sooo, brave fellow," he crooned, stroking the big beast's arched neck; it was sweating, sensing the tension of the men about.

He swung into the saddle, armor clanking; each knight-brother slid his poleax into the carrier beside the rear wheel and bestrode his machine. The banner followed, and the formation fell in behind him in column of fours as they pedaled north and then east, towards the Jerusalem Gate. Few civilians watched from the windows of the half-timbered houses or shops on either side; some built in that style in the old days for the tourist trade, more since because it was a fairly easy style to imitate with the tools available in the post-Change world. Most of the remaining townsfolk had gone through the tunnel the other way, carrying the ill and the young children.

Those who lined the streets were the first rank of the town and country militia, who would follow him. The second and third ranks—women, the old men, all commanded by the Sisters—would hold the town walls, and the Abbey. He didn't think the enemy could take the town, even so. He was absolutely certain they couldn't take the Abbey, but if he lost this force, there would be little left . . .

The faces of the men waiting to follow were tight and grim for the most part; they were fighting for their homes—for their families, the fields that they worked and the workshops where they labored, and for freedom in a most immediate and concrete sense.

And because they trust me, they follow me as I hazard everything on one throw of the dice. Lord who blessed the centurion, if I lead these Thy people astray, let mine alone be the fault and mine the punishment. Give them victory, O Lord, I beseech You, he thought one last time. *They fight for all that a man rightfully holds dear: for their women and children, for the graves of their fathers and for Your Church. Yet Thy will be done, not mine: for Thy judgments are just and righteous altogether.*

Signing himself: *Mary, pierced with sorrows, all those who fall today are born of woman. Madonna, intercede for us, now and at the hour of our deaths!*

At the gate, the keepers waved to show the road was still clear and the enemy still in their camp to the north. He raised a steel gauntlet to give the signal. Within the blockhouse and towers, gears ratcheted as the portcullis and its mate went up. The inner gates swung back.

As they did, one of the militiamen suddenly shouted, breaking the thick silence: "For Father Dmwoski! Jesú-María!"

As he rode out onto the drum-hollow boards of the drawbridge, the cry broke from twelve hundred throats: *"Jesú-María!"*

The first fence went over with a long crackling as the steel-clad chests of the barded destriers struck it. The boards meant to confine cows and sheep were little hindrance to the heavy horse, but it slowed them; here and there a mount went down, a brief shriek of man and beast under the pounding hooves. Then they struck the asphalt of the roadway, more slippery than bare ground beneath steel horseshoes.

It wasn't until they hit the second fence that even the first rank were really aware of what awaited them—and it wasn't the backs of the broken, fleeing rabble they expected to ride down and skewer like lumps of meat. Instead long steel points bristled towards their horses beyond the fence, and near nine hundred bows were drawn to the ear, at a range where shafts would smash through shield and armor. Despite the roaring clamor, a silence seemed to fall for an instant that stretched like winter taffy.

Juniper saw Emiliano Gutierrez then, under his banner and raising his visor with the expression of a man who wakes from dream into nightmare. Beside her, as if from a great distance, she heard Sam Aylward say in a conversational tone: "And when you ride against the Mackenzies, you nasty little booger, *keep your visor down*!" Then in a great shout: "Let the gray geese fly—wholly together—*shoot!*"

The Marchwarden dropped his lance and shrieked as the arrow sprouted suddenly from his eyesocket . . .

"Blow the rally!" Jabar Jones shouted, reining in his horse.

He shook the blood out of his eyes; the helmet and coif had saved him from having his face transfixed, but not from a long gash on his forehead where a flap of skin hung down to show naked bone. The taste of his own blood was like tarnished copper in his mouth, the taste of defeat.

The curled trumpet screamed. Knights and men-at-arms pulled up their mounts, the horses panting and dribbling foam, those that weren't bucking or squealing from the pain of arrow wounds; one went over in a roar of metal as he watched, but the rider got free, staggered erect despite the weight of metal, and took the reins of a riderless horse that another led over to him.

Three hundred twenty, he rough-counted.

Back south by the road over which the charge had gone— both ways—the Mackenzies were coming forward again, each of them with their spear-shovel in hand. They planted them well forward, in their original position.

And then they stood, waiting. A murmur grew from them, then a chant, as they shook their bows overhead:

> *"We are the point—we are the edge*
> *We are the wolves that Hecate fed!"*

The baron of Molalla ground his teeth; pain and fury blended into an intolerable knot below his breastbone. Almost, he shouted *charge!*

"No," he muttered to himself.

A scout pulled up in a spurt of gravel. "My lord!" he shouted, pointing westward towards Mount Angel. "The monks—all of them, out of the city gates without warning! What should we do?"

Sutterdown, Willamette Valley, Oregon
March 8th, 2008/Change Year 9

"The Lord Protector won't be happy," Sir Buzz Akers said, as the last of the officers left the tent.

"He's not the only one," Conrad Renfrew said, stepping out of the pavilion and pulling on his mail-backed gauntlets.

The camp had been full of desperate, disciplined motion since the courier arrived and Renfrew gave his orders; now the headquarters support staff threw themselves at the big command tent, knocking down poles and folding fabric. Little was left of the encampment that had held twenty-five hundred men, save the ditch and bank; the supply wagons waited drawn up in columns down the principal street, and the troops themselves in neat formations with their unit banners before them, ready to mount horse or bicycle. The air was thick with bitter chemical smoke as the napalm stores went up in flames, the black pillar of smoke trailing away to the north in the warm wind that had sprung up overnight. High above, hazy white clouds drifted through a sky gone blue from the bright rim in the east to the lingering night in the west, the last stars just now fading as the sun rose opposite them.

"I thought Dick Furness was going to cry and cut out his own heart when I told him to torch the stores," Renfrew added, with a grim smile contorted further by the scars that seamed his face. "But we're traveling light—west to the I-5, north to Oregon City. If we can, we'll cover whatever fugitives from Emiliano's force managed to make it out."

He looked at the sky again. The peach orchards would be at their peak in the Hood River country now, and from the tower of Castle Odell he could see them scattered like blocks of pink froth between the plowlands. And April would be even better, as the cherries and pears came into bloom; he could smell them a mile off. His wife Tina loved them, and had the place stuffed with flowering branches; the scent lingered for weeks afterwards.

"So, we lost despite our numbers, my lord?"

Renfrew shrugged and set the helmet on his head. "We haven't won," he said. "But neither have the enemy—they haven't knocked us out of the game, not if I can save this army. We still have more men, and we have the castles to fall back on. They've just pushed us back to the start-line and cost us a campaigning season."

And you're right. The Lord Protector will not be pleased. But Norman Arminger is going to get a piece of my mind.

CHAPTER EIGHTEEN

Norman Arminger had wanted to hold a full meeting of the War Council, in a presence room where he would sit on a throne of sable granite and gold. Sandra had talked him into using this chamber, high in the Dark Tower but much more informal, with a window that looked down over the gardens outside the keep, and plain except for the carpet, table and chairs . . . and the black stone of the walls. Those were partly covered in maps. Only three sat there; herself, the Lord Protector of the Association, and its Grand Constable. Fresh spring air poured through, smelling of cut grass; the scent mingled with that of the rhododendrons in their shallow bowl in the center of the table, but it was not enough to cut the curdled psychic stink of rage and fear under the arched groin-work of the chamber's ceiling.

"What I did," Conrad Renfrew said, "was bring my troops back intact and pick up a thousand or so of Emiliano's, including a lot of his knights and men-at-arms. Thus preventing a *defeat* from turning into an *absolutely catastrophic* defeat that would have left us open to invasion or revolt."

Arminger gripped the arms of his chair. "Conrad, you told me that you didn't think the Mackenzies could get around north of you."

"No, I didn't think they could do that," the Count of Odell

said. "Not over those trails. Bold move. Very risky. It paid off, for them."

"Which means that while you were standing looking at Sutterdown they got around behind you *and ass-fucked you!*" Arminger snarled; his fist hit the table surface with a dull thudding sound—it was four inches of solid teak.

Renfrew's hideously scarred face was calm, the blue eyes impassive. "That's one way of looking at it," he said. "Or you could say that I'm the only commander you sent out this spring who didn't get his army either beaten up like Alexi or completely wrecked like Emiliano."

"That's *my lord*, when you address me," Arminger grated.

Ever so slightly, Sandra's eyes rolled towards the ceiling. Renfrew shook his shaven head.

"No, here with just us three it's *Norman* from me to you, Norman," he said. "Look, I've been carrying water for you since the day of the Change, when you and Sandra came bopping in and talked me around. You didn't make me Grand Constable because I was a complete fucking idiot, did you? So try listening to me for once. Try listening to *this*."

The Grand Constable was in military dress but not armor; black leather pants, shirt, and a black tunic with his own arms on it inside the outline of a heraldic shield—sable, a snow-topped mountain argent and vert. He reached inside the neck of the baggy woolen garment and produced a sheet of paper. The calluses on his fingers scratched on it as he spread it out.

"This is the minutes of the Council of War, back in February. *We're leaving our left flank open for sixty miles,* quote unquote. *We're attacking three ways at once, thus carefully throwing away the advantage of superior numbers,* quote unquote. *We should have Alexi stand on the defensive and tie up the Bearkillers without getting the Corvallans hot and bothered, and invest Mount Angel with six thousand men, even if it takes a year,* quote unquote. Because then it wouldn't *matter* what the God-damned kilties did. Instead *you* got greedy, and yeah, *we* got collectively ass-fucked. The above is the voice of the only man on the Council with the balls to tell you what you need to know, Norman."

Arminger controlled his fury with an effort of will that brought a bead of sweat to his forehead; the smell of it was a faint, rank musk. "Corvallis was supposed to be neutralized," he said in a flat voice. "Alexi's report is pretty clear that he had the Bearkillers back on their heels until that happened."

Sandra spoke for the first time, her voice like cool water. "We *did* have the Faculty Senate neutralized. What happened was that the Corvallans who wanted to fight us just strapped on their armor and jumped on the bicycles and started pedaling north. Unorthodox, illegal, unconstitutional . . . but there you are."

Renfrew slapped the table, a gunshot sound as his palm struck dense, oily wood only a little harder. "Yeah. Precisely. Which happened because we tried to take away the buffer between them and us. Made our protestations of peaceful intent look pretty much like complete bullshit, didn't it? OK, yeah, they always *were* bullshit, but did we have to make that entirely plain to the most wishful wishful thinker? And all that effort we put into cultivating Turner and Kowalski? *They'll* be lucky not to get lynched, and there goes years of work."

Arminger jerked to his feet, a move with none of his usual feline gracefulness. Then he stalked over to the tall, narrow window, looking down across the lands that acknowledged him ruler. His hands writhed together behind his back, but when he turned at last his face was calm.

"What do you recommend?" he said. He turned his head slightly. "Both of you."

"That we pull in our horns," the Grand Constable said promptly. "Inside our own borders we've got enough manpower still to fight off anything the other side can throw at us, easy. We're bigger and we've got interior lines and strong fortifications—which is why we've been squeezing so hard from the first to get the damn castles built. In a year or two we can convince the Corvallans that we're really just little lambs, baaa-lambs, and that they should sell us the rope we use to hang them; they're almost as gullible that way as people were before the Change. Then we attack the Free Cities League, and digest it, and *then* we see what's possible next. You're not going to conquer the world all at once, Norman. But if we stick out our dicks again *right now,* and if we have a couple of inches trimmed off *again,* like Alexi did or even worse the way Emiliano did, God alone knows what might happen. The Free Cities might have a slap at us, for starters. And a lot of our farmers would rise the minute they thought we were losing our grip."

Sandra nodded. "That'll be true until the last people who grew up before the Change die. And we do have to worry about the Free Cities, darling."

Arminger looked at his wife. She spread her hands on the table. "My dear, they're quiet now because we frightened the daylights out of them last year and broke down a lot of their irrigation canals, not because they love us. The problem with that is what happens if they *stop* being afraid of us. Which is true more generally, too, you see."

"I hate to say—" Renfrew began. "No, let's be honest. I *love* to say 'I told you so,' and I told you we could forget about the Willamette for a while and take the Yakima, because the Free Cities League was isolated from anyone else—they're too far away for Boise to support them effectively. That would have given us a base to take the rest of the Palouse country, which is good wheatland. I know you've got a hard-on for the kilties and Mike Havel, Norman, but let's not get irrational about this."

Suddenly Arminger smiled; it was an amused, rueful expression. "I *do* tend to get obsessive," he said. "And they've been driving me absolutely mad for years now; the more so as things have gone so well everywhere else. I confess to a *very* strong desire to see them suffer, and that's one of the perks of being the overlord, isn't it? All right, we'll make up some face-saving thing about the Grand Constable 'saving the host' and stand on the defensive, at least until after harvest. Then we'll see. We can talk a little at dinner tonight, Conrad. Right now I'm going to go to the sparring room and hit things for a while. Better still, I'll hit *people.*"

Silence fell with the lord of the Association gone. After a long minute Sandra Arminger tapped the papers before her into neat piles. "Well, that was easier than I thought it would be," she said in a tone as neutral as the spring sunlight.

Conrad Renfrew nodded. "Norman's being reasonable."

Their eyes met, with a common, unstated disquiet.

In the corridor outside, Norman Arminger snapped his fingers. A messenger in black livery knelt.

"Find Sir Joris Stein," Arminger said calmly. "Tell him to attend me in the Salle d'Armes of the Dark Tower guardroom, immediately."

The Mackenzies would be celebrating. Time for them to feel a little grief.

The Silver Tower looked west from Castle Todenangst's keep; the pearly granite that sheathed it had come from a number of banks in Portland and Vancouver and Oregon City.

In popular slang, it was known as the Spider's Lair. Sandra Arminger thought that extremely amusing; in fact, Tiphaine wouldn't have been surprised if the consort hadn't started the necessary rumors herself. She took a deep breath and walked past the guards at the arched entranceway, nodding to their stamp and crash of metal since she was in civilian garb.

My first time as a member of the nobility, she thought. *Granted, the lowest rank of the nobility, but it's still a big change. And don't forget who* got *it for you.*

The same gray-and-silver theme was continued within, when you came to the upper chambers that were Sandra Arminger's private quarters; off-white marble floors, silvery silk hangings with the occasional tapestry for contrast, cool restraint in the furniture, only the Oriental rugs providing a blaze of colors—there was an experimental workshop in Oregon City which was patiently laboring to duplicate the best Isfahans for her. The air smelled slightly of jasmine and sandalwood; from the opened windows she could hear the evening sounds of the great fortress-palace, guards tramping, faint music in the distance, wind flapping a banner, the *skree-skree-skree* of a hawk in the mews. Gaslights kept the interior light, and recessed hot-water radiators made it pleasant despite the chill of the spring night.

And the only problem is the damned cats, Tiphaine Rutherton thought, quietly nudging one aside as it tried to chew on her boot; she was mildly allergic to them, but *nobody* dissed the consort's felines.

I wish she'd drown the nasty pug-faced Persian monstrosities. And they always shed on your clothes when you're wearing black. Well, not my problem anymore.

She bowed deeply, and one small, elegant hand gave her leave to sit.

"My husband, Lady d'Ath, is a very capable man," Sandra Arminger said after a moment's silence, leaning back in her chair on the other side of the table and stroking a blue-eyed cat curled up in her lap. "Very forethoughtful, in many respects—did you know he had a plan of this castle made *before* the Change? However, like even the greatest men, he has a few weaknesses."

Tiphaine Rutherton bowed her head, a slight, silent gesture. A servant slipped forward noiselessly and filled her cup with herbal tea. She'd really have preferred wine, and it was late enough—after eight and after dinner—but admittedly they needed clear heads for a task so delicate that nothing could be said explicitly even in strict privacy. She also knew that there was no point in speculating until her liege gave her more information; trying to get ahead of the consort in a guessing game was a short route to gibbering madness or a very nasty shock, or both.

Instead she let her mind drift, passively ready to absorb information or act suddenly and without hesitation, otherwise free-associating. She spared the servant a glance; it was the same girl they'd taken to Corvallis back in January, and it was typical of Lady Sandra that even a trusted operative like Tiphaine wasn't entirely sure what her capabilities were or what she was tasked with besides pouring tea, except that it was much more than that. It no longer felt like disloyalty to notice that the girl was extremely pretty; she'd sworn vengeance for Katrina Georges, not eternal celibacy.

One of Norman Arminger's "weaknesses" was shagging anything that moved, as long as it was in its teens, female, and good-looking, like this one. In the old days he'd certainly had dozens of them running around in extremely skimpy outfits; she could remember the tail end of that, before the consort and the Church talked him out of it, amid the general settling down after the wild years. That wasn't a reputation that hurt him with most of the Association warriors, quite the contrary—being a "real three-ball man" was an advantage with them, if not with Pope Leo.

Pigs, she thought, hiding a slight sneer; but it had never been a matter of much concern to her and Kat, since the Lady Sandra protected *her* Household quite thoroughly.

Rumor also said that the consort helped hold them down for him on occasion. She found the image rather disturbing; it was odd to imagine the Lady Sandra involved in anything so sweaty and . . . complex.

And I'm fairly certain she has absolutely no interest in women, Tiphaine thought; she and Kat had both had a mild, Platonic knight-and-fair-lady crush on her for much of their teens, and she'd made it gently but unmistakably clear that it had better stay that way. *She seems to like them better than men as daytime company, though.*

Sandra's lips turned up. "I trained you well," she said. "Waiting patiently for me to say too much, are you?"

Tiphaine chuckled, as her mind snapped automatically back to the here and now. "Actually, my liege, I was just noticing the slight differences in the way you speak to me now that I've been ennobled. It's much more subtle than the way most of the court has reacted."

"Bravo!" Sandra said, her eyes sparkling, and made as if to clap. "Although on occasion a flood of words can be a disguise as efficient as silence. In any case, take a look at these.".

She used one finger to slide a folder across the table. It had the Eye stamped on the cover, and was bound with black ribbon. The blond woman opened it, and flipped rapidly through typewritten pages and hand-drawn maps. As she did, her pale brows rose farther and farther. When she'd finished she closed the file and spent a moment running the data through her mind, and considering implications.

"I gather that the official announcement of *setbacks* in the grand Crusade of Unification was a bit of an understatement," she said dryly.

Sandra snapped her fingers, and the servant-girl slid forward again, taking the file away and locking it in a cabinet disguised with a birch wainscot. She laid the key before Sandra and stepped back; the ruler picked it up and toyed with the little metal shape as she spoke, her eyes focused somewhere far away.

"This war is over," she said flatly. "Bungled into wreck. It was bad enough that those Corvallan 'volunteers' saved the Bear Lord, but losing our *second* Marchwarden of the South in the space of a year is embarrassing. Emiliano . . . what's the warrior expression? Screwed the pooch? I'm afraid 'looks good with an arrow through the head' is becoming a qualification for that job."

Tiphaine's lips compressed to hide the chuckle that almost startled out of her.

Sandra nodded and went on: "The Grand Constable managed to save most of our forces, but the net result is that we're back where we started, with no territorial gains or plunder to compensate for our losses—including, unfortunately, many knights and members of significant families. The Lord Protector is . . . annoyed."

"And your policy, my liege?"

"To avoid throwing good money after bad. As I said, my husband is a very capable man, and very determined; he wouldn't be where he is otherwise. Unfortunately he's also stubborn, which is the flip side. And he's extraordinarily vindictive. So am I, of course, but it's less . . . personal, shall we say. I make a point of not letting it interfere with serious matters."

Tiphaine nodded soberly. She'd heard nothing that she hadn't figured out for herself, parts of it long ago, but the fact that Lady Sandra was willing to tell her, and in so many words, was an important fact in itself.

"So what do you want *me* to do, liege-lady?" she said.

Sandra smiled wryly. "I want you to keep my options open," she said. "By taking up that little property of yours; it needs the fief-holder's foot, as the saying goes. And I'd like you to entertain some guests there. No need to have daily propinquity give dear Norman ideas. Or His Holiness."

Dun Juniper, Willamette Valley, Oregon
March 11th, 2008/Change Year 9

"O Goddess gentle and strong, protect him," Juniper said, feeling the blood drain from her face, tasting the acrid sourness of vomit at the back of her throat, smelling her own fearsweat. "I hadn't thought Sandra hated me so much, or would be willing to torment a child."

"Wait a minute," Nigel said.

Juniper looked up. It wasn't the sympathy in his voice that made the cold nausea in her gut subside a little, but the sharp common sense.

"Would you mind reading that to us again, Lady Juniper?" he said.

This was semiformal; they were in the third-floor bedroom-loft-office of her Hall, sitting near the north-face hearth that held her personal altar as well, with a mandala and images—a tile plaque of Cernunnos playing the flute, and a blue-robed Lady of the Moon. A low blaze crackled in the small hearth and dispelled some of the damp chill of a spring night. Lanterns cast yellow-red light over bookshelves and desk, filing cabinets and ritual tools, her rolled-up futon and the big vertical loom down at the edge by the dormer windows. The loom held a blanket she was working on, in zigzag stripes of cream white, taupe, cinnamon brown and a darker brown that was almost black, the natural colors of sheep's wool. She was weaving it on two levels, so that her eight-heddle loom could produce a stretch eight feet across; it had been intended for Rudi's bed . . .

Sam Aylward was there, and Chuck and Judy Barstow, and Eilir and Astrid and their men.

And Nigel is mine, she thought, drawing a deep breath. *Trust him.* She read the report again.

"The day after her investiture and oath of fealty, Tiphaine d'Ath left Castle Todenangst for her Domain; this caused some surprise. A closed carriage accompanied them, and Rudi Mackenzie and the Princess Mathilda were not seen afterwards in the Castle."

"*And the Princess Mathilda* is the operative phrase here, my dear," Nigel said, a hunter's expression on his face. "She knows what close friends the children are. Surely she wouldn't risk her own relationship with her daughter so soon after getting her back. She most certainly would not send her along to a place where Rudi was to be mistreated—if she planned that, she'd separate them."

And Mom, it was Sandra who announced that Rudi should be treated like a prince, Eilir signed. *All the accounts agree on that. She couldn't lose face by reversing herself in secret.*

"You have a point, so," Juniper said slowly, feeling her mind begin to function again. The loss had hit her much harder here at home, where every board and window shouted memories of Rudi. "I thought . . . this Tiphaine is an assassin, and she hates us so bitterly. . . ."

"I don't know about that," Alleyne Loring said, brushing the downy yellow mustache on his upper lip with a fingertip. It was a habit he'd acquired from his father, and Juniper found it peculiarly endearing. "I had the impression that she hated Astrid, specifically, and others only in relation to her. Eilir, of course, and myself, and John. Not that she wouldn't be willing to kill anyone she was told to, but that was the *personal* element."

Even then, a corner of Juniper's mind noticed something; when the Lorings had arrived in Oregon a year ago, young Alleyne had usually referred to the other Englishman as "Hordle" or "sergeant," for all that they'd been companions since childhood—some peculiar English Frodo/Samwise thing, she supposed. Now it was just "John". . . .

Our American egalitarianism at work, I suppose, she thought. *Or the Clan Mackenzie's ways.*

She thought for a moment, then asked: "I didn't see much of Tiphaine Rutherton—and particularly not together with Sandra Arminger—or fight her. What's your take?"

Eilir hesitated, then signed: *I think it's some sort of sick guru-chela thing with those two. I got the impression she'd trained her—and Katrina Georges—for a long time. Not their warrior training, but mental disciplines.*

Astrid nodded. "She was very, very good in the warehouse. Movement as fast as anyone I've ever seen, beautifully fluid, and she was *thinking* every second—good improvisation and use of externals. And when we talked later, she fooled me completely."

And me, Eilir said. *Sorry, anamchara, but you're not as good at reading people.* Astrid nodded, unfazed; that was a truth they both acknowledged. The deaf woman went on: *Doesn't the report say that the two of them were taken in by Sandra Arminger right after the Change?*

Juniper nodded. "They were Girl Scouts, oddly enough . . . I think, given what I've learned of her over the years, that Sandra Arminger delights in her own cleverness. And what better way to mark it than fashioning . . . shaping . . . very clever people herself? So that they develop their minds and become formidable in their own right, yet she remains the center of their universe. She would not hesitate to hurt Rudi to suit her own purposes, or even simply to hurt me. But I think Nigel is right; she would not throw an advantage away to gratify cruelty, nor would she ever act on impulse."

She gave a short, bitter laugh. "And it is my best hope, that my son is in the hands of such a person."

Alleyne nodded. "What intelligence do we have on this Ath place?"

Sir Nigel coughed discreetly. "It's the land Arminger tried to buy us with, last year, Alleyne. Ath is the name of the castle he mentioned . . . a small one, he said, if I recall correctly."

The younger Loring's eyebrows went up. "They didn't stint young Tiphaine's plate," he observed. "That's better than four thousand acres, and those lovely vineyards, with a big tract of woodland in the Coast Range tacked on."

Sam Aylward spoke up, startling them all a little: "Roit you are. They're smart enough to reward success. What was that saying the old-time general used, sir?"

Nigel frowned in thought. Then: "Ah, yes. *To command armies, it is sufficient to pay well, punish well and hang well.*"

Judy Barstow spoke: "We have some people in the villages near there. A small coven, though the High Priestess died last year. Perhaps we could get information from them, if any are on the castle staff. There's a traveling liaison, a peddler and his family . . ."

Aylward took up the thread: "And when we do, we can see about getting young Rudi back—perhaps Mathilda as well."

Juniper surprised herself by shaking her head: "Not Mathilda. We were wrong to keep her so long. Remember the Threefold Law. And we . . ." She swallowed and made herself go on. "We needn't be in a desperate hurry. Sandra Arminger would rather corrupt than kill, and she's very patient. She'll need to be; my Rudi isn't one to be corrupted easily!"

"Right you are, Lady," Aylward said grimly. "But we'd best remember that she isn't the only player at the board. There's her husband."

Astrid nodded. "The Dúnedain Rangers will do all they can to rescue Artos . . . Rudi," she said.

Eilir nodded vigorously. Sam Aylward thought for a moment, then nodded himself, with a rueful sigh. "A youngster's job, right enough."

When all had left, Juniper Mackenzie extinguished the lights and knelt before the altar, hands crossed upon her breast. She took a moment to empty her mind, then opened herself to the night—to the crackle of fire and the smell of fir burning, to the wind that brought the living forests into the room, to the distant murmurs of sound that faded into the creaking, rubbing, crackling stillness of the mountain forests. When she launched her will, it was like a spear—and like the cry of every mother, to the Mother: *Save my son!*

Castle Ath, Tualatin Valley, Oregon
March 15th/16th, 2008/Change Year 9

"Welcome to your domain of Ath, my lady," the steward said.

He was middle-aged—in his late thirties—and looked as if he'd be more comfortable in a suit and tie than the tabard and tunic of ceremony, but post-Change clothes were the prestige dress in the Association's territories. His eyes went wide as he recognized the gold chain around her neck and across the breast of her hauberk, made up of linked sets of letters reading PPA; that could only be a gift from the Protector's own hand. Swallowing, he went on: "I am Richard Wielman, the

Lord Protector's steward for this domain of Ath these last nine years, and yours as well if you wish."

"Thank you, Goodman Wielman," Tiphaine Rutherton said as she leaned a hand on her saddlebow.

A slight smile lit her face as she looked up at the gray bulk of the fortress, sharp against the bright blue sky, and took a deep breath of fresh country scents, cut grass, turned earth, fir-sap, wood smoke, and just enough of horse and manure to add a little pungency. Then she turned her attention back to Wielman; a good estate steward would make *her* work a lot easier, and this one had actually been a farm manager *before* the Change, and knew bookkeeping as well. He'd probably want to keep this job, but there were plenty of landholders who'd snap him up if he left.

"I examined the Exchequer records at Castle Todenangst, and you appear to have done a fine job. I was particularly pleased with the price you got from those Corvallis merchants for the spring wool clip. I'm sure we'll get along well," she said.

The man bowed again and babbled thanks, then pulled himself together and introduced his wife and children and the other important staff; Father Peter, the priest; the bailiffs of the three manors, the head stockman and the vintner . . . All of them looked nervous; the offices on the estate were in her gift now, even the clerical ones if she didn't mind a head-butting session with the local bishop, and she might not want the same men holding them.

Ath was on a hill not far south of the town of Forest Grove and a little west of old Highway 47, just where the Coast Range began rearing out of the Tualatin Valley in green forest-clad heights, walling off the Pacific. Orchards and groves of filbert and walnut had covered it before the Protector's labor gangs came, and still mantled the lower slopes. The castle itself was of a simple design the Association had put up by the dozens as the vacant lands were resettled, and then handed out to knight and baron; unlike many, it hadn't been enlarged. In the southeast corner of a walled enclosure stood a rectangular tower whose outline was about the size of an ordinary suburban house, but four stories tall; smaller round towers stood at the other three angles, one of them sporting a metal windmill whirling at its peak to keep the reservoir filled. The gate ran in beside the main keep, with portcullis and drawbridge, and a dry moat full of barbed wire and angle iron surrounded the whole; the wall itself was crenellated and half the main keep-tower's height, and it enclosed an acre and a half.

North and east and south the castle commanded a broad view of land where patches of cloud-shadow drifted over smaragdine brightness in an infinite variety of greens, dappled by occasional squares of red-brown plowed land. It was good to be back from the wild lands and the dead cities, back among the fields that fed mankind. Fingers of higher, tree-clad ridge stretched out into the rolling farmlands; those were busy now with ox-teams and people planting barley and oats and potatoes, and sugar beet for the new factory in Forest Grove.

My barley, my oats, and my potatoes. My cows, and wheat, and vineyards . . . my farmers, for that matter, Tiphaine thought.

It was pleasing and daunting and exciting at the same time. And the Lord Protector and Lady Sandra certainly hadn't been cheap about it; there were barons without much more than this, and most ordinary landed knights had a lot less.

It can be sort of disorienting when you finally get what you've been aiming for. I'm twenty-three. What do I do now? Do I want to be . . . oh, Mathilda's right hand and her Grand Constable and bone-breaker when she's Lady Protector?

On south-facing slopes peach trees were in blossom; sheep grazed beneath on the crimson-clover sod. Swaths of the grassland below the castle walls were bright with yellow daffodils. Down by Carpenter Creek a mile northward, horses and black-coated cattle drifted through the meadows; southeast lay a big block of vineyard drawing square regularity over rumpled land. A hamlet of frame cottages with ditch and bank around it stood on the south side of the roadway that led west to the castle gate, and anxious-looking civilians and their families in their best tabards stood there, waiting to greet her—those would be the castle service staff, most of whom lived outside the wall in normal times. The castle garrison and *their* families were inside the gate, in the courtyard, the men drawn up in ranks for inspection.

Or would I rather just sit here and enjoy my life? Get in some hunting and hawking, read a few books, play my lute, drill the troops . . . maybe find some nice girl and settle down to quasi-clandestine bliss?

A six-year-old in double tunic and tabard with ribbons in her hair clutched a bouquet of early wildflowers and daffodils eked out with ferns, and what was probably her brother led a pretty, plump and spectacularly well-groomed lamb with a bow around the neck; their parents discreetly pushed them forward.

The steward grew formal once more, going to one knee for an instant: "Lady, I deliver to you the estate."

He had a big book of accounts under his arm, and touched it reflexively as he rose. "You have forty-six hundred acres of field, pasture, orchard and vineyard, and pannage and forest rights and rights of venery in the mountains; fishing rights at Henry Hagg Lake; three villages and the castle settlement; two hundred thirty-two families of free tenants, bond tenants and peons, eight hundred and ten souls in all; two gristmills, a sawmill and a fulling mill, a tannery—"

"Thank you, Goodman," Tiphaine said; that was what you called civilian commoners of just below Associate status. "I *did* read the accounts. We'll go over them together in the next few days, and I'll be riding around the estate to familiarize myself, and to settle Sir Ivo and Sir Ruffin on their fiefs. Now, I presume my quarters are ready, and those for my guests?"

She indicated the carriage that followed in her train, a four-horse closed model built before the Change for the tourist trade. These days it was a symbol of wealth and power sufficient to make anyone thoughtful; modern equivalents weren't nearly as comfortable yet unless you had the limitless resources of the Lord Protector or his consort.

"Yes, my lady, as the message instructed; and we've been preparing a feast. If I may say so, the quarters in the Montinore manor are much more comfortable. I've had what gear I could brought up here as your messenger instructed, and we've been working hard on putting things in order, but the castle is simply . . ."

"More suitable in a time of war," she pointed out. "And my guests are Princess Mathilda and Rudi Mackenzie."

Wielman's eyes bulged. "The princess . . . *here,* my lady? And the son of the *Witch Queen*?" He recovered quickly and bowed, sweeping a hand sideways; it wasn't his place to question her. "Please, my lady, enter and take possession."

Tiphaine swung down from the saddle, the skirts of her hauberk clashing against the shin-guards. "I'd better accept the bouquet and the lamb first. Wouldn't do to disappoint the moppets."

At least they don't have a choir, she thought as she jerked her head slightly to the man behind her. She didn't exactly dislike children, but preferred them past the age of reason and in the background at that. When you wanted to play with something, a dog was usually better, and it didn't grow up to be surly and ungrateful.

Ivo walked his horse forward to hand a wrapped cloth bundle to one of the garrison. The soldier took it and trotted away; a few instants later the cords along the tower's flagstaff worked, and the banner broke out at the top.

"Sable, a delta or over a V argent," the steward said respectfully, as her new arms took the air over her citadel for the first time, silver and gold and black. "What is the symbolism, my lady?"

"V for the Virgin Mary, of course," Tiphaine answered gravely.

I thought Lady Sandra would do herself an injury laughing, she thought. *And she suggested a pair of crossed keys with a fist beneath them, middle finger extended, that would be only a little more explicit . . . going to be lonely leaving the Household. Even more lonely.*

It had been half a year since Katrina died. They'd been together since the day ten years ago when their Girl Scout troop was left in the Cascades by the Change; they'd made it back to Portland together, and together they'd managed to penetrate the Protector's security. He'd wanted to kill when two starving fourteen-year-olds woke him up in the middle of the night and demanded a job, with the bodyguards none the wiser. Lady Sandra had laughed then, too, and said no, that they would be far too useful to waste.

Always together until Kat went off to rescue the princess.

Since then she'd learned that you didn't die of loneliness. You even got used to it, and the pain of being abandoned faded to a dull ache. The need for revenge didn't, though.

Well, that's something I know I want to do. Someone else *is going to die of my loneliness, and Kat . . . I know* just *who.*

CHAPTER NINETEEN

Castle Ath, Tualatin Valley, Oregon
March 16th, 2008/Change Year 9

"This is sort of cool," Rudi said. "I like this better than Todenangst already."

Then he looked over at the girl beside him. "And your folks really didn't want to send you away, you know. They're just busy. That happens with my mom sometimes, and your mom and dad have a lot more to look after."

Mathilda wiped her forearm over her eyes and smiled. "Yeah, I know. Sometimes it just *sucks* when your parents have jobs like that, doesn't it?"

"Oh, *tell* me," Rudi said. He waved at the huge dappled stretch of countryside. "This is great, though."

"Well, I think it's even better from the Dark Tower at Castle Todenangst," Mathilda said judiciously. "But this isn't bad."

"That's the only thing I really don't like about home," Rudi said. "Even from the gatehouse towers, all you can see is the meadow and the mountains. But that's sort of the point—it's hard to get at."

Mathilda frowned slightly. "Then why do our castles have such great views?"

"I remember something Sir Nigel said," Rudi said. "Castles aren't just for stopping someone attacking you. They're bases to go out and fight people and control places, and for that you have to see the ground around."

"We sure can!" she grinned, tapping the heavy tripod-mounted binoculars.

They'd graced some tourist lookout-point once. Now they were part of a surveillance and message system that linked most of the Protectorate's castles, from here to Walla Walla and north to Puget Sound.

"Yeah, it's like being a god or an angel or something, with these."

They had a box to stand on, which let them reach the eye-pieces, and a helper—what they called a varlet here—to move the tripod around for them.

The forty feet of the tower and the two hundred and fifty of the hill gave a splendid view of a countryside that was subtly different from what he was used to, looking like a painting tinted with old gold as the sun dipped towards the Coast Range westward. He could see two villages from here, with their houses and barns, worksheds and mills, surrounded by truck plots. Farther out each had a set of five large fields; winter wheat, spring oats or barley, roots like turnips or potatoes, and two in clover for grazing and hay. Strips within each marked family holdings; there were meadows beside the rivers, and the vineyards and orchards mostly where pre-Change convenience had put them; manor houses had a big farm attached, the demesne. The main roads were well kept; potholes patched with asphalt, gravel and grading maintained on the smaller ones.

A train of ox-drawn wagons loaded with unknown boxes and sacks passed in the middle distance, heading south towards the railway stop there. Heading north was a troop of half a dozen horsemen; he looked through the glasses and saw it was a knight in bright tunic and tooled leather with golden spurs on his heels and a peregrine on his wrist. Beside him was a lady riding with divided skirts and embroidered leggings showing beneath, as gaudy and as haughty, bearing a goshawk; as he watched she unhooded it and the bird mantled, wings splayed for an instant before it leapt skyward in a torrent of strokes.

Rudi sighed; and again when he pivoted the binoculars westward. Barely two miles in that direction was trackless forest. Literally trackless since the hand of man was withdrawn, as lumbering roads were overgrown, and clearcuts sprawled into impenetrable tangles of undergrowth taller than a man through which Douglas fir and hemlock and red cedar saplings pushed. He could . . .

Nah. Make a realistic threat appraisal, the way Unc' Sam does. I'm a kid. Sure, I'm really, really good in the woods for a kid my age, but they've got some real *woodsmen here. And Lady Tiphaine isn't just good, she's* scary. *They'd catch me and then they'd lock me up all the time. If someone does come to rescue me, that could screw everything up. The Luck of the Clan will help me, if I'm smart and wait for the Lord and Lady. Gotta be like Coyote, always waiting for the right moment for a trick.*

The top of the tower was a featureless rectangle, fifty-five feet by forty-five, covered in thick asphalt paving, broken only by the trapdoor and a metal chimney in the middle of the eastern side, and by the turntable-mounted throwing engines crouching under their tarpaulins at each corner. They walked over to the western edge and looked down, Mathilda sitting casually in the gap between two merlons, with Rudi leaning by her side. The fighting platform on the inside of the circuit wall ended a dozen feet short of where it joined the tower's second story; the gap was covered by removable footbridges that ended in thick steel doors. A full-scale metal drawbridge joined the ground floor of the tower to the courtyard over a ditch bristling with sharpened, rust-reddened angle iron that surrounded the tower-keep on the inside. The drawbridge was down now, and the gates wide open, but two spearmen stood by the entrance.

Houses and barracks and workshops lined the inside of the wall, along with a chapel, all built in thickly plastered and whitewashed cinderblock, plain and serviceable; there were paved pathways, but most of the courtyard was graveled dirt. Savory smells came from the kitchens; scullions bustled in and out, and outside over pits full of white-glowing oak coals two yearling steers turned on spits, along with shoats, sending wisps of blue smoke skyward as cooks basted and brushed. Others rolled barrels up pairs of beams thrust slantwise through cellar doors. There was a cheerful bustle in and out through the main gates; relief was in the voices as well, for nobody had lost their post, and the new seigneur had ordered a feast on a scale that showed she wasn't the sort to squeeze every silver dime until it squeaked. The tenants and peons would pay for all in the end, but at least the staff would get a good feed out of it.

A female knight was very rare, but not enough to be bizarre or totally unheard-of, even as a fief-holder. And this one had the prestige of rescuing the princess, and capturing none less than the son of the Witch Queen, and having the favor of the Lord Protector and Lady Sandra.

Tiphaine d'Ath was busy at something else, over by the pells and targets where the castle garrison trained. Rudi grinned, and Mathilda did too: one of the men-at-arms froze in midstroke. Even at this distance they could tell how his face went white as new cheese under a weathered tan. The razor tip of his new liege-lady's sword rested very lightly against the throat of his mail coif; a slight push would crush his larynx, or even pierce the mail—she used a sword with a lighter blade and a longer point than most in the Protectorate.

"Not bad," she said, stepping back. "But you can all use some work with the blade, particularly the pointy bit on the end. A hint: it's supposed to go into the other guy. Any of you infantry care to try a bout? You'll have to use a sword sometimes as well as crossbow and spear."

Sir Ivo and Sir Ruffin were grinning as well, where they stood with their shields slung over their backs and their crossed hands resting on the pommels of their own drawn blades. None of the men-at-arms had been able to beat either, even Ruffin with his not-quite-completely recovered left arm, but some of them had lasted more than a few seconds. Then the new Lady of Ath had offered a hundred rose nobles and a promotion to anyone who could beat *her*. . . .

"Tiphaine made them all look like dancing bears," Mathilda giggled.

"Yeah. She's *good*," Rudi said; he blinked away a memory of Aoife's neck suddenly running red, and her eyes going wide in shock. "I think maybe Aunt Astrid's better, and maybe

Lord Bear, but maybe not. And she's smart, too. Now they'll all go around boasting about what a swordswoman their new liege is."

Mathilda gave him an odd look. "I thought she was just making them look silly, and they'd hate it," she said.

"Well, yeah, she made them look like clowns. But they don't . . . you know . . . *feel* silly if she's Scathach come again with a sword," he said, blinking a little; he'd thought it was obvious. "Warriors are like that. If their leader can beat *them,* they want to believe they can beat anyone else easy, and that makes them feel sort of proud. It's a bit funny when you say it out loud, but that's the way it works, I guess here too."

"Yup," she said thoughtfully. "And I suppose 'cause Tiphaine's a girl, she has to show that she's better than anyone real quick."

"Well, yeah, around here, I suppose so. Dumb."

"I wonder if we could get her to tutor us with the sword, while we're here?" Mathilda said, still thoughtful. "Mom said we'd have a tutor for book stuff soon but she didn't say anything about phys-ed. I want to be real good. Like you say, it'll be handy someday. And it's fun anyway."

Matti's no dummy, Rudi thought with approval. *A Chief has to think of things like that.*

"Her friend Katrina was your tutor, wasn't she?"

"Yup," Mathilda said. "Arms, gymnastics, and riding. I don't know if she was *that* good—" She nodded towards the exercise ground. "I was only just eight back then, you know, too little to know much. But she and Tiphaine used to spar a lot, and people would come to watch. They did all sorts of things together."

"Like Aoife and Liath," Rudi said absently.

Down below, the row of spearmen and crossbowmen were respectfully declining more practice bouts with Tiphaine d'Ath; several of them were smiling as they did so. She nodded to the two knights, and both of them attacked immediately, not wasting time on preparations beyond unslinging their shields. He leaned over the parapet and wished he were a little closer, absently hooking a hand into the back of Mathilda's belt as she bent forward as well.

There was a fast, violent clash, steel-on-steel and beating in sharp cracks on the big kite-shaped shields, and then Ruffin's blade went flying as a shield edge slammed into his forearm just above the wrist. People dodged the pinwheeling length of sharp metal; sparring with real battle swords was a bit of a show-off thing. But even then they kept looking as Tiphaine drove Ivo before her; at last he leapt forward, trying to knock her back shield-to-shield, and she spun like a dust devil, tripped him neatly and tapped the point of her blade between his shoulders before helping him up.

"Well, not *really* like that," Mathilda said; then her brows flew up in shocked surmise.

Rudi looked up at her. "Oh? I *thought* it was probably like that—I can usually tell things about people, you know. But I can't be sure, 'cause I never, like, saw them at the same time."

She frowned, and looked over to see that the varlet was out of hearing distance. When she spoke it was quietly: "You'd better not tell anyone else you think that," she warned. "You could get her into a *lot* of trouble."

"Oh? Oh, yeah. Sure, no problemo. Tiphaine's not so bad."

Mathilda hesitated. "I'm sorry about Aoife and Liath. They were great, and . . . I sort of think it was my fault. If I hadn't gone under the trees—"

Rudi let the grief flow through him and past him. "It wasn't your fault, Matti. I mean, we were right there, only a mile and a half from the gates of the dun. Who could have known? Even Uncle Dennis just said not to go beyond the watchpost, and we didn't get that far. Tiphaine and her bunch pulled it off really slick."

The garrison cheered and shouted as they watched the brief, spectacular match, then formed up again; Tiphaine addressed them with her sword blade resting on her right shoulder, and the other hand on her hip, shield with its new blazon hanging off her left by its *guige*.

"Sir Ivo and Sir Ruffin are damned good. I won't settle for anything but the best in my *menie*," she said. "So you're all going to be working hard from now on. When the call comes, you're going to be facing pikes and crossbows or Bearkiller lances or Mackenzie longbows, not wooden posts and targets.

Anyone who doesn't like the idea can go hire on with someone else, like maybe as bouncers at the Slut and Brew in
Portland."

That got a general laugh, and blades flourished in salute.
"And now let's get cleaned up before the feast; I don't know
whether this gambeson is trying to drown me or marry me,
and if I get any hungrier I'm going over there to hack that cow
apart personally. Dismissed!"

She sheathed the sword without looking down, then passed
weapons belt and shield to one of the varlets. The smile was
off her face as she turned to look up at the tower top; the wall
was casting shadow over the courtyard, but her hair still
burned bright in a stray beam.

Yeah, gonna have to be real *careful,* Rudi thought, ducking
back. *She doesn't fool easy.*

Then his stomach rumbled; it had been a long while since
the picnic lunch in the carriage. Mathilda punched his
shoulder.

"Let's get ready for dinner," she said. "I'm clemmed."

"You're gonna have to stop talking like that," Rudi said as
they walked over to the head of the stairs. "You sound like a
kiltie!"

The great dining hall was the whole ground floor of the keep.
With no resident lord, it had been used as an armory and
storehouse until now, and spears and crossbows still stood
racked around the inside of the massive concrete walls. The
slight tang of oiled metal was now overlain by the sweet scent
of burning fir and the savory smells of roast beef and pork,
chicken and duck, vegetables and spiced gravy and fresh
wheat bread. There were no openings in the two walls that
faced the outer world, and only thin slits for firing through on
the pair that overlooked the courtyard through thick ferroconcrete. The inside walls were plain apart from whitewash,
and the concrete floors hastily covered with mats of woven
straw. Open gates and portcullis let in air grown a little chill
with the spring evening, but the stars were many and bright
save where the moon hung on the horizon. Torches burned in
brackets outside, mostly for show; the bonfires in the court-

yard gave both light and warmth to the commons feasting there on tables set on the drawbridge and close by it, sending flights of sparks drifting skyward.

A fire in the great inner hearth kept the room warm despite draughts, thigh-thick fir logs crackling and booming on the iron dogs and making an occasional spit of sparks and sending out a strong, wild scent. Gasoline lanterns hanging from the ferroconcrete beams that crisscrossed above kept it bright; draughts flickered the only hanging in the room, the new banner of Ath hanging behind the high seat. The tables were set up in a T, with chairs at the upper end and benches lower down. Tiphaine sat at the center of the top bar; Mathilda and Rudi had the honor seats on her right, with Ivo and Ruffin and their soon-to-be wives just beyond; the priest of Ath, Father Peter, sat on her left along with the captain of the men-at-arms and his wife and two of their older children. Beyond the big gilt ceremonial saltcellar that marked off those of lower rank sat the ordinary men-at-arms and their families, below them the other soldiers of the garrison, their families, the primary officers of the estate and *their* families.

The steward was on his feet, directing carvers and servers and pourers with a white wand in his hand; a yearling shoat with an apple in its mouth stood on one stand, and a quarter of beef on another, smoking and cooling a bit before the carving.

Father Peter was a slightly plump young man with a friendly-looking face; he stood and said a long grace, ending with a blessing on the Lord Protector, the Defender of the Faith, and Pope Leo. When he sat again the new overlord of Ath stood in her turn. Silence fell amid the crowded tables, and an instant later from those outside the tower gate as well, broken only by the crackle and pop of burning resinous wood. When she spoke, it was in a clear cold voice that carried without being particularly loud.

"The Portland Protective Association, through the Lord Protector and Lady Sandra, have granted seizin of this domain of Ath and its manors to me and my heirs, as tenants-in-chief, with the right of the high justice"—which meant she could hang—"the middle"—which meant she could imprison and flog—"and the low." That meant fines and extra service.

"To all the folk of the Domain of Ath I promise fair justice and good lordship, defense against attack to the limit of my strength, and punishment of wrongdoers. From them I expect due loyalty and service. I will take what the law of the Association allows, neither more nor less."

She gave a quick sidelong glance at the two knights who would hold part of it for her, and then down the table at the garrison and the officers who would carry out her will.

"And so will everyone else," she said, a slight note of warning in a tone gone flat. "I will not tolerate insolence from underlings; nor will I tolerate their mistreatment by any in my service, whether on the rolls of the Association or not."

After a moment's delay there was a cheer from the lower table, and from those seated outside. Tiphaine judged the tone and cocked an eye at the steward, who kept his face carefully blank; doubtless he was reassessing any scams he had running. She went on: "While I'm at it, we have the Princess Mathilda here as our guest, entrusted to the care of the Domain of Ath by the Lord Protector himself. This is an honor I'm sure we'll all strive to deserve."

You'd better, her tone added. *Every one of you.*

"And also with us is Rudi Mackenzie, son of the Chieftain of the Clan Mackenzie—"

She hesitated as Rudi came to his feet and bowed slightly to her. "Thank you, Lady d'Ath," he said, his treble loud and steady. "I also honor the Lady of Ath for her care of me in . . . ummm . . . difficult circumstances. I swear by . . ." He cocked an eye at the priest. ". . . by my holy things and by hers that I will not try to escape from her lands until the war ends, or my people come for me, so long as I stay here with the princess."

There was silence and a murmur after that; Tiphaine bowed, but the pale gray eyes narrowed slightly in the strong-boned impassive face; he knew she'd noticed the careful reservations in his oath.

"Thank you, young lord. As you mentioned, there is unfortunately war between the Association and the Clan and its allies at present. Therefore our other guest will be treated with all respect, but let no man allow Rudi Mackenzie beyond the gates of this castle, save with my immediate leave on each occasion, and with such escort as I order."

But I bet I wouldn't have been allowed out of the tower at all if I hadn't promised, Rudi thought, keeping any satisfaction off his face.

Tiphaine inclined her head again, beckoning to a guard and murmuring in his ear before she raised her glass and went on: "To the Portland Protective Association, to the Lord Protector, to my liege the Lady Sandra. May God and the Saints have them in their keeping. And to our spiritual father, Pope Leo, and to Holy Mother Church, our guides on the path of salvation."

Everyone rose and lifted their glasses; except Rudi, of course, who politely stood but left the small glass by his plate. Tiphaine raised one pale brow and shrugged very slightly as she saw the untouched wine.

Ruffin's voice boomed out in the pause that followed the toast: "And to our noble liege and good leader, Tiphaine d'Ath, God bless her!"

"And on that note, let's eat," Tiphaine said, and sat down to cheers.

A hum of conversation followed, and the steward's voice: "My lady, here we have a soup of pickled clams, black cod, and smoked dried shrimp with scallions, mushrooms and ginger," he announced. "With it, we have a chilled pinot gris from your manor of Montinore, and beaten biscuits with new butter."

"Mmm, thanks!" Rudi said to the servant who put the bowl before him. He blew on a spoonful and swallowed; Dun Juniper wasn't well placed for fish, except mountain trout. "That's *good.*"

The server was a friendly-looking girl in her late teens, slender, with long black hair and clear blue eyes and freckles across high cheekbones above a tip-tilted nose; she seemed a little surprised that he'd talk to her, and gave him a broad white smile before she moved on. She wore a double t-tunic, the longer green one to her ankles and the shorter russet-colored over-tunic to her thighs, both of good wool woven in a herringbone pattern, and over both a black linen tabard embroidered with the new arms of the Lady d'Ath. The belt under it was embroidered cloth as well, and skillfully done.

Tiphaine noticed the clothing as the servant ladled soup into her bowl, glancing aside and then up at her face, and then at the tabard again.

"That's fine needlework, girl," she said. "Your own hand?"

Rudi listened without seeming to. That was a trick his mother had taught him; you just let the information flow in, without straining or trying to stop it in your head. And he was in a place where he had to know everything he could, for his life's sake.

"Yes, my lady, thank you," she said, casting her eyes down after meeting the landholder's for a moment.

"And done quickly, to get my arms on the tabard with only a few days' notice."

The girl looked up again and smiled shyly. "People are always telling me I should slow down, so they'll be something weft when old age looms. But I just needle them more, so they lose the thread."

Tiphaine d'Ath gave a snort of startled laughter, then looked at the tunics. "The pun's bad but the weaving's good. Is that yours as well?"

"My own and my sisters', my lady. My mother wove before the Change, and she taught us."

"What's your name? Are you with the castle staff?"

"I'm Delia Mercer, my lady; my father keeps your mill in Montinore village as free tenant, and I serve three days a week for half the year as part of my family's boon-work. Usually in the manor house there."

Tiphaine made a noncommittal sound and nodded, and the girl moved on. When she had, the Association noble turned to the cleric on her left.

"Having that girl serving at table is a waste, Father Peter," she said. "I noticed that some of the bond-tenants and a lot of the peons here don't have enough to wear, if they're in rags when the new lord shows up. We grow enough flax and shear enough wool, from the books; I want every family to have enough to wash and dry a set while they're wearing one. Two

sets of working clothes and a best outfit for Church or weddings or funerals; nothing fancy, but not rags either. And un-
derdrawers. Filth breeds disease and I won't tolerate it on my
land. Men without warm clothing can't work as well in bad
weather, either."

"Very true, my lady. The free-tenants and many of the bond-
tenants already do well enough, but the rest, and the peons . . .
The, ah, policy of the steward was to sell most of the demesne
yield of wool and flax to realize the profit to the domain in
cash."

That meant it had been the Lord Protector's policy, probably,
unless the steward wanted the sales to produce a cash flow so
he could subtract a share. Tiphaine ate a biscuit and then crumbled another in her fingers as she thought.

"False economy, and against the Association's local self-
sufficiency policy. Plus, typhus is no respecter of persons, and
besides, it's a waste not to have the peon girls working at
something in the slack seasons. I'll buy the extra spinning
wheels and looms in Forest Grove or Portland if we don't
have a carpenter who can make them, and we can run classes
when the harvest's in; we'll use one of the tithe barns. From
the look of it, Delia's mother would be a good teacher."

"I'm afraid she's dead, poor soul. Late last year. I think it
was cancer, but I'm not sure. It was a hard passing. Her father
borrowed more than they could afford for drugs—for the
pain, you see." The priest crossed himself. Tiphaine repeated
the gesture; there wasn't much anyone could do about cancer
these days, except pray.

The priest went on: "And . . . the family is not the most pious
in the domain. Not that I have anything specific to say against
them, but I sense mental reservations."

"Is there much dissent here, then?"

"No, no, nothing too bad—I don't think there's a coven or
anything of that nature. A little grumbling now and then. I
think it's a wonderful idea, my lady, but perhaps some
other . . ."

Tiphaine shrugged. "Father, the cure of souls in my villages
is your business, and the parish priests' under your guidance.
But the worldly welfare of this land and its people is now *my*

concern. We could have her and her sisters give the lessons in weaving and spinning to the peon girls—it takes ten spinners to keep a weaver supplied, anyway. The cloth might even be good enough to sell, which would give the poorer families something profitable to do with their winters, and enrich the domain as well. You'd know who would be suitable . . . we'll discuss it on Monday. I'd like to have a regular conference with you, the steward and the Montinore bailiff anyway."

Rudi didn't follow all of that, but it was interesting. The soup plates were taken away. The steward's voice boomed out again, and they were replaced by plates of small skewers of chicken and duck, grilled with a spicy-sweet plum glaze and served over noodles in a spicy cream sauce, and on the side fresh bread spread with garlic-butter paste and lightly flame-grilled. The carvers' great knives flashed down in the center of the hall, almost long enough to be shortswords and sharper, since they didn't have to worry about turning an edge on bone. The plates came by with meat and steamed vegetables and potatoes, and the same girl served him.

"Gravy, young sir?" she asked.

"Yes, please," he said; that went well with potatoes roasted in the dripping. He especially liked the crunchy bit from the outside of the roast, and they'd used some sort of tingly hot sauce on the young pig.

Delia poured gravy from a ladle . . . and as she did, she drizzled it in a pattern he recognized, then poured more to hide it.

Rudi's eyes went wide with shock. "*Thank* you," he said, and cleared his throat, reaching for the salt shaker to cover his start.

The girl moved on. Matti looked around, still grinning from a joke Sir Ivo's leman Debbie had told her. Her cheeks were flushed. The children had only the one full glass of wine before it was replaced with apple juice and water, but hers had gone to her head a little.

"Oh, it's so *good* to be back with my own people, Rudi!" she said; then put a hand to her mouth. "Oh, I'm sorry!"

"Nah, don't worry, Matti. You could handle it, so I guess I can."

Dessert was ice cream, and little round pastries baked with sliced brandied pears in their centers, the glazed flaky crusts around that drizzled with chopped hazelnuts. Rudi ate two and was thinking wistfully about another one—there was something in it that was *really* good and brought out the taste of the fruit, probably some sort of spice that wasn't available outside the Protectorate any more.

The rest of the company hadn't switched to water, except for the priest, and things were getting a bit more uproarious than they would at most Mackenzie gatherings, except on special occasions. Which this was, of course, but . . .

Occasional snatches of song came from the lower tables, and roaring choruses from outside in the courtyard. Tiphaine was moving with her usual feline grace, but it looked as if she had to think about it a little, and occasionally a feral grin broke through her calm front as she looked around.

Yeah, she's realizing it's really real, Rudi thought judiciously.

The priest asked a question. Tiphaine shrugged. "God knows," she said. "We got a good swift punch in the nose from the kilties and they killed the Marchwarden, and the damned Corvallans showed up to help the Bearkillers, I'll tell you that much. Whether we'll come back for a second round and try—"

Then she frowned and stopped and went on more carefully. "—is of course up to the Lord Protector, however his servants may have failed him."

To cover the remark she signed for more wine. Delia bent over her shoulder with the decanter, and whispered something in her ear as she did; the seigneur of Ath gave another startled snort of laughter and then smiled down into her glass before she replied, equally quiet-voiced, nodding as she did so.

Just then Mathilda's nurse waddled forward and bent to touch Tiphaine's shoulder. The blond woman with the pale eyes started, then stopped her hand moving towards her dagger.

"Oh, yes, you're right. Time for the children to get to bed. Party's getting a bit rough for the kiddies."

She stood, leaning one hand on the table. It took a minute

and then a shout to produce a drop in the roar of noise, a valkyr call that might have cut through the noise on a battle-field; Ruffin's girlfriend was sitting on his lap now, feeding him bits of pastry between her lips, and things were less deco-rous elsewhere.

"To the Princess Mathilda, our Protector's heir!" she called, and a blast of cheers answered until the great concrete room rang with the echoes.

Mathilda rose and everyone bowed. That was the signal for all the youngsters to withdraw, some carried asleep by their mothers, and the priest left as well. Rudi rose and brushed himself with his napkin; the tunic he was wearing was some sort of silk stuff, and it caught crumbs something fierce. Bend-ing that way let him catch what Tiphaine muttered to herself after the toast; he had very good ears.

"And I hope when it's her turn the snippy little bitch does a better job than her Daddy's doing right now."

Ooooh, he thought, as they turned past the guards and up the darkness of the spiral staircase. *I bet she'll wish she hadn't said that, if she remembers it.*

The two floors above the hall were the lord's private quar-ters; Mathilda was yawning and her nurse puffing and wheez-ing by the time they reached the fourth level just below the tower top, which held the guest suites. She waved good-bye to him as they went into their rooms; he heard a muffled squeal from hers that sounded like . . . *a kitten!*

His own chambers had tile over the concrete floor, wallpa-per with a floral pattern, a nice-looking rug and a small fire-place currently banked but sending out comfortable warmth. There was also a little bathroom with a toilet and sink and a shower that had hot water if you asked an hour ahead of time; it struck him as a bit superfluous. The castle had a perfectly good bathhouse of the type Dun Juniper used, with shower and hot and cold plunges—two, in fact, one with fancy fixtures for the lord and his family and another in plain concrete for the commons.

The bedchamber also had a table of some shiny, carved wood with writing gear and a good lamp—lit right now—and cupboards and bookshelves, with stuff he and Matti had picked out before leaving Castle Todenangst. That included a lot of his favorites and a couple by Donan Coyle he'd never read himself—*Sir Guilliame,* and *The West-Country Rising,* which Sir Nigel had told him about. Someone had put a glass of milk and a plate of raisin-oatmeal cookies beside the big four-poster bed; he stretched and yawned and reminded himself to thank whoever did it.

People around here don't say thanks enough when someone does something nice for them, he thought. *The Threefold Law is going to smack some of them good and hard, if they don't watch out.*

And over by the window . . .

His breath caught, and he walked over, stepping up on the footstool beneath it. The opening was narrow, too narrow for a grown man to get through even if the wall hadn't been four feet thick, and shaped like a V with its broad side in the room and the narrow part looking out—there was a hinged glass window, but it was an arrow-slit and nothing else. *He* could have gotten through it, with a little squeeze, but there was no point—it was nearly forty feet down onto sharpened steel, where the inner moat separated the keep from the courtyard. He'd checked that first thing this afternoon.

But in the brackets beside the window was a bow; *his* bow, neatly strapped in its leather carrying case, with his quiver and dirk, just the way they'd been when he was taken prisoner, when Aoife died.

He put his face against it, drawing in the familiar scent. Tears rolled down his face and onto the soft breyed leather. After a while they stopped, and he went into the bathroom to splash water on his face, and then to brush his teeth and undress. Then he took the candle and holder from beside the bed, lit the wick at the lamp, turned that out and carried the candlestick over to a bookshelf on the north face of the room.

He made a space for it after sketching the sign of Invocation, then knelt and watched the candle, making himself breathe until he really felt things—how tired and full he was, how the carpet was prickly under his feet, how people outside were singing as they danced around the bonfires; something like "Life is a lemon/And I want my money back," whatever that meant. His mind went quiet as he imagined ripples spreading in a pond, smoothing themselves out until there was only the glassy water, still and silent but with shapes moving in the depths.

After a while he began to chant himself, softly:

"Your Sun is gone and Your Moon will follow;
Mother-of-All, my thanks for the day given me to weave;
Father and Lord, for the strength to follow Your path—"

When he blew out the candle and got into the bed, he was asleep before he'd finished arranging the pillow.

Tiphaine Rutherton woke and winced, throwing her left forearm over her face; then she smiled, letting it grow into a grin as she remembered that she was now Lady Tiphaine *d'Ath*, baronet. Things got hazy after she arrived yesterday afternoon, but she remembered *that* quite well.

The title had a very nice ring to it, even when her head felt like an Inquisitor had a steel band around the temples and was turning the tightening screw, and the dim light of the narrow window stabbed through closed eyelids. Not to mention the vague nausea . . . Then she winced again, when the effort of smiling made her temples pound even worse. She didn't do this often, but the sensation wasn't exactly unfamiliar either. Her bladder suggested that getting up was fairly urgent, however much she hated the thought.

Oh, God, a band of Eaters crapped in the fur that's growing on my tongue. I didn't drink that *much, did I?*

She cautiously removed her arm, blinked gummy eyes open and saw an empty wine bottle on the bedside table. That led her gaze down to the floor; another bottle lay on its side on the rug peeping out from under a tunic.

That's cherry brandy, *half full. God, I was mixing my drinks! I shouldn't drink that much, even at a celebration. I do impulsive things when I drink too much and I can't afford to be reckless.*

She rolled over, coming up to one elbow; the mattress was too soft and she'd have to do something about . . .

A fan of tousled black hair rested on the next pillow, with bright blue eyes peering out through it. Delia the seamstress brushed back her locks, smiled up at Tiphaine and wiggled her fingers.

"Hi!" she said. "You snore, my lady."

That wasn't my tunic I saw, either.

Tiphaine closed her eyes again, then flopped back and stared at the bed canopy above her. *Oh, God.* The room smelled of lavender sachet inside the stuffing of the pillows, fresh sheets, snuffed lamp wicks, perfume, stale wine and, slightly but definitely, of sex.

Then her eyes opened wide, despite the too-bright dimness; the memory of leading a conga-chain came back to her in flashes of exhilaration and whirling torchlight, dancing around the castle courtyard, then up a stair and around the curtain-wall fighting platform.

"Look, I did *ask* you to go to bed with me, didn't I?" she said.

Because my self-esteem might not survive the shock if I just threw you over my shoulder and went reeling up the stairs like Sappho the Cimmerian. And it would sort of deconstruct my don't-abuse-the-peasants speech, although that looks like a happy smile you've got on. Plus it wouldn't do my reputation any good to get into a fight with the Church right after getting the estate. Oh, please, God, tell me I wasn't that stupid with the senior priest of the Domain watching!

Delia laughed, a sort of gurgling chuckle, and came up on one elbow in her turn. "Actually, my lady—"

"Oh, hell, we're in the same *bed.*"

"—my lady . . . Tiphaine, I asked *you* if you wanted to see the designs I put on my underwear, since you liked my needlework so much," she said. "You let me in by the postern wall-gate."

"Ah."

"You even said, *That's really lovely embroidery on the hem, I like the flowers,* before you pulled my drawers off, too. Then you said, *Pretty as an orchid* and—"

"Ah."

"I won't tell Father Peter if you don't." Then she put a hand over her mouth to stifle a laugh. "I'm *sorry,* but you were so cool and elegant at first and now you look so . . . so *rumpled.*"

Tiphaine smiled again despite herself, made another non-committal *ah* sound, swung her legs down and stood. She steadied herself against one of the bedposts and squinted at the sun glinting through glass into the big bare room through the narrow window-slit. If she remembered correctly, that one faced east—and if she remembered correctly, the sun rose in the east, too. In which case it was still fairly early; there was barely a gleam there, and it still looked rosy.

As if to confirm it, a rooster decided to tell the world he owned it. That set off a chorus of them, mostly sounding a bit farther away, doubtless from coops in the hamlet outside the castle gates. She repressed an impulse to put her thumbs over her ears and walked in a straight line to the arched doors of the bathroom; blinked around at the unfamiliar facility for a moment, turned up the lamp, used the toilet, ran a big sink full of cold water and immersed her head, then drank several large glasses despite a minor rebellion from her stomach—hangovers were mostly dehydration. Of course, the rest of it was toxins. A groping hand found a bottle of aspirin, and she followed a few of those with still more water and dunked her head again.

I look like a debauched dandelion, she thought, regarding the dripping image in the mirror.

Her face was surrounded by tangled wet tufts of blond hair pale enough that even water couldn't darken it much. She raked at it with her fingers to get some of the sleep-snarls out, and wished she could cut it shorter than the pageboy bob. Then she kneaded her neck muscles with her thumbs to get the blood flowing again, working hard. She also smiled at herself as memory of the recent past returned; it didn't make her body feel any better right now, but it put the sensations in perspective.

That was really nice, mutually so. There were certain aspects of enthusiasm impossible to counterfeit. *You are not only the most deadly warrior in the Association, you are not only the newly ennobled holder of this castle and fief, you are one hot babe, Tiphaine d'Ath!*

She felt a degree of smug self-satisfaction, and a little relief. The last couple of times she'd been to bed with anyone, it had been sort of sad; the absolutely last time a month ago she'd been so miserably blitzed beforehand that she woke up next to a *guy,* which had meant not only serious yuk-*euuww! euuww!* cootie-shudders whenever she thought about it but mad panic while she waited to see if the bunny died. This had been just . . . very nice.

I guess I've got rock-star charisma and my own groupies now. In the last months before the Change she'd had a desperate crush on Melissa Etheridge, and long involved fantasies about saving her from a stalker or a speeding truck. *Is that a hickey on my neck? Yup. At least it's the only one that'll show when I'm dressed. I think I like this girl. Shy, she ain't.*

She took another drink of water, and then after considering the taste of the stuff in the glass she reached for her toothbrush. She needed it badly and with mouthwash to follow; either that or a corpse-eating plague rat had died in the pipes some time ago. Most of the furnishings in the lord's quarters of Castle Ath were very sketchy, because the Protector had used Montinore manor house when he visited the area, but the bathrooms had been installed during the original construction as the labor-gangs went from site to site, with fittings salvaged from luxury homes in the Portland area. This was all marble tile and creamy whiteness and faucets of polished bronze, big fluffy towels on racks of rare hardwood and etched glass panels around the shower stall. Someone had put scented soap out, as well as a wide range of toiletries; there was even pre-Change toilet paper, or a good imitation. And there was *hot water* on tap, as much as she wanted all to herself, something only a fief-holder could have these days.

Should I invite Delia in for a shower? Regretfully—and cautiously—she shook her head. *Not enough time. I need to sweat the poisons out soonest, anyway.*

She still felt a little more human as she returned to the bedroom drying her hair on a towel. Delia was up, pulling on her second tunic and belting it, which looked interesting as she stretched and bent.

I must be recovering. Youth, health, lots of exercise and no vices, that's the ticket. Well, no vices except pouring cherry brandy on top of pinot noir sometimes.

Tiphaine's smile had less of a wince in it this time. "Sorry we don't have time for a snuggle, Delia, but you'd better run before people see too much. You're a sweet girl, and I don't want you getting in trouble."

The young woman came over and embraced her; the kiss was even more interesting than the view and went on for a while.

"Father Peter's not a sheet-sniffer like some. He doesn't notice stuff unless you make him. Besides, I know you'll protect me, my lady Tiphaine."

Nobles, even the few gay ones, didn't end up before an ecclesiastical morals court very often; the military caste wasn't going to let the Church get *that* much power. Still, *not very often* wasn't the same thing as *not ever. . . .*

"Sweetie, my power here is vast and my liege-lady's power in the realm is vaster still, but the Hounds of God are no joke, and they and Father Peter work for the same boss, and the Hounds *are* sheet-sniffers. Keep that lovely mouth shut about this and everything will be fine, OK?"

"Until next time?"

"Right. Now scoot!"

Tiphaine opened the door and checked the corridor both ways before the girl slipped out; it was windowless and very dark. There were a couple of empty rooms on this floor and no resident servants or established routine as yet, and it wouldn't be much trouble for Delia to slip out looking as if she was dusting or fetching or something. Then she dressed herself, rummaging in the unfamiliar closets and their mostly new contents for a familiar drill outfit of quilted tunic in coarse gray patched linen, and scuffed black buckskin pants stained with white patches of sweat-salt. After that she stamped her feet into her boots, and buckled padded leather support straps on her wrists.

The temptation to tidy up before she left was strong—she was compulsively neat, and hated leaving Delia personal things to the care of others. That was an eccentricity she could get away with, when those quarters were one small chamber or less wherever the Lady Sandra was in residence, which was all even a fairly prominent member of the Household could expect. But picking up after herself would be perilously close to *dérogeance,* here at home in her own fief. The temptation to shower first was even stronger, but she pushed it down.

Got to punish myself for carelessness, she thought, buckling on her sword belt and walking down the stairs, left hand automatically on the hilt to keep the chape on the end of the scabbard from bumping on the stone. *Besides, I'd just be getting all sweaty again right away.*

She'd been right about it being early; things had been put to right a bit the night before, but the morning cleanup in the hall was just getting started. She walked out, blinking at the increasing brightness and returning her own nod and salute to the clank and crash as the gate guards slapped spears against shields.

Note to self: get all the shields repainted, soon. My arms, quartered with Lady Sandra's.

The day outside was just on the brisk side of cool, with the smell of dew on dusty concrete and dustier gravel still strong, but there were no clouds in the sky and it felt like it would be a perfect spring day when the sun was a little higher and dispelled the shadows within the courtyard. A scent of old smoke from the bonfires lingered, but the scorched circles had been swept up, and the firepits outside the kitchens were being shoveled clear as she watched, the ashes carted away in big plastic trash barrels for leaching into lye and making soap. A train of two-wheeled oxcarts dumped loads of split firewood there—boon-work dues, by the way the drivers turned around at once and got going towards their own affairs—and scullions began to stack the billets against the kitchen walls. Birds pecked at the ground, and flew up in swirls when someone came too close, particularly when it was one of the patrolling cats. She'd given orders that none of those were allowed over the inner drawbridge into the tower, and her sinuses already felt better than they ever had in the Household.

Wielman the steward was bustling towards the Keep gate with a crew, looking nervous as a man herding cats, probably because it was a scratch gang and he was doing two men's jobs; or possibly nervous because he now had a superior resident full-time, and one with enough time to keep a close eye on him. He stopped when she turned towards him, obviously anxious to get to work but unable to dodge a conversation, and his laborers halted behind him in a wave of curtseys and bows.

Delia needed time and distraction to get clear . . . which was a pain in the ass; nobody except a *very* strict priest would so much as blink at a tenant-girl slipping out of a *male* nobleman's room in the morning, except for an admiring chuckle.

"Splendid welcoming feast last night," she said. Then she smiled slightly. "Haven't enjoyed myself so much in months."

"Thank you, my lady. We're all at sixes and sevens, of course, with so little notice of your arrival—you should have a *domestic* steward or a butler here at the castle, if you're going to take up residence, so I can concentrate on my own work where my offices and the records are. I can move some people up from Montinore and my wife has a young cousin who'd suit."

"Do that," Tiphaine said. "I leave it in your capable hands, Goodman."

Meaning, don't bother me with details, and yes, getting jobs for your relations is a legitimate perk, as long as they don't screw up too badly.

Aloud she went on, lest he get too enthusiastic: "Just enough staff that I can offer suitable hospitality: the cook we had last night will do fine, some assistants, and as many cleaners and maids and such as are needed to keep things tidy. Some of them can commute up from the manor until winter at least, it's only two miles by bicycle. Or you could hire some of the soldiers' wives."

"Very well, my lady, but the Protector and his guests always brought their own body servants on visits," he went on. "Do you have an, ah, valet, or lady's maid who'll be arriving? Or should I find someone suitable from the domain?"

Tiphaine shook her head. "I don't need someone to hand me a towel or comb my hair."

Some people thought that was a status symbol; she considered it a waste of scarce labor. A tenant-in-chief who was a

mere baronet could get away with that much informality,
though a baron couldn't. She'd need a squire or two eventually, of course, but that was something entirely different.
Squires were apprentice knights, and supposed to be of good
family. Which so far meant related to someone lucky enough
to get into the Association early on. She had Katrina's elder
brother's kids in mind for that, particularly since he'd been
killed out east last year fighting the cowboys and they didn't
have a landed inheritance.

"Ummm—" The steward cleared his throat and seemed,
without actually doing it, to glance discreetly aside as he lowered his voice. "But surely you'll at least need someone to
look after your wardrobe full-time, my lady? The more since
you'll have, ah, two sets. Repairs, replacements, cleaning . . . I
was thinking of the miller's daughter from Montinore village;
her name is Delia. She's an excellent needlewoman by hand
or sewing machine, she can weave figured work on the loom,
and she's used to household ways and manners. She could use
the valet's room that gives off the lord's chamber."

Tiphaine gave him a cool, considering glance, tapping her
fingers on her sword hilt, head tilted to one side.

Clever. Dangerously so, she decided, her eyes narrowing
and lips thinning into an expression that had been the very
last thing a number of men ever saw, starting in her fourteenth
year. This time it said: *I'll know exactly who's responsible for
any rumors.*

She'd get in trouble if she just had the men-at-arms hang
him for no particular reason; fines from the Court of Petition
and Redress, penances from the Church. . . . Casual killing had
gone out of style since the wild early years, at least where
middle-class types like Wielman were concerned. But when
you added all that together she wouldn't have nearly as much
trouble as *he* would, dangling from a noose on the gallows
down the road and putting on a dinner party for the crows
and ravens until his bones dropped off one by one.

One part of taking reasonable precautions was thoroughly
intimidating any subordinate who even *dreamed* of knuckling
his way up the greasy pole by a threat of outing her.

So much went by in a flicker as she kept up the stare. A few seconds later a little sweat showed on Wielman's forehead, and he dropped his eyes.

Good, now you know better than to try and blackmail me.

"You're right," she said. "She'd be very suitable. See to it. Deduct an adult's boon-work from her family's dues and put her on the rolls as a free retainer. I'm going to start spinning and weaving classes for the peon women later this year; she could handle that, and possibly her sisters as well. Set up a loom-room here in the castle or down in Montinore when you get the time, and see about ordering more spinning wheels and equipment—locally if you can, in Forest Grove if you can't, in Portland as a last resort. And in the meantime, send to market for some cloth, and we'll make a start—enough to keep us going until we get production ramped up. I'm not going to have my workers looking like scarecrows. Delia can oversee the sewing, too."

Putting Delia in charge of those projects would be a sensible thing to do even if they didn't get along otherwise.

But I think I'm going to really like that girl, and not just when I'm in a state of lustful, drunken horniness; she's cheeky as a sparrow, she's not afraid of the priests, and she made me want to laugh even when I had a hangover. Plus she's awesome cute, and I think she likes me, not just the career prospects.

As he bowed his head and turned to go with a murmured *of course, my lady,* Tiphaine contemplated the square of raked, rolled gravel in front of the barracks with less than enthusiasm; it held a dozen upright oak posts six feet tall, resting in metal sleeves set into the ground, and climbing frames, some of them dangling knotted ropes. Then she went into the salle d'armes; Ath wasn't big enough to have separate ones for different ranks. The one it did have occupied the ground floor of part of the barracks block built against the west side of the court, opposite the tower-keep and the gate. Inside was a big, bare room with a wooden floor, rolled mats against the walls, some gymnastic equipment, weights, a few Nautilus machines and mirrors on one wall, with a corkboard on another carrying a map of the castle and the patrol paths around it, and a duty roster.

People slightly older than herself told her that dojos had been like this before the Change. She didn't remember, since she hadn't studied the martial arts then, though she'd been a state-level gymnast and track-and-fielder in middle school. Today she began with a series of stretching exercises and *kata*.

Now I know what it's going to be like to be seventy, and arthritic, she thought after a moment. But she gritted her teeth and persisted, then did a routine on the parallel bars and vaulting horse, and some tumbling on the mats, stopping now and then to drink from the water fountain.

After the sweat started and joints and tendons loosened a bit she ducked into the ready room and picked up a blunt practice sword and heavy wicker training shield—a middling-sized four-foot shield, since she was tall for a woman and about average for a man. Then she went back outside, setting the shield's bandolier-like *guige* strap around her neck. That took part of the weight, and she could use it to sling the kite-shaped defense over her back with a quick readjustment.

Tiphaine took stance in front of one of the six-foot posts, left foot advanced, left fist up under her chin, which put the upper arc of the shield just under her eyes and the point at about knee level; the convex triangle almost completely covered her body. The sword went up overhead, hilt forward.

"Ya-*hi!*" she shouted from the bottom of her lungs, and attacked. *"Haro!"*

A chip of tough oak flicked out, even though the practice sword had neither point nor edge. It was also a lot heavier than her real blade, but that was all to the good—a woman had to work harder to build upper-body strength, and train harder to maintain it, one of life's manifold injustices. Eighty minutes later she stepped back and let the rounded tip of the sword fall to the ground, propping the hilt against her body and working her hand and shaking it. Every impact on the unyielding hardwood jarred back into her wrist and arm, and the hand felt as if someone had driven a wagon loaded with bricks over it; she was breathing deeply but not panting, and her sodden clothes clung as if she'd waded through a river.

The experience was familiar, and pleasant enough normally; she'd done at least as much and usually much more six days in seven since her fourteenth year. In Lady Sandra's Household, she'd usually done hours of classwork afterwards, too; the consort insisted on her personal retainers getting book-learning as well.

While she caught her breath she looked around, and found the castle had thoroughly come to life. Two men-at-arms and a double pair of crossbowmen trotted out through the main gate on routine patrol against bandits, lances in rest and crossbows across backs; spearmen and more crossbowmen paced their rounds on the fighting platform, or watched from the towers. Bread was baking in the kitchens, and the rich, earthy smell made her acutely aware of being famished. Iron rang on iron in the smithy, and a grinding wheel made a tooth-gritting sound as it bit into metal. Carpenters' hammers knocked; children and dogs ran about, and mothers called to them from the windows of their apartments. Two girls with broad straw hats and skirts kirted up carried a load of laundry in through the gates between them in a big wicker basket with handles on either side, and a wagon full of cut fodder followed. The doors of the chapel were open, and Father Peter's housekeeper swept it out, giving Tiphaine a curtsey as she noticed her gaze. She was a buxom young woman with café-au-lait skin set off by the—expensive—saffron of her tunics and headdress, which made the new overlord of Ath wonder slightly about the priest's lack of interest in sheets . . .

And a number of the garrison were working out; many of them looked more the worse for wear than she'd felt when she woke. Tiphaine had only a vague throb of headache now, and a hot shower and breakfast would cure that. One of the diligent ones was Sir Ivo.

"Hi," she said as he stepped back and rested his blade over one shoulder; he'd put his hauberk on for the drill, which was conscientious of him. "Where's Ruffin?"

The young knight grinned at her and pointed the sword towards the second story of the barracks. The two and their lemans had slept there in cubicles usually occupied by the senior married men-at-arms, since Mathilda and Rudi were in the keep's guest suite; everyone had bumped the one below him out of their quarters, until a couple of rankers ended up on hay in the stables.

"Maybe the arm's still bothering him. But I doubt it. They

got thin partitions up there, my lady," he said. "It sounded like he and Joyce were celebrating *again*."

"Christ Jesus, I hope for her sake he brushed his teeth first," Tiphaine said, and they both laughed; you didn't get dainty in the field.

Then she looked critically at the garrison troops at practice. "You know, Ivo, the men-at-arms weren't half bad hand-to-hand, and the infantry's drill is OK and none of them are really fat, but some sure got tired 'way too fast. That'll get you killed as easily as not knowing the counters when it's for real—no rest breaks. We need to schedule more aerobic conditioning and sweat them hard."

"Yeah, no dispute, my lady. But remember a lot of them have been out here in the ass-end of nowhere since the castle was built."

"This isn't the ass-end of nowhere. Barony Chehalis is."

Ruffin chuckled; neither of them liked the Stavarovs. "OK, this is within wiping distance of the ass-end of nowhere. It's too far north to skirmish with Bearkillers most times, and too far west for Mount Angel or the Mackenzies, and too far south for a levy against the Yakima towns. And these guys, they're old men. Some of them are thirty, or even more."

The remark made perfect sense in their trade. Endurance got harder to keep up after your twenties, but there was more to it than that. Men who'd come to the warrior's life as adults after the Change were rarely really first-rate by the standards of the generation who'd trained since puberty.

"They're what we've got and I want their stamina built up," she said. "I'll run 'em up and down the stairs to the walls in armor for a couple of hours every second day. Any of the footmen who can't take it, we'll give early retirement. And find some tenant's kid to train as a replacement. There's always some who don't want to spend the rest of their life staring up the ass of a plow-ox. Also, I want to get them working on unconventional stuff, not just fighting in ranks. Mackenzies are too damned good at sneaking around."

"*Tell* me," he said fervently. "We'll have to check on the ones settled on the manors with me and Ruffin, too. Likely they're worse than this bunch and spend most of their time farming their fiefs-in-sergeantry."

He paused, and almost shuffled his feet. "Ah, my lady, I want to say thanks again, for giving Debbie and me our chance. I'd have been glad to get something east of the mountains, even, much less prime land like this. Sorry if I was, you know, a bit of an asshole to start with."

"You got over resenting the position I pee in, Sir Ivo," she said, slapping him on the arm with the flat of the practice blade. "Joris didn't get over it and you may notice *he's* not here."

Despite the fact that he could take you or *Ruffin, easy,* she did not add. *You two I can trust. Joris . . . I'd trust* him *to win in a fang-in-ass competition with a rattler.*

Aloud she went on: "And hell, I've been known to do a convincing imitation of the aforesaid orifice myself, from time to time. *Hel*lo!"

That was prompted by the appearance of Rudi Mackenzie and Princess Mathilda. They were in children's versions of practice gear, padded gambesons of thick, quilted linen and small helmets with barred face-shields and boiled-leather protectors on elbows and knees. A ripple of silence followed in their wake as they walked through the gates and over to the practice ground, and a ripple of curtsies and bows for Mathilda's rank. In a way it was a damned nuisance to have them here while she was trying to settle in and get a feel for the place; in another it was a tremendous honor and responsibility, of course.

That's Lady Sandra for you. Do well, and you get rewards— and more work. I've learned a lot from her, not least how to handle people. And of course, it's not only more work, but a chance to get in good with the heir, and it must be part of her plans for Mathilda, too. Wheels within wheels within wheels.

The two had shields and swords suited for their size as well, from the armorers at Castle Todenangst; except for the size and the lack of point or edge on the blades, they were better gear than many knights could command. Tiphaine and her vassal leaned on the hilts of their weapons and watched. Boy and girl did their stretches, then began practicing strikes and counters on the air.

"Hey, not bad," Ivo said quietly to her. "The Protector's kid is good, but the kiltie brat is better. He's got the right instincts, too—just throws the switch and goes for it. I mean, he'd have killed me dead with that dirk if the jacket hadn't been lined with mail on the torso. And Ruffin's shield-arm still isn't quite right."

Tiphaine grinned, and spoke in the same undertone as she watched: "The princess is pretty good, though. A good friend of mine"—the grief echoed, but a little less strongly each time—"was tutoring her before she was kidnapped last year, and I dropped in on it now and then. She was promising then and it looks like she kept it up."

"Yeah," Ivo said critically as they switched to sparring.

Both the adults leaned a little closer; that was both more interesting and more dangerous, hence requiring more supervision. Tiphaine pursed her lips. Neither showed much of the usual childish awkwardness or beginner flailing—most kids couldn't free-spar with any profit until they were a year or two older than these, not having enough hand-eye coordination. What they were doing was very basic, of course, but the blows were still light, but they were moving beautifully; she'd seen plenty of trainees of twelve or thirteen who did no better. Mathilda had made serious progress since the raid that kidnapped her, rather than going back, and she suspected trying to keep up with Rudi was part of that.

The male knight nodded and confirmed her unspoken judgment: "It's not that Mackenzie sword-and-buckler stuff, or Bearkiller targe-and-backsword. Someone's been teaching them both our style, or something close to it."

"That'd be the Englishmen," Tiphaine said. "The Lorings. I saw them work out last year when they were staying with the Household. They're good, both of them; the young one was *really* good."

"Yeah—watch it, kid! Careful with the princess!"

Mathilda staggered, wobbling loose-jointed after a strong backhand cut went *boonnggk* across the side of her practice helmet.

Rudi Mackenzie waved acknowledgment, then went over to his partner and steadied her, his own blade under his left arm.

"You OK, Matti?"

"Sure. Wow! I didn't see *that* coming!"

"You gotta remember how the helmet blocks things in the corner of your eye," Rudi said. "Sir Nigel taught me this trick on how to keep moving your head—want to see it?"

"That's enough for the morning," Tiphaine broke in firmly. "Time for a shower and breakfast. At your ages too much is as bad as not enough. You can overstrain your bones and tendons."

The children nodded obediently, and helped each other out of the gear and bundled it up neatly. Mathilda looked at her guilelessly. "Could you give us some lessons, Lady d'Ath?"

Tiphaine grinned back, more genial than most who knew her a little would have thought likely. "I think I could squeeze that in, Princess, for you and your friend there. Now let's go get cleaned up."

It certainly beats washing with river water scooped up in a helmet, and half the army copping a look, she thought a few minutes later, looking around at the bathroom of her suite with unbleared eyes as she stripped off the sodden practice outfit and turned up the wall-lamp. *What's this?*

This turned out to be liquid soap scented with lavender and rosemary. Unlimited hot water of their very own was a luxury that few enjoyed these days, which was why most places had some sort of communal bathhouse; Tiphaine soaked until the last tension left her neck muscles and then walked back out into her bedchamber wrapped in a big fluffy towel.

It had been thoroughly cleaned up while she was under the spray, and the rest of her baggage unpacked. Her field armor stood on a stand in one corner, and her parade set beside it, very similar except that the hauberk and coif were made from burnished stainless-steel wire, and the helm and vambraces and greaves from chrome-plated metal—harder to work, and thus fiendishly expensive. There were fresh sheets and a new coverlet on the big four-poster bed, a set of riding clothes laid out, and fresh sachets of dried flowers scented the air. A fire was laid ready to light in the swept and scrubbed hearth of the fireplace, and the glass wall-lamps had full reservoirs; right now the tall, narrow window/arrow-slits provided enough light, unless you wanted to read.

Her pictures had also been set out by the bedside. There was a small silver-framed one of her parents and brother, whose whole neighborhood had vanished in one of the first great fires before she got back to Portland. And a fold-out set of three of her and Katrina; one in their Girl Scout uniforms, another taken not long after they entered Lady Sandra's Household, still looking like they had ten pounds between them and starving to death, and a last one six years old, of them both in hauberk and helm, when they'd turned eighteen and been sworn onto the Household rolls as full members and Associates of the PPA. They looked very solemn in that, with their arms around each other's shoulders.

Or so she'd thought, when an expressionless Lady Sandra took the picture, with the very last priceless frame of Zeiss film for the camera. In fact Katrina was holding two fingers up in rabbit-ears behind Tiphaine's helmeted head.

And nobody told me until it was developed!

Someone had also left a golden daffodil on the pillow, with a red ribbon around it tied in the shape of a heart, and another in front of the pictures. Tiphaine picked up the one on the pillow, clipped the stem with her dagger, tucked it behind one ear, and went down into the Hall, smiling quietly to herself and tucking the knot into a pouch at her waist.

I really think I am going to like that girl.

Ruffin and his Joyce had joined the party there, and Ivo and Debbie; they were deep in wedding plans, and Mathilda was listening raptly; the two women rose to give Tiphaine a curtsey before diving in again. Rudi looked frankly bored, and was focusing on his food. She didn't blame him. Debbie was an amiable ditz, in her opinion, but at least smart enough that you didn't *always* want to gag her with her wimple after five minutes of conversation. Joyce was good-natured and loyal and had cheerfully put up with the hardships court and camp held for the leman of a man-at-arms, and was admittedly eye-

stopping, sexpot gorgeous in a big-eyed, big-hair, buxom way
that had never appealed to Tiphaine. She supposed the
woman was very attractive overall, *if* you weren't put off your
feed by the very thought of having sex with someone whose
IQ was about the same as a large dog's.

*Say a golden retriever, but with the added disadvantage of
being able to talk and doing it nonstop, mostly about the
puppies—pardon me, children—she wants. How on earth
does Ruffin stand it? Ah, well, breeders . . . somebody has to
do it,* she thought indulgently, and returned their greeting
with a nod.

Everyone gave an odd glance at the flower behind her ear,
which was not the sort of gesture she usually went in for, but
nobody commented as she took the high central seat and a
servant brought her breakfast from the dishes kept warm over
spirit-lamps on a sideboard; four eggs, a dozen rashers of
bacon, fried green pickled tomatoes, hash browns and toast.

They're good sorts, Ivo and Ruffin, she thought. *It didn't
even occur to them they could dump their girls and find better
matches, now that they've got manors in fief. And I can trust
them to back me come what may. Lady Sandra knows how to
pick 'em.*

She sat down and began eating with growing enthusiasm;
the cook had heard that she liked her eggs over easy but the
whites *weren't* liquid; the bacon was Canadian-style; the hash
browns had bits of chili and onion; and best of all her stomach
had settled back to normal. Even the chatter wasn't too bad,
if you unfocused your ears and just heard it as a happy babble, like a mountain brook.

"We'll get you two settled in today and show you to your
fiefs," she said to the knights, mopping at a yolk with some
toast. "And you can swear me homage on Sunday after morning mass. Then we get busy. Sitting on the veranda watching
the tenants work isn't on the schedule, and hunting can wait
until after wine-harvest. You've got competent bailiffs, and
your good ladies can see to setting up housekeeping and finding cooks and shopping for household gear on their own."

They nodded; Ruffin gave a mock-theatrical groan and
then winked at Joyce, who bounced up and down in glee at

the thought of being turned loose in the vast warehouses of salvaged luxuries the Association kept for its elite. Several of the nearby males paused to look over at the results of the bouncing, even confined in a cotte-hardi.

Christ have mercy, Tiphaine thought; one of the few things she and Katrina had disagreed about was whether shopping was fun in itself, or just more fun than standing naked in a hailstorm while juggling live squid.

That switched the conversation from weddings to home improvement; Tiphaine did her best to blur it into background noise, and signaled the servant for another plate. The manors they'd be swearing service for had been in the Protector's demesne since the area was resettled in late fall of the first Change Year, and the spring of the second. That meant a good bailiff, probably picked originally because they knew something about raising food. Norman Arminger had raked the survivors for such from the day he announced his Protectorate, and sent out raiding parties to capture/rescue as many farmers as he could before they were eaten out by the refugees, or just eaten plain and simple, so they could instruct the ignorant urban survivors who made up most of the labor pool and future peasantry—that was one reason for the simple system of five fields per village. But the manor houses themselves would be bare inside, empty and waiting.

When her plate was empty likewise, Tiphaine cleared her throat and spoke: "Yes, Joyce, you can probably get a gold chandelier and a swinging love seat and a four-poster."

The younger woman recognized the tone and fell silent, still smiling. Tiphaine went on: "Ivo, Ruffin, what *I* want is to get the *menie* in order. Right now what we've got is sorta-kinda good enough to keep one of the Grand Constable's inspectors from blowing through the roof and ordering floggings all 'round. Just. Sorta-kinda is not good enough for *me*. Next time the *ban* is called, the Domain of Ath is going to put the sixty best-trained fighting-men in the Association at my horse's tail if we have to kill them all to do it."

They nodded enthusiastically, being men who took their profession seriously. "Is that why the Lord Protector picked this fief for you, my lady?" Ivo asked. "He knew you'd slap the garrison into shape and do it quick?"

"That was probably one of the reasons," Tiphaine said judiciously. "Believe me, there's always more than one reason behind the Protector's decisions, and at least four behind Lady Sandra's."

"Can Rudi and I come along on the ride, Lady d'Ath?" Mathilda asked.

She'd either learned or inherited her mother's way of making a request sound like an exquisitely polite but definite command nobody could dream of disobeying. Unlike her mother she didn't have the might of the Protectorate to back it up . . . yet, but she would someday, which was a good thing to keep in mind. Rudi said nothing, nibbling on a piece of toast and doing his best to be beatifically uninvolved. Tiphaine looked at him narrowly.

Well, it would be the best way to keep an eye on him, she thought. *He did promise, and I think he takes it seriously. Plus keeping him cooped up and going stir-crazy would be the best way I know to make him mad enough to try and run. Of course, he also wants to get to know the area in case he gets a chance to escape within the wording of that reallllly careful promise. But I can't turn Mathilda down without a good reason, and it'd make trouble to make him stay here if she went.*

"Sure," she said.

Mathilda clapped her hands. Rudi smiled, and the gray-green eyes glowed in the shadowed dimness of the tower's hall.

CHAPTER TWENTY

Near Dallas, Willamette Valley, Oregon
April 2nd, 2008/Change Year 10

"Thanks," Michael Havel said, gripping Alleyne Loring's hand. "Christ Jesus, but I wish I was going with you!"

The little party of Dúnedain and Bearkillers waited in the gathering shadows beneath the edge of the trees, some already mounted, some holding their mounts' reins. Westward the sun sank over the Coast Range, casting their shadows towards the croplands. Eastward a strategic hamlet stood a mile away, behind its ditch and mound and stone-and-concrete wall, with an A-lister's fortified steading not far off, within mutual supporting distance. As he shook hands with the Bearkiller lord Alleyne saw a bright blink of light from those walls as a militiaman's steel caught the dying light. The rich smell of plowed earth came on the wind, mingling with the fresh fir-sap scent of the great forests westward, and the horse-leather-wool-oiled-metal scent that meant *action*.

"We'll get him back, sir," Alleyne said, giving a squeeze back.

The word came naturally; this was a man you had to respect, even if he was a bit of a rough diamond. His wife, on the other hand, was a stunner—not better-looking than Astrid, which wouldn't be humanly possible, but more *human*. Her blue eyes were steady on his as she nodded; then she stepped forward and gave him a hug, which was pleasant enough even though she was wearing a mail hauberk. Like the rest of the

Rangers, the young Englishman was in mottled camouflage-patterned clothing of green and brown, with a brigandine covered in the same material, and a war cloak rolled behind his saddle. They all carried sword and bow, but this mission could only be done by stealth and speed, not hammer blows.

"I pray to God you do," Signe Havel said sincerely. "And take care of my little sister, too." She looked at the others. "All of you take care."

Havel went on: "I wish you could take more supplies, but you're right to limit the load. Still, it's better than a hundred and fifty miles by the paths you're going to be following, and the mountains can be cold and wet this time of year."

There were a dozen of them, and only half as many pack horses, beside the riding animals. Alleyne smiled. "By now I've spent enough time in your Oregonian forests to feel quite at home, I assure you."

"Yeah, well, the Coast Range isn't quite the same as Silver Falls," he said.

Astrid stirred where she stood contemplating the sunset. "That's *Taur-i-Mithril,* or in the Common Speech—"

"—Silver Falls State Park," Havel said, smiling his crooked smile. "You take care too, Sis. Get the kid, and get out."

"We will," she said, and Eilir and John Hordle nodded. "And it's time to go. We want to get as far as we can before moonset."

Havel nodded. Alleyne swung into the saddle and turned his mount westward, touching it into a fast walk and bending his head as they passed beneath the branches of the oak at the head of the trail. A last look showed him Michael Havel staring after him, and pounding his right fist into the hollow of his other palm.

Village of Montinore, Tualatin Valley, Oregon
April 8th, 2008/Change Year 10

"Come and hear!" Estella Maldonado said. "Come and buy! Come and laugh!"

She circled the wagon dancing and rattled the tambourine

in the air as her mother played her fiddle from the driver's seat, and her brothers juggled cups and eggs and daggers, flinging them high to catch the evening sun. They were slender, dark-haired, olive-skinned young men, dressed *gitano*-style in dark pants and baggy shirts, boots and spangled vests, with kerchiefs bound around their hair and big gold hoop earrings, and daggers—just barely of legal size—thrust through their sashes. She was younger—twenty to their twenty-two and -three—and wore a silk kerchief herself, but her strong black hair flowed waist-long behind it; a flounced scarlet skirt swung around her calves as she swayed her hips, and a red bodice thrust her full bosom up into the low-cut, embroidered white blouse, enough to show an enticing amount without quite bringing down the wrath of some village priest. Her jewelry was gaudy and abundant and quite genuine; it was a convenient way to store the family assets . . . and fun.

"Come and buy! Come and laugh! Come one, come all, people of Montinore Manor!"

The tinerant wagon—the legal term for its owners was *licensed itinerant*—was a simple box with a curved sheet-metal roof, but gaudily painted. Light trucks had furnished the wheels and springs; four red-and-white oxen drew it. Right now they were lying down and chewing their cuds unconcernedly while her father walked around the vehicle and unfolded the sides. Another much like it followed; that was their sleeping quarters and for baggage, with the family's one horse hitched behind the door in the rear, and a tin chimney through the roof.

Rogelio Maldonado opened the cargo wagon up in cleverly arranged stepped metal trays on both sides, a staircaselike arrangement that reached almost down to the muddy surface of the village green. There was a tempting smell from bottles of perfume, and from trays of spices—curry powder, dried chilies, ground sage and sesame seeds; there were rock candy and crystallized ginger; toys and picture books and tops; cloth in bolts and little cakes of wild-indigo essence and saffron and madder. Ribbons and precious cotton sewing thread (and the newer, distinctly inferior linen variety for those who could not afford it) shared space with buttons and vied with tools and pans and pots and a few luxury foods like potted shrimp and pickled peppers and jams. There were also the miniature anvil and hammers and punches, last and awls, that proclaimed the travelers to be tinkers and shoemakers and repairers of leather goods as well. Bundles of wildflowers hung from twine set along the sides of both wagons, in the first stages of drying to make sachets.

A crowd was already gathering from the homes and cottages along the single patched asphalt street of the settlement below Montinore Manor, drawn from wheel and loom and garden hoe and workbench by the noise and the gear and the prospect of a break in the dull round of days. There were three hundred souls in the village, a little more than average, most of them here on the Saturday half-holiday . . . *holiday* meaning for most it was time to do for themselves and their families instead of the landholder. A few in the crowd were probably servants from the manor or castle from the embroidered tabards, and a pair were off-duty soldiers in the padded gambesons usually worn below armor for protection, and now keeping their owners warm against the spring evening. She looked around, deliberately waking her memories; when you moved every couple of days that was necessary, or you could get lost because your mind used its map of some other familiar place.

Yes, there was a glimpse of white off to the north and west, over low, rolling hills covered in leafy rows of vines—the manor house, a pre-Change mansion that had been the center of a vineyard estate. A little more west of north, and the brutal exclamation point of the tower of Castle Ath reared over a low hill, flying the black-and-red of the Lord Protector and the more complex heraldry of the new baronet; mountains green and forested rose beyond, and to the west. That was all demesne land. South more vineyards, east the old railroad tracks and the five open fields where the tenants had their strips of land, looking more settled every time they visited as the trees planted along their edges grew.

Hmmm, Estella thought, considering as she danced. *They're better-dressed than last time. Especially the peons.*

More shoes, too. And the place looks tidier, the church has been painted. As we heard, there's a new broom here . . .

The fiddle squealed on as Papa unrolled the awnings above the slanted steplike trays of their goods. He claimed to have a little *gitano* blood, but it was probably not true, though she and her brothers looked the part—which in his rare moments of candor he admitted was what you got when you crossed Sonoran mestizo with small-town Arizona Anglo. The half-believed claim had gotten them help that let them live through the Change—she remembered little of that, since she had been barely ten—and nowadays some of the other tinerants were the genuine article, and it was the fashion among the rest to imitate it. Hiding in plain sight; if you were suspect and despised because you were a tinerant and a gypsy, you'd be less likely to be suspected of witchcraft.

Other than size Montinore village was similar to hundreds of others in Portland's territories, which was no accident; they were built to a standard pattern out of the Lord Protector's history books. The church was brick, and a few of the free-tenant houses were pre-Change, ordinary frame structures covered in clapboard. Others had been moved here, hauled with ox-teams or disassembled and rebuilt. The peon cottages were all new-built from salvaged materials, one room and a loft, with a toolshed and chicken coop attached. Each house was on its own garden plot, a long narrow rectangle stretching back from the road; the tenant farmhouses had barns and byres attached on their larger allotments. There was a mill here, built on a water-furrow from a dam on the creek a few hundred yards away; the wheel wasn't turning right now. The bailiff's house stood near it, and the miller's, the two best in the village with the priest's cottage right behind.

"Come buy!" Estella shouted again. "Come buy!"

Suddenly an off-duty soldier grabbed her around the waist from behind, hands groping at her breasts. "*I'll* buy!" he said, laughing.

You think that's funny, pig? Let's see how you laugh at this. But no, better not be too emphatic.

Fortunately he wasn't wearing his hauberk, which would

make it easier to reach behind and grab *so* . . . and then he howled and let her go.

"That would be renting," she said sweetly, as he bent and rubbed at himself and laughed—it had been more of a playful tweak than a real wrench-and-twist. "Ask someone else, soldier, and don't believe all the stories you hear about tinerant girls."

Then the steward was there holding his white staff, with the fat bailiff in tow; she let the tambourine fall silent along with the fiddle. Both were looking more sour-faced than usual, and the bailiff's even more loathsome son looked more like a sulky boar than he had the time before.

"You have your permit?" Wielman said.

Her father bowed—the whole family did, except for Estella and her mother, who curtsied. Then he produced the stamped, signed authorization they had for travel and petty trade; it was countersigned by a bishop and several priests, all of them deceived by the ostentatious piety of the Maldonado family. Such permits were something the PPA gave out only grudgingly, and only because they knew that otherwise swapping and barter would go on underground.

Which they do anyway, Estella thought. *Along with a good deal else, by the Lord and Lady!*

"You can stay four days and nights," he said at last, after checking that the signatures were up-to-date and taking the bag of "gifts" her father offered, along with the regulation fee; the bailiff got another. "We have a new lord . . . lady . . . here, so be careful. I don't have the right of the High Justice, but she *does.*"

And nobody would care if she used it on tinerant trash, Estella thought, grim behind her smile.

Later that night Estella walked away from the bonfire where a sudden *ah* from the gathered crowd said her brother Carlos had swallowed the sword. They had done well today, in coin and in supplies and barter—the miller had sold them three bolts of the lovely woolen twill that his daughters wove and two great sacks of shelled filberts in return for a set of big metalworker's files salvaged from the ruins of Olympia, and they'd picked up enough flour, spuds and flitches of bacon and hams to last for two weeks in trade for sundries. Tomorrow they would start repairing pots and making shoes. . . .

And speaking of the miller and his daughter, she thought with a smile. *It will be good to see Delia again. I could use cheering up, and she is fun.*

Delia waited behind the millrace scaffolding, where deep shadow made the night even blacker, and the fires and noise were comfortably distant; if anyone noticed she'd gone from the crowd around the wagon, they'd suspect the reason, though hopefully not the person, for she'd cheerfully flirted with half a dozen, including the undiscouraged soldier. Water gurgled by overhead, making the spring night chilly and damper than elsewhere, with a scent of wet earth and soaked wood; Estella pulled her shawl over her shoulders.

But she can get us in the mill, which has a nice comfortable pile of grain sacks, she thought with a warm glow of anticipation.

They exchanged the murmured recognition signals, as much to cater to the younger woman's sense of drama as from real need—both had been raised witches—and the ritual kiss of greeting; both were tailored to be meaningless to someone outside the hidden Coven network. When she tried for a real kiss, though . . .

Estella laughed ruefully at the dodge; a relationship conducted at month-long intervals just didn't have a long shelf life.

"Well, you've found someone at last," she said, taking the other by the hands and giving them a squeeze. "Alas!"

"Yes, I have . . . can we still be friends? You're not angry?"

"Of course we'll be friends! We always were, for years before we were lovers. And I always said I couldn't be here for more than visits, remember. We were lucky to have what we had; the memory will always be warm."

Delia grinned in the darkness. "Well, now maybe *I* should be angry! Aren't you sad at all? Disappointed?"

"I'm heartbroken, *mi corazón.* Have they hitched you to the bailiff's son, with his pig face and little curly tail?"

Delia laughed. "As if! I'd be sobbing on your shoulder and asking for comfort if *that* had happened! And you, heartbroken? You've probably got a girl in every village."

"Only half a dozen," she said, with some exaggeration. "Boys in one or two," she went on, and laughed at the other's grimace. "Purist! But tell me who, then. I hope you're not being careless!"

The girl was practically dancing with delight. "You'll never guess!"

"Of course not; that's why I asked."

Delia leaned forward and whispered in her ear. "Tiphaine . . . d'Ath!"

Estella felt her eyes go wide in shock, unseen in the darkness. She grabbed the other by the shoulders. "She didn't hurt you?" she asked sharply, then shook her head. "No, evidently not—"

"Oh, Estella, it wasn't like that at all. I practically dragged *her* off!"

A soft whistle. "Dangerous! You couldn't be sure she wouldn't turn you over to the priests!"

"Well, it was a bit scary at first. She *looked* sort of . . . forbidding, you know? Beautiful, but like a sword blade would look if it walked. But I felt prettier when she looked at *me,* so I took a chance. She's sweet, and was so lonely—her friend who'd been with her forever died last year."

Yes, killed trying to kidnap Lady Juniper's son, Estella thought. *And this one succeeded, and left some of our brothers and sisters dead behind her.*

Slowly, she went on aloud: "*Querida,* you are taking a big risk here. Think how the soldiers are, think how all the castle people are, like rattlesnakes in a bucket. Because this woman likes to make love with you doesn't mean she loves you."

"It isn't just that. When we're alone we talk about our lives, and play games—she's teaching me chess—and laugh, and she plays the lute and we sing . . ."

Estella winced at an unexpected stab of jealousy, as much for the privacy and safety as anything else; it was easier to arrange your life when you had your own castle. *Not that I would have one on a bet!*

"Darling, she's an Associate. She has been an Associate since the Change, in the Protector's Household—"

"The consort's."

"She was still raised to kill people for a living, and take what others grow and make, by threat of death and pain. The Associates are the sword arm of the Church, and the Church burns witches. Nice is not something the Portland Protective Association are very good at; killing and taking, that is what they do. Think what might happen if you two quarreled, or you yourself changed your mind . . ."

"No, really, she's not like most of them! Not just to me— she's starting a spinning and weaving school for the peon women, with me and Rose and Claire to teach, and she's buying the equipment—and she spent *fifty rose nobles* on cloth, so people wouldn't have to wait until then to have decent clothes, and she's gotten Wielman and the bailiff and Keith the Pig under control so they're not squeezing people nearly so bad, and she keeps the soldiers in line. And hardly anyone's been whipped or put in the stocks unless they really deserved it."

That's all interesting, but it doesn't necessarily mean she's nice, just smart *and foresighted, Estella thought. Let's not argue. I recognize the tone. This poor girl has fallen hard. I hope she is not hurt too badly, but such is life. We must not let it endanger the Craft . . . but it could work to our advantage, as well. She will hear things and see things she would not otherwise.*

"And she's like an older sister to the Princess Mathilda— Mathilda's nice too—and to Rudi. I gave Rudi the pattern—"

"How?" Estella asked sharply.

Delia giggled. "In some gravy, so nobody else could see— he wouldn't have himself, if he weren't so sharp. We haven't said a word beyond that, but he knows, and it makes him feel better. His poor mother must be so worried, and he's homesick and lonely sometimes, but like I said, Tiphaine treats him like her own family."

"That will be a relief to Lady Juniper. We can pass it on . . . never mind how. And if we must, we can have you pass a message to him. The risk, though! He's still not quite ten years old.

That's why we don't tell children about the Craft until they're older than that, and able to keep secrets."

"Not with Rudi. He's a wonderful kid, so brave! And smart too. He's teaching me my letters, well, how to read them better, and he tells lovely stories about how the Mackenzies live. And you can see the Lord and Lady walk with him, all the time, not just at the special times."

She hesitated. "Can we have an Esbat while your family are here? Since Mom died"—her voice caught for a moment—"we haven't had a High Priestess, and nobody else knows all the things she did, not here or in the other villages. She was teaching me, but I hadn't learned nearly as much as I need. Dad was so sorry we couldn't have a passing rite for her. We couldn't find her books, either."

"Good!" Estella said. "If you can't find them, the Hounds of God can't either."

Delia nodded, completely serious for the first time in their meeting. *Excellent,* Estella thought. *She may be eighteen and infatuated to giddiness, but she knows that is a matter of life and death.* Aloud, the tinerant went on.

"I'll talk to my parents, and see what we can do. But first you must tell me all about Rudi; where he's kept, and what he does each day. Leave nothing out." She sensed a hesitation. "This is for the Old Religion, and for the Queen of Witches."

"Well . . . OK. I don't suppose it can hurt."

Near Cherry Grove, Tualatin Valley, Oregon
April 10th, 2008/Change Year 10

Astrid tapped him on the sleeve. *There,* the gesture said.

Alleyne could see it too, the faint shimmering blink of a campfire ahead, wavering through half a mile of forest and brush and a gathering ground-mist that muffled the strong, musty scent of rotting leaves and fir needles and cones. He stroked the soft blond stubble on his chin—shaving while moving fast and secretly through the woods wasn't very practical—and compared the lie of the land about him to the map in his head, then nodded.

Astrid made a sound beneath her teeth, held up two fingers and tapped them to right and left, and half-glimpsed figures spread out and moved forward. The nighted forest was not quite pitch-black, but fairly close to it; they'd left their war cloaks behind with the horses farther up the slope of Mt. Richmond for the sake of speed and quietness. Here the unpeopled mountains that stretched west to Tillamook and the ocean met the cultivated eastern lowlands in a maze of twisting valleys. The one ahead was called Patton—not, he thought, for the general—and held the upper stretches of the Tualatin River. There was a village called Cherry Grove a few miles to their west, lately rebuilt on the pre-Change ruins because there was a good fall of water for a mill. Its fields stretched eastward along the valley this mountain overlooked on either side of the river, and there the contacts they were to meet should be camped. They'd picked the location because the little hamlet on the edge of the mountains had no manor and no garrison to speak of. That made it a little safer, but not much.

So that campfire is them . . . or they were discovered, and it's an ambush. Well, no time like the present.

Astrid and he eeled forward. The hillside had been logged off recently enough that the trees were only fifty or sixty feet high above them, and there was plenty of bush; even after better than a year gone he was still conscious of how different the sounds were from an English wood at night, sharper and harsher, with more buzzing and clicking of insects. The birds were surprisingly similar, though he missed the nightingales. They ghosted downslope; once a red fox leapt aside in panicked surprise as they passed from tree to tree, and shot off with a crackle of leaves under churning paws. He grinned to himself at that, since it was like meeting an old friend from Hampshire. As if to remind him where he was, from somewhere in the northern darkness came the appalling, rowling screech of a cougar, probably just after it dropped on a passing deer, or perhaps in disappointment after it missed.

They went to their bellies a hundred yards from where woods gave way to the scrubby pasture where the wagons waited; beyond that was a road, and beyond that a field of some sort—probably grain, from the strength of the scent of wet earth. A few dogs lay around the fire, and a pot bubbled above it, and something roasted on a wooden spit close beside it; that was the best way to do small game, and let you catch the drippings in a pan. The smells made his stomach cramp, since they'd had nothing but cheese and waybread today.

A last halt, and Eilir and John came in on either side, quiet and slow. The big man put his mouth next to Alleyne's ear: "Nothing. We've got scouts out on all sides now."

Astrid smiled and rose. *"Mae Govannen!"* she called.

The figures around the fire rose; one spilled something in his haste, and began an abortive snatch for a hunting bow.

"I hadn't expected them to come for the heavy gypsy quite so much," John said to him quietly as he passed to get a refill from the pot.

Alleyne made a subdued noise of agreement; the rabbit stew was taking most of his attention, nicely thick with peas and onions, and fresh bread as well. It was true, though. He'd met a few real Rom before the Change, and some since in Gibraltar, and they generally weren't nearly so much like a Romantic-era operetta, all headscarves and earrings . . . Of course, a few clans of an extremely traditional variety had survived in remote Carpathian valleys, and they'd drifted westward since to get away from ongoing chaos and warfare there, where the die-off hadn't been quite as complete as it had in the lands west of the Elbe.

And this gentleman and his wife are rather obviously ordinary Americans of Mexican and what-they-call-Anglo-here descent, he thought. Bits of mispronounced Romany notwithstanding . . . *Is there anybody in this country who isn't putting it on?*

"Te avel mange bakht drago mange wi te avav po gunoy," he said with malice aforethought. And it was true; luck was all they needed, and they were in a bit of a dungheap. *Mind you, we need a great* deal *of luck.*

Mr. Maldonado looked slightly panic-stricken, then shrugged, looking trapped by the circle of firelight that wavered on the gaudily painted wagons to either side.

"I'm afraid I have only a little of the old language," he said, and his wife gave a wry smile.

Eilir winked at him from behind the man's back. *And we're not actually Numenoreans,* she seemed to be saying. *But it's fun, so why not?*

Turning back, he caught a twinkle in Astrid's eye; you could never be quite sure . . . and he remembered King Charles and the smock frocks and Morris dancing. Perhaps it was a seeking after reassurance, given the terrible shock of the Change and its aftermath.

The younger Ms. Maldonado unfolded a map and a sheaf of notes. *She* looked the part; she might have stepped out of a tavern in Gibraltar, in fact, with that creamy olive skin and lush figure, the pouting lower lip—

Astrid elbowed him in the side, and he grinned, a little apologetically. The young woman went on.

"This is the layout of Ath castle; the barracks, the inner Keep, the guest rooms where the princess and Rudi sleep. And I have the patrol and guard schedules."

"Excellent," Astrid said. "You must have good sources inside the castle . . . no, don't tell me, I don't need to know."

Estella Maldonado shrugged interestingly, with something oddly wry in her smile. "Sources *very* close to the top," she said.

"Hmmm. We could come in from the west," Hordle said, tracing one thick finger over the paper. "Around this big lake—"

"Hag Lake," Estella supplied. "People seldom go there, particularly this early in the year. It's said to be haunted by a hag who cursed a band of Eaters after the Change—"

Castle of Ath/Hag Lake, Tualatin Valley, Oregon
April 15th, 2008/Change Year 10

"I just want you to find me charming and wise;
I just want you to find me somewhere inside—"

Tiphaine let the tune die, leaning back against the pillows with a calf over her knee, idly strumming the lute, watching

Delia sew for a moment before she spoke: "You know, sweetie, your dress sense is a lot like Lady Sandra's. At least, you pick the same sort of stuff for me that she used to tell me to wear when I was in the Household. Black with white and gold accents for me, brown and russet and silver for Kat—Kat had dark hair and fair skin and blue eyes, like you."

Bright morning light streamed in through the narrow eastern window; sunrise and sunset were the best-lit times in the tower bedchamber. The air was cool and fresh, made more so by the sprays of cherry blossom in vases on tables and mantelpiece and the headboard of the bed.

Delia replied as her fingers moved deftly with needle and thread and fine cambric linen: "So, what's she really like? Lady Sandra, I mean?" she asked, holding the fabric up. "Besides having good taste in clothes. I brought her some hot rolls once, that my mother baked, when the consort was visiting Montinore Manor. I was really nervous, I was just fourteen then, and she said *thank you* very nicely. I thought she was wonderful."

Lucky you didn't meet her husband, then, Tiphaine thought, surprised at the surge of protective anger she felt. *Hey, I guess I really* do *like her a lot.*

The girl continued: "Is she really sinister and cruel and evil, the way the stories say?"

Tiphaine reached over and took a stem of raw asparagus from a bowl by the table that also held the first snowpeas of the season, and crunched on it, savoring the fresh, intense, nutty-green flavor, like eating springtime, or what she imagined fresh grass tasted like to a horse. She looked at the file of accounts tossed aside on the bedcover; they kept saying *you're in the nobility now, tra-la,* anyway; that didn't make them less boring but it did help.

"Sinister? Yup, in spades. But I wouldn't say *cruel,* exactly," Tiphaine said thoughtfully. "She's certainly pretty evil, though."

She tuned the lute and played a trickle of notes. Now, how to sum up Lady Sandra . . . slither of minor key, plangent, fading to something soft and wild . . . you couldn't really get fingering complex enough. A harpsichord might be better for it.

Delia considered the loose-sleeved linen shirt critically, bit off a thread and stuck her needle in the pincushion. "There!"

She rose from the chair beside the swept and empty hearth and handed the shirt to Tiphaine. The design around the neck and down the seam of the sleeves intertwined the letters PPA and the new arms of Ath, the black and gold and silver stitching neat and precise.

"Did she treat you and your friend badly?" the younger woman went on, turning to one of the cupboards as if to hide the flash in her eyes. "Is that how you know she's evil?"

Tiphaine smiled at the indignation in her tone as she set down the instrument and bunched the linen. "Nope!" she said through the fabric.

Then, as she pulled it down, laced up the three-quarter opening in front, buttoned the cuffs and tucked the tail into the new black doeskin riding breeches she was wearing: "She took me and Kat in, protected us from everyone, got us training and education that nobody else would have. Taught us plenty herself, too. Being around Lady Sandra sort of forces your wits along, like starting this asparagus early under glass frames."

Delia smiled over her shoulder as she sorted through the clothes with quick, skilled fingers. "Then she's really a nice person underneath, like you."

"Oh, I'm pretty evil too, sweetie. I'm just nice to *you,* which isn't the same thing at all."

Delia laughed; so did Tiphaine. *Though she's laughing because she thinks I'm teasing, and I'm laughing because I'm not.*

"If she's so evil, why did you work for her?" the seamstress said.

"Well, since I'm evil too, it sort of makes sense . . ."

Delia made a rude gesture with two fingers and stuck out her tongue. Tiphaine went on, more seriously: "It's my duty; she's my liege-lady, and I owe her, big-time, so honor requires it. Plus in this world we've got you're either on top of the heap or on the bottom, and I prefer to be the one on—"

She stopped: Delia was looking at her with an exaggerated innocent-surprise rounding of the eyes, making a rosebud of

her lips and laying one index finger on it, the picture of astonishment.

"*Stop* that!" Tiphaine said, laughing in earnest now. "I am
not that bossy in bed!"

She threw a stem of asparagus; the girl caught it and ate it,
then tossed back the thigh-length sleeveless jerkin she'd
picked out for the seigneur of Ath. It was black-dyed fawn-
skin, even slighter and more supple than doe-leather, finished like soft suede and lined with thin silk; the delta and V
of her arms was done on the front in gold and silver thread,
with a mandarin collar closed by a gold button. Tiphaine
pulled it on and tugged it into place, swung her legs over
the side of the bed to buckle on her boots, slung the lute over
her back on its ribbon and walked over to the floor-length
mirror.

"Ohhh, *not* bad," she said, and tossed back her shoulder-
length hair, still slightly damp from the shower. "Not bad at all."

"You are one babelicious chick-magnet, Tiphaine d'Ath,"
Delia said, with a chuckle. "And that outfit looks very sinister
and . . . andyrowgenerus?"

"Androgynous," she supplied, turning and preening slightly.
"And no it doesn't. I never was boyish, even at fourteen, just
athletic."

To herself: *She's so smart I forget she can't read very well,
sometimes. I must do something about that.* Formal education
for people below the Associate level wasn't illegal, just sort of
seriously frowned on except for bright children picked for the
Church. *Nobody would really mind with a miller's daughter,
though.* It wasn't as if she was a peon; the family trade required literacy and arithmetic. So would supervising the domain's cloth-making enterprise.

The seamstress-weaver nodded critically, circling behind
her, examining the clothes with professional skill and tugging down a hem, then went on with a thoughtful finger tapping at her jaw: "Well, it looks nice and sinister and *evil,*
which I suppose is *good,* since you say you're evil and all.
And it does so look andyer-iogenous to me. I mean, nobody
could mistake that gorgeous ass for a guy's, but you could

bounce a rose noble off it, and the way the jerkin sets off your shoulders and legs against the tuck of your waist and the bosom—"

Tiphaine nodded: *I suppose it* does *look that way, these days. It's sort of a different effect now that most women don't wear pants very often.*

Delia handed her the sword belt—her second-best one, with monochrome tooling rather than inlay and a cut-steel buckle, since she was going out for a ride and a picnic, not to a festival—and she put it on, settling it fashionably just above her hips and just below the waistline. The sword was new, made to her preferences by the best war-smith in Forest Grove and layer-forged from fillets of mild steel and tough alloy; double-edged but relatively slender, with a yard of blade tapering to a long, vicious point, checked-ebony hilts and a silver fish-tail pommel. She speed-drew it and did a quick figure-eight flourish, making the air hiss as she neatly snipped off a spray of cherry blossoms and cut it in half again before it fell an inch. Then she sheathed the sword again with a sweet *tiinngg* as the quillons kissed the metal rim of the scabbard.

"Beautifully balanced," she said with satisfaction, tucking one bunch of the flowers behind her own ear and one behind Delia's; the miller's daughter was wearing her hair in braided coils over the temples. "I don't *care* what the Period Nazis say; the fifteenth-century model is just way more effective against anyone wearing decent armor than those Franco-Viking meat cleavers."

She grinned reminiscently. "One time Conrad Renfrew— this was at a tournament, I'd just cleaned up the intermediate foot-combat event—asked me if I didn't have any respect for the Norman broadsword. He was sounding sort of indignant, and I bowed and told him, *My lord Count, if I ever have to butcher an ox, the broadsword shall be my* first *choice.*"

Delia sighed and began to dress herself; her interest in swords roughly matched Tiphaine's in furniture. Looking at the asparagus and snowpeas, she said: "Mind if I have the rest of these?"

"Sure, sweetie. I was only eating them because they're

fresh," Tiphaine said. "You know, I remember a few things from before the Change—"

"That's more than I do," Delia said, pulling on knitted hose made for riding, with leather inserts on the insides of the thighs, what Tiphaine had heard Sandra call a bastard cross between pantyhose and a sweater.

She paused to eat a stick of the asparagus. "All I really remember is the Change, the way it hurt inside my head, and then being hungry and afraid and Mom and Dad hiding us. I used to remember more, but it gave me bad dreams. And then the Association came that fall . . . at least we had food, and we went to work helping to build the mill."

Tiphaine shuddered slightly; she had certain memories of her own about those first months that she'd *like* to be able to forget, and the dreams had gotten less frequent but never gone away entirely. Particularly what had happened to Ms. Darroway, their troop leader, when she got an infected cut on her leg after leading them in fighting off a bunch of would-be Mountain Men who thought a Girl Scout troop was a gift from God. Things had gotten really bad after the wound went gangrenous and she died, until Tiphaine and Kat took off on their own . . .

With an effort of will, she shook herself back to the present: "Well, what I was going to say was that I really like the taste of cherries, you know—"

She stopped and made an exasperated sound at the other's wide-eyed expression, then laughed; it was hard to look guilelessly surprised when naked to the waist and holding a stalk of asparagus between the teeth, but Delia was bringing it off.

Tiphaine extended an arm and index finger at her: "You were not! Not, *not*!"

Delia curled her tongue around the asparagus, bit the stalk in half with a flash of white teeth, gathered the pieces into her mouth without using her fingers and then slowly licked her lips, keeping up the innocent stare in the process.

"God, that has *got* to be the most lascivious thing I've ever seen!" Tiphaine shook her head, slightly dazed. "Anyway, back then you could get fresh fruit out of season, even if you were just an ordinary person; I remember my mother buying peaches and grapes and things at Christmas. Now I'm rich and I can't have cherries until June. Not even the Lord Protector and the Consort could."

The seamstress finished pulling on her own tunics; for riding, the longer undertunic was split, with a flap that could be buttoned over to close it when on the ground. That and the leggings were the respectable female's solution to riding astride, though some Associate-rank women wore men's clothing for the purpose and a few used a sidesaddle, which was the only way you could back a horse and wear a cotte-hardi at the same time. Lady Sandra's opinion of *that* was short and pungent, and she'd outright forbidden them at court, with the Protector's backing because sidesaddles weren't period. Of course, cotte-hardis weren't eleventh century either, more like fourteenth, but they'd become firmly established before Norman Arminger noticed.

Against fashion, even tyrants struggle in vain, she thought.

"So," Delia said, putting on her own belt, which had a knife with a legal four-inch blade, the universal tool of the countryside. "If Lady Sandra's sinister and evil but really sort of nice, what's the Lord Protector like?"

The smile died on Tiphaine's face. Wordlessly she extended her hand, palm up, then slowly curled the fingers into crooked predator talons that quivered with the tension in her tendons and strong wrist.

Delia swallowed, silent for a moment. "It's sort of hard to remember sometimes that you're . . . one of . . . *them.*"

"Them?" Tiphaine asked.

"The castle-folk—Association people."

Who, we both know very well, aren't too popular with a lot of commoners, Tiphaine thought.

She didn't answer, but instead took a moment to put on her hat, the usual rolled-edge affair with a long palm-broad tail of black silk down one side, and Lady Sandra's livery badge of the Virgin and the Dragon at the front in silver. Today she turned the tail up under her chin and pinned it on the other side, which would keep it from flying away completely in a high wind or a gallop.

Tiphaine's mouth quirked when she spoke. "You should

have thought about that before you asked me to take a look at your embroidered underwear, sweetie. *I* might have been cruel as well as evil, you know, and you'd have been stuck with me regardless."

"I didn't think so." Delia's spirit bubbled back. "And it was you or Keith, the bailiff's son; his dad had been dropping these awful, heavy hints and Keith wouldn't go *away,* and my dad's scared of them, they're the bailiffs, after all. And he has pimples and crooked teeth and bad breath and he's mean and his father's worse, and oh, God, he's boring!"

She picked up her own Chinese-style straw hat and mimed throwing up in it. "Besides being a guy."

"Well, *I* don't have halitosis or pimples, and . . ." They kissed.

After a moment Delia sighed. "I don't like having to *hide,* though. We wouldn't have had to do that before the Change, would we?"

Tiphaine laughed grimly. "OK, someday I'll have to tell you about being the 'Designated Homo-Loser-Goat' in Grade Nine at Binnsmead Middle School, 1997–8. I wanted the world to end—and then it did!"

The excursion party was forming up in the courtyard when Tiphaine and Delia came down; Rudi, Mathilda, two men-at-arms and four mounted crossbowmen, and a varlet with the two packhorses that carried picnic panniers, fishing rods and her lute, spare clothing in case it got cold . . . The rest of the midmorning bustle of the castle was well under way, the noisiest part of that being Sir Ruffin leading most of the garrison in full battle kit on circuits that involved running up the inner stairs to the top of the wall and around and down and up again, over and over, clash and clatter and clank. Ruffin waved to her as he passed, face streaming sweat; the rest kept their heads down and concentrated grimly on putting one foot ahead of another, panting like bellows . . .

At least none of them are falling down and puking now, she thought. Although two had quit over the past month, and been replaced with farm-boy recruits, both of whom were shaping well despite some—unstated—trouble with their families.

"I was out to Hag Lake myself once before," Mathilda burbled to Rudi. "We went sailing; it's real pretty. My dad says it has the best spring trout fishing anywhere near here, too."

Rudi nodded. "Is it called *Hag* Lake after the Wise One?" he asked.

Mathilda frowned. "I'm not sure," she said. "I don't think so, not here."

Tiphaine grinned to herself. It had been named *Henry* Hagg Lake, after a politician, when the stream was dammed back in the seventies; of course, that was before she'd been born. God alone knew what local folklore would make of it eventually, back-filling from the suggestive name with a legend; Lady Sandra called it mythogenesis.

"They say—" Delia began.

It was a good idea of Lady Sandra's to get the brat away from Castle Todenangst or Portland, though. And away from the Holy Father; it's painfully obvious Rudi just never learned to watch his mouth. That was amazing in itself, if you'd been brought up in the Household. *I'd hate to see him get—*

Then she stopped for an instant, surprised. *You know, that's the truth. I would hate to see the Mackenzie brat get hurt. How odd.*

> *Master, lead your Hunt tonight*
> *Bathed in the Lady's silver light*
> *Earth, Air, Fire and Water*
> *Ride in Your train—*

Rudi whistled rather than sang as they rode; it was a hymn to the Horned Lord, so it might not be too tactful to use the verses here where they followed a face of God they thought jealous. Mathilda, who didn't know the words, whistled along with him as she caught the tune; Delia, who did, joined in. Then they all started to do counterpoint, topping each other until they were laughing too hard to go on.

It was easy to laugh, on a bright morning like this, with the sun breaking off on polished metal and bright on dyed cloth as pennants snapped, and he had a good little Arab under him—though nothing like Epona of course—one of a pair

Mathilda's mother had brought out last week in a brief whirl-
wind visit . . .

Matti's still happy with it, he thought. *And I miss Mom and
home* so much. He squared his shoulders. *Well, you're a warrior of the Clan. Act like it!*

They rode northward down towards Carpenter Creek from
the castle gate, along a dirt road that ran through sloping orchards of pear and peach, plum, nectarine, cherry and apple.
All were in some stage of their blossom-time now, in a froth
of pink and white, drenching the mild spring air until they
were almost giddy with the scent and the buzzing of countless bees, and petals drifted over them like snow with every
gust of wind. The crimson clover beneath the trees was in
blossom too, and the grassy verges by the side of the road
were thick with wildflowers, the daffodils fading but camas
bright blue, chicory the darker color of the eastern sky at
sunset; taller bracts of henbit reddish purple, all thick with
hummingbirds and sphinx moths feeding on nectar.

Birds of all kinds swarmed, familiar friends from Dun Juniper; a red-tailed hawk watching them pass from the branch
of a roadside tree, the majesty of a bald eagle wheeling high
overhead, jays calling raucously from the bright new leaves of
the cottonwoods and alders and bigleaf maples beside the
stream, pintail ducks on the spring-swollen waters that tumbled down from the low mountains to the west . . .

They turned upstream, in a clopping of hooves and clink of
horse harness, creaking of saddle leather and the rhythmic
rustling chink of chain mail, the bright morning sun casting
their long shadows ahead of them. Past the orchards the field
on their left was plowed and harrowed dirt, raked every two
feet with furrows where a team was planting quartered potatoes, along with dollops of fertilizer. That was familiar from
home too, and the oxcart full of the seed stock and another
bigger one of stable-muck, and even the cauldron bubbling
over a fire.

The workers who had been at it since dawn weren't homelike at all; glum and quiet, though they'd stopped to eat the
morning meal, a score of scarecrow figures—even those who
owned better clothes now didn't wear them for field work.

Many wore pre-Change clothing, ranging from rags to overalls still fairly intact, if frequently patched. They stopped and rose and bowed or curtsied at the sight of the lady of Ath and her party, leaving a litter of spades and hoes and buckets where they'd been sitting.

Rudi winced at the look they gave the well-dressed riders and the armored men behind them; he recognized hopeless fear and throttled anger, and something like dull awe among the teenagers, and even the young children brought along so their parents could mind them as they worked. A few looked excited at the break in routine—except for a couple still at their mothers' breasts, of course. One ginger-haired, pug-nosed young man of about twenty was rather cleaner than most and much better dressed, in modern Portlander linsey-woolsey breeches and shirt, t-tunic and knit cap; he had a broad smile that didn't reach his eyes as he swept the cap off and bowed, and his nostrils showed like caves.

Tiphaine reined in and turned her white courser aside; Rudi noted how its hooves sank silently in the soft turned earth once they were off the packed dirt and gravel of the roadway, and how much deeper the destriers of the mail-clad men-at-arms did as they followed; the crossbowmen spread out behind them in a semicircle, leaving him and Mathilda and Delia to peer between. A couple of short spears and the bow allowed free-tenants—no stave longer than four feet, no pull heavier than thirty pounds—leaned against one of the carts. That and farm tools would do against coyotes, dog packs and sneak thieves; there were no bandit gangs within striking distance, and tigers would rarely attack a group of humans, though they were dangerous to lone travelers in the wild. A few bundles or backpacks lay there as well, one with the heel of a loaf sticking out of the cloth wrapping, another with a dead rabbit beside it, probably shot on the way to work in the gloaming before dawn and intended for lunch. It wouldn't go far among twenty.

"This field is demesne land," Tiphaine said, in that water-over-smooth-rocks tone. "And these are tenants doing boon-work, aren't they? And you're Keith Anton, son of the Montinore bailiff?"

He nodded and bowed profoundly, cap in hand. "Yes, my lady," he said, the same fixed smile on his face. "I'm overseeing the planting of this field for you."

"Then stop grinning and hand me up a bowl of that and a spoon," she said crisply, flicking the riding crop she held in her right hand towards the cauldron.

The young man looked surprised, but he ran to obey. "Not bad oatmeal porridge," she said, handing it back to him after a considering mouthful. "There's some milk in there."

One of the fieldworkers, an older man with a graying brown beard, spoke: "There wasn't before you got here, miss. Uh, my liege."

A man-at-arms sitting his mount behind her stirred, and lifted the butt of his eleven-foot lance from the ring riveted to his right stirrup-iron.

"Watch your manners, dog!" he barked, the voice blurred and menacing through the mail coif whose flap covered his mouth; only his eyes showed, dark and angry on either side of the helmet's nasal bar. "And keep your place!"

Tiphaine held out a hand in a soothing gesture as the farmers cringed. "Easy, Bors, easy. His village hasn't had a resident lord. They're old-fashioned. You can't expect them to know modern manners yet."

She turned her face back to the tenant-farmer, who was looking as if he wished the earth would swallow him, or as if he wished very much he'd kept his mouth shut.

"You don't say *my liege* . . ." Tiphaine paused and raised a brow.

"Uh, S-s-steve Collins, mmm, Lady Tiphaine. Bond-tenant."

"—to me, Collins," she went on, and used the crop to point around at the armed men behind her. "*They* say 'my liege,' and their families do. They're Association warriors and my vassals, my *menie,* my fighting-tail. You bond-tenants just say 'Lady Tiphaine' or 'my lady d'Ath,' or 'your worship.' I prefer 'my lady,' plain and simple. Now go on."

The man licked his lips; he had glasses on, clumsily patched where one earpiece had broken, the hinge replaced by a lump of sugar-pine gum. "Uh . . . I hold sixteen acres on Montinore, and my due is three days a week on the demesne, and this is the first month in the last ten years we haven't done our boon-work hungry. It used to be just oatmeal and water and salt, and only two bowls of it in a damn long day at that. Anything extra you brought yourself. Now it's better and we can get seconds. I think this . . . Keith . . . and his father had some sort of deal cooked with the steward, Wielman, to keep what we should have gotten, until you came and they were too scared. Thanks, uh, my lady d'Ath."

"You're welcome, Collins." She turned to the bailiff's son. "I'm not going to ask too many questions about what happened before I took seizin of the fief," she said carefully. "But the law says that peons, and tenants doing boon-work, are entitled to be fed twice a day when they're working demesne land, fed 'full and sufficient' meals."

He bobbed his reddish-sandy head and his hands made unconscious washing motions around each other.

"Yes, your . . . my lady. You can see, there's plenty for everyone here, good and hot, and a barrel of clean water. And a break at nine for breakfast and an hour for dinner at one-thirty, and a rest every couple of hours, and nobody kept past the time you can tell a white thread from a black."

She nodded. "That's all very well, Goodman, but men aren't horses; you can't expect them to work all day on oats. I don't want a harvest-home feast laid on every day—

An anonymous snort said that the harvest feast hadn't been much to talk about, either. Tiphaine ignored it.

"—but there should be soup or stew for midday, lentils or beans or barley with vegetables and some meat in it for the taste—sausage, or salt pork, or chicken. And a two-pound loaf of whole meal for each grown worker, and butter and cheese. And some beer; enough for a pint or two each. It's your family's responsibility to organize things like that; it's what you give for the reduced dues. See that it's done starting tomorrow. Draw on the Montinore manor storehouses as needed."

"You should check on whether he does it, my lady," Delia called suddenly from the rear. "He'd skin a louse for the hide, that one, and his dad's no better."

Keith Anton evidently hadn't realized who it was behind the iron wall of the men-at-arms and under her broad-brimmed straw hat; he went white as he recognized her, flushed, started to say something, then looked at the ground again, crushing the cap between strong, calloused fingers.

"Look at me, man," Tiphaine said quietly. When he did: "Do *not* let me hear that I've been disobeyed, or you'll get a whipping and a day in the stocks, with your father beside you. Steal from me and it'll be worse. Understood?"

"Yes, my lady d'Ath. I'd never disobey my overlord, your worship."

"No, I don't suppose you would," Tiphaine said.

She lifted her voice slightly to take in the other workers, who stood staring at her wide-eyed. "Now listen to me; I'm your overlord, not your mother, or a priest. But I intend that the law shall be followed—to the inch. Tattletales who waste my time will go away sorry and sore, but whoever has a legitimate grievance can come and tell me about it. Understood?"

There was a mutter of agreement and bobbing nods. Rudi thought a few of the smiles were even genuine this time.

The party moved on; two crossbowmen riding well ahead, then Lady Tiphaine, then the two men-at-arms, Bors and Fayard—Association people tended to have strange names, he'd found, something about an old Society custom—then him and Matti and Delia, and then the varlet with the packhorses, and two more crossbowmen bringing up the rear.

Delia was beaming—she rode with the children, of course, and was theoretically there to serve them, for propriety's sake by local custom. She called out: "My lady!" Tiphaine turned in the saddle. "I thought you said you were evil?"

"I didn't say I was *stupid,* girl," she replied, grinning for a moment before she turned back to the front again; it made her rather stern face light up and look younger than her twenty-four years.

"When my lady said she'd give us good lordship, she meant it, your highness!" Delia said happily to Mathilda, who liked her. "Things are going to be a lot better here now! We needed a real lord, one who could keep people like Keith and his father and the steward honest."

Mathilda nodded agreement. "My mom and dad can pick

them," she said proudly. "My mom raised Lady Tiphaine in her own Household, you know."

When the others looked at him, Rudi said carefully: "She's certainly very smart. She knows what she's doing."

Which had the advantage of being truth that wouldn't hurt anyone's feelings, particularly not people he liked like Matti, and Delia was nice too, and a Witch here where it was a hard and dangerous thing to be. But . . .

Who's going to keep a lord honest if they don't want to be? People shouldn't have to cringe like that. It's not right, he thought, remembering the raucous assemblies of the Clan. *Nobody's scared when Mom talks to them . . . not like that, at least. And they shouldn't have to lick someone's hand like a frightened dog just for not being treated badly. Tiphaine isn't as bad as she could be, but she shouldn't be able to do that. The Law should be above everyone.*

Tiphaine looked over her shoulder again and gave him a raised eyebrow and a quirking smile. She'd heard, even two horses away and with all the clatter, and she'd known what he meant. Rudi made a small thumb-to-nose gesture and she shook an admonishing finger at him, then turned back.

The plowed field gave way to a meadow with forested hills rising on either side, like lobes stretching down towards the creek; he shook off gloom as he and Mathilda and Delia laughed at the antics of the lambs. Then they turned southward—left—onto the forest tracks. At first there were abundant signs of humankind, stumps and woodchips, the tracks of oxcarts and horses, an old gravel-pit overgrown with brush and half-full of water green with algae, and a four-by-four light truck abandoned ten years ago, overgrown. Birds exploded out of the rusted hulk's broken windows as they passed, small and blue-headed with mauve underparts.

Nobody was there right now, and soon the scented green twilight glow of untouched deep woods closed around them, mostly tall second-growth Douglas fir, grand fir and western hemlock in rough-barked brown columns seventy feet high and better, their branches meeting overhead. He could see off a fair distance, though there was undergrowth; yew with its orange sapwood showing through gaps in the loose purplish bark, the delicately contorted branches of vine maple, nodding sword fern taller than he was; bushy Indian plum with its bunches of hanging white flowers, yellow violets and fawn lily with its golden core and rose pink blossoms. Insects darted through, their wings catching in an occasional slanting ray of sunlight, dragonflies soaring among them like glittering cobalt blue flying wolves; a squirrel ran like a streak of living silver-gray up a tree trunk and around it, then peered back at him, chattering anger.

Sorry, little brother, just passing through, he thought. *Peace between us now.*

Aloud to Mathilda, he went on: "You know, it's odd how you can tell morning sunlight from afternoon even in thick forest. Even if you don't know which way east or west is."

"Yeah," Mathilda answered. "It's sort of . . . *newer,* somehow, in the morning. Brighter even when it isn't."

Delia was simply clinging to her saddle—she rode badly, and had been put on a contented old plug that would walk obediently with the other horses—and looked around in awe. He'd been shocked to learn she'd seldom been beyond the edge of the forest, though she'd lived near here since she was his age.

And her a member of a coven! he thought. *Of course, we haven't had much chance to talk about that. And she has to keep it* real *secret. I bet she can't even tell Tiphaine. That must hurt.*

He'd always found people in love a bit ridiculous—even Mom and Sir Nigel, who were more sensible about it than most, got all spoony.

But then, I'm too young to really know about it. Never make fun of the Lady's gifts! Bad luck, bad luck, three times three, bad luck. Mock them now, lose them later!

He made a gesture of aversion, the Horns pointed down. They broke out of the tall forest, into what had been a clearcut before the Change and had burned in a wildfire since; now it was spring meadow like a living carpet before the horses' feet. Tiphaine whistled and pointed for them to turn, and they rode upward, through grass high enough to brush the horsemen's stirrups, full of tall blue lupine and yellow western buttercup. The wind was in their faces, strong with the scent of the forests that rolled from here to the Pacific, when they came over the sharp crest of the hill and into the path of a herd of elk walking the other way.

Rudi and Mathilda whooped to see them, thirty or so big fawn-and-brown animals, and Delia clapped her hands. The crossbowmen whooped on another note, and began to unship their weapons as the herd milled for an instant, then turned and flowed away like a torrent of water downhill, squealing and barking as they went and showing the yellowish patch on their rumps.

"No," Tiphaine d'Ath said. "Not this time of year. They're mostly pregnant females, and skinny with winter. Wait until autumn, Alan, and I promise you some sport."

"There were a couple of nice fat yearling bucks and does, my lady," the corporal of the crossbowmen grumbled, but slung the weapon again. "There's nothing like fresh elk liver right out of the beast and onto a fire in the woods."

Tiphaine began to neck-rein her horse around, then suddenly stopped with her clenched right fist thrown up for a halt.

"Quiet!" she said sharply.

Everyone fell silent, the loudest sound a wet crunch as a horse bent its neck to tear off a mouthful, and the wind through the trees. Rudi closed his eyes and let his mind go quiet, with nothing to get in the way of his senses . . . something . . . no.

"Alan, did you hear anything just then?" she asked, her voice crisp. "A horse, maybe?"

"No, my liege," he said, shaking his head; he was an older man, a year or two past thirty, and a hunter in his spare time.

Tiphaine shrugged. "Maybe a cat walked over my grave." She grinned. "In which case I should have sneezed, not shivered."

They rode on through the meadow, and through more forest ranging from saplings to something near old growth, and then the glittering surface of the lake showed through the trees, hundreds of feet below. It was roughly a rectangle, running three miles from northwest to southeast, with tongues of water stretching into the hills that gave it the shape of a distorted gingerbread man. They had come seven miles at a gentle walk on the winding trails—Delia for one would have fallen off at anything faster—and it was a little before noon. Water glinted like hammered metal beneath them, save where the shadows of clouds drifted over the lake and turned the color intensely blue. They rode down to the water, where there was a recently repaired dock, a gazebo, and an aluminum canoe left upside-down beneath it. Mostly the shores were very steep, forested hills running straight into deep water.

"So, what'll we do first?" Rudi said happily. "Swim, fish?"

"Can I just *sit* for a while?" Delia said, rubbing her thighs in between unloading folding chairs and pillows. "Sit on something soft that doesn't move, that is. I don't see why you castle people like riding so much, my lady."

The soldiers grinned, but didn't say the things they usually would. Rudi was glad. He didn't mind bawdy humor even when he didn't see the point, and there was plenty of it back home, but here it had an edge he didn't like at all, or fully understand.

Tiphaine smiled slightly. "If we're going to swim, we should have a fire ready for when we get out. The water's cold."

They built one a little way up the shore—the soldiers and the varlet had to take turns going well away for their dip, and stand at a distance with their backs turned while Rudi and the others came up out of the water to warm themselves near the fire.

"Why?" Rudi asked, throwing off the towel and reaching for his clothes.

"Because they're men," Mathilda said.

"Well, so am I," Rudi said reasonably.

"No, you're a boy. It's all right until your voice breaks. And they're commoners, even if the warriors are Associates. We're nobles."

"I'm not," Rudi said. "Delia isn't either."

"Well, you're *sorta* like a noble—I mean, your mom's the Chief of the Mackenzies, right? That's like being a count or something, so you're a viscount."

"No, being Chief is *not* like being a count!" he said indig-nantly.

"I know. I *said* sorta like. And Delia can be here because she's a servant, and a girl."

"Oh. Weird," Rudi said. "You've got some really strange *geasa* here, Matti. And Delia's here to fish and swim and play with us, isn't she?"

"Oh, no, young lord," Delia said—grinning as she came out of the water and wrapped herself in a towel. "I wouldn't dream of doing anything so presumptuous."

"Insolent wench," Tiphaine said calmly, following her to the fire.

Rudi finished dressing and galloped his horse up and down the shore with Mathilda by him, then came back to the pier; they hobbled the mounts and threw a Frisbee around for a while before they got out fishing rods and folding chairs. Tiphaine was already there, with a fair-sized trout hanging in the water with a sharpened twig through its gills. The two cast their fly-lures out, and settled down to watch the water as the last shreds of morning mist burned off it, enjoying the *plop* of occasional fish jumping, the flight of wildfowl over the water and up into the steep green trees . . .

"So, this is fly-fishing," Delia said, after a few minutes. "When does something happen?"

"Something *is* happening," Tiphaine said from her recliner, making another cast. "We're fishing."

"It looks a lot like sitting staring at the water to me, my lady," she said. "We could do *that* at the millpond."

She got a book out of the picnic baskets and began reading aloud, pausing whenever anyone got a bite. Rudi pricked his ears with interest even though she stumbled over a word now and then; it was something like the older old-time stories, and there were even witches in it—though not good ones. And the names . . .

"Isn't that name a lot like yours, Lady d'Ath?"

"It's the same. When I was entered on the Association rolls I took a new one; a lot of people do that."

"People in the Clan do, too, when they're Initiated."

Tiphaine nodded. "And they had the same custom in the

Society, I think, except that back then they kept the old name too. Mine was . . . Collette, originally. We picked the new ones out of a hat."

"It's a pretty name, my lady," Delia said.

"Yes, Lady Sandra thought so. But the character named that in the book is totally lame; all she does is get raped by a bandit named Joris, have a baby—who eventually *kills* Joris when it grows up—and then get massacred by some peasants. I would have picked Herudis or better still Lys, but in the book Lys is a witch and that wouldn't be . . . prudent. I think those books would be on the Index if they weren't favorites of the consort; she even had them reprinted. She named half the younger set in the Household out of them, it's quite a fad."

"Shall I get the food ready?" Delia said, looking a little uneasy. "The fire's down to nice hot coals."

Rudi pitched in to help, ignoring the girl's objections when she tried to shoo him away; Mathilda looked a little guilty, and helped the men-at-arms clean the trout. Evidently anything to do with wild game was sufficiently noble, and Rudi got away with helping—just—because a picnic was like *field* cooking, which a warrior could do if servants were short.

Weird people, he thought again. *Work is work. Everyone has to work, or should, or how do things get done?*

The food was hamburgers in folds of waxed muslin, ready to be peeled off onto the grill, fresh pork sausages with sage and garlic, rolls and onions, a salad of pickled vegetables and early greens, and a honey cake with dried fruit and nuts in it. They added the trout, lightly brushed with butter, which was the best part of all, the flesh white and flaky and delicate. Bors—the senior man-at-arms—grinned at Rudi as he loaded a tray with food to take to his men.

"I'm glad it's Lady d'Ath who got the fief," he said. "Even though she's working us until we drop. I thought it was sort of funny, at first, you know, a woman as lord. But she's tough as nails, and she knows how to look after the troops—I know nobles who wouldn't have thought to bring anything along for the rest of us, or just cheese and bread. Maybe that's why they wanted the little princess here with her, to learn that sort of thing."

"A Chief or an Armsman has to look after the warriors first," Rudi said seriously. That was something all his teachers agreed on. "He should never rest or eat in the field before they do, or sleep warm and dry when they can't."

The soldier gave him a grave, approving nod. Rudi took his plate to sit beside Mathilda on the pier, looking out over the blue, unrestful water, where the wind cuffed white from the chop. He tucked in; the morning and the swim had given him an appetite, and some types of food always tasted better cooked over an open fire in wild country. After he'd satisfied the first pangs of hunger and was addressing a piece of cake he noticed . . . something.

What is it? he thought.

Tiphaine had been standing as she ate a hamburger, looked eastward towards the earth dam that held back the waters of Hag Lake, with a frown on her face. Rudi followed her gaze; there *were* a lot of ducks and geese taking to the sky there. Suddenly she flicked the remains of the food into the water and walked over to her courser, tightening the girths and slipping the bridle over its head.

"Bors!" she said, swinging into the saddle and reining around. "Fayard! Alan! Get everyone ready."

She set the horse at the upslope northward. Rudi felt a strumming inside, as if he were a string of the lute that lay abandoned by the lounger. The man-at-arms and the crossbowman did what they'd been told, with a quick, rough efficiency; Delia's eyes were wide with concern, and Mathilda's sparkled with excitement.

"What is it?" she said.

Rudi shook his head. Tiphaine had spurred up through a belt of light forest and out onto open meadow. That made her doll-tiny with nearly a mile's distance, and hard to see through the trees; he could see her coming back all right though, because she did it with reckless speed and casual skill. When she pulled up by the remnants of their fire her face had gone tight and hard, the ice gray eyes as blank as glass.

"Abandon the packhorses," she said calmly. "Armed men headed this way, a dozen of them, most of a *conroi*—lancers in Protectorate gear, moving fast. And they've got the covers still on their shields."

Bors swung into the saddle. "*All* lancers?" he said. "I'd have thought some crossbows would be a good idea, here, for support—it's a bit broken."

He didn't seem surprised; the Protectorate's nobility had their own internal feuds, and raid and skirmish weren't unknown by any means.

"Not if they're after the princess," Tiphaine said. "They wouldn't risk hurting her; the Lord Protector would keep anyone who did that alive—for months and months after they wanted to die. Now let's see what we can do about getting her away."

The man-at-arms grinned; Rudi could see a little fear in his eyes, but it was way back. "I knew life would get less boring once you took over, my lady."

Astrid of the Dúnedain held up her hand. "That's fighting," she said, as the small column stopped.

Alleyne's head turned; his hearing was about as good as hers. The harsh, flat, unmusical clamor of steel on steel carried a long way; the banging of sword on shield nearly as much, with shouts and the screams of men in pain. It was difficult to tell exactly where the sound came from, except northward; the winding trail and the steep ridge on either side played tricks with sound, and so did the deep forest all about. They looked at each other and nodded, reaching for the helmets at their saddlebows.

This is too close to the place they're holding Rudi, she thought. *There are no coincidences.* And aloud: "Go!"

Rudi drew his bow and shot his last arrow. The shaft bounced off a man's helmet, and made him flick his head back instinctively. The impact wasn't enough to hurt, but it distracted him. . . .

With Tiphaine d'Ath before him, that was quite enough. The sword moved with a deceptive smoothness, darting out and back like the snap of a frog's tongue. A trail of red followed it through the air, and the man-at-arms staggered backward with his metal-backed gloves clapped to his face, dropping sword and shield. He fell and began to shriek as he rolled down the hill, the weight of his armor pulling him faster and faster until he struck a tree, grasping its roughness like a drowning man at sea, still pawing at his ruined eye. Then she was backing again as the other two pushed doggedly uphill, toiling, using their shields to hold her off. Metal on metal; she leapt backward and up, a broadsword hissing under her boot soles. . . .

"Here!" Mathilda cried. "I've got it spanned!"

Delia took a long breath and accepted the crossbow Norman Arminger's child had taken from beside the fallen Alan. It was heavy, too heavy and long for a child to aim, but the weaver's arms and shoulders were strong from long years at the loom and wheel. What made Rudi bare his teeth was the desperate clumsiness of her grip. In fact—

"Duck!" he yelled.

Tiphaine did, spinning aside from a thrust and out of the path of the bolt. The *tung* of the steel bow releasing was not over when the crack of impact sounded, and one of the enemy screamed a curse and threw his shield aside; the thick, heavy missile had gouged far enough into it to wound his left forearm.

"Oh, Goddess, I nearly shot her!" Delia moaned.

The mistress of Ath slid forward again, moving to her left into the man's now-shieldless side. He turned desperately to keep his face to her, but blocked his comrade at the same time. Their swords struck, sparked, slid down to lock at the guards. The dagger in her left hand punched up with the twisting drive of her arm and shoulder and hip behind it, the narrow point breaking the links of riveted mail under his short ribs. The man went to his knees and clutched at himself. She skipped back once more; the slope was more gentle now, flattening to the hilltop meadow. The last man-at-arms began a rush, then stopped and ducked back beneath his shield as he met the smile and glacier eyes and realized that the odds were now even. That made him slip, the long grass crushed into slippery pulp under his boot soles, holding him for an instant while he scrabbled for balance and his weight pinned the bottom edge of his kite-shaped shield into the dirt. Tiphaine bounced back with a long running lunge, and the point went home over the shield and into his face with a crackle of breaking bone and shattering teeth.

Rudi wheeled at Delia's scream. Another armored man had her, his left arm clamping her close behind his shield and the right holding the edge of a sword to her neck; he recognized the china blue eyes—Joris Stein. None of them had noticed his approach from the rear.

"Bravo, Tiph," he said as she freed her blade with a jerk and wheeled, poised in a perfect stance. "You're *good,* and I'd be the last man to deny it. Checkmate, though. This black-haired piece of peasant ass is your squeeze, isn't she? Can't fault your taste; she smells *fine.* It's true what they say; blonds like us have more fun."

Tiphaine straightened, flicking the sword and dagger to the sides, shedding a spatter of red from the blades; she was panting deep and slow, sweat and red blood running down her face, her own from a nick on one cheek mingling with sprays from others.

"I should have known," she said. "That was always your idea of misdirection; have somebody else grab them by the nose while you snuck up to corncob them."

"And you were always too subtle for your own good, Tiph. This time my approach worked, though, didn't it?"

"Not quite yet," she said. "What's the word, Joris?"

The knight's face moved; you could tell he was smiling behind the coif. "Simple. I'm here for the witch-brat, dead or alive—preferably alive. The Lord Protector wants him, and as a loyal vassal you'll hand him over, right? Do that and you get your fucktoy back intact. I think that's important to you, Tiph; you were always the sentimental type."

"Compared to you, I suppose I am . . . which is a judgment on both of us, when you think about it."

"And you get to keep the princess, so you don't look *too* bad."

"You've got a written decree?" she asked, her voice that cool water-flowing-on-rock tone again.

She walked towards him as she spoke, with her hands out to

either side and the blades pointing down, looking at him from beneath pale brows with eyes the color of ice at the edge of a winter pond. Each step was delicately precise. Calmly, she went on: "Somehow I don't think you do, seeing as you just pitched into us without warning, and I don't think those were Household regulars. Not unless Conrad's letting the standards slip."

"Of course there's nothing in writing. *And not one step closer.* I know exactly how far you can lunge, all right? We sparred often enough."

"Where *did* you get that *conroi* of so-called men-at-arms, though? Clown school?" she asked, halting, seemingly casual and relaxed.

Joris shrugged, and Delia took a sharp breath as the sharp edge dimpled the white skin of her throat. A tiny, slow trickle of blood started.

"They were the best I could get on short notice, for a job like this, who wouldn't ask too many questions. Still, they were good enough to soak up crossbow bolts. And now that you and your trusty vassals have conveniently killed them, I don't even have to split the money."

"Well, I *do* have an explicit order from the consort to keep Mathilda and Rudi here. Orders from *my* liege. Who's also yours, last time I looked."

Joris tensed, and his voice went from friendly conversational to a snarl for an instant: "You always got the plum jobs—she always favored you and Kat! It wasn't *right*!"

"Well, Joris, that was because she knew if a situation like this ever did come up, you'd be the one who'd rat her out for a higher offer."

"I suppose you can't be bought?" he spat.

"No, you're the one who can't be *bought,* Joris. That's the problem. You can only be *rented.* And she's not going to be happy with you for putting her daughter right in the middle of a running fight, either."

"That's why we didn't do any shooting."

"Oh, that'll make it *all right,* then."

"The Lord Protector's orders take precedence," the knight said, cheerful again. "Also, unless you hand the witch-brat over—I'll be leaving him to the Hounds, by the way, so the Lord Protector gets a pass from the missus—I'm going to cut your little bed-buddy's throat, and I don't think you're into necrophilia, right? Not really practical considering the anatomy."

"No, you're not going to do that, Joris," she said.

"Why not?"

"Because if you did kill her, you still wouldn't get the boy, and I'd kill *you* very slowly instead of quickly."

"I'll take my chances," Joris said. "I wouldn't like to face you on even terms, *Lady d'Ath*, I admit it. You're fucking unnatural in more ways than one. But me in full harness and you in that fancy riding outfit? Yeah, I like *those* odds. The armor and shield make up for the speed, and I've got you beat on strength and reach."

Mathilda spoke, her voice hot with anger. "You'd better let her go, Sir Joris."

The blue eyes flickered to her without the least particle of attention being diverted from Tiphaine. "This is a very bad woman, Princess," he said. "They both are. You'll understand when you're older."

The girl's temper overflowed and she stamped her foot, immediately regretting the gesture, face flushing brick red and burying her hands in her hair. "I'm *nine,* not *four,* you oaf—nearly ten! I'm old enough to remember your face and I'll see you broken on the wheel someday unless you *let her go*!"

Joris laughed, but there was the slightest edge of uncertainty in it. Rudi knew what he must do. He shouted as he ran in, and the bow was in his hands like a spear. Like a spear he thrust it up at the knight's face, aiming for his right eye. The response was automatic, when the shield was pinned immobile by the woman he held behind it; he cut backhanded at the threat to his face. The sword flicked out, the heavy blade moving with the blurring speed of a strong man's trained wrist and shoulder. It cracked through the tough yew and flashed within a fraction of an inch of Rudi's nose, even as the boy threw himself flat with a yell. That saved him, but it put him flat on his back as the longsword drew back to pin him to the ground like a butterfly on a board. What was left of the bow cracked uselessly against the shin-guard as he flailed it at the walking armored tower.

Skrinngg.

Tiphaine's sword came down across Rudi's body, like a slanting rafter. It bent under the impact of Joris' heavier blade, but the fine steel sprang back and the man's weapon buried itself in the dirt. Joris wrenched at it with desperate strength, and in the same instant used his shield in a slamming blow against her. That wasn't as effective as it might have been, with a suddenly screeching and madly clinging Delia on his arm, but Joris Stein was very strong. And with Tiphaine d'Ath at less than arm's reach he was striking for his life, as a man might lash out when he discovered an adder coiled under his pillow.

She had leapt headlong to cover Rudi's body, with no choice but to sacrifice balance. Now the double blow of shield and sword knocked her own blade from her hand, and sent her rolling half a dozen paces with Delia falling on her with a squawk.

Rudi lay on the ground, clutching as if it were his mother as well as the Mother. Black wings seemed to flap about him, gauzy as veils, more solid and vaster than worlds. A deep thudding came from the soil as the blade was wrenched free and rose to kill, like a great heart throbbing . . .

Crack!

The hooves would have killed an unarmored man. They hurt Joris Stein badly, even in the diamond instant of concentration, when every dream of fortune and rank seemed to be glittering just beyond the point of his sword. He dropped as the great black mare reared again, her forefeet milling like a deadly circle of steel war-hammers, bugling out her challenge. Curled beneath his shield he felt the frame crack and the tough plywood shatter as the pile-driver feet stamped downward with half a ton of bone and muscle behind them, the loops coming free of the inner surface as it broke.

"Epona!"

Rudi shouted it, a trumpet-call of rage and joy. The horse dropped to all fours and trotted over to him, and he threw his arms around her neck, lost in the grassy scent as she nuzzled him against her side.

Tiphaine leapt even as the horse attacked, landed rolling and came erect with her sword back in her hand; she whipped it through a quick figure eight as Joris rose. Rudi took two steps back, leapt himself, grasped the big horse's mane and pulled himself over her withers. And shouted for sheer exhilaration as he felt her move beneath him: "*Free! Free!*"

Joris Stein had his own sword; he shook his ruined shield free and drew his dagger with his left hand, wincing a little as he forced the wrenched muscles to work. He dropped into stance.

"You know," Tiphaine said in that cool voice as she walked forward, "I never liked you, Joris. And you've just come onto my land, slaughtered my vassals, threatened to cut my girl-friend's throat and tried to kill a little kid I was ordered to guard."

She smiled a slow, stark smile. "But hey, you know what they say—all's well that ends well."

"I'll see you rot in Hell!"

"Undoubtedly. But we won't meet there today, I think. Usually it's just business, but I'm going to *enjoy* this. Let's get it on."

"Go, Epona, go!" Rudi called. "Find them!"

Astrid Larsson trotted up the hill. The wreckage of the fight was on either side; men dead, men wounded and moaning or trying to patch their injuries. A trained eye could see how it had gone—the charge, the volley of crossbow bolts and then the savage running scrimmage up the winding pathway, the defenders falling one by one. For the last fifty yards it had been *one* defender, and her eyes went a little wide as she read the evidence of scuffed soil, bodies, sprays of blood on the trunks of the thinly scattered Douglas firs, a sword left where a desperate dying stroke had driven it into a trunk as deep as the blood-channel down the middle of the blade. The heavy iron scent of slaughter was as familiar as the sap and musty scuffed earth and duff of the forest floor. Eilir pointed with the tip of her bow, moving from one sign to another, and John Hordle's lips shaped a low whistle.

Then Astrid's head snapped up at the rapid thudding of hooves. It was very steep here for a horse, even one as agile as her Asfaloth or her soul-sister's Celebroch; that was why they'd dismounted a ways back. Alleyne gave a shout of exultation as Epona halted and pawed the earth with one hoof, but the face of the titian-haired boy on her back was strained and set.

"Follow me," he said. "Quickly!"

"Wait—" Astrid said, but the big horse turned in place, graceful as a cat, and plunged away back uphill.

The four looked at each other. The rest of the Dúnedain were beating the woods all around . . . and there was no choice at all. They bent their heads and ran up the forty-degree slope, banishing exhaustion by an act of will. The trees thinned still more, turning to an open meadow that tilted from steep hillside to sloping plateau, blue distance opening around them as they passed from the shadows of the trees into knee-high grass starred with flowers and dotted with prickly Oregon grape. There were more dead men, more wounded, and two figures that still fought—one in armor, the other in white linen and black leather, with pale hair swirling around her shoulders. As the Dúnedain approached the armored man reeled back, his sword turning circles in the air as it flew away from a wrist half severed by a drawing cut.

The blond woman's sword moved with a speed that only those themselves experts could follow. The man screamed and screamed again.

"That's for finking out Lady Sandra," Tiphaine d'Ath said in a panting snarl as she struck in a blurring flurry, every blow lethal but none instantly so. "*That's* for risking the princess. *That's* for trying to kill Rudi. *That's* for hurting my girl, you son of a bitch!"

The man tottered and fell to his knees, moaning and clutching at his wrist.

"And *this* is for the character in that stupid fucking book!"

He tried to scream once more, but the sword transfix-

ing his throat through leather and mail had cut the voice
box, and his eyes alone spoke as the blood swelled
through his mouth and clenched teeth in a growing tide.
When the blade withdrew with a twist he fell and beat his
mail gauntlets on the ground for an instant, then slumped
limp. Grass and blue lupine waved in to hide most of the
metal-clad shape.

Tiphaine d'Ath, Astrid thought, and felt herself smile as she
raised her bow. *Rudi back with us and you here to kill. This is
a good day!*

The Association warrior stood and let her breathing slow,
eyes flicking from face to grim-held face, seeing implacable
Fate in each. Then she spread her arms, sword and dagger held
loosely, the spring breeze flicking wet elflocks of her pale hair
around her face.

"It's a good day to die," she said, preparing for a final leap.

"No!"

A girl Astrid didn't recognize sprang in front of Tiphaine,
trying to cover her body with her own; she was full-grown
but younger than Astrid herself by a few years, wide blue
eyes desperate, long black hair falling past her shoulders.

"No, don't hurt her!" The girl's hands moved in signs. "I'm
with the Coven, you've got to listen to me—don't hurt her!"

The drawn bows remained unwavering; at this range any of
them could shoot past without injuring anyone but their target. Astrid's eyes flicked to Eilir, and she nodded—the claim
was true, then. That didn't mean they shouldn't dispose of so
dangerous an enemy, of course.

"She saved Rudi's life!" the young woman went on.

"She did," Rudi said, calming Epona with a hand down her
neck. "Twice."

Mathilda nodded vigorously, laying down a crossbow far
too big for her. "She did! Joris was going to kill him! Tiphaine
jumped and got her sword between them and Joris missed,
but then he nearly killed her too."

That's different, Astrid thought as Tiphaine urged the black-
haired girl aside.

"Go see to the princess, sweetie," the noble said to her.
"These people and I have unfinished business."

Astrid closed her eyes for an instant. *Threefold,* she thought with a sigh of regret, and lowered her bow. The others did as well, Hordle with a low almost-grumble of protest and a roll of his eyes.

"Tiphaine d'Ath," the Lady of the Dúnedain said. "I owe you nothing for your friend Katrina's death; that was honest war. But we do stand greatly in your debt for saving Rudi. Take a life for a life then, and count us quits. I am not eager to deal out death in judgment."

Their eyes met for a long instant, ice gray to silver-blue. Then the Protectorate noble shrugged; she drew her sword blade through a cloth and sheathed it.

"You can't have the princess back," she said carefully. "Not while I'm alive to guard her."

"We don't want her. Lady Juniper's orders are to leave her in her mother's care. You're not in a position to make conditions, though, are you?"

The other's lips quirked a little. "Oh, I was going to challenge you to single combat. Now, *that* would have been interesting."

"Yes . . ." Astrid said, with a momentary pang. *Like Éowyn and the Lord of the Nazgûl before the walls of Gondor.* "Except that I wouldn't have accepted. Duty would forbid."

"With its shrill, unpleasant voice." Tiphaine bowed her head slightly and sighed. "It's time to let Kat's ghost go, I suppose. Take the brat, then. He's a good kid, but sort of spooky . . . and that horse is worse. And a favor for a favor; you'd better hurry. I got one of my men out before the fight started, and there'll be a rescue party heading this way fast."

The Dúnedain nodded, and silently turned to go. Rudi took his hat off and waved it at Mathilda. "See you, Matti!" he called, and then whooped as the great horse pirouetted and followed.

As the hooves faded in the distance Tiphaine took a deep breath, suddenly conscious of how distant shrieks of pain cut through birdsong and the sough of wind through forest and meadow. Some of them would be her men, and the others should be given mercy.

"We'd better get to work," she said, turning towards the head of the trail. "We might be able to save some of the wounded; Joris and his merry band didn't have time to finish them."

Mathilda nodded, standing silent and forlorn, staring after the path Rudi and his rescuers had taken. Delia cried silently into her hands.

"Hey, sweetie, come on," Tiphaine said, touching her on the shoulder, urging her forward. A hug wasn't really practical, considering what coated her hands and face and much of her body. "Work to do."

Delia looked up. "I told them all about the castle, and where Rudi was—"

"Yeah, but they weren't the ones who tried to kill us and him, were they?"

"I betrayed you!"

"Funny, I could have sworn you just now jumped between me and four drawn bows," Tiphaine said gently. "And you stayed, when you could have gone with them. Just don't deliver any intelligence reports on me in future, OK?"

"I'm . . . I'm a witch."

"I won't tell Father Peter if you don't."

A curled trumpet sounded through the hills from the north, a harsh urgent scream: *We're coming! We're coming!*

"Good," Tiphaine murmured. "They'll have medical supplies and a doctor with them."

And soon Joris' head will be off to Castle Todenangst pickled in a tub, with a report nailed to it which ought to cover my ass fairly thoroughly at court unless the Lord Protector wants to break with Sandra, which I doubt. And Rudi's going back home, probably Mathilda too, and the war will start again after harvest, but there's the summer to live through first. And for the first time in a while, I'm actually looking forward to that.

"You're not angry? You don't want to punish me?" Delia said doubtfully.

Tiphaine grinned, tired and triumphant. *And most of all, I'm still alive.*

"Well, if you *insist,* I could spank you a little," she said.

And administered a gunshot slap to the appropriate location. Delia yelped and leapt, startled back into functionality.

"Come on. Get that cloak and start cutting it into strips."

CHAPTER TWENTY-ONE

"Last one!" Michael Havel yelled through a mouth dry and gummy and far too full of chaff.

He turned with the wheat sheaf on the long, slender tines of the pitchfork and did what had given the implement its name originally, pitching the thirty-pound weight of grain and straw up onto the canvas conveyor belt, heads-first. The air around the machine was full of dust and powdered chaff, the harsh dry smell of it, and of the canola oil used to grease the metal parts.

Then he stepped back and stretched, feeling the good-tired sensation of hard-worked muscles, leaning on the six-foot shaft of the fork, blinking at the sun—it was still six hours to sunset, and they'd gotten a lot done today.

And it's a relief to do something besides another *round of practice with the saddle-bow or that goddamned lance.*

Off twenty feet to his right six hitch of horses walked in a circle, pulling a long bar behind them. That turned the upright driveshaft on its deep-driven socket base, and the big flywheel attached to it; a great leather belt stretched off to another on the side of the threshing machine in front of him. Six yards of engine rattled and clanked and groaned on its truck-wheel mounting, giving off a mealy scent of grain and hot metal. The sheaves disappeared up the conveyor belt. Chaff and straw came out one long spout pitched high towards the top of the great golden mound of it already there. Threshed grain poured out of another, into coarse burlap sacks that turned plump and tight as they filled. Teams labored there in disciplined unison; some dragged the full sacks aside, some sewed them shut with curved six-inch needles and heavy hemp twine; others shouldered the sixty-pound bags and ran to heave them into wagons for the horses to haul away towards the granaries.

One month's bread for an adult in every sack, Havel thought with satisfaction, scraping sweat off his forehead with a thumb and flicking it at the yellow stubble underfoot. *All nicely stowed away where nobody but us can get at it.*

Signe was working there, the needle flashing as she fastened a sack with a neat, tight stitch, and the muscles moving like flat straps in her arms. Threshing was dirty work; bits of chaff and awn flew through the air like thick dust. There were two currents of thought on how to handle it, besides the kerchiefs most kept over their mouths. Some bundled up, and endured what got beneath layers of clothes and chafed; that also made the heat worse, of course, and it was near ninety today—very hot for the Willamette Valley, though he could swear the weather had warmed up a bit since the Change. Havel's wife followed the minimal-clothing-frequent-washing-down school, and was wearing an ancient pair of faded cutoffs and a halter, her skin tanned honey-brown, the curve of her full breasts and her strong shoulders liberally specked with chaff and bits of straw sticking to the sweat, her eyes turquoise gems in the sweat-streaked mask of her face. She caught his eye on her and looked up, grinned, touched the tip of her tongue to her upper lip in promise, then darted forward to claim the last sack.

I'm not the only one looking, he thought happily; the male who didn't give Signe Havel a second glace was either very gay, or nearly dead. *But I* am *the one who gets to sleep with her tonight.*

A cheer went up all across the great sloping field as the threshing machine's tone changed, and the last grain slid out of the spout in a dying trickle. This was the Larsdalen home-farm—he could see the vineyards start where the land rolled upward a bit west and, just barely, the towers of the gate over some trees in the distance; hills swelled upward on either side, and the Coast Range showed along the edge of sight. Most of the people working this stretch of land dwelt behind the wall there; they'd just harvested a good bit of what they'd eat over the next year as bread and biscuits and pie crusts and beer. There were dozens of them, too, even Aaron Rothman and a helper over there under the infirmary tent, dealing with the cuts and bruises and sprains that went with farming.

Sorta complimentary that his boyfriends always look like me, Havel thought, watching a black-haired young man carefully opening an autoclave that sat over a small, hot fire and handing the instruments within to the doctor. *Weird, but complimentary.*

The Family was out in force well: Ken Larsson here with a couple of his apprentices, keeping the machinery in working order; Eric over there keeping the horses going . . .

His daughter Ritva came up with a ladle of water. Havel rinsed out his mouth, spat, coughed, spat again, then drank three dippers-full and poured one over his head.

"Oh, to hell with it," he said, and took the bucket from her sister Mary and upended it over himself, glorying in the way the wash of coolness spread across his bare torso; he was stripped to the waist save for the checked neckerchief.

On the whole, life is pretty damn good.

The girls laughed and ran back towards the water cart. Other children helped with that, or keeping birds off the grain; ones a bit younger just ran around shouting with the dogs, or minded the toddlers and infants lying on blankets in the shade of the trees along the road. A mist of dust lay above the road's gravel, as more loaded wagons headed up the gentle slope towards Larsdalen. Still more folk busied themselves with cooking over open fires and portable grills, and setting up the long trestle tables; as Eric shouted *whoa* and the big draught-horses stopped a waft came from there, smelling of roasting meat and French fries in oil, and loaves and pies brought down hot from the Larsdalen ovens and cooling on racks covered in muslin. There were big tubs of sweet corn boiling, too. That was one of his favorite foods and a rare seasonal treat, hard to grow to seed in this land of mild summers, and his mouth watered at the thought of it. Someone tossed him a peach, and he bit into it, letting the juice run down his corded neck. There was a creek across the road and the field there, too. They'd all go and splash themselves clean before they sat down to dinner.

Hello, Grandpa, he thought; his grandfather Väinö had bummed around as a teenager back just before Pearl Harbor, working harvest gangs in the Dakotas and Minnesota, a few years before combines completely replaced older methods. *This is a lot like the stories you used to tell—except no steam traction engine to run the thresher, of course.*

A ripple went through the crowd. Havel's head came up as well, and his eyes flicked towards where the weapons were stacked. But it was a single rider coming down the road from the east, the white road smoking behind the galloping hooves. He swerved and took the fence, a young man in mail vest and helmet, a Bearkiller scout-courier.

"Lord Bear!" he said, pulling up in a spurt of clods and dust. "Dispatch!"

Havel sighed, reversed the pitchfork and stuck it in the dirt, and took the envelope. When he looked up from reading it he saw three dozen sets of eyes on him, amid an echoing silence where the *Chi-KA-go!* of a flock of quail was the loudest sound.

"All right, folks," he said. "We're in for a fight, but we knew that was coming. Arminger has called up his men, *ban* and *arrière-ban,* with the rally-point as Castle Todenangst, for no later than two weeks from now. So there's no reason at all not to enjoy the supper . . . but first, I'm going for a swim."

Dun Laurel, Willamette Valley, Oregon
August 23rd, 2008/Change Year 10

Dun Laurel was the newest of the Clan's duns, a village of a hundred and twenty souls surrounded by a ditch and palisade, northwest of Sutterdown and established only last year. The Hall at the center of it was a smaller copy of Dun Juniper's, done in frame and plank rather than logs, but it also had a conference-room-cum-office on the loft floor, with a hearth and altar on the northern wall. It still smelled of sap from new-cut wood, as well as the bunches of rosemary and lavender and sweetgrass hanging from the rafters overhead, and the alcohol lanterns showed only a beginning made on the carved and painted decorations Mackenzies loved. The location near the northwestern edge of the Clan's settled lands, and the relative newness, made it the best place for Lady Juniper to meet the delegates from the Protector's territory. The sun had set, and they would leave before it rose, slipping back into the tangled scrub and tall grass with Mackenzie or Ranger guides.

The dozen men and women sitting across from her and her allies were all free-tenants or itinerants back home; it was simply too difficult for bond-tenants or peons to move around. Several were High Priests and Priestesses of clandestine covens; medieval Europe might not have had an underground cult of witches except in the perverted imaginations of the witch-finders, but the Protector's realm most certainly *did*. Others were simply those who were willing to take risks to get out from under the Association's gang-boss feudalism. All of the farmer majority were from the eastern side of the Valley, Molalla and Gervais and the others; the baronies north of the Columbia or west of the Willamette were simply too far away, and had had too little contact with the Clan.

They were serious people; eight men, four women, all fairly well clad and well fed, but roughened and weatherworn by lives of hard outdoor work, and all over thirty though few were much older than her; the terrible years hadn't been kind to the elderly, or even the middle-aged. Juniper looked from face to face before she spoke: "Our sympathy you have—but sympathy is worth its weight in gold. I'm troubled, to be frank. On the one hand, now we face the full weight of the Portland Protective Association. Corvallis is with us this time, as well as the Bearkillers and Mount Angel, and we can match their numbers, but that is mostly ordinary folk against professional killers. If you were to rise behind them, our chances of victory would be greatly increased, but I must tell you frankly that there is not much hope of our defeating the Protectorate so thoroughly that they will be overthrown at home, at least not most of them. That *could* happen, but it is not likely. Our realistic hope is to beat them so badly that they will leave us alone."

The underground leaders looked at each other. Their spokesman was an itinerant, one Rogelio Maldonado, a dark man with a red bandana tied around his hair and the raggedy-gaudy clothes that folk in his trade affected. His English held only a slight Hispanic lilt.

"Lady Juniper, for what other reason than winning our freedom would we rise? We wish you well, we hope you win, but if we fight, it will be for ourselves and our families. I speak for all of us, not just those who follow the Old Religion, who have a special tie to you. But even they . . ."

Juniper inclined her head. *What reason indeed?* she thought. There were times when the things she had to do as Chief troubled her sleep, but her responsibility was to her Clan . . . though also to right, and the Threefold Law.

"If this is not a wonderful or a certain chance of overthrowing the Association, it is still the best you are likely to have. They have stripped the garrisons of every castle to the bone."

Maldonado nodded in his turn; his thick-fingered hands, calloused and marked with burn scars, spread on the polished wood of a tabletop salvaged from a government office in Salem, the hands of a man who handled reins and rope, awl and waxed thread and solder. The frieze of carved ravens around the edge of the table was new, not very well carved but done with naive forcefulness.

"There is the word, Lady Juniper: castles. We might drive the soldiers and men-at-arms left behind after the *arrière-ban* back into the castles, they are few and not the best fighters, but we cannot *take* the castles. In the castle granaries is the harvest, and the seed grain. We will starve before they do, as it was in the days right after the Change, when Arminger held the grain elevators and cargo ships, and used the food as a whip to force submission. That is what made us obey him in the first place, as much as his fighting men. And that is without the field army ever returning . . . which you say it will?"

"Some of it," Juniper said. "Even if we break them."

"We thank you for smuggling us weapons, but still, we cannot face armored men-at-arms in open country as you can."

Juniper nodded. "No. But if you control the ground *outside* the castles, even for only a short time, many of you could flee. We are willing to take in thousands, the Bearkillers likewise and Corvallis even more. Our harvest was good, and there is land here—and more southward, towards Eugene—fine land lying empty and waiting to be tilled."

Another of the would-be rebels spoke, a thickset farmer with a gray beard: "That's wild land, grown up in bush. And if we run, we can't bring much in the way of seed or stock or tools with us, damn-all but what's on our backs. It would take us years to make farms, and more years to earn what we'd need to *start,* and we'd be laborers until then, maybe all our lives. Like peons."

"No," Juniper said. "You would be free—a man can be poor, and yet free. Or possibly, if we damage them badly, you can force the Association members to give you better terms at home."

She lifted a hand. "I am not saying this is very likely, or that fleeing your homes is not a counsel of desperation."

Those old enough to remember the times before the Change also remember the dying times just after it, she thought. She did herself, and the early Clan had been far more fortunate than most. *They remember the bandits and the Eaters, and the raw terror of starvation. On the other hand . . .*

"In another ten years, or twenty, doing *anything* will be much harder," she said.

They nodded. The farmer stroked his beard. "Yeah. My own grown kids hate the castle-folk, right enough. But they don't . . . the old world isn't *real* to them; they get bits from movies or TV confused with what really happened, Captain Kirk with President Clinton, and things like elections aren't even fairy tales. They don't hate them the *way* I do. And the bastards don't let us have schools. I try to teach the kids in the evenings, but it isn't the same."

Juniper sighed. "I can only ask for your help, not require it," she said. "You must consult your hearts and each other."

A woman with burning eyes spoke: "My village *will* rise, as soon as we hear the knightboys've marched. We're just not going to put up with it any more! Rapes, beatings, never enough to eat, working every day until we drop down with exhaustion! They don't even obey their *own* laws, and those are bad enough!"

"Mine *won't* rise," another said. "We . . . I remember my youngest dying in the first Change Year, and sneaking away to bury her so nobody would dig the body up to *eat* it. Things are bad but my children are alive . . . and I have a grandkid born this year."

"We've got to work together!"

"We *can't* work together, not when we've got to sneak around, and . . . well, you know as well as I do. Some people tell the Associates things—or the priests, it's the same thing."

"Please!" Juniper said, and the budding argument died. "As I said, it's your decision. We will try to give as much help as we can, whatever you decide to do."

Astrid exchanged a few words with Eilir in Sign, then spoke herself: "We Dúnedain Rangers will help smuggle more arms to those who wish them. We moved much captured equipment from Mount Angel up into the hills after the battle there this spring. If you want it, talk to us afterwards—individually, to reduce risks. And we're too few to be of much use in the great battles, so we'll be able to send small parties north to guide fugitives, and do as much as we can to protect them. We've done that before, on a small scale. Perhaps we can do it now on a greater one."

Juniper leaned back and let the talk proceed. Her gaze stole to the altar, and the figures there; the Mother was a simple, stylized shape in a blue robe, but the Lord was shown with Coyote's grinning face. She closed her eyes a moment in prayer; wishing for the cunning of the one, and the compassion of the other.

Because I must lead all my people out to war, she thought. *Help me!*

Somewhere out in the burgeoning wilderness beyond Dun Laurel's walls and fields, a coyote howled in truth . . . or was it a wolf?

Castle Todenangst, Willamette Valley, Oregon
August 30th, 2008/Change Year 10

Norman Arminger looked down from the Dark Tower and smiled with pride at the iron might his word had called into being. He knew he must be doll-tiny on the balcony to the vast host stretching along the east-west roadway to the north of the castle, but the roar of sound that greeted his upraised fist was stunning even at this distance. Blocks of gray-mailed troops stretched to either side across the rolling countryside, a long glitter of summer morning sun on their spears and lanceheads, flashing from the colors of banners and painted shields, blinking as bright on the river behind them as it did on edged metal. The surging wash of voices gradually focused into a chant rippling across miles: *"War! War! WAR! WAR!"*

The smile was still on his face as he turned from the little balcony and into the War Council's chamber. Armored nobles and officers waited around the great teak map table, helms under their arms or on the wood as they looked down, memorizing the last details of their tasks. The black-mailed knights of his personal guard stood around the walls of the big semicircular room, motionless as ever. And the Grand Constable was stuffing some papers into a leather pouch.

All but the guards turned towards him and bowed; he waved a hand in permission, and the groups began to break up and file out. Renfrew waited for the last.

"We're about as ready as we could be," he said when they were alone except for the guards. "Ninety-two hundred of our own men, twelve hundred from the Duchy of Pendleton, and a siege train that'll make any wall sit up and take notice ... except Mount Angel, of course; we'll have to starve that out."

"Glad to see you happy about it, Conrad," Arminger said jovially.

"I'm not, my lord Protector; any victory will be at heavy cost. But if we're going to do it, this is the way to do it. They'll have about our numbers, with the contingent Corvallis sent, but our men are superior in a stand-up fight, in my opinion. If we break their main army, it'll split up—it's a coalition, an alliance. Then we can reduce them one by one."

"Exactly," Arminger said, thumping him on one mail-clad shoulder; it was like whacking a balk of seasoned hardwood.

"There is one thing," Renfrew went on, and Arminger felt his smile die a little. "We've been receiving reports of internal disorder. Attacks on supply wagons, even a few cases of arson—tithe barns and manors torched in the night. Perhaps some of the light cavalry—"

"Conrad, Conrad, that's why we build all those castles— even if they're ferroconcrete instead of real stone. Nothing a few farmers or *Rangers* can do can really hurt us. You were the one talking about concentration of force. I'm not going to detach any troops until we've beaten the main enemy army and laid Mount Angel under tight siege."

"Yes, my lord Protector. That was the strategy I called for this spring."

The shaven head bent and the hideously scarred face was hidden for a moment. One thing he'd always found a little irritating was how the white keloid masses made it hard to read the Grand Constable's expressions, and his voice was very controlled. They were silent save for the rustle and clink of their armor as they walked over to the elevators.

Arminger grinned to himself as the operator cranked the doors closed and pulled the cord that ran through floor and ceiling, ringing bells far below where convicts waited in a giant circular treadmill. The lurch and then the smooth counterweighted descent were like something out of the old world. His amusement was at a memory; the first time he'd ridden the elevator, Sandra had concealed a couple of musicians on the roof over his head and had them do a creditable imitation of elevator music from pre-Change days, Glen Campbell's "Wichita Lineman." He'd nearly jumped out of his skin. . . .

Renfrew snorted laughter when he mentioned it, though of course he'd been in on the joke beforehand.

"It's the look on your face I'm remembering, Norman," he said.

The exit was in the ground-floor chamber, a great circular space used for dances and speeches, cocktail parties and meetings of the House of Peers, with the Eye set into the floor in mosaic. Today it echoed to the tramp of the guards as they fell in and followed him out onto the broad semicircle of steps facing the inner courtyard. The castle staff drawn up there cheered him; Pope Leo and the clergy were down at the castle's main gate, waiting for *their* moment, smells and bells at the ready. What halted him was Sandra in her light cart, and the closed four-horse carriage that would take Mathilda away for the duration.

She left her mother's side and began to run to him, then stopped and came on at a pace of stately dignity. Arminger composed his face to the same solemnity, hiding the burst of pride he felt. *My little girl's growing up,* he thought. *Soon she'll be a great lady, another Eleanor . . . or Mathilda.* That thought was prideful itself, but a little painful as well; soon she wouldn't be a little girl, either, and that perfect trust would be gone.

Mathilda went down formally on one knee for an instant, taking his hand and kissing it. "God give you victory, my lord father," she said; but she kept hold of the hand as she rose, and walked at his side as he came over to her mother.

Who may be a little irrational wanting to send Mathilda farther from the fighting than Castle Todenangst; this is the strongest hold in the realm, he thought. He looked into the brown eyes of his wife, as always seeming secretly amused. *On the other hand, maybe she isn't. Best to trust Sandra's instincts.*

He shoved aside the memory of a time a few months ago when he *hadn't* trusted her instincts. That had been a screwup . . . and the sight of the Baronet d'Ath heading the escort that would take his daughter west brought those memories forcibly back. Perhaps Sandra had made that appointment to rub his face in it . . . but he'd earned a little of that. And Ath was sufficiently distant to be away from the main action in this war, which would be on the eastern side of the Valley, and its seigneur could be trusted not to take too much advantage of having the heir to the Protectorate behind her drawbridge.

Unlike, for example, Alexi. Or Jabar, who still cherishes hopes for his son I've decided to frustrate.

"Lady d'Ath," he said, as she too knelt and kissed his hand. Like all her gestures, it was impeccably smooth. "We give you a great trust. It is good of you to volunteer for it, sacrificing glory and advancement in this war for the benefit of the Association."

Her smile surprised him a little. "Caring for the princess is a pleasure, not a duty, my lord Protector," she said; her voice wasn't quite the cool falling-water sound he remembered from past years; it had more resonance in it, somehow. "And I'm content with the good estate you've given me. Let others have their chance at glory and reward now. I've taken a new motto for my House of Ath: *What I have, I hold.*"

He nodded, beginning to turn away.

Conrad spoke: "I wish we had your *menie* with us, d'Ath. They've improved drastically since you took the fief."

"Despite the losses," Sandra cut in; yes, she was needling him a bit.

"Dad, Mom, why can't I come along too?" Mathilda said suddenly. "Mom's going. With Lady Tiphaine to guard me, I'd be safe behind the army. If I'm going to . . . I'm going to have to go to war, someday, right?"

Arminger laughed aloud, and repressed an impulse to tousle the reddish-brown hair above the fearless hazel eyes.

"Yes, you will, Mathilda, but not quite yet. For now, you have to do as your mother and I say. And when I win this war, I'll bring you back the world for a toy!"

Her stiff decorum broke for a moment, and she threw her arms around his armored chest. "Just bring yourself back, Daddy!"

CHAPTER TWENTY-TWO

Field of the Cloth of Gold, Willamette Valley, Oregon
September 3rd, 2008/Change Year 10

"Folks, we got a problem," Mike Havel said. "We've got
to step back and look at the bigger picture instead of getting
caught up in the details."

He looked around the table under the awning. Abbot
Dmwoski was silently telling his beads. Apart from that, the
leaders were looking at him with nothing more than a raised
eyebrow or two; none of them were what you'd call the nervous sort.

"Well, we've got a murtherin' great battle to win," Sam
Aylward said after a moment.

"No, that's not it. We've got a great murdering battle to
fight, and *that's* the problem."

Havel took a deep breath and pointed northward, across
the rolling plain, blond stubblefields and pasture drowsing
under the August sun, the stems of the cut wheat glittering in
a manner that had already given the former Elliot Prairie
north of Mount Angel its nickname with the thousands assembled there. The enemy encampment was just on the edge
of sight; mounted scouts from both sides patrolled the empty
fields between, adding their mite of dust to the smells of dirt
and not-very-clean bodies, frying onions and hay and sweating horses, smoke and leather, sun-heated canvas and oil and
metal. He waved aside some flies; no way to avoid them, with
so much livestock in one spot.

"Arminger's *there,* with just over ten thousand men. We're *here,* with just over ten thousand too."

He pointed skyward. "He's got aerial recon, and we don't, so we're not going to turn somersaults and come down on both his flanks at once; this army doesn't have enough unit articulation or triple-C to do that sort of thing anyway. This is going to be a slugging match, toe-to-toe, last man standing wins. We've got more infantry and it's better, but he's still got about twenty-five hundred knights and men-at-arms, plus the light horse, and they outnumber our cavalry by six, seven to one. So we're talking our pikemen . . . and pikewomen . . . walking forward with a rain of napalm bombs landing on their heads, to say nothing of the dartcasters and crossbows, and then facing the men-at-arms."

"We've beaten his cavalry before," Eric Larsson said defensively.

"Yeah, brother-in-law of mine, we have, when we managed to make him or whatever goon was in charge do something spectacularly stupid. Or when they underestimated what riding forward into an arrowstorm from our Mackenzie friends was like. That's not going to happen here; for one thing, Renfrew's in charge of that army and he's not stupid. The monks and the Clan made him retreat last time, but nobody's ever managed to sucker punch him. All Arminger has to do is walk up to us and start hitting us with a hammer, and he's a pretty good hammer-hammer general; Conrad Renfrew's better."

He drew in another breath. "I figure if we *win,* we're going to be real lucky to leave here with six thousand people still breathing—and a lot of those'll be crippled for life, burned, legs and arms ending up on a pile outside a surgeon's tent. If we lose . . ."

Havel shrugged and smiled his crooked smile. "Well, we don't have to do a count on that because we will be so totally fucked it isn't fucking funny."

Dmwoski frowned, but nodded. Nigel Loring snorted, but did likewise. "You have some idea, my Lord Bear," he said in that excruciatingly cultured English voice.

It went a little oddly with the kilt and plaid he was wearing today; that was probably a lot more comfortable than the armor most of the rest were in.

Havel nodded gravely and answered: "Yeah, I do. A lot of those barons and knights out there would rather be home, fighting the Jacks . . . why were they called Jacks? Never mind. They've got an uprising behind them and from what the Dúnedain say it's getting worse every day. The only reason they're not completely baboon-ass about it is because their families are in nice safe castles, but they're spooked. They want to fight us and get it over with and go home and unload some whup-ass on the revolting peasants. What's holding them here? Norman Arminger, is who. He's bossed them so long they can't imagine not obeying him, not really."

"You're saying that Arminger is the *Association's* weakness," Alleyne Loring said thoughtfully.

"Yup. He's what makes it an offensive force instead of a bunch of quarreling gangbangers in armor with delusions of chivalry. Remove him—"

"Sandra Arminger is smarter than her husband," Juniper objected.

"And Conrad Renfrew is a better general," Signe said.

"Yes. But *neither of them is the Lord Protector*. He's the one with the . . ."

He hesitated, looking for a word, and Nigel Loring smoothed his mustache with one finger. "The *baraka,* the charisma. He's their founder. Their creator, in a way. You think we should assassinate him, then?"

The Englishman looked at his son, at John Hordle, at Eilir and Astrid sitting as leaders of the Dúnedain Rangers.

"Oh, God, no. Not an assassination. Sticking a knife in his back would be the one thing that would rally them all behind Sandra as Regent and Renfrew as warlord; they'd rule with Arminger's ghost as their false front, which would be just like fighting him only without the hang-ups that cripple him."

"Ah," Juniper said, her green eyes going wider. "You want to kill his *myth,* not just the man. I should have thought of that. It's hidden depths you have, Mike. But how?"

"Bingo, Juney. As to how . . . so, we're agreed he's *their* weakness. Now, what's *Arminger's* big weakness?"

"Sweet young girls?" someone said, and there was a chuckle.

Havel smiled himself, but shook his head. "Norman Arminger's big problem is that inside the big bad warlord is a suburban geek weenie," he said. "I thought so when I first met him a bit more than ten years ago—he reminded me of a D&D freak and would-be badass whose nose I broke behind the bleachers in high school. When his inner pimply geek takes over, he's the dumbest really smart man you'll meet in many a long mile."

He nodded at a banner standing in the rear of the pavilion, captured during the last week's skirmishing, the black-and-scarlet folds hanging limp.

"I mean, the *Eye of Sauron*? The *Dark* Tower? Give me a break! Look at the way he took the Association's setup out of his favorite books—and I mean the storybooks, too, not just the history ones he'd claim he used. He didn't put in all that pseudo-medieval Camelot-from-Hell crap because it was a useful way to build his power; you can tell because he put in the parts that weaken him, too, not just what he needed to please the Society types. He put it in because deep inside the warlord is the professor and deep inside *him* is the pimple-popper who thought Knights in Armor were *so* cool. The same guy who couldn't get a date until his freshman year and hated all the girls who turned him down, so he still likes raping teenagers; every new victim is revenge on the ones who laughed at him and his hard-on. And so the Association he's built has one great big juicy weakness we can exploit—a way we can make him walk with open eyes into a trap, because if he doesn't the cracks he engineered into his own system would split it wide open. He can't change it now, not now that it's had time to set, not overnight."

His eyes went to the bear-topped helm standing with his armor on its rack. "That's the problem with calling in a myth. It may start out as an obedient little doggie, but pretty soon you've got the wolf by the ears."

"What precisely are you saying now?" Juniper asked; Signe's eyes were wide with the same alarm.

Mike Havel smiled a hungry smile.

*   *   *

"My lord Protector, an enemy envoy under a white pennant wishes to speak with you," the knight said. "It's a man of high rank."

Norman Arminger looked up from the map table and finished his coffee; unlike most he preferred it just on the hot side of lukewarm and always had. The smell reminded him of the Tasmanians who'd brought the first beans this part of the world had seen since the Change. That was a pleasant memory, particularly the way they'd died . . .

He wished now he hadn't added the big map of the Association's territory, the one with red pins for Jack uprisings; that looked unpleasantly like a case of measles, and he could see every nobleman's teeth set on edge when they came into the tent and glanced at it.

But it'll be over soon. The monks and those crazy pseudo-Celts and the Bearkillers and Corvallans can't keep that hodgepodge of a non-army together for more than another week or two, and unlike the Conqueror or Roger I, I don't have to worry about mine starving or dying of typhus. They have to come out and attack us. We'll crush them so completely we'll be able to go home, put the Jacks down once and for all and then sweep to the gates of Corvallis before the year's over.

"My lord?"

He shook his head and forced his mind to quiet. "A man of rank? Who?"

"Lord Eric Larsson, sir. He comes with a white pennant and asks leave to address you."

A prickle of anticipation ran down Arminger's spine. Silence fell within the command tent; Sandra folded the file she was reading and sat up on the lounger, and the Grand Constable stopped talking to the supply officer. Half a dozen barons whispered to each other, a rising ripple of sound until Arminger raised a hand.

He looked out at the sunlit fields, smiling at a world golden and ripe; the command tent was on a low rise, the closest thing to a hill this flat farmland had.

This has to be a desperation move on their behalf, he

thought. *And if it's the Bear Lord's brother-in-law, I'd better make it a public audience for maximum effect.*

"Admit him under promise of safe-conduct," he said, turning and walking to the chair behind the big table.

It was light, a thing of straps and cunning hinges, but broad enough that he could lounge arrogantly with his chin on the thumb and forefinger-knuckle of one hand. A rising murmur came from the great camp outside as the A-lister with the tall scarlet crest on his helmet rode through the lanes between the tents. Everyone knew who the Bear Lord's brother-in-law was . . .

Which means I have to be very careful, he reminded himself. *There are things our knights take seriously, particularly the younger generation. Charming, but sometimes inconvenient. Who'd have thought it would take on so quickly?*

The younger man drew rein outside the command pavilion and dismounted, hanging his helm on the saddlebow of the horse. Arminger made a single spare gesture, and the guards at the entrance uncrossed their spears and braced erect.

Formidable, he thought, reading the man through the war harness with practiced ease; it wasn't much different from an Association man-at-arm's gear, anyway.

Six-three, a bit taller than me, and a hundred and ninety, just a little lighter. Trained to a hair, in his late twenties . . . at his peak or close to it. I wouldn't care to fight him, but luckily I don't have to. He'd be an interesting match at a half-time game. A few starving wolves, perhaps, and him fighting them naked.

He had a gauntlet in one hand. Arminger's brows went up; and suddenly Sandra was at his side, leaning over slightly to whisper in his ear, her voice a sibilant hiss: *"Kill him! Tell them to kill him! Don't let him say another word—kill him now!"*

"Don't be absurd," he said quietly, and she choked off her words with a bitter sound like a frustrated spitting cat. "Kill him with the whole camp watching? I'd lose so much face I'd never recover."

Men were crowding around the perimeter of the command pavilion's circle of space now; they didn't push against the guards, but they were pointing and murmuring. Many looked delighted at the break in the boredom; many, especially the young knights, looked exalted. The yellow horse waited on dancing feet, its hide gleaming like polished bronze, and it attracted its share of admiration in a camp where the pursuit of horseflesh was a common obsession.

Arminger made another gesture. The guardian knights wheeled aside, and Eric strode up the stretch of crimson carpet. He halted on the other side of the table with an impeccable bow—low enough to acknowledge he was greeting a sovereign.

"Lord Protector Arminger," he said crisply.

"My lord Eric Larsson," Arminger replied. *Most of our nobility acknowledge A-listers as our equivalents,* he thought. *Can't hurt to do the same. It'll all be very theoretical soon, anyway.* "Has your master reconsidered my offer? What message does the Bear Lord send to me?"

As he spoke, he suddenly wished that he hadn't let his taste for archaic vocabulary betray him. He might have known that a Larsson would have a solid education in the classics. Eric's face showed a little of his sudden glee, but that was to be expected in someone still young.

"What does the Bear Lord send unto you? Defiance," the emissary said. "Add unto this, contempt, and slight regard."

And he hurled the gauntlet down on the table. Unit markers went flying from the surface of the map, some of them striking Arminger in the face. Almost, for an instant, he did what his wife was still silently willing he should. When he spoke he slowly stood upright, forcing his teeth apart.

"Be glad you're an ambassador, boy. I can't kill you now. When the battle comes, there will be no such restrictions."

Larsson smiled. "You refuse the challenge?"

"Sovereigns don't accept challenges from their inferiors. Tell your master that."

One yellow eyebrow went up. "Oh, my lord Protector, it isn't *my* challenge." He raised his voice: "The Bear Lord calls the Lord Protector to account for his many crimes, and will meet him between the armies tomorrow in single combat, with any weapons the Lord Protector may choose, to the death."

Norman Arminger felt his face go gray. It wasn't fear—fear

of ordinary physical danger was not one of his weaknesses. It was the realization ...

I can't say no, he thought, thinking of the young lion eyes on him. *Not here, not now, not with all my men assembled and with the uprising back home. They'll accept anything but what looks like cowardice. The old gangers as much so as the new crop of knights, for only slightly different reasons.*

"I *told* you to kill him!" Sandra whispered fiercely.

"And I will," he answered. "After I kill the Bear Lord, tomorrow."

He turned his head, conscious of her slight moan, and met Eric Larsson eye-to-eye. "Tell the Bear Lord that the Lord Protector of the Association will meet him tomorrow with destrier and armor, shield and sword and sharpened lance, at noon between the armies. This fight to settle our differences as men, and not to bind our armies; and there will be a general truce until sunset."

"Agreed, my lord," Eric Larsson said.

He bowed again, made a precise turn and walked out to his horse. It had waited with perfect discipline until he returned; it swiveled in the instant his foot found the stirrup, and he rode it into a canter as it left.

Field of the Cloth of Gold, Willamette Valley, Oregon.
September 4th, 2008/Change Year 10

Signe handed him his lance. Mike Havel looked down at the fierce, beautiful face with its little nick at the bridge of the nose and smiled.

"Thanks," he said. "See you in about half an hour, I think."

"*Kill* him, Mike," she said.

"Hey, that's the general idea, *alskling,*" he said, his smile growing into a grin. "We'll be out of this stinking armor and back in bed at Larsdalen inside a week."

"That's a date, buster!" she said.

The other leaders were there, but they left the last words to his wife; he nodded to them and set the lance-butt on the toe of his right boot. There was no point in using the scabbard behind his right hip; he wouldn't be taking his bow to this encounter.

Yeah, gotta beat him on his own terms for this to work properly.

It was almost precisely noon, the sun overhead to minimize advantage to either side. And it was a hot day for the Willamette country, in the eighties; clouds were piling up on the western horizon over the distant Coast Range, like taller mountains of cream and hot gold to match the blue-white Cascades. Soon the fall rains would start, softening the land for the fall plowing and planting; right now the last sun of summer baked pungencies out of earth and horse and man. Dust puffed up under hooves.

A low rumbling spread across the front of the allied army; everyone who didn't have inescapable duties was out today, drawn by dread and fear and hope, protected by the truce. It built to a roar as he cantered Gustav out into the open space. The Protectorate's force was there as well, a dark line across the stubblefields a mile north. Their cheering was more regular, and as their lord emerged from under the black-and-scarlet banner they started beating their spears or the flats of their swords against their shields, a rumbling like ten thousand drums, stuttering through air and ground, bone and flesh. From the south the roaring of Havel's supporters grew louder too, not wanting to be outdone. He surprised himself with a chuckle as he recognized the OSU fight song in that chorus of screeches and bellows and chantings of his name.

The two men cantered forward, meeting midway between the armies; the roar was still loud, but muffled to the point where ordinary voices could be heard. Arminger's coif didn't cover his mouth; not surprising, since he'd be planning on giving orders in any fight he was in; the Lidless Eye was on his shield, and on the forehead of his conical black-enameled helmet, making him look like a caricature of evil. They each leaned their lances forward and tapped the shafts together ceremoniously before raising them upright again.

"Ten years since we last met, isn't it, Havel?" Arminger said.

Mike grinned. "Ten years since I suckered you the last time, Norman," he said.

There were lines graven on the angular face across from him that hadn't been there back when he'd come through Portland so soon after the Change; partly just age, but partly stress too, he judged. It couldn't be easy staying on top of that snake pit he'd built.

I'm going to kill you, he thought coldly. *Not least because you're still playing a game, college boy. I'm a working man, and fighting's just another job I do to keep my family fed and safe.*

There were none of the melodramatic threats or boasts he half expected, the I'm-going-to-rape-your-wife-and-feed-your-children-to-dogs; the man had learned control since they last talked. Though of course he'd be quite capable of *doing* anything of that sort.

The Lord Protector simply nodded. "One of us, I think, will not leave this field alive," he said, and turned his horse.

They continued until they were about a thousand yards apart. This was no tournament with rebated lances, or even à outrance, and there were no heralds or trumpeters. Each horse reared and came down moving fast, building speed in lines of dust across the reaped grain stalks. The black-armored figure grew with shocking speed, only a pair of eyes visible on either side of his helm's nasal bar, and the shield expertly sloped. Arminger wasn't a kid jagging out on testosterone and dreams of glory; he was a man not long past his physical peak, trained to a hair and immensely experienced.

So, gotta think outside the box, went through him as the lancehead came for his life.

Then: *Crack!*

He caught the lance on his shield, just. The force of it punched him back and sideways, out of the saddle. The ground came up and hit him with stunning force, and he tasted blood. Doggedly he shook off pain and struggled to his feet, spitting to clear his mouth. A half-dozen yards away Norman Arminger struggled to free himself from the wreck as his horse sank and threshed and screamed, with three feet of lance driven into its flank; the broken stub protruded just in front of Arminger's left knee. Havel took a step forward, and hissed at the sensation in his left leg and hip; it was like nerves being stretched out naked and scraped with serrated knives. He made himself move nonetheless, the backsword coming out as he advanced, the targe on his left forearm.

"Pain is weakness leaving the body," he muttered to himself. "*Shit.* Let's go, Marine."

The lord of Portland managed to get himself free of the high, massive saddle, but at the cost of abandoning his shield beneath it; the Bearkiller would have been on him while he pulled and tugged otherwise. He drew his heavy dagger with his left hand instead, holding it point-up with his sword overhead, hilt-forward. His eyes fixed on the limp Havel couldn't quite keep out of his walk.

"You swine," Arminger said with quiet sincerity. "You aimed at my horse. Deliberately!"

The northern army seemed to share its lord's prejudices; a huge chorus of hoots and groans came from them. Laughter and roaring cheers came from the allied host behind him.

"Why is it," Havel said, grinning, "that you evil bastards always get indignant when you find out you don't have a monopoly on ruthlessness? It's only a horse, Norman—and you're better than I am with a lance. If God had meant us to be lancers, He'd have given us hooves."

"*Haro! Portland!*"

"*Hakkaa Paalle!*"

The longsword flashed down. *Crack* and the curved leather of the targe shed it, but he didn't overbalance, and the smashing punch of the Bearkiller's backsword caught on the dagger. The hilts locked and they strained against each other for an instant, face panting into face in a perverse intimacy.

Christ Jesus, he's strong! Havel thought, as they disengaged and Arminger blocked a cut at the back of his knee, turning the longsword from the wrist like a ribbon-saber. *Got the edge on me there, only by a bit, but it's there.*

He'd counted on better speed and endurance, but the wrench to his hip was slowing him, draining away agility. The other man's lack of a shield would help—he couldn't just tuck his shoulder into it and try and overrun with a rush. It balanced out . . .

They circled, Arminger moving on the outside of the curve, Havel turning on his right heel. Engage, a flurry of strikes, back. The Portlander was breathing harder, sweat runneling down his face, but Havel felt the weight of his armor too. Try a stepping lunge for the slit in the hauberk exposed by the lack of a shield—

The hip betrayed him, and Arminger's dagger knocked the point wide. He snarled and reversed the strike, slamming the pommel of his sword up at the other man's armpit. The strike hit, but not quite on the nerve center, and the armor and padding muffled it. Arminger's fingers flew open, and the dagger went flying, but the arm wasn't disabled; he grabbed at Havel's shield, dragging it down and pinning that arm as their swords locked. Swaying, pushing, and he hooked an ankle around the bigger man's and *pulled*.

They crashed to earth, side-to-side. Arminger wasted an instant trying to shorten the sword and stab; the edge grated over Havel's hauberk, and then he raised it high to hammer the pommel down.

Crack.

Something gave in the left side of Havel's chest, and the coldness of it radiated out into his body like cracks in ice on a winter pond. But he'd dropped the long sword and had his dagger out now, and as the brass ball on the pommel crashed down on him again he let the rest of his body go limp and focused, draining the strength into his right arm. And *thrust,* the will a point of rage and effort like the knife, and the narrow point punched into a ring of the hauberk and broke it, sank deeper.

Crack.

The pommel struck in the same place, and Havel's mind went blank for an instant in a sheet of icy white fire. Arminger fell forward onto him, gauntlets scrabbling at the wheat stems. Havel pushed, pushed again, slowly and laboriously climbed to his knees. He took up his sword and used it to climb erect, right hand only—the left was limp, and the whole upper left side of his body was coming and going in waves that washed out farther and farther.

The Lord Protector looked at him, and one strengthless hand

fumbled at the dagger driven up under his short ribs. He tried
to speak, or perhaps only to scream. Havel took a staggering
step, and placed the point of his backsword on the coif at the
base of the other man's throat, and leaned all his weight on it.

"Signe," he wheezed. "Mary, Ritva, Mike . . . Rudi."

Something crunched beneath the steel. Havel's hand
slipped away and he went to his knees. Blackness.

Aaron Rothman was bending over him, fingers infinitely gentle in their probing. Tears were falling into the stubble on the
doctor's face.

Mike Havel said nothing, squinting against the sun. He felt
clear-headed, but weak, and there was an enormous weight on
his chest that was just this side of pain. Gradually he grew
aware of other faces around him—Signe on one side and Juniper on the other, looking unaware of each other for once,
Eric Larsson and Will Hutton, Luanne. More stood at a distance, silent, waiting.

Definitely not good, he thought, and tried to raise a hand. It
took considerable effort; someone took it, Signe.

"Arminger's dead," she said, knowing what he'd want to be
certain of. "Some of his men are leaving already."

He sighed, and turned his head to the doctor. "The word,
Aaron."

"Oh, God, Mike, I'm sorry, I'm so sorry, there's not a
damned thing I can do that wouldn't kill you quicker—ribs,
heart—if I had a pre-Change trauma room, maybe—"

"The *word.*"

"Maybe ten minutes, maybe an hour. That's all I can say."

"Well, that sucks!" Mike Havel said, and started to laugh,
then controlled it; not a good idea if his shattered ribs had
punctured things inside, and there were a few last things to do.

"Aaron, you're a good guy and a good friend. Help look
after my kids, will you? Face it, you were born to be an uncle!"

The doctor turned away and fell to his knees, sobbing into
his hands. Havel looked up; there was a tree casting some
shade, they must have carried him back on a stretcher, and the
light dappled his face, dazzling glimpses of sun and blue
through shifting green.

Pretty damn good world, he thought. *Right to the end. This isn't a bad way to go, not bad at all. I've seen and heard a lot worse.*

Then he pushed heavy eyelids up. "Hey, *alskling,*" he said.

Signe leaned forward; her hands felt very warm as they gripped his, which meant his was getting cold.

"Alskling," she said back, her eyes searching his.

"Look after the kids, and tell 'em I loved them; God knows it's true enough. Tell 'em I wish I could have seen them grow up. Never expected to be a dad . . . that was more fun than anything except you. Help look after the Outfit. Couldn't have done it without you, kid."

"Goddamit, Mike, don't leave us!"

He grinned, feeling the fierce beat of her will even then. "We're both hammers, you and I, that's our problem—and Lord, didn't we make some lovely sparks together! Remember when we fought those bandits in the ruin, and it turned out to be a porn-video store? And I said *I still live,* and you thought it was Tarzan, and it was John Carter?"

Sleep was calling; she was nodding, crying and laughing at the same time. He went on: "Just . . . keep in mind . . . all the problems aren't nails, OK? And you're twenty-eight. That's how old I was when I met you the day of the Change, and my real life was just starting. Don't make this the end of yours."

She kept hold of his hand; the words got softer despite his best efforts.

"Will," he whispered. The weathered brown face leaned towards him. "You're boss of the Outfit for now. Don't forget that election come January. Listen to Signe and Ken and Eric and Luanne and all, but you're ramrod. Always . . . thought you should be . . . back at the start, remember? And you wouldn't take the job."

He nodded and set a hand on Havel's for a moment, where his wife gripped it. "I'll do my best, Mike. Mighty big boots to fill."

"Eric." The blond head so like his wife's bent. "Brother . . . you always had my back . . ."

His eyes closed. A moment later he opened them again, watching all of them start. Then it was too much effort to speak; he'd managed all the essential things.

You did pretty good, Marine, he thought, as the bright light faded above. *You found Signe and made some great babies with her. You fought that bastard Arminger to a standstill for ten years and then killed him. You got a lot more than you thought you would, when the plane's engines cut out over the Bitterroots.*

It all became a tumble of images, and then suddenly his thoughts were clear for an instant:

I was father to the land. I saved my people. I was . . . King.

"By . . . earth," he said, more of a movement of the lips than a thing of throat and air. "By . . . sky . . ."

Another breath, and it did hurt a little now. The next was harder. The women leaned over him, the mothers of his children. He blinked once more. His own mother, her black braids swinging as she rocked his hurt away. She was singing to him:

> *"Manabozho saw some ducks*
> *Hey, hey, heya hey*
> *Said 'Come little brothers, sing and dance';*
> *Hey, hey, heya hey—"*

CHAPTER TWENTY-THREE

Field of the Cloth of Gold, Willamette Valley, Oregon
September 5th, 2008/Change Year 10

Juniper Mackenzie woke with a start. The tent was dark, but dawn had broken outside; Nigel's bedroll was empty, and there was a stale cold smell, slightly fusty, that she associated with war. She scrambled into kilt and shirt, socks and shoes, then buckled and belted her plaid as she stood outside, breathing in freshness and wood smoke and cooking smells. A flight of geese went over high above, the first of the year heading south and sounding their long song.

The memory of sorrow clutched at her, like a hand at her throat as she heard the keening among her people, rising and falling and then rising again into a saw-edged wail of grief, the heavy silence from the orderly rows of the Bearkiller camp, the Latin chanting from the chapel-tent of the warrior monks. Nigel turned and she leaned into him, hugging fiercely.

"He was a brave man," he said. "I've never met a braver."

Her head nodded against the rough surface of his quilted tunic. "He was the father of my son."

Then she took a deep breath, and another, standing and raising her head proudly, accepting the strength of his arm without leaning on it.

"And . . . he was the given sacrifice that goes consenting; the King who dies that the people may live," she said. "I knew it from the beginning, but I didn't . . . he always laughed at the myths."

"Even when he stepped into one," Nigel said. "And now he's become legend himself."

He shook himself, and she smiled despite her sadness as she felt him put on practicality like a well-tailored suit, even if it was a little threadbare at the cuffs.

"We heard some fighting from over there last night," he said.

He nodded northward towards the Protectorate's camp ... a Protectorate without a Lord Protector, now. Smoke rose over it, more than cookfires could account for.

"And according to the Rangers, a block of about five hundred of them is leaving right now—for the baronies along the Columbia, we think; they're worried about the Free Cities and the Jacks. We may not have to fight that great murdering battle after all."

"And our folk?" she asked, knowing the answer.

"Grieving, but not downhearted. I wouldn't like to face them in a fight now."

"Indeed!" she said. To herself: *With Mike's spirit behind the blade and the bow? No, no, and no three times!*

They stood in line for porridge and bacon, and ate without tasting. The noise of grief died down, but not the reality of it, as the day dawned blue and dreaming over the golden stubblefields around them. Juniper felt herself moving in a shell of quiet, making herself attend to things—reports from spies, the camp disputes and pettiness that nothing stopped. Less than an hour later, a knight galloped out from the Association's camp with a white pennant snapping on his lance. Waiting with the other hastily assembled leaders Juniper was astonished to see the marks of tears and grief on the man's haughty young face as well, as he sat his curveting horse like one born there.

Well, she chided herself. *And if there had never been a one who loved Norman Arminger, the man could not have done so much ill or ruled so long. And now he must account for all his deeds before the Guardians, in the place where Truth stands naked and lies are impossible, and choose his own course to self-forgiveness.*

"I am envoy from the Lady Sandra Arminger, Regent of

the Portland Protective Association for the Princess Mathilda," he called.

O-ho, it's Regent she is now? Juniper thought with a return of the cold calculation a Chief must be able to pull on like a garment; from the corner of her eye, she saw Signe's valkyr face close like a comely fist. *I wonder what the others over there think of that?*

"She and her loyal Grand Constable, Count Renfrew of Odell, would come and speak peace with the other rulers gathered here," he went on; was it her imagination that there was a slight stress on *loyal*? "She and he will come alone, if they have your pledge of armistice and safe-conduct from now until her return."

Eyebrows rose. That was a major concession; it was also a show of strength, that she could come unguarded and with what must be her main supporter along . . . and also a sign of trust, of sorts. Sandra Arminger had always been a good judge of other people's scruples, even if she didn't have any herself.

Will Hutton spoke, his hard Texan drawl skeptical: "Anythin' else, boy?"

The knight's lips grew tighter, but he inclined his head. "Do you speak for this assembly, Lord Hutton?"

"I speak for the Bearkillers, by Mike Havel's last words," he said. "These others are the leaders of free communities. We'll consult."

Even then, the Protectorate knight sneered a little. "The Lady Sandra says that she would speak first with Lady Juniper Mackenzie, Chief of the Clan Mackenzie, and then with your leaders in council."

Signe looked daggers at the Mackenzie chieftain, but Will Hutton smiled. "Wouldn't be tryin' to sow a little distrust here, would she? Sure. There's nothin' she can say to Juney that Juney won't tell us all. We'll meet her at the command pavilion over to there." He pointed. "Whenever you're ready."

"At once."

The knight ducked his head, and wheeled his horse so abruptly that it reared as it turned; then it landed with a puff of dust from among the reaped wheat stems and galloped northward once more.

Well, Juniper thought. *Well, well, well!*

"Probably best this way," Will Hutton said quietly as they walked towards the big open-sided tent. "We Bearkillers 'r too sore with it now. And Mike died so we wouldn't *have* to fight that big battle."

"He was the father of my son," Juniper replied, her tone equally quiet. "And I loved him too, Will."

The older man nodded. "Figure so. But you didn't live with him day-in-day-out."

Unwillingly, she nodded . . . *And Mike knew what he was doing when he gave Will the power. Signe would be too blinded by her rage.*

Evidently "at once" meant what it said. "Alone" was something else; it included a driver for the light two-wheeled horsecart that Sandra rode in beneath a parasol, and a maid-servant on a little rumble seat behind, and a groom to hold Conrad Renfrew's horse. The former consort sat erect and elegant; Renfrew dismounted first, standing at the wheel to hand her down from the vehicle as it bobbed on its springs.

Signe was close. The consort nodded to her. "We're both widowed today," she said. "Let's see if we can keep too many more from sharing the condition."

The tall, blond, young woman in armor looked down her straight nose. "My husband was a great and good man," she said coldly, then stopped herself with an obvious effort.

Sandra nodded, the black mourning ribbons fluttering on her white headdress and framing cold pride. "And mine was a monster. But that, Lady Signe, doesn't mean I loved him any less than you did yours. And now if you'll excuse me . . ."

She swept into the command pavilion as if it were a gazebo in the grounds of Castle Todenangst, waiting an instant while the servant unfolded a chair and small side table and set out refreshments, even pouring coffee from a thermos.

Juniper followed and sat across from her, studying the face and form she'd never seen so close before. The Protector's widow sat half-turned in her chair; sunlight from outside the pavilion and through the striped cloth made the pale colors of her cotte-hardi and headdress glow in the dimness inside the tent, the mourning ribbons like shadows across the brilliant white, a subdued glitter of lapis and silver from the buttons. The air smelled of hot canvas and crushed grass and coffee; Sandra sipped, apparently as relaxed as she'd have been in a castle solar, and picked up one of the little watercress sandwiches with the crusts cut off, nibbling.

"Well," the Chief of the Mackenzies said at last, into that silence and Sandra's slight catlike smile. "What do you have to say for yourself, then?"

"That I protected your son, when my husband would have killed him," she said promptly, and the smile grew slightly. "Several times, in fact."

Juniper winced slightly. *True enough and there's no getting around it. Still . . .*

"You're not a good person at all, really, are you?" she asked, genuine curiosity in her voice.

"No, I'm not," Sandra agreed, and shrugged. "And you are, and yet you won anyway. Unfathomable are the works of God." A pause. "And many are the marvels, yet none so marvelous as humankind."

"You agree we've won?"

Another shrug. "Well, somewhat. A chunk of our army has melted away. What's left isn't big enough to fight you, the Grand Constable tells me, although it would cost you many lives to overrun us and we could probably get away even if you tried. Besides, how long will your farmers stay here, when there's work to do at home? They came to stop us invading their land, and that's . . . no longer on the program."

Juniper looked aside. Conrad Renfrew was standing like an armored fireplug in the open. Eric Larsson was not far away, glaring at him. The Association's general looked at him, shrugged and walked over. The younger man bristled like a wolf at a stranger on his pack's territory, then nodded reluctantly and answered whatever it was the count said.

Sandra went on: "But the Grand Constable is loyal to me . . . and Princess Mathilda. It's quite extraordinary, but he has no wish to be Lord Protector himself."

"Ah, but some others do."

"But they can't agree on a candidate, and none of them alone has anything like the strength of the combined loyalists.

We can *all* go home, haul up our drawbridges, and wait—the harvest is in the storehouses behind our walls and gates. And in a little while, after you're tired of sitting outside the moat and making rude gestures, you'll have to go home to your farms and villages too, before we taunt you once again."

Her face was calm but her eyes twinkled; Juniper fought down an answering smile as Sandra went on.

"For that matter, if you split your army up to watch castles, Conrad tells me there are things he could do which might reverse the whole result. And Pope Leo is still talking about a Crusade, you know. He has quite a popular following."

Juniper smiled herself, grimly. She was prepared for that, and there was an edge in her tone when she replied: "But speaking of farmers, before we have to go home we can pay *your* farmers a visit. We don't have to take castles. All we have to do is take the farmers who want to go with us . . . and then you can set your men-at-arms to plowing your fields, and follow along with a bag of wheat slung around your neck, sowing the good earth yourselves."

The wimpled head nodded. "There is that. But if you really wanted to do that, you wouldn't be talking to me now, would you?"

Juniper sighed. "We can't make you tear down your castles. We can't occupy your territories and make you reform that dreadful system you've established. We *can* wreck you, but only with much loss of precious life and a risk of the same to ourselves, and what was left of you would still be a deadly threat. We can't cross the Columbia at all, and much of your strength is there these days. Yet we can't just let you put the Protectorate back together as it was, either—you're smarter than your late, unlamented husband, bad cess to him, the creature. You wouldn't make the same mistakes."

Sandra Arminger's small left hand closed on the arm of the chair; she made it relax, but there was something in her eyes, like a red spark moving in the depths.

"I'm less ambitious than Norman was," she said carefully. "And I know when to stop. My primary goal is to pass his inheritance on to my daughter, intact."

"That's probably even true. However, you're also just as

vindictive as he was, if far more subtle. I'm not going to rely on your loving kindness and better nature, so."

Sandra gave a small snort of laughter. "Granted. I don't *have* a better nature. So?"

"So, we—the Mackenzies, and I'm sure we can persuade everyone else—will recognize you as Regent of the Association, against the time of your daughter's majority, which will be when she's twenty-six. We will even help you enforce it against any noble who disputes your claim—we need a single authority to deal with, not a mass of robber barons raiding as the whim takes them."

"But," Sandra said. "There's always a 'but.'"

"There are conditions. Several of them, in fact."

At her raised eyebrow, Juniper went on: "First, you must withdraw from the territories in the Pendleton area you occupied last year. We'll agree not to occupy them either."

A sigh. "We've already ordered the garrisons there to withdraw; we needed the men. And with so many nobles and even heirs dead, there isn't the demand for new fiefs anymore. Agreed. They're a bunch of hicks and boors out there anyway."

"Next, you have to renounce any claim on our lands and recognize all the free communities as equals. Peace on the border."

"Agreed," Sandra said at once. "You *have* won this war, after all. I warn you that Norman couldn't control what every baron did in detail, and I won't be able to do so either, but I will try."

"And promises are worth their weight in gold," Juniper said; she was a little surprised when Sandra chuckled and made a gesture of acknowledgment.

"And you will decree, and have the decree read in every domain, castle, manor and village, that any resident of the Protectorate is now free to leave, now or at any time in the future, without bond or let, taking their personal property with them."

"*Ah.*" Sandra Arminger closed her eyes for an instant. "Now, that's the big one. *That* would be difficult to sell to the barons."

"Better lose some than lose all," Juniper said ruthlessly. "Not all would go; I imagine a lot of the free tenants and even some of the bond-tenants would stay. They've put their lives into that land, after all, and leaving would mean starting over again penniless, without land or stock. They can't carry their farms on their backs. But you'll have to stop squeezing the rest so hard, and that's a fact, and get rid of those iron collars, if you want any of your peons to remain. They're already penniless and abused to boot, the which they wouldn't be in the south."

"Which means we'd have to cut back on the army," Sandra observed. "We couldn't afford it any more."

"Exactly, unless your nobles preferred to sacrifice their standard of living." Sandra made a rueful twist of the lips that wasn't quite a smile, and Juniper went on: "*That* is how we can trust your word; you won't have that great standing army hanging over our heads like a hammer anymore. I suggest you settle the ordinary soldiers on farms and call them a militia— or whatever piece of old-world foolishness you choose to hang on it, fiefs-in-ordinary or whatever suits your fancy."

Sandra's left eyebrow went up again, and she silently looked at Juniper's kilt and plaid and the raven-feathers in the clasp of her flat Scots bonnet. Juniper fought down a smile.

And if she weren't a cruel, murderous bitch who's evil to the painted toenails I could like this woman, sure. She had an uncomfortable feeling that the other could read the thought, as well.

"Anything else?" the consort—now the Regent—said.

"There's to be a yearly meeting of all the communities, to consider grievances and settle disputes."

"Where?" Sandra asked curiously.

"Corvallis. They're further from you and have fewer feuds. Also, later people from south of there may wish to join."

Sandra nodded thoughtfully, looking at the dignitaries scattered around the field outside the pavilion. Turner and Kowalski were there with a clutch of other Corvallan magnates. Juniper could see the calculations of political advantage going through the other woman's brain.

But two can play at that game, my lady Regent. Any number can, in fact. It's not my favorite sport, the game of thrones, but I like it better than the game of swords.

Sandra nodded. "Agreed. A . . . oh, God, let's not call it a United Nations, shall we? That would doom things from the start."

"We could simply call it the Meeting."

"A yearly Meeting at Corvallis, agreed. And that's all?"

"By no means. There's the matter of Mathilda."

Sandra Arminger went very still. She took another sip of the coffee and put the cup on the folding table with its surface of mother-of-pearl and gold.

"Yes?" she said, her voice full of pride and danger. "There's something about my daughter you don't like?"

Juniper smiled; it wasn't even an unkindly expression. "On the contrary. She's a sweet girl, and nobody's fool, and we agree without dispute she's to be your heir. So much do we all love her that we'd insist on her company, for, shall we say, six months of the year."

Sandra's basilisk glare went blank and opaque; Juniper could see twisting pathways behind the dark brown eyes, like one of those old Escher prints, and felt dizzy for an instant. To help the process of thought along she gently pointed out: "And Rudi is very fond of her, so. And she of him."

The pathways were joined by gears, meshing in silent smoothness. Sandra smiled, a somewhat alarming expression.

"There is that. It would be cruel to part the children, and I'm quite fond of Rudi, as well."

Which I think is even true, Juniper said to herself.

"Two months, though, not six. Her name is Mathilda, not Persephone."

Juniper forced down a startled chuckle. "Five," she said.

"Three."

"Four."

"Agreed, four," Sandra said. "Provided, of course, that Rudi spends four months with *us*."

She held up a hand to stop Juniper's startled retort. "I can't agree to anything that will make most of my barons . . . or their widows, now . . . abandon me. Letting their laborers leave at will is bad enough. If I send my daughter as a hostage with-out you doing the same, it's a symbol of humiliation and de-feat, and it will be the straw that breaks the back of their pride. You have to give them a gesture of respect and hope."

Juniper sat and wrestled with herself. She knew that Sandra Arminger was enjoying every moment of her internal tor-ment, which made her end it the sooner: "Done. Mathilda will come to us at Mabon and stay until Yule; Rudi will return with her and come back to us at Ostara. And when they're old enough, they can visit as they please, of course."

"Whittled it down to a bit *under* three months, when you had to wear the other shoe, eh?" Sandra said. Then: "Agreed. And each to bring a suite of no more than six with them. No religious pressure on either."

"Oh, agreed."

Sandra finished her coffee and said musingly: "I'll send Tiphaine d'Ath and her little friend the witch along with Mathilda. They'll enjoy that, and I've wanted to poke Pope Leo in the eye for some time now, not to mention trim back his pretensions a bit. . . ."

She extended a hand. Juniper took it and they gave one firm shake before releasing. A murmur rose from the crowd outside, and the two women looked at each other.

Juniper sighed. "Now we have to make them think it was their own idea."

"Just so. Strange, isn't it, that it's always more difficult to talk people *out* of killing each other than *into* it?"

Larsdalen, Willamette Valley, Oregon
September 6th, 2008/Change Year 10

The funeral cortege made its slow way up from the gate of Larsdalen, the pennants of the lancer escort and the manes of the horses fluttering in the warm wind from the east, a wind that smelled of baked earth and drying grass as much as wood smoke or massed humanity. Michael Havel's body rested on the flat bed of a two-wheeled wagon drawn by four glossy horses; his charger followed behind, boots reversed in the stirrups. The brown-and-scarlet flag of the Outfit was draped over the coffin, and his unsheathed sword and bear-headed helm rested on it. Silence ran under the sough of the wind, under the crunch of gravel beneath feet and hooves, despite the huge crowd gathered; every adult of the Outfit who could come had, and many had brought their older children to see the passing of the first Bear Lord.

The day was cruelly bright on the white and yellow of the great house and on the gardens, but the lawns were covered right to the edges of the flowerbanks that trembled in sheets of gold and purple. To the edges, but not beyond, for Bear-killers were an orderly and disciplined folk, and today they came to mourn. Flowers brought from their own homes flew out to land beneath the horses' hooves, roses and peonies and rhododendrons, until the destriers seemed to tread on a carpet or a spring meadow. Hats came off in a wave as the coffin passed by behind its escort of mounted A-listers led by the dead man's brother-in-law, and heads bowed. They remained that way in respect as the family passed behind: the dead man's wife and children, his sister-in-law, Ken Larsson and the rest.

Signe walked behind the cart, Mike Jr.'s hand in hers; the boy was sobbing quietly in hopeless bewilderment, knowing that something very bad had happened, and that he couldn't bawl the way he needed to or ask: *When's Daddy coming home?* Mary and Ritva were old enough to understand; their tears were more silent, but more bitter. Signe herself walked like an iron statue from a Viking myth, in A-lister panoply but with the crest of the helmet under her right arm dyed black. Today you could see what she would be like when the last of her youth left her.

He's gone, she thought.

The knowledge was there, but her mind couldn't really take it in. *Ten years, and suddenly he's gone. He's gone. He'll never smile at me that way again, mostly on one side of his mouth, and I'll never look over in the morning and find him rubbing his face the way he always did right after he woke up. None of it, ever again.*

She remembered his eyes, that first time when he'd walked

into the room in the airport: cool and polite and showing no sign that he was mentally undressing her, which she'd known damned well he was. *Cute, but a spoiled rich kid* had been visible if you knew how to read men, which she had even then. It had driven her wild . . . and then the terror when the Piper Chieftain's engines had cut out, and the way his face had turned to a slab of granite as he wrestled with the controls.

He's gone. Forever.

Her son's small hand tugged at hers, and she looked down. His hair was hers, white now; it would be corn gold when he grew. But the eyes were his father's, slanted and gray as Lake Superior water on an overcast day, and so were the promise of cheekbones and small square chin.

But my kids are here. His kids too. Everything isn't gone. Not yet.

The cart creaked to a halt on the terrace that held the house. Signe turned, picked her son up and handed him to Will Hutton. The older man's face was graven too, grief and strength in the brown eyes. They widened a little in surprise as the blond boy was put in his arms. The child's own went around his neck, and the tear-and-snot-streaked face was buried in the crook of it.

That immobilized him as she vaulted up into the cart and stood beside the coffin; she stood for a moment, and then touched two fingers to her lips and bent for a moment to press them to the polished wood.

Then she stood, looking out over the sea of faces below, and filled her lungs.

"Bearkillers!" she shouted. A murmur, then hushed silence again, with a soughing sound like some great beast breathing quietly as it waited.

"Bearkillers, Michael Havel is dead!"

There was a fringe of A-listers along the edge of the great crowd nearest the roadway and the house; nobody grudged them the position today. Many were bandaged; some were on crutches; a few were in wheelchairs, pushed along by friends or kin or retainers. The least she saw anywhere were the grave, shocked faces that wondered: *what will become of us now?* Some of them wept; a few covered their faces with their hands and sobbed unashamed. Nor were the A-listers the only ones.

I hope you can see this, alskling, *wherever you are,* she thought, with a moment's wistfulness. *They always respected you, but now they know they loved you too.*

Then she pushed down tenderness. Mike had fought his fight; hers was still to be won.

"When the Change came, I and my family were flying over mountains. A lot of people died that day. How many didn't die, who were in the air when the machines failed? Michael Havel saved our lives."

She let one hand point for an instant to the man holding her son. "This is Will Hutton. You know him; a strong man, and a wise leader. But Mike Havel rescued him too, and his wife and daughter—rescued them and me and my sister from bandits out to rape and rob and kill."

She looked over the rapt audience, feeling their eyes like a huge wind bearing her up. The real wind blew a strand of her yellow mane into her eyes, and she brushed it aside with memories of terror and helplessness.

Mike taught me. I was never helpless again. I never will *be helpless again. Nor will our children.*

"Who among all of you *didn't* he save? He found you here and there—starving, hiding, hiding from Eaters and bandits and warlords, hiding from each other, in basements and culverts and little hollows up in the hills, all of you waiting to die like the rest or get hungry enough to do the forbidden thing. Who brought you together and made you into the Outfit, where nobody's alone and everyone has brothers and sisters who'd die for them? Who was it taught you how to fight and made you strong? *Who?*"

"Lord Bear," a man said near the front, in an almost conversational tone. Others took it up: "Lord Bear. Lord Bear. *Lord Bear!*"

Now it was a thunder, echoing off the walls behind them and the great house behind her. The house that had been owned by her blood for more than a hundred years, and that looked out over the land that fed her children, its wheat and fruit and meat the stuff of their bones and blood. She raised a hand again.

"Who was it brought you to this good earth? Who was it found you seed grain and tools and stock? Who gave every family their land, and made fair laws, and kept them, and saw that others kept them too? Who made the Brotherhood of the A-list, so that we'd have guardians always ready and you could plow and reap in peace, knowing you'd keep what you grew and made? Who was always ready to hear a grievance, and give those who needed it a helping hand . . . or a kick in the ass, if they needed that? *Who?*"

"*Lord Bear! Lord Bear! Lord Bear!*" Fists were in the air, and drawn blades, men shouting it like a war cry even as the tears ran down their faces.

"I'm not the only one who lost a husband in this war," she went on more quietly, when the sound had died down to a rumble.

The tone brought that to a new hush, and now they were straining to hear what she said. At the rear there was a mumbling as her words were repeated and passed backward.

"I'm not the only one who has children who will grow up without a father. My daughters, my son, the child I'm carrying beneath my heart right now, they've lost the man who loved them, who held them and told them stories. They're crying for him, like all the other children who lost someone dear to them."

Several of her family looked at each other, startled. *Well, I wasn't sure I was pregnant again until about last week.*

A long sigh went across the crowd, and she spoke into it: "But Mike Havel was special. It isn't just my children who've lost a father. My husband was father to this land, to all the people of the Outfit . . . landfather, they said in the old days. He was our landfather. When the enemy came from the north with all their numbers to take our homes and make slaves of our children, who led us out to fight them? Who made our plans? Who was in the front of every battle? Who killed the tyrant Arminger with his own hand, and preserved our freedom and our lives?"

She bent and then raised the helmet and its snarling covering over her head in both hands. "When this wild thing came to kill, who stood fearless between the beast and his folk, though its claws tore his face and his own blood poured out on the earth? *Who killed the Bear, Bearkillers? Who was the lord who died for his people?*"

"LORD BEAR! LORD BEAR! LORD BEAR!"

This time she let the thunder build until her ears rang with it and it pounded at her chest like huge soft hammers, and then let it die away until she replaced the helm on the coffin with gentle reverence.

They're mine, she realized, when she looked at them again. *And I'm theirs. I've never felt like this before . . . did Mike?*

She motioned Mary and Ritva up into the cart; Will handed her the boy. The girls stood straight on either side of her; Mike Jr. rode her hip, knuckled an eye and then looked out over the crowd fearlessly. He'd never been a timid boy.

"The Bear Lord is dead. Will you keep faith with the one who gave his life for you? Will you keep faith with the blood that he spilled out for you, the blood that runs in his children? When the time comes they can take up his work. Will you choose one of them to wear the Helm of the Bear Lord in his place?"

The noise wasn't words, not this time, but it was certainly agreement. There was a roaring guttural undertone to it, as well: *Let anyone who wants to say* no I won't *run far and fast!* She noticed even then that her brother and *his* wife had their swords drawn, and were shouting as loud as anyone.

Is this what Juniper feels, when she makes magic? Signe let herself smile a little before she continued.

"Bearkillers, with his dying breath the Bear Lord named Will Hutton as his deputy, to rule in his stead until his children came of age and a new Bear Lord could be chosen by you, the free people of the Outfit. You know Will Hutton; a fighting man our enemies and the wild folk fear, and a wise and honest one as well. He was always Mike Havel's strong right hand and close councilor. The Bear Lord put the authority in his hands, and to advise him Mike set me, and my brother Eric, Will's son-in-law, and Luanne his daughter and my sister-in-law, and his wife Angelica, and my father Ken and his wife

Pamela. People of the Bearkiller Outfit, is it your will that this be so?"

Will stepped up to stand by her side before the sound of acclamation died. He turned his head slightly to whisper into her ear; they were about the same height. "You might have told me about this first, honeypie."

"And then you might have said no to the arrangements," she said back with a wintry smile. "And this is what Mike wanted . . . or at least, it's what I think Mike would have wanted."

"And now I can't do otherwise without it lookin' as if I was out to trample down his memory and his kids'. Folk'll remember *this* day for a good long time, that's certain-sure. What your daddy calls makin' myths. Mike, he did marry him up a smart one, didn't he?"

"Hey, Unc' Will, you don't believe those stories about dumb blonds, do you?"

"I used to, truth to tell, but now I got me a tow-haired Swedish grandson and he's as smart as a whip," he snorted. "I won't say which side of the family he got it from."

She blinked then, shocked that the tears she'd fought back were still waiting. *I can't cry now. Later, but not now.* "Oh, God, Unc' Will, I miss him!"

He nodded, gave her shoulders a brief squeeze, then stood straight beside her and waited for the noise to die, blocky and strong and looking out at their people with shrewd eyes dark in his weathered, coffee-colored face. The crowd fell quiet bit by bit.

"Mike Havel was like a son to me," he told them shortly. "I'm grieving with you."

He crossed himself. "I hope he's with God now . . . or that he doesn't have too long a spell in Purgatory. God knows and we all know he wasn't a perfect man; he wasn't the prayin' sort, and he had him quite a temper, and he was a bad man to cross, a hard man to his enemies. Hell, folks, if y'all find a perfect man, come runnin' and tell me—I ain't going to nohow waste my time looking around for one, except Jesus his own self."

A burst of startled laughter cut across the crowd's mood; when he went on they were coming back to the light of common day, from that other place where Signe had led them, even as sun and winds and shadows fell towards the west.

But that's OK, she thought. *They'll remember it the more strongly because it wasn't long. I don't think it* could *be long, or we'd burn out. Common day is where we live. That other place . . . it's for visiting and coming back.*

Hutton went on: "But Mike Havel was a *good* man, as good as any I ever met. He stood by his friends and his kin and his given word, and he wasn't never afraid of nothing in all the world. There was no give in that man, and no steppin' back. *Sisu,* his old-country folks called it, and Mike had all there was to have. Everything around us here today is his work. Now he's gone."

He put his hand on the head of the boy Signe carried for a moment.

"But like Signe said, his kids are still with us. They say our children *are* the future, and that's God's truth; I've got grandkids and I hope to see *their* kids before I go. Mike Havel wasn't afraid to die, for his kids, or for yours, for our future. That's right and fitting; it's a man's work to fight and die for his fam'ly, and it's his pride. But it's also a man's pride—or a woman's—to *work* for his kids and their future. You know that; you work every day to grow the food they eat and make the clothes they wear. We've got work ahead of us, Bearkillers. The Outfit has to fix up what this war tore down, and we're going to have lots of people moving south. Some'll be honest and hard-workin' folks who'll want to join up with us. They won't have much, but they'll have their hands and their backs and the guts to use them—and remember how we got our start, from people just like them. Others won't be honest, and likely we'll have to fight again.

"So today we bury Mike Havel, and we'll remember him the way he'd have wanted—what he did for us, and what we did with him leadin' us. Then tomorrow, we get to *work*."

Signe Havel nodded as she stepped down from the cart, and

the coffin-bearers came forward. Her eyes flicked eastward for a moment.

All right, she thought. *Your son is his too, and you've got an inheritance for him. But this is for* mine, *and the children of their children.*

EPILOGUE

Dun Juniper, Willamette Valley, Oregon
September 22nd, 2008/Change Year 10

"Not much longer," Nigel Loring muttered to himself. "You can do it, Nigel—not much longer!"

Juniper Mackenzie laughed aloud as the crowd filed up the mountainside towards the *nemed,* the Sacred Wood, and felt her feet trying to skip a dance beneath the steady pace. She'd made the trip so many times; alone sometimes to speak with the Mighty Ones and the landwights, with her Coven before the Change, and even more since—in sunlight and dark clouded night, by moons that shone on spring flowers or white as salt on winter snow, but seldom with a crowd as joyous as this, as the couples went up two by two. The path wound back and forth up steepness, through towering Douglas fir where summer's last heat baked out the resin scent like strong incense, past hardwoods whose yellowing leaves glowed even as the sky began to darken ahead over the snowpeaks eastward that made a wall to the world. Squirrels streaked chattering along branches, wings were thick overhead as the flocks went south ahead of oncoming winter, and somewhere in the distance a wolf howled.

"Nigel, you're going up this path to be married, not executed," she chided gently, squeezing his sword-hardened hand in hers. "You're supposed to *enjoy* this, you know! And you're looking so indecently handsome I could ravish you on the spot, sure."

He did, erect and slim, trim and graceful in kilt and ruffled shirt, the plaid belted and pinned at his shoulder with silver plaques bearing the five roses of the House of Loring, gifts from Major Jones over in Corvallis.

Rudi went by, skipping nimble as a goat on the rough verge of the trail, at the head of a pack of boys his age doing their best to induce maternal despair as they plunged on heedless of carefully arranged finery. Juniper's eyes followed him for an instant, as the bright red-gold hair shone in the cathedral dimness beneath the flat Scots bonnet.

Thank you, Mike, she thought. *Thank you for my son, and for the sweet night when we made him, in that time of terror and despair. Thank you for your strength, and your kindness, and for saving us all. Horned Lord, he'll be so surprised there beyond the Gate! Guide him home to the lands of Summer beneath the forever trees, and be a friend to him, for here among us he walked in Your forms: the wild Lover, the wise Father, the strong Warrior who wards the folk.*

The shade of the great trees gave breaths of cool grace between bursts of sunlit summer warmth, like autumn casting a shadow through time before itself, and the beams of light that slanted through them made a green-gold glow that seemed to explode on bushes of late Cascade azaleas, their last blooms frothing white and filling the air with their sweet-tart citrus perfume. Glimpses westward where the path and the forest allowed showed blue distance and yellow-brown stubblefields, sunset flashing from river and pond, and the thin spires of smoke that marked the hearths of humankind, all nearly lost against the sinking sun. Earth was warm and dry beneath her strong, bare feet, duff and fir needles prickly, the fallen leaves rustling and crunching, even the swirl of her robe across her insteps like a caress. The circlets of silver bells she'd strapped about her ankles chimed in chorus with those the other women wore. Her neck felt bare without the torque, but that was for a reason this day.

She and Nigel went with wreaths on their heads as well, pink fireweed and scarlet gaura, daylilies creamy white and lavender, orange rose mallow. Drawn by the nectar, moving flowers—California Sister butterflies, black and orange and silver—fluttered about their heads.

"You look like Silenos the father of fauns dancing with the wood-nymphs," she whispered into Nigel's ear.

"My dear, *you* look like a dancing wood-nymph. My *son* looks like a young Apollo with Artemis on his arm. Even John Hordle is managing to do a credible imitation of Hercules with your lovely daughter as Hebe. *I* look like a complete middle-aged idiot, or at least I feel like one."

"You're being *English* again, my darling."

He grinned at her, the wreath a little askew once more. "Something to that. I felt the same way the first time, you see, even though it was only dress uniform and not this kilt."

"You could have worn a robe, too," she said, just to see him shudder theatrically.

The others followed, wreathed as they were for the joining. Eilir and John Hordle were just behind Nigel and Juniper—he'd complained that he felt like a bull at a county fair and bellowed like one when Eilir nodded in calm agreement, stately in her robe and *airsaid*. Alleyne and Astrid followed, both in long robes of fine white linen as well as garlands, looking like the Fair Folk come again in their tall blond handsomeness—though she'd bristled like a great cat with silver-blue eyes blazing at the sight of Tiphaine d'Ath in Mathilda's train, the Protectorate warrior quietly bristling right back. Others followed them in turn; Judy and Chuck's Dan, beside lanky brown-haired Devorgill the huntress, her long bony face transfigured into beauty, and many another. There was nothing like the memory of a war just past to put a hand on shoulder and say: *hurry*.

But now we have peace, she thought. *And new beginnings.*

"I'm sorry we were too busy at Beltane," Nigel murmured.

"Mabon is a good time for handfasting too. It's a season of fruitfulness, isn't it?" she said, and laid a hand on her stomach for an instant. "I wasn't going to tell you just yet, but I want you to be as happy as I this moment, my darling nervous one."

For a moment his reserve cracked into incredulous joy, and she laughed at the sight; and again at how quickly again a tinge of worry crept in. He would always be concerned for her, and that was like welcoming light burning through a window on a winter's night, when you'd traveled through sleet in darkness.

"My beloved, I'm a mother twice over, remember, and neither birthing gave me the slightest problem, and Judy is the best midwife in all the Willamette country. Have some confidence! Shall we name her Maude?"

His brows went up under the wreath; she reached out and straightened it.

"It . . . it . . ." He stuttered for a second, and she basked in the look he gave her. Then he won back to self-mastery, as this man of hers always would. "It, ah, might be a boy."

"No, somehow I don't think so." She looked at him slyly, green eyes glinting from under her fox red brows. "And I'm a witch, you know."

To herself: *And there's power in names. All our loves return to us, my poor, strong, stoic darling. We and they are braided together, the dancers and the Dance.*

More flowers starred the sides of the pathway, planted by nature or patient hands. Today there was an arch of roses over the place where the pathway gave onto the flat knee that stood out from the mountainside.

Music played as they emerged from the close hush of the forest into the open wind and the vast blue distances of the mountainside clearing; flutes like that wind given form, the sweet eeriness of the uilleann pipes—the great hoarse war-drones were put aside for this—a harp, a rattle of bodhran-drums, and a choir of girl-children singing:

> *"A Bhennáin, a bhúiredáin, a bhéichdáin bhinn*
> *Is bhinn linn in cúicherán do ní tú 'sin ghlinn."*

"Antlered one, belling one, you of the sweet-tongued cry, we love to hear Your song in the glen," Nigel murmured, surprising her for a moment.

The High Priestesses and High Priests waited for them there, robed, crowned with the Moon or masked with the muzzle and stag antlers of Cernunnos, with opal and silver and tricolored belts, staffs and wands in their hands; Dennis solid and smiling beside his Sally, Judy and Chuck as familiar as they'd been so many years, Melissa Aylward grave and matronly with a twinkle breaking through now and then and Larry Smith the shepherd doing his game best beside her, Tom Brannigan and Mora all the way from Sutterdown.

Behind them scores of friends waited on the meadow and around the pool, Sam Aylward with his arm in its sling, looking on with pride—and relief, she thought, that *he* wasn't wearing the stag-mask . . . even Eric Larsson and his Luanne and Will Hutton and Angelica from over in the Bearkiller territories, both given special dispensation by Abbot Dmwoski. They grinned and waved; Juniper answered in kind, and even Nigel did as well. Smiles were well-omened on a day like this.

Children raced around, or stood importantly holding their pieces of the ceremony, her own Rudi among them, and his friend Mathilda standing back looking envious. Adults passed canvas *chagals* of wine from hand to hand—it was Mabon, wine-harvest, after all, and there was an occasional shout of "Io, Io, Io, *evoii*!"

She took one and squirted a mouthful in a single stream past her lips, tasting the blood of Earth, wild and strong; then she passed it on and threw her arms around Nigel for a long, lingering kiss, ignoring the whooping and cheers and bawdy good wishes shouted in the background, for those were also luck-bringing.

The great circle of oaks stood ready, rough-barked columns thicker than her body and a hundred feet tall, the tattered late-season lushness of their leaves making an arch around the Circle itself, streaked with old-gold yellow as they caught the setting sun high above. Today they were draped and joined with ropes of garden blossoms and great wreaths at the Quarters as well. The same light glinted on the spring-fed pool beside the *nemed* and the place water tinkled downward over rocks, glowed on the nodding flowers of the alpine laurel that grew thick around it, deep pink bowls above the low matted leaves.

Juniper gave Nigel's hand a final squeeze. Then she caught her daughter's, and she her *anamchara* Astrid's, until all the women were linked. The music grew wilder, and they danced out to the spring, the laughing crowd giving way before them and following in their wake as they coiled around the waters with feet skipping on the soft, dense turf amid a chime of silver bells, their unbound hair tossing beneath the flower-wreaths. Juniper lifted her strong soprano in a high wordless note for an instant, and then they sang together as they danced:

> *"Sister of Waters*
> *Daughter of Light*
> *Dreamweaver, spelldancer*
> *On scented air*
> *Teach me Your magic*
> *That I may this night*
> *Make love like fine music*
> *Both glorious and rare—"*

Then solemn quiet fell, as Judy cast the Circle and admitted the celebrants: "I conjure you, O Circle of Power—"

Salt and water and incense smoke and steel, and the crackling of fire in the central hearth of the *nemed*. The other pairs of High Priest and Priestess stood at the Quarters, and the ritual went forward.

"—as in the Beginning, so it is now. As above, so below. The Two are One."

Juniper took up the torque, and Nigel bowed his head as she spoke and placed it around his neck. "As symbol of my love, I give you this token. I will comfort and honor you in all our days."

He was smiling as he rose and took the torque he'd made for her in his hands; smiling more deeply with his eyes than his lips.

"As a symbol of my love, I give you this token. I will honor and protect you in all our days."

They each took a taper and lit the offered candle, and faced the altar as the High Priestess brought the ribbons from the cauldron. Her face was still graven with sadness, but there was happiness there as well when she met her friend's eyes.

I wish Aoife could be here too, and her Liath, Juniper thought, and knew the thought shared. *They were brave and glorious and full of life and love. But they're together in the Summerlands, and we'll see them again, even if we call them by different names.*

Judy bound the ribbons about their crossed wrists.

"Ribbon of white, for the Maiden and the Son; new life and beginnings. Ribbon of red, for the Mother- and the Father-of-All; growth and change. Ribbon of black, for the Wise One and the Keeper-of-Laws; death and the silent rest that comes before renewal. Can you walk this path together; bound by the freedom of your choice; to be as one, yet also Two; your love the fire that warms without destroying?"

"I can," Juniper murmured softly, and turned her hand within the loose circle of the ribbons.

Nigel's fingers gripped hers, and his voice was firm as he answered: "I can."

Judy removed the ribbons and placed them on the altar knotted together. Then she lifted the chalice and cried: "By the Lord and the Lady, I call down blessing on these two. As the Lord and Lady join in the Sacred Marriage from which springs all creation, so are they joined. By the power of the Goddess, as Her priestess, I decree it. Blessèd be!"

The antlered man joined her, hands touching on the chalice. "By the Lady and the Lord, I call down blessing on these two. By the Chalice and the Blade, they are joined. By the power of the God, as His priest, I decree it. Blessèd be!"

As the pair drank, Judy laid a broom on the ground before the altar, the rough twig besom scratching on the flagstones. "Over the broom and into new life!"

They joined hands and leapt over it; then Nigel gave a shout of laughter and caught her up as if she were weightless, twirling her around and bearing her away to the side where they'd wait while the others came before the altar. When he put her down again she sank forward with her head against his shoulder, feeling the strength of the arm around her shoulders, the scent of flowers and wool and faint, clean male musk.

Nigel shifted, and she opened her eyes. Rudi was there,

looking up at her with that heartbreaker grin. Then he turned it on her husband, and said quietly: "Can I call you Dad now? I never had a dad, not really. Uncles aren't the same. But you're the one I'd pick to be father."

"Yes, son, you can."

"Good. See you later, Mom, Dad!"

He slipped away, and Nigel's eyes twinkled at her. Juniper watched the others approach the altar, waiting quietly content. At last Chuck stood forth and called to them all:

"Rejoice, beloved! The God and the Goddess are honored in all celebrations of joy and love. This ceremony is accomplished—so mote it be!"

"Always," Juniper murmured, turning to look into Nigel's blue eyes; they blinked back at her in their nest of fine wrinkles.

"Always, my dear. While the Gods allow."

People were filing forward to light the torches that would guide them home; sunset was an arch of crimson and hot gold in the west.

She looked up sharply at the *ahhhh!* that ran around the Circle. A raven came out of the western light, first a dot and then a wingspan wider than she'd ever seen in that breed.

It circled over their heads and landed on the altar itself, and shocked silence descended, a silence so complete that breathing was the loudest sound under the fire-crackle, and she could hear the rustle of its feathers, and the scritching of its claws; one set of talons on the stone, the other on the hilt of the ritual sword. Rudi was there, and he sank to his knees before the altar.

A whisper of sound went through her: her own voice, near ten years gone. "And in the Craft, I name you *Artos*."

Then Rudi spoke himself; clear, yet without any stress, as if he spoke to her rather than the great black bird whose wings near enfolded him. And he smiled, a smile full of joy, and fearless youth.

"Of course, Mother. Whenever You call for me, I will come."

Juniper blinked. She saw her son, the child she had carried and nursed and loved, here in the dawning of his days. The raven's wings moved, slowly, once and twice and again, and its beak dipped forward. Despite herself she caught her breath in fear; that flint-hard dagger could take out an eye in a single motion. And peck it did, a quick sharp stab, but all that left was a single drop of blood between his brows.

And then she saw him still, but not the child she knew, or in the *nemed*.

Instead the wings beat about another face, the face of a man in the first flush of his grown strength, jewel-cut strong-jawed handsomeness, with a bleeding slash on his forehead that he dashed at with one impatient hand, scattering clotted drops into his glory of curling red-gold hair. His mouth was stretched wide in a shout that was like the expression in his blue-gray eyes, a cry terrible and fierce and beautiful. His black horse reared beneath him, and in his right hand was a sword held aloft with more red drops flying from its sweep—a great, straight double-edged thing with a crescent guard and staghorn hilt, its pommel a glowing opal gripped in spreading antlers, like the head of Cernunnos raised against the Hunter's Moon.

Behind him she could sense banners, the moon and horns of the Clan, and others besides. Around and about him a great bare plain, and mountains rearing above it bleak with winter's snow; a shadow of pike and lance and painted faces yelling; the sound of battle, screams of human and horse-kind, and the iron clangor she knew all too well, the massed whicker of arrows and the harsh snarl of steel on steel.

As the horse reared and the sword shone in the light of another setting sun a growing chorus sounded, louder even than the threnody of pain. A roar from thousands upon thousands of throats, beating like the heart of some great rough beast, or like the Pacific surf once, when she'd stood on a cliff in a time of storm and felt the living rock tremble to the blows of Ocean.

"Artos! Artos! Artos! Artos!"

Juniper closed her eyes and shuddered for an instant; above the chant and woven with it, she heard the words she'd spoken in this very *nemed* at Rudi's Wiccaning, or which Someone had spoken through her as she lifted her infant son over the altar:

> *Sad winter's child, in this leafless shaw—*
> *Yet be Son, and Lover, and Hornéd Lord!*
> *Guardian of My sacred Wood, and Law—*
> *His people's strength—and the Lady's sword!*

When she opened them again her Rudi knelt before the altar, watching the raven sweep aloft and vanish into the blaze of the setting sun, mouth and eyes open in wonder. Red light washed over it, from the direction that held the Gate of the Summerlands, and back into the dying sun.

Juniper stepped forward, putting her arm around the boy's shoulders as he rose. "I . . . I think I saw something, Mom," he said slowly, looking at the drop of blood on his questing fingers.

She nodded and stroked his hair, then looked up at the people and spoke, her voice soft-seeming but pitched to carry:

"Now indeed, I am thinking that this is a sign, and a wonder."

Folk looked at her, and to her—and blinked, and shook themselves a little, and began to breathe once more. Eilir's eyes stayed wide, and Astrid's; they had seen something as well, then. The others were uncertain; only a fleeting moment had passed, after all, less than a minute between the raven's landing and its departure. Most had been aware of nothing else.

Juniper smiled at them all, feeling weight lifting from her shoulders and a return of everyday happiness. Suddenly she was hungry, and eager for feasting and dancing and love.

"But my best beloved—" She looked at Nigel and smiled again; at her daughter and new son-in-law, at Astrid and the others. She held out her arms in what might be the gesture of blessing, or a welcoming. "All my beloved ones, look around you. Isn't *everything* a sign and a wonder?"

She put her hands on her hips then, and her grin had an impudent, urchin glee. "So let's take the feast prepared, not to mention enough music and wine to grow tiddly but not soused, and the nice soft bridal beds, and the season of our happiness. The story never ends, but our part in the tale does, for a while, and I'm in the mood for some happy-ever-aftering! We earned it, as the Gods themselves know!"

The Latest in the Series

THE SUNRISE LANDS

by S.M. STIRLING

A generation has passed since The Change that
rendered technology inoperable around the world, and
western Oregon has finally achieved a degree of peace.
But a new threat has risen in Paradise Valley,
Wyoming. A man known as The Prophet presides
over the Church Universal and Triumphant, teaching
his followers to continue God's work by destroying
the remnants of technological civilization they
encounter—and those who dare use them.

S.M. Stirling

THE PROTECTOR'S WAR

It's been eight years since the Change rendered technology inoperable across the globe. Rising from the ashes of the computer and industrial ages is a brave new world. Survivors have banded together in tribal communities, committed to rebuilding society. In Oregon's Willamette Valley, former pilot Michael Havel's Bearkillers are warriors of renown. Their closest ally, the mystical Clan Mackenzie, is led by Wiccan folksinger Juniper Mackenzie. Their leadership has saved countless lives.

But not every leader has altruistic aspirations. Norman Arminger, medieval scholar, rules the Protectorate. He has enslaved civilians, built an army, and spread his forces from Portland through most of western Washington State. Now he wants the Willamette Valley farmland, and he's willing to wage war to conquer it.

And unknown to both factions is the imminent arrival of a ship from Tasmania bearing British soldiers...

"[A] VIVID PORTRAIT OF A WORLD GONE INSANE."
—*STATESMAN JOURNAL* (SALEM, OR)

Available wherever books are sold or at penguin.com

S.M. Stirling

DIES THE FIRE

It all started when an electrical storm over
Nantucket produced a blinding white flash,
causing all electronic devises to cease to function
across the globe. Now, without computers,
telephones, engines, or radios, the world is
plunged into a darkness humanity is not prepared
for. In the Pacific Northwest, some are banding
together, while others are preparing for conquest.

Praise for the novels of S.M. Stirling:

Available wherever books are sold or at
penguin.com

S.M. STIRLING

From national bestselling author
S.M. Stirling comes gripping novels of
alternative history

Island in the Sea of Time

Against the Tide of Years

On the Oceans of Eternity

The Peshawar Lancers

Conquistador

"FIRST-RATE ADVENTURE ALL THE WAY."
—HARRY TURTLEDOVE

Available wherever books are sold or at
penguin.com

THE ULTIMATE IN
SCIENCE FICTION AND FANTASY!

From magical tales of distant worlds to stories of
technological advances beyond the grasp of man, Penguin has
everything you need to stretch your imagination to its limits.

penguin.com

ACE
Get the latest information on favorites like
William Gibson, T.A. Barron, Brian Jacques,
Ursula K. LeGuin, Sharon Shinn, and Charlaine Harris,
as well as updates on the best new authors.

ROC
Escape with Harry Turtledove, Anne Bishop,
S.M. Stirling, Simon R. Green, Chris Bunch, Jim Butcher,
E.E. Knight, and many others—plus news on the
latest and hottest in science fiction and fantasy.

DAW
Mercedes Lackey, Kristen Britain, Tanya Huff,
Tad Williams, C.J. Cherryh, and many more—
DAW has something to satisfy the cravings of any
science fiction and fantasy lover.
Also visit dawbooks.com.

*Get the best of science fiction and fantasy
at your fingertips!*